Unmasking the Heart

A Honeysuckle Creek Novel

Macee McNeill

Copyright © 2021 by Keena Arrowood
All rights reserved.

This is an original work of fiction. All characters, names, places, and incidents are products of the author's imagination or are used fictitiously. Any resemblance to actual persons, living or dead, businesses, companies, events, or locales is entirely coincidental. No portion of this book may be used, reproduced, scanned, or distributed in any manner without the written consent of the author, excepting short quotations used for the purposes of review or commentary about the work.

ISBN: 978-1-09836-139-6
eBook: ISBN 978-1-09836-140-2

Books
by
Macee McNeill

<u>Finch Family Series</u>

Once and Forever

Unmasking the Heart

DEDICATION

To Graham, my oldest son,

I wish every little girl could have a daddy just like you.

Love you always!

ACKNOWLEDGEMENTS

Thanks to:

My fabulously supportive, always entertaining husband who still hasn't read a single one of my books.

My amazing family for listening to me talk. And talk. And talk…

Jann, Carla, Esther, and Jenny for reading my manuscript. Thanks for the encouragement and the suggestions.

The real Nurse Carol. Thank you for sharing your medical expertise and for helping me write about Devin's condition. (Even though it was *your* idea to give the poor man a broken femur.) You are a wonderful friend.

Lauren, because you are the most positive person I know. Period.

Christina—always kind and infinitely patient—and the rest of Bookbaby's amazing staff.

God, for His endless blessings.

She warned him

not to be deceived by appearances,

For beauty

is found within…

--Beauty and the Beast

Contents

PROLOGUE	1
CHAPTER ONE	8
CHAPTER TWO	18
CHAPTER THREE	24
CHAPTER FOUR	30
CHAPTER FIVE	41
CHAPTER SIX	48
CHAPTER SEVEN	55
CHAPTER EIGHT	70
CHAPTER NINE	77
CHAPTER TEN	91
CHAPTER ELEVEN	98
CHAPTER TWELVE	108
CHAPTER THIRTEEN	118
CHAPTER FOURTEEN	123
CHAPTER FIFTEEN	128
CHAPTER SIXTEEN	135
CHAPTER SEVENTEEN	153
CHAPTER EIGHTEEN	165
CHAPTER NINETEEN	178
CHAPTER TWENTY	184
CHAPTER TWENTY-ONE	195
CHAPTER TWENTY-TWO	204
CHAPTER TWENTY-THREE	214
CHAPTER TWENTY-FOUR	223
CHAPTER TWENTY-FIVE	234

CHAPTER TWENTY-SIX	244
CHAPTER TWENTY-SEVEN	263
CHAPTER TWENTY-EIGHT	275
CHAPTER TWENTY-NINE	283
CHAPTER THIRTY	293
CHAPTER THIRTY-ONE	302
CHAPTER THIRTY-TWO	319
CHAPTER THIRTY-THREE	325
CHAPTER THIRTY-FOUR	332
CHAPTER THIRTY-FIVE	336
CHAPTER THIRTY-SIX	341
CHAPTER THIRTY-SEVEN	349
CHAPTER THIRTY-EIGHT	361
CHAPTER THIRTY-NINE	373
CHAPTER FORTY	380
CHAPTER FORTY-ONE	388
CHAPTER FORTY-TWO	396
CHAPTER FORTY-THREE	405
CHAPTER FORTY-FOUR	415
CHAPTER FORTY-FIVE	428
CHAPTER FORTY-SIX	440
CHAPTER FORTY-SEVEN	451
CHAPTER FORTY-EIGHT	465
CHAPTER FORTY-NINE	477
CHAPTER FIFTY	484
CHAPTER FIFTY-ONE	498
CHAPTER FIFTY-TWO	504
CHAPTER FIFTY-THREE	522
CHAPTER FIFTY-FOUR	530
CHAPTER FIFTY-FIVE	541
EPILOGUE	551

PROLOGUE

Belize City, Belize
June 2017

Kenneth Wade was the luckiest man alive…at least in his own narcissistic estimation. Not only had he, unwittingly, stumbled upon his boss' very illegal drug operation, but he had figured out how to use his discovery to increase his already substantial income.

Blackmail.

It was a brilliant plan. And he was a brilliant man.

Kenneth rolled down the window by his seat in the ramshackle bus. He hoped the dilapidated transportation held up long enough to get him and the rowdy group of tourists he was traveling with to their zip-lining excursion. Hot, dry air blew in his face as he leaned his head out the window to see why the bus wasn't moving.

"Ken-ny," his companion whined, tugging on the sleeve of his polo shirt. "You're messing up my hair."

He pulled his head back into the bus to deal with yet another complaint from the well-endowed redhead. Her eyes went wide with horror. As he turned back to the window, another bus whizzed by inches from where his head had been. Kenneth's mouth fell open in shock, a wave of heat running through his body. For a moment, he teetered between passing out and throwing up; then his senses relaxed and his heartbeat returned to normal.

"Oh, Ken-ny," the redhead sobbed, throwing her arms around his neck, clearly relieved.

The man sitting in the seat across the aisle leaned toward them. "You're pretty damn lucky," he observed. "That bus almost took your head off."

He was a typical middle-aged tourist in his wide-brimmed Panama hat, bright blue Hawaiian shirt, cargo shorts, and brown sandals. His features, while pleasant, weren't remarkable. In fact, there wasn't a single memorable thing about him, except the coldness in his gaze. And the fact that he seemed almost disappointed that Kenneth's head was still firmly attached to his shoulders.

Kenneth couldn't help but feel annoyed by Joe Tourist's intrusion into what should have been a private moment between himself and the weeping woman in his arms. Who knew where such emotion might lead? He had yet to experience all that Calliope had to offer.

He met the sexy tease in one of the ship's dance clubs on the first night of the cruise. It took three days of intensive effort to convince her to spend the night. The hot little redhead had finally succumbed to his considerable charms the previous evening, eagerly accompanying Kenneth back to his suite.

But, then, the oddest thing occurred. While she was in the bathroom "getting more comfortable," *he* had fallen asleep on the couch. He still didn't understand how that had happened. Maybe the drinks she had ordered for them were too strong. She told him she fell asleep right after he did. That made him feel a bit better.

Joe Tourist was still leaning toward them, waiting for Kenneth to speak.

"You're right about that, Mr....?" Kenneth inquired politely.

"Smith," Joe Tourist said. "You can call me Mr. Smith."

Kenneth pasted a superior smile on his lips. "You're right about my luck, Mr. Smith. I just might be the luckiest man in the world."

"Is that so?" Mr. Smith said, with veiled interest. "And why is that?"

Kenneth grinned into the admiring eyes of the redhead. "You tell him, Calliope."

The redhead gazed at Kenneth adoringly before turning her glowing countenance on Mr. Smith. "It's true," she gushed. "Kenny has tons of money and he's just found out something naughty about his boss." She let out a high-pitched giggle and started talking in a little-girl voice. "Now, his Bossy-Wossy wants to give Kenny-Wenny even more money to keep Kenny-Wenny from telling his Bossy-Wossy's naughty-waughty little secret."

She leaned back against Kenny as she talked, and he clasped his hands around her waist. He gazed down on her considerable assets, straining against her tiny bathing suit top. For someone who had to be in her mid- to late-thirties, Calliope's body was remarkably alluring. She had the looks of a supermodel and the sensual maturity of an experienced woman. How could one man possibly be so lucky?

"That sounds a little bit dangerous," Mr. Smith remarked.

"Not dangerous." Kenneth shook his head smugly. "Brilliant. And not only that…"

"You mean there's more?" Mr. Smith asked with an edge of sarcasm.

Calliope giggled again. "Kenny won a free cruise. You should see his suite. It's two levels—and *so* fancy. He even has a butler. And then he found two complimentary tickets for a free zip-lining excursion. Can you believe that?"

Mr. Smith raised his eyebrows. "Impressive." He sat back in his seat without another word.

He's jealous. Kenneth was rather pleased by his own assumption. It also helped him to understand Mr. Smith's cold, malice-filled eyes.

The bus started moving again. Kenneth spent the rest of the journey making promises—expensive restaurants, fabulous jewelry, an endless expense account—to the woman who so obviously idolized him.

MACEE MCNEILL

The view from the platform was spectacular. There was no arguing with that. The rain forest spread out below them—a lovely green canopy—sultry in the intense heat, like the woman behind him. Kenneth leaned closer to study the zip line they would be gliding down. It looked sturdy enough, stretching into the untamed forest then disappearing in the rich vegetation. He figured the whole setup was safe. Hell, the ratings for this particular zip line company were almost all five-star. He had checked before deciding to take advantage of the passes for the excursion. Kenneth Wade was nobody's fool.

He peered over the railing. The ground was a long way down. For the first time since he had found the zip-lining tickets in his suite, he hesitated. His stomach wasn't feeling quite right. Maybe it was the drinks from the night before, or maybe it was something else.

"What's the matter, Lucky?" Mr. Smith jeered.

Out of all the tourists on their bus, only Mr. Smith had followed them up to this platform—a fact Kenneth found incredibly annoying.

The aggravating man continued his taunt. "Lose your nerve?"

"Of course not," Kenneth snarled, turning around to face his tormentor.

Mr. Smith's face wore a smug smile, as if the sole reason for his existence was to emasculate unsuspecting males in front of infatuated females.

"Do you want *me* to go first?" the irritating man asked slyly.

"Oh, Mr. Smith! You're sooo brave." Calliope's eyes were glued to the man in wide-eyed admiration.

That was all it took. "Hook me up," Kenneth said to the zip line employee who was waiting patiently on the platform. Nobody was going to mock Kenneth Wade like that. *Nobody*. He would show the infuriating bastard he had what it takes—*and* walk away with the girl. But the triumphant grin he flashed over his shoulder at his heckler was met with a blank stare. Kenneth turned back quickly, strangely unnerved by the expression in Mr. Smith's dark eyes.

When the employee finished fastening his harness, Kenneth looked behind him again. Calliope and Mr. Smith were standing side by side. Watching him.

Kenneth shook off a strong feeling of foreboding. He gave the redhead his sexiest, most devil-may-care grin. "I'll be waiting for you at the end," he said with more confidence than he felt.

She did not return his smile. "Bye-bye, Kenny," she said with a wave of her perfectly manicured hand.

Kenneth watched as that hand and the redhead attached to it drew farther and farther away. He decided that her curious response was the result of nerves…or, well, *something*. They would sort it all out later. She'd be crazy to walk away from Kenneth Wade. He was the luckiest man alive.

Calliope and Mr. Smith didn't move when they heard the first scream. They waited until the third before crossing the distance to the edge of the platform. From there, they could easily see Kenneth Wade's lifeless body lying amid the rocks of a small stream on the rain forest floor. His twisted form was surrounded by an ever-growing number of tourists who had been waiting below for their own chance to zip line. Their enthusiasm for that endeavor, at the moment, was understandably diminished.

"He's dead."

Those words came from the competent-looking man who was the first to reach the unfortunate victim. Loud voices and the sound of someone crying reached their ears.

Calliope turned her back to the scene unfolding on the rain forest floor. "He was a swine," she said, her voice falling comfortably into a foreign accent of indeterminate origin. She walked to the back of the platform near the steps the three of them climbed a few minutes ago. Only *two* of them needed those steps now.

Calliope turned around and propped her back against the railing. She held out her hand. Palm up.

Mr. Smith grinned in admiration, highly amused by her callous attitude. He couldn't place her accent, either. The woman, whoever she was, was a consummate professional.

For the sheer pleasure of reminding Calliope who was really in charge, Mr. Smith deliberately ignored the greedy redhead's out-stretched hand. He approached the zip line employee first. The silent man was both efficient *and* patient…two qualities that deserved to be rewarded. Mr. Smith reached into his pocket and pulled out a folded envelope. He unfolded it and held it out to the man in front of him.

"Pleasure doing business with you…" Mr. Smith hesitated. According to the nametag on his shirt, the man's name was Artan. "Pleasure doing business with you, Artan."

A ghost of a smile appeared on the man's expressionless face. "Name's not Artan," was all he said before taking the envelope and heading down the steps. Mr. Smith watched until Not-Artan disappeared into the rain forest as quickly as the envelope had disappeared into the pocket of his jeans.

He turned back to Calliope. She looked bored. She was watching him through narrowed eyes, seemingly oblivious to the chaos that had erupted below. She was ice-cold. He chuckled as he handed her a second envelope he pulled from his pocket.

"Thank you, Calliope," he said, watching with appreciation as she folded the envelope twice and tucked it between her ample breasts stuffed into her bathing suit top. "It was a pleasure doing business with *you*."

"I chipped a nail."

She glared in the direction of Kenneth Wade's body as if he were solely responsible for ruining her perfect manicure.

Mr. Smith nodded. "Is your name really Calliope?" He couldn't resist asking.

"Is your name really Mr. Smith?" she responded, acidly, her eyebrow raised.

They studied each other in silence. It seemed they had a lot in common.

Another shout from below interrupted their moment. Not-Really-Calliope shrugged and headed down the steps without a backward glance.

After giving the redhead a few seconds, Mr. Smith followed. He couldn't be more pleased. Their operation was a success. Winning the "free cruise" had prevented Wade from keeping his scheduled meeting with McCallum Industries' head of legal affairs, Devin Merritt. Whether Wade's threat to tell Merritt everything he knew was legitimate or merely his first attempt at blackmail would forever remain a mystery. As of this moment, Merritt knew nothing of their illegal activities. And, Wade—their greatest liability—had been eliminated.

Mr. Smith couldn't wait to get back to the cruise ship. He deserved a little vacation.

Once he reached the rain forest floor, he made sure to blend in with his fellow tourists as their tour guide rounded them up to return to the bus. Mr. Smith carefully averted his eyes as he passed the scene of the accident.

Life was about choices, he mused. The cocky, ambitious man who thought he had it all figured out now lay lifeless on the ground. Like the mythical Icarus, he had chosen to fly too close to the sun. And, like Icarus, he had paid for his choices with his life. A tragedy of human nature, Mr. Smith decided.

In spite of possessing an almost maniacal confidence in his own abilities, Kenneth Wade's luck had finally run out.

CHAPTER ONE

Newport, Rhode Island

Devin Merritt felt his phone vibrate in the pocket of his pants, momentarily distracting him from the game he was playing in his head. Deciding what kind of animal each person in the crowded bar resembled had been amusing—at least for a little while. After identifying a pair of laughing hyenas, a couple of promiscuous gazelles, and several empty-headed peacocks, however, what had started out as a welcome escape quickly devolved into a meaningless, repetitive exercise. The rest of the crowd he neatly divided into two groups: buzzards and sloths. The buzzards hovered around waiting for some useless prey to die so they could eat it, and the sloths didn't care.

He felt his phone vibrate again. Fortunately, he didn't have to depend on his hearing; the pounding beat from the speaker behind him obliterated all other sounds. He probably would be deaf before the end of this interminable evening, anyway, if he chose to remain in his current position. Still, he hesitated. If he moved anywhere else in the room, he might be cornered again by the nervous-looking loser who was leaning against the bar…O'Connell, or something like that.

The annoying man appeared genuinely shocked that Mrs. O'Connell had decided—after discovering his involvement with not one, but *three* different women—to sue him for everything he had. Devin's firm assertion that he was a contract lawyer who did *not* specialize in divorce cases had fallen on deaf ears. According to the illustrious Mr. O'Connell, "One lawyer is just like another." The man was eyeing him speculatively, even now, seemingly desperate for free legal advice. There was no doubt that in the animal world, as in the human one, Mr. O'Connell was an ass.

From his vantage point, Devin idly studied the groupings of Newport's self-absorbed second tier. Their ultimate desire, of course, was to join the glittering throng at the pinnacle of high society…to be absorbed by the elite. He had to give them credit for their single-minded devotion to that goal, even while he abhorred their methods. If they turned such intense focus away from themselves and toward some worthwhile cause—feeding hungry children, for example—they could do a lot of good. Instead, these ambitious social climbers used each other shamelessly in their uphill battle to reach the top of the food chain. Was it any surprise that the lucky few who actually made it to the upper echelon of high society did *not* become beacons to light the way for those still clinging to their…their what? Devin always hesitated at this point in his musings.

What, he wondered, was the proper term for the myriad relationships swirling around him? *Friendship* was a stretch because it implied genuine caring and concern for others. The relationships before him exhibited a distinct lack of either attribute. Perhaps *association* was the best word. Association…with emphasis on ensuring oneself was the user. *Not* the used.

Devin's eyes moved from group to group. Yes, he thought. Association was the best term for what he saw. In spite of those associations, however, the fortunate few—those who successfully bridged the great divide—rarely gave another thought to those left behind. They were very careful, instead, to rid themselves of any lingering connections.

His phone vibrated again. Devin sighed and stood up so he could fish it out of his pocket. His eyes were drawn to the large group of women, and a few men, almost directly across from him. He watched the gorgeous blonde in the white, gauzy halter dress work her magic. The silver specks embedded in the expensive material of her designer original shimmered as she tossed her head and let a delicate giggle emerge from her throat, making her a vision of living, breathing starlight. No wonder the entire group was hanging on her every word. She was a master of illusion, pulling everyone within her orbit under her spell. Everyone, that is, but him.

As if privy to his thoughts, the blonde glanced across the space that separated them, lifted her hand gracefully to her carmine lips, and blew him a kiss. Every head turned his way, watching—with varying degrees of longing and envy—as Devin raised his palm into the air, closing it as if catching the carefree kiss. His eyes never left the glowing blue ones that bored into his as he slowly brought his fist to his lips. He saw the flare of satisfaction in the woman's eyes before she carefully covered it with wide-eyed innocence. As her rapt audience returned its attention to her lovely face, the spellbound men and women saw only her abject adoration.

Devin carefully schooled his features so the distaste he felt wasn't visible. It really didn't matter. They weren't looking at him anyway. Still, on the outside chance that someone decided to give him a second glance, *he* could not be the one to diminish the vision *she* wanted to create. This was what she expected of him, what she wanted, and what his life had become.

He was trapped in an unending 24/7 illusion. He didn't get weekends and holidays off, or even time off for good behavior. Sometimes he wished he was still like the poor suckers across from him. It had actually been easier when he was her willing victim instead of what he had become.

Now, he was her unwilling hostage, forced to play the role of the fool in a farce of her own making. Mallory had shattered every illusion he'd ever had with regard to her—and most of the ones he'd had about himself. He saw her for what she was…unending drama in a dress that was too sheer, too short, and slightly inappropriate for the occasion. He saw it all—and much more— because the woman across from him was, unfortunately, his wife.

She latched onto him with the hope of reaching the uppermost realm of societal power. She assumed—because his last name was Merritt and because he held the prestigious position of head of the legal department of McCallum Industries—that he was well on his way to ruling the upper echelon and enjoying all the benefits thereof.

She should have done better research, he thought with savage satisfaction. Yes, he was a member of the Merritt family. And, yes, Merritt Brothers was a very successful law firm. *But*—and this was the important part, the part Mallory was incapable of understanding—the Merritts were, first and foremost, a *family*. They were far more likely to spend a Sunday afternoon playing a backyard football game than a Saturday night at a flashy gala.

And, although Devin agreed that he had an incredible job, he valued his friendship with the enigmatic CEO, Blane McCallum, far more than any power or prestige that came with the position. If during the course of his life Devin had *ever* been like one of the purely selfish creatures currently occupying the space across from him, he was well over it.

Perhaps Mallory had sensed something of a kindred spirit in him, he thought, with a modicum of self-disgust. Otherwise, she would never have taken a chance on Devin Merritt. Or perhaps—and he preferred this option—what initially attracted her had been purely superficial. How typical that would be. Plain and simple, she liked the way they looked together. His close-cropped auburn hair, light gray eyes, ruggedly masculine face, and strong, athletic build created the perfect foil for her delicate beauty. All of the Merritt cousins shared similar features, but it was universally acknowledged that Devin was the best-looking of the family. His good looks coupled with a high-paying job and impressive stock options made him quite a catch.

So, Mallory had gambled, but—although her wager had won her a lovely townhouse, a flashy Porsche 718 Boxster GTS convertible, and unlimited access to Devin's bank account—it still wasn't enough. In other words, no resident of Martha's Vineyard or Kennebunkport had invited her for the weekend. Those doors remained firmly closed.

That's not to say that Mr. and Mrs. Devin Merritt didn't make an occasional foray into the world of the elite, but those ventures occurred only when Devin's boss was required to attend an event and invited them to go along. McCallum Industries' CEO was as unimpressed by society functions as Devin was. Blane McCallum vastly preferred spending his time in the small town of Honeysuckle Creek, North Carolina, with his lovely fiancée.

Devin wouldn't be at all surprised if Blane decided to move part of McCallum's North American headquarters to North Carolina in the near future. As a matter of fact, he expected it. Relocating to North Carolina would topple the carefully erected tower of Mallory's social ambitions, depriving his wife of the only path to her lifelong goal. Was *he* wrong to look forward to such an explosive development? He couldn't help but wonder. He was not proud of the fact that the mere possibility gave him a tremendous sense of satisfaction, but there it was.

Something in Devin's life needed to change. That much was clear. Mallory was becoming more demanding, making his marriage more difficult. He felt like a puppet attached to the strings of a controlling master. He would love to walk away from his ill-fated union right now—to hell with losing half of his assets. But—because of his damned signature on the damned addendum to the damned pre-nuptial agreement—if he walked away, Mallory would get full custody of their daughter.

Only his cousin, Roman, knew what had possessed him to sign such a ridiculous document. Roman *knew*. And Mallory, of course. *And* the slimy attorney she had hired. According to the prenup, if Mallory decided to exit their marriage, she wouldn't get a single dime of Devin Merritt's considerable assets.

Devin sighed. He doubted anything on earth would coerce Mallory into giving up her gilded lifestyle. Since he *couldn't* leave, and she *wouldn't* leave, it appeared they were at an impasse.

Why, then, didn't he do something to make her want to leave? Cut off her funds? Sell her Porsche? Cancel her weekly mani/pedi appointment? The answer was easy. He knew she would wage a spectacular custody battle if he did. Mallory was a convincing actress; there were no guarantees he would win custody of their daughter in a court of law. Chances were, the legal effort would result in joint custody, at best. He wasn't willing to take a chance that his little girl might end up at the mercy of a selfish, neglectful mother, even part of the time.

So, where did that leave him? The answer was obvious. Devin was trapped in a net of his own making—woven of poor judgement and bad decisions, with a few threads of pure stupidity. He couldn't leave Mallory... and he couldn't give her any reason to leave him. It didn't matter how many times he had to give in to Mallory's demands, or how often he had to bow to Mallory's will. It didn't matter what he had to do. He would *never* allow his little girl to be taken away from him.

UNMASKING THE HEART

Devin grimaced. Well, there wasn't anything for it, he decided, trying to be philosophical. He had no choice but to ask, even though he already knew the answer. So certain was he of the outcome of the conversation he was about to have that he paused a moment to arrange for an Uber. Then, he crossed the room, reluctantly, motioning for Mallory to join him at the edge of her group. She excused herself with a smile, but Devin could tell that it was forced.

"What is it, Devin?" she asked in the singsong voice he had come to dread.

"Mallory, did you tell Diana that we would be home by nine-thirty?"

"Of course not," she said evenly, glancing behind her to see whether or not they had an audience. They did. Of course, they did. This particular crowd was totally attuned to Mallory's every emotion.

She looked like an angel, with her luxurious waves of white-blond hair framing nearly perfect features. She wouldn't like the "nearly perfect" part. She would be furious that Devin ascribed to her anything less than the highest pedestal of physical perfection. Her imperfections were subtle, becoming more and more obvious to him the longer they were married. The high cheekbones and elegant nose that he had so admired once upon a time, now gave her a distinctly reptilian look. When combined with eyes that tilted slightly at the corners and her penchant for hissing when displeased, she reminded him of a snake…A poisonous snake. To put it plainly, after four and a half years of "wedded bliss" his wife reminded him of a hissing cobra. If he had a choice, he admitted to himself, he would rather be married to a sloth.

Still, Devin gave Mallory another chance to tell the truth. "Are you sure you didn't tell her nine-thirty?"

Mallory's answer was exactly what he expected. "If I had told Diana nine-thirty, we would already be at home, darling. *She* must be mistaken." Her baby blue eyes were wide and limpid, exuding an air of innocence.

Yet, he knew she lied. Devin sighed. If he handled this the wrong way, well…he still remembered the scene from last time. He hadn't been back to his favorite restaurant since, and that was three months ago. Dealing with

Mallory was like walking on the edge of a knife. It didn't matter where he stepped, he was going to get cut.

"Mistaken or not, Diana needs to leave," he said firmly. "She has a meeting with her publisher tomorrow. It's important."

He watched Mallory's eyes grow cold. Her expression swiftly changed from radiant to calculating.

"It's a shame that Amalie's nanny is more devoted to *herself* than to the precious little girl in her charge," she said loudly, with a convincing break of emotion in her voice.

With a quick glance at their rapt audience, she threw herself against his chest in a dramatic show of despair. She clung to Devin for a few moments more, as if the very act of pressing her lithe curves against him gave her all the power. Maybe that had once been the case, but—unbeknownst to her—she had lost that ability four years ago, when Amalie was born.

Mallory placed both hands against Devin's chest and gazed up at him adoringly. He braced himself for the performance she was about to give. His wife was nothing, if not predictable.

"Devin," she whined, prettily. "Why do *we* have to leave just because Diana says so? She works for *us*, not the other way around. *We're* paying her to do as *we* say, not to do what she wants." Mallory's red lips twisted into a practiced pout, her eyes growing impossibly wide. Her lashes fluttered delicately.

Devin focused on keeping his breathing even and his voice low and soothing. "She works *for* us, Mallory. She's not our slave."

Mallory pushed away from his chest, crossing her arms in front of her. "Is Amalie already asleep?" she asked.

"Yes, I suppose she is."

"Well, why can't Diana go ahead and leave? She can lock the door behind her. Amalie never wakes up during the night, anyway, and she won't even know she's by herself."

Mallory looked so certain he would accept her solution that Devin almost lost his composure. Even though her reaction was typical, a hot surge of anger swept through his body at the thought of his beloved daughter alone and helpless in their big townhouse. What if she called for him and nobody came? Devin closed his eyes for a minute, refusing to address Mallory's selfishness. When he opened them, he forced himself to reply calmly, "I'm going home to our daughter. I would appreciate it if you joined me."

"I'm not going anywhere."

Mallory looked at him with a gleam of triumph, thrilled that she finally had the right to a little drama.

"Fine," Devin said, holding back the first response that leapt to his lips—something along the lines of *I don't care if you ever come home, you selfish bitch*—saying instead, the more acceptable: "I'll go home to Amalie and you can stay here as long as you like."

He pulled the keys out of his pocket and held them out to her, unwilling to walk the five steps that now separated them. "Take the keys," he said, dangling them from his fingertips. "I already ordered an Uber."

Mallory's beautiful features twisted into a snarl, her voice growing louder with each word. She had the full attention of the room now. As usual, she would make the most of it. "I can't believe you're just going to leave me here all alone. You're letting a four-year-old come between us! Can't you see what she's doing to us? She's stealing your love, bit by bit, and ruining our marriage! Can't you see it, Devin? That child is tearing us apart!" Mallory covered her face with both of her hands, completely consumed by her own performance.

As if on cue, Desiree Hampton, Mallory's best friend, rushed to her side. Devin watched his stricken wife throw herself into her friend's arms, sobbing on Desiree's shoulder. He absently noted that it wasn't easy for Mallory to reach her ally's shoulder, due to the presence of Desiree's overly large bosom. The woman's breasts were as fake as her bleached blond hair and botoxed lips.

Desiree glared at Devin. "What kind of a man lets the *nanny* make his decisions for him? Poor Mallory deserves so much better," she growled through puffy lips. "If you care anything about your marriage, Devin, you better start looking for a good boarding school for your little brat as soon as she turns six." She continued her rant, looking exactly like an enraged blowfish: "Go home, Devin. Go home to your *daughter*. You've made your choice!" She grabbed the keys from his hand then led a sobbing Mallory toward the ladies' room.

Complete silence gripped the room, broken only by the rapidly receding sound of expensive high heels tapping against the wood floor. Someone said something in a low voice, and gradually the noise returned to its previous volume. Devin hadn't moved. In spite of a few sympathetic expressions on the faces of the sloths (and one of the gazelles), no one had come to his defense or the defense of his daughter. No one seemed to find anything remotely wrong with what Mallory or Desiree had said. He was sickened by the entire display, by the sheer self-absorption they exhibited so effortlessly.

Devin turned his back on them. Without saying anything to anyone, he walked out of the club.

After several minutes of uninterrupted pacing, Devin had calmed down enough to call Diana. She answered on the first ring.

"Dev, is everything all right? When you didn't text back, I was afraid…"

She paused to give him a chance to respond. When he didn't, she continued:

"Oh, drat, I'm sorry Dev. I knew I shouldn't have texted you. Mallory promised you'd be home by nine-thirty. I swear. We talked about it right before you left."

He could tell by her voice that she was upset. Poor Diana. She and her brother, Roman, had always been his favorite cousins. He hated putting her in the middle of his impossible situation. But he needed her. So did Amalie.

"Diana."

"I should have waited for you to get home. Then I could have…"

"Diana," Devin said again, "it isn't your fault that I'm married to a selfish, irrational…" Just then he saw a blue sedan approaching. "Uber's here. Hang on for a sec."

He stepped off the curb and walked into the street to wait. But instead of slowing down, the driver of the sedan deliberately sped up, heading straight for him.

"What the hell?"

Devin jumped back onto the curb to avoid the speeding car.

"What's wrong, Dev?" Diana's voice sounded alarmed. "What's happening?"

Before he could reply, the sedan jumped the curb and plowed into him. Devin was immediately hurled headfirst into the wrought iron fence that separated the outside patio area of the club from the sidewalk. Devin's right eye exploded in white-hot, searing pain that seemed to burn across his face. Then, seconds later, he felt nothing at all.

The next moment, the blue sedan backed up and sped off into the night.

"Dev! Dev! What's going on?"

Diana's frightened voice could be heard loud and clear: it reverberated from the phone lying on the ground beside Devin Merritt's motionless, bleeding body.

"Dev! Are you all right?" The worried voice filled the silence. "Devin! Answer me right now!"

But instead of the voice for which Diana was praying, she heard a woman scream, followed by the sound of running feet.

"Call 911!" somebody said.

"I think he's still breathing..." said another.

And finally, "Oh my God. Look at his face!"

Diana clutched the phone to her chest as her heart sank in terror.

A few seconds later, a blue Prius pulled up to the curb. A man climbed out and walked toward the scene of the accident. He glanced at the crumpled body on the ground, quickly averting his eyes from the mangled remains of the man's face.

"I'm looking for Devin," he said, loudly, to the gathering crowd of onlookers. "The one who ordered the Uber."

CHAPTER TWO

The metallic taste of blood in Devin's mouth was the first sign that something was seriously wrong. That, and the indecipherable murmur of voices, like so many bees buzzing around him. He didn't move or try to open his eyes. As his torpor slowly faded, he realized he was awake…really awake, and somewhat clear-headed. He wasn't still lolling around in the hazy place he had been stuck in for days.

Or was it weeks?

Months?

Damn. It could be years for all he knew. Maybe he had a long, white beard and a couple of grandchildren by now. Or maybe not, he thought, quickly dismissing that sobering idea.

He tried to remember what had happened to send him into this stupor in the first place. Without moving, he managed to take inventory. He was definitely lying in a bed, but it didn't feel like his comfortable mattress, so he wasn't in his bedroom.

He couldn't smell Mallory's overapplied perfume, so he wasn't in her room at home. He could count on one hand the number of times he had actually slept in her bed anyway. Hmm…this was bad. This meant his spotty memories of an accident weren't a dream at all. Surmising the truth wasn't difficult. He was in the hospital. He tried again to remember exactly what had happened to put him there.

He thought of Mallory's spectacular scene at the club and his decision to go home without her. He had ordered an Uber—and then, the Uber had jumped the curb, coming straight at him and…

Well, hell, he thought in amazement. That had to be it. He had been run over by an Uber. What a great conversation starter that was going to be.

He drifted for a minute, pondering this bizarre scenario. He had never before heard of anyone being run over by an Uber. *Had* anyone else ever been run over by an Uber? Was he the only one? Or was it a common occurrence? Maybe people got run over by Ubers every day. Maybe it was something nobody talked about. Maybe the company was staging a giant cover-up.

Well, they had picked the wrong man this time, he thought with determination. Devin Merritt was going to blow this story wide open. If, that is, he still had all of the necessary parts to do so. He decided to check, bracing himself for the possibility of extreme disappointment.

His brain appeared to be intact, judging from his ingenious theory of an Uber cover-up. A functioning brain was good, he figured, finally forcing himself to evaluate his present situation. He could move his toes…yeah, all ten…and his fingers, too. He wiggled them back and forth, aware that the buzzing sound of voices nearby suddenly grew louder after that. Strange. The fact that his limbs were all accounted for *and* in working order was a plus, wasn't it? He hoped so, anyway.

Devin's face felt uncomfortably dry, as if moving his nose or opening his mouth might shatter it into a thousand pieces. A dull throbbing echoed in his head. He focused on that part of his skull for a few seconds, deciding the throbbing wasn't too bad. Nothing he couldn't stand. He had suffered worse headaches from listening to Mallory drone on about why she needed to spend more money, or some other nonsense.…

He listened carefully to the murmur of voices around him, becoming aware that someone was holding his left hand. He strained his ears, forcing himself to lie perfectly still. If he moved, if he opened his eyes, he would have to face the reality of just how injured he really was. And he had a feeling it was bad. He wasn't sure he wanted to know, but, that voice—some desperate quality in that voice—called to him. He forced himself to do as it asked.

"I swear I felt his fingers move. Look, Robert. Look at his eyelid. See. He's coming back to us. Dev...Devin, wake up, honey. Please wake up."

It was no mystery who was squeezing his hand. Devin had known that sweet voice from the cradle. "Mom."

A sharp pain shot from his mouth to the crown of his head, causing him to hiss at the excruciating sensation. He cracked his left eye half open—something was covering his right—fighting the bright midafternoon light to keep it from closing. The blurry image of his mother swam in front of him, gradually coming into focus. She was smiling. The same sweet smile he had counted on all his life.

"Welcome back, honey." She beamed at him. "You gave us quite a scare."

Even though she had lived in Rhode Island and New York for more than twenty years, Allana Merritt—South Carolina-born and -bred—had never lost her Southern accent. Her habit of calling everyone "honey" was a source of endless amusement to her family.

"Amalie..."

Devin whispered in agony, tensing as the effort drove another laser-sharp streak of pain across his face. He searched his mother's eyes, finding some comfort there.

"She's with Diana. They're staying with us. Mallory is too distraught to..."

Her voice faded as Devin closed his eye in relief.

His baby was safe. For now. He pinned his mind on the image of his blond, blue-eyed baby girl who loved big hairbows and the color pink, who talked to stuffed animals and dolls, who was determined to be a princess when she grew up. That little girl needed her daddy to make up for a mother who wasn't worthy of the title.

Amalie needed him, so here he was. He was a medical mess—of this he had no doubt—but he was still here.

Devin sensed a movement on his right side; then his other hand was enfolded in a firm grip. His attempt to see past the bulky bandage was unsuccessful, but he was pretty sure who stood beside him.

"Dad?"

Again, a sharp stab of pain shot up toward his forehead. He closed his eye for a minute and tried to breathe until the pain subsided to a bearable ache.

"It might be better if you try to talk without moving your mouth," his father suggested.

Robert Merritt had always been Devin's rock. Nothing fazed him. Absolutely nothing. Contract negotiations worth millions of dollars. Unexpected pregnancies. Nothing. He was level-headed and logical. The voice of reason. Totally unflappable. Devin registered mild unease when he felt the slight tremor in the grip his father had on his hand.

"You mean like a ventriloquist?" Devin asked, without moving his lips. *Pretty good,* he mentally congratulated himself, except it was hard to say *ventriloquist* without moving his lips. He knew a healthy dose of irony underpinned his thought, but anyway, his dad was right. He didn't feel any shooting pain, only the same dull throbbing in his head that had been there since he opened his eyes...Well, eye. Speaking of which: "So...Dad?"

Robert moved closer, sitting on the bed, within Devin's range of sight. "Yes?" his father asked gravely, as if he knew—and dreaded—what was to come.

Devin's heartbeat accelerated. He had to know. He concentrated on keeping his breathing even and not moving his lips. "Dad, how bad is it?"

Robert hesitated, glancing at Allana. Devin didn't miss the silent communication between his parents. He just wished he understood it.

"Truth, Dad," he whispered. "Please."

Robert took a deep breath and gripped Devin's hand with both of his own. "You've lost your right eye, Devin."

Well, that explained the bandage; but from the look on Robert's face there was more. Devin peered into his father's eyes expectantly.

From the methodical way Robert explained Devin's condition, it sounded as if he had repeated the words a hundred times. He probably had. "The doctors managed to save your left eye; hopefully, your vision will be completely unimpaired. Your nose is broken, your right orbital bone is shattered, and your left one is cracked. You have multiple, deep facial lacerations. You will need extensive plastic surgery as soon as the swelling goes down." Robert's grip was firm on his son's hand. "Your right femur was broken—you've already had surgery for that—and you fractured four ribs. You also suffered a hefty concussion, but the bottom line is…You. Are. Alive. And we are blessed."

Robert squeezed Devin's hand before letting go. He stood from the bed then walked toward the light side of the room, out of Devin's vision—he had probably walked over to the window. But his son had seen the suspicious moisture gathering in the corners of his father's eyes. Well, that was a first. Devin had never—*never*—seen his father shed a tear.

He was both surprised and touched by Robert's loss of composure. Still reeling from discovering the full extent of his injuries, Devin tried desperately to lighten the mood. "Well," he quipped through stiff lips, "at least my contact lenses will be cheaper."

Of necessity, he had learned to use humor to take the sting out of any bad situation. Heaven knew he had had a lot of practice during the last four years of his miserable marriage. He clung to that well-honed coping mechanism now.

"Oh, De-e-ev," sobbed a female voice—which could belong only to his sister. He would know that sound anywhere. She had cried dramatically, at the slightest provocation, throughout her teen years. Devin felt just a tiny bit of brotherly guilt at the memories of deliberately provoking those tears… just for fun. But, back then, he had made certain *nobody* else made her cry.

"Lydia, you're here, too? Who else is hiding over there?"

Devin tried desperately to see. The realization that this wasn't a temporary impairment settled heavily on his mind.

"If you wanted time off, all you had to do was ask." The voice belonged to Blane McCallum, CEO of McCallum Industries, and Devin's boss. "I mean, this is extreme…even for you." Blane suddenly appeared at the corner of Devin's vision. "Some people will do anything to get out of a little work."

As the usual victim of Devin's teasing, Blane was taking advantage of the chance to get a little back. He was grinning, but his eyes were kind, and filled with genuine concern.

"What are you doing here? You're supposed to be wearing kilts and teaching Grace to play the bagpipes…or eat haggis…or doing something else Scottish." Wow. That was a lot of words without moving his mouth. Devin was impressed with himself. He was getting pretty good at this ventriloquist thing. Maybe he could get his own ventriloquist's dummy…

Blane raised his eyebrows at the man in the hospital bed who was a good friend as well as an employee. "Where would *you* be if I was lying in that bed?" he asked, softly, crossing his arms. Blane then explained that he and his fiancée had cut short their month-long trip to visit his family and ancestral home in Edinburgh as soon as they found out about Devin's accident.

"Scotland. I'd definitely be in Scotland," Devin lied, but there was gratitude in his eye.

Just then the appearance of the doctor made further conversation impossible. The next half hour was full of questions—which Devin did his best to answer without moving his mouth—and an endless amount of poking and prodding—which Devin did his best to tolerate without groans of pain emerging from his lips.

CHAPTER THREE

The cottage was nearly invisible, tucked behind heavy shrubbery, but sited close enough to the shore to warrant a spectacular view from the second-floor balcony. Strategically perched at the end of the point, it was sufficiently isolated to discourage visitors, but convenient to Douglas' Bellevue Avenue mansion. As usual, Douglas had chosen well.

The money Douglas had embezzled from his nephew's trust fund, in addition to the enormous amounts he had stolen from his father's accounts, had enabled him and Calli to finance their small-time criminal activities for years. And, eventually, to make big-time contacts. Over the course of the previous decade, their fledgling efforts in the illegal drug trade had become a well-oiled machine commanding a worldwide market. For the past four years, the lovely cottage had served as the strategic headquarters for their criminal operations. And as their own secret love nest. Thinking of that made Calli smile.

Even the accidental—and rather unfortunate—discovery of Douglas' thievery five months ago had not hindered their illegal operations. It only forced them to be more careful. And creative. It was no surprise when Blane forced Douglas to step down as president of the North American branch of McCallum Industries as soon as he discovered his uncle's perfidy. What *was* surprising was Blane's decision *not* to fire his disgraced uncle. Per the request of his beloved grandfather, Fergus McCallum, Blane reassigned Douglas to a lesser position in the company.

Calli both admired and disdained the sappy, old man's unending loyalty to the man who was robbing him blind. Fergus' plea for his wayward son played right into their hands. Douglas was able to assume his new role as a model employee while retaining his reputation as a devil-may-care playboy.

Douglas' never-ending pursuit of pleasure was fodder for the tabloids, celebrity talk shows, and social media. His hedonistic lifestyle supplied him with a number of labels: *Legendary lover. Notorious womanizer. Smooth Operator. Lady-killer. Player. Philanderer. Sybarite.* Of all the monikers, *lady-killer*, in Calli's opinion, was perhaps the most appropriate, for a variety of reasons. Calli tolerated the infidelity because it was the perfect cover. Douglas' one-night stands might be necessary to distract anyone from inquiring too closely into his other activities, but Calli didn't have to like them. Douglas' longtime lover, however, realized that ignoring his sexual proclivities was one of the requirements of maintaining a relationship with a very complicated man.

Calli looked at the clock on the bookshelf. Bill was late. Again. Anyone who callously disregarded his own instructions, acted on his own, and screwed things up this badly should, at the very least, have the courtesy to be punctual. Shouldn't he? Apparently not, Calli thought, sarcastically. Because, according to his own over-inflated ego, Bill wasn't just *anyone*, now was he?

Calli blew out a breath of frustration. This wasn't the first time that Billix Watson had gone rogue. The little bastard had been a liability since the night seventeen years ago when he bungled his first assignment. Drowning twelve-year-old Blane McCallum should have been easy. Not only was Bill bigger and stronger than the younger boy, he also had two accomplices—fellow students of the Herbert M. Ward School for Adolescent Boys. The job was a no-brainer if—and it proved to be a very big "if"—Bill and the two other morons had followed Calli's carefully orchestrated instructions.

But Billix Watson rarely followed Calli's instructions to the letter. Then or now. The cocky son of a bitch decided, on that particular night, that it would be more fun to beat the hell out of Blane *before* throwing him into the pond.

Bill's impulsiveness *could* have turned a simple "accidental" drowning into a murder scene. And there was no doubt he would have taken Calli down with him. Straight to prison. Fortunately, the other two boys understood the legal implications and refused to go along with Bill's asinine idea.

The entire situation blew up in Calli's face, anyway, when Douglas discovered what was going on behind his back. Funny how he already knew all the details *before* he confronted Calli with them. Whoever could have told him? No mystery there. Calli was still bitter about Bill's betrayal. To say Douglas reacted badly was an understatement. *No one* was allowed to conduct an operation without Douglas McCallum's knowledge and approval.

Instead of showing his appreciation for Calli's thoughtful attempt to spare him years of serving as the pathetic orphan's guardian, Douglas was livid. He was angrier than Calli had ever seen him. Before or since. Frighteningly angry. And Calli still had the scars to prove it. They served as a permanent reminder of the folly of crossing Douglas McCallum.

Calli glanced at the clock again. Twenty minutes late. Billix Watson was an inconsiderate asshole. And an unreliable screwup. He was becoming more of an encumbrance every day. And, shockingly, Douglas refused to admit it.

Fifteen-year-old Bill had been greedy and heartless. According to Calli's observations, he had not improved with age. Thirty-two-year-old Bill had no conscience, no sense of humor, no observable personality. He was remorseless and ice cold. Douglas, however, was of the firm conviction that Bill's loyalty to him was absolute.

It was Calli's personal opinion that Bill *was* absolutely loyal to one person. But that one person was Bill, not Douglas McCallum. Thus, Bill fell under the category of *high-risk employee*. And everybody knew that the best way to deal with a high-risk employee was to eliminate him. Or her, as the case may be. It wasn't anything they hadn't done before. They had successfully eliminated Kenneth Wade. Why not Billix Watson?

Because, to Calli's eternal amazement and disbelief, Douglas always said, "No." And that was *all* he said. "No." There were no embellishments. No excuses. And no explanations. Just *"No."* Calli didn't have the slightest idea why the mere suggestion of ridding the company—and the world—of the psychotic presence of Billix Watson was met with such complete resistance. Douglas wouldn't fire him outright. He wouldn't give him a permanent assignment in another country. And he flatly refused to order a hit on the man.

Even when Calli admitted to being frightened of Bill's unpredictability, Douglas only laughed. He *laughed*. And that laughter stung. One word from Calli had *always* been enough to make any difficult employee disappear. Permanently. But not Bill. And the worst part was, Douglas expected Calli to deal with the loathsome devil.

This time, though, Bill's actions had angered Douglas. And the insufferable ass couldn't possibly argue. The orders Calli was going to deliver came from Douglas himself.

The door to the office flew open, smacking against the wall: another classic example of Bill's carelessness. The dark-haired man immediately strutted in and plopped down on one of the midcentury modern chairs in front of Calli's trendy desk.

"Nice tan, Calli. Enjoy your trip?" Bill Watson's expressionless eyes belied the sincerity of his greeting.

"What the *hell* were you thinking?"

It was the only greeting Bill deserved. Calli sat down behind the desk, deliberately using it as a barrier. Being in the same room as the unpredictable man sprawled so casually in the chair did *not* inspire feelings of security. Nevertheless, Calli continued: "Our goal was accomplished. The problem was eliminated. Or so I thought…until I got back. Now, it seems *you've* created another problem, so I'm asking you again. What the hell were you thinking?"

Bill smiled smugly. "You got rid of Problem Number One. I got rid of Problem Number Two. Simple as that." He almost preened with self-indulgent pride. "Come on, Calli, admit it. *You* know you're impressed, and maybe a little sorry you didn't think of it yourself?"

Calli exploded. "I didn't think of it because I, unlike you, have a brain. Taking care of Wade was easy. He thought we had met his demands. We threw in a free cruise to seal the deal. We added in a zip-line excursion and he couldn't believe his good luck. It was easy to make it happen…Sketchy company, a little cash in the hands of a couple of locals, tragic accident. No questions—and no more Wade. Problem solved. But you, *you*..."

"Me? What do you mean *me*?"

Bill sat up, leaning a little forward. Calli definitely had his attention.

"What did *I* do?" he asked, warily. "Hit and run. Stolen car ditched and burned. Merritt's dead. Problem solved." As he ticked the points off his fingers, his confidence had returned. "You have to admit that Douglas will be happy when *he* finds out."

Calli looked at the ceiling, summoning the patience to make the arrogant little bastard understand. "First of all, Wade cancelled his meeting with Merritt after the payoff, so Merritt doesn't know anything. Second, Merritt isn't dead. He's in the hospital. Third, your whole setup looks deliberate, like attempted murder. It's only a matter of time until the questions start—and then...I hope to God you covered your tracks."

At Calli's words, Bill leaped to his feet, pacing around nervously. "Merritt's not dead? What is he...a cat with nine lives? He went straight into that fence. Damn it all to hell! Which hospital is he in? I'll go there now and pull his plugs or rip out his tubes or smother him with a pillow. Whatever I have to do...."

"No. You. Will. Not. You will listen to *me*, you brainless moron. You are, once again, overlooking one important fact." Calli paused for effect. "*You* aren't in charge of anything. You work for me. For *me*." Calli stood up, letting the words sink in before delivering the final blow. "You've really screwed things up this time, Bill. Douglas is *extremely* upset about this situation with Merritt."

All the bluster left Bill's face as he stopped pacing and faced the desk. "Douglas is upset? With *me*?" Standing in the middle of the room he looked like a sullen child...a very menacing child capable of untold violence.

"Douglas is upset with the *situation*," Calli said, carefully, holding out an envelope to the capricious chameleon across the desk. "*You* are leaving tonight for Mexico. You will lay low until you hear from me."

Billix took the envelope and looked inside. "A plane ticket?" he asked, stupidly.

"To Mexico. You can hide out at the compound until this thing with Merritt blows over. You're leaving tonight."

"Yeah...tonight."

Bill shoved the envelope into the back pocket of his jeans.

"Remember, don't do anything until you hear from *me*." Calli walked to the door and opened it, relieved that the interview was finally at an end. "Don't do anything on your own. Don't even think about doing anything on your own." Calli took a deep breath, glad to have the upper hand once again.

Bill walked to the door, pausing to stand uncomfortably close. "Yeah, I understand," he said softly, menacingly. "Hey, Calli, do you know why I like killing people myself?"

Calli remained perfectly still, looking mutely into eyes as cold as ice.

"It's the power," he said, placing his hands around Calli's throat, his thumbs pressing gently. "Just like that"—he jerked his thumbs hard, shutting off Calli's windpipe—"and it's over." He removed his hands just as quickly, his smile as chilling as his words. "See you around, Calli."

Then he was gone.

Calli staggered back to the desk, completely unnerved by what had just happened. Getting rid of people was an unfortunate necessity, not something to be enjoyed. Finding pleasure in the act, well...that was just unstable. What a huge relief to know that the disturbing man would be on a plane headed for Mexico in a few hours.

The phone rang twice before Calli glanced at the screen. Douglas...of course. Right on time.

CHAPTER FOUR

When Devin opened his eyes the next morning—*eye*, he soberly reminded himself—it was to find the face of his cousin.

"Diana," he said.

Pain rippled across his face. He automatically raised his hand, still surprised to feel the rough, jagged edges of the healing lacerations. He closed his eye, breathing deeply as his fingertips lightly brushed the lines that crisscrossed his once-smooth visage.

Ventriloquist. Ventriloquist, he reminded himself. *I am the ventriloquist, not the dummy.* Holding on to that reminder, he opened his eye. "Diana, sorry about that. Can't move my mouth."

"It's okay, Dev. You don't even have to talk if you don't want to. I'm just so…" Her voice broke a little and she looked away, trying to regain her composure. "I'm just so glad to see you, but…" She turned back to him and glared. "I'm still so mad at you. You scared me half to death. Your phone was connected the whole time. I heard the car hit you. And I kept calling your name, but you didn't answer. And then I heard people screaming and someone yelling to call 911. All I could do was listen. And cry. It was awful. And now…now I could just, I could just…Oh, Dev…" And she burst into tears, covering her face with her hands.

Devin was stunned at his cousin's show of emotion. She was crying. Real tears. His wife "cried" all the time, but he couldn't remember the last time *her* tears had been genuine. Real tears on Mallory's part might mar her perfect makeup. He felt a sheen of moisture in his own eyes…*Eye.*

When the sobbing let up a bit and Diana seemed a little calmer, he wracked his brain for something to say to make her feel better. "Di-an-a," he said, mimicking his Aunt Lucinda's intonation, to the decibel.

Diana's head came up, and she smiled, shakily. "Oh, Dev, you do that so well. Nobody can imitate Mom the way you can." She grabbed some tissues from the bedside table then disappeared into the bathroom to mop up.

Her face was a little splotchy when she returned a few minutes later: the delicate freckles covering her nose and cheeks stood out a bit more than usual. Her auburn hair was pulled back in a loose ponytail, the waves and curls under control for now. Her heavily fringed gray eyes were filled with compassion, but when she spoke, it was in the efficient way he recognized… employee to boss. In other words, she used her nanny voice.

"Now, I want to talk to you about Amalie. She's had a good week with the family. Uncle Rob and Aunt Allana have been here at the hospital most of the time, but Mom and Dad and Uncle Gary and Aunt Naomi have switched off."

Devin couldn't help but interrupt. "Is the whole family in Providence? Who's running the firm?"

His family was amazing. They really were.

"Nobody else is here, although they've been calling every five seconds to see if you're any better. 'The Boys' are taking care of the practice. Luckily it's a light week in Alexandria and nothing's going on in New York."

The Boys referred to Diana's brother, Roman, and Gary and Naomi's two sons, Lance and Connor. Devin had left the family law firm to work for McCallum Industries, just as his father before him. But Devin expected that, eventually, he, too, would return to the family business.

The four cousins would forever be called The Boys, it seemed, even though Roman had just turned thirty, the same age as Devin. Lance was thirty-seven while Connor would turn forty in September. Devin figured it would get a little confusing if The Boys ever managed to produce any boys of their own. So far, however, that was a nonissue.

Diana continued talking, knowing she had to proceed carefully. "So, as you can imagine, between the six of them, Amalie's having a wonderful time. But she misses you—and, Dev, she's worried. She really wants to see her daddy, and I thought…"

"No."

"But, Dev…"

"*No*, Diana." Devin's tone was flat and final. "She doesn't need to see…this."

Diana sighed. "It isn't going to matter, Dev. She's going to love you no matter what."

"*No*, Diana. Not yet. She may be ready, but I'm definitely not."

"All right, then." Diana knew better than to argue with a man who couldn't move his mouth. She would keep trying, though, in the coming days, because this was important for Amalie. "We've taken this week off from schoolwork. She colors in the princess book you gave her almost every day, and she sent you this."

Diana reached into her bag and carefully withdrew Amalie's latest project. She held the picture up for Devin's inspection.

It was from *Beauty and the Beast*. Devin tried not to think of the irony of Amalie's choice. He was currently experiencing a great deal of empathy for the Beast. Amalie's picture was of Belle and the Beast reading a book together. His baby girl was meticulous with her crayons, taking great pride in her neatness and ability to color inside the lines.

Devin studied the picture with his one eye. "For a four-year-old, I'd say that's pretty impressive. She uses those crayons better than I could."

"She's very good with her color choices, too. You may have a little artist on your hands." Diana turned the page over. "Don't miss this part."

Devin saw the letter *I* at the top of the page and the letter *U* at the bottom, with *AMALIE* scrawled underneath; but he squinted, with difficulty, at the center of the drawing. "What's that red blob in the middle? A pizza?"

"It's a heart, Devin. For love. It says, 'I love you.' Duh. Why would she write 'I pizza you'?" Diana sniffed in disgust before she realized Devin had been kidding. "Oh, ha ha," she said, shaking her head. "I'm so glad you haven't lost your awful sense of humor." She started to put the picture back in her bag.

"No, don't put it away. Hang it up somewhere so I can see it."

She looked around, spotting the dresser in the corner of the room. "Which side do you want to see?" she asked.

"The side with the pizza, please," Devin said.

He watched Diana fuss with the picture until she was satisfied. Then he braced himself for the next part of the conversation. "So, it sounds like I've had a lot of visitors," he said.

She sat down beside his bed. "You have. Besides the family, Blane has been here every day, sometimes twice. Grace has come, too. She's also helping out with Amalie; I forgot to tell you that. And three of the admins from McCallum stopped by yesterday to bring you the daisies over there." Diana grinned. "They were hilarious. Also, the phone rings constantly—people want to know how you are. We've even gotten a couple of calls from Scotland. People seem to like you, Devin. I can't think why."

Although she was teasing him, and he knew it, she couldn't quite meet his eye.

They had talked around the elephant in the room long enough.

"So, Diana, I don't suppose that..."

Diana interrupted before he could even say the name of his errant wife. He was a little surprised by the vehemence of her response. "No, Devin. Mallory hasn't been here. She just hasn't been able to tear herself away from her social calendar. Her doctor says that she has suffered such a trauma that she *must* stay on a regular schedule, for the sake of her mental health."

"*She* has suffered such a trauma," Devin echoed in disbelief.

"Yes, poor thing. Her husband was injured, didn't you know?" Diana's voice oozed with sarcasm. "It's been sooo difficult for her. She's in such a state that she can't properly fulfill her motherly duties." Diana gave a *very* fake cough and raised her eyebrows. "Like there's ever been any chance of her doing that in the first place. Honestly, Devin, I was fully prepared to stay with Amalie at your house around the clock, or to take her somewhere else by force. It didn't matter what I had to do. No way was I going to leave 'Malie with your sorry, self-obsessed excuse for a wife. I don't trust Mallory alone with that little girl for two seconds. And neither do you." Diana had shifted from sarcasm to fierce protectiveness without taking a breath.

Devin thanked God once again for the series of events that had led to the hiring of Amalie's nanny. Diana was the best thing that could have happened to his little girl. And to him.

A new visitor knocked lightly on the door. Blane popped his head into the room as Diana finished her tirade. "Am I interrupting or…"

Blane paused, taking in Diana's red face and defensive posture.

Diana shook her head, smiling ruefully. "Come in, Blane. We were just discussing the absent Mrs. Merritt."

Blane grimaced. "Seems to me that absence is a blessing. She's the last thing Devin needs to deal with right now." Blane's distaste for Devin's spouse was written plainly on his face. "Grace had an interesting conversation with Mallory when she went to pick up some more clothes for Amalie this morning. Interesting in a bad way. My lovely fiancée was all fired up when she got back to the apartment." He glanced at Diana. "Get Grace to tell you about it. She's in the waiting room with Rafe at the end of the hall. The nurse on duty today isn't as forgiving as the one from yesterday. 'Only two visitors to the room at a time, please.'" Blane mimicked the new nurse's high-pitched voice. "She talked to me like I was five years old." He shook his head sorrowfully.

"In other words, 'Get out, Diana. Rafe and I need to talk to Devin privately.'" Diana stood from her chair and headed for the door. "No problem. I know when I'm not wanted. Hmph."

She left the room, tossing her head in a sassy gesture that made Blane grin. Devin grinned, too…in his head.

Rafe Montgomery was fascinating…one of the most fascinating people Devin had ever met. His official job title at McCallum Industries was personal assistant to the CEO. He was, however, involved in almost every aspect of the company, particularly in the area of security. He had a keen mind and a sharp wit, and he was unconditionally devoted to Blane. That same devotion, thankfully, extended to Blane's family and friends. Devin had spent many an enjoyable hour picking the brain of the complex man who seemed to know a little something about everything.

But who was Rafe Montgomery? Was that even his real name? Was he ex-CIA, ex-SIS—or MI6, as the British preferred to call it—or a member of some other country's elite organization? Was he in a witness protection program, or hiding out as a fugitive? Devin wasn't exactly sure, and he wasn't alone. Blane had privately admitted as much the last time Rafe disappeared on one of his "errands." The fact that Blane—who was twelve years old when he met Rafe—still had no answers was a slight conciliation to Devin. Both of them knew, however, that Rafe was unequivocally trustworthy, in spite of—or perhaps because of—the hidden secrets of his past. No doubt about it: they felt better when he was around.

As soon as Rafe walked into his hospital room, Devin knew his appearance was no ordinary social visit. In his early seventies, Rafe was still strong and impressively fit. His alert gaze missed nothing as his eyes darted around the room, assessing its acceptability. When he relaxed his focused inspection, Devin relaxed, too…but only momentarily. Rafe turned his intense perusal on the man in the bed. He seated himself in the chair that Blane now vacated.

The sudden understanding of why the chair had been placed in that exact location hit Devin hard, nearly stealing his breath. The chair was on his left side, he realized, because that was the side with his good eye. With his *only* eye, he reminded himself, soberly.

"Tell me everything," Rafe said, in a voice that brooked no argument.

Devin turned both palms over, raising his hands slightly. He mentally shrugged his shoulders, his sore ribs hindering actual movement. "I was run over by an Uber."

Silence. His statement was met by blank looks from Rafe, staring at him from the chair, and from Blane, leaning against the wall.

Finally, Rafe looked at Blane. "What kind of drugs are they giving him?"

"Tylenol during the day. He's refused anything stronger except at night." Blane nodded his approval.

Devin cleared his throat. "I'm right here. Why don't you just ask me?"

Rafe grimaced. "Because your first answer sounded a little bit like you were out of your head." He paused, studying Devin's expression. "I guess it's possible that you don't know…"

"Know what?" asked Devin uneasily. He was starting to have a bad feeling about the conversation….

"You were *not* run over by an Uber," Rafe said. "Your Uber was supposed to be a blue Prius. You were hit by a blue sedan."

"Prius. Sedan. I only knew that it was blue and headed to the right pick up spot. I was on the phone with Diana and, um…a little upset at the time."

Devin made this admission grudgingly. Now that he thought about it, he should have checked the model of the car that was picking him up. That was just common sense. *Thanks a lot, Mallory.*

"Ah, and I'll bet your lovely viper, Mallory, had something to do with the upset." Rafe nodded. "I understand a little better now. You usually aren't that careless."

"Thanks…I think."

Devin mentally furrowed his brow, congratulating himself on his newfound ability to include mental facial expressions in his regular conversations. He was going to make one hell of a ventriloquist.

"So…who hit me?" he asked.

"That's what we're trying to find out. The sedan was stolen from a parking garage several blocks away. Cameras on the bank—two buildings down from the place where you were hit—show that the driver waited until you came out of the restaurant. As soon as you reached the sidewalk, he—or she—came straight at you, making no effort to slow down. Then he—or she—sped away immediately after hitting you. After the accident, the car was abandoned in a remote field outside of town and set on fire, obviously in an effort to hide any evidence."

"Wait a minute."

Devin gasped, forgetting not to move his mouth. The pain was still a surprise but seemed to fade away more quickly this time. He paused a moment, watching as Rafe and Blane exchanged another look.

"What do you mean the driver waited for me to come out?" he asked. "You sound like you're saying it wasn't an accident. That someone hit me deliberately. That someone tried to kill me."

"That's exactly what I'm saying," Rafe said, calmly. "Someone tried to kill you, and we want to know who and why. Is there anyone you can think of that would like to—"

"Get rid of me? Do away with me? Wipe my name from the face of the earth?" Devin said. "With the exception of Mallory and, possibly, her dear friend, Desiree…no." Devin couldn't think of a single person who would want him dead. He had mentioned his wife and her friend as a jest, but Rafe's next comment wasn't funny at all.

"We've already checked both of them and eliminated the possibility," Rafe said, seriously.

"You've got to be joking," Devin said in surprise.

"I assure you, Devin, I am not joking. We've checked your cell phone, work computer and email, your personal email, and every business contact you've had in the last month."

Rafe had been busy. That answered Devin's question regarding why he hadn't heard from him since the accident.

"Did you find anything?" Devin couldn't quite believe this was actually happening. It was one thing for someone to want him dead. It was another thing, entirely, not to know who wanted to kill him. He suddenly sat up in bed, ignoring the throbbing pain radiating from his torso. "Amalie," he hissed. "Someone has to protect Amalie! Please, Rafe…." He was sweating from the torture of the sudden movement, black dots dancing in front of his eyes—eye—and in the throes of sudden nausea.

Blane took a step toward him, but before he could reach the bed, Rafe stood up and gently pushed Devin back onto his pillow. He gripped Devin's shoulders and met his eyes, compassion in his voice. Rafe had had his own little girl, once; now he spoke to Devin as only a father could. "Amalie was the first thing we took care of, Devin. That's why she's staying with your parents. It's easier to keep a twenty-four-hour watch on her there. I promise you, she's completely safe."

Devin relaxed against the pillows, willing his heart to slow down and his stomach to settle. Rafe helped him to drink from the half-filled cup of ginger ale sitting on the table by his bed. Devin would have preferred brandy or scotch or whiskey or…hell, why not champagne? It wasn't every day that a man found out someone wanted him dead. When he opened his eye, he found himself under the intense scrutiny of Rafe and Blane.

"Should we call for the nurse?" Blane asked Devin, anxiously.

"No…no. I'm all right. Please, just tell me the rest. Tell me all of it."

He braced himself and waited for Rafe to continue.

"What do you know about a man named Kenneth Wade?"

Devin thought for a few moments. "Kenneth Wade? I don't think I…Wait a minute. I do know that name. He's from the North American office, from the acquisition department. Very pushy. He called me several times demanding a meeting. He didn't *ask* for a meeting, he demanded one. I finally told Karen to put him on my calendar just to get him off my back. The day before the meeting, he cancelled on me. I guess you guys already knew all that from my emails. I was going to follow up this week, but…" His voice trailed off. *I was run over by an Uber.* Devin sighed. He liked that version of his accident so much better.

"Kenneth Wade took an impromptu cruise to Cozumel and Belize over the weekend. He flew out of JFK the afternoon before your meeting was scheduled. On Monday, he went on an excursion…zip-lining or something. Anyway, there was an accident. The harness broke and he fell. He's dead." Rafe didn't say anything else for a moment.

"Well," said Devin into the silence. "Isn't that a coincidence?"

"It very well could be," said Rafe. "We're trying to figure out if his death and your 'hit and run' are related. As of today, we can't find any connection, other than the cancelled meeting."

Nobody spoke for several seconds.

Finally, Blane broke the silence. "We have a suggestion, Devin. Well, it's really more than that. We strongly recommend that you have your next surgery in North Carolina, at Duke Hospital in Durham. It's one of the best facilities in the country for facial reconstruction. Between surgeries, you can recover in Honeysuckle Creek, at Heart's Ease. We have superior security there. We can protect you while you heal."

Blane's childhood home was a beautifully renovated plantation house surrounded by horse pastures and a substantial creek on three sides. It was quiet, peaceful, and secure…the perfect place for Devin to recover from his ordeal, both physically and mentally.

"And Amalie?"

For now, Devin wanted to spare his little girl the stress of his recovery. He might change his mind, but he doubted it. He wanted her to stay right where she was…safe, secure, and innocent of the ugliness surrounding his accident. Or should he call it an attack? He couldn't quite bring himself to say *attempted murder*, even in his head.

"Amalie and Diana can join you when you feel up to it. Mallory, too, if you wish," Blane added, politely.

Rafe didn't say anything, just crossed his arms and let out a disgusted, "Hmph."

"Mallory?…'Quiet and peaceful'? Doesn't sound like her kind of place. You're watching over her too, aren't you?" Devin felt almost guilty for his belated inquiry into his wife's safety. Almost.

"Mallory refused to relocate to your parents' house with Amalie," Rafe informed him. "She said it would be too much for her nerves. So, we're watching your house, too." Rafe raised his eyebrows. "Her nerves seem fine so far, according to Emmanuel, the lucky man currently assigned as her bodyguard. Excessive shopping trips are the only things he's recorded as odd so far." Choosing not to comment on Devin's heartless spouse, he continued briskly, "So, Devin, how do you feel about the plan?"

Rafe's expression was so full of pity that it made Devin a little uncomfortable. "Why do I have the feeling that—even if I say 'no'—it's not really my choice?" he asked ruefully. "I bow to your superior wisdom, Yoda. I trust your judgement, and Obi-Wan's over there." He glanced at Blane. "I willingly put myself in your hands." His *Star Wars* references broke the tension, causing Rafe to chuckle.

Blane grinned. "Good answer. Because we've already made the arrangements. We're leaving tomorrow."

CHAPTER FIVE

Honeysuckle Creek, North Carolina
August 2017

*D*arcie Finch studied herself in the mirror. The reflection looking back at her was flawless. Her features were perfectly symmetrical. No freckles or moles dared mar her smooth, glowing complexion. Elegantly sculpted brows arched over darkly mysterious eyes accented by thick, inky lashes. Her gorgeous smile was perfectly formed by a pair of rosebud lips and straight, white teeth. Her ears were delicate shells. Her exquisite visage was enhanced by shiny hair of the darkest midnight black, pulled into a smooth knot at the top of her head.

She had never had braces on her teeth. She didn't need glasses or contacts, being blessed with perfect vision. Her hair always cooperated, even in the thick humid heat of a long Southern summer. She didn't have to diet to maintain her enviable figure. She had a genuine love of physical fitness, running in particular. As a matter of fact, she had to make an effort to consume extra calories so she wouldn't lose weight. (She preferred to keep that particular bit of information to herself…for obvious reasons!) Her makeup routine rarely consisted of anything more than a good moisturizer and a little mascara. In other words, Darcie didn't try to be beautiful. She just was.

Her beauty wasn't the kind to go unnoticed, either. Oh, no. No such luck for Darcie Finch. She was a showstopper or, at the very least, a traffic stopper. She wasn't proud of it, but it was true. She had actually stopped traffic while walking down Main Street in the town she called home. Twice.

Honeysuckle Creek was located in the foothills of North Carolina, conveniently close to the Blue Ridge Parkway. Over the last two decades, it had transformed itself from a sleepy farm town—with an economy based on tobacco and dairy cows—to a popular tourist destination. The number of boutiques, restaurants, and unique specialty stores continued to grow and diversify, to the delight of locals and visitors alike. The crowds were heaviest on weekends and during the fall of the year, due to the draw of the beautiful autumn foliage. But there was always a steady stream of visitors…visitors who had never seen the goddess that was Darcie Finch.

The locals, for the most part, were used to Darcie. She adored them for their loving indifference to—what she had dubbed for years—her *problem looks*. Strangers, however, were a different story. She could handle the children. They tended to gaze up at her with awestruck expressions, asking if she was a princess, or a good witch. Always a *good* witch. Bad witches were ugly. Everybody knew that.

The reactions of the female set varied. Sometimes, they were sweet, their admiration quite genuine. But, often—more often than she would have liked—they looked down their jealous noses at her, making cruel comments she couldn't help but overhear. Out of necessity, she had developed something of an immunity to the barbs of the "mean girls."

At this point in her life, it was the men that bothered Darcie the most. Those close to her own age were the absolute worst. It wasn't all of them. And, fortunately, it wasn't all the time. To be fair, she had met a few nice guys here and there. The majority of them, however, acted like she was the sweet shop's treat of the week. The older she got, the less patience she had with their pathetic attempts to gain her attention, particularly when they assumed that—because she was attractive—she didn't have a brain in her head. The persistent fellow who didn't get the message was in for an impressive set-down, politely administered, of course. Darcie was raised in the South, where being polite was an unwritten law. If the speaker crossed the line separating *complimentary* from *inappropriate*, however, he did so at his own risk. She had inherited her great-grandmother's wicked tongue, and she didn't hesitate to use it.

She still remembered the day she made the decision to be more than merely a pretty face. It was during a visit from Martha Fremont, one of the caretakers—she didn't want to be called a *librarian*—of the Honeysuckle Creek Public Library. She was the scary one, the one who didn't understand how impossible it was for children to be quiet in a library.

On that particular day, Miss Fremont was soliciting funds for the children's wing of the library. She was also dropping unsubtle hints to Darcie's mother, Juli, as to the behavior of *Juli's* children in the sacred portals of the library. Hints Juli was adept at picking up on. It was rather like a one-sided tennis match, with one opponent refusing to return a volley.

Had Darcie realized that her mother's visitor was Miss Fremont, she would never have run into the room. Her nine-year-old face fell in dismay.

Juli, however, looked incredibly happy to see her. After pulling Darcie into a gentle hug, she kept her arm around her daughter's waist, refusing to let go.

When Darcie looked up in surprise, she saw the determination behind her mother's sweet smile. She sighed a nine-year-old sigh, relaxing against her mama. When Mama had that look on her face, her word was law. Darcie knew that she wasn't going anywhere. Together, they faced the nemesis of the children of Honeysuckle Creek.

Juli fixed her silent daughter with her best teacher gaze. "Say hello to Miss Fremont, Darcie."

"Hello, Miss Fremont," Darcie repeated dutifully. She added, "You old bat," in her head. She had a feeling her mama was doing the same thing.

"Miss Fremont was just telling me how much she enjoys it when you and your brother and sister visit the library," said Juli, politely, putting a positive spin on the details she had just received.

Darcie didn't say anything.

"Darcie," Miss Fremont replied. "I haven't seen you in the library for a few weeks. I'm pretty sure that you have a couple of over-due books by now." She cut her squinty gaze in Juli's direction. Her mouth was screwed up with distaste, as if she was sucking on a lemon.

Darcie thought she looked like a prune.

"See that you take care of that for me, will you, Juliette?" It was not a question, but a demand.

Juli nodded her head graciously.

Miss Fremont had been the librarian since Juli learned to read. Miss Fremont had once accused six-year-old Juli of spilling coffee on a brand-new copy of The Cat in the Hat. Her accusation was ridiculous for two reasons. The book had already sported a dried coffee stain on page 12 the first time Juli opened it. And, most importantly, little girls didn't drink coffee. It was common knowledge, however, that Miss Fremont was never without a cup of coffee in her hand.

That bit of information exhausted the patience of Mrs. Sofia Hanover, Juli's grandmother. Sofi had never liked the uppity Miss Fremont much anyway. The blistering set-down Miss Martha Fremont received that day from Mrs. Hanover, in the Honeysuckle Creek Public Library, was the stuff of legend. After more than twenty years, no love had been lost between Juliette Finch and the arrogant woman seated on her couch.

Miss Fremont looked Darcie over from head to toe, then sighed, heavily. "I declare, Juliette, your children are as different as night and day."

Juli asked, cautiously, "What do you mean, Miss Fremont?" Her arm tightened around her daughter: an unconscious gesture of support.

Darcie knew that in the librarian's eyes she was the least favorite of the Finch siblings, probably due to Miss Fremont's nasty cat, Mr. Kittypaws. That was actually his name. Mr. Kittypaws. How could anyone do that to a cat? No wonder he was so angry. How was Darcie supposed to know that the scraggly thing wasn't allowed outside the exalted domain of the public library? What was she supposed to do? Let it hiss at her and give her arm another long scratch? She was only trying to be friendly, but the cat scared her. So did her big brother's ominous prediction of the deadly case of Cat Scratch Fever she had surely acquired from her first attempt to befriend the creature. So, she had opened the library's front door and watched as the cat put his scrawny tail in the air, prancing outside and scurrying right up a tree.

Miss Fremont had to call the fire department to rescue her nasty cat. And nothing Darcie did after that could get her back in the librarian's good graces.

"Well," Miss Fremont said, smiling coldly at Darcie. "Joey is such a wonderful athlete. It seems like he plays well in every sport, and Grace is so talented. She can sing and dance. It's amazing, really. I love to see her in her little school and church plays."

Miss Fremont paused, malice dancing in her squinty eyes. "As for Darcie, well…" She paused, again, as if she was struggling to think of an area in which Darcie excelled. "Hmm. I guess Joey is the athletic one. And Grace is the talented one. And Darcie, well…Darcie is the beautiful one." She said beautiful as if it was an accusation. The vindictive woman sighed heavily. "It's a pity she'll never be anything else. Just another pretty face." Her smile turned cruel at the surprised look on Darcie's face.

Direct hit.

Juli rose from her seat as if the house was on fire. "Just look at the time," she gasped, desperately, even though no clock was to be seen anywhere in the room. She wasn't even wearing a watch. "Thank you for stopping by, Miss Fremont. I'll talk to Joe and let you know about our donation."

She practically pulled Miss Fremont out of her seat and propelled her across the family room, rushing her into the hall. She opened the door and walked onto the porch with the librarian. Juli, clearly, wanted Miss Fremont out of her house, far from her daughter, before she spoke her mind. As soon as they stepped onto the porch, Darcie's gentle mother gave the haughty librarian a tongue-lashing the hateful woman would never forget.

"Miss Fremont," Juli began. "Let me make one thing crystal clear. You *do not* get to put a label on *my* children. Do you understand me? You *do not* get to decide who is athletic or talented or beautiful. My children are all of those things, but they are so much more. They're smart and funny and capable." Juli leaned closer to Miss Fremont, whose mouth was hanging open in disbelief.

It was very unattractive.

Juli stared at the woman for a few seconds until Miss Fremont closed her mouth. Then she spoke very clearly so the caretaker wouldn't miss a word: "And added to that, they are kind. Something that they didn't learn from their local librarian, I might add. They would never go out of their way to hurt someone. Maybe it's time you took a page from that book."

Miss Fremont opened her mouth to reply but was denied the chance of a rebuttal.

"Have a nice day, Miss Fremont."

Juli slammed the door and turned around, intent on repairing any damage that had been done to her baby. She nearly tripped over Darcie, who was standing right behind her.

"Oh, Darcie. Oh, honey, I'm sorry. I didn't know you were behind me."

"You made her leave," said Darcie, in awe. She had heard the whole thing.

Juli was pink-cheeked and a little breathless. "Well, of course I made her leave, the old bat. She can't come into our house and talk to you like that. She isn't any nicer than she was when I was a little girl." She gathered her thoughts. "Don't call someone an old bat, Darcie. It isn't nice."

"Mama," said Darcie, throwing herself into her mother's waiting arms. "I don't want to be the beautiful one. I want to be good at something, too." She thought about it for a minute. "If Joey is the athletic one and Gracie is the talented one, then I want to be the smart one. Mama, can I be the smart one?"

"You already are," Juli responded, tears in her eyes.

"I am?" Darcie asked, breathlessly. "How can you tell, Mama?"

"Because you, my dear, have already figured out that what you look like on the outside isn't as important as what you are like on the inside."

Darcie never forgot that day or her decision to be *the smart one*. As she got older, she realized that her athletic brother and talented sister were extremely intelligent in their own right. She also discovered that she had her own athletic and musical skills. But she never lost the desire to excel.

Her academic focus paid off. She received the Morehead Scholarship, graduating Phi Beta Kappa from the University of North Carolina, with a double major in history and political science and a minor in public policy analysis. She chose to attend law school at UNC, in part for the familial connection as well as the fact that she loved the university and the town of Chapel Hill. She couldn't resist the opportunity to spend three more years there after graduation.

And, now, she was a third-year law student at the top of her class with several post-graduate opportunities lined up in front of her. The best—and current frontrunner—was the invitation she received only yesterday from the Merritt Brothers Law Firm in Alexandria, Virginia after completing her summer internship at the firm. But, even after all of her hard work and success, the majority of people never looked past her beautiful face.

Darcie was tired, so very tired, of trying to avoid false overtures of superficial people. No matter how plainly she dressed or wore her hair, she never seemed able to fade into the background. She garnered attention whether she wanted it or not. She had heard the same words all her life: flawless, incomparable, gorgeous, exquisite, stunning, ideal complexion, perfect figure, mesmerizing eyes, a dream walking. What did they mean to her? Absolutely nothing.

There were other words…words that mattered. Smart, capable, kind, compassionate, talented, clever, creative. Those were the words she craved. She couldn't care less about appearances. She was interested in substance.

Darcie sighed as she finished washing her hands, pausing long enough to wrinkle her nose and stick out her tongue at her perfect reflection. Taking a deep breath, she traded her temporary sanctuary—the ladies' room of Jack's Restaurant—for the coffee-to-go counter.

CHAPTER SIX

After placing her order for a Cinnamon Whip Latte, Darcie took a seat on the narrow bench by the door. She smiled and waved at several friends she knew eating breakfast across the restaurant. The sight of familiar faces filled her with warmth. She was glad to be back in her hometown, even if it was only for a few days. Relaxing against the bench, she enjoyed the chance to check her email and skim her Twitter account while remaining relatively undisturbed.

Darcie was addicted to Jack's coffee. There was no other way to explain it. Home fewer than twenty-four hours—and here she was. Oh, well, she rationalized. There were worse vices than steaming, fragrant, cinnamon-tasting bliss. After the intensive internship she had just completed, she had earned a few cups of Jack's signature Cinnamon Whip Latte.

Her first internship with Merritt Brothers took place the summer after her junior year in college. It involved, for the most part, hours and hours of research. She also made lots and lots of copies. Occasional orders to pick up at the local coffeeshop had been thrown in for good measure. She didn't mind, because being a part of one of the most successful law firms on the East coast made starting at the bottom worth the effort.

Darcie's second internship at Merritt Brothers, however, had been a completely different experience. Fresh from her second year of law school, she was assigned to Roman Merritt, who specialized in family law. Being Roman's intern left her with zero free time. She rarely went back to the apartment she shared with her brother, Joey, without taking work with her.

That didn't stop any of the other lawyers, however, from "borrowing" her on a number of occasions. She was surprised to find herself in high demand. And, for once, it was because of her professional abilities. While being respected for her brain was indeed gratifying, it was also exhausting. Darcie hadn't left Alexandria once the whole summer. But she *had* gotten the chance to spend at least part of one day with each of the partners at Merritt Brothers. And, she had worked with several of the younger lawyers, including Lance and Connor Merritt, and her own brother. The previous morning, the partners at Merritt Brothers extended an invitation for Darcie to return for a formal interview after her law school graduation. According to Joey, that request was practically the same as a job offer. To Darcie, it seemed that all of her hard work was coming to fruition. Her future goals were finally within reach.

"Hey, Darcie!"

Her reverie ended abruptly, followed by the realization of how ridiculous she must look staring into space, with a silly smile on her face.

"Hey, Zack!"

Darcie warmly greeted the grinning young man. She had known Zack all his life. She was, in fact, one of the few babysitters brave enough to return to the Kimel household more than once. Taking care of the youngest of the four Kimel brothers had been a significant challenge. Zack was tall and skinny, still growing into his lanky frame. His usually unruly brown hair was neatly trimmed in a newer, shorter style. Darcie noticed Zack wasn't wearing his ever-present baseball cap. Despite his youthfulness, he exuded the confidence of a young man who had all the answers, even though the ink had barely dried on his diploma. He handed Darcie her coffee with a flourish.

As the son of hard-working parents, Zack had spent his eighteen years growing up in the high-energy atmosphere of Jack's. His parents poured every ounce of their time and energy into making the restaurant worth a detour to passersby. Jack's reputation for cookies and pancakes—*"The Place for Snacks, Packs, and Stacks"*—did not disappoint. Jack's older brothers—Jack, Jr.; Eli; and Newton ("Newt," for short)—were completely devoted to the family business. After his parents produced three children who were perfect cookie-cutter likenesses of their father, Zack came as something of a shock. He was an unexpected surprise—his mother's explanation—born when Newt, his closest brother in age, had just turned eight. Zack's family adored its youngest member. They really did. But Zack was…different. Oh, he loved the business, was proud to be a part of it, and equally proud to be a Kimel. But he was the first to admit he never quite fit in.

It was Zack's private opinion that his beloved family's devotion to cookies and pancakes bordered on the obsessive. As a result, he had carved out his own unique place in his family tree. He was the cutup. The quintessential class clown. The goofy guy always good for a laugh. Zack's persona allowed him to hide his sharp, observant mind under the guise of super-slackness and chronic boredom.

During his senior year in high school, however, Zack had come into his own. The positive changes the young man had made over the past year were due, in part, to his involvement with the Honeysuckle Creek Academy's Show Choir and theater program. Under the tutelage of the academy's theater teacher, Evander Mayfield, and Darcie's sister, Grace—Zack's long-suffering English teacher—Zack gained confidence in his own abilities. He also became a protégé, of sorts, of Grace's fiancé, Blane McCallum, and Grace's ex-fiancé, Roger Carrington. Zack's neat haircut and appearance could be attributed to his mentors' positive influence. Dating sweet Emma Lewis had been the final piece of the puzzle.

Darcie could see that her little Zack had grown into a fine, young man. She surreptitiously wiped an unexpected tear from her eye, after making sure no one was looking. She was ridiculously soft-hearted, a little-known fact she tried very hard to hide. It wouldn't do for someone to report that Darcie Finch had been crying at Jack's. Small town gossip was to be avoided at all costs.

MACEE MCNEILL

Darcie glanced up to check the time, her eyes drawn to the giant chocolate chip cookie clock that had hung behind the counter for as long as she could remember. She watched its eyes move back and forth with every *tick tock*, wondering why looking away always proved so hard. She had twenty minutes before she was supposed to meet her sister at the bridal shop. And, today, she was determined to be on time. Punctuality was one virtue in which she was sadly lacking.

Her peaceful interlude was broken when a man she had never seen before walked into Jack's. He studied the menu and ordered his coffee before looking around for an open seat. He was of average height, with sandy, brown hair, probably in his early thirties. He glanced at her with a smile. Motioning to the other end of the bench, he raised his eyebrows, inquiring as to its availability. She nodded slightly, quickly looking back at her cell phone. Her instincts went on high alert.

He seated himself at the end of the bench. "That smells delicious," he said, giving her another friendly smile.

"Excuse me?" Darcie said, trying to remember what kind of lotion she was wearing so she wouldn't wear it in public again.

"Your coffee. It smells delicious," he said smoothly.

"Oh, my coffee," Darcie smiled, feeling a little foolish for automatically assuming he was talking about her appearance. "It's Cinnamon Whip Latte," she volunteered. "And it tastes as good as it smells."

"You can change your order, if you want," said a voice from behind the bench.

Zack had appeared out of nowhere, busily cleaning off one of the tables that had just been vacated.

"I think I will," said the stranger, rising from the bench. He returned a minute later, sitting closer to the middle this time. He placed his arm along the back of the bench, his hand nearly touching Darcie's shoulder.

"Say," he began, smoothly.

Darcie looked up, cutting her eyes from his hand to his face and back again. He got the message, bending his elbow to lessen the proximity of his hand.

"Say," he began, turning toward her again. "Has anyone ever told you that you are drop-dead gorgeous?"

Well, that took a little longer than usual, Darcie thought. *But here we go.*

She looked the stranger straight in the eye and lied through her teeth. "No," she said, evenly, "no one has ever said anything even remotely like that to me ever before in all my life. *Ever.*" She deliberately finished with a strong emphasis on the last word. She looked back down at her phone, hoping she had successfully concluded her part of the conversation.

Darcie heard Zack clear his throat as he moved to the table closest to her, busily wiping the already pristine surface.

"Well, now, that's a shame," the stranger purred. "I can't stand for a beautiful woman to be unappreciated." He paused, leaning closer and lowering his voice, "Listen, honey, I've got some time. Maybe we could go somewhere…"

Ok, Creepy Stranger. That's enough. Warning bells resounded in Darcie's head. *Your luck just ran out.* She opened her mouth to tell him exactly what she thought of his invitation, only to be interrupted.

"Hey, Darcie."

Zack's voice broke in just in time to save the stranger from Darcie's scathing reply.

"Listen, dude," the stranger growled, oblivious to the fact that his dignity had just been spared. "Don't you have anything else to do but clean that table?"

"Why no, sir," Zack said, innocently. "Here at Jack's we strive to incorporate cleanliness into every aspect of our job. Thank you for noticing." Zack stepped to Darcie's end of the bench. "I forgot to tell you that Bubba called and left a message for you." He was looking hard at Darcie, encouraging her to go along with him.

"Bubba?"

Darcie hesitated, not sure what Zack wanted her to say.

"Bubba, your *hus-band.*" Zack tilted his head, giving her a knowing look.

"Oh, that Bubba," said Darcie, nodding her head.

"You mean there's more than one?" the stranger asked, a confused expression on his face.

"In a town this size in the South?" Darcie said smugly. "You have no idea." She turned expectantly to Zack. "So, what did dear Bubba have to say?" she inquired pleasantly.

Zack turned to the stranger. "Bubba…that's her husband," he explained.

"I gathered that," the stranger said, and rolled his eyes impatiently. He leaned back, crossing his ankle over his knee, much to Darcie's amusement.

"You ought to see old Bubba," said Zack, warming to his story. "He's a cop with huge arms. Man, you have never seen arms like Bubba's. And his legs… like tree trunks. He has a bad temper, too. He's the kind that punches first and asks questions later, if you know what I mean." Zack punched the palm of his hand with his fist. "Do you?" he asked.

"Do I what?" The stranger was thoroughly annoyed.

"Do you know what I mean?" Zack asked with a grin.

Darcie smirked. She knew it was rude, but she couldn't help it.

Zack turned his attention back to Darcie. "Anyway, old Bubba said you didn't have to wait for him. Said he was on a call. Been looking for some guy who's harassing women. They found the guy. So, don't you worry about that. But apparently, he—the guy, not Bubba—had some kind of an accident while Bubba was apprehending him. They're waiting on the ambulance right now. Or was it the coroner? I can't remember. Anyway, old Bubba has to go fill out some paperwork and change his shirt because of the blood stains, so he's gonna be late."

"Cinnamon Whip Latte for Harold." Zack's middle brother, Eli, was working the coffee takeout..

" 'Harold'?" Zack chuckled, raising his eyebrows at Eli. He flashed some sort of signal behind Harold's back as he stood to retrieve his coffee. Zack's brother nodded once in understanding.

Harold cast one last regretful glance at Darcie as he walked by. He hesitated for a split second until his eyes strayed to Zack, who punched his palm with his fist again. That seemed to make up Harold's mind. He picked up his coffee from the counter then headed out the door, bringing the cup to his lips as he reached the sidewalk. Poor Harold never got to enjoy his delicious Cinnamon Whip Latte, however, because the lid of his to-go cup had mysteriously detached itself from the container. He ended up wearing his coffee instead of drinking it.

The closed door might have prevented Darcie from hearing the curses that followed, but she did enjoy watching Harold throw his cup on the ground and stomp down the street as he headed to his car.

"Za-ack," said Darcie, using the same tone she had used as his babysitter all those years ago. But, this time, she was smiling. "You know I could have taken care of him myself, don't you?"

"I know," said Zack. "But Darcie…I sort of owe you."

"Owe me?" Darcie was puzzled. "What do you mean?"

"Well." He shrugged, looking a little embarrassed. "You were the only babysitter that came back." He gave her a crooked, little grin before walking to a new table full of customers, enthusiastically resuming his role of server.

CHAPTER SEVEN

*D*arcie was still smiling when she arrived in front of the newest boutique in town, Looks By Lou. She paused with her hand on the door handle. The sleek pewter was intricately fashioned to look like ribbons tied in a bow. No surprise there, Darcie thought. She expected nothing less than pure elegance. This was Lou's shop, after all.

No wonder Lou was so bossy when they had been little girls playing with their Barbie dolls. Lou had a vision, even then. And now, she had designed Grace's wedding dress. Darcie's grip on the handle tightened as a wave of emotion swept over her. What was wrong with her today, anyway? Gracie was supposed to be the emotional sister, she reminded herself. She took a deep breath, pinning a cheerful smile on her face. She flatly refused to walk into Lou's shop with tears in her eyes. The observant blonde would tease her forever.

Lou Ann—*Lou,* to her friends—understood Darcie in a way no one else did. She, too, was blessed—or cursed, as Darcie was fond of saying—with beauty queen looks. Lou was blonde, blue-eyed, and tall, with legs that went on forever. She had a sharp tongue and an acerbic wit that, these days, was largely self-deprecating. She knew her strengths and weaknesses and was unfailingly honest…a trait Darcie appreciated. With undergraduate and graduate degrees from the Savannah College of Art and Design, Lou Ann Boggs was the total package.

Growing up, Darcie always thought of Lou as an honorary member of the Finch family, a kind of surrogate sister. Lou had been a fixture in her life as long as Darcie could remember. Even though she was Grace's best friend, she was Darcie's friend, too. Until one day she just...wasn't. Not only did Lou end her friendship with Grace, she went out of her way to be nasty to her ex-best friend.

Hurt and disappointed by Lou's defection, Darcie leapt to her sister's defense at every turn, proving herself a formidable adversary to the spiteful Miss Boggs. But, thankfully, after seven and a half years of unfortunate estrangement—for which Lou Ann willingly took the blame—all was forgiven. Grace and Lou's friendship was stronger than it had ever been. Darcie hadn't realized how much she missed the blue-eyed blonde until Lou was back in their lives.

Darcie glanced up to see those blue eyes—and a pair of familiar green ones—peering, quizzically, at her through the glass door. The owner of the gorgeous green eyes, her beloved sister, turned her wrist so that Darcie could see the time on her elegant watch. *Nine-fifteen. Oh great.* She was late. Again.

Grace and Lou opened the doors for Darcie, one standing to either side, before she had a chance to enter on her own.

"Greetings, oh, *Queen of Punctuality*," Grace intoned, solemnly. She swept her hand dramatically and bowed her head in mock deference.

"Glad you could make it," Lou said, dryly, watching with satisfaction as Darcie's delighted gaze swept the room.

"Oh my gosh, Lou! This place is beautiful!"

From the muted gray walls, tiled floor, and soft, flowing window coverings to the sparkling light fixtures and carefully chosen furnishings, Lou's shop gleamed with elegance and sophistication. "This is a lot better than that cardboard box with the popsicle stick dressing rooms that you made poor Barbie use. You've really stepped it up."

Lou grinned. "Come here, you." She held out her arms, and Darcie returned her hug, glad the days of awkward politeness lay behind them.

"Good to see you, baby sis." Grace received her own quick hug. "Isn't this place amazing? I couldn't wait for you to see it."

"Sorry I'm a little bit late. I made a *new friend* at Jack's. It took some gentle encouragement to send him on his way, with a little help from Zack, of course. And my imaginary husband, Bubba."

Darcie held up her empty coffee cup, raising her eyebrows in an unspoken question.

Lou pointed to a dark gray trashcan, which added considerable flair to the area beside the front door. Darcie got rid of her cup. Leave it to Lou to have stylish trashcans, she thought.

"Awww. That's so cute," Grace said, responding to Darcie's news with a grin. "Zack loves you. If he didn't, he would have given the guy your home address and cell number. Right, Lou?"

Lou glared at her smiling friend, moving toward the antique desk on the right side of the shop.

"Oh, Lou, he didn't," Darcie gasped.

"Oh, but he did. Multiple times." Lou shrugged her shoulders. "But I probably deserved it."

While teaching at Honeysuckle Creek Academy, Lou had struggled with Zack's behavior; he was her least favorite student. Their constant battles were somewhat legendary. Their relationship, however, had evolved over the past six months. Now, Zack would do anything for *Miss Lou*. Lou had resigned from her teaching job at the end of the school year to pursue her dream of opening her own bridal and dress shop.

"So, you're married to Bubba, huh? *My* imaginary husband's name is Roy." Lou nodded her head in perfect understanding. "At least yours has a name with two syllables. Mine is plain ol' Roy. He's an ex-Navy SEAL, now a firefighter. And he is, apparently, quite fit."

Darcie smiled. "Bubba has legs like tree trunks and a bad temper."

"Roy once lifted a car to save a man who was trapped underneath. And he holds the Navy SEAL record for holding his breath under water," Lou added.

They looked at each other, in silence, each wondering why Zack had thought to include that seemingly irrelevant detail.

"I have no idea…" Lou said, in response to their unspoken question.

"The way Zack's mind works is…unexpected," said Grace. "You can't imagine what reading his essays was like. It was exhausting."

"What's your imaginary husband's name, Gracie?" Darcie asked her sister.

"Seriously, Darce?" Grace laughed, in genuine surprise. "I don't need one. Guys don't hit on me. I'm too 'girl next door.' They just ask me for directions and things like that."

"She doesn't need an imaginary husband. She's getting a *real* one," Lou whispered loudly to Darcie, with a wink.

Grace was smiling a secret, happy smile as they headed through the archway that led to the dressing rooms. They entered the large, inviting space that was used for fittings. In the middle stood a slightly raised platform facing a wall completely covered by a single gigantic mirror. The rest of the walls were also covered with mirrors, strategically placed to allow a client to see herself from every possible angle. A mirror was even mounted to the ceiling.

"Wow!" Darcie exclaimed, stepping onto the platform and spinning this way and that, studying her own reflection. "No way to make a bad decision in here. This is as real as it gets."

"I don't want any woman to buy a dress without realizing *exactly* how she will look in it from every angle." Lou opened the door of the largest dressing room on the left. "All right, Gracie Marie, here you go. Let me know if you need any help fastening anything."

Grace went into the dressing room, then poked her head around the door with narrowed eyes. "Hey, what is all this extra stuff? It looks like a lot of pieces."

Lou sighed. "Just trust me, Gracie. This is a fitting, remember?"

"Oh yeah." Grace bit her bottom lip. "I guess I'm a little nervous." She disappeared into the dressing room again.

Lou and Darcie exchanged a knowing smile. Blane would adore his "Green Eyes" if she wore a trash bag to their wedding, but they understood why she wanted everything to be perfect.

The phone rang. "Get comfy, hon." Lou winked. "You know she's going to take forever."

She gestured to a dainty plush sofa in the corner across from Grace's dressing room before disappearing through the archway.

Darcie sat down to wait. From her vantage point she could see a glass case against the interior wall of the shop, full of tiaras of every shape and size. She knew Grace would be wearing the antique tiara and veil worn by almost every McCallum bride for the past one hundred and fifty years. Grace would look beautiful with a tiara, but Darcie, well... no way in hell was she ever putting another tiara on her head. Absolutely. No. Way.

She had enough of that nonsense four years ago. She still wasn't sure how she had been able to endure an entire year of wearing the crown of Miss Honeysuckle Creek. Oh, she did her best to smile and sparkle at every event and personal appearance. The people of Honeysuckle Creek deserved her best. So, that's what she gave them...her best. She even participated in the Miss North Carolina Pageant. And, though she still couldn't believe it, she made the top five. But that didn't mean she enjoyed it.

Of course, she managed to keep that bit of information to herself. More or less. Nobody else knew how much she detested her own pageant queen persona. Nobody, that is, but her sister. And her brother. And her parents, of course. And her great-grandmother. And her best friend from high school. And all of her college friends. And...Well, pretty much everyone who cared about Darcie knew that wearing that tiara had been a struggle for her.

No queen was ever as thrilled to crown the next Miss Honeysuckle Creek as Queen Darcie Finch. She almost cried from sheer relief as she pinned the sparkling tiara on Michelle Drummond's strawberry-blonde curls. Watching the new queen wave to the enthusiastic crowd, Darcie felt as if a weight had been lifted from her shoulders. She embraced her former Queen status, happy to fade into the shadows of her newfound freedom.

To this day, she had never told anyone, not even her beloved family, why she entered the pageant in the first place. The real reason for her year of misery—the only reason—had just answered the phone in the other room... Lou Ann Boggs.

Darcie stumbled onto the conversation completely by accident. She was waiting to pick up lunch for her dad and Will—the Parker half of their law firm, Parker and Finch—at the Honeysuckle Creek Diner, when she heard the honeyed drawl of Lou Ann Boggs. For some reason, Lou Ann—she didn't go by plain old Lou anymore—had adopted a fake Georgia accent during her time at the Savannah School of Design. Darcie couldn't stand it. Her friend had turned into someone she no longer recognized...or liked. She had never asked Grace what happened to end her friendship with Lou, because talking about it upset her beloved sister. And because Darcie had been a little afraid of the answer.

The arrogant blonde seated on the other side of the divider was surrounded by three girls Darcie privately dubbed her minions. The old Lou wouldn't have been caught dead with the shallow and gossipy trio of mean girls, but Lo-ou A-ann seemed right where she wanted to be.

"There is no wa-ay that Gracie Marie will sign up for Miss Honeysuckle Cre-ek, Liz," Lou Ann drawled, "I've be-en training for this title all of my li-ife and she knows that she could nevah beat me."

The other girls at the table nodded enthusiastically.

"She ca-an only dre-am of being as pretty as you, Lou Ann," Liz Grubbs added, trying to imitate Lou Ann's fake drawl, and failing miserably.

"Nobody's as pretty as you are, Lou Ann," Leslie Cline agreed eagerly.

"Grace couldn't even keep her own boyfriend from wandering. Could she, Lou Ann?" Cassidy Meadows asked smugly.

"Hush, Cassidy," Lou Ann said quickly, looking a bit uncomfortable. "That is a-ancient history. Surely, we ca-an find something better to ta-alk about than poor, little ol' Gracie Marie." She paused for the benefit of her avid listeners. "Bless her little hea-art," she added, in a voice dripping with insincerity.

The other three giggled, happy to follow Lou Ann's lead, and the conversation drifted to additional details regarding the upcoming pageant.

Darcie remained riveted to the spot. So that was it. That's why the friendship ended. Grace's boyfriend, Roger, had cheated on Grace with Lou Ann. It all made sense now. Damn. Darcie had never even thought of that...had never imagined that Lou Ann would betray her very best friend. Even though it had happened four years ago, the newfound knowledge still stung.

Lou Ann only got worse after that, full of careless comments and hurtful words for Grace and anyone else who got in her way. What a witch she had become! That was the moment when Darcie realized that the witch was right. Lou Ann Boggs would become Miss Honeysuckle Creek, even though she was the last person to deserve it. She would win the title. There wasn't anyone who could beat her, unless...

The official meeting for the current crop of contestants was getting ready to start. According to the rules for the Miss Honeysuckle Creek Pageant, any female resident between the ages of eighteen and twenty-five was eligible to participate. Participation, however, was limited to one year only. Once a contestant signed up, she forfeited the option to change her mind. She could back out, but she wouldn't be allowed to sign up again, except if she withdrew due to an extreme medical emergency or the like.

The pageant officials had created strict rules for contestants back in the seventies. This was due to the fact that Donna Mae Leinbach entered the pageant seven years in a row before finally winning—according to general consensus—out of sheer pity. The gossips still talked about poor Donna Mae every year at pageant time. Small towns had long memories.

Truetta Sinclair, pageant coordinator, was having a bit of difficulty quieting down the eleven chatty and excited young ladies in the room. "Ladies, please! I know you are all terribly excited to be embarking on the path to Miss America.... She paused for effect. "And as a former Miss Honeysuckle Creek myself, I understand and applaud your enthusiasm. But, ladies, we must have a degree of decorum."

Just then the door flew open, foiling Mrs. Sinclair's attempt to enforce propriety. All eyes turned as Darcie Finch—breathless from another unsuccessful attempt to be punctual—hurried into the room. She made a beeline for the only empty seat, two down from Lou Ann. "I'm so sorry, Mrs. Sinclair," Darcie said, bracing herself for a lecture on tardiness. Mrs. Sinclair was famous for her lectures—and her inflexible rigidity—when it came to the pageant.

Mrs. Sinclair, however, beamed at Darcie. "Welcome, Miss Finch! We are delighted that you have decided to participate this year."

While Mrs. Sinclair continued the meeting as if nothing had happened, several of the girls exchanged surprised glances.

"Darcie," Lou Ann hissed, leaning back in her chair.

Darcie waved, enjoying the fact that Lou Ann looked furious.

Leslie Cline—in the seat between them, and, as always, oblivious—moved her head just then, completely blocking Darcie from Lou Ann's view.

"Move your head, Leslie!" Lou Ann whispered.

"What?" Leslie asked, clearly puzzled.

"Move. Your. Big. Head." Lou Ann's glare could have melted an iceberg.

"Oh, Lou Ann," Leslie gasped, her eyes filling with tears. "Do you really think I have a big head?"

Mrs. Sinclair narrowed her eyes over the top of her glasses. "Miss Boggs? Miss Cline? Is there a problem?"

Leslie burst into tears. "Lou Ann thinks I have a big head," she sobbed, standing and running from the room. One of the other pageant board members went after her.

Lou Ann pressed the heels of her hands into her eyes for a second, before clasping them together tightly in her lap. She met Mrs. Sinclair's gaze with a bright smile. "No, ma'am. No problem. Just a little misunderstanding."

"We don't have misunderstandings in the Miss Honeysuckle Creek Pageant, Miss Boggs." Mrs. Sinclair spoke with all the force of a drill sergeant. "Please make sure that it doesn't happen again."

"Yes, ma'am," Lou Ann said, politely.

Although her nemesis didn't look at her again for the rest of the meeting, Darcie understood how a cornered gazelle must feel…waiting for the lion to pounce. No worries, she encouraged herself, as she silently prepared for the inevitable confrontation. She could handle Lou Ann Boggs. She was doing this for her sister, after all, and that made her fierce.

When the meeting ended, Lou Ann turned to find Darcie waiting. "Why are you here?" *Lou Ann asked, not trying to hide her disdain.*

"Why, whatever do you mean, Lou Ann?" *Darcie asked sweetly.* "I want to be Miss Honeysuckle Creek, of course. Why else would I be here?"

"Did Gracie put you up to this?" *Lou Ann's blue eyes were full of venom.* "Is she trying to get back at me?"

"No, Lou Ann," *Darcie said, in disgust.* "Gracie doesn't even know I'm here. She's the nice one, remember? She's the one who's kind and forgiving, even though you do your best to hurt her at every opportunity. She would never try to keep you from being Miss Honeysuckle Creek, but…"—*Darcie threw down the gauntlet*—"…I will."

Darcie looked Lou Ann straight in the eyes, gratified when her rival flushed and looked away.

"Good luck with that, Darcie." *Still not meeting the righteous glare of her opponent, Lou Ann put her nose in the air and flounced away.*

Darcie had never before, or since, used her beauty as a weapon. But she approached that pageant like it was a battlefield, arming herself to the hilt. She practiced diction with her mother, interview skills with her father, stage presence with her sister, and everything else with Maggie Parker. Maggie, her mother's best friend, was herself a former Miss Honeysuckle Creek. And Darcie practiced the piano…a lot.

She wore makeup, gorgeous gowns, and managed the most fabulous looks with her hair. *And* she won. She had the satisfaction of watching Lou Ann Boggs receive the title of first runner-up. But Darcie also locked herself in to a year of personal appearances, parades, ribbon-cuttings, and preparations for the Miss North Carolina pageant, all while trying to maintain her GPA and study for the LSAT. It hadn't been an easy year, but she had learned a lot about herself—and about the price of vengeance.

And now, it was as if none of it had ever happened. Here they were, waiting for Gracie to try on the wedding dress designed by her best friend Lou, just like they had always planned. Life was funny that way. Still…

Lou returned from the interior of the shop and flopped down beside Darcie. Sinking into the couch, she stretched her long legs out in front of her.

"Late night?" Darcie asked, with a smile.

"Late night choreography." Lou grinned. "Since Gracie's traveling with Blane, Evander asked me to help out with the summer musical. I'm not as good as Gracie, but I'm all he has."

In addition to his job as theater teacher at the academy, Evander Mayfield directed musicals and plays for the town's very active community theater program.

Darcie still wasn't used to the return of the sincere and humble side of Lou. She hesitated, then jumped in with both feet. "Ummm…Lou, I really feel like I need to apologize…you know…for the Miss Honeysuckle Creek thing. I know you really wanted it, and I didn't. I just entered the pageant because I overheard you at the diner talking with your minions about Grace and…"

Lou breezily waved a hand in the air. "Don't you dare apologize, Darcie. You won fair and square; and, seriously, I was pretty high up on the bitch scale then. You said it yourself. I even had my own minions. If I was Miss Honeysuckle Creek, I might never have been able to get myself under control. I owe you a debt of gratitude on behalf of the whole town."

They sat in comfortable silence for a moment. "You would have won, you know," Lou confided.

"Won?"

"Miss North Carolina." Lou smiled at Darcie's disbelieving expression. "One of the judges cried."

"What?"

Darcie was stunned.

"One of the judges cried," Lou explained patiently. "After the interview. When you told them you wouldn't accept the title if you won because of 'prior obligations to pursue your education.'"

"How do you know this stuff?" Darcie asked, impressed in spite of herself.

Lou laughed at the question. "Seriously, Darcie? My mom spent years dragging me from pageant to pageant when I was growing up. I was on the circuit for half my life. I know *everybody*."

Darcie was shocked by Lou's phrasing. "'Dragging you around'? I thought you loved doing pageants."

Lou shook her head ruefully. "I loved the clothes, but the rest of it…not really my thing." She grinned. "It was worth it, though. Honestly, I'd never seen such gorgeous dresses in my life. The gowns were to die for. I came home with hundreds of ideas."

"That makes perfect sense." Darcie nodded. "I just never realized—"

She was interrupted when Grace pulled open the dressing room door. "All right, you two," Grace said, "I'm ready."

She carefully walked to the platform, turning to face them. "How do I look so far?" she asked anxiously.

It was the plainest gown Darcie had ever seen. There wasn't a pearl or a bead or a sprinkling of lace to break up the expanse of white satin. The shape of the gown was flattering, she admitted, desperately searching for something positive to say. The off-the-shoulder bodice showed her sister's lovely shoulders and arms to good advantage, and the drape, well…it made Grace's small waist look even tinier. But it was so far from what Darcie had expected that she was a little at a loss for words.

"Perfection," Lou said. "It fits you to perfection, but…" She shook her finger in warning.

"I know." Grace laughed. "Don't gain or lose a pound. Yes, ma'am." She gave her friend a little salute. Then she turned hopeful eyes on her sister. "What do you think, Darcie?"

"Umm…" Darcie looked from her sister's happy face to Lou's satisfied smile. "It's…umm…not exactly what I expected, but, it's…nice." She gave a weak grin, sinking a little farther into the couch.

Grace bit her lip, looking worried. "Don't you like the shape? I thought…"

Lou, who had been studying Darcie's reaction, burst out laughing. "She thinks this is it, Gracie Marie. She thinks this is your whole dress."

They were laughing at her, but Darcie was too relieved to care. "You mean there's more?" she asked.

Grace smiled, gently, at the look on her sister's face. "Oh, Darcie, do you really think I would get married without lace, pearls, and tulle?"

Lou speared Darcie with a glance. "All right, genius, are you ready for the rest?"

Without waiting for the answer, she went into Grace's dressing room. She returned with her arms full of…what else? Lace, pearls, and tulle. Yards and yards of tulle.

"Come and make yourself useful," Lou instructed Darcie.

Darcie helped Lou pull part of the fluff over Grace's head, holding the pins while Lou went to work. The designer muttered to herself as she rearranged the layers, folding this part down and pulling that part up until she was satisfied. Then she told Grace to close her eyes, turning her around to face the mirrors so she could get the full effect.

From her awkward position—on her knees, facing away from the mirrors and covered with a mountain of material—Darcie couldn't see much of anything. She *could* see that the lace and beading on the skirt were exquisite. That part, at least, was perfectly aligned with the picture she had in her head of what her sister, the bride, was supposed to look like.

Lou held out her hand to help Darcie stand so she could face the mirror at the same time Grace opened her eyes.

Lou gave the word. "All right, Gracie Marie. Open your eyes—and if there's anything you don't like or want to change…"

Lou's voice faded away as Grace gasped.

"Oh, Lou, it's perfect!" The bride started blinking her eyes rapidly, overcome with emotion. "I don't know what to say. I never imagined…"

Darcie was in awe. Her sister was radiant. Her gorgeous green eyes sparkled with unshed tears. Her face was alight with joy. Grace was beautiful, with her glowing skin and long, brown hair. She was tiny—barely five foot two—but perfectly proportioned, with a lovely figure. Her subtle beauty was often overshadowed by her sister's movie-star looks, an unintended rivalry Darcie had always regretted. Rather than allowing themselves to fall prey to sibling jealousy, the sisters had formed a strong bond. They were extremely protective of each other. Each possessed a fierce pride in the strengths and accomplishments of the other, and a steadfast loyalty.

The fit and flare style was perfect for Grace, showing her assets to their best advantage. The drape of the yards of sheer material was airy and light, flowing down from the elegant bodice like a delicate waterfall of lace. The strategically placed beading sparkled. The entire dress glowed like a magical work of art.

Grace glowed, too, with joy…so happy in her full bridal splendor that it almost hurt to look at her. Darcie's vision blurred with tears.

"Oh, Darce," Grace said, holding out her arms to her first and forever friend.

Lou joined them on the platform, her own eyes wet with tears. The three shared an emotional moment that ended in laughter. Lou's enthusiastic embrace overbalanced the Finch sisters, sending all three to the floor in a mountain of lace, tulle, and pearls. After checking for damage and finding none—Lou made a quality product after all—they helped Grace out of her soon-to-be-completed gown.

UNMASKING THE HEART

Because Lou had another appointment at eleven-thirty, Grace and Darcie found themselves alone on their hometown sidewalk. They happily decided they were long overdue for a "sisters only" lunch.

"What about the tearoom?" Grace asked. "We haven't been there in a long time."

Darcie looked at her watch. "Do we need a reservation?"

"Ooh, I didn't think about that. We can always—"

Grace's phone rang. She pulled it out of her purse, glancing at the number.

"Hang on a minute," she said. "It's Blane. That probably means they're back at Heart's Ease."

Darcie knew that the other half of "they" was Devin Merritt. Devin had been recuperating at Blane's estate between hospital stays for the past two months. The injuries he sustained from his horrible attack required multiple facial reconstruction operations and plastic surgeries. As if that wasn't enough, he was also dealing with physical therapy for his broken femur. At least the medical part of his ordeal was almost over. Devin's follow-up for his final plastic surgery was in a couple of days. After that, he would return to Providence to begin intensive occupational therapy.

Darcie's heart went out to the poor man. He had been through so much. She was glad his parents were coming to stay with him at Heart's Ease so he wouldn't have to spend the rest of the week alone.

Grace and Blane were flying out later that afternoon, headed to the McCallum ancestral castle in Scotland. Blane's aunt and uncle were hosting a massive engagement party for their only nephew and his lovely fiancée on Saturday night. Darcie was meeting Joey in New York at the end of the week to catch their own flight. She was looking forward to her first trip to Scotland. McCallum Castle was only about fifteen or so miles from Edinburgh. Darcie hoped to visit the city and to see as much of the beautiful Scottish countryside as possible.

Grace motioned to a nearby bench located in the shade. Darcie nodded, following her sister so Grace could take her call. Darcie tried to mind her own business, but she couldn't help overhearing.

"Hi hon! Is Devin all settled? I'll be there as soon as we have lunch. Do you want me to bring you anything, or has Mrs. Hofmann already—" Grace paused as her lovely smile became a frown. "What? Oh, no! Stomach bugs are the worst. And the whole family at once? That's awful!" She glanced at Darcie, a worried look on her face. "No, of course they can't travel. I'll just wait and come on Thursday night, with Darcie and Joey. No, it's okay. I'd feel awful leaving him all alone, especially since he can't see. Too bad Mom and Dad are already in London."

"What's wrong?" whispered Darcie.

"Hold on a minute, Blane." Grace turned to her sister. "Devin's whole family has a stomach bug…his daughter, Robert, Allana, even his nanny. His parents can't come to stay with him. So, I'm just going to wait and go with you and Joey."

Darcie shook her head. "No, you're not. I'll stay with Devin. You need to be in Scotland with Blane. I'm not supposed to leave until Thursday, anyway."

Grace looked so hopeful that Darcie had to smile. "Oh, Darcie, that would be great, but are you sure? I don't want you to feel awkward. You've never met Devin, have you?"

Darcie shrugged. "I'll meet him now. He'll probably sleep most of the time anyway. Besides, he has a nurse round the clock, right? I won't have to do anything except be there in case something weird happens. It'll be a nice vacation."

"Oh, Darce, you're the best."

Grace picked up her phone to tell Blane the news as Darcie basked in her sister's smile.

Grace had been through a lot in the past two years. She deserved to enjoy every part of her engagement, and her wedding. And Darcie was happy to help. That was her job, wasn't it? She took her responsibilities as maid of honor seriously. Besides, Heart's Ease was spectacular…*and* there was a pool. How bad could it be?

CHAPTER EIGHT

*I*t was going to be awful.

Absolutely awful.

Mr. Devin Merritt was the most difficult man Darcie had met in a very long time. Maybe ever. She couldn't wait for the next two days to be over.

Stomping down the hall after their first unfortunate encounter, she reminded herself why she was going through with this glorified excuse for a babysitting job. She couldn't think of anything else to call it. She was doing this for Grace. And her beloved sister was worth any amount of trouble. Even if the trouble came from the cynical and sarcastic Mr. Devin I-Know-Everything Merritt.

Granted, the man had been the victim of an attempted murder, she reminded herself. Not only had he lost an eye, but he was, unfortunately, scarred for life. Darcie started to feel a little bit guilty. She usually kept her cool under fire, but there was something about Devin Merritt that seriously strained her self-control.

She stopped outside the kitchen to get her emotions under control. She was determined to rise above Mr. Merritt's sorry attitude. She would be the better person. She could do this. Darcie Finch didn't back down from a challenge.

It hadn't started out badly. On the contrary, she had actually been looking forward to making the acquaintance of another member of the Merritt family. The Merritt Brothers Law Firm reminded her a lot of her father's own firm, Parker and Finch. Oh, it was a lot larger, but the camaraderie, crazy inside jokes, and obvious affection the family Merritt held for each other made her feel right at home. Devin was apparently a great favorite with his cousins. During both of Darcie's internships, they had regaled her with all kinds of funny stories about Devin's antics. And his *glorious* sense of humor. *Hmph*, Darcie thought. Talk about a disappointment.

She arrived at Heart's Ease around three-thirty that afternoon, stopping for a few minutes to chat with her old friend, Mrs. Hofmann. The elderly cook had been baking scrumptious memories in the kitchen of Heart's Ease since Darcie was a little girl.

She was also delighted to discover that she knew the home healthcare nurse. Carol Cavendish had worked for Darcie's great-grandfather, a beloved, local physician, until he retired. Her son, James, had been one of Darcie's best friends since elementary school. Darcie had staunchly defended the shy, awkward youth until he had grown into his own gangly limbs. Carol would always be grateful to Darcie for dragging her son to the Junior Prom as her date—he never would have gone otherwise—and helping him to polish his latent social skills.

Carol adored Darcie. She had always hoped more than an ordinary friendship might develop between her son and the beautiful girl who looked beyond James' nerdy exterior to the heart that beat beneath. Her wish, however, never came to fruition. James was currently a second-year medical student at Emory University in Georgia, a fact that made his good friend, Darcie, very proud.

After fortifying herself with a cup of tea, Darcie left her haven, turning down the short hallway behind the kitchen. She followed the sound of her future brother-in-law's voice to the large first-floor bedroom in the back corner of the house. She stopped just before the doorway.

The bedroom was an ideal location for anyone who enjoyed a lovely view. Its wide, back windows looked out over the beautifully landscaped English garden; a charming bay window on the side revealed the glorious roses that had once been the pride and joy of Blane's mother.

The bedroom was cheerfully decorated in shades of pale green and white. Sheer white curtains billowed gracefully from decorative curtain rods. The quilt that covered the bed was also white, with a delicate floral design. The window seat underneath the bay window was done in a pattern of complementary green and white stripes; several plump green and white pillows were tidily arranged at the foot of the window.

It was a beautiful room. Unfortunately, the man lying in the bed couldn't enjoy it.

Darcie took in the arrangements of the room—Blane stood at the foot of the bed, his back to the door—before turning her full attention to her obligation. He lay in the bed, propped up by several pillows. Broad shoulders in a snug-fitting T-shirt hinted at an impressive physique, although the rest of Devin Merritt was covered by a light sheet. He had a strong-looking chin and perfectly formed lips, but the rest of his face was swathed in bandages. He couldn't see a thing, Darcie realized with a start. Even though the surgery had been a success, he must be scared to death. Devin's entire world had changed without warning. Darcie felt sorry for him, suddenly glad she could be of help.

"No, it isn't the same thing, Devin."

Blane was obviously trying to explain something. Darcie quietly stepped into the open doorway.

"Carol works for Home Healthcare. I need someone else to be here who's family, someone I know I can trust to make the right decisions and contact the right people, if necessary. It will make me feel a whole lot better about leaving." Blane paused, raking his hand through his hair, a sure sign he was agitated. "But listen, man, you know I don't want you to be uncomfortable. So, just say the word and I'll change my own plans."

"Hell no, Blane," Devin hissed through his teeth. His skin still felt tight from the recent plastic surgery around his eyes. "You've done enough for me already. Go to your engagement party. *One* of us needs to be happily married."

Darcie cocked her head to one side. She had forgotten hearing that the poor man's wife hadn't once visited him in the hospital. Even her kind-hearted sister, Grace, said Devin's wife was awful. Darcie was filled with sympathy and compassion, determined to do whatever she could to ease the burden of Mr. Devin Merritt. Her noble intentions, however, lasted exactly as long as it took for the man in the bed to open his mouth again. After hearing his next few sentences, she realized how unfortunate it was that the bandages didn't cover his mouth, too.

"But there's got to be somebody else…a little, old grandmother, somebody's maiden aunt. Hell, Blane, the checkout girl at the Walmart would be a better choice." Devin's voice was filled with frustration. "I mean, of all the people you could get to be my babysitter, you had to get a second-year law student? And a female one, at that?"

"Actually, Darcie just *finished* her second year of law school," Blane explained, patiently. "So, technically, that makes her a third-year law student." He blew out a breath of frustration. "Look, Devin. Darcie is smart. She thinks on her feet. She can handle any situation that might come up, and, under the circumstances, she's our only choice. We can't let too many people know that somebody tried to kill you, at least until we find out who the driver was that hit you."

"A third-year law student. Oh wow. That's so much better." The sarcasm practically dripped from his tongue. "How do you know she won't open up the whole place to the media or start her own YouTube channel?"

"Because, Devin, I trust her. Implicitly. And you can, too." Blane was adamant. "You already know your family loves her."

"Yeah, most of them loved Mallory, too, in the beginning, and you know how well that worked out for everybody." Devin was out of patience. The lack of control he had of his own situation—not to mention his temporary lack of vision—was starting to get to him. Spending the next two days answering ridiculous questions from a starry-eyed idealist or stroking the ego of a self-promoting prima donna made him long to return to the mindless joys of anesthesia.

Blane looked at his Rolex. He glanced behind him to make sure Darcie wasn't overhearing Devin's less-than-grateful speech. Much to his regret, his fears were justified. She was standing behind him, propped against the doorway with her arms crossed. Her eyebrows were almost touching her hairline in outrage.

Blane's eyes widened warily at the expression on her face. "Umm…Dev," Blane hedged, turning back to his hapless friend. He was glad Devin couldn't see the desire for rebuttal glowing in Darcie's dark eyes.

"Which is she?" Devin continued, blissfully unaware of the coming storm.

"Dev, umm…"

Looking very apologetic, Blane half-glanced back at the door, watching Darcie out of the corner of his eye.

"Which is she, Blane…enthusiastically naïve or arrogantly condescending?"

With those words, Devin sealed his own fate.

Darcie straightened, walking into the room to stand beside Blane. She had had enough unwarranted judgement on the part of Mr. Devin Merritt. The man didn't even know her, he had no right to make assumptions. It was time to put him in his place. Or, at the very least, to make her presence known.

"Only *two* choices, Mr. Merritt?" she said. "You don't have much of an imagination, do you? Lucky for you, I do…and I think I'm going to switch it up. I think I'll go with, hmm…let me see…how about enthusiastically condescending?"

Her unexpected entry into the conversation was met with complete silence.

Two things crossed Devin's mind. The first was that the speaker had the sexiest voice he had ever heard. Its slightly husky cadence rolled over him like warm velvet, wrapping around his senses. The hair at the back of his neck stood up. He felt goose bumps rising on his limbs. He had *never* responded to anyone's voice the way he responded to this one.

His second thought was that the voice he had just heard was filled with a sarcasm that eclipsed even his own. *Well, hell,* he thought. *I've done it again.* He had put his foot so far into his mouth that he was going to choke to death. Slowly and painfully.

Blane attempted to break through the awkwardness. "Umm…Darcie, this is Devin Merritt, McCallum's head of legal, and my good friend."

He waited a second or two for Darcie to respond.

She didn't.

Blane cleared his throat and continued. "And umm…Devin, this is Darcie Finch, a third-year law student at your alma mater, my future sister-in-law, and your…" His voice trailed away as he looked at Darcie hopefully.

Darcie refused to say a word. She just crossed her arms again, waiting to see if Mr.-I-Look-Down-On-Law-Students-Like-I-Was-Never-One-Myself could dig out of the giant hole he had just dug himself.

Well, damn. What am I supposed to do now? Devin wondered, a little desperately. He hadn't meant to offend Darcie Finch. Really, he hadn't. He reached for humor, as he always did. "What's she doing?" he asked Blane in a loud stage whisper.

Blane whispered back: "Her arms are crossed and she's glaring at you."

"I can feel her glare," Devin quipped, making an effort to break the tension. "She's not shooting lasers out of her eyes, is she?"

Blane's lips twitched, but he added, gravely, "No lasers, but I wouldn't put it past her. She's only looked at me like that one time. I swore that day I'd never do anything to make her do it again."

"When was that?" Darcie asked, curious in spite of herself.

"In the barn," Blane explained, turning to her, "when you thought I made Gracie cry."

"Oh yeah." Darcie nodded. "I remember that."

"I didn't, by the way," Blane said.

Darcie looked a bit confused. "Didn't what?"

"Make Gracie cry." Blane grinned.

"I know that," she said, tossing a half smile to the man who, a few minutes before, proclaimed his absolute trust in her. "I'm allowing you to marry her, aren't I?"

Devin almost smiled. *Impressive, Miss Finch,* he thought, approvingly. *Familial loyalty* and *a quick comeback. Two points in your favor.* "Nice to meet you, Miss Darcie Finch," he said, making a belated attempt at politeness. Or was it because of his strong desire to hear her voice again?

"Hmph!" was all he received for his efforts.

The silence stretched again, broken by the chiming of the antique grandfather clock in the hallway.

"Well, it's four-thirty," Blane said, unable to tamp the genuine relief from his voice. "Time for me to pick up Grace. Take care of yourself, Devin, and try to find your likable side. I know it's in there somewhere under all of those bandages."

Blane's effort at a joke was met by a disbelieving "Hmph!" from his future sister-in-law.

"Ay, Ay, Cap'n!" Devin made the effort to salute, but his bandages made his small attempt at humor all the more pitiful.

Blane motioned for Darcie to step into the hallway with him.

"Darcie," Blane began, gently. "He's been through some serious trauma. You might want to consider giving him a break." He raised his eyebrows, silently pleading for understanding.

Darcie sighed. "All right, Blane, I'll try. I know he's your friend, although at this moment I can't figure out why. I'll try to give him the benefit of the doubt. But"—she raised her voice so Devin was sure to hear—"he's running a little short on the charm I've heard so much about." She paused for emphasis. "Bless his charmless, little heart," she added, enthusiastically, in her most condescending tone.

CHAPTER NINE

So, here she stood in the hallway an hour later, holding a heavy dinner tray and stalling. *Get on with it, Darcie,* she told herself. Taking a deep breath, she swept into the room. "Time for dinner," she said, trying to sound as cheerful as possible. She placed the tray on an adjustable table borrowed from the Honeysuckle Creek Medical Center.

"Thank God."

Devin made an awkward attempt to adjust his pillows so he could sit up a little more. He succeeded only in sliding sideways. "The Voice" was back, and he was determined to make amends. He was more than a little embarrassed by his earlier outburst. Miss Darcie Finch was right. He was known for his charming and witty personality. However, the sheer frustration of his own situation—compounded with the knowledge that Amalie and his entire family were sick—well, it was almost too much.

He had lashed out at one of his best friends. *And* he had insulted an innocent bystander, one who was only trying to help. Definitely not on point for Devin Merritt. She had certainly put him in his place, though. He liked the fact that she stood up to him. She hadn't treated him like a broken man who had to be handled delicately. She had given him what for, and he respected that. He was perfectly able to adjust his position and his pillows himself. But for some unknown reason, he remained slumped sideways, waiting to see what she would do.

Darcie leaned over, putting her arms on either side of his muscular shoulders. She helped him to straighten his torso while efficiently taking care of his wayward pillows. The episode happened so fast that Devin might have been able to convince himself that the hint of perfume in the air—sweet and exotic, like some rare, tropical flower—was a figment of his own overactive imagination. Almost.

Helping Devin sit up left Darcie slightly breathless. Her heart pounded erratically. Good Lord. She hadn't done anything but touch his shoulders. Granted, the man did have an impressive pair, she tried to rationalize. But still. She had seen shoulders before. Lots of times. *But you've never reacted like this,* she informed herself. It was a little disconcerting. If she had anticipated her unexpected physical response, she would have left him slumped on his pillows. And fled the room.

As it was, she was stuck. The man had to eat, didn't he? She struggled to shake off the last few seconds as she wheeled the table over to the bed. She adjusted it, making sure it was the right height and distance from Mr. Impressive Shoulders. She berated herself, all the while. *Okay, Miss Looks-Don't-Matter. Since when do you react to a pair of shoulders like a hormonally depraved sixteen-year-old, especially considering what a stellar impression he made an hour ago? Stop being such a hypocrite.*

"What's on the tray?" Devin asked eagerly, distracting her from her internalized lecture.

Darcie studied the plate for a moment, trying to discern the best way forward. The plate was round, like a clock. Of course. "French fries at two o'clock, peanut butter and jelly sandwich at six. It's cut into little pieces, and—"

"What kind of fries?" Devin couldn't stand the suspense. This was his dinner, after all.

Darcie had seen those fries before. "They look like the ones from the diner."

"The ones with seasoned salt?" he asked hopefully.

She almost smiled at his single-minded culinary quest. "Yes, I think so." He was so different now, sort of appealing…in a boyish way. She was starting to feel like his babysitter.

The rapid-fire questions continued.

"What kind of jelly?"

She peered at the pieces of sandwich. "Let's see…Looks like grape to me."

"Grape is good. But, what about the bread? White or wheat?"

"Wheat."

"And…" Devin prompted.

"And what?" she responded, a little confused.

"You said, 'and', but you didn't finish."

"That's because you interrupted me," she admonished.

"Oh. I'm sorry." His lips came together to form a childish pout.

Darcie nodded in response.

"I said, 'I'm so-rry!'" He enunciated the words in a loud voice, as if Darcie was a very, very old lady. Old and senile.

"You don't have to yell. I heard you the first time. And I nodded my head." Darcie gasped as his reality hit her hard. "Oh." *Way to go, genius,* she admonished herself. *He can't see you.* She blew out a defeated breath. *Worst. Babysitter. Ever.*

Devin took complete advantage of her mistake. "Pretty frustrating, huh? Imagine how I feel. Left all alone. Starving in my bed. Waiting for someone to take pity on me and bring me food, even though she may not like me very much."

He stopped talking and waited, striving to look as pitiful as possible.

"You have a buzzer," Darcie said, calmly, refusing to take the bait. "All you have to do is ring the buzzer; someone's always at your beck and call. Twenty-four seven."

Devin tried harder. "But, that's so demeaning…forcing someone to do something against her will. I want someone to bring me my dinner out of the goodness of her heart. Out of the pure desire to help a fellow human being who's down on his luck." He was rather proud of his dramatic performance. He waited, breathlessly, for her response.

"I think I understand why someone tried to kill you," Darcie said slowly.

His shout of laughter surprised them both. Even though it didn't do much for his stiff face, he had trouble suppressing his smile. *Touché, Miss Finch*, he thought. *So, you aren't immune to a little needling after all.*

Devin was beginning to enjoy this encounter. "Let's see. I have a delicious peanut butter sandwich with grape jelly, cut into squares at two o'clock. And tasty fries from the diner, covered with seasoned salt at six." He said it wrong, deliberately, just to see if she was paying attention. "Surely there's something at ten o'clock. I hope it's jello. Please, Miss Darcie Finch, third-year law student, don't keep me in suspense."

"Your fries are at two and your sandwich is at six. And at ten o'clock you have…" She paused, deliberately heightening his suspense. "…Jello!"

"Hurray!" said Devin, enthusiastically, using his four-year-old daughter's favorite exclamation. "Is it cut in little squares or is it flat in a bowl?"

Darcie almost laughed. "Little squares."

"Yes." Devin raised a fist in the air and pulled it down quickly. "What kind of jello?"

"It's red."

"But what kind is it? It could be cherry or strawberry or raspberry." He changed his mind. "No, not raspberry. Raspberry jello is blue." He straightened his lips into a line, a sure sign that he was thinking.

"What are you? Some kind of jello connoisseur?"

"Just hungry," Devin said, happily.

"You seem different than before. Are you bipolar by some chance?" Darcie asked gently.

"Nope. Just happy about my dinner."

"Maybe it's the anesthesia," she said encouragingly.

He wanted to chuckle, impressed with the way her mind worked. He liked verbal sparring with The Lady of the Glorious Voice. He liked Darcie Finch.

Darcie knew she should offer to help him with his dinner, but she was a little unnerved by her earlier reaction to him. And to his shoulders. Just the thought of feeding him his dinner made her heart beat faster. She gave herself a mental shake. *Get a grip, Darcie. You're supposed to help him,* she reminded herself. *The poor man can't see, for goodness sake. Helping him with his dinner is the least you can do.* Still, she hesitated, not wanting to make him feel awkward. And—she was honest enough to admit—not wanting any unnecessary contact. Gathering her courage and taking a deep breath, she asked, delicately, "Do you want me to…umm…feed you?"

"Do you *want* to feed me?" Devin asked wickedly.

"No!" said Darcie, too quickly.

He had certainly turned the tables on her. Who felt awkward now? She was a little rattled.

"I mean, let me know if you need help. Otherwise, umm…enjoy your dinner."

She left the room quickly, trying to make sense of the Devin Merritt she had just encountered: the gorgeous man shoulders and the little boy excitement about his dinner. She was at a loss to reconcile *that* Devin Merritt with the one who had passed judgement on her sight unseen. She headed to the kitchen, hoping to settle her nerves, leaving the conundrum to enjoy his jello.

Two hours later she was back, magazine in hand, determined to do her duty. She had enjoyed eating dinner and visiting with Nurse Carol, who seemed grateful for the company. Darcie had *not* spent those two hours hiding in the kitchen. She was in *no way* trying to avoid her responsibility to Blane's friend. Or to Blane's friend's shoulders. At least, that's what she kept telling herself. Devin didn't need much help, anyway. According to Carol, he made it clear that he didn't want someone hovering around him all the time.

So, why was she currently standing outside Devin's door, her hand primed and ready to knock? Why did she feel compelled to check on the man? She refused to delve too deeply into her own motivation, choosing, instead, the most obvious reason. Because she had promised. That's why. She had promised Blane to look after his friend, to make sure he had everything that he needed. Blane was counting on her and she wouldn't let him down.

Still…she hesitated, lowering her hand. Maybe it would be better if she checked on him in the morning. That had been her original intention. If there wasn't anything for his nurse to do, then how could Devin possibly have any need of Darcie? He couldn't. He didn't. That's why the best thing she could do was to go into her own room, read her own magazine, and mind her own business.

But she wasn't going to do that, was she? Of course not. And why not? Because, try as she might, Darcie Finch couldn't seem to leave well enough alone. That's why she had purposely walked down the hallway past her own room until she ended up in front of Devin's. That's why she was currently staring at his door and feeling ridiculous.

She took a deep breath, raising her hand again.

The fact that her hand refused to knock on the door was becoming something of a problem. Part of her hesitation had to do with a single unanswered question. Who currently occupied the bed inside? Was it the semicharming—she would give him that—Dr. Devin Jekyll? Or was it the arrogant and annoying Mr. Devin Hyde?

She was almost hoping for Mr. Devin Hyde because he was easy to dislike. Some little voice, somewhere in her head, kept warning her that it wasn't a good idea to like Dr. Devin Jekyll too much. That was odd. She was sure she had no reason to be wary of the man. She knew his family, and he was a good friend of Blane's. That should be enough, but…

"No, damn it." Devin's anguished voice pierced the quiet of the hallway. "This cannot be happening. This absolutely cannot be happening."

Darcie grabbed the doorknob, flying into the room. "What is it? What happened? What's wrong?"

She looked around for chaos, disaster, or—horror of horrors—blood. But all she saw was Devin lying in the bed, looking exactly as he had when she left the last time. Only without the jello.

"He struck out," said Devin, disgustedly. "Struck out looking…on the third out with bases loaded. Can you believe that? No way we're going to win now."

Darcie grabbed the corner of the dresser, her heart pounding. "Baseball," she gasped, "You're watching baseball."

"Well, not exactly," Devin said. He gave an overly dramatic sigh, gesturing to the television on the wall opposite his bed. "More like listening."

"Sorry." Darcie mentally kicked herself for being so insensitive. Again.

"What did you think I was talking about?" His mind suddenly registered the voice…that glorious voice. "Say, you're not the nurse." His lips quirked. Who cared if the Mets lost? He had The Voice. "Did you miss me, Darcie Finch?"

"Of course not," she said, desperately, already feeling a little off-balance. "I was…umm…on the way to my room. I heard you yell so I came to see if you were okay."

He stifled a chuckle. "Good try, Darcie Finch, but your room is at the other end of the hall. No way you could hear me yell from there." He grinned, obviously pleased. "Don't worry. I won't tell anybody that you missed me. It'll be our little secret." He had no idea why he couldn't resist teasing her, only that he seemed unable to stop.

"I actually thought you might need some company," she said, with great dignity. "But since you're listening to a ballgame, I'll just…"

"Stay, Darcie Finch, please. It's the seventh inning stretch and I'm soooo lonely." He tried to look pitiful…but then it dawned on him that he really didn't have to try. How could he possibly look more pitiful than he already did?

The *please* was the only thing that kept her from fleeing the room. "Oh, all right. I'll just sit over here on the window seat and read my magazine. You can listen to your game when it comes back on."

He could hear her moving pillows and getting settled. He got a whiff of the flowery scent she wore, but, sadly, she didn't say anything else. He listened to the announcer sing "Take Me Out to the Ballgame." The military quartet was halfway through "God Bless America" before Devin had his first genuinely brilliant idea since the night of his attack. If he asked her to read to him, he could listen to her voice...an immensely better option than listening to the Mets lose their game.

He waited until the end of "God Bless America." He didn't want to be disrespectful, after all. He turned off the television with the remote control, having memorized the function of each button weeks ago. "So, what are you reading, Darcie Finch?" he asked pleasantly.

"A magazine," she said flatly. After regaining some of her equilibrium, she was determined not to give him any encouragement.

"What's the name of your magazine?" he asked.

"It's called, 'Mouth of the South,'" she said, hoping her continued refusal to elaborate would discourage his interest.

It didn't.

"What's that about?" he persisted, enjoying the fact that she was getting a little impatient.

She paused. He heard her inhale and let her breath out slowly. "It's about what people eat at the South Pole."

Yes, he thought, gleefully. *Got you, Darcie Finch. Let the games begin.* "Oh, like penguins."

She was horrified. "No! Not like penguins. Penguins are too cute to be eaten. More like fish."

"Some fish are cute," he objected.

"No. Fish are not cute. Fish are scaly and slimy. That is, unless you have a different definition of cute than I do."

"Nemo was cute," Devin said, defensively. "And Dory was definitely cute."

Darcie gave up. "I guess you're right. Fish from cartoons are cute."

Devin waited, but it seemed as if nothing more would be forthcoming. So, he tried again. "What about the North Pole?"

"What about it?"

"Does it say anything in your magazine about what people eat at the North Pole? They eat reindeer, I think. Don't you think so, Darcie Finch?

Don't you think they eat reindeer at the North Pole?" Devin could almost feel her irritation.

"Good Lord! You have got to be the most annoying person I've ever met."

Darcie finally gave Devin the reaction he had been waiting for. Her velvety voice rolled over him as he savored his small victory.

She continued, briskly: "You know as well as I do that my magazine is not about the South Pole, or the North Pole for that matter. It's a magazine about Southern cuisine."

Devin chuckled delightedly. This was the most fun he had had in years.

Darcie, however, was busy berating herself again. *I can't believe I just yelled at a man recovering from surgery. What is wrong with me?* She took another deep breath, bracing herself for more questions, but none came. She glanced at Devin, hoping he had fallen asleep. That's when she noticed the devious little smile flirting with the corners of his mouth. *Why, that sneaky little rat,* she thought. *He's trying to rile me up for the fun of it.* She smiled, then, in spite of herself. She had a brother. She had played this game before.

A few seconds later he started in again. "Darcie Finch. What's your article about?"

"Pie," she said calmly.

"Pie?" He actually sounded like he didn't believe her.

"You know, one or two crusts with some kind of filling. Chocolate, apple, cherry, pecan..." She ticked them off on her fingers one at a time.

Devin held up his hands in mock surrender. "Okay. Okay. I get it. Pie. So, why are you reading about pie, Darcie Finch?"

"Because I make them." She said it like it wasn't a big deal, like every third-year law student made pies.

Devin was impressed. His teasing quest was getting interesting. "From scratch?"

"Uh-huh. I've been baking since I was a little girl. We—Mama, Grace, and I—use any excuse to bake. Mama bakes cakes, Gracie bakes bread—"

"I've had Grace's bread," Devin chimed in. "Blane hides it in the second drawer of his desk. Don't tell him I know."

"I won't." Darcie chuckled. "Anyway, I make pies."

"My grandmother makes pies, too. She lives in Charleston, and she always makes me a chocolate chess pie for my birthday." Devin paused, savoring that delicious memory. "Will you make me a pie, Darcie Finch?"

She finally understood why people said he was charming. She was starting to enjoy talking to Devin. She had to fix one thing, though. "Why do you keep calling me Darcie *Finch*? You don't have to say *Finch* every single time. Plain, old Darcie is fine."

"You don't seem like a plain, old Darcie to me. What do you look like anyway?"

He could feel the change in her demeanor from across the room. Her voice took on an icy edge. "I'd rather not talk about my looks."

Well, hell, he thought. *How was I supposed to know that she's sensitive about her looks? It's not like I can see her.* He grasped at the last thing he had said before she went all ice princess on him. "Why do I call you Darcie Finch? Because it's fun to say Darcie Finch. DAR-cie Finch. Dar-CIE Finch. Darcie FINCH." He demonstrated how each syllable could be emphasized.

"You are ridiculous."

Maybe he was, but her voice was a little warmer. He ran with it. "So, Darcie Finch, what's your middle name?"

"Sofia."

"Darcie Sofia Finch," he said, mulling it over for a minute. "Darcie. Sofia. Finch." He frowned. "I don't like it."

"What do you mean, you don't like it?" She was indignant. "You don't have to like it. It's not your name. Anyway, my middle name comes from my great-grandmother. And you better not tell *her* you don't like it. She's formidable."

"So, you're a lot like her then?" he asked innocently.

"Hmph." That was her only reply.

"It's not that I don't like the name Sofia," he explained, "Darcie Sofia Finch just isn't as much fun to say as Darcie Finch."

"Hmph."

"Tongue-tied, are you?" he asked, perceptively.

"Of course not. Why would you say that?" She was definitely getting her spirit back.

"Because when you can't come up with a reply you just...*hmph.*"

Darcie crossed her arms in denial, even though she knew he couldn't see her. "I do not!"

"Oh, yes, you do, Darcie Finch."

"Hmph!"

He raised his hands, palm up, in a gesture of innocence.

"Well, what's *your* middle name?" she asked, choosing to ignore his observation.

His lips quirked up at the edges again. "Devin," he said.

She glared at him in disbelief. "Not really."

"Really," he echoed smugly.

"It figures." She huffed in frustration. "What's your first name, then?" she asked, refusing to give up.

Devin sighed heavily, bringing a smile of anticipation to Darcie's face. Finally. She was onto something.

"My first name is Laurence. Laurence Devin Merritt." He braced himself for her response, but she surprised him.

"That's not so bad. I thought you were going to say Jehoshaphat or something like that. Where does Laurence come from?" she inquired.

Now it was his turn. "Seriously? You were an intern for the whole summer and you've never heard about the Merritt name conspiracy?"

"Nobody said a word," she said solemnly.

"Well, then, what I'm about to tell you will make your middle name look pretty good." He settled comfortably against his pillows. "My grandmother Merritt was a Berry before she got married. Her first name was Mary."

"Mary Berry?" Darcie asked. "I bet she was glad to get rid of that and become Mary Merritt. Oooh...that's almost worse."

"May I continue?" Devin asked politely.

"Of course. Sorry."

"Anyway, Grandmother Mary had two sisters…my great-aunts Carrie and Sherrie." He paused for her reaction.

"Mary, Carrie, and Sherrie Berry." She shook her head in disbelief. "Were they triplets, by any chance?"

"No."

"Are you making this up?"

She was observing Devin carefully to see if she could detect any sign indicating he was setting her up as the victim of an elaborate joke.

"No. None of these names have been changed to protect the innocent," he stated.

"Please continue."

"As you wish." Devin cleared his throat dramatically. "Before they got married, the Berry sisters made a pact. They promised—to the everlasting detriment of their unfortunate offspring—to continue the rhyming tradition with their own children. So, Great-Aunt Carrie had two girls…Jeri and Teri. And Great-Aunt Sherrie had a boy, Harry, and a girl, Dairia."

"Oooh! Let me guess!" Darcie interjected excitedly. "They called her Dairi."

"Exactly," Devin said, with approval.

"Your cousins…were they scary, or very, very hairy?" Darcie was giggling so hard she couldn't get any more words out of her mouth.

"Of course they weren't scary. This is my family I'm talking about."

Devin was thoroughly pleased with his ability to make Darcie Finch laugh. As a matter of fact, he was enjoying the sound of her throaty giggle a little too much.

He continued his tongue-in-cheek defense. "And they weren't hairy, either…at least not the women. Well, except for Cousin Jeri."

When he said that, Darcie broke into laughter so contagious he couldn't help but join in. At that moment Devin realized he was feeling much better—much more like himself—in spite of the fact that his face was a little too stiff for so much joviality.

When they finally got themselves a bit under control, Devin started again. "So, anyway, my grandmother had three boys."

"Oh, no!" Darcie gasped. "There's more?"

"By this time, most of the rhyming names were spoken for, so she improvised. She chose Garrett, known as…"

"Gary," Darcie supplied quickly.

"Barrett, known as…"

"Barry. Garrett and Barrett Merritt. Wow." Darcie was impressed in spite of herself.

"And"—Devin held up one finger—"Laurence, known as…"

"Larry." Darcie's eyes narrowed. "Wait a minute. Your dad's name is Robert."

"Well, you see, my dad is kind of the rebel of the family. He has blond hair instead of auburn, hazel eyes instead of gray…stuff like that. Anyway, you know how most of my family graduated from the University of Virginia?" he asked, just to make sure.

Darcie nodded, caught herself, then added, helpfully: "I'm nodding, just in case you were wondering."

"I figured. Anyway, Dad got the Morehead scholarship to UNC, and when he got there, he introduced himself to everyone as Robert or Rob. To the family, though, he'll always be Larry."

"My dad and Blane's dad were both Morehead scholars. I guess that's how they met your dad." Darcie was putting all of the pieces together now.

"Wait a minute, Darcie Finch, weren't you a Morehead scholar, too?" Devin seemed to remember that bit of information.

"Funny that you and I were at Carolina at the same time and never met each other," she mused, glossing over her own accomplishment.

He had a feeling she did that frequently. He was noticing lots of things about The Lady of the Lovely Vocals. "Did you live on campus?" he asked. "I started out in Hinton James my freshman year and then…"

For the next two hours, they traded college stories about their beloved University of North Carolina. They were surprised to discover they had actually been to quite a few of the same games and school events. They also talked about their childhood escapades and adventures.

Time flew by as they chatted in mutual enjoyment until Nurse Carol came in to take Devin's vitals and administer his meds. "You seem to be feeling better," she remarked as she approached the bed.

"Must be the excellent company," Devin said, truthfully.

Darcie smiled, thoroughly pleased with the compliment. "Awww...stop." She walked toward the door, feeling lighter and more relaxed than she had in a long time. "Hope you get some rest." She turned to the nurse. "Have a good night, Carol."

"You, too, Darcie," Nurse Carol said. Then she turned to take Devin's temperature. "Sleep well, Darcie Finch," Devin slurred, Nurse Carol's thermometer already in his mouth.

"Good night." Darcie paused for effect. "Laurence."

CHAPTER TEN

The music swelled and ebbed, rolling over him in a continuous wave. Each chord lilted and swirled, covering him in a blanket of peace so comforting and soothing that...

Oh, my God. I must be dead.

It was the only possible explanation. He was dead. He had died overnight.

Devin didn't move as he assessed his situation. Heavenly music. The sweet smell of roses. Yes, he surmised. It all made sense. He lay still listening to the music, thankful for the scent of flowers instead of hot, flaming sulfur. He was definitely dead.

Or, maybe not.

There was one earthly problem that wasn't resolved. He still couldn't see. He had spent enough time in church in his youth—and, more recently, with the audio Bible that Blane had given him—to assume that if he was really in heaven, he would be able to see.

That Bible had been a literal godsend.

"You should probably start with the Book of Job," Blane had said. "Listen to that one all the way through, though. It does have a happy ending."

Job lost everything…his wealth, his family, even his health. What Devin didn't remember, however, was a happy ending for the poor man. He was intrigued, both by the possibility that Job found life after trauma and that one of his best and most respected friends was encouraging him to read about it. It had been a long time since Devin's mind had traveled in that direction. But God had let him live, so he figured the least he could do was to reacquaint himself with his Maker.

Devin's thoughts flowed around him as the music continued. A series of intricate runs and delicate trills added to the richness of sound. He drifted, so immersed in the melodies, that he almost forgot he was…dead?

Maybe he was lying in his coffin. The roses he could smell were part of the elaborate casket-piece and wreaths that his family and friends had prepared in response to his untimely demise.

He couldn't hear anyone weeping, though. Surely there would be weeping.

But not from Mallory.

She would probably have difficulty containing her delight. He could almost see her in a very expensive and—true to form—slightly inappropriate black dress. She would wear an enormous black hat. With a veil, like she was in some kind of music video. She would cling to Desiree's arm as she approached the casket, holding a stark, white handkerchief in her hand. He could almost hear her fake-sobbing, just loud enough so everyone's eyes would be glued to the tragic figure of the beautiful—and, thanks to him, very rich—young widow.

Ridiculous.

The image of a triumphant Mallory was so unsettling that Devin cautiously stretched his arms out on either side, as far as they could go. He was both pleased and relieved that he couldn't feel the wooden sides of a casket. He raised his arms up until his palms touched. With a sigh of relief, he relaxed into his comfortable bed, bringing his arms back down to rest on either side of the mattress. He blew out a breath, still a little unnerved by the past few minutes. He decided, then and there, that he wasn't taking any more prescription pain medicines at bedtime.

The music soared to its passionate conclusion, followed by a peaceful silence. Devin could feel a slight breeze, bringing with it the strong fragrance of roses. He listened to the birds scolding one another. The windows were open in his room, taking advantage of a day of low humidity, a rare occurrence in a Southern summer. He heard the sound of footsteps and deliberately tamped down the hope that they belonged to The Voice.

He had spent quite a lot of time last night pondering the puzzle that was Miss Darcie Finch. On one hand, she was confident and unafraid to say what was on her mind. Sometimes, to his unending amusement, she said the first thing that popped out of her mouth. She was going to have to work on that absent filter a little bit to become a successful lawyer. He could just imagine her spouting out her thoughts to a judge. Oh, she would make an impression, all right. She might, also, end up in contempt of court.

She was kind, though. Compassionate. Genuine. And, well…funny. Not just funny. Oh, no. Darcie Finch was hilarious. Her stories of growing up in the small town of Honeysuckle Creek were a riot. He had laughed so much last night that his sides were a little sore. For the first time in several weeks, it wasn't because of broken ribs. That part was unexpected.

After their first unfortunate meeting, he had assumed she would be aloof and all-business. *Enthusiastically condescending*, in other words. Nothing could be farther from the truth. She thought he was funny, too. He could tell. Her uncontrolled giggles—he wished they didn't sound so sexy—were a dead giveaway.

He cursed his temporary absence of vision. He wanted to see her laugh, giving in to her hilarity with total abandon. He wanted to watch the emotions flit across her face, as he had imagined last night. He was getting so good at imagining his own facial expressions that, now, he was starting to imagine hers. The images were hazy, of course, because he didn't have any idea what she looked like. He wanted to see her. He wanted to see Darcie Finch, but the bandages currently covering his face made that desire an impossibility.

Under such dire circumstances, he would be happy with a description… any description. That, however, was a problem. He remembered the way she turned all icy and cold when he asked what she looked like. No way was he going to ask her again. His curiosity, however, was rapidly becoming an obsession.

He could only assume that there was something wrong with her, at least in her own opinion. He wondered if she was ashamed of her weight or the shape of her body. Had she been picked on or teased by other children when she was growing up? Maybe she was chosen last for games in PE. If so, he wanted to go back to her elementary school and find anyone that had dared to torment her and, well...he didn't know what he would do. He only knew that he felt as protective of Miss Darcie Finch as he did of his cousin, Diana, and his very own daughter. And nobody was going to mess with either one of them.

Maybe she was like some of the radio personalities whose voices didn't match their bodies. That was a possibility. Well, he didn't care. He didn't care what Miss Darcie Finch looked like. He liked her, just the way she was. He had had enough of beautiful people who were in love with themselves.

His good mood faltered with that thought. Yes, he thought, darkly. He knew all about people like that. After all, he had been married to one for four and a half very long years.

"Good morning, Sleepy Head. Rise and shine."

The Voice was back—and not a minute too soon. Her velvety tones chased away his dark thoughts, leaving behind a sharp feeling of anticipation.

"Rise and shine?" he asked, trying to hide some of his eagerness.

"That's what Daddy always says. Basically, it's his way of saying, 'Get yourself out of bed and be happy about it.'"

She set the breakfast tray down on the tray table.

"And are you?" he asked.

"Am I what?" she asked, cautiously.

"Happy about it."

"Well, of course I am. Aren't you?"

"I'm happy about my breakfast."

She laughed. "I swear. You have a one-track mind. I don't know how you persuaded Mrs. Hofmann to make this stuff for you. It's completely devoid of nutrition."

"But completely delicious," Devin said, enjoying the teasing disapproval in her voice.

"You are going to have to double your workout if you keep eating all of these carbs," she advised.

"Nope," he said happily. "I'm one of those lucky people with a super-high metabolism. Sometimes I have to eat extra carbs so I won't lose weight."

"Oh my gosh, me, too." She fussed with the tray table, carefully sliding it into position. "I don't say that out loud very often, though. People like us aren't very popular with the general population."

People like us. Devin liked being an *us* with Darcie Finch, even though it completely ruined his theory about her looks. She couldn't possibly be overweight if she had high metabolism. *Hmm.* It made him wonder. He knew her siblings. Her brother, Joey, was a good-looking guy. And Devin had always thought Grace was a little hottie, although he didn't say that around Blane unless he was trying to irritate him.

What if Darcie was the ugly sister? The horse-faced one? What if she looked like the *other* end of the horse? That was a possibility. It would explain her unwillingness to talk about her looks. Poor Darcie Finch. His heart went out to the kind-hearted woman who was helping a relative stranger with his breakfast. The good gene train must have passed her by just like his Cousin Jeri…the hairy one. Well, he didn't care what she looked like. He liked Darcie Finch. He liked her a lot. He got a whiff of that tropical flower scent she wore as she adjusted his tray table. She always smelled so nice.

"What time is it, anyway?" he asked. His bandages made it hard to tell.

"It's ten-thirty," she said.

"Ten-thirty? I haven't slept this late since college." He had enjoyed his best night's sleep since the accident.

Darcie lifted the lid off his breakfast. "Listen carefully," she instructed in a no-nonsense tone. "French toast at two o'clock. Mrs. Hofmann says it has lots of cinnamon-sugar and that it doesn't need syrup. It's cut into strips. You also have four pieces of bacon at ten o'clock. She seems to think you're starving."

"I am," Devin interjected, his lips tipping up on either side. "I think Mrs. Hofmann has fallen in love with me."

Darcie couldn't help but smile at that. "Don't kid yourself, Laurence. She treats everybody that way." She cleared her throat. "And, now, if I may have your permission to continue…"

"Permission granted."

"Thank you. There are mandarin orange slices at six o'clock. Those were my idea. At least you can have some natural sugar."

"Awww, Darcie Finch, I'm touched by your genuine concern for my welfare." Devin reached for his oranges at six o'clock. He bit into the first slice. "You must have fallen in love with me too," he said, wickedly.

"Hmph!" was her only response.

As Devin continued eating, he could hear Darcie moving around the room. She was opening the blinds…picking up the pillows he had knocked onto the floor during the night. He was quite the active sleeper. He ate his breakfast, completely distracted by the presence of The Voice. She began humming something in her rich, silky timbre…something he had heard before. After several minutes, he figured it out. It was the same song he had listened to earlier, when he thought he might be dead. And that could mean only one thing: The Voice was also The Music. He silently digested this astounding information, along with his last slice of bacon.

Nurse Carol breezed into the room. "And how is our patient feeling today?" she asked in a cheerful voice.

"I'll get the remains of his breakfast, Carol," Darcie volunteered. She added mischievously: "I think he's done all of the damage he can do, unless he's going to eat the tray, too."

Devin heard the sound of the wheels on the tray table stop and the clink of dishes as Darcie picked up the tray.

Nurse Carol began her examination. "Did you sleep better last night, Devin?"

"I did," he said sorrowfully. "Until the most awful noise woke me up this morning." The dishes rattled a little as Darcie paused on her way to the door. He hoped she was listening.

"Awful noise?" Carol asked with some concern.

"Yes," Devin answered with relish. "Someone was banging on the piano. I thought that racket would never end." He heard Darcie's swift intake of breath. "I guess you heard it, too. It was awful. Whoever was doing it obviously has no sense of rhythm or musical ability." He tried to look serious but couldn't tamp the grin that was tugging at his lips.

The dishes rattled again, with more force.

"Hey, Nurse Carol," Devin said in an exaggerated whisper. "What's she doing right now?"

"She's glaring at you," Carol whispered back, getting into the spirit of things.

"Is she trying to decide whether or not to start throwing dishes?"

"No." Carol paused, considering. "I think she's trying to decide *which* dish to throw first."

"*Hmph.*" Darcie made sure she was extra-loud this time, rattling the tray while stomping out of the door.

Silence descended. Carol continued her examination of her patient. Suddenly the sounds of intricate musical runs echoed down the hallway, followed by a series of horribly off-key chords. Devin mentally applauded Miss Divine-Talent's musical message. He understood exactly what she was saying. He understood it loud and clear.

CHAPTER ELEVEN

Half an hour later—with a little help from Nurse Carol—Devin was freshly showered, dressed, and sitting in a chair instead of in his bed. He was a little surprised to discover that The Voice had agreed to escort him around the yard for his morning exercise. "Do you really think that's a good idea?" he asked Nurse Carol, slightly concerned about retaliation for his little musical joke.

"It was her idea," Carol said, thoughtfully. "I was telling her about how well you did yesterday when she just volunteered right out of the blue."

"She'll probably escort me right into the creek," he said with a shudder.

The Voice chose that exact moment to walk into the room. Of course.

"I have to be honest with you, Laurence," Darcie Finch said. "The thought has crossed my mind."

Devin's nerves immediately shifted to high alert, more from her unexpected entrance than her thinly veiled threat. He was never quite prepared for the effect her voice had on his senses. Her warm tones wrapped around him like a blanket.

Carol laughed as she gathered her things and headed for the door. "Good luck, Devin. There are extra-absorbent towels under the sink in the bathroom, just in case. I hear they're perfect for soaking up creek water."

"Thanks, Carol," Devin replied. "I'll be sure to remember that." But in truth, he was pleased to have another chance to match wits with The Voice. "All right, Fantastically-Talented-Yet-Kind-and-Forgiving-Lady-of-the-Ivory-Keys," he said. "I'm ready if you are."

He stood up, holding on to the chair and grinning in spite of himself. He took a moment to savor the fact that, after two months, he no longer needed to use a cane. He considered that little triumph his personal reward for taking his physical therapy very seriously. He was looking forward to this unexpected excursion with Darcie Finch.

His anticipation, however, had little to do with the great outdoors and everything to do with the plan he had devised last night before falling asleep. It was a sneaky plan, but a plan nonetheless. And he refused to apologize for that. However, he needed to be in close proximity to his target in order for his plan to succeed. Darcie had unknowingly supplied the opportunity by offering to take him on his walk. Today he would try to solve the puzzle of the Problem Looks of Darcie Finch.

He held out his arm, eager to get started. "I am completely at your mercy."

Just then his phone rang, effectively silencing the sassy retort about to spring from Darcie's lips. "I'll see who it is," she said, instead. She picked up his phone from the nightstand between the bed and his newly vacated chair.

He sat back down, feeling a stab of dread. Every time his phone rang, the likelihood increased that it would be Mallory. He hadn't personally heard from her in...what? Two weeks? Or was it more like three? He knew she would call only if she wanted something. As the date for Blane's engagement party drew closer, he was pretty sure he knew what that something would be. There was no way *that* particular conversation was going to go well. No way in hell.

What's the matter, Merritt? he asked himself sarcastically. *Afraid of having a cozy, little chat with your loving wife? You know she only wants what's best for you.* He almost groaned at the enormous exaggeration. *Joke's on me,* he silently jeered. During his folly of a marriage he had learned to live with one indisputable fact: Mallory wanted what was best for Mallory. Everyone else was a distant second place. Every. Single. Time.

Darcie noticed the way Devin leaned forward in his chair, as if preparing for battle. "It's Diana. Do you want me to put her on speaker phone?" she asked uncertainly.

"Yes, please," Devin answered, feeling the tension drain from his body as he relaxed back in his chair.

Hmm. It was easy for Darcie to surmise that Diana *wasn't* the person he didn't want to talk to. Interesting. She stored that little fact away as she pressed the button, carefully placing the phone back on the table between Devin's chair and the bed. "Do you want me to leave?" she whispered.

"No, no," he said absently. "This won't take long."

Darcie sat down on the edge of the bed to wait.

"Hi, Diana. Is everything all right?"

Diana's cheerful voice responded quickly, "Hi, yourself. Everyone is feeling much better here. I'm just calling to check on you."

"Me, too, Nanny Di," a childish voice added. "I'm calling, too. Hi, Daddy! I miss you!"

Devin didn't try to hide the joy that little voice produced. "Hi, Amalie. I miss you, too. How are you?"

"I'm fine, Daddy, but Iggy has a stomach bug. He's been very sad. Nanny Di says that he has to stay in bed until he feels better. Do you have a stomach bug, too?"

"No, 'Malie. I don't have a stomach bug, but I hope Iggy feels better very soon." Devin turned to Darcie. "Iggy is her stuffed iguana," he said.

"Who are you talking to, Daddy?" Amalie asked shrilly.

"I'm talking to Miss Grace's sister, Miss Darcie."

"Hi, Miss Darcie!" Amalie's excited voice took over the conversation. "I like Miss Grace. She's nice. And I like Mr. Blane. He's silly. And I like Atticus. He's a funny dog and Mr. Blane calls him Atta-boy and he sits on Mr. Blane's foot. And I saw Mr. Blane kiss Miss Grace when I was behind the curtains in the dining room and…"

"Am-a-lie," Diana interjected. "You aren't supposed to hide behind the curtains. Spying on people isn't very nice."

"I wasn't spying," the little girl denied earnestly. "I was there first, playing with Iggy, and Mr. Blane pulled Miss Grace into the room and shut the door and kissed her, and then I jumped out and yelled, '*Boo!*' and Miss Grace squealed and then her face got really red and Mr. Blane helped me find my daddy. Remember that, Daddy?" Amalie's voice ebbed and flowed; Devin pictured her dancing around the room as she talked on the phone.

"I do," said Devin, trying not to laugh out loud. "I bet Mr. Blane remembers that, too." He mentally winked at Darcie, but, unfortunately, she had no idea. Or maybe she did. He thought he heard her smother a giggle.

"Are you playing with Miss Darcie, Daddy?" Amalie asked.

"Your daddy can't play yet, Amalie," Diana explained. "He has to get well, first."

"Poor Daddy." Amalie's sweet voice was full of childish compassion. "I wish I could play with you, Daddy. Why is Miss Darcie there?"

"Miss Darcie is my…" Devin hesitated. *Nurse's helper? Meal advisor? Piano-playing, sweet-smelling, sultry-voiced, funny-as-hell* what? Leaning toward Darcie, he asked, a little desperately, "What are you?"

"Hi Amalie!" Darcie spoke up, quickly, moving closer to the phone. "I'm your Daddy's…um…babysitter," she finished, taking advantage of the chance to retaliate for Devin's musical dig earlier that morning.

"Babysitter!" Amalie squealed happily. "Nanny Di, Daddy has a babysitter!"

Devin—and his babysitter—heard her infectious laughter loud and clear.

"Ooh, that's a good one, Darcie. Lord knows he needs a babysitter." Diana was thoroughly enjoying herself. "I try my best, but he's pretty much a hopeless case."

"I'm right here," said Devin, causing both women to burst out laughing.

"Daddy, Daddy! Guess what?" Amalie cried excitedly over the commotion. She didn't give Devin a chance to guess. "Gamma Ollie and Papa

Rob bought me a new princess dress." When Amalie was learning to talk, "Grandma Allana" had come out as "Gamma Ollie." The name stuck.

Devin sighed. "Di-a-na, *another* princess dress?"

"But it's a pink Sleeping Beauty dress, Daddy. Gamma Ollie says that I can wear it for Halloween. Hurray!" Amalie's enthusiasm was almost tangible.

"And what girl, in her right mind, would say no to Gamma Ollie?" Diana asked ruefully. "Certainly not this girl. Gamma Ollie bought a few princess dresses for me when I was little, too."

Darcie was enjoying herself immensely. Amalie obviously had her daddy wrapped around her little finger. Their exchange was providing her new insight into the character of Devin Merritt. Even though she couldn't see his eyes, his very expressive lips revealed a whole range of emotion—from paternal pride to reluctant disapproval to unwilling acceptance. It was evident: he loved his little girl.

Darcie pondered Devin's part of the conversation so far. His initial response to "another princess dress" revealed his I-don't-want-to-raise-a-spoiled-brat side. That was good, Darcie decided. She equated most of society's problems to overindulgent parents who gave their children too many material objects and too little personal time and attention. She liked the fact that Devin was involved enough in his daughter's life to know that, sometimes, it was all right for Amalie's grandparents to spoil her. That revealed his I-want-my-daughter-to-be-happy-but-within-reason side. The entire exchange reminded Darcie of her own childhood and her beloved father, Joe Finch, whose unconditional love and support still wrapped warmly around her.

"Miss Darcie, Miss Darcie!"

Darcie was jerked from her reverie by the urgency of the childish voice. "Yes, ma'am?"

"Do you like princesses, Miss Darcie? I *love* princesses! My favorites are Cinderella and Sleeping Beauty. I already have a Cinderella dress. It's blue. I like blue, but I like pink better. Do you like pink, too? Nanny Di says that I am pretty in pink. Are you pretty in pink, too? Who's your favorite princess,

Miss Darcie?" Once she got started, Amalie couldn't seem to stop peppering her new friend with questions.

Darcie was absolutely enchanted. She loved to talk to children. She thought, carefully, before answering, to be sure that she covered everything. "I like blue *and* pink, Amalie, but my mama says I'm pretty in red, so I like to wear red dresses."

"Ooh! I like red, too. What about the princesses?"

Amalie was excited. Grown-ups weren't always this much fun on the phone. Especially mommies. Amalie's mommy *never* wanted to talk to her on the phone. She liked talking only to grown-ups, like Miss Desiree. Amalie liked talking to Miss Darcie. She was fun, like Nanny Di.

Darcie didn't disappoint the little girl. "I like princesses, too, Amalie. Grace and I used to dress up when we were little, just like you. My favorite princess is Jasmine, but I like Cinderella, too. I always wanted my brother, Joey, to dress up like Aladdin and play with us, but he wouldn't."

"Boys are funny like that," Amalie commiserated, in a grown-up voice. "My daddy plays dress-up sometimes. He likes to play Pretty, Pretty Princess with me. He looks silly wearing the earrings. One time for Halloween, he was Prince Charming and…"

Devin interrupted, trying to save what was left of his dignity. He could hear Darcie's throaty giggles, so it was probably too late. "All right, Amalie, that's enough information for now. Maybe you can tell Miss Darcie more fascinating stories some other time."

Diana spoke up. "I, for one, have thoroughly enjoyed this conversation, but we need to go have lunch."

"Daddy, are you going to be a monster for Halloween?" Amalie asked, without her earlier exuberance.

"A-ma-lie, don't you dare," Diana said, forcefully.

Devin tensed, his hands clutching the arms of the chair. "Why would I be a monster for Halloween, Amalie?" he asked, carefully.

Amalie's voice quivered a little. "Because Mommy said that the accident made you look like a monster, so you won't need a costume for Halloween."

"A-ma-lie Rose! Hush!" Diana admonished her small charge. "I told you not to repeat that."

But her words came too late. Devin sucked in a gasp of pain. The sheer cruelty of Mallory's comment, delivered in the innocent voice of his child, stole his ability to speak. His grip tightened on the chair until his knuckles were white. Darcie was horrified by the exchange. What would Devin say? How could he assuage his child's innocent fears without lying about the reality of his injuries? She watched him with concern. He was, seemingly, paralyzed. Even worse, he was gripping the arms of his chair as if it was a lifeline. He was obviously devastated by his wife's careless words.

Darcie was outraged. How could the evil woman put such thoughts into her own child's head? Darcie liked to give people the benefit of the doubt, she really did. However, she decided, then and there, that Mallory Merritt wasn't worthy of being the mother to such a delightful child. Or to any child, for that matter.

She also decided that Mallory didn't deserve to be married to a man like Devin Merritt. Darcie hadn't known him very long. Had it really been less than twenty-four hours? During their brief period of acquaintance, she had watched him deal with traumatic, life-changing injuries. It would only be natural for him to give in to despair and depression. Instead, he had earned her reluctant respect, no small task after her initial impression of him.

His acceptance of his unforeseen circumstances, his philosophical humor, and his determination to enjoy everything he had left—from eating breakfast to teasing Darcie about her music—well, that kind of fortitude made a lasting impression. She clearly saw that Devin adored his daughter, another point in his favor. She had heard plenty of negative comments about his wife from his family as well as her own. His wife had issues. Serious issues. That much was readily apparent.

Darcie dropped her polite filter to address the situation before her. Devin was a good man…and his wife was a bitch. Plain and simple. The fledgling lawyer inside of her was itching to help free this man and his little princess from the clutches of the Evil Witch. Darcie had always been a shrewd judge of human nature. *Except for yesterday*, she reminded herself ruefully. She had seriously misjudged Devin Merritt during their first meeting. But with regard to Devin's heinous wife? Darcie was confident her impressions were spot-on, falling in line with the sentiments of those she knew and trusted implicitly.

Was it possible for people to change? she asked herself, trying to be fair. Of course, it was. Two perfect examples were Lou Boggs and her sister's ex-fiancé, Roger Carrington. But, those two were from the friends-turned enemies-turned-friends-again category. That was different. Sometimes good people lost their way. It was a shame, she decided. But, unfortunately, it happened. That wasn't what Devin's situation was about at all.

Darcie placed Devin's bitchy wife in the category of diabolical creatures who were bad to begin with and who only became worse with time. She felt very strongly that Mallory Merritt fit the category perfectly. In the span of a single phone conversation, Darcie realized that Devin had her loyalty, and Mallory, her contempt. In light of these revelations, there was no way she could stay quiet. No way at all.

Darcie leaned closer to speak directly into the phone. "It's not true." The words burst from her lips, begging to be repeated. "Amalie. Listen to me very carefully. What your mother said…it's not true."

"Daddy doesn't look like a monster?" Amalie whispered.

"Of course, he doesn't." Darcie was adamant. "Your daddy had a very bad accident, but he does *not* look like a monster."

"Are you sure?" Amalie asked, hopefully.

"Why, I'm sitting right here, looking at him. Of course, I'm sure. Your daddy absolutely, positively, does *not* look like a monster." Darcie let out a breath of relief, noting that Devin had relaxed a bit. At least he wasn't gripping the arms of his chair anymore.

Back in Providence, Amalie thought about what Miss Darcie had told her. She glanced at Nanny Di, whose eyes were full of warning. Amalie looked away, thinking furiously. Miss Darcie's favorite princess was Jasmine. And she liked to wear red. Miss Darcie was Daddy's babysitter…and Daddy wouldn't have a bad babysitter. So Amalie decided to believe Miss Darcie instead of her mommy.

Amalie knew that Mommy lied a lot. Mommy *liked* to lie. Amalie had overheard Nanny Di tell Gamma Ollie that Mommy was a *lying bitch*. She didn't quite know what that meant, but she knew it must be very bad. Amalie knew that *she* wasn't supposed to say *lying bitch* out loud because she had said it once—and Nanny Di told her it wasn't nice. She was glad that Daddy didn't look like a monster, but, if Daddy didn't look like a monster, then…

"What does Daddy look like?" she asked.

In Devin's bedroom, Darcie started, straightening her back in alarm. "What?" Amalie wasn't going to let it go. Good Lord. The child was a little Darcie Finch in the making.

"Am-a-lie Rose." The warning tone was clear in Diana's voice.

Amalie ignored her nanny. "If Daddy doesn't look like a monster, then what does he look like?"

"He looks like…" Darcie said the first words that came to her mind. "A pirate. Yes," she continued, confidently. "He looks like a pirate. When you see him, he'll have some pretty cool scars on his face. He might even wear an eye patch."

Darcie sat up straight again, slowly releasing her breath. She glanced at Devin. His lips had lost their grim line and his jaw wasn't clenched as tightly as before. *Please, please, please.* Darcie lifted her eyes to heaven. *Please let that be the right thing to say.*

"Hurray!" squealed Amalie. "My daddy looks like a pirate! Oooh, Daddy! Can I be a pirate, too? Can I wear your eye patch? Nanny Di, can we buy a pirate costume? I want to be a pirate for Halloween. Daddy and I can go trick-or-treating together. Please, Nanny Di, please!"

Diana was laughing again. "Ask your daddy."

"Daddy, can I get a pirate costume?" Amalie begged, in her little girl voice. "Please."

"How can I say no to that?" Devin asked, pleased that he didn't sound as shaky as he felt. "Diana, please take my daughter to the store, immediately, and buy her a pirate costume." Gone was the tense stillness he had exhibited only moments before.

"Hurray!" Amalie yelled in Providence. "Let's go right now! I'll get Iggy!" She started to run from the room but stopped at the sound of Darcie's voice.

"I thought Iggy had a stomach bug," Darcie said, matter-of-factly.

Amalie paused, thinking it through. But Darcie's comment had just earned her Devin's undying admiration. How had she remembered such a small detail after the trauma of the last few minutes?

"Iggy will be all better when I wake him up from his nap," Amalie replied. "Right, Nanny Di?"

"I'm sure that Iggy will be well enough to go to the costume store," Diana agreed, wryly. "Amalie, don't forget to say goodbye to Daddy and Miss Darcie."

"Bye, Miss Darcie! Bye, Daddy!" And she was gone.

Diana continued the conversation without missing a beat: "Darcie, you are a genius," she said enthusiastically. "I could have killed Mallory for putting that idea in Amalie's head. I didn't know what to do. And, just like that, you've turned it into the best thing ever. Thank you *so* much, even though I have to go back to the costume store. Again."

"I'm sure Devin will give you an afternoon off with a free manicure thrown in as a reward for your dedicated service," Darcie said, slyly.

"That's so nice. Thank you, Devin." Diana was trying to sound serious but failing miserably. "Bye, Darcie. You're the best babysitter he's ever had. I may need to hire you again some time. Bye, Devin."

"Thanks, Diana."

Darcie disconnected the call. She watched Devin lean his head against the back of the chair. He looked exhausted.

"I'm going to give you time to rest and eat lunch before we go outside," Darcie decided. "I don't want you passing out in the garden. I'd hate to have to drag you back to the house."

He heard her leave the room. A difficult hurdle—one that he had been dreading—had been crossed. Instead of being frightened of Daddy the Monster, Amalie was excited about Daddy the Pirate. None of his family—or friends—had known what to tell Amalie about the changes in his appearance. No one except Darcie Finch. She had met the problem head-on and conquered it for him. He would be grateful to her for the rest of his life.

"Yo ho, ho, Darcie Finch," he said aloud, raising his hand in tribute.

CHAPTER TWELVE

*T*he Avarice *rocked in the night breeze as the ship's deck filled with pirates. Devin watched as Mallory—sporting a short-skirted pirate dress with a ridiculously low neckline—swung her cutlass menacingly.*

"Avast, ye mateys!" *she screamed.* "Bring the lass aloft. It's time to feed the fish."

"Ay, ay, Cap'n!" *A second pirate—looking suspiciously like Desiree, but sporting a full beard—left the foredeck to do Mallory's bidding.*

Pirate Desiree returned moments later dragging a struggling, little girl by the wrist. The girl was dressed in a pink princess dress. She wore earrings that looked just like the ones from the Pretty, Pretty Princess *board game. And she was carrying something in her hand.*

Devin couldn't seem to make out what it was. His vision was clear one minute and blurry the next. He tried to rub his eyes. That's when he realized his hands were tied behind his back. His vision cleared suddenly, and he was able to observe that he was tied to one of the masts of the giant pirate ship. Now, he could easily make out what the little princess was holding in her hand, and the sight made his heart beat frantically. It was Iggy the Iguana, and that could only mean…

"Amalie Merritt. Ye chose the landlubber, that son-of-a-biscuit-eater." As she spoke, Mallory pointed her cutlass toward Devin before turning the full force of her fury on the young girl in front of her. "Ye betrayed us—and for that, ye must walk the plank."

Devin struggled to free himself, but to no avail. He tried to spit out the gag tied securely over his mouth, but he could only watch...helpless to aid his daughter.

Suddenly, Amalie let go of Iggy. That loyal iguana latched onto Desiree's hairy leg, freeing Amalie from her grasp.

"NOW!" yelled a rich, velvety voice.

As though on command, the moon burst forth from behind a thick cover of clouds. Devin made out the hazy outline of a second ship as it drew close alongside the Avarice. A gang of lithe, fearsome corsairs—ladies, every one of them, adorned in red princess dresses—swarmed the deck of the Avarice, attacking Mallory's crew.

He recognized Diana, rushing toward him, with Amalie's hand fastened securely in hers. "Thank God we got here in time!" she said feverishly. She immediately went to work untying his gag.

Amalie held Iggy once again as that ferocious beast made short work of Devin's bindings. The iguana emitted a loud burp as he swallowed the last piece of rope. Amalie giggled.

"Hurry!" Diana whispered.

They crept, unnoticed, toward the gunwale and the safety of the longboats waiting below. They were going to make it.

Suddenly, a lone pirate stepped in front of them, blocking their way. Diana gasped.

Mallory!

Her eyes were blazing with hatred, her hands were covered with blood, but her skin was nearly flawless. Not even a single hair was out of place.

She took a step toward their little group. Her four-inch red heels clicked loudly against the old boards of the wooden deck. "The only way ye three be leavin' this vessel is over me cold, dead body."

What happened next was a blur. Literally. Devin couldn't see anything but a blurry flash of red. The next thing he knew, Mallory was shark bait.

"Well, shiver me timbers," said The Voice. "Princess Amalie, you are safe. And you, too, Cap'n Laurence." *As she leaned over the gunwale, a pale, moonbeam illuminated her lovely figure. She was clad, like all the rest, in a red princess dress. Devin waited, in an agony of suspense. Finally, he would see her face. Finally.*

She turned around, slowly. Devin couldn't believe his eye. On top of her elegantly sloped shoulders rested, not the face of a lovely pirate queen, but the head of a horse.

Well. That was unexpected.

The sound of squeaky wheels of a borrowed tray table pulled Devin back to the real world. Clearly, somebody needed to invest in a can of WD-40, and soon.

He moved his neck from side to side, trying to escape the remnants of his unnerving dream. Several thoughts lingered.

First, it had probably been wrong for him to enjoy seeing Mallory go overboard. But he had enjoyed it…a lot.

Second, he would never be able to look at Desiree again without seeing her bearded pirate face and hairy legs. Those images would be a perpetual source of amusement for him.

The third and final consequence of his short nap was an even stronger determination to find out what Darcie Finch looked like.…He liked to work puzzles. He liked putting all of the pieces together—he was pretty good at it. Usually. But not so with the puzzle of Darcie Finch. He was absolutely certain she was hiding something from him. And he wanted, desperately, to find out what that something was.

The Voice did not reappear with his lunch tray, allowing him to take full advantage of his time with Nurse Carol. Asking a few pointed questions, Devin learned that Darcie was a great favorite of Carol's. Apparently, Darcie had defended Carol's socially awkward son for years. While defending him, she had taught him to stand up for himself. The ability to stand up for himself gave him the confidence to apply to med school. Applying to med school changed his life. And on and on and on...

Devin gained the impression that Darcie was some kind of superhero in disguise. He could almost see her. Standing on a mountain with her hands on her hips. Her cape billowing out behind her. A gigantic *DF* emblazoned on her chest. Darcie Finch. Defender of the weak. Crusader for the less fortunate. Friend to the friendless. Yes, he thought. He could almost see her. Except for the fact that he couldn't see her because *he didn't know what she looked like!* And the not knowing was driving him crazy.

He heard Carol tidying up the tray. Apparently, his time with his informant was growing short. *What the hell?* He was feeling reckless. He might as well just come right out and ask her.

"So, Nurse Carol, I was wondering..." Devin tried to appear as nonchalant as possible. "What does Darcie look like, anyway?"

"She didn't tell you what she looks like?" Carol asked, a smile in her voice.

"No, she didn't. She just said her looks were a *problem*."

Carol didn't say anything.

Devin blew out a breath. "Well?"

"Well, what?" she asked innocently.

Devin felt as awkward as an adolescent. "Are they a problem? Her looks, I mean?"

"I suppose they could be." Carol thought for a moment. "Listen, Devin, I know Darcie pretty well. If she didn't tell you what she looks like, then it's probably because she doesn't want to talk about it. Enjoy your walk. I'll see you later."

Devin mentally said goodbye to his lost opportunity. *Well,* he thought. *It looks like I'm going to have to get my information straight from the horse's mouth.* That unfortunate phrase—coupled with the ridiculous dream he had earlier—struck him as so hilarious that he was still chuckling when The Voice reappeared.

"Ahoy, matey," she said.

Darcie's pirate cant startled Devin, making him wonder if he was still dreaming.

"What are you wearing?" he asked, urgently. If she said a princess dress...

"Shorts and a T-shirt," she said quickly. "Why?"

"No reason. Just wondering."

Thank goodness his bandages were coming off tomorrow. Spending so much time inside his own head obviously wasn't healthy.

He liked the pirate idea, though. He would enjoy being a pirate so much more than his original post-accident plan of becoming a ventriloquist. A pirate could move his mouth when he talked. That was a definite plus. He could do this. He could embrace his new persona.

Devin Merritt, Pirate.

Or, even better...

Devin Merritt, Pirate-Lawyer.

Maybe, he thought, he could do commercials for Merritt Brothers while wearing his eye patch. The idea was unexpectedly appealing. So caught up was he in the vision of his new life as a pirate that he failed to reply to Darcie's happy pirate greeting.

"Umm...Devin?" Darcie hesitated, unsure if the man in front of her was asleep or awake. "If you don't want to take a walk right now, all you have to do is tell me."

"Oh, I want to take a walk. The real question is, do you?" Devin's suddenly buoyant spirits threatened to spill over. "Arrrre you ready?" He hoped so, because he was about to have some fun with Darrr-cie Finch.

The pirate cant continued into the hall, out the side door, and into the rose garden. "How arrre we doing, Darrrr-cie Finch?"

"Arrre we in the yarrrrd yet?"

"Don't try to arrrgue with me."

"Will you read me some arrrticles later?"

"Maybe, you can turn on the radio and I can listen to some ARRR'n B."

"What have I done?" Darcie asked, pleased that her usually absent filter had prevented her from blurting out: *I've created a monster!* That would have been the worst possible thing to say after their earlier conversation. So, she encouraged his nonsense. It was impossible not to laugh at his unbridled creativity, anyway, and she figured that Devin the Pirate might need to blow off a little steam.

"Tell me what everything looks like, please, Darrr-cie Finch," Devin requested, finally running out of words that started with or contained *arrr*.

"Well, we just walked through the rose garden. It's absolutely gorgeous...." She made sure to keep her descriptions vivid and thorough to help him create a picture in his mind. He looped his arm through hers, bringing his muscular frame in close proximity. By focusing diligently on the quality of her narration she avoided being distracted. At least, that's what she kept telling herself.

They had scarcely reached the banks of Honeysuckle Creek when Devin put his brilliant plan into action. He deliberately lost his footing, stumbling for a minute. Darcie immediately grabbed hold of his waist, one hand on either side. She tried to steady him to prevent them both from ending up on the ground. They weren't close enough to the creek for a dunking, but if she lost her grip and he staggered the wrong way...

Overjoyed by her reaction to his premeditated stumble, Devin allowed his arms to settle around her waist. Taking shameless advantage, he leaned into her. For several moments, his body was plastered against hers, giving him the chance to test his theory. His hunch was correct. There wasn't an ounce of excess fat on her body, unless she had very large feet.

What he wasn't at all prepared for was the sensation he felt holding her in his arms. Their brief embrace gave him more to think about than the ratio of her body fat. He became aware of her perfect proportions, the supple muscles in her back as she fought for balance, and the way they fit together.

In other words, that brief moment had the impact of a lightning strike. He was suddenly more aware of this woman than he had ever been of any woman in his entire existence.

Devin's overheated brain struggled to focus on a safer topic. He ended up pondering the unknown size of Darcie's feet as she fussed over him. Once he was steady on his feet again, she took a step back. She was breathing hard, and he regretted having frightened her.

Even as he applauded himself for the successful outcome of his quest, Devin felt a degree of trepidation. On one hand, he had established that The Problem Looks of Darcie Finch had nothing whatsoever to do with the shape of her body. On the other hand, he was already regretting their brief contact. The soft touch of her hands at his waist was now permanently imprinted in his memory.

Darcie was stunned as well. She had never experienced anything like the exhilarating—but simultaneously terrifying—moment in Devin Merritt's arms. The situation was made worse by the knowledge that any attraction she felt had to begin and end right there. He was married, she told herself.

Married.

Damn it.

She let out a sigh of relief when Devin had regained his footing. She felt a little lightheaded, attributing her uncharacteristic shortness of breath to the shock of his hard body pressed against hers. Darcie had never—*never*—been so drawn to a man in her life. Every instinct was screaming for her to put some distance between them, but what was she supposed to do? Run away and leave him standing alone in the middle of the back lawn of Heart's Ease? Alone and unable to see? Of course not. So, she stepped back as far as she could while still giving him an anchor to hold on to. His hand remained on her bare arm. She hoped he wouldn't notice she was trembling.

Devin was in big trouble. He racked his brain for a distraction…anything to keep his mind from the soft, warm woman who was the perfect fit for him. The fact that he could feel her trembling beside him didn't help. He was fighting the almost irresistible urge to pull her back into his arms. Making a valiant, last-ditch effort to return to their precollision camaraderie, Devin blurted the first words that came to his mind: "What's your shoe size, Darrr-cie Finch?"

His question was random and unexpected. The perfect distraction.

"My shoe size?" She was completely puzzled and a little suspicious of his motives, but grateful, too. The haphazard question, somehow, restored her equilibrium. "Why do you need to know my shoe size?"

Devin almost groaned. "No reason." Pretty lame question for someone who was supposed to be clever *and* witty. *Way to go, you idiot.* She was probably looking at him like he was some strange creature from another planet. That supposition went a long way toward cooling his ardor. Maybe he could ask Nurse Carol to find out Darcie's shoe size for him, he mused. Unless he could learn this small, but important, detail, he was doomed to dream of a beautifully proportioned lady pirate with the head of a horse and very large feet.

Darcie finally relented, seeing no harm in supplying such an innocuous piece of information. She was actually thankful for something to talk about. "I usually wear a seven or a seven and a half, depending on the make of the shoe."

"Seven or seven and a half," he echoed, realizing that he knew absolutely nothing about women's shoes. Her revelation was no help at all. "So…" He gave up all attempts at subtlety. "Does that mean you have big feet or not?"

Darcie wanted to laugh. This had to be their most ridiculous conversation yet, and that was saying a lot. "I believe my feet are correctly proportional to the rest of my body." She paused before saying, politely, "Thanks for asking."

Devin snorted in appreciation and relief. It appeared his dream horse/woman had normal-sized feet.

"Arrre you ready to go back?" she asked, relieved that those few uncomfortable moments were behind them.

"Ay ay, Cap'n," he answered, winding his arm around hers as he turned them toward the house. He was feeling rather proud of his fail-safe sense of direction...until she gently turned him around to face the opposite way.

"Larrr-ence." Her velvety tones were full of amusement. "The house is this way."

They walked for a few seconds in comfortable silence.

"Darcie Finch," said Devin, thoughtfully. "Has anyone ever told you that you have a gorgeous..."

Darcie felt her entire body tense in disappointment. *Please don't say it,* she begged silently. *Not you. Not one of the few people who doesn't seem to care what I look like. Please don't say it.*

"...speaking voice?" Devin finished, oblivious to Darcie's distress.

Darcie gritted her teeth. "No," she answered automatically. "No one has ever said that I have a gorgeous...What?" She paused for clarification.

"Has anyone ever told you that you have a gorgeous speaking voice?" Devin repeated patiently.

"Why, no," she said, truthfully, shocked and humbled at the same time. "No one has ever said that to me before. That's probably the best compliment I've ever gotten. Thank you."

"You're welcome," said Devin, touched by her gratitude. Had no one ever given her a compliment before? He was a little angry on Darcie Finch's behalf. Was she the neglected Finch sibling, overlooked because she wasn't blessed with the good looks of the rest of the family? Was he one of the few who had discovered her amazing qualities?

"Watch the steps," Darcie instructed, leading him through the outside door and back into his room. She turned him carefully, placing his hand on the arm of the chair. "Okay. You can sit down now."

He sat, surprised that his legs were a little weak. He was, it seemed, more than ready for a rest. He was equally ready to put some distance between himself and Miss Darcie Finch. He needed some time alone to figure out why he was so drawn to her. In less than a day, they had formed a bond. A connection. An understanding that was incredibly satisfying on a deeply personal level.

Something, however, had shifted between them on their walk...an increased awareness of each other on a level deeper than he had previously understood. Given his circumstances—his precious daughter and his miserable excuse for a wife—Devin had to find a way to prevent that awareness from making itself known. On every level. He refused to put a name to the swirling cacophony of emotions Darcie inspired. He knew better than to examine those feelings too closely. He allowed himself only to acknowledge their existence. And to remind himself that for a man like him, those feelings were very, very dangerous.

Darcie, too, felt the need to get away. "I'm going to run some errands this afternoon and stop by the house to finish packing for my trip," she announced, brightly. Too brightly, in her own estimation. It was time to make her escape. Devin's compliment—so unexpected and so genuine—was doing funny things to her heart. While she was filled with gratitude for his sincerity, she was, also, honest enough to admit that she was enjoying his words a little too much. As a matter of fact, she was enjoying everything about Devin Merritt a little too much.

Darcie decided it would be wise to stop dwelling on those pointless feelings. She would, instead, concentrate on the gratitude she felt for such a rare and genuine compliment. She resolved to do something for Devin and his adorable, little girl. Her heart ached when she thought of all they had been through and all that was to come. "I'll be back later," she said decisively, heading for the door. She had a lot to accomplish.

Before he could stop it, Devin's mouth outpaced his brain. "I'll miss you, Darcie Finch." Even as he said it, he knew he shouldn't have. He got no reply.

CHAPTER THIRTEEN

*H*oneysuckle Creek's successful transition from sleepy farm town to popular tourist spot was due, in part, to the high quality and variety of shopping and dining options in town. Interestingly enough, some of the most popular businesses had been around for years. Re-creating themselves to appeal to each new generation allowed them to thrive.

A perfect example, one of Darcie's favorite stores, currently bore the name Sweet Life. Since the 1920s, the business had been owned and operated by a branch of the once prolific Broad family. The store was originally known as Broad's Medicine Shop, Honeysuckle Creek's first pharmacy.

The Broad family's lack of originality in naming businesses spilled over into several other less successful ventures, including the ill-fated Broad's Horse-drawn Carriage Company, the unfortunate Broad's Typewriter Repair Shop, and the short-lived Broad's Disco Clothing and Accessories.

Many Broad family businesses had come and gone. However, the descendants of Edward Lee Broad—the founder and original owner of the medicine shop—learned to change with the times. After two successive generations failed to produce a pharmacist, the Broads made the most of other familial strengths. Broad's Medicine Shop evolved into Broad's Soda Shop in the mid-forties, Broad's Sweet Shop in the fifties, and Broad's Sweets and Treats in the seventies. Its present configuration, Sweet Life, had come into being in the late nineties. In Honeysuckle Creek, innovation was the key to longevity.

Sweet Life sold homemade candy, but that simple description of their confections was quite an understatement. The sheer variety of sugary treats—lovingly and stylishly displayed—made the store a treat for the eyes, as well as the taste buds. Knocking out the wall they shared with the store next door—the now defunct Broad's Video Rentals—allowed Sweet Life to expand their business. In addition to candy, they offered an amazing array of gift baskets, and items with which to fill them. The promise of "designer quality baskets while you wait" made a frequent visit to Sweet Life a must for visitors and locals alike.

Darcie couldn't help the little girl feeling of anticipation that swept over her when she opened the door and inhaled the delicious aromas. After packing for Scotland and making a pie, she was ready to enjoy herself. She had asked her great-grandmother to take the pie out of the oven for her so she wouldn't have to rush. Feeling more in control—more like herself than she had in the past twenty-four hours—she entered the shop.

Before the door had fully closed, an excited voice squealed, "Darcie Finch!"

She was immediately ambushed by seventeen-year-old Leticia Broad. The raven-haired teenager had been crowned Miss Honeysuckle Creek Junior Miss the same ill-fated year Darcie wore her crown. They had appeared at a number of the same events and, despite the difference in their ages, struck up an alliance.

Thirteen-year-old Letty hadn't enjoyed her stint as royalty any more than Darcie. She adored softball, not crowns. With a little coaching from Darcie, Letty had been able to convince her parents to let her follow her true passion. Mr. and Mrs. Broad made the right decision. In a few weeks, Letty would begin her senior year at London County High School, a traditional powerhouse in 4A softball. The talented, young lady had already accepted an athletic and academic scholarship to attend East Carolina University.

Darcie returned Letty's embrace. She was proud of Letty for standing up for herself and finding a way to follow her heart. Letty was a fierce competitor on the field, making only one error during the last two seasons as starting shortstop on her high school team. She was also a girly-girl: she had never played an inning without mascara and a gigantic bow adorning her perfectly braided hair. Letty was true to herself. Darcie respected that.

Mr. Broad cleared his throat loudly from behind the candy counter. He raised his eyebrows at his daughter-employee. Then he winked at Darcie.

Letty stepped back from her friend, trying to be professional. "What may I help you with today, Miss Finch?" She was poised and confident, but her eyes were dancing.

"I need two gift baskets, please," Darcie responded, adding conspiratorially, "And I would appreciate your assistance, Miss Broad."

"This way, please."

Letty motioned for Darcie to follow her through the arched entrance that led to the next room.

Behind a long counter an amazing array of baskets, each neatly numbered and labeled, hung from large hooks on the back wall. Individually packaged ribbons of all kinds of fabrics, styles, and colors were displayed on the walls on either side of the counter. They hung from smaller hooks, each identified by a letter of the alphabet.

Darcie chose a small, white basket for Amalie and a medium-size, pale green basket for Diana. Amalie's nanny, she decided, deserved a treat, too. After choosing the baskets, the fun began. She and Letty prowled through rows and rows of shelves. Each shelf was filled from top to bottom with bins of all sizes. Each bin had a full-size, color picture of the contents, grouped by themes to make choices easier. Beautifully filled, decorated baskets stood on display at the front of the store.

If customers needed advice or simply couldn't make up their minds, a comfortable nook afforded a bit of privacy for personal consultations. Although the area was currently vacant, Darcie had seen lines of desperate gift-givers more than once, usually the day *before* Valentine's Day, Mother's Day, and Christmas. The women of Darcie's acquaintance always had a good giggle over the fact that the lines were almost always filled with men. To be fair, an occasional gift-impaired woman dotted their midst, but it was rare, indeed.

For the next twenty minutes, Darcie and Letty enjoyed themselves. They managed to choose just the right gifts in spite of their animated conversation. Darcie chose lotion, shower gel, and a couple of those cute, fizzing bath bombs—currently all the rage—for Diana. Because she didn't know if Diana liked strong scents, she picked lotion with a subtle hint of peach. The pale green and peach bottles looked pretty in the green basket. She also found a purse-size notepad in the same color palette. And a matching pen.

For Amalie, she chose a child-size bottle of pink bubble bath that smelled like strawberries. She also added a tiny tube of strawberry-scented lip balm and a big, pink hairbow. She wanted to include a little toy, too; so she was delighted when she found a pink teddy bear. In a happy coincidence, she discovered a black-and-white pirate costume that fitted the bear perfectly. It included little black pants, a black-and-white striped shirt, a black bandanna to wrap around the bear's furry head, and, of course, an eye patch. In a word, it was adorable.

After a brief stop at the back counter to select the perfect ribbon—pink for Amalie, a delicate peach for Diana—Darcie followed Letty back to the candy room. Mr. Broad helped her choose the appropriate sweets: a little bag of pink, gummy bears and six pink lollipops tied with a ribbon, for Amalie, and an assortment of Sweet Life's delicious fudge for Diana.

After paying for her gifts, Darcie handed the baskets over to Mr. Broad. He attached the ticket to each and sent them to the back. "Would you like to wait for these, Darcie?" he asked.

"No, thanks. I'll come back in about an hour."

Mr. Broad nodded. "We'll have them ready. Thank you, Darcie."

"These are going to be perfect. Thank you, Mr. Broad." She winked at Letty. "By the way, I couldn't have chosen such perfect gifts without help from your fabulous employee. I really think she deserves a raise," Darcie announced, enjoying Mr. Broad's pleased chuckle.

With a final hug for Letty and a smile for her proud papa, Darcie left the shop. On the way to her Jeep she checked the time on her phone. Her pie needed to come out of the oven in four minutes. By the time she pulled out into the late afternoon traffic, she was very thankful that Grandma Sofi had agreed to take care of that particular chore. As much as she would like to pretend otherwise, she wanted the pie to be the best pie Devin the Pirate had ever eaten in his life.

CHAPTER FOURTEEN

The rich smell of chocolate chess pie greeted Darcie as she opened the front door of the beautiful Victorian home where she had lived all of her life. Honeysuckle Creek's historic district boasted an impressive collection of architectural treasures. Almost every house retained its late-1890s charm, giving visitors the impression that they had stepped back into another century. Darcie's ninety-one-year-old great-grandmother, only slightly younger than the house, was waiting for her in the kitchen.

Sofia Bertolli Hanover was perched on a comfortable bar stool with her arms crossed and a suspicious gleam in her dark eyes. She looked effortlessly elegant in a light purple pair of slacks, a matching floral blouse with sheer sleeves, and her ever-present pearls. Her gray hair was twisted into a knot at the back of her neck, and her posture put Darcie's to shame. She raised her eyebrows in greeting, glancing at the counter and the cooling pie, before fixing her eyes on Darcie again. The questioning look she gave her great-granddaughter made full disclosure a foregone conclusion.

Darcie ignored the strong urge to turn around and run.

"Bella," was all Grandma Sofi said, nodding her head regally. Her foreign accent seemed particularly strong today. Although she was capable of speaking with only a hint of her European upbringing, she enjoyed using her accent to make a point or command attention. More often than not, she used it to ferret out information.

Uh-oh. Darcie knew what was coming. Time to employ a few time-proven defensive strategies. She wasn't the least bit intimidated by her formidable great-grandmother. In fact, Darcie was usually quite adept at avoiding a full-blown interrogation. She tossed her purse on the counter and gave her redoubtable relation a kiss on the cheek. She quickly leaned down to properly adore her parents' golden doodle, Romeo...and to avoid Grandma Sofi's inquisitive gaze.

"Romeo, are you putting on weight?" Darcie asked as she scratched her canine brother behind his furry ears. Darcie delighted in teasing her great-grandmother about her substantial contribution to Romeo's "fluffiness." Grandma Sofi loved the golden doodle to distraction and was prone to slip him treats, an act she vehemently denied whenever she was caught. Darcie's underlying motive, however, was to keep her all-too-observant great-grandmother from asking too many questions.

"Ah," said Grandma Sofi, nodding her head. "It is because he is spoiled, no? Too many treats. Too much Romeo. I have told him this, but he does not seem to care." She stroked Romeo's soft head as Darcie stepped back, pleased to have drawn Grandma Sofi's attention away from the pie.

"Tell me about the pie, Bella. I do not think it is for me or for this beast," she said, indicating the dog. Romeo was currently tapping her leg with his paw to remind her that she wasn't finished patting his head. "You would not make it for yourself and you cannot take it to Scotland. You made this pie for the man with one eye, no?"

"His name is Devin," Darcie said, with a sigh. "He lost his eye several weeks ago in an accident." It was nearly impossible to avoid providing Sofia Hanover with information. She should have been an army interrogator. Darcie hopped up onto the bar stool next to her great-grandmother and prepared to comply.

Grandma Sofi pinned her with a look. "And what has this *Devin* done to deserve one of my Bella's pies? Hmm?"

Darcie started at the beginning, relating everything that had happened in the last twenty-four hours. Well, she thought, a little guiltily, *almost* everything. She deliberately left out the part about Devin's stumble and their brief, but all too memorable, bodily contact. She certainly didn't need Grandma Sofi's insight into that particular encounter. She had, thus far, managed to avoid analyzing those feelings herself.

"He gave me a compliment, Grandma Sofi…a genuine, honest-to-goodness compliment."

Grandma Sofi studied Darcie, seeing, as always, a portrait of the young woman that she, herself, used to be. "You get lots of compliments, Bella, and they do not please you. What makes his compliment so very different than the others?"

"He complimented my speaking voice, Grandma Sofi. My speaking voice. That's something that has nothing to do with my physical appearance. He's never seen me because of his bandages. He has no idea what I look like and he doesn't seem to care. I know *you* understand exactly how much that means to me," Darcie said, softly. She paused, studying her great-grandmother. "Please tell me that you understand."

Sofia Bertolli had been a rising opera star—lauded for her beauty as well as her talent—before Nazis forever changed the course of her life. "Oh, Bella, your beauty is a gift. But you can only see it as a curse. It does not matter anyway. The old saying is true, 'Beauty is in the eye.'"

"I know, Grandma Sofi. I know." Darcie sighed. "'Beauty is in the eye of the beholder.' I've heard that before." The fact that her great-grandmother had started out by quoting things did not bode well for Darcie. Grandma Sofi invariably garbled old proverbs and sayings until they were almost unrecognizable. Sometimes, however, the wise, old woman made more of a point by mixing things up than not. Darcie and her siblings were fairly certain she did it on purpose.

"Beholder? No, Bella, no one is holding anything. Beauty is in the eye… the good, the bad, or, sometimes, a bit of both. You see it all when you look into someone's eyes. What is on the outside…poof, it is gone. But the inside…" She nodded wisely. "That is eternal."

Darcie tilted her head to the side. Her great-grandmother had always called her Bella. She called Joey and Grace by their given names, but Grandma Sofi had never called her youngest great-granddaughter anything but Bella.

When Darcie discovered—at the tender age of nine—that the word *bella* meant "beauty" in both Spanish and Italian, she was very disappointed. She marched across the backyard to her great-grandmother's house. Grandma Sofi had opened the door to be confronted by a very serious young lady.

"I prefer to be called Darcie instead of Bella from now on, please," Darcie said politely.

"And I prefer to call you Bella. From now on."

Grandma Sofi, just as politely, forever shut the door on Darcie's request.

Neither Grandma Sofi nor Darcie had ever mentioned or even made a reference to that particular conversation. But Darcie was feeling reckless. How could her very own great-grandmother call her *Beauty* while renouncing the importance of physical beauty in the same sentence. It just didn't make any sense.

"Grandma Sofi..." she began.

"Yes, Bella?"

"Why do you call me Bella?"

Grandma Sofi lost her serious expression as her face broke into a gentle smile. "Finally, you ask. I call you Bella because you look exactly like my sister."

"Your sister?"

Darcie couldn't have been more surprised. She knew that Grandma Sofi had an older sister who had died during the war, but she had never heard her great-grandmother talk about that time in her life.

Darcie racked her brain, finally able to remember. "Your sister's name was Isabel?"

"That's right," said Grandma Sofi. "But I always called her..."

"...*Bella*," they said together.

Grandma Sofi nodded. "You look exactly like her. You always have."

Darcie was a little confused. "But I thought I look just like you, Grandma Sofi."

"My sister and I...we looked very alike. It was almost as if we were twins, but we were not." She paused, studying Darcie. "She was taller, like you." She winked at her mirror image. "And she was older, by two years." She shrugged her shoulders in her charmingly European way. "I was the little sister, too, you see?"

Darcie laughed. She couldn't help it. She had just gotten the answer to one of the greatest mysteries of her life, and the revelation was completely unexpected. She hugged her great-grandmother. "I love you, Grandma Sofi."

Grandma Sofi returned her hug. "And I love you, Bella." Before Darcie could relax, her great-grandmother returned to her original concern. "So, this man with one eye has a mind that can keep up with yours, no? Not an easy thing, Bella. And he loves his daughter, but, not so much, his wife."

Darcie couldn't hide her shock. "But, how did you know..."

Grandma Sofi shrugged. "Your parents talk. I listen."

"Oh," Darcie said, tonelessly. Why was she not surprised?

Grandma Sofi continued undeterred: "You know this man with one eye for less than a day, yet you make him a pie?" She paused, an odd expression on her face. "Guard your heart, Bella."

"Grandma Sofi," said Darcie, firmly. "I haven't known Devin long, but he's a very brave man. In very difficult circumstances. I admire his courage. In my opinion, he deserves a pie and that's all there is to it."

With an emphatic nod, she slid off the stool and went into the pantry to look for a cardboard pie box.

"Twenty-four hours with Archie Hanover was all it took," Grandma Sofi informed Romeo. He gazed back at her with calm understanding. She looked at the doorway through which her beautiful great-granddaughter had disappeared. "Guard your heart, Bella," she whispered.

CHAPTER FIFTEEN

Devin hadn't felt so restless since his accident. The Voice had deserted him, apparently. He was frustrated with his inability to see. Tired of sitting in the same chair. Sick to death of listening to podcasts. And audiobooks. And sports broadcasts. He was—for lack of a better description—bored out of his mind.

For a while he toyed with the daring idea of removing his bandages himself. What could be the harm of ripping them off his head and tossing them in the nearest trashcan? Surely a few hours wouldn't make that much difference. The doctor was going to take them off in the morning anyway. He managed to talk himself out of the idea after a meticulous accounting of the pros and cons. He ended up with three more cons than pros, so that was the end of that.

He drummed his fingers on the arm of the chair. The house was perfectly quiet. There was no gorgeous piano music or rich laughter to break the stillness. Time seemed to stall. His forced inactivity was driving him crazy. He could barely sit still. The nervous energy pulsing through his body was making his skin crawl.

He felt the overwhelming urge to scream at the top of his lungs in an effort to break the unending silence of his present isolation. Or he could laugh...maniacally, like the villain in one of those old black-and-white movies. After mulling over those two brilliant ideas, he quickly decided against either one. At this point, he wasn't at all interested in winning a free trip to the mental institution of his choice. But *choice* rhymed with *voice* and that just brought him full circle to the root of the problem. The center of his discontent. The Voice. Or absence thereof.

Devin found himself wholly focused on the whereabouts of his missing obsession. What could she possibly be doing? Why was it taking her so long to pack? Was she taking her whole wardrobe on her trip to Scotland? Or—and this was a sobering thought—was she tired of hanging out with a one-eyed man swathed in bandages? No, that one couldn't be right, he argued. Darcie Finch wasn't like that. She would never treat anyone that way. Of that he was certain. She was probably somewhere doing good deeds. Helping the poor. Defending the downtrodden. Feeding the hungry.

Well, hell, he thought as he realized the irony of his own words. All of these hospital bills and visits with doctors weren't helping his wallet any. He was feeling pretty downtrodden at the moment. And he was hungry. No, he was starving. So, where was his superhero now? Where was Miss Darcie Finch?

He heard footsteps coming down the hall. Was it her? Could it be? Was she here to save his day?

"Hi, Devin," said the cheery voice of Nurse Carol. "I bet you're hungry."

Devin's momentary hope disappeared like a puff of smoke. Nurse Carol was bringing his dinner, not The Voice. *Damn, damn, damn.* He tried not to think like that, but he couldn't help it. He liked Nurse Carol. He really did. She was nice, but...she couldn't distract him from the disturbing knowledge that tomorrow was The Day.

Tomorrow he was going to see his new—and permanent—face. He hadn't thought about the removal of his bandages since yesterday. That was when The Voice informed him, in her melodious vocals, that she had chosen to be *enthusiastically condescending.* Darcie Finch kept the apprehension at bay. But, without her, it threatened to overwhelm what good sense he had left. His anxiety was, even now, clawing to break free. And, worse than that, he felt himself on the verge of losing the battle. He was almost frightened to discover that—for the first time in his well-fed life—he had actually lost his appetite. What could have happened to his babysitter? Where the hell was she?

He heard the sound of the tray table being wheeled toward his bed. "Sorry your dinner is so late, but you napped until nearly six," Carol informed him. "Mrs. Hofmann didn't want your food to get cold, so she waited until you woke up to start making it. She really went all out on account of it being your last night here. I'm sure you're getting tired of finger foods for every meal, but your ordeal is almost over. By this time tomorrow, you'll be able to eat whatever you want."

Carol's voice was as encouraging as ever, but Devin struggled to find a positive reply. Her next sentence, however, changed everything.

"Darcie just got back a few minutes ago. She's bringing a few things in from the car. Then she'll be here to check on you."

"That's nice," said Devin, trying to sound disinterested, and failing completely. He attacked his finger foods with gusto. His previously nonexistent appetite had suddenly returned with a vengeance.

Carol wanted to laugh. Darcie was the perfect choice for keeping her patient's spirits up. Devin actually seemed quite taken with the delightful Miss Finch. Their constant sparring and repartee sounded very much like that of an old married couple.

Carol frowned. She had grown quite fond of her patient over the past two months. Too bad Devin already had a wife; he and Darcie were perfect for each other. She found the entire situation a little sad. And—as if the poor man didn't have enough to worry about—apparently his wife wasn't a very good one. Her continued absence was telling.

As if Nurse Carol had conjured the demon, however unintentionally, Devin's phone rang. The ever-efficient nurse picked up the phone from the nightstand. Her pleasant greeting was followed by a few seconds of silence. "It's your wife," Nurse Carol gently informed him before returning the phone to the nightstand. "I'll put her on speaker phone."

Devin couldn't object. His mouth was too full. He was doomed.

Carol quickly vacated the room. Suddenly, Devine found himself alone with the slightly nasal tones of the last voice he wanted to hear.

"De-vin."

Her singsong tones were the equivalent of flashing lights at a railroad crossing. Trouble was careening toward him. If he didn't get out of the way, he would find himself flat on his back with a pair of pointy high heels in his chest.

In other words, Mallory wanted something.

"Hello, Mal," he said, evenly, bracing himself for the worst.

"When are you getting home tomorrow?"

Her voice, dripping with sugary sweetness, grated on his already overtaxed nerves.

"'Devin. I miss you sooo much. I can't wait to see you again,'" he improvised, saying all of the things she should have said, but didn't.

She made a pouty sound and blew out an impatient breath. "Oh, Devin, really. Stop being such a child. This whole situation has been difficult enough without you making it worse."

"Have you had a difficult time, Mallory? I'm *so* sorry my accident has been *so* hard on you." He pumped as much fake sincerity as he could into the false phrases, knowing that pacifying Mallory would make the conversation end that much sooner.

Somewhat mollified, his wife continued: "I need to know what time I should be ready to go to the airport."

Devin was shocked. "You're going to meet us at the airport?" Such a gesture would be completely out of character for a selfish woman like Mallory.

She made a frustrated little sound, as if Devin had the same brain capacity as Iggy, the stuffed iguana. "Of course not, Devin. I don't have time for that. I just want to make sure that I'm ready in time for us to make our flight."

"What flight?"

He felt like his head was stuffed with wool, making him unable to follow her conversation. A detached part of his brain registered the strong smell of cinnamon. That was odd.

"Our flight to Scotland, of course, for the *engagement party*."

She enunciated the last two words as if he wasn't capable of comprehending them at regular speed.

Devin was speechless for a few seconds. She couldn't possibly be serious.

"De-vin!" She all but yelled into the phone. "De-vin Merritt!"

He had reached the end of his restraint. "You cannot be serious."

"Of course, I'm serious. I don't want to miss this party. It's one of the most important parties of the year. All kinds of celebrities will be there, and lots of media coverage."

"Mallory," Devin said, tonelessly. "I just had facial reconstruction surgery. I am *not* in any condition to fly to Scotland."

"Ooooh, I'm so sorry, sweetie."

Her tone oozed fake sincerity. From prior experience, Devin knew the worst was yet to come.

"You're right, of course," she crooned. "It will probably be better for you to stay at home and rest. I'll call Desiree and see if she wants to go with me."

Devin's jaw was so tight, he felt like it might crack. So, that was her plan. She already knew he wouldn't be able to go. And Mallory, being Mallory, had devised a scheme so that she could go to the party *without* her husband—but *with* her very best friend.

Devin moved his jaw back and forth to loosen it up. He almost smiled. He was going to enjoy the next few minutes. "I'm sorry, Mallory, but Blane cancelled our plane reservations after I had the accident. He knew that I wouldn't be ready for such a long trip. I'll be able to go to the wedding, of course, so don't worry about that."

Mallory sputtered. "But, but…the party…"

Devin could tell she was unprepared for his refusal. He waited silently, certain she wasn't going to give up without a fight.

Sure enough, she quickly regrouped.

"But, Dev, Blane is your friend," she said, using the same sugary sweet tones from the beginning of the conversation. "Surely one of us should be there for his special night. What if he never forgives you? And what about Grace? I'm sure she'll be devastated. We've gotten to be such good friends, you know."

Devin almost laughed at that last bit of fiction. His wife barely tolerated Grace. For some unknown reason, she saw Blane's fiancée as some sort of rival...probably for the attention Mallory considered her due.

According to Blane, Mallory had all but demanded that Grace find a spot for her as a bridesmaid in the wedding party. Her request had been politely, but firmly, rebuffed by the astonished bride. Mallory was still irate that Grace had dared to tell her no.

"It is a shame to miss such an important event," Devin said, smoothly. "But it can't be helped. I know that Blane and Grace understand completely."

His initial satisfaction at foiling her plans was, unfortunately, short-lived.

"This is all your fault, Devin Merritt!" Mallory exploded. "I can't believe you didn't even think to ask Blane if I could go without you. You're the most selfish man I've ever met!"

Mallory's words slammed into him with all the force of a head-on collision. Selfish? Him? Sitting in a chair that was not his own. In a house that wasn't his home. Alone. His face covered with bandages. A world of uncertainty in front of him. No, he wasn't feeling very selfish.

"It's always all about *you*, isn't it?" Mallory continued, warming to her rant. "You. You. You. What am I supposed to tell Desiree? She's already packed, and she'll be so mad at me. You're a complete beast," she snarled. "No, not a beast. You're a *monster*. That's exactly what you are...a *monster*! I'm married to a *monster*."

A monster? Devin recoiled from the word, stunned by the viciousness spewing from his phone. His heart had begun to beat heavily. His fingers closed around the arms of his chair in a death grip. She was wrong. She had to be wrong. He wasn't a monster. He was a pirate. Wasn't he?

"That's why you don't want to go to the party," Mallory continued, exulting in her own power to wound. "You're afraid to show that hideous face of yours. You'll probably *never* want to leave the house again. You know, Devin," she hissed, triumphantly, "it might have been easier for you if you lost *both* of your eyes instead of just one. Then you'd never have to see yourself at all." She figuratively plunged the knife into his back, twisting it cruelly. "It's worse for *me*, anyway. You only have to see your *monster* face when you look in the mirror, but I have to look at it for the rest of my life."

With that final blow, Mallory ended the connection.

Absolute despair took her place.

CHAPTER SIXTEEN

*D*arcie couldn't move. Her feet might as well have been glued to the floor. She knew she should have turned around and fled the moment she stepped into the room, but the maliciousness of Mallory's words wouldn't allow it. She couldn't bear for him to face the dragon alone, even if he remained unaware of her presence. So, she stayed and, by staying, she became privy to the whole unfortunate conversation.

Her heart went out to the man, sitting in silence, in the wingback chair directly in front of the door. He hadn't moved since his wife callously ended the call. He was gripping the arms of the chair, his knuckles white with tension. His breathing was shallow, and he looked like he might explode any minute.

Darcie panicked. What should she do now? Should she stay? Or should she sneak out? Could she sneak out before he figured out she was standing there? Her emotions were all tangled up. A horrible sadness for Devin warred with a raging anger at Mallory Merritt.

Darcie would never have believed anyone could be so insensitive and vicious if she hadn't heard it for herself. And Mallory was Devin's *wife*. She was supposed to be right beside him, making things better. Instead, she was heartless. Cold-blooded. Almost inhuman. The things she said were devastating. Absolutely devastating.

Darcie's vision blurred. She blinked to clear it, surprised to find her cheeks were wet with tears. She quietly set the to-go cups of coffee she was holding on the dresser by the door. After wiping her cheeks with the tips of her fingers, she took two silent steps toward the hallway.

Just then, Devin reached the end of his control. With a sweep of his arm, he sent his dinner tray flying off the rolling tray table. The sound of shattering china and glass filled the room. At the same time, he kicked the rolling table as hard as he could, propelling it toward Darcie and the open doorway. She squeaked in surprise, leaping out of the way, as the table disappeared into the hall. She didn't move, hoping she hadn't given herself away.

"How much did you hear?" Devin asked, in a resigned tone.

Darcie froze. She all but stopped breathing.

"Darcie Finch. I know you're in this room. I can smell you."

He could *smell* her? Was that a good thing? Darcie wasn't sure. She sniffed the air. Cinnamon. Her eyes flew to the dresser. The two not-so-innocent to-go cups were there, sharing their overly strong aroma with the world. Cinnamon Whip Latte. Jack's troublemaking coffee had given her away.

"How much did you hear?" Devin asked again, in a controlled voice she hadn't heard him use before.

Darcie sighed. "A little."

She moved then. The urge to do something useful was too strong to resist.

He could hear her scrambling around the room, picking up dishes and broken pieces of glass. And the remains of his dinner. "Dar-cie Finch," he repeated, through gritted teeth. "How much did you hear?"

She didn't know what to say, so she didn't say anything. If she didn't answer, maybe he would stop…

"Answer me, please."

Darcie's sigh was deep and heartfelt. "All right, Devin. If you must know, I heard everything. The whole horrible conversation." Her rich voice actually shook a little. "And, well, I…I don't understand."

"You don't understand what?" he asked patiently.

"Why did you marry her?" Darcie asked, softly. "She doesn't deserve… you don't deserve…" She couldn't seem to say all that needed to be said, so she finished lamely: "I don't understand."

Devin laughed, without humor. "Don't you see? No, you wouldn't, because *you* have integrity. My dear Darcie Finch, she used what is called *the oldest trick in the book*."

"She got pregnant on purpose," Darcie whispered, horrified, finally putting the pieces together. Amalie was four years old, but Devin and Mallory had been married for only four and a half years.

"Strangely enough, she told me on the night I planned to break it off with her. Her timing was perfect."

He raised his hands to his head as if he wanted to run his fingers through his hair in frustration. His shoulders slumped in defeat when he touched the bandages.

Darcie wanted to cry again. Instead, she walked over to sit on the side of the bed. If he wanted to talk, she would listen. It was all she could think to do.

Devin took a deep breath. He was going to tell her. He was going to tell Darcie Finch the whole sordid story. Well, almost. There was one part he never intended to tell anyone. Ever. But he was going to tell her everything else. And why was he going to tell her? Because she was Darcie Finch, and there was just a tiny, minute outside chance that she might understand. That was worth the risk.

Devin took a deep breath. "Mallory played me, Darcie. She played me so well, I still have trouble believing it. In the beginning—as much as I hate to admit it—I was completely ensnared by her face. By her beauty. By the whole pretty package." Devin hesitated, as if he also hated to say it. "I just couldn't see straight. Roman told me to slow down. He begged me to be careful, but I wouldn't listen."

Devin paused, wishing he could see Darcie's face. What was she thinking? Was she, even now, wishing she was somewhere else…somewhere far, far away from Devin Merritt? As always when he thought about the early days with Mallory, he nearly writhed in self-disgust. What a damn fool he had been.

"She deceived you, Devin," Darcie said softly.

"Yes, but it didn't help that I thought I knew everything. Roman was the only one who had any clue as to what she was hiding under her pretty mask. Everyone else—Mom, Dad, Lydia…hell, the whole family—was as charmed as I was. Mallory can be quite convincing when she tries."

"I'm sure she can," Darcie agreed soothingly. Her rich voice was warm and comforting.

Devin cleared his throat. Darcie didn't sound like she thought he was a complete idiot. Heartened, he continued: "As time went by, I saw flashes of her manipulative nature, her selfishness, and plenty of the other flaws she's so careful to hide. More and more of our relationship was about what *she* wanted, what *she* needed. I was spending a lot of my time trying to please her. And even more time trying to appease her. I learned all kinds of tricks to keep her happy. It was exhausting. Finally, I decided that I had had enough. I made up my mind to end our relationship."

"Good for you," Darcie said in approval. "Except, it was already too late, wasn't it? What happened?"

"The night I told her…well, I figured she would cause a scene. She's very good at causing scenes."

"Hmph."

Devin almost smiled. A world of censure lay inside Darcie's *hmph*.

"Yes," Devin agreed. "I feel exactly the same way. Anyway, I asked Roman to show up at the same restaurant, just in case things got out of control.…"

Every detail of the night that had forever altered the course of his life was permanently etched in his brain.

MACEE MCNEILL

"I have something to tell you, Mallory," Devin said, having found his courage somewhere between the salad course and the entrée.

"Oh, Dev," she said. Her smile was radiant. "There's something I have to tell you, too." Her eyes glittered in the soft candlelight.

Later, he would realize that they glittered with the thrill of victory, with the triumph of finally achieving her true goal. And with greed.

"I'll go first." Devin and Mallory said at the same time.

She giggled softly, stretching out her hand across the small table to cover his.

He nodded in acquiescence, automatically steeling himself for what she was about to say.

"You're going to be a father," she announced. She dabbed at her eyes, daintily, with her cloth napkin, wiping away imaginary tears.

Devin was stunned. Absolutely. Stunned.

He lost the ability to speak. His thoughts were jumping around his brain like frogs on caffeine. His eyes met Roman's across the room.

Roman's look of confusion quickly changed to worry, then to anger. He watched in amazement as Mallory jumped from her chair and threw her arms around Devin.

"Isn't it wonderful news?" she squealed, loud enough to catch the attention of every patron in the restaurant. "I knew you'd be thrilled. Just think, Devin! A baby! We're going to have a baby!"

The audience of restaurant goers broke into spontaneous applause. Mallory—overjoyed to find herself at the center of attention—was actually quivering with excitement.

Devin managed to lift his arm enough to pat her, weakly, on the back. His pitiful gesture seemed to satisfy her because she sat down in her chair again.

It did not, however, bring an end to the one-sided conversation at their table.

Mallory, of course, had a lot to say. "We have to pick out a ring and plan the wedding as soon as possible before I start to show. I don't want to look like *a pregnant bride, waddling down the aisle. And then, there's my wedding dress. I really want to go to New York, to that store that's on TV. I want to say 'yes' to the dress. And, oh, Devin, we'll have to find somewhere to live. There are some new townhouses for sale in Newport. One of those might be perfect."*

She couldn't seem to stop talking. That was fine with Devin. It meant he didn't have to say a word. How fortunate for everyone, he observed, with a curious sort of detachment, as he was currently incapable of speech.

He listened to her chatter while he ate his dinner, nodding at the appropriate times. He smiled for the picture—taken by their server—that would be posted all over social media by the next morning. He shared a complimentary congratulatory dessert with Mallory. He even pulled out her chair after paying the check. He did all of these things on autopilot.

He was numb. Completely numb. He was also trapped...tangled in the web of a very accomplished spider. With no way out.

They passed Roman—still seated at his table—as they left the restaurant. Out of the corner of his eye, Devin saw him raise his glass in salute. Devin nodded in response but didn't miss the look of triumph that Mallory threw at his cousin.

As they waited for Devin's Porsche to be brought around, Mallory nudged him with her elbow. He looked down into blue eyes, the color of a summer sky.

"Okay," she said, teasingly. "Your turn."

"My turn?" He raised his eyebrows, uncomprehendingly.

"You let me go first, silly. Now, it's *your* turn. What is the important information *you* wanted to tell me?" She waited, expectantly.

"Mallory," Devin said, honestly. "So much has happened tonight that I haven't the slightest idea."

He waited a few seconds for Darcie to speak.

She didn't.

The seconds turned into a minute. Then two. He knew she was waiting. He knew what she wanted to know but was too polite to ask. Finally, he couldn't stand it any longer. "I know you're wondering why I'm still married. Why didn't I give my baby legitimacy; then get a divorce at the first opportunity? Why would I live in the same house with someone who says the things Mallory says and acts the way Mallory acts?"

"No, that's easy." Darcie crossed her legs underneath her on the bed. Devin's situation was complicated. She may as well get comfortable. "You do it for your daughter. Obviously, you're afraid you won't win custody if you go to court. You're not willing to risk the chance of Mallory gaining sole—or, even, partial—custody of Amalie. That makes sense and is exemplary, considering what your life must be like. And, considering what you probably have to do to keep the peace. I imagine there's some heinous clause that Mallory's lawyers worked into the prenup, making it difficult, if not impossible, for you to walk away."

Once again, she had surprised him. Devin recognized, from Darcie's detached tone, that she was analyzing the situation like a lawyer with a new case. Joe Finch would be proud, Devin thought, dejectedly.

His fledgling lawyer continued, almost without pause: "Since you come from a family of very competent and experienced lawyers, I'm assuming that they've gone through your prenup with care. Probably more times than you can count. But—and this is significant—even the combined minds of Merritt Brothers Law have been unable to find a way out. That's a double-edged sword, since they're probably the ones who wrote the majority of the prenup in the first place. In addition, I presume that the reason for the error has to do with *you*. Due, perhaps, to some noble desire on your part to placate the mother of your child, thereby reducing stress and ensuring a healthier pregnancy. I also assume that your *family* takes the blame for allowing the loophole *against* their better judgement. Although, in reality, the mistake is the sole property of one, Devin Merritt. In other words, Counselor, you're trapped. And you don't have anyone to blame but yourself." Darcie took a deep breath before asking, "How close am I?"

Devin's admiration was tinged with the bitter taste of despair. "Well done, Miss Darcie Finch, third-year law student. Your assumptions are, unfortunately, spot-on. Care to continue?"

Darcie cleared her throat. "I think that you're planning to wait until Amalie is old enough to choose with whom she wants to live. When that time comes—if she chooses you—you will file for divorce on the grounds of irreconcilable differences."

Her final summation was delivered in a crisp, business-like manner. She was professional and concise and very different from the Darcie Finch of the last twenty-four hours.

Devin sighed. He missed his sassy babysitter and wondered, wistfully, how to make her reappear. "All correct. But…all of that was *before* the accident. At present, I am a *monster* who—to avoid the misfortune of looking upon my now hideous visage—would be better off completely blind. Or so I'm told." He was trying to be amusing but failing miserably.

"It isn't true, you know," said Darcie, softly.

"Which part…the fact that I am a *monster*? Or that I would be better off blind and unable to see my *monster-ness*?" Devin asked, politely.

"Stop it."

"Stop what? If I'm going to be a *monster*, I'm going to be a damn good one. I'm going to embrace my *monster-ness* and…"

"*Stop. It.*"

Darcie couldn't sit there, acting as though she didn't care, for one more second. Unfolding her legs, she slid to the floor. After covering the space between them, she knelt in front of Devin. Since he was still gripping the arms of the chair, she placed her hands over his.

He jerked slightly at her unexpected touch, surprised by her offer of comfort. Something about her soft, warm hands, coupled with her tropical flower scent, loosened the knot that had formed in his stomach. A little.

Darcie was on a mission. She was determined to eradicate this *monster* nonsense once and for all. She squeezed his hands. Every word she said came straight from her heart.

"*You* are not the *monster*, Devin. The only *monster* is the woman you married." Devin remained silent, but at least he didn't try to pull away. She continued in a soothing voice: "*You* are a good man, Devin. *You* love your daughter enough to sacrifice your own happiness for hers. She loves you, too. I heard it in her voice when she was talking to you."

Darcie studied the unmoving form of the man in front of her. He still hadn't said anything, but he was listening. She could tell. So, again, she continued: "You treat your cousin Diana like a friend instead of an employee, which makes you an excellent boss, as well as cousin. And, you're a good friend. I know this because Blane chooses his friends very carefully, and here you are, in his house. He trusts you, and, believe me, that speaks well of you."

She was making progress. The pasty color was gone from his face—well, what she could see of his face—and his breathing was slow and even. "Your family adores you," she continued, relaxing a bit. "Your cousins talked about you all the time while I was doing my internship. 'Devin has the best sense of humor.' 'Devin is the best contract lawyer you've ever seen.' 'Devin has good instincts.' 'Devin is—'"

"The best looking of all of the cousins," Devin interrupted, sarcastically. His voice had taken on the guise of a reporter on the nightly news. "And in an ironic twist that no one saw coming, Devin Merritt—known far and wide as the best looking of the Merritt boys—has lost that distinction, opting, instead, for a monster's face in place of his former good looks." He heard Darcie draw in a quick breath.

"Stop it, Devin. Stop it right now."

Her voice broke on the last word and he heard her sniff, almost as if…

"Darcie Finch, are you crying?"

He whispered the question in disbelief. She was feisty and determined and strong, but she was…crying? Over *him*? He turned his hands over and laced his fingers with hers.

Darcie's hands clung to his. "You listen to *me*, Devin Merritt. You are not a *monster*. Say it."

"You are not a *monster*," he repeated, obediently, trying to humor her. Anything to stop her tears.

Her grip on his hands intensified. "Stop it." She was deadly serious now. "Say 'I am not a *monster*.'"

"I am not a *monster*," he intoned.

"Say it again," she demanded.

"I am not a *monster*."

"Say it like you believe it. Damn it."

She squeezed his hands, determined to reach him. Darcie was stubborn. She refused to let him hide behind a mask of his own making. The second he started using his looks as an excuse, he would lose himself. She flatly refused to let that happen.

"I. Am. Not. A. Monster."

He said it forcefully, finally allowing her strength and conviction to flow through him. She *did* understand. Thank God. Darcie Finch understood. At that moment, Devin stopped fighting. He finally allowed Darcie to pull him away from the yawning hole of despair and doubt that was threatening to swallow him. He felt an incredible relief.

Of course, Darcie understood, he fathomed. She had *problem looks*. Hell, for all he knew, she really *did* look like a horse. But—in typical Darcie fashion—she hadn't let that stop her. She had overcome whatever her issue was. She had become…more. That was it. Darcie Finch was just…*more*. And, suddenly, he realized that he wanted to be more, too. She was right. He believed her. He wasn't a *monster*. He really wasn't.

Oh, his face might look a little different when the bandages came off tomorrow morning. But the essence of who he was—his character, his intellect, his personality, all of the qualities that made him Devin Merritt—remained unchanged. Nothing could take that away without his permission. He alone had authority over what kind of person his future self would be. It was *his* decision. Would he let his circumstances control him? Or would he take control of his circumstances? From where he was sitting, only one acceptable option presented itself.

"I want you to make me a promise," she said, still clinging to his hands.

He could feel her arms shaking. "Anything, Darcie Finch." Her genuine concern and regard for his welfare filled a corner of his heart he'd never even realized was empty.

"When Mallory says the word *monster*, I want you to think, '*I am not a monster*.' Every. Single. Time. Please promise me," she begged. "I don't want her to get into your head again."

"I promise that I will think '*I am not a monster*' whenever she says the word *monster*. Hell, I may even say it out loud. That would throw her. Or maybe I'll say, '*I'm not the monster. You are.*' How about that, Darcie Finch?" He was determined to ease her mind any way he could.

She squeezed his hands, finally satisfied. "You are a good man, Devin Merritt. Don't ever forget that."

He wasn't sure, but he thought he detected a smile in her voice. He knew enough about Darcie Finch to know she didn't mince words when she was serious. She—Darcie Finch—thought he was a good man. He felt such a depth of gratitude he didn't even know how to express himself. With the simple act of offering her hands, she had given him a precious gift…something to hold on to, something true and strong. The words she made him say embedded themselves into his brain, replacing the fear of rejection and the uncertainty of returning to his old life…his pre-accident life.

If people turned away from him because of his face, well then, good riddance. If they broke their connections with him because they couldn't handle his new look…that was on them. But Devin was going to make damn well sure it wasn't because he gave them any other reason. In other words, he would do everything in his power to be the man Darcie described. A loving father. An excellent boss. A good friend. And the person his family needed him to be. Darcie's words were an encouragement and a challenge rolled into one. Still holding her hands, he raised them to his lips, pressing a kiss to each one. He lowered their hands again. Finally, giving hers a gentle squeeze, he released them.

She was profoundly moved. The spontaneous gesture was devastating in its simplicity. He didn't mean it as a romantic gesture; and she didn't take it as such. It was so much more than that. Darcie was acutely aware of the soul-deep bond that had sprung up between them so quickly. She suspected that Devin was aware of it, too. Their connection was rare, even a little frightening.

How could this have happened in such a short time? Twenty-four hours. Yet, Darcie felt she had known him forever. She understood this man in an elemental way, one she had never experienced with anyone else. The touch of his lips had only intensified their blossoming connection. She struggled with the instinctive realization that such a bond was dangerous, for a variety of reasons. Not the least of which was the wedding ring on Devin Merritt's left hand.

As the silence lengthened, Darcie grew somewhat frantic, wanting to break the spell. Finally, she did the only thing she could think of. "I brought you some coffee and some cookies, but you can't have the cookies until you have some dinner." She started for the door. "I'll go and make you a sandwich."

"Darcie Finch."

His voice was relaxed again, infused with a teasing note that had been missing during their fraught exchange.

"Yes," she said cautiously.

"Why did it take you so long to come back? What were you doing?"

Devin asked the question against his better judgement. Did he *really* want to know what she had been doing? What if she told him that she had been meeting someone? Someone special? Someone with two eyes and a handsome face? He stopped himself, remembering the promise she had required of him. *I am not a monster.* He had given his word to Miss Darcie Finch. He would not break it.

She jumped on the change of topic, striving for normalcy. "I finished packing, made a pie, went shopping, and had a lovely visit with my great-grandmother," she said, ticking each item off on her fingers. "I had gift baskets made for Amalie and Diana, picking out a few things I thought they might like. The baskets are on the table in the kitchen. I also bought three packs of cookies from Jack's when I picked up the coffee. Be sure and share them with your family. Two packs are assorted, and one is all chocolate. I didn't know if you like raisins or not, so…"

"I don't," Devin said. But he couldn't resist adding, "I'll give the ones with raisins to Mallory."

Darcie ignored that comment. "I didn't get any cookies with raisins. I can't stand them." She shivered. "It's like eating chewy, little bugs!"

He laughed. "Thank you, Darcie Finch. I'm sure Amalie will be thrilled. She and Diana will enjoy their baskets very much. I promise to try to share the cookies with the family...if there are any left by the time that I get home."

She had deliberately glossed over the part about the pie, just to see if he was paying attention.

"Wait a minute," he said, suspiciously. "Did you say pie?"

Darcie laughed. "Why, yes, I did say pie."

"Darcie Finch, did you make me a pie?"

"Chocolate chess," she confirmed.

"Darcie Finch, I think I love you," Devin said, happily.

Darcie gasped. She couldn't help it. Her heart started to beat erratically.

Devin froze in shock. *What the hell did I just say? Idiot,* he reprimanded himself. He opened his mouth, desperate to fill the awkward silence. "What kind of coffee is it?" he blurted out.

"Excuse me?" she asked in confusion, still reeling from his unfortunate phrasing.

"What kind of coffee did you bring me?" he repeated, determined to return to their teasing camaraderie.

Her tense muscles loosened just a little. "Cinnamon Whip Latte from Jack's. It's my favorite. I got you a decaf." She turned, determined to leave this time.

"Darcie Finch."

"Uh-huh?"

"May I have my coffee?" he asked, innocently.

"What? Oh, of course," she mumbled. "Sorry."

Good Lord. She sounded as flustered as she felt. She even had trouble with the coffee, nearly tipping it over before she got her shaking hands under control. Finally, grasping the cup with both hands, she carried the vexing latte to its equally vexing recipient. She realized too late that she was going to have to touch him. She nearly groaned aloud. She should have grabbed both cups of coffee and run out of the room when she had the chance. Squaring her shoulders, she approached, calling herself every kind of a fool.

"Be careful," she chided. "It's still hot."

She took his hand, pressing his fingers around the cup. She tried to ignore the tingling sensation in her own fingers, but she couldn't ignore his swift intake of breath. As soon as he had a good grip, Darcie fled.

He listened to her retreat, his heart beating in time with her feet as her steps echoed down the hall.

During the few minutes she spent chatting with Nurse Carol in the kitchen, Darcie chose to keep information regarding Mallory's phone call to herself. Devin's response to the call, and her own response to Devin, seemed too personal to share. While making his sandwich she deliberately left the crust on the bread. She wasn't quite sure why. Maybe it was some form of quiet rebellion against the unwanted emotions he evoked.

When she returned to his room, fifteen minutes later, it was as if their earlier encounter had never happened. Devin was relieved, but—if he was honest—a little disappointed to see she had recovered so quickly. His own heartbeat had yet to return to normal. In any case, it seemed that his bossy, no-nonsense babysitter was back.

She returned the tray table from the hall, its wheels protesting loudly. She insisted that he eat the peanut butter and jelly sandwich she, herself, had made. She mumbled about people who attacked innocent bystanders with tray tables. She fussed about people who threw trays. She grumbled about people who destroyed other people's belongings. She never stopped talking as she swept the remains of broken glass and china into a neat pile by the door. She made sure that her words were loud enough for him to hear.

Devin's sandwich *wasn't* cut into little squares this time. She *hadn't* cut off the crust, either. But he decided it was in his best interest not to mention the omission.

Darcie swept the mess into the dustpan, collected his empty tray, and disappeared into the hall again.

In her absence, Devin had an epiphany. He couldn't wait to torment her fine mind with his latest discovery.

Darcie recovered her usual aplomb by managing to convince herself she would feel the same connection to *anyone* in Devin's situation. As a matter of fact, she was sure there was some kind of medical term—a *syndrome* or something—for what sometimes happens between a caregiver and a patient. It was all perfectly normal. Nothing to worry about, she informed her heart. She took a deep breath and exhaled very slowly. *Normal. All of this is perfectly normal*—or so she thought.

She hadn't been back in the room for five seconds before Devin the Pirate proved her wrong.

"Darcie Finch," he stated, in a firm voice. "You are a hypocrite."

Her eyes flew open in surprise. "Excuse me?"

She must have misunderstood him. Nobody had *ever* called her a hypocrite before. *So much for normal,* she thought ruefully.

"You are a *hy-po-crite*," he enunciated carefully.

She was shocked and a little hurt. "Why would you say that?"

"Because, my short-sighted friend, you spent a lot of time convincing me that the way I look doesn't make me a monster. But *you* can't seem to deal with your own—in your words—*problem looks*." He crossed his arms smugly.

Uh-oh. Darcie knew she was in trouble. "Devin, umm…it's not quite the same thing."

"Oh, really?" he asked, clearly doubting her words.

"Really."

"Then, what do you look like?"

He had her now. There was no way she was getting out of it.

"Hmph."

"Oh, no, you're not getting out of it with a *hmph*." He shook his head emphatically. One corner of his bandage flopped down over his nose.

Darcie reached out and carefully pulled the bandage up, patting it back into place. She didn't need his bandages to come unwrapped. Letting him *see* the answer to his question before she had a chance to explain was *not* a good idea. "It's just that I'm…I'm…" She couldn't say it, not without sounding arrogant.

"You're what?" He let out a sad, little laugh. "You can tell me, Darcie Finch. I'm the last person in the world who would ever judge you."

She sat down on the bed. She was going to have to tell him. "The problem with my looks is sort of the opposite of what you're thinking. The problem isn't that they're really bad."

He tilted his head to one side, as if pondering this unexpected remark. "Go on."

"Well, they're actually really, really good." She sounded almost apologetic. "Too good."

"I don't understand." Devin sounded skeptical. "How could your looks be too good?"

Darcie sighed. She was going to have to say it. "You see, Devin, I'm what people around here call a beauty."

"A beauty," he repeated.

"You know. Perfect face. Perfect hair. Perfect figure. A beauty."

For someone who was describing herself in the most flattering terms possible, she sounded almost annoyed.

Darcie continued to elaborate in a bored voice: "People call me stunning, dazzling, indescribably beautiful, drop-dead gorgeous, and—don't forget—unforgettable."

"Drop-dead gorgeous," he said, tonelessly. He still didn't seem to understand.

"I look like a magazine cover, Devin. Like a movie star. Miss America. A princess."

He didn't say a word.

"That's it. I look like a princess."

There. She had said it. She had confessed all. Now she wondered what he would say. Would he make fun of her for thinking she had a problem? Would he hate her because her problem was completely the opposite of what he was dealing with? Would he call her a hypocrite again?

"You see, Devin, people can't get past my looks. They don't *want* to know Darcie Finch. They just want to look at the pretty princess. It's very difficult—" She was going to say it was difficult to know who she could trust, but he interrupted before she could finish.

"Don't say another word, Darcie. Please. If you don't want to tell me what you look like, then just say so. But don't make things up. It's demeaning. You're better than that." He was emphatic, and a little fierce.

Darcie gasped, in surprise. "But…" He didn't believe her. He really didn't believe her.

The impact of what he said next was magnified by her sudden realization.

"Don't say another word. You made me listen to you and now you're going to listen to me," he began. "I don't care what you look like. I don't care if you have the head of a horse. Hell, I don't care if you look like an iguana. I don't care if you have one eye or three. And do you know why I don't care? Do you?" He paused, determined to make her understand her own worth. "Well, I'll tell you why. It's because you, Darcie Finch, have a beautiful soul. And that's all I need to know." It was true. Every last word was true, damn it. Whether she believed it or not.

Darcie closed her eyes, trying desperately not to cry. Since when did she cry every five minutes anyway? She was humbled, grateful, and taken completely off guard. Before she could even try to thank him, however, for the most precious words ever spoken, Nurse Carol bustled in for Devin's bedtime check.

The nurse looked at Darcie in surprise, taking in the scene and drawing her own conclusions.

Darcie, her eyes full of tears.

Devin, for the first time, at a loss for words.

Carol hesitated. "I can come back later, if that would be better."

"No, no. I'm going to bed anyway," Darcie managed to get out. Her usually silky voice sounded slightly strained to the nurse's ears.

As Carol pretended to search through her bag for the stethoscope that was already hanging around her neck, Darcie slid off the bed. She stepped close to Devin, putting her left hand on his shoulder. She touched his face, softly, with her other hand, just below his bandages.

He didn't move. His entire being was focused on the feel of her soft palm against his jaw. Her light, tropical flower scent floated on the air.

She spoke quietly, for his ears only. "There's an envelope in the box with your pie. In that envelope is a picture of me." She sighed. "You see, I didn't want you to find out what I looked like until you got to know me. You don't have any idea how much your words mean to me right now, but I think you'll understand when you see my picture. Thank you, Devin, for saying them to me." Her voice broke a little. She forced herself to continue, trying to do for him what he had done for her. "When the doctor removes your bandages, remember that you are a pirate. And pirates embrace their scars. Don't forget what I said. You made me a promise and I expect you to keep it. I know that you're going to be all right." She kissed his cheek. Well…actually—because of the bandages—her lips fell closer to his chin. Her palm lingered as she stepped away.

"Thank you," he said, sounding a little hoarse.

Devin resisted the unbearably strong urge to reach for her hand. He forced himself to crawl out from under all of the tangled emotions that were doing their best to smother him. "Good night, Darcie Finch."

"Goodbye, Laurence."

As she left the room, her velvety tones wrapped around him for, what he feared, was the last time.

CHAPTER SEVENTEEN

Providence, Rhode Island
Two months later

*D*evin logged off and closed his laptop. All he had to do was wait for Diana and Amalie. Rafe was already at the airport. Blane was going to meet their little party there after stopping by his apartment to collect the rest of the things a groom might need on his wedding day.

Devin tried to tell himself that seeing the Boss-man happily wed to his lady love was responsible for his sharp sense of anticipation. He tried to tell himself his excitement was a consequence of embarking on his first real vacation weekend since returning to work. He tried to tell himself his nervous energy resulted from the fact that he would finally have a chance to spend some extra time in the beautiful town of Honeysuckle Creek. He tried to tell himself that pigs could fly, and that birds swam in the sea. But he wasn't buying any of it.

The real reason he felt more alive today than he had in weeks was due to the prospect of renewing his acquaintance with a certain member of the wedding party. The maid of honor, in fact. The enigmatic Miss Darcie Finch. The *beautiful* Miss Darcie Finch.

Devin had never been more surprised than he was on the day he discovered that Darcie was actually telling the truth. He chuckled as he opened his desk drawer. Carefully lifting the drawer divider, he pulled Darcie's photograph from its hiding place. He couldn't forget the impact of seeing that photograph for the first time. It made the first glimpse of his own post-surgery face almost anticlimactic.

Sitting on the examination table as the doctor painstakingly cut away his bandages, Devin held Darcie's words close. They wrapped around him like a protective blanket. Darcie understood—and because of that, he wasn't alone. Amazing how much of a difference one person's understanding could make.

That's why he was so hell-bent to return the favor. He had tried to be supportive by giving her the opportunity to unburden herself. But, apparently, her looks were a bigger problem than he had realized. So much so that she had lied to him. That stung. It really did.

"I look like a magazine cover, Devin. Like a movie star. Miss America. A princess."

Or so she claimed. Yeah, right. The majority of the world would love to have a problem like that. Oh well, it didn't matter. Not really. Not to him, anyway. It didn't change the way he felt about her. She was still Darcie Finch…superhero. Besides, he would know what she looked like soon enough. If the doctor ever finished with him, he would open the envelope with the photograph that would answer all of his questions. It was waiting in the passenger seat of Roman's rental car. At least, that's where he thought it was.

Thank God for Roman. He had arrived at Heart's Ease earlier, the sole family member who had missed the cookout and escaped the stomach bug. Roman was always supportive, without being overly-demonstrative. And he was very much family. A warm hug followed by a firm pat on the back said what his cousin could not. He was full of information about the family and the practice. His steady discourse was designed to distract Devin from his looming day of reckoning.

Even now as the bandages loosened, Roman stood somewhere in the examination room. He had firmly refused the opportunity to escape. He was probably leaning against the wall with his arms crossed. Roman was a master of the casual stance, managing to look relaxed even in the midst of a crisis. It was a skill that was a benefit in and out of the courtroom. That was Roman, Devin thought, gratefully. Always above and beyond.

As the last of the bandages fell away, Devin blinked at the bright light flooding his sensitive pupil. One hurdle crossed.

He could still see.

Thank God.

Gradually—when everything else came into focus in the examination room—he was able to meet Roman's questioning gaze with a nod. Roman expelled a tense breath—one he had obviously been holding—to nod in return.

The doctor walked Devin through a thorough vision test before pronouncing himself satisfied. He went to the counter and picked up a large hand mirror, returning to Devin's side. "Mr. Merritt," he asked. "Are you ready to see the finished product?" His expression turned serious as he added, "The redness will fade with time. However, the damage went several layers deep. Some of it was so severe, that it was impossible to erase the scars without risking permanent nerve damage. I speak from experience when I say you will get used to your scars over time."

The doctor's words, while not overly encouraging, only increased Devin's curiosity. What would he see when he looked into that mirror? It dawned on him then: both Roman and the doctor could already see his face. Neither one of them had so much as flinched in horror. That was a good sign, wasn't it? Yes, Devin decided. It was a very good sign.

The doctor continued: "You must also keep in mind that we haven't fitted you for your eye yet. It will take several more weeks before the healing of your socket is complete. After that, we can get to work. Getting a new eye will completely change the way you look. Until then, you should wear a patch." He glanced at Roman, then back to Devin. "Tell me when you're ready," he said, kindly.

"I'm ready," Devin said, even as he silently reminded himself, *I am a pirate.*

All of his adult life he had been called a handsome man. His wavy auburn hair fell across a strong brow. His thick eyebrows arched over light, gray eyes. His eyelashes made the females of his family extremely jealous. His nose was straight, and his perfectly formed lips were accented by his sculpted jawline. He had a rugged, masculine face...the kind of face that made women want to get to know him better. Or so he had been told.

After the doctor handed him the mirror, Devin held it up to study his new reflection. His auburn hair was still wavy. His brow was still strong. But several large and sharply defined scars stretched from his hairline to his left ear. For some reason, he had envisioned the scars only in relation to his missing right eye. Those scars ended, as he had anticipated, in his empty eye socket. The others, well...they were a surprise. One of those scars stretched across his left eyebrow—mercifully bypassing his eye—to his left cheek, ending near his ear. No one had mentioned how close he had come to losing his other eye. He silently thanked God for that gift.

"A pirate embraces his scars," Darcie had said. And he had to admit that his were pretty impressive. One of the scars cutting through his left eyebrow made it quirk up in the middle. The overall effect gave him a look of disbelief, as if he were on some perpetual quest. Not a bad look for a lawyer-pirate. Or should he say pirate-lawyer? Either way, he decided, he could deal with it.

His nose, although swollen, was straight. That was good. And it still worked. He sniffed just to make sure. That was good, too. Even his empty eye socket wasn't as awful as he expected. He would be getting an artificial eye in a few weeks, anyway. And wearing an eye patch wasn't the worst thing. Every pirate knew that. Speaking of which...

He put the mirror on his lap. "Can I have the eye patch?" he asked.

The doctor handed it over, instructing him as to the proper angle to provide for maximum protection.

When he finished, Devin picked up the mirror. *There,* he thought with satisfaction. *That was more like it.* The combination of the black eye patch, his scars, and his longer than normal hair gave him a rakish, buccaneer look. He really did look like a pirate.

"Well, hell," said Roman, looking completely disgruntled as he leaned against the wall, his arms crossed over his chest.

Devin looked at him curiously. "What?"

"You're still better looking than me, even with one eye," his cousin said ruefully, shaking his head. "Damn. It just isn't fair." Then, he grinned.

The doctor, too, looked relieved. His worried face broke into a smile.

Devin couldn't help but grin back.

A short while later, Devin was seated in the passenger seat of the rental car. He was riding shotgun with Roman just like he had done so many times before. It was as if nothing had changed, and yet…everything had changed. Learning how to live with one eye was going to be quite an adjustment, according to the doctor. Dealing with things like distorted depth perception, driving, and even an act as simple as pouring a glass of water would require the use of an entirely new skill set. He was looking at a long sequence of occupational therapy sessions. The challenges were many, the doctor said, but not insurmountable.

It was a sobering discussion. Devin was momentarily distracted from any thoughts save those of his resolve to confront all obstacles awaiting him. He was determined to resume as normal a life as possible.

Roman stopped for gas on their way out of town. While his cousin was filling the tank, Devin looked out the window. He had been deprived of sight for so many weeks that he needed a few moments to reacquaint himself with the world. Grass. Trees. Sky. Cars on the highway. Yep. Everything was blessedly normal. That was comforting, somehow.

As he turned his head to monitor Roman's progress, his eye fell on the little, white envelope lying half on—and half off—the console. He reached for it, but his fingers failed to grasp the slippery thing. Damn, he thought. This was going to be harder than he expected. On his second try, he managed to pick the envelope up, more by feel than anything else.

He carefully tore one end of the envelope open. The photograph inside fluttered to the floorboard of the car. Facedown, of course. Devin bent to retrieve it. He gave a little growl of frustration as he failed, once again, to grab something on his first try. He bent over with both hands, somewhat mollified when he felt the edge of the photo. He picked it up. His heart was pounding in his chest. His hands were shaking as he turned the photograph over. Would Darcie have a horse's head or...?

He couldn't take his eye off the photograph. A radiant beauty queen smiled up at him. She was stunning, all right. A raven-haired princess...complete with crown. There was no way in hell the woman in this photograph was Darcie Finch, he decided immediately. No woman blessed with such exquisite perfection of face would ever complain of problem looks. No woman in her right mind, anyway. And Darcie Finch was most definitely in her right mind.

He blew out a defeated sigh. What could Darcie possibly have to gain by perpetuating such a myth? Was she so certain that he would reject her after seeing how she really looked? He couldn't believe she hadn't been able to trust him with the truth, even after all they had shared. He looked at the photograph again, surprised at the degree of hurt he felt. Was it a photograph of someone Darcie actually knew? Or was it just some random person taken from some random website? He tossed the offending photograph toward the console in disgust, mentally berating himself for his failure to win the trust of Darcie Finch.

Roman got back into the car, sensing instantly that something was wrong. "Problem?" he asked, studying Devin's annoyed expression.

"What could possibly be wrong?" Devin replied with a little more sarcasm than he intended.

"Easy, man," Roman responded. "Sorry I asked." His eyes fell on the photograph. "Hey, why do you have a photo of Darcie Finch?"

Devin was stunned. "A photo of...?"

It was impossible. Purely impossible. No way did Darcie really look like that. No way at all.

"That's not Darcie Finch. It can't be."

Roman reached for the photograph, picking it up on the very first try. Devin couldn't help but notice.

"Yeah," Roman confirmed. "Definitely Darcie Finch. I thought she helped take care of you for a couple of days."

"She did, but I couldn't see anything," Devin explained. "The bandages? Remember?"

"Oh. Well, that makes sense." Roman shook his head regretfully. "Hate it for you, though. She's a looker."

Devin studied the photograph in his hand for the hundredth time since that day in the car. Or was it the two hundredth time? Honestly, he had lost count. He still had trouble believing that the goddess who gazed back at him from that photograph and the woman who giggled at his jokes, called him a pirate, and baked him a pie—a delicious pie, at that—were one and the same.

He felt like the victim of a colossal joke. Where was his Horse-Faced Dream Girl? That was the photograph he had expected to see. Not this glorious vision. No matter how he tried, he couldn't quite believe it. He had even done some of his own research just to make sure. He looked at digital photographs online and even scrolled through old articles from the *Honeysuckle Creek Gazette*. He knew it was true. His eyes—eye—knew what it *saw*, but it was hard to convince his brain.

It made Devin wonder how he, himself, would have behaved if he met Darcie Finch under ordinary circumstances. He had a feeling such a meeting would not have revealed himself in a particularly flattering light. He was fairly certain he would instantly have assumed that such a gorgeous woman was going to be vain, demanding, and spoiled. And fake. It was almost a given: she would be fake. Even worse, he would have treated her along the lines of his assumptions. All because of her appearance. And why was that? he asked himself.

He knew the answer as well as he knew his own last name. His assumptions—every single one—were the result of his miserable excuse for a marriage. No one could argue that Mallory was a beautiful woman. Blond hair. Blue eyes. Glowing complexion. Her fragile essence brought to mind an angel come to earth. Devin grimaced. Angel? More like a demon from hell. She was also vain, demanding, and spoiled…and that was on a good day.

In addition, his *beautiful* wife had *beautiful* friends, all equally consumed with their own beauty. They were experts at using their appearance to exploit, demean, or crush other less fortunate human beings. Not to mention the painstaking—and incredibly expensive—lengths to which they would go to maintain that beauty. Devin, however, had learned the hard way that their beautiful masks were just that. Masks. And behind those masks they hid selfish hearts. Or no heart at all in Mallory's case.

Darcie Finch, however, was a revelation. Removing her beautiful mask revealed a beautiful heart. And a beautiful soul. Devin knew deep in his own soul that, this time, his assumptions were spot on. He also found it very satisfying to admit—after seeing Darcie's photograph— that his *beautiful* spouse couldn't hold a candle to the ravishing Miss Finch. Unfortunately, Darcie had to deal with crap all the time from people who judged her *only* by her appearance. Hence Devin's new understanding of what the term *problem looks* actually meant to Darcie Finch. He got it now. He really did. Her gorgeous face was as much a mask as his scars and eye patch. Both effectively blocked all but the most discerning from seeing the reality behind the mask. They had a lot in common, he and Miss Darcie Finch.

He couldn't help but appreciate the irony of his own role reversal. Now he—formerly so quick to judge—was forced to deal with the judgement of those who couldn't or wouldn't look beyond his monster mask. *I am not a monster,* he repeated to himself. Saying the words was automatic now. Funny how hearing the word *monster*—and he heard it often—didn't make him flinch anymore. He owed it all to one beautiful woman with the courage to look through his bandages…straight into his heart.

And, tonight, he was going to see her with his own two—Devin grimaced—with his own one—eye. But, what about *her*? Would *she* be glad to see him, too? He hoped so. Still, he couldn't help but wonder if the twenty-four hours that meant so much to him was just another day in the life of Darcie Finch, superhero? He knew what she looked like now. She wasn't just some blurry image in his head. His Pirate Queen didn't even remotely resemble a horse. She was, he decided, magnificent. Devin didn't even feel guilty for thinking about her so much. Lord knew that his own wife didn't want him. Never had, really.

Oh, Mallory still wanted things. She wanted plenty. She wanted his name. His money. His connections to rich and powerful people. His money. Especially, his money. But she didn't want him. She had no desire for any kind of emotional relationship with him.

Unsurprisingly, she didn't want any kind of physical relationship, either, not since the accident. That omission was telling, because sex was the *only* thing their marriage had ever had going for it.

Since Devin returned home, however, he had been nothing but thankful for her lack of interest. He had no wish to resume relations with his cold-hearted wife. Sex was a tool Mallory used to manipulate, to coerce. It was her greatest weapon. And she was good at it. Exceptionally good. She could make a man believe he was the world's greatest lover. That no one else could possibly make her feel the way he did. Oh, it was always quite a performance, one he had fallen for more times than he could count. But, in the end, it was just that. A performance. Sex. Nothing more. It was never about love.

The ability to love someone other than herself was an intrinsic quality sadly absent from Mallory's genetic makeup. Devin and his wife had *never* made love. They just had sex, and, then, only when Mallory wanted something. Or when she was pretending to be sorry about something. Or when she wanted him to change his mind about something. They had never once had sex as a result of genuine desire or an overabundance of feeling. Or any feeling at all, save lust.

These revelations weren't new. Devin had the deficiencies in Mallory's character figured out by the time she induced him to sign that farcical prenup. When he finally realized what was happening, it was already too late. He was trapped, and he couldn't do a damn thing about it. After a whirlwind wedding, he had a baby girl he loved—and a wife he didn't. The worst part was he couldn't have one without the other.

UNMASKING THE HEART

Amazing how twenty-four hours with Darcie Finch made more of an impact on his life than four and a half years with Mallory. Every time Mallory said the word *monster*—and she said it a lot, especially during those first few weeks—he remembered his promise. And Darcie Finch.

I am not a monster. That was all it took to make him feel like Darcie was right in front of him. Speaking in her gorgeous voice. Holding his hands in hers. Helping him to go on. And—Devin always smiled when he got to the next part—smelling like tropical flowers. He just couldn't forget her. And he was grateful. So damn grateful. He wanted to tell her, in person, that her support had made all the difference.

Gratitude. Pure gratitude. Nothing more. It was all he would allow himself to feel. He could live with that rationale, he told himself, as long as he didn't delve into it too closely. Under such extenuating circumstances, he forgave himself for the number of times Darcie crossed his mind during the day. And during the night.

Devin drew in a deep, cleansing breath then let it out slowly. Tonight, he would finally see the remarkable Darcie Finch for the first time. He couldn't, however, help but feel a degree of trepidation at the knowledge that *she* would also see him.

Devin replaced the photograph under the drawer divider. Not a moment too soon. He had scarcely closed his drawer when the door to his office burst open.

"Daddy!"

Amalie's voice broke Devin's reverie as she ran into his office. She threw herself into his lap, already beside herself with excitement.

"Daddy! Are we really going to ride on Mr. Blane's plane? And go to his house? And see his horses? And am I *really* going to be in the wedding? When do I get my pretty dress? Can I have wedding cake? And see Miss Grace's dress? And play with Atticus? Mommy's not coming until tomorrow, and she's mad. She says it's all Miss Desiree's fault. She says Miss Desiree cares about herself too much."

After that revealing statement, Amalie busied herself by opening Devin's desk drawer to look for gum.

"The ultimate irony," he said, softly.

Mallory had perfected the ability to find flaws in others while seeing none in herself. Upon realizing that Desiree's yearly charity auction had been scheduled for the same night as the rehearsal dinner, Mallory threw quite a fit. It was spectacular. Devin had watched the whole thing in awe, glad that, for once, he was not the recipient of his wife's glorified temper tantrum. She whined. She wheedled. She wept, but to no avail. Desiree wouldn't budge. Mallory had promised to help, and help she would. Devin felt like a fly on the wall during their heated exchange. Neither woman acknowledged his presence to any degree, but the fireworks were fascinating.

Eventually, Mallory gave up. She agreed to help with the auction on Friday night. She would fly to Honeysuckle Creek on Saturday morning, giving Devin an unexpected day of peace. He owed Desiree a debt of gratitude. He really did, as well as an apology. Try as he might, he couldn't stop picturing her with the bearded face and hairy legs from his dream. He felt slightly better about that mental image only because he knew Desiree couldn't care less about raising funds for childhood hunger. She sponsored the auction every year solely for the glitz and glamour, and the opportunity to hobnob with the fabulously wealthy.

Amalie found what she was looking for in Devin's desk. At Devin's nod, she popped a piece of sugar-free, dentist-recommended gum into her mouth. After giving it a few chews to soften it up, she started again: "Daddy, Nanny Di says that you will let me stay up late and that you will dance with me at the 'cepshun.' " She slid off his lap and twirled around the room. "Daddy, what's a 'cepshun'?

Diana appeared in the doorway. "Reception," she corrected, gently.

"Re-cep-shun," Amalie repeated, carefully.

Devin chuckled. "A reception is the party after the wedding ceremony. Mr. Blane and Miss Grace's will have lots of food, music, and dancing." He stood from his chair and approached his daughter, holding out his hands. "Amalie Merritt, may I have this dance?"

Her smile grew impossibly wide as she performed a childish curtsey. "Oh, yes," she said, putting her hands in his.

As they moved back and forth to the music in Amalie's head, Devin glanced at Diana. "Has she been this excited all day?" he asked.

Diana nodded ruefully. "Since her feet hit the floor. I have to admit, I'm a bit frazzled. I'm glad it's finally time to go."

That admission, coming from Diana, was saying a lot.

"Diana, you are a saint," Devin told her, gratefully. "We're going to grab lunch on the way and meet Blane and Rafe at the airport. Hopefully, between the three of us, you can get a little break."

"That sounds wonderful." She held out her hand to her young charge. "C'mon, 'Malie. Let's go freshen up before lunch."

"I don't need to *freshen up*," Amalie responded, with a puzzled look. "I just need to go to the bathroom."

Devin laughed as Diana sighed, shaking her head. "That's what *freshen up* means, Amalie. It's a polite way of saying that you are going to the bathroom."

"Oh." Amalie took Diana's hand and skipped to the door. "But, Nanny Di, what if I say *freshen up* and somebody doesn't understand? What if they…" Her voice faded into the corridor.

Devin smiled as much at his daughter's enthusiasm as at the prospect of enjoying the next twenty-four hours. Mallory-free.

CHAPTER EIGHTEEN

Their arrival at Heart's Ease, Blane's beautiful estate, held all of the joy—and some of the awkwardness—of a family reunion. Devin, Diana, and Amalie followed Blane into the entryway of his impressive home. Rafe, mumbling something about security issues, opted not to go inside with them. He disappeared the minute they climbed out of their car. Devin was so accustomed to Rafe's mysterious disappearances he scarcely noticed.

They were warmly greeted by Grace and her parents, Joe and Juli Finch, as well as their best friends, the Parkers. There were hugs all around. And, just as Devin expected, quite a fuss was made over Amalie, the only child in the wedding.

Devin already knew Will Parker—Joe's law partner—but he had never met Will's vivacious wife, Maggie, who was directing the wedding. Will introduced their two grown sons, Ric and Dom, as well as their seventeen-year-old twins, Penelope and Phoebe. Devin smiled at the girls. He shook hands with Ric, but before he could find out if Dom's handshake was as firm as his brother's, Amalie squealed at the top of her lungs. She hopped up and down, pointing through the archway to the staircase on the west side of the grand foyer.

All eyes turned to see Atticus, Grace's three-legged dog, carefully descending the stairs. As soon as he reached the bottom, he turned into a brown ball of fur, hurtling toward the excited, little girl. It took a few minutes to untangle Amalie and Atticus from the meeting of their own personal mutual admiration society. In the end, the scruffy canine happily seated himself on Blane's foot while basking in Amalie's enthusiastic adoration.

Talk then turned to the out-of-town guests. "Mom, Dad, and Lydia will be here midmorning tomorrow," Devin volunteered, in response to their queries. "And Mallory, of course," he added, trying—and failing—not to make it seem like an afterthought. "She's on the same flight with them. I mean, they're coming at the same time. Together."

Not by choice, he added silently, remembering his sister's displeasure at discovering she was assigned the seat beside her irksome sister-in-law. In coach. Their parents had been upgraded to first class, but Lydia was stuck. Devin couldn't help but be amused at his sister's creative—but quite possibly illegal—suggestions to remedy the situation. In the end Lydia decided to purchase a pair of noise-cancelling earbuds and make the best of it.

Maggie smiled at Amalie. "I'm sorry your mommy couldn't come with you to the rehearsal dinner. I'm sure you'll be excited to see her tomorrow."

"Nanny Di says my mommy is a selfish bitch," Amalie replied, rubbing Atticus' tummy. The contented canine had rolled over onto his back, wrapped in blissful oblivion.

Devin glanced at Diana, noting that all of the color had drained from her face. Her light gray eyes were wide with shock. He knew that she would *never* intentionally say such a thing in his daughter's presence, even as he silently acknowledged that the epithet his daughter had used to describe his wife was the truth.

Maggie had a stunned expression on her face. The loquacious redhead was momentarily speechless…a rare and precious occurrence, according to her husband.

The small group exchanged glances. Nobody knew quite what to say.

Finally, Joe broke the silence. "Is that so?" he asked, in a mild tone of voice. He didn't appear the least bit startled to have heard such unexpected words come out of the mouth of a four-year-old girl.

"Amalie. Rose. Merritt," Diana gasped, when she had finally regained the ability to speak. "I have *never* said anything like that to you." Tears had begun to form in Diana's eyes, but she refused to let them fall. She was determined to make her point.

Amalie stood up when Diana used her full name, a worried frown on her face. The little girl was anxious to defend herself. "You didn't say it to *me*, Nanny Di. You said it to Gamma Ollie," she explained. "I was playing with Iggy. Iggy heard you and then he told me."

"Amalie, were you hiding behind the curtains again?" Devin asked, in a stern tone.

"I was just playing with Iggy. We were there first," Amalie said. "Is Iggy in trouble?" she asked anxiously. Her lower lip trembled as crocodile tears filled her blue eyes.

To her family's surprise, Phoebe came to the rescue. She approached Amalie with a conspiratorial smile. "Iggy?" she asked. "Are you talking about Ignacio Iguana? Do *you* know him?"

Of the twins, Phoebe was usually the quieter girl, content to remain in the background. But because the gentle teenager was already planning for a career in elementary education, she was very familiar with the series of children's books Diana had written.

Amalie nodded in response to Phoebe's questions. "This is Iggy," she said, seriously, indicating the stuffed iguana she carried backward under her arm. Iggy's tail stuck out the front, his head hung behind him.

Phoebe reached out to shake Iggy's tail. "Hello there, Mr. Iguana, sir. It's nice to meet you."

Amalie's good mood was instantly restored. "That's his tail, silly." She giggled, turning the iguana around so Phoebe could meet him properly.

Phoebe took Amalie by the hand. "Let's go introduce him to my sister, Penny."

She towed the little girl toward Penelope, who was standing, mercifully, out of earshot of the adults.

Diana turned to Devin. "I am *so* sorry," she said. "I should have known better than to say anything about Mallory without checking behind the curtains first. I *never* meant for Amalie to overhear." Then Diana raised her chin as she faced the others. "I apologize to all of you."

It didn't escape anyone's notice that she wasn't apologizing for her words. She was apologizing for the fact that her words were, inadvertently, overheard by an innocent child. And repeated.

She looked so upset and embarrassed that Devin felt sorry for her. "It's all right, Diana," he said. "It could just have easily been me. We both know Amalie has a habit of hiding behind the curtains."

Blane nodded in understanding. "Grace and I learned about the curtains the hard way."

Grace's face flooded with the loveliest shade of pink. "Hush, Blane," she said, unable to keep her eyes from dancing. Her charming reaction brought smiles and chuckles from the group, quickly diffusing the tension.

Devin was glad Amalie remained blissfully unaware of the romantic nature of the interlude she had interrupted that day in his library.

Maggie spoke up quickly. "Don't worry about a thing, Diana. You're among friends here." She patted Diana's shoulder encouragingly.

Juli nodded in agreement. "Maggie's right. We *do* understand."

Diana smiled gratefully.

Maggie had spoken the truth. They *were* among friends, Devin thought, thankfully, as his little group followed Grace up the curving staircase. When they reached the balcony, they turned left into the guest wing. As Grace showed them to their rooms, Devin wondered what his Pirate Queen had been like at the age of four. He had a feeling that being the father of a young Darcie Finch had more to do with Joe's calm acceptance of Amalie's words than with all of his law cases combined. He also had the feeling that he should be trying harder to rid himself of his ever-present preoccupation with the sister of the bride.

After depositing his suitcase and garment bag in the beautifully appointed suite to which he had been assigned, Devin was eager to reacquaint himself with the rest of Blane's childhood home. It had been his home, too—in between surgeries—for the two months following his attack. Even though he had been confined to a wheelchair at the beginning of his recovery, and had been sightless at the end of it, Devin felt at ease navigating the vast layout of Heart's Ease. He was rather pleased he didn't need the help of the small, laminated map that was included in the welcome basket in his room. He invited Amalie and Diana on his impromptu tour because he knew how much they would enjoy the beautiful house and grounds. The plantation house was always impressive, but now—all dressed up in its pre-wedding splendor—it was magnificent.

Heart's Ease was an extensive estate. Visitors entered the estate house through the giant front doors and stepped into a rounded entryway, sporting a convenient powder room beyond a large arch in the east wall and a coat room through a doorway in the west wall. The curved chamber was one of the first additions Blane's parents made after their purchase of the huge house.

After crossing the entryway, guests took two steps down—through a graceful archway—onto the black-and-white parquet floor of the grand foyer. Elegant sofas and chairs were arranged in groups to allow visitors a chance to gather. An impressive stone fireplace on the west wall stood at the ready to chase away the chill of any October day. Typical of North Carolina's predictably unpredictable weather, however, the temperature that day was supposed to top out close to seventy-eight degrees. Lighting the fire in the beautiful fireplace would have to wait.

The large open foyer was flanked on either side by curving staircases that led to the second-floor balcony. Double doors, beneath twin archways, graced the east and west ends of the balcony, leading to the family wing and guest wing, respectively. The largest set of double doors in the middle of the north wall opened to an impressive library. The room was bordered by a three-sided balcony that overlooked the ballroom. The books stood neatly stacked on floor-to-ceiling shelves that ran the length of the walls. An elegantly carved railing provided onlookers a breathtaking view of the ballroom below. Looking down—on what was obviously the site of the reception—Devin watched the Heart's Ease staff and the catering crew busily preparing the space for the following night's festivities.

After visiting the stables, Devin was glad to return with Amalie and Diana to the main house and enjoy afternoon tea. Dinner—which wasn't until seven-thirty—seemed very far away. They eagerly passed through the twin columns in the west side of the grand foyer to enter the formal dining room. An expansive spread—complete with coffee, tea, little sandwiches, scones, and a few sweets—had been set up by the staff.

Amalie chattered nonstop, nearly overcome by the thrill of seeing real, live horses back at the stables. After perusing the beverage choices, Diana asked one of the servers for a drink for the smallest—and most excited—member of the wedding party that did *not* contain caffeine or sugar. Mrs. Hofmann, herself, came to the rescue, bringing a nice, calming cup of warm milk. Devin, Diana, and Amalie filled their plates with a substantial snack before returning to the grand foyer. Plates in hand, they settled themselves near the fireplace on the most child-friendly sofa in the room. True to expectations, within thirty seconds of taking her seat, Amalie spilled her milk on the black, leather sofa. Diana, ready with extra napkins, quickly averted the crisis.

From their vantage point, Devin and Diana were able to see all of the guests as they entered the grand foyer. There wasn't any doubt: Southern hospitality was alive and well in Honeysuckle Creek. Each newcomer was greeted effusively before being sent directly to the dining room. The atmosphere became more and more festive as the afternoon wore on. Blane and Grace had survived a great deal of personal heartbreak and tragedy along the way. Seeing the devoted couple, so happy and so very much in love, was cause for celebration.

Blane's grandfather, Fergus McCallum, along with Fergus' son, Ian, and Ian's wife, Alina, had traveled all the way from Scotland to attend the festivities. After introducing them to Diana and Amalie, Devin spent a few minutes in conversation with Ian and Fergus about last month's board of directors' meeting.

Blane waved, catching Devin's attention from across the room. Devin excused himself to join McCallum Industries' CEO. Devin had always known that he was incredibly fortunate to work for Blane McCallum. Not only was Blane a good boss, he was also a good friend. That had never been more apparent than in the last few months.

During the days and weeks after the attack, Blane had given Devin the greatest gift imaginable. He treated him no differently *after* the accident than he did *before*. Blane made it clear he expected Devin to get back to work as soon as possible. That expectation, alone, gave Devin something on which to focus besides himself. Even in the early days, Blane kept Devin informed and involved him in the day-to-day decisions of McCallum Industries. Blane's obvious confidence that Devin would return to his position, still capable of performing at a high level, propelled his recovery. The CEO flatly refused to fill Devin's position, even temporarily. He opted instead to rehire Devin's dad, Robert Merritt—McCallum's former head of legal—as a consultant.

Blane epitomized flexibility, making it possible for Devin to work as much or as little as he wanted when he returned to Providence after his final surgery. As CEO, Blane demanded excellence from all of his employees, especially those closest to him. He made it quite clear he expected Devin to perform at the same level he had maintained before the attack. Such high expectations from his boss helped to remind Devin that a damaged face did not equate to a damaged brain. If Blane believed in him, then why wouldn't he believe in himself? Once Devin realized that he was just as capable on the job as he was before the attack, he relaxed. And did his job.

On a personal level, Blane continued to trade jokes and friendly insults with Devin, just as he always had. He was patient, supportive, and encouraging as Devin took time off for physical and occupational therapy. In spite of Devin's numerous medical challenges, Blane treated his friend with dignity. Not pity. That was the part Devin appreciated the most. Blane didn't seem to notice Devin's disfigurement—or if he did notice, it didn't matter.

Nevertheless, Devin tried to back out as one of Blane's groomsmen. He jokingly told Blane that he didn't want to steal the limelight. In reality,

Devin hadn't wanted to ruin the wedding photographs. His polite attempts to withdraw from the wedding party met with vehement resistance from the groom himself. Blane scoffed at his friend's feeble excuses. He declared that he didn't choose his groomsmen for their pretty faces, and that Devin's tux had already been ordered. After that, Devin got the message. If the groom thought Devin's face was a nonissue, then it was. A. Non. Issue.

"How are you holding up, Boss-man?" he asked with mock solemnity, gripping Blane's hand in a firm handshake.

"About as well as can be expected," Blane replied. "Under the circumstances." He didn't even try to hide the grin on his face.

Before Devin could reply, Joey Finch, brother of the bride—and of the maid of honor—joined the pair. "Good to see you, Devin," he said, holding out his hand in a friendly gesture.

Devin shook hands, trying—and failing—not to notice how much Joey resembled his still absent sister. Same dark hair. Same dark eyes. Same smile. No tropical flowers, though. That was a scent Devin couldn't seem to forget.

Joey indicated the groom with his head. "Blane is nauseatingly, sickeningly, disgustingly happy. Don't let him tell you otherwise."

Devin shook his head sadly. "I know. I'm afraid it's too late for Blane." He continued, much to Joey's amusement: "I warned him over and over, but, well..." He shrugged. "Here we are."

"*I* believe you," Joey, the quintessential bachelor, said, with an overexaggerated shudder. "The word *groom* isn't even in my vocabulary."

A man with dark, wavy hair joined the conversation. "Aw, leave the poor groom alone, Finch," he said to Joey. "He's got enough to worry about. Ball and chain, and all that." He turned to Devin, holding out his hand. "I'm Roger Carrington."

"Devin Merritt," Devin responded, shaking Roger's hand. He didn't know the whole story of how Roger Carrington, the bride's ex-fiancé, had become a member of the wedding party. But Devin did know enough to understand that Carrington played an instrumental role in Blane's courtship of Grace. Whatever it was that Roger did, it had earned him Blane's respect and undying gratitude.

"Nice to meet you, Devin," Roger said. "Don't pay any attention to Joey," he added, grinning. "He's just afraid all of this will rub off on him and send him spiraling toward the altar."

Joey coughed, pretending to choke. "Spiraling toward the altar, Carrington? Me?" He laughed, shaking his head. "Not. A. Chance. Weddings are for *other* people. People like my soon-to-be brother-in-law, Blane," he said with a grin.

While he was talking, a tall, radiant blonde and a giant of a man—who bore a striking resemblance to Denzel Washington—wandered over.

Joey continued, indicating the new arrivals: "And like these two. Lou. Evander. This is Devin Merritt."

"Nice to finally meet you," Lou said, holding out her hand with a friendly smile.

"Lou and Evander taught with Grace at Honeysuckle Creek Academy," Joey explained.

"That's right," Evander confirmed, also shaking Devin's hand. "But now, Lou has become an entrepreneur." His voice was filled with pride. "*She* designed the wedding dress."

"Shh!" Lou teased, covering Evander's mouth with her hand. She cut her eyes toward Blane. "We can't talk about *The Dress* when *he's* around."

"You mean *you've* seen it?" Blane asked Evander, clearly surprised by this news.

"Of course, he's seen it," Lou soothed, patting Blane's arm. "I had to get a man's opinion. Don't worry, Blane," she teased. "You'll see it soon enough."

"I've seen it, too," said Joey, appearing a little offended. "Why didn't you ask me for my opinion? I'm definitely a man."

"You're her brother," Lou answered, wrinkling her nose. "Your opinion doesn't count."

They were still laughing—all except Joey—when a young man with neatly trimmed hair planted himself beside Devin. He wore a friendly smile, and a blazer that was just a little too small for his lanky frame. He didn't wait to be introduced. "You must be Devin," he said, holding out his hand. "I'm Zack."

"Nice to meet you, Zack," Devin replied, surprised at the confidence the young man displayed. And the strength of his grip.

Since graduating from high school and turning eighteen, Zack had embraced every aspect of his fledgling adulthood. He thoroughly enjoyed addressing his former teachers, and every other adult he knew, on a strictly first-name basis.

His eyes were full of mischief as he punched Roger in the arm. "Hi, Dad. Can I borrow the car?" he asked, casually.

Roger's expression registered pure horror. "I am *not* your dad," he said to Zack, looking at the grinning young man as if he had lost his mind. Roger immediately turned to Devin. "I am *not* his dad."

"That's not what you said last night, Dad," Zack contradicted him happily.

"He has a point, Raj," Evander agreed, his eyes full of mirth.

"What are you two talking about?" Roger asked them. He turned again to Devin, clearly at a loss. "I don't know what they're talking about."

"We're talking about when Zack finally let you win a game of pool last night," Evander explained patiently.

"He didn't *let* me win," Roger told Devin, shaking his head.

"Oh, yes, I did," Zack chimed in, confirming Evander's accusation. "I let him win," he said to Devin. "Old Dad's not quite as good as he thinks he is."

Roger frowned. "Why do you keep saying that? I am not your..."

"Think hard, Raj." Evander's big voice shook with laughter. "Remember how you kept asking him, '*Who's your daddy?*' *Who's your daddy?*' "

Roger could only nod.

Evander grinned. "Well. I guess he figured out who his daddy is."

Roger was completely disconcerted. "Oh, for the love of..."

Joey cut in. "What time does this rehearsal thing get going, anyway?" He checked the time on his phone.

"Maggie said six o'clock," Lou offered. "Can't wait to get started, huh?"

"Can't wait to get finished," Joey said. "I've got a date."

"You've *always* got a date," Roger pointed out, happy the conversation had turned to somebody else.

"Look who's talking." Joey turned the spotlight right back on Roger without supplying a single detail of his own. "Who are *you* bringing to this fiesta?"

"Umm…well…" Roger shrugged his shoulders, carelessly. "Lou, I guess. We're usually each other's fall back."

The toe of Lou's elegant high-heel shoe began to beat a tattoo on the floor as she glared at her desperation wedding date. "Excuse me, Mr. Carrington," she said in vexation. "I do not recall being asked."

Roger cleared his throat as the tapping continued. "Well?" he asked politely. "Will you be my date?"

Lou smiled gleefully. "Sorry, Raj," she said politely. "I'm afraid that ship has sailed."

Roger was thoroughly confused. "What's that supposed to mean?"

Lou's smile became smug. "I already have a date."

"Who?" he asked in disbelief.

"Me," Evander said, laughing at the look of surprise on Roger's face. He turned to Lou, offering his arm. "Miss Boggs, shall we?"

"Why thank you, Mr. Mayfield. I'd be delighted."

Turning her nose up in the air, Lou Ann allowed Evander to escort her to the dining room.

Zack threw his arm around Roger's shoulder. "I think she picked him because he's a better dancer than you are, Dad," he said, philosophically.

Roger shook off Zack's arm, straightening his shoulders. "Evander does *not* dance better than I do. And I am not your…"

"C'mon, Dad," Zack interrupted. "You'll feel better after you have a snack."

Roger didn't say a word. He didn't have to. His glare said it all as he turned and headed for the dining room.

"Nice meeting you, Devin," Zack said, cheerfully. "I better go and grab a bite, too. Wouldn't want poor Dad to eat alone." His comical wink was pure theatre.

Devin and Blane shared a grin, watching Zack's confident stride as he went to hunt down his favorite victim.

"He's quite a character, isn't he?" Devin asked. "He seems to keep Carrington on his toes."

"Yeah," Blane agreed. "Zack keeps all of us on our toes, especially Roger. He drove Gracie crazy when she was his English teacher."

Devin chuckled. "I can imagine."

"Speaking of my lovely bride..." Blane said, unable to hide his eagerness. "I know she wants you to meet the rest of the female contingent..."

"So, we better get over there right away," Devin finished with a chuckle.

He followed Blane to the far side of the room, observing the way Grace's green eyes lit up as she saw them approach. Devin privately marveled at her response. Grace looked like she hadn't seen Blane in months even though it had only been a few minutes.

The only way Mallory would look at me like that, Devin thought, *was if I was holding a bag full of money. Or, maybe, diamonds. Yeah,* he decided. *Diamonds would do it.* Devin tried to force that thought out of his mind. He tried not to be cynical about his situation. But maintaining a positive outlook was proving to be quite difficult, especially in the presence of such a happy couple. He felt his good mood falter as they approached the women gathered around the bride.

Devin managed to be polite and—in his own estimation—somewhat charming as he was introduced to Grace's college roommates, Haven and Charlotte, and to Ana Martin, a former teaching colleague and friend of the bride. To his relief, not one of the attractive, young women cringed upon seeing his scars. They had obviously been well prepped.

He didn't want to assume that was the case, but he couldn't help it. He had yet to shake the slight sense of dread he felt when meeting someone for the first time. He had learned, however, that the best course of action was to forge ahead as if his *monster face* looked like everybody else's. He had discovered that only the smallest-minded people had trouble getting past his appearance. And, he decided, who wanted to talk to them, anyway?

He pretended to enjoy the lively conversation of the ladies for a few minutes. What he really wanted to do, however, was to stand by himself against the wall, brooding about his rotten marriage and why it made his intense desire to see the absent Darcie Finch such a problem.

After a decent interval, he excused himself to check on Amalie and Diana. He discovered his daughter chattering away to Blane's aunt Alina, who appeared to be enjoying herself immensely. Diana winked as he approached.

"And that's why I *really* need a pony," he heard Amalie say.

He exchanged an amused glance with Diana over his daughter's blond head.

"Hi, Daddy!" Amalie exclaimed excitedly. "Miss Alina has a whole stable full of horses in Scotin. She says if we come to visit, she'll take me riding. Can we?" she pleaded. "Can we, Daddy? I want to go to Scotin. I want to ride horses with Miss Alina."

"Scot-land," said Diana.

"Scot-land," Amalie repeated, obediently.

"I'm going to get some tea, Amalie," Alina said, gently. "We'll talk more about horses later." She rose from her seat at the end of the sofa.

"And about Scotin, Miss Alina? Can we talk about Scotin?"

"Scot-land," said Diana.

"Scot-land," echoed Amalie.

"Of course, Amalie." Alina nodded. "I have lots more to tell you about Scotland." As she passed Devin, she paused to lay an apologetic hand on his arm. "Sorry about that," she said so only he could hear.

"Don't worry," Devin replied. "Every little girl wants a pony eventually. It's inevitable. I'm just thankful it's a pony and not a unicorn. That's what she asked for last week."

Alina smiled as she went in search of the teapot.

CHAPTER NINETEEN

*A*malie stood up. "Nanny Di, I need to freshen up," she said loudly. "That means go to the bathroom," she added to Devin and the group at the end of the sofa. The group was made up entirely of men, of course.

Diana sighed. Thankfully, with the exception of Blane's uncle, they all were fathers, and even Ian didn't try to hide his amusement. Diana smiled back, ruefully, and relaxed a bit. What a kind group of people, she thought. They genuinely seemed to enjoy Amalie's comments. It was nice not to have to worry about being reprimanded for every word that came out of Amalie's mouth. Devin knew Mallory was frequently unpleasant to Diana, but he had no idea how bad things really were on a daily basis. Diana refused to add to his impossible situation by complaining. At least she was allowed to go home at night and most weekends. Poor Devin was stuck.

Diana took Amalie's hand and escorted her small charge on her necessary errand.

Devin's thoughts, however, lay far from Mallory and Rhode Island. He found himself musing over the fact that Amalie's words about *freshening up* had kept him from wondering when Darcie Finch would appear. For a whole thirty seconds. Devin took up a position beside the fireplace, thankful to have a few minutes to himself.

As he glanced around the room, he realized that Darcie and Rafe were the only people he could think of who were still unaccounted for. He chose to dwell on the absence of the latter, thereby keeping his thoughts from the impending arrival of his Pirate Queen. Doing so felt a great deal safer.

Rafe was probably outside on the estate somewhere, checking on security. That brought to mind the—as yet unresolved—nature of the attempt on Devin's own life. Unsolved after four months. Devin was still ruminating on the conversation that had taken place between himself, Rafe, and Blane a few hours earlier, during the flight to Honeysuckle Creek. He couldn't quite decide how he felt about it.

"I'm not going to mince words, Devin," Rafe began. "After four months, we are no closer to figuring out who hit you with that car—or why—than we were the day it happened. The police decided pretty quickly that it was a random act. After so many weeks without another attempt on your life, the men I've had investigating are inclined to agree."

"But?" Devin prompted.

"Why do you think there's a but?" Rafe asked, watching Devin carefully.

"Because you didn't say anything about yourself or your own opinions."

Devin unconsciously braced himself for what Rafe might say.

"What do you think, Rafe?" Blane asked his mentor. "We both know you well enough to trust your instincts. What are they telling you?"

"In short, I don't believe the attack—and, gentlemen, it was an attack—was in any way random. I believe somebody needed some insurance."

"Insurance?" Devin was more than a little confused.

"I think this all started when Kenneth Wade contacted you and demanded a meeting," Rafe said patiently. "From what you said, he wasn't forthcoming as to the subject of said meeting. He just demanded to be put on your calendar. This leads me to believe that he had discovered something—probably some kind of illegal activities—either taking place at McCallum Industries or involving a McCallum employee. I am inclined to favor the latter."

"And he was trying to tell me about it," Devin interjected, somberly. "And he was killed for it. Poor guy." This was a sobering bit of information.

Rafe held up his hand. "While it's a shame for anyone to die under those circumstances..."

Blane interrupted before Rafe could continue, "Is it possible he found out about Douglas' embezzlement?" He referred to last winter's horrific discovery that his uncle Douglas had been stealing from the McCallum family for years. Blane felt that his grandfather's wish not to prosecute was a mistake then, and he was even more sure of that now. "Wade worked in the same division and could have stumbled on some old records," Blane said hopefully.

"Perhaps Wade found proof of the embezzlement of monies from your trust fund, Blane, and wanted legal advice regarding what to do with that information. It's not likely that he found anything new. We've blanketed everything Douglas has touched since the original discovery of the thefts. There aren't any irregularities in any of Douglas' accounts, and everything in which he has been involved for the company has been flawlessly executed. In short, he's been an exemplary employee."

"If my accident—attack—wasn't about the discovery that somebody was embezzling the trust fund, then what could Wade possibly have planned to tell me?" Devin wanted answers to all of his questions, even though he was fairly certain he wasn't going to like them.

Rafe cleared his throat. "Getting back to my original statement..." Here he paused to direct his eagle-eyed gaze toward Blane. That look reminded Devin of one his friend might have received when he was about twelve years old. *Don't interrupt me again, it said.*

Blane acknowledged his mistake with a nod and a grin.

Rafe grinned, too, for a moment before he continued, soberly: "While it is a shame for anyone to die under these circumstances, it is highly likely that the poor guy—as you call him, Devin—was trying to make a buck rather than help the company." Rafe sat back in his chair and crossed his ankle over his knee. His relaxed position belied the intense focus he was giving the conversation. "Would *either of you call it a strange* coincidence *that Wade made a large cash deposit into a new account before leaving for his cruise? Or that the deposit occurred the day before your scheduled meeting?"*

"Blackmail," Blane said, nodding his head. "That makes sense. He was blackmailing someone about what he had discovered. Otherwise he would have reported a business irregularity to the security division. We don't have any record of him refusing to follow protocol before, do we?"

"No," Rafe said. "It appears that, until this incident, he was a model employee."

"Nothing like a little financial opportunity to bring out the worst in a model employee," Blane added, soberly. "But, Rafe, I still don't understand why Wade decided to turn to Devin."

Devin nodded in agreement. "Why come to me at all if the information didn't have anything to do with McCallum Industries?" he asked. "What could Wade possibly have been hoping to accomplish?"

"What if Wade stumbled onto something that involved the company? Or—a more likely scenario—what if he found out someone in the company was involved in some shady activity that was making him or her a whole lot of money? You underestimate your own reputation for integrity and honesty, Devin, if you can't see that you were the perfect choice. What if getting an appointment with you was a threat, done solely to convince the person—or persons—he was trying to blackmail that he was serious?" Rafe was laying down the framework of his own suppositions. "Telling you would have been like telling the police, because if Wade wouldn't call the police, you would have made the call yourself. What if he went to somebody else first and told them he was going to tell you? What if that person wanted to keep him quiet?"

"And what if that person wasn't sure if Wade told me or not?" Devin suggested. What Rafe said was starting to make sense.

"Then killing you would have been a form of insurance for the guilty party," Rafe said, nodding his head. "But it quickly became obvious that Wade didn't tell you, because nothing happened. No investigation. No uncomfortable questions. Nothing. This leads me to believe that you are no longer in danger for two reasons. First, it's been four months. The guilty party believes that he has gotten away with whatever he is, or was, doing. So, you have ceased to be a player in the game. The second reason is that no one seems to realize that your accident was anything other than a random attack. I've even heard rumors that it was a terrorist attack of some sort, and that it was being looked into by Homeland Security. If another attempt is made on your life, however, it will validate the fact that someone wants you dead. Then, the authorities will have to deal with it and the person, or persons, responsible will risk being discovered."

"So, as things stand, the best thing that Devin, and all of us, can do is to act like Devin was the victim of a random accident," Blane said.

"Exactly." Rafe folded his hands together. "That's exactly what I want you to do. Leave the rest to me."

"What does that mean?" Devin asked, throwing his hands in the air in frustration.

"It means that, unless we find out otherwise, you, and your family, are safe. But, my friend, don't let your guard down. That goes for you, too, Blane. Don't assume that this thing is over. Immediately after the wedding, I'm going back to Belize to see if I can find out who hired the man who tampered with the harness on the zip line that killed Wade. If we can find out who, then maybe we can find out why."

"Damn it," Blane said forcefully. He needed a change of scenery. He stood from his seat to check on the pilot.

Rafe opened his laptop and started typing.

Devin leaned back in his own seat, wondering for the thousandth time, who was behind his attack. His face bore the evidence of someone's malice. And, while he was relieved Rafe thought the danger was over, Devin was afraid quite some time would pass before he stopped looking over his shoulder whenever he went outside. Even without any evidence to the contrary, he couldn't keep his suspicions from going back to one man—the embezzler-turned-exemplary-employee—Douglas McCallum.

After watching Amalie smell all of the different lotions in the powder room, Diana found Devin holding up the wall beside the fireplace. She joined him as Amalie sat on the floor to play with Iggy. His eyes met hers, questioningly. She grinned at him, obviously enjoying the controlled chaos currently at large in the room. The Honeysuckle Creek crowd was a boisterous bunch. They were obviously devoted to each other though seemingly unable to resist a constant litany of good-natured wisecracks and teasing. This form of lunacy hearkened to a gathering of the Merritt clan, making Devin and Diana feel right at home.

Devin looked around for the bride and groom, but Blane and Grace were nowhere in sight. That, he quickly decided, was none of his business. He checked his watch again. The rehearsal was supposed to start in fifteen minutes. Fifteen minutes. A quarter of an hour. His wait would soon be over. No way would Darcie Finch be late for her own sister's wedding rehearsal.

CHAPTER TWENTY

*D*arcie checked her GPS with satisfaction. This time, she was *not* going to be late. She wasn't even going to be right on time...the same thing as being late, according to Joe Finch. She was going to be five minutes early in spite of—she might add—the stop-and-go traffic caused by that wreck on Interstate 85. Five whole minutes. It might not be much to some, but to Darcie it was a major accomplishment. She would almost call it a breakthrough.

She relaxed for the first time that day, enjoying the scenery of the two-lane country road. Autumn was a beautiful time of year in her hometown. The leaves were gorgeous—deep red, brilliant yellow, blazing orange—a breathtaking display set against the backdrop of a magnificent sunset. She was sure the view from Heart's Ease would be just as glorious. The ceremony was going to be spectacular. She could just imagine...

Darcie's eyes narrowed. No. No. No. It couldn't be. Just a few more miles, she thought. So close. She was so very close....

"This cannot be happening," Darcie groaned. She realized, at that moment, that she was talking to herself. Out loud. But, at this point, it didn't matter. There wasn't anyone to hear her. She refused to believe what was right in front of her—that...*thing*...in the middle of the road—until it was, well...right in front of her. Or she was right behind it.

A tractor.

A harmless, little tractor.

A harmless, little tractor moving at the blinding speed of two miles per hour.

And—horror of horrors—that little tractor was being driven by one of the Porter brothers. Jeremiah or Hezekiah? She never had been able to tell them apart. One of them was driving while the other one rode high up on the fender.

She might not have been able to identify which Porter was which, but she knew the exact moment whoever was driving the tractor had recognized her. Darcie watched as the driver relayed the information to his brother. She returned their excited waves with a reluctant hand.

The Porter brothers were sweet. No doubt about that. Not bright, but sweet. They would do anything for anybody. They were a good-hearted pair. Honest and hardworking. But they didn't have enough sense to come in out of the rain. And they certainly didn't have enough sense to pull off the road to let a car pass.

The country road was filled with twists and turns. Darcie was doomed.

She forced herself to relax, settling back into her seat. She flatly refused to give in to the clawing need to pass that tractor…in spite of the double yellow line and the curving road. Her urgency—she was honest enough to admit—was not based solely on the desire to avoid the comments and heckling that always accompanied her tardiness. She was used to that. Truth be told, she deserved it. She *was* late a lot. It was a habit she really needed to get under control. No, that wasn't what was making her more than a little anxious.

The real problem stemmed from the fact that she was finally going to see *him*. Without his bandages. She was going to look into his eyes—oops, eye—and he was going to look back. He would see her. *Really* see her. He would see her face, not just her *beautiful soul*, as he had so eloquently called it. His precious words, and the circumstances in which they were uttered, were something she would never forget. She would always be grateful, no matter what happened in the next thirty minutes. Or hour. Or…who knew how long? That depended entirely on the Porters.

As the tractor continued to crawl up the road, Darcie continued to wonder. What would it be like to see him again? What would she say? More importantly, what would *he* say? Would they fall back into their effortless relationship of two months earlier? Or would finally seeing each other be like meeting a stranger?

Darcie *almost* hoped for the latter. She *almost* hoped that Devin had gone home to an apologetic and regretful wife. A wife who had seen the errors of her ways. A wife who was waiting to welcome him home with open arms. Darcie *almost* hoped that their marriage had grown stronger because of their adversity. She had *almost* prepared herself to meet Devin's beautiful wife. To watch his wife hanging on to his arm. To see her gaze adoringly at the man she had married. Darcie was *almost* ready to wish Devin well. To forget all about the twenty-four hours they had shared.

Almost.

Almost was the definitive word here, because Darcie had to admit there was a small part of her—well, maybe not so small—that hoped…What did she hope? The good Lord knew she had pondered *every* nuance of *every* conversation they had *ever* had. More than once. Or twice. Or five dozen times, in the last two months. At least once a day. But who was counting?

She knew that she had no right to spend so much time thinking about another woman's husband. But—and it was a big but—she couldn't quite shake the feeling that Devin Merritt needed her. And if that feeling was true, well…what? That unanswerable question explained her shaking hands. It explained why her stomach felt like one great, big tangled up knot. Because, if Devin's wife still thought he was a monster. If she hadn't changed. If their marriage had continued to deteriorate, creating a mockery of their wedding vows. Well, then, Darcie would…

Here she paused because she couldn't complete the sentence. She didn't know what she would do. She only knew that turning her back on Laurence Devin Merritt was going to be extremely difficult if he needed her.

Six o'clock. On the dot. Devin's already frayed nerves were unraveling more and more by the minute. He was still holding up the wall beside the fireplace. Ric Parker was sitting in the middle of the sofa closest to the door. His brother, Dom, had draped one leg over the arm of the same sofa. Joe and Juli Finch were hovering around the entryway, while Joey held vigil by the window.

"And who do you think is going to be the very last person to get here?" Joey asked aloud, to no one in particular. He had been complaining steadily for the last fifteen minutes. After a brief pause, he answered his own question. "*My sister*, that's who. *My sister* will be late for her own funeral," Joey stated adamantly.

Dom stood up from the arm of the sofa, abandoning his role of casual observer. "In her defense," he said, glancing at Joey. "There was a three-car pileup on 85 before the I-40 split. Even if she left early, that would hold her up."

So, Darcie Finch has a defender, Devin mused. *That's good. I'm glad. Very glad. Absolutely ecstatic.* Devin tried to keep his thoughts of a benign nature. He even tried to believe them.

"And I'm *sure* that she left early," Joey muttered. Pulling the sheer curtains back, he peered, morosely, toward the empty driveway. "Just like she *always* does."

"What's your problem, Little Joe?" asked Ric, leaving the comfortable sofa to join Joey at the window. He looked over Joey's shoulder easily, being a full four inches taller.

Blane and Grace reappeared just in time for Grace to answer Ric's question. "My big brother has to pick up his date," Grace explained. "Between the rehearsal and the dinner, for some unknown reason."

"So why didn't he pick her up *before* the rehearsal?"

Ric winked at Grace, taking advantage of the chance to torment one of his oldest friends. Messing with Joey was something Ric enjoyed immensely but was rarely home long enough to do.

Grace shrugged, flashing her fiancé a mischievous smile. Blane's turn.

Blane couldn't resist the opportunity. "His date probably couldn't get ready that early. She's going out with Joey Finch. *The* Joey Finch. She's getting her nails done. Or maybe it's her toes. Or she's getting a new tattoo. Something like that. Joey always did like those high-maintenance women."

"What's wrong with getting your nails done?" asked Lou, holding out her newly manicured nails. She and Evander had just joined the group.

Evander shook his head, sorrowfully. "Like Blane said, *high maintenance women*."

Lou turned her shiny nails into claws and hissed like a cat at her detractor.

Evander's big, booming laugh echoed through the room as Lou turned those claws on him. He caught her wrists in his hands. What started as a mock wrestling match ended in a fluid waltz around the outer edge of the room.

Devin chuckled. The wedding party and friends continued to remind him of his own family. Lots of insults and jokes intermingled with lots of laughter and genuine affection. It was all in fun, and he was happy to be a part of it. He would be even happier, he admitted, if he wasn't so damn edgy.

Joey continued to bemoan his fate. "Why is Darcie always late? I've spent half my life waiting on that girl. See why I call her The Princess?" He enjoyed calling his sister by the childhood nickname she had always despised. He sighed mournfully before continuing his soliloquy. "I'm here." He pointed to himself. "And The Brat's here." He pointed at Grace, who scowled upon hearing her own childhood nickname. "Mom and Dad are here. But one member of the family *is not here*." Joey looked at his father, seeming genuinely perplexed. "Dad, please enlighten me. From whom did my ever-delightful sister inherit her propensity for tardiness?"

"Well, don't look at me."

Joe Finch angled his head toward his wife, who was deep in conversation with the wedding director.

Poor Maggie. She looked as edgy as Devin felt.

Joe fixed his eyes on Juli, grinning as if he knew all her secrets and relished every one.

Feeling his eyes upon her, Juli caught the look that she knew so well. She stopped talking in midsentence. Her eyes narrowed suspiciously. "What did you just say about me, Joe Finch? I know that look and I'm betting that whatever just came out of your mouth is either untrue or an extreme exaggeration."

"Your firstborn just asked me why his beloved, baby sister is chronically, consistently, inevitably late. And I laid the blame, my darling wife, at your tiny, little feet." Joe tried to look serious, but the twinkle in his eyes gave him away. He liked nothing better than verbal jousting with his lovely wife, who always gave as good as she got.

"Now, wait just a minute," Juli began, but before she could come up with an appropriate defense, Joe interrupted her with his own coup de grâce.

"Now, now, Juliette, simmer down. Even you have to admit that you carried Darcie two weeks past your due date. I believe this perpetual tardiness is an inherited trait. After looking at all of the evidence, it becomes clear that our daughter's penchant for arriving late to any and all occasions is totally your fault."

Juli's mouth flew open in surprise. She put both hands on her hips and glared at her husband. "And how is it *my* fault? It's not like I had any say in what day the baby was born. It's sort of up to the baby. That is an extremely weak argument, Counselor."

"Oh, Lord," Joey moaned. "The Princess was late for her own birth."

Ric was beyond amused by the conversation. "What gives, Little Joe? Who is this girl you have to pick up and why is she such a big deal?"

"It's a new girl. From out of town." Grace fluttered her long eyelashes.

"She's not really from out of town," Joey objected. "She's from Clover Gap." The community was an unincorporated township about twenty minutes west of Honeysuckle Creek.

"Oh, I get it," Ric said, trying to appear serious. "Little Joe's already been out with every available girl in Honeysuckle Creek, Greater Ashwell, *and* Squirrel Knot. Now he's going to work his way through the London County girls." Ric grinned at the *go-to-hell* expression on Joey's face. "Better watch out for those county girls, Little Joe. I've heard they're pretty wild."

"It took him *two whole days* to wear this one down, so she would agree to go out with him," Grace added, helpfully. She bent down to straighten the one remaining ear on her dog's head. It was flipped upside down, making Atticus look even more diabolical than usual. "Joey has to go out with her fast, before she finds out what he's really like."

"But it's *always* a new girl, isn't it? I mean, Little Joe isn't one for repetition in the land of love, is he? Or," Ric paused, dramatically. "Has he…gasp… changed?" He put his hand over his chest and bounced his palm up and down, mimicking a beating heart.

"Oh no," Grace said, giggling. "He hasn't changed."

"I'm right in front of you," Joey interjected. "I can hear every word you're saying."

"Then it's still the same, old thing." Ric nodded wisely, as if Joey hadn't spoken. "It's *always* a new girl because *nobody* will go out with him more than once."

"Damn, I've missed you, Ric," Joey growled sarcastically. "How I look forward to the day when you come back for another visit, say in ten or twelve or *fifty* years."

"Little girl in the room, Joey; watch your language," Lou sang out as she danced by in the arms of Evander. "Shame on you."

Devin glanced around for Amalie, not surprised to find her dancing with Iggy in the corner of the room. She seemed completely oblivious to anything but imitating the prowess of Lou and Evander.

Everyone seemed to be enjoying themselves except Darcie's defender, Dominic Parker. Instead of joining in the fray, he stepped toward the entryway, pulling out his cell phone. His distraction gave Devin the opportunity to study the man. Dom wasn't overly tall—maybe around five foot eleven—with short, brown hair and a muscular frame. Devin would describe him as pretty ordinary looking, in a nonthreatening sort of way. *Seems like a good sort*, he thought. Probably a family friend. An old, family friend. A perfectly harmless, old, family friend.

When she reached the top of the hill, the road to Heart's Ease would be in sight. Of course—at the rate the Porters were moving—it could be hours before she reached the turnoff. So close and yet, so very, very far away. She was near enough that if worse came to worst, she could always stop the car and run to the rehearsal. In a dress. And high heels. *Great idea, Darcie,* she admonished herself.

She raised her hand to wave at Jeremiah—or was it Hezekiah?—for the five hundred and twenty-seventh time since coming up behind them.

It was nice of Dom to call and check on her, she thought. She made it a rule never to use her phone while driving, but, given that she had been coasting along at the intoxicating speed of two miles per hour, she decided to live dangerously. Good, old Dom. He had been one of her best buddies since they lay side by side in the church nursery.

His call, however, made her brilliant plan of slipping into the house through the side door and coming out of the kitchen—as though she had been waiting there all along—completely obsolete. It wasn't very impressive as far as plans went. Sadly, though, it was all that she had been able to come up with. Probably because she was being slowly poisoned by the fumes from the ancient piece of farm equipment in front of her.

Darcie sighed. Her plan probably wouldn't have worked anyway.

Amalie Merritt glanced at Daddy. He was watching one of the men with the funny blue eyes. Nanny Di said they had turkey eyes, but Amalie didn't think they looked like turkeys at all. The men with the turkey eyes liked to laugh. Amalie was glad. She liked to laugh. Daddy liked to laugh, too. Daddy was a pirate and he was always glad to see her, even though he could see her with only one eye now. Poor Daddy. He had been watching the man with the turkey eyes talk on the phone. Daddy wasn't smiling anymore. She wondered why.

She looked at Mr. Joey, standing by the window. Mr. Joey wasn't smiling, either. He was looking out of the window, waiting for the princess. Mr. Joey had been waiting on the princess for half of his life. He said so. Mr. Joey really wanted to see the princess. The men with the turkey eyes thought that was very funny. They laughed at Mr. Joey until he said a bad word. Amalie pretended not to hear the bad word, because she knew that Daddy would tell Nanny Di to take her somewhere far away from Mr. Joey, so she wouldn't hear any more bad words. She didn't want to go far away. She wanted to stay right where she was, so she could see the princess.

The pretty lady with yellow hair fussed at Mr. Joey for saying the bad word. Amalie liked the pretty lady and the big man she was dancing with. They were nice. She wanted to dance like them, so she spun around and around with Iggy. She stopped spinning, but her head didn't. She sat down on the floor. Iggy wasn't a very good dancer. Poor Iggy. Dancing with Iggy wasn't as much fun as dancing with Daddy. And Daddy had promised that she could dance with him at the 'cepshun.'

Dom finished his conversation and returned his cell phone to his pocket. He looked supremely satisfied, even pleased by whatever information he had obtained from the person on the other end of the line. He moved so quickly that Devin couldn't avoid meeting his eyes. Dom met his gaze for a split second, nodded his head as his lips quirked up into a friendly smile. He moved past, without giving Devin a second thought, obviously on a mission.

Ordinary looking, my ass. Devin had finally gotten a good look at Dom's defining feature, the turquoise eyes he inherited from his mother. Those eyes, so deeply blue, transformed his ordinary face into something that women would be panting after. He hadn't noticed Dom's eyes when they met, having the distraction of the happy reunion of Amalie and Atticus to deal with. Devin was completely irritated at Dominic Parker for being, not only good-looking, but for being…something to Darcie Finch. He was also irritated at himself for caring.

Dom moved to stand behind Joey at the window. "Darcie's almost to the entrance of Heart's Ease," he announced in a clear voice. "She would have been here fifteen minutes ago, but she got stuck behind—"

"The three-car pile-up on I-85," Joey interrupted over his shoulder.

"No, the Porter brothers," Dom said.

Joey's eyebrows shot up in genuine shock. Dom was unable to keep his face straight at Joey's look of abject amazement.

"The Porter brothers?" Joey said. "The Porter brothers can drive? You're sure about this? They finally got their driver's licenses? They actually have licenses to drive?"

"Yeah, terrifying isn't it? She's been behind their tractor since she turned off the highway." Dom grinned at Maggie as she came over to find out what was going on. "Did you hear that, Mom? Darcie's stuck behind a tractor driven by your favorite brothers."

Maggie grimaced. "Oh, no. Don't tell me."

She closed her eyes as Dom confirmed her worst fears: "Yep. Jeremiah and Hezekiah Porter. Or maybe it's Hezekiah and Jeremiah Porter. I never could tell them apart."

"That's because they're interchangeable. Oh, dear Lord, poor Darcie." Maggie closed her eyes again. "It would never dawn on the Porter brothers to pull over and let her pass. They only have one brain cell between them on a good day and they usually forget and leave it at home."

Maggie was nothing if not blunt. She sighed and changed the subject. After all, the less said about the Porters, the better. "Looks like your troubles are over, Joey. Your sister will be here soon, and we can start this rehearsal."

Devin took a minute to process what had just happened. So, the person that the Defender was talking to was none other than Miss Darcie Finch. Devin didn't understand why that news annoyed him so very, very, much, but it did. It bothered him terribly. *He* should be the one calling to check on her, not Old Blue Eyes over there.

The fact that such a thought would even cross his mind was unsettling. Why did he feel so protective of a woman he had only known for twenty-four hours? She was obviously held in high esteem by the man with the turquoise eyes. A man who was looking out for her. All of these things should have made him feel much better and less concerned for the well-being of Miss Finch. Regardless of the revelations, and in spite of the fact that the Defender appeared to have Darcie's best interests at heart, Devin decided, then and there, that he had no use for the man. No. He didn't like Dominic Parker at all.

Joey dropped the curtain and turned away from the window, but not before Devin saw the little red Jeep coming around the last curve.

"All right, Maggie," Joey said. "Since The Princess has *finally* decided to grace us with her presence, let's get this party started."

A few minutes later, Devin heard the general greetings and conversations near the door indicating that she...The Voice, The Music, Superhero Darcie Finch...had arrived. He stayed right where he was, near the fireplace. He felt he needed the firm support of the wall at his back. When she stepped into the grand foyer, he would be able to see her before she saw him. He needed to buy a little time. The sound of her husky laugh was already causing his heart to beat a little too fast. It was time to renew his acquaintance with his Pirate Queen.

CHAPTER TWENTY-ONE

*D*arcie couldn't have been happier when she realized that Pastor and Mrs. Faircloth were in the car behind her. She didn't even try to sneak in through the kitchen. She just fell in behind the good reverend and his wife, chatting with the pair as if she hadn't a care in the world. And it was a fortunate thing, too, because a small mob had gathered in the foyer to greet them.

"I told Stephen we should have started earlier, but he had to finish watching another rerun of *NCIS*. It's his favorite show, you know. Anyway, I was afraid we would hold up the whole rehearsal, but then we got behind Darcie, and I knew that you wouldn't start without her."

Mrs. Faircloth hadn't stopped talking since she got out of the car. According to her husband—the long-suffering and patient Pastor Stephen—she hadn't stopped talking since she was born. He might have said as much under his breath as he passed the parents of the bride.

"Amen, brother," said Joe Finch, with such sincere empathy that his own talkative wife stepped backward and kicked him in the shin with her dainty foot. Accidentally, of course. Joe didn't miss a beat as he stated, smoothly, "God has blessed us both"; but he made sure that he moved well out of the range of the shiny, black high heels of his innocent-looking spouse. He also made sure she couldn't help but notice his overly exaggerated limp.

Juli couldn't quite hide the little smile that flitted around her mouth.

"Darcie-girl," Joe addressed his tardy daughter. "I was getting ready to form a search party." His words were stern, but his eyes were kind as he reached for her.

"I'm sorry, Daddy," Darcie said, sincerely, as she was pulled into a hug by her irrepressible father. "I would have been on time, but I got *Portered*."

Joe chuckled as he pulled back far enough to give her a fatherly look of approval. Nobody ever had a more attractive daughter, but it was of Darcie's sharp mind that he was most proud. Darcie didn't miss much.

Tonight, the simmering energy that always lurked just below the surface of her handsome father was well contained. His looks were deceptively mild, but Darcie knew the worst thing anyone could do was to underestimate the man. His loyalty was fierce. His love was unconditional, and he was always two or three moves ahead of just about everyone. She knew him well enough to know that he was up to something. "Why are you limping?" she whispered.

"I got *Julied*," Joe whispered back with a wink, causing his daughter to nod wisely.

"Oh, then you probably deserved it," Darcie answered with her own wink. She left his side to embrace her mother.

Juli's green eyes were shining with mischief as she enveloped her youngest daughter in a warm embrace. "You know him well, my dear," she said, giving Joe a challenging look that promised a reckoning later, a promise her husband seemed to relish.

The Finch children had learned long ago not to pay too much attention when their parents exchanged such a look. Juli and Joe had a language all their own, full of spoken words and unspoken gestures incomprehensible to anyone else. Thinking about it too hard became embarrassing when Darcie and her siblings were adolescents. That's when they started to understand why Juli's hair was all mussed and her lips slightly puffy after spending thirty minutes in Joe's office with the door locked.

"*I was just asking your father a question,*" Juli would say, and that was the end of that.

The older Darcie got, the more she had come to admire—and envy—her parents' marriage, and to long for that kind of intimacy for herself. Seeing her sister's relationship with Blane McCallum blossom into love had caused her own heart to feel a bit empty. Spending any time thinking about her own unattached state still caught her off guard because—until the past year—she had been so focused on academic and professional achievement, she had neglected Darcie Finch, the woman.

At this point in her life, she had almost achieved all of her professional goals, and then…what? What was next for Darcie Finch? What did she want? What did she really want? *I really want to get through the next few minutes without making a fool of myself when I see Devin Merritt,* she admitted. *Or when he sees me.*

Juli studied her youngest daughter, her lovely green eyes full of questions. "Makeup, Darcie?" she asked gently.

Darcie was surprised by an unfamiliar feeling of intense paranoia. "What's wrong, Mama? Is it too much? Do I look overdone?"

"No, no, of course not," Juli said quickly. "I wasn't criticizing, just a little surprised. I was prepared for our usual…um, discussion about that." She smiled, her eyes lighting up with pleasure. "You look absolutely beautiful."

Darcie relaxed. Her resistance to wearing makeup—or doing anything extra that would call more attention to her looks—was the subject of ongoing debate. Juli always encouraged her to have the confidence to shine. To a degree, she had. Darcie's fierce desire to be known for brains instead of her beauty, however, often overshadowed her mother's advice. She felt some of her confidence return. If Juli said her makeup looked all right, then it did. Her mother didn't lie. She wasn't one to placate her daughters, even if they sometimes wished she would. Darcie suddenly realized that Juli was studying her closely, her eyes full of unanswered questions.

"Oh, Mama, I couldn't very well wear yoga pants and no makeup to my sister's wedding rehearsal. I mean, I am the maid of honor." Her laughter was a little forced and her explanation came out a little too fast to be completely believable.

Juli raised her eyebrows, but, taking pity on her daughter, let it go. After squeezing Darcie's arm, she joined her waiting husband to accompany the pastor and his wife to the site of the ceremony outside.

Darcie watched them go, absently noting the way Joe took Juli's hand. The look her parents exchanged was one of perfect understanding. What was wrong with her? She couldn't remember *ever* being so aware of her parents, or so conscious of their relationship. The wedding atmosphere must be affecting her brain. Already.

As Juli disappeared down the hallway beside the kitchen, Darcie breathed a sigh of relief. Her reprieve from Juli's sharp eyes, however temporary, was still a reprieve. Hopefully, Darcie could pull herself together a bit before she was, once again, under the microscope of motherly concern.

She couldn't very well tell Juli the truth. *"By the way, Mama, I wore makeup because Devin Merritt hasn't ever seen me, and I want to look as fabulous as possible for him. I know he's married, but...."* No, she couldn't tell her mother that. She couldn't tell anyone because, well…because it made her sound like a homewrecker, and that was something she flatly refused to be.

Darcie paused before proceeding down the twin steps into the grand foyer. Her eyes skimmed the room briefly, noting a flurry of movement as the wedding party ambled toward the hallway beside the kitchen.

"'Bout time you finally showed up," Joey growled, appearing on her right, his words in seeming opposition to the mischievous look on his face. He planted a brotherly kiss on her cheek, laughing when she swatted at his arm.

"Looking good, Darce."

That was from Dom, on the left, who pulled her close for a quick hug. "You didn't have to get all dressed up just for *me*. And is that makeup? Darcie Finch is wearing makeup?" He put up both hands in front of his face as if to ward off a blinding light. "Where are my sunglasses when I need them?"

Darcie bumped him with her hip, managing to push him off the top step. Dom stumbled, laughing, into the grand foyer. She shook her head at his antics as she stepped down into the room. Even while joking with her brother and one of her oldest friends, she was carefully searching the faces still in the room. She had yet to lay eyes on Devin Merritt. Where was he?

Why didn't she see him anywhere? He was one of the groomsmen, so he had to be there somewhere. Unless—her heart jumped in fear—he had decided not to be in the wedding. But he would still be there, even if he wasn't in the wedding party, wouldn't he? Maybe he was already outside…*with his wife*. That scenario left a bad feeling in her stomach. *Maybe I'm an idiot*, she thought, trying not to care.

Through sheer force of will, she managed to calm her overactive mind long enough to tune into her other senses. She took a deep breath, struck with a sudden awareness. *He* was in the room somewhere. She was certain of it. She could feel it. Her senses absorbed the sensation of being under someone's intense scrutiny. It was coming from her left. *He* was watching her. She was almost certain that when she looked to the left, *he* would be there. She started to turn, bracing herself for the impact, only to be confronted by a four-year-old angel. The little girl had long blond hair and big blue eyes. She was clutching a stuffed iguana under one arm. She blocked Darcie's way as effectively as an armed guard. Darcie was enchanted.

Amalie smiled. This was the princess Mr. Joey had been talking about. She was sure of it. The princess was finally here. She was the prettiest princess Amalie had ever seen. Prettier, even, than the princesses in her coloring books. This princess was wearing a red dress. It wasn't a long dress, but it was beautiful all the same. And she was wearing red shoes. Amalie decided that she wanted a red dress and red shoes, just like the princess.

The princess smiled at her. *Hurray!* The princess was nice like Nanny Di and Miss Grace and Miss Juli. And the princess looked happy to see her. She wasn't frowning and telling her to go play in another room like Mommy. Mommy was always grumpy. Amalie was glad that Mommy wasn't here. If Mommy was here, she might be mean to the princess. Thinking about Mommy made Amalie frown. She had an unhappy thought. What if she was wrong and the beautiful lady wasn't the princess? Amalie had to know. She had to be sure. "Are you the princess?" she asked in an anxious whisper.

Darcie looked puzzled. "The princess? Oh, sweetie, what makes you think that?"

Amalie's smile drooped a little. She pointed to Joey, who had both hands in his pockets. He was studying the crown molding in the ceiling as if he was its architect. "Mr. Joey said he was waiting for the princess to get here."

"Oh, he did, did he?"

Darcie understood instantly. Mr. Joey. *It figures.*

"Mr. Joey has been waiting for the princess for half of his life," Amalie explained helpfully. "That's a really long time to wait."

"Has he really?" Darcie asked. "My, my, half of his life? That *is* a long time to wait, isn't it, Mr. Joey?"

"Not so long," Joey muttered, as he continued to study the ceiling.

"He actually said that he had *spent* half of his life waiting *on* the princess," Dom clarified, happy to do his part to irritate Joey whenever possible.

Darcie felt a little hand tug on her arm. She stopped glaring at her brother's back and looked down into the angelic face of the child, who was, undoubtedly, Amalie Merritt. There was so much excitement in those blue eyes and so much hope, tempered with a tiny bit of doubt.

Amalie whispered, "Are you *really* the princess Mr. Joey was waiting for?"

Who could be so cruel as to crush the dreams of a child? Not Darcie Finch. She was no dream crusher. "Of course, I am. If Mr. Joey says I'm the princess, then it must be true. Right, Mr. Joey?"

Joey laughed weakly, tugging at his collar, which was suddenly too tight. "Right, *Princess*. See you in a few." He made his escape, strolling across the parquet floor and disappearing into the hallway.

Amalie, however, wasn't easily convinced. "Wait a minute." She put her hands on her hips, clutching the iguana by the tail. She studied Darcie's hair suspiciously. "If you're *really* the princess, then where is your crown?"

"You mean I'm not wearing it?"

Darcie gasped in mock surprise, putting her hands on her head to feel around for her missing crown. She had such an expression of comical surprise that Amalie dissolved into giggles.

Darcie shrugged her shoulders. "It must be in my suitcase." She crouched down until she was on eye level with the little girl, holding out her arms.

Amalie returned the impromptu hug enthusiastically.

She was so adorable Darcie couldn't help but laugh.

Amalie ran to Diana. "Nanny Di! Nanny Di! Guess what? I hugged the princess." She grabbed Diana's hand. "Come on, Nanny Di! Come and meet the princess! Maybe she'll hug you, too!"

Diana followed the little girl, smiling at the woman who, once again, had handled a delicate situation perfectly. "Hello, Darcie. It's nice to see you, again."

"Good to see you, too, Diana."

"Darcie? You're Miss Darcie?" squealed Amalie, overcome with excitement. She couldn't help it. She didn't have to try to be quiet here. Nobody fussed at her for being too loud except her mommy—and her mommy wasn't coming to the "her-sal." Oh, this was even better than she could have imagined. The Princess was Miss Darcie!

Amalie looked at the beautiful lady in awe. She liked Miss Darcie. Miss Darcie talked to her on the phone. Miss Darcie sent her the pretty basket and the bear dressed like a pirate. Miss Darcie liked to wear red, and her favorite princess was Jasmine. Miss Darcie was Daddy's babysitter. Meeting Miss Darcie was even better than meeting some other princess because Miss Darcie was her friend.

"Can we go to the 'her-sal', now, Miss Darcie?" she asked, excitedly, taking Darcie's outstretched hand.

"Re-hear-sal."

Diana crouched down to pick up the iguana her small charge had dropped in all of the excitement. This way, she wouldn't have to look for it later.

"Re-hear-sal," Diana said, again, holding Amalie's other hand.

"Re-hear-sal," Amalie repeated, carefully, as she skipped between Diana and Darcie.

As they made their way across the room, Darcie finally glanced to her left. *He* was leaning against the wall, a slightly stunned expression on his face, as if he couldn't quite believe what he was seeing. She didn't allow herself more than a glance, fighting the urge to stop and stare. She got the impression of broad shoulders—oh, those shoulders!—encased in a perfectly fitted sportscoat. She got a tantalizingly brief glimpse of auburn hair, not quite as long as she remembered. One important detail, however, burned itself into her mind. *He* was wearing an eye patch. Her pirate had returned.

She met his eye. "Hello, Laurence," she said. It was all she could manage.

Devin didn't move. He stayed where he was, watching his daughter, his nanny, and his Pirate Queen disappear, together, down the hallway.

The fact that she didn't wait for him to speak was fortunate. He couldn't have said a word if his life depended on it. He was frozen, mesmerized by his first official sighting of the goddess, Darcie Finch. He was helpless to break the spell and unable to formulate a one-word reply. An entire sentence would have been completely beyond his current capabilities.

Her hair was dark and lustrous and, probably, as soft as silk. He wondered how it would look spread across her pillow. Its smooth waves framed a flawless face. Her dark eyes glowed against her porcelain skin, and her lips were beautifully formed. He didn't want to dwell too much on those lips. After his appreciative gaze had taken in her perfect figure, he realized that thinking too much about any part of Darcie Finch's anatomy would likely get him into deep, deep trouble.

He tried to concentrate on her dress. It was made entirely of red satin, covered with red lace. Her delicate cap sleeves, rounded neckline, and knee-length skirt, while stylishly elegant, would be considered modest if worn by anyone else. On her, it was evocative, inspiring all kinds of thoughts a happily married man should steer clear of. Unfortunately for Devin's good intentions, his marriage was barely tolerable. He found his baser self and his integrity locked in a battle to the death. Even her shoes were sexy, damn it. How was he supposed to deal with that? He was only human, after all. No wonder she said she had *problem looks*. They were a problem all right. For him.

Devin jumped as a hand fell on his shoulder. He was physically unable to see anyone approach from his right side, so it always felt like a surprise attack. Maybe he should start wearing a sign, he mused. Something like…*Warning. Permanently out of order. Please use other side.* Or maybe he was an idiot.

"Breathe in and out. You'll feel better in a minute."

This sage advice came from Dominic Parker, the one person from whom Devin didn't want sympathy. Or understanding. Or anything else. Dom continued, oblivious to Devin's discomfort. "It happens to everybody, man. Hell, it even happens to me from time to time, and I've known her all my life. It's kind of like jumping into a cold lake on a hot day. The shock of it takes your breath at first, until you get used to it." He removed his hand after an empathetic squeeze. "Don't let her know, though. She hates that kind of reaction," Dom advised, as if he, personally, knew everything there was to know about Miss Darcie Finch.

Dom started walking to the hallway; Devin strolled alongside him. Even though Devin was slowly regaining his wits, he still wasn't able to formulate a reply.

Dom didn't seem to notice anything unusual. He just kept talking…about Darcie Finch. "I mean, she looks gorgeous all of the time. Even after a workout or a day at the beach. Even when everybody else looks like absolute crap, but tonight isn't even fair. She's wearing red. She should never be allowed to wear red. It should be illegal." Dom grinned at the silent man beside him. "Don't you think so, Devin?"

"Yeah," Devin agreed. "Illegal."

His mumbled words seemed to satisfy Dom, who walked toward the outside door, opening it for Devin as they stepped into the rose garden.

"Have fun," Dom said, cheerfully. "And, by the way, Mom comes across all tough and bossy, but she's a real pushover. See you later."

Devin watched him walk across the garden to join his brother near the back of the rows of white chairs that were set up on the lawn. Dom was a nice person, full of helpful and kind—though unsolicited—advice and a friendly smile. He was obviously someone who was completely comfortable in his own skin and wished the same for everyone else. It appeared that he was, also, completely comfortable with Darcie Finch.

Devin's mind finally started to function again.

Damn, I hate that guy.

CHAPTER TWENTY-TWO

The ceremony would take place at the gazebo on the side lawn. On the western side of the gazebo was a lovely copse of dogwood trees dotted with red maple and pine. On the eastern side, a wide expanse of lawn. The gazebo itself overlooked the creek. Across the rushing waters, the heavily wooded area was on fire with the colors of autumn. It was hard for Devin to imagine a more perfect spot for an outdoor wedding, especially since the weather was cooperating beautifully.

As the rehearsal got underway, Devin decided that Maggie was either the most organized person on the planet or she had been a drill sergeant in another life. He was inclined to choose the latter. In less than ten minutes, she had the boisterous group standing in two perfect lines on either side of the bride and groom.

As she carefully marked each spot with a tiny bit of white chalk, she gave each person explicit instructions as to his or her specific responsibility during the ceremony. These instructions were accompanied by a look each member of the wedding party understood completely. The wedding was serious business. If any one of them did anything other than follow her instructions to the letter there would be dire consequences. Devin noticed that even the irrepressible Zack was doing exactly what he was told.

He noticed other things, too. He noticed how the light reflected on Darcie's hair, making it gleam in the setting sun. He noticed how perfectly the red of her dress looked against the backdrop of colored leaves. He noticed her graceful stance and poise. He noticed her studying him, surreptitiously. He also noticed how, when he glanced her way, she averted her gaze to avoid being caught.

"And now, I need my flower girl," Maggie said, motioning for Diana to bring Amalie forward. Diana and a few other observers were seated in the chairs closest to the front. "All right, Amalie, you get to stand right here beside your daddy."

Devin saw Amalie glance at Darcie then back at Diana in indecision. Diana nodded her encouragement.

"Miss Maggie," Amalie said. "I like your turkey eyes." She smiled happily.

"Why, thank you, Ama…you like my what?" Maggie looked at the little girl in confusion.

"Tur-quoise," Diana said, trying not to laugh.

"Tur-quoise," Amalie repeated, dutifully. "Miss Maggie, I like your tur-quoise eyes."

Maggie's in-charge demeanor melted into a pool of sweetness. "Oh, Amalie, thank you so much. I like your pretty blue eyes, too."

She held out her hand. Amalie put her small hand into it. They had taken only two steps when Maggie felt a little tug on her hand. She leaned down so she could hear better.

"Miss Maggie," Amalie whispered. "May I please stand with Miss Darcie and the girls?"

Maggie wouldn't have changed one part of her perfect wedding plan for anybody else, but who could say no to this adorable little flower girl with the selfish bitch of a mother? Maggie remembered what the child had revealed earlier all too well. Mallory Merritt was in extreme danger of getting an earful from Maggie Parker…after the wedding. "Of course, you can, honey. You come right over here." Maggie changed direction. "Having all of the girls together is a wonderful idea." She winked at Amalie.

Diana exchanged a look with Devin. *Good luck with that one when she's sixteen*, the look seemed to say. Devin privately agreed. He was, however, charmed by the reactions of the bridesmaids as they welcomed their new addition.

Darcie took the little girl by the hand, introducing Amalie to each of the women whom she didn't already know. Haven and Charlotte, Grace's favorite college roommates, bent down, one by one, to give Amalie a warm hug. Ana, the bride's longtime friend, touched Amalie's nose, saying words that drew a delighted giggle from the excited child. Devin's little flower girl was beaming by the time she reached the bride. Grace and Amalie were old friends, and after a few minutes of whispered conversation and a kiss on the cheek, Amalie returned to her place between Darcie and Lou. She said something to those two that made them laugh. All three of them waved at Devin. Amalie even blew him a kiss.

Devin's eyes met Darcie's, which were brimming with laughter. They shared a moment of pure sweetness. The bond was still there. He could sense it. The connection was broken when Grace said something to her sister, causing her to look away. But Devin had felt it...that strong pull he had never felt toward anyone but Darcie Finch.

Maggie went to work on the bridesmaids, giving the men a chance to relax a bit. Joey, as the best man, was standing alongside Blane. The rest of the groomsmen were arranged by height. This placed Devin between Evander and Roger. Zack stood on the end. The arrangement also put Devin in the middle of everybody's conversation.

"So, where'd she get the line chalk?" Roger asked to nobody in particular.

"From Coach Hollister," Evander supplied helpfully. "He had some left from last season." Coach Hollister was the baseball coach at the academy.

"Great idea," Roger said. "Unless it rains."

"It wouldn't dare," Zack chimed in. He had a history with the indomitable Mrs. Parker.

"What was that, Mr. Kimel?" Maggie inquired of her former student. She was on her knees, marking Ana's place in line, but she gained their attention with a swift turn of her head. Her all-knowing gaze swept over the groomsmen, making sure every man in line knew she was listening to every word.

"I said the weather's going to be fair, Mrs. Parker. No rain for this wedding." Zack improvised, quickly, with his most-disarming smile. "And, might I add, Mrs. Parker, you're doing a great job over there."

Maggie didn't reply. She simply turned back around to finish her instructions to Ana.

"Nice save, Zack," Evander grinned.

"Damn, that was close," Zack said, under his breath, wiping imaginary sweat from his brow.

"Yeah," Roger nodded, for once in perfect accord with his protégé. "She was my teacher, too. Four times."

Zack couldn't believe it. "You failed Spanish four times?"

"No, you idiot," Roger said. "I took every Spanish class that was offered, levels one through four."

"I never made it to Spanish Three," Zack said, mournfully. "But it's pronounced *idiota*. Even I know that," he added, with a superior smirk.

"Shhhhh!"

That came from the giggling bride with a dainty finger on her lips.

"She's still trying to keep you out of trouble, Zack," Joey added, shaking his head. "And she's not even your teacher anymore."

"She'll always be my teacher," Zack declared, loyally, shaping his hands into a heart before pointing at his favorite.

Grace responded in kind. Blane gave Zack a warning stare before punching his palm with his fist. Zack made another heart and pointed at Blane, causing Grace to dissolve into more giggles.

"I'm glad this rehearsal is so entertaining," Maggie said wryly, as she finished positioning the bridesmaids. "Now, we are going to practice going out and then…"

"The rehearsal will be over," Joey interrupted, cheerfully.

"We will practice coming in, since we haven't done that yet," Maggie continued, as if Joey hadn't said a word. "Grace and Blane will turn around after the kiss…"

"Can we practice the kiss?" asked Blane, hopefully.

Grace gently elbowed Blane in the ribs. "Blane, hush."

"No, you may not," said Maggie, moving right on. "Pastor Faircloth will present the new Mr. and Mrs. McCallum…"

"That's us," Blane said, waggling his eyebrows at Grace.

"Shh," Grace hissed. She and Blane were currently on the top steps of the gazebo.

Maggie valiantly continued: "…And they will start walking down the steps and up the aisle. Darcie and Joey will meet each other in the spot at the bottom of the steps after Grace and Blane…"

"Don't be late, Princess," Joey quipped as Darcie wrinkled her nose and stuck out her tongue.

Maggie refused to quit. "…Lou and Evander will move into Darcie and Joey's places. Lou will take Amalie with her. They will wait there for Devin. When Grace and Blane reach the third set of chairs—and tomorrow the first two sets will be marked with flowers—Darcie and Joey will move forward."

"This is like being on the Homecoming Court in high school," Lou said. Maggie was in charge of that, too.

"Exactly," said Maggie, with approval. "Just pay attention and follow the person in front of you." Maggie called out the pairings: "Lou and Evander. Amalie and Devin. Haven and Roger. And Zack, you'll walk out with Charlotte *and* Ana…one on each arm."

"You mean I get two girls?" Zack asked, enthusiastically. He punched Roger in the arm. "Who's your daddy now?" He looked so pleased that everyone burst out laughing. Even Maggie couldn't contain her smile.

UNMASKING THE HEART

After practicing everyone's exit, entrance, and exit again, Maggie pronounced herself satisfied. Joey left immediately to pick up his date; the rest of the wedding party lingered to enjoy the deepening twilight before heading to the rehearsal dinner.

Maggie spent a few extra minutes working with Grace, Darcie, and Lou. Something about fluffing the train of Grace's dress and holding each other's flowers. Amalie watched the proceedings with so much interest that Devin had the feeling a request for a bridal costume would be forthcoming. A few minutes later, his little girl still stood chattering nonstop to Darcie, moving along with the speed of a tortoise on race day. Everyone else had meandered inside, leaving the stragglers on the far side of the darkening rose garden.

"If we don't do an intervention," Devin said to Diana, "we'll get to the rehearsal dinner *after* the wedding."

Diana merely smiled. She walked over to see if she could encourage Amalie to pick up the pace a bit. She whispered a few words in Amalie's ear. The excited little girl started skipping to the house, tugging Diana by the hand.

"Daddy! Nanny Di says we get to eat gooms cake! She says it might be chocolate!"

Cake...the magic word. Diana was a genius.

Amalie, with a puzzled look on her face, stopped skipping. "Nanny Di, what's gooms cake?"

Diana laughed. "Groom's cake."

"Groom's cake," said Amalie, still puzzled. "But, Nanny Di, what *is* groom's cake?"

Diana began her explanation, making sure that Amalie kept moving. For the first time, Darcie found herself alone with Devin.

She watched the retreating figures with a smile. "She's a treasure," she said, her voice as rich and velvety as he remembered it.

So are you. Devin knew better than to say what he was thinking. He put his hands in his pockets instead. "Which one?" he asked, because he had to say something.

"I was talking about Amalie, but Diana is a treasure, too."

Darcie started walking toward the house. Devin ambled along beside her.

The late-blooming roses were almost gone at this point in the season, so the lush aroma he remembered wasn't there to drown out Darcie's perfume. That sweet scent was as light and delicate as he recalled. It reminded him of the last time he stood in this garden with this woman. The fragrance of tropical flowers swirled around him as the narrow pathway forced them closer together. He blamed sensory overload for the reckless words that emerged from his mouth. "So…" he paused on the path, facing her. "What do you think?"

She looked up at him, assuming he was talking about the rehearsal. "I thought it went pretty well, considering. I mean, getting that group to be serious about anything for five minutes was quite an accomplishment. Maggie's good. She's the perfect director. I also think…" She trailed off at the expression on his face, wrinkling her nose in confusion. "Why are you looking at me like I'm not very bright?"

"I wasn't talking about the rehearsal," Devin said, a hint of superiority in his tone. How could someone as smart as Darcie Finch misunderstand what he was talking about?

Darcie didn't like his condescending attitude one bit. "Well, what then?" she asked, giving him a chance to explain himself.

"What do you think about *me*? I mean, about my face?" Devin's nerves were getting the better of him as he blundered on: "You've been staring at it for the last thirty minutes, so I just figured you would have an opinion." Devin nearly groaned aloud. *Way to go, Mr. Smooth.* Nothing like a little unnecessary sarcasm to pave his way.

"Oh," Darcie gasped, a bit taken aback. *Idiot,* she scolded herself. *Of course, he wants to know what I think about his face. How insensitive can I be?* She took the time to give him an honest appraisal, trying to ignore the anxious expression in his eye. She could tell her answer was vitally important to him.

A few unruly locks of his auburn hair drooped onto his strong forehead, probably displaced by the light breeze during the rehearsal. The patch covered one of his eyebrows, but the other brow quirked up in the middle. She would have smiled at that, if his lovely, gray eye wasn't watching her with such intensity. Several deep scars sliced across his forehead from his hairline to his left ear. A few smaller ones—harder to see from a distance—interspersed themselves among the larger ones. She had wondered about the wrought iron fence that had done so much damage to Devin's face. The spires must have been of varying heights. That would explain why some of the scars were deeper than others. There was no discoloration or redness, and the skin around those scars was smooth. That was a good thing, wasn't it? She didn't like to think about the horrible pain he must have experienced, so she forced herself to move on with her perusal.

She couldn't see his eye socket because of the patch, but she could imagine what that looked like. She couldn't, however, imagine learning to navigate life with only one eye. What kind of courage did it take to wake up to such a challenge every single day? She knew from Blane that Devin had a prosthetic eye implant, but that he wasn't pleased with the way it looked. Or the way it moved. He much preferred wearing the eye patch. She could understand that. It gave him a little edge of mystery. *Mystery?* She nearly scoffed at her choice of words. Who was she kidding? That eye patch was unbearably sexy. Just looking at it was putting all kinds of inappropriate-because-he's-married ideas in her head. She might revisit those ideas later—if she decided she could handle them—but for now, she forced herself to move on.

The right side of his face from the patch down was unscathed. Even his nose appeared to have escaped permanent scarring, probably because it was broken on impact. No one would ever know that now, because his nose was straight. Or, at least it looked straight to her. His lips were rugged, masculine perfection. She felt a delicious shiver run down her spine. His chin was strong, maybe a little too strong. Stubborn man.

"I like it," she said. "It suits you." She started walking again.

Devin couldn't move. He was stunned by her words. Absolutely stunned. What was wrong with her? He had endured her scrutiny for what felt like forever. How could she give him such an answer with a straight face? Couldn't she see his scars? His eyepatch? His hideously disfigured disaster of a face? And if not, then what the hell was she looking at? Once again, she had surprised him. He caught up with her, taking hold of her arm and forcing her to stop. She looked up at him inquiringly.

"Darcie, I…" He had no idea what it was he wanted to say.

Now it was her turn to be surprised. He had *never* called her solely by her first name. It made her a bit wary.

"Darcie Finch," he said again, slowly. "I only have one eye."

"I know," she said softly, a bit relieved that he had added the *Finch*.

"And my face is covered with scars," he added, turning his head from side to side so she could get a better look in the fading light.

She nodded in agreement. "I know that, too."

He took a deep breath, trying to remain calm. "And, yet, you still say…"

"It suits you. It's like…" She hesitated, trying to find the right words. "It's like your character is showing on the outside. Like you've triumphed over evil. It's actually quite attractive."

There. She'd said it.

The eye patch and scars were striking enough but combined with his natural dignity—and those shoulders—well, *attractive* was putting it mildly. *Devastating* was a better description, she decided.

He didn't look at all happy with her words. In fact, he looked downright exasperated. "You, Miss Finch, obviously have no idea what you're talking about," he managed to say through clenched teeth. "This is, without a doubt, the most ridiculous conversation I have ever had."

There. He'd said it.

"In. My. Life," he added for emphasis, just in case she didn't get his point.

"Ridiculous?" She was instantly vexed. Devin Merritt had the ability to irk her faster than anyone, even her brother.

"Not just ridiculous, Miss Finch, but the *most* ridiculous conversation in which I have *ever* participated. With anyone. And keep in mind that I have a four-year-old daughter."

"Hmph," Darcie breathed, crossing her arms in irritation. "Well, Mr. Merritt, I can see that the past two months haven't improved your *delightful* disposition."

"Nor your powers of observation," he responded.

"Hmph," she huffed, in sheer frustration, stomping off toward the house.

"Tongue-tied, are we?" he called after her, unable to keep from enjoying the way her legs looked in those bewitching, red heels.

She stopped stomping. He was, she determined, *the* most provoking man on the planet.

Devin felt the full force of her glare as she turned to blister him with her reply. He was spared only because the side door of the house opened just then. Dominic Parker poked his head out.

Of course, Devin thought, nearly throwing his hands into the air in defeat. Who else would it be but Darcie's damned defender?

"Come on, Darce," Dom called. "The bus is already waiting. I don't know how much longer I can hold your seat." He grinned at Devin before disappearing back into the house.

Darcie turned her back on Devin, tossing her head as she flounced inside without another word.

As he watched her go, the last hard knot of bitterness—one he barely knew he was still harboring—unfurled within him. It dissolved into nothingness. And in its place, bloomed hope.

Darcie paused in the hallway, trying to slow her breathing. It wouldn't do to appear flustered in front of Dom and company. They knew her too well to let it go.

She certainly hadn't anticipated *this* Devin Merritt, the one from their very first meeting. She had, foolishly, expected Laurence instead. She *should* be disappointed, but the emotions coursing through her body were a far cry from disappointment. In spite of the frustrating end to their first conversation in two months, she was exhilarated. Instead of wanting to wash her hands of Devin Merritt, she found herself eager for their next confrontation. She had expected to feel pity or sympathy, but instead, all she felt was sharp anticipation. Something must be wrong with her. Pasting a smile on her face, Darcie hurried to join the rest of the wedding party.

CHAPTER TWENTY-THREE

*D*evin couldn't wipe the grin off his face. It had nothing to do with Amalie's running commentary or Diana's equally entertaining remarks. No, he was grinning because he felt *alive*. More alive than he had in two months. Despite their rather inauspicious reunion, he could hardly wait to match wits again with his Pirate Queen. She was feisty, that one, and full of passion. Far from being burned by the fire glowing in her dark eyes, he had gloried in her incendiary gaze, reveling in the heat that danced between them. There was no doubt: when they were together, the sparks flew. He was torn between the fear of, and the desire for, an actual conflagration.

"*I like it. It suits you,*" she had said. He was astounded by those six words. They stripped him of his carefully constructed defenses and made him feel vulnerable. Was it any wonder he had lashed out as he did? Coming from anyone else, he would have laughed it off, but from her…well, he knew she spoke the truth. She was honest, above all else. The words that came out of her mouth were sincere. Only Darcie Finch could look at a man with an eye patch and a disfigured face and see character. She had a way of viewing the world that was uniquely Darcie and incredibly appealing.

The woman in question was already seated with Dom Parker in the second seat from the front of the chartered bus that was taking them to the rehearsal dinner. Joe, the conscientious father of the bride, reserved the bus as both a courtesy and a precaution because the dinner was being held at a local vineyard. The curving, two-lane road that led to Dogwood Hills Winery was challenging enough for those unfamiliar with the area. By the time the dinner was over, it would be pitch black in the hill country.

Darcie's color was still high when Devin finally climbed aboard the bus. He couldn't help but notice that little detail, his eye were automatically drawn to her. He also saw the way his Pirate Queen averted her head—prettily, of course—when he passed by to join his daughter and her nanny.

Diana and Amalie clambered out of their chosen seat—two rows behind Darcie—so he could slide in. It was just like his thoughtful cousin to choose a seat so that his good side—the one with his eye—was beside the window.

"Don't squash Iggy!" Amalie squealed, pointing to her father's feet.

Devin froze, just in time to avoid stepping on his daughter's favorite stuffed animal. Looking down, he saw Iggy's substantial tail poking out from under the seat. He leaned over, congratulating himself for picking up the troublesome iguana on the first try.

"Hurray!" Amalie said, scrambling onto the seat beside Devin.

Diana joined them, chuckling as she sat down. Devin sat, too, with Iggy in his lap. He didn't recall the impertinent iguana's name being on the invitation to the rehearsal dinner, but Iggy was notorious for crashing important events.

Before they even turned onto the main road, Amalie was sitting in Devin's lap, gazing out the window. Iggy was safely out of sight, napping in Diana's giant purse. Devin tried looking out the window, too, so he wouldn't have to watch the animated conversation Darcie was having with her seatmate, Dom. To be fair, they were also talking with Grace and Blane—in the very front—and Lou and Evander, who were sitting in the seat in front of Devin.

Sitting behind the genial giant gave Devin the chance to watch his lovely obsession without the chance of discovery. Amalie viewed the whole trip as an exciting adventure. Her childish chatter was guileless and endearing, adding another level of security to his quest. He watched Darcie's facial expressions, enjoying the way her eyes flashed when she made a point. He chuckled as he heard her familiar *hmph*. Not once, but three different times. Somebody was definitely giving Darcie a run for her money. When the light had all but faded—helped along by low-hanging trees on either side of the road—he closed his eyes. Even in the cacophony of chatter, picking out the warm tones of Darcie's velvety voice was easy.

Twenty minutes into their journey, Amalie squealed with excitement. "Look, Daddy! Look, Nanny Di!" She pointed out the window.

As the bus slowed around a sharp curve, Devin saw three deer illuminated in the headlights. A buck and two does stood placidly beside the road, as if they had nothing better to do than enjoy the comfortable temperature. He felt a sharp stab of envy as clarity returned. What was he doing? He had a child. And he had a wife, of sorts. *And responsibilities,* he endeavored to remind himself. He was blessed with a plethora of responsibilities. He had no right to sit there mooning over Darcie Finch as though she was the answer to his prayers.

And what about Darcie? He forced himself to answer that question. She had law school. And this Dom character. And who knew what else? Or *who* else? His best option—really, his only option—was to leave it alone. To leave her alone. He resolved, at that moment, to put his Pirate Queen out of his mind.

Devin gazed out the window into the darkness. He had to make sure he stayed away from Darcie Finch, before it was too late. Even though he knew in his heart that it already was.

The property known as Dogwood Hills boasted not one but two of the area's most popular attractions. The winery was located at the top of one hill; its sister operation—an elegant five-star bed and breakfast—rested at the top of the other. The twin hills provided an unmatched view of beautiful Dogwood Falls, the pride of Honeysuckle Creek. Acres of grape vines covered every available space as far as the eye could see. The Old World European atmosphere coupled with the beauty of the North Carolina foothills made for a heady combination.

The Dogwood Hills Winery was modeled after one of the oldest wineries in Tuscany, Italy—Capezzana: its main building sported the same whitewashed walls and green shuttered windows. The winery also boasted a beautiful outdoor courtyard, perfect for lunch or dinner in warmer weather. Due to the falling autumn temperatures, Blane and Grace's rehearsal dinner was being held in the gorgeous banquet hall on the second floor.

The owner, Carlo Giannini, purchased the land nearly fifteen years earlier. Italian by birth, he was a distant relative of the Contini Bonacossi family of winemakers. By specializing in sweet wines, Carlo had found his niche. The winery's reputation for consistently excellent vintages made Dogwood Hills a favorite destination of wine connoisseurs. Over time, Capezzana also earned an outstanding reputation in the culinary world, hosting its week-long cooking school four times a year.

Those who had never visited the winery or seen its main building were delighted at their first glimpse of the lovely structure. Tonight, Carlo and his wife, Valentina, were waiting for the guests in front of the archway that framed the wooden front doors. They graciously greeted the group themselves, making it clear that Blane was one of their favorite customers. Valentina gave the guests a brief walking tour of the building before showing them into the dining room.

Blane's aunt and uncle were transparently delighted to host the rehearsal dinner for their only nephew. Alina welcomed everyone with a touching enthusiasm, unable to hide her happy tears. Ian followed with the surprise announcement that each guest would be allowed to choose a bottle of wine at the end of the meal. His words were met with appreciative applause, getting the evening off to an excellent start.

Devin was glad to see that Rafe was seated at the head table in his rightful place…beside his daughter. To protect his family, and for reasons relating to international security, Rafe had spent years hiding his true identity. Only recently had he finally given Alina permission to reveal that he was her father. Her glowing face was evidence of the joy she felt in sharing the special evening with him.

Ian, his Scottish accent heightened by the emotion of the moment, introduced Blane's grandfather to give thanks. Fergus bowed his head; the rest of the gathering followed suit. His musical brogue began: "Our most kind and gracious Heavenly Father..." Fergus' prayer of family, faith, and forgiveness was filled with thanksgiving and joy. His spoken "amen" was echoed around the room.

Devin found himself at a table with Diana and Amalie. They were joined by Maggie's youngest brother and his wife. Forty-seven-year-old Stephen and forty-year-old Jennifer had almost given up on having a child of their own. But, after years of infertility treatments, their prayers were finally answered. Their good-natured baby girl had been born the previous Thanksgiving. She was seated between them, eating Cheerios and babbling nonsense words. Amalie was so enchanted by little Audrey that Diana finally switched the little girl's seat with Stephen's, so she could entertain her new friend between courses. The children behaved beautifully...which worked out well for everyone.

For the next two hours, the guests were treated to one delicious culinary experience after another, accompanied by three complimentary wine selections. The already buoyant atmosphere was pleasantly enhanced by the arrival of the poached shrimp and scallop appetizer. A leafy green salad with homemade dressing arrived next. The two main courses—spinach-stuffed ravioli and herb-crusted beef with creamy horseradish sauce—received rave revues from Devin and the dining companions at his table.

The winery's considerate staff supplied Amalie with carrots and ranch dressing as an appetizer, macaroni and cheese instead of a salad, and chicken nuggets and fries for the entrée. They also brought her milk and apple juice in tiny, plastic wineglasses whenever the adults were served a new vintage. Devin was very appreciative of their thoughtfulness.

He was not, however, appreciative of the seating arrangement. Darcie had been placed at a table with Dominic Parker. Their dinner companions included: Roger Carrington, Ana Martin, and Joey and his date. Even though Darcie appeared to be having a wonderful time, he caught her sneaking stealthy glances in his direction. More than once. When their eyes met, she quickly looked away, but a few minutes later, she was at it again.

Devin understood completely. He was fighting the same battle.

He was enjoying his conversation with Stephen, but that didn't keep his mind—or his eye—from wandering. Every time Dom touched Darcie's arm or leaned in to say something, Devin felt a wave of possessiveness. Every. Single. Time.

I am not jealous, he thought. If the phrase worked for his monster face, maybe it would work for his heart. *I am not jealous,* he reiterated, trying to concentrate. *I am not a monster. I am not a jealous monster. I am not monstrously jealous.* His internal litany continued. Fortunately, Stephen was a big talker; Devin had, by now, lost the gist of their conversation. After a few minutes of calming repetition, Devin started to feel a little more in control. That was until he saw Dom lean over to whisper into Darcie's ear.

I am not monstrously jealous, Devin thought, determinedly. But it was no use. The green monster dug in its claws, refusing to be dislodged. *Like hell I'm not.* Devin's fingers turned into fists before he could prevent it. *I am one hundred percent, irrationally, monstrously jealous of damn Dominic Parker.* He felt better after admitting it, but only for a few seconds. He knew, logically, that he had no right to feel anything even remotely like jealousy, but there it was. He tried to step back and remind himself that Darcie was off-limits. He told himself that he really didn't know her that well, anyway. He tried to convince himself that he was imagining any reciprocity of sentiment on her part. But it wasn't working, because he *did* know her. He just…did, and because he was unequivocally sure *she* felt the same way.

It finally dawned on Darcie—midway through her leafy green salad—that every ounce of her composure, self-control, and self-confidence had disappeared. Along with the last shreds of her sanity. Yes, she decided, she had clearly lost her mind. There was no other way to explain her behavior on that cursed bus. She had been in trouble from the minute Devin appeared in the doorway. She made it a point not to look at him as he passed her seat.

Ignoring him, however, did not lessen her awareness of him. She felt the intensity of his stare all the way to the winery. To make matters worse, she was barely able to resist staring back. On top of that, she uncharacteristically lost her train of thought several times, struggling to complete her sentences. Once or twice she actually stopped talking midphrase. By the end of what was surely the longest bus ride in the history of humanity, the ever-observant Grace was regarding her sister with a degree of concern. Dom looked downright suspicious.

But Darcie's troubles didn't end once she stepped off the bus. Oh, no, they didn't end at all. Once dinner started, the overpowering presence of Devin Merritt made drawing a comfortable breath a distant memory. It didn't matter that he was sitting two tables away. Even at that distance she felt his intoxicating proximity bubbling through her like the finest champagne. Thank goodness she hadn't ended up at his table. She could just imagine what a spectacle she would have made of herself. Unable to hold her fork. Unable to move. Unable to speak. Unable to do anything but stare at the object of her fascination.

Darcie was struggling.

Once the initial adrenaline rush of their earlier encounter wore off, she realized that her hands were shaking. Not only that, but she was unable to collect her thoughts. No, that wasn't exactly true. She was collecting lots of thoughts, but they were all about Devin Merritt. The effort she was making to stay focused during the conversation at her table was exhausting. She tried to laugh and comment at the appropriate times so that no one would notice her distraction. Everything would have been so much easier if she wasn't sitting with her brother. And her best male friend. Both of them were overly intuitive, especially when it came to her.

Darcie had to get out of the dining room for a minute before she freaked out completely. Freak out? Her? Darcie Finch didn't freak out. As a rule, she was calm and controlled and...*I am freaking out*, she thought, desperately. What had possessed her to say those things about Devin's face? It was obvious that he didn't want to hear them. He thought she was joking. She was sure of it and...*Oh, damn it*, she swore. *He caught me looking again.*

She quickly glanced down, trying to focus on the patterns of twisted vines embroidered on the elegant ivory tablecloth. She tried to listen to what Dom was saying, something about the Carolina Panthers' defense. She tried to recite the Gettysburg Address in her head. She tried to... *Stop looking. He must think you're a lunatic.*

Maybe she was, she mused. After all, she let the man's daughter believe that she was a princess. What sane person tells a lie like that to a four-year-old? *But Amalie was so cute,* Darcie argued with herself, *and she really wanted me to be a princess.* Maybe Devin's daughter *needed* a princess in her life. The good Lord knew she already had a wicked witch.

Another possibility crossed her mind. What if Devin and his witch of a wife had gotten through their rough patch? What if their marriage now stood on solid ground? That would be a good thing, right? A wonderful thing. Darcie tried to believe that statement, but her logical mind wasn't buying it. If their marriage was so very wonderful, where was Devin's wife right now? Why wasn't she sitting with her precious child? Why wasn't she basking in the glow of being Mrs. Devin Merritt? Who in their right mind wouldn't want to do that? *Stop it. Stop it. Stop it.* She became aware that everyone at the table was regarding her in silence.

"Darcie," Joey asked in an uncharacteristically gentle tone of voice. "Are you all right?"

"Of course," she said, carefully. "Why do you ask?"

She met their puzzled expressions, striving to appear calm and unaffected.

"Because you just put butter in your coffee," Dom explained.

She glanced down to see the rapidly melting pat of butter spreading out on the surface of her coffee. "I guess I'm just a little distracted," she said, making the flimsiest excuse imaginable. "My sister is getting married tomorrow."

Her watchers relaxed a bit. There was gentle laughter around the table. Dom patted her hand cheerfully. Ana winked. Roger shook his head, grinning with the superior air of a male in the presence of yet *another* emotional female. Joey's date appeared confused, a permanent condition, if Darcie judged correctly.

General conversation resumed for everyone, with one exception. Darcie's big brother. Her very astute, very observant big brother. Joey Finch was watching her from across the table. That did it. Darcie stood, determined to put some distance between herself and Joey's piercing gaze. She felt his eyes boring into her back as she made her escape.

Devin saw Darcie stand. No surprise there, he noted, sarcastically. How could he miss her doing anything when he couldn't keep his eye off her? As he watched, she leaned down to say something to her brother. Joey nodded, covering the hand she had placed on his shoulder with his own. Darcie didn't even glance in Devin's direction as she passed his table, but his eye followed her as she opened the door to the outside balcony. It seemed to him that her hand fumbled with the door handle a bit before it opened. He turned back to his dinner companions only when her alluring red heels disappeared into the shadows.

"Why is Miss Darcie going outside, Daddy?" Amalie asked innocently. Her outspoken question echoed Devin's unspoken thoughts.

"She's probably going to see the falls," Stephen replied helpfully. "They're all lit up and pretty spectacular at night. You should take Amalie to check them out," he suggested. His idea fell right in line with what Devin was thinking.

"Can we, Daddy? Can we go see the falls with Miss Darcie?" Amalie had latched onto the idea with her usual enthusiasm. "Please, Daddy! Please!"

Devin smiled. "Absolutely." He stood up to help his daughter out of her chair. Diana started to rise, but Devin waved her back. "I've got this." He didn't want to interrupt Diana's lively conversation with Jennifer. And—for reasons he hoped no one else would notice—Devin was more than happy to take care of this particular outing himself.

With Amalie skipping beside him, he made his way to the door and stepped outside. The patio was deserted with the exception of the corner farthest from the balcony doors. Leaning on the railing with her back to him—her slender figure framed by a spectacular display of natural beauty and colored lights—was his Pirate Queen. All alone.

CHAPTER TWENTY-FOUR

*D*arcie leaned on the railing with her arms loosely crossed, her gaze on the waterfall's bubbling base. Suddenly, she felt his presence, the way she had earlier in the grand foyer of Heart's Ease. How was such a thing possible? The nerves at the back of her neck were tingling. Actually tingling. Goose bumps appeared on her arms and legs. She took a deep breath and tightened her grip, holding the railing as if the floor of the balcony might drop out from under her any second. She almost wished it would. She wasn't ready yet. She wasn't ready for...*this*. She had no idea what to say, no inkling how to start a conversation.

Darcie's thoughts were interrupted by a blessed little voice. "MISS DARCIE!" Amalie yelled over the sound of the falls. "MISS DARCIE! LOOK AT THE PRETTY LIGHTS!"

They were not to be alone, then. Thank God. Darcie turned around with a big smile on her face for the excited, little girl. Amalie ran straight to her new friend, Iggy's stuffed tail bouncing under her arm. Darcie held out her hand, allowing the little girl to tug her toward the overlook. It was preferable, at that moment, to facing Amalie's father.

The platform extended about fifteen feet past the edge of the balcony. The distance from the top of the falls to the churning pool below was nearly seventy-five feet. The viewing platform stood halfway between the top and bottom of the falls. Strategically placed colored lights, continually blinking on and off, gave an observer the feeling of floating in the middle of a fireworks display. The effect was mesmerizing.

Standing on the overlook, Darcie and Amalie were close enough to feel the spray of the falls bouncing off the rocks below. Listening to Amalie's childish chatter afforded Darcie a moment to steady herself. "You should see the falls in the daytime, too, Amalie. They are just as pretty without all of the lights."

"Will you bring me back to see them, Miss Darcie?" Amalie asked. "In the daytime?"

Oops. Darcie realized her error too late. She hesitated, not wanting to make a promise she wasn't able to keep. "You can see the falls from the other side, too," she said, hoping to distract Amalie without answering her question. "It takes a couple of hours to hike up there." Darcie pointed toward the top of the falls, before continuing: "But the view is worth it."

Devin appeared at the railing on Darcie's right. "Maybe we can all come back and see them together sometime," he added, smoothly.

"Did you hear that?" Amalie asked her stuffed iguana excitedly, ignoring the adults. "Oooh! Look at the green lights, Iggy!" She rushed over to the opposite side of the observation deck.

"Thank goodness for the glass," Devin said, nonchalantly, referring to the panels of clear plexiglass that ran from the top of the railing to its base. "Whoever designed this balcony had kids like Amalie in mind."

He had placed himself on Darcie's right side, she realized, so he could see her.

Darcie gathered her courage, slowly lifting her eyes to his face. His forearms rested on top of the railing. His hands were lightly clasped. He was leaning in, one foot slightly behind the other. His casual stance belied the intense expression in his eye.

Think this time, Darcie admonished herself. *Think before you speak.* And she tried. She really did, but…

"I shouldn't have said what…" Darcie blurted out.

"I'm sorry for the way I…" Devin said, at the same time.

They shared a smile, which went a long way toward breaking the tension.

"Me, first," Devin began. "What you said to me earlier…I wasn't ready for it. You really caught me off guard. I've come to expect the usual platitudes. You know: *What scars?* Or, *I didn't even notice until you mentioned them.* Both of those…outright lies."

A frown marred Darcie's lovely face. "That's terrible," she said.

"And there's always: *Your face doesn't look that bad.* Or, *I'm sure you'll get used to it,*" Devin continued, watching her reaction.

Darcie's face was flush with emotion. "That's pretty noncommittal. Acceptance and denial at the same time."

Devin agreed, touched by her reaction. "I hadn't thought of it that way, but you're right. Then, there's always, *You're still the same person on the inside.*"

"Blah, blah, blah," Darcie said disgustedly.

"And the ever popular, *It's your new normal.*"

"I hate that phrase. It's so overused."

"Yeah." Devin sighed, his eye on the falls. "Anyway, I guess I just wasn't expecting you to—"

"Like it?" Darcie asked thoughtfully. "You have to admit that it's better than the bandages."

"I guess so," Devin agreed. "I also should have remembered that I asked for the opinion of Darcie Finch, so I should have known to expect the unexpected."

"Because of my filter." Darcie nodded. She knew her shortcomings well. "Or lack thereof." She sighed.

Devin turned to face her. "Because of your honesty. Because I can trust you. You aren't going to lie to me to make me feel better, even out of kindness. If you say you like it, then you like it." He looked her over from head to toe as if questioning her sanity. "No matter how twisted that makes you." The wicked grin on his face told her he was kidding.

"Hmph," she said, turning her own gaze to the falls.

They settled into a comfortable silence, watching the reflections of the lights on the rushing water. Peace settled between them, as well as a bone-deep understanding that began setting off alarm bells in Darcie's head.

Devin's thoughts were of a similar nature. *This feels right*, he realized. *Too right. Too comfortable. Too easy.* What the hell was happening between them?

"Miss Darcie!"

Amalie dropped Iggy and rushed over to Darcie. She was hopping up and down in excitement.

"Iggy says that you're a real princess. I think you're a real princess, too. Do you know how we know? Do you, Miss Darcie? It's because of the photograph. The photograph in Daddy's drawer. You're wearing a crown. I've seen it and so has Iggy." She hugged herself in excitement. "Miss Darcie is a real princess, Daddy! I knew it!"

Darcie was shocked. And flattered. And, suddenly very, very warm. Her photograph was in Devin's desk drawer? Why did he keep her photograph? She assumed he would have thrown it away in disgust after discovering the exact nature of her *problem looks*. But, apparently, he hadn't. And he obviously didn't know that his baby girl had seen it.

Devin's face mirrored her surprise, coloring with his own embarrassment. How could he have been so careless? *Damn it.* He almost groaned. He should have known better than to keep Darcie's photograph. It was asking for trouble…trouble he couldn't afford. Who knew when the same little tidbit of information would randomly pop out of the mouth of his own little princess? He averted his eyes from the expression on Darcie's face. She was completely stunned, speechless for once.

"Amalie," he said. "I'm afraid that Miss Darcie isn't really a princess."

The little girl's face fell, tugging at Darcie's heart. Before she could say anything to make Amalie feel better, Devin took matters into his own hands.

"Darcie's not a princess," he informed his daughter. "She's a queen. A real live beauty queen."

Amalie's eyes filled with excitement. "Really, truly, Daddy?"

Devin nodded, measuring Darcie's reaction. She was staring at him in amazement, her dark eyes wide with surprise. Satisfied, Devin continued:

"But she likes to keep it a secret, so we can't tell anybody else about that photograph. Okay, Amalie?"

"Okay, Daddy!" Amalie was thrilled. "Hurray!" she exclaimed. "A secret queen is so much better than a boring, old princess." She raced back to tell Iggy, having no idea of the impact her innocent remarks had left on the secret queen herself.

Darcie's expression was one of complete disbelief. "I can't believe you still have my photograph. I figured you would have thrown it away as soon as you looked at it."

"I almost did at first," he admitted. "I didn't believe it was you. I thought it was a photograph of somebody else. That you were lying to me. That you couldn't bring yourself to trust me with the truth. I have to admit I was rather hurt. When you talked about your 'problem looks', I assumed you were unattractive," Devin confessed. "With a face like a horse."

Darcie chuckled, her rich tones lingering in the air. "Why a horse? Why not a giraffe or a hedgehog?"

He ducked his head, looking like a little boy. "I had a dream about…"

Darcie was charmed. "About…" she encouraged.

Devin sighed, resigned to confess all. "About pirates. Lady pirates."

"Lady pirates?" Darcie's dark eyes were dancing.

Devin cleared his throat. "Yes," he said, with great dignity. "Lady pirates. You were a lady pirate and…well, you had the head of a horse." Devin shrugged his shoulders as if he couldn't believe it either. "So, I assumed it was true. I also thought you had really large feet." He added that little detail as an afterthought.

Darcie's eyes widened. "Large feet? That's why you asked me what size shoe I wore?"

Devin smiled, pleased she remembered their conversation. He remembered every word.

"How did you find out I was telling the truth?" she asked, curious to discover the rest of the story.

"Roman asked me why I had a picture of Darcie Finch. And I said, 'That's not Darcie Finch.'" Devin shook his head. "He told me I was wrong. He felt sorry for me because I *hadn't* been able to see you. He told me you were a looker. And Darcie"—Devin hesitated before he added softly—"he was right."

Darcie closed her eyes, holding up both hands in supplication. "Don't say it. Please don't say it. I thought you, of all people, would understand."

Devin understood all right. He understood all too well. And now, it was time for Miss Darcie Finch to understand. "Look at me, Darcie," Devin said, seriously. "Give me one eye at least."

She took a deep breath and opened two.

"I do understand." He touched the top of his eye patch. "I understand completely. But *you* need to understand something, too. I've earned the right to say it. And you…well, you've certainly earned the right to believe it. You. Are. Beautiful."

Darcie's knees went weak. Her breath caught in her throat. It meant something when Devin said it. It actually meant something. A lovely, warm feeling bloomed around Darcie's heart. She was drowning, watching the colored lights reflect in his fathomless gray eye.

"I couldn't throw your photograph away," Devin admitted, a bit reluctantly. "It was like my talisman…my good luck charm. It helped me to remember I was a man. Not a monster. I didn't know how bad it was going to be, Darcie." The intensity of his voice deepened. "I had no idea how much I was going to need those words. I didn't realize how hard I would have to fight to feel normal again. I honestly don't think I could have gotten through it without your voice in my head. I wanted to thank you." He paused for a moment, as if he didn't know what to do next. "So, um, thank you," he said humbly.

Filled with compassion, she reached out instinctively, placing her hand on top of his on the railing.

Her touch ignited some long-dead fragment inside him. He wasn't sure what to call it. Something akin to a bolt of electricity rushed through his body, filling him with a profound sense of wonder. He had never felt anything even remotely close to the raw heat he felt now—never with anyone else in his life.

And he very much doubted that he ever would again. Only with *her*. She filled the gaping hole in his heart. She was *The One*.

Standing by the beautiful waterfall, with the lights reflecting the greater beauty of the woman by his side, it was all so clear. So very simple.

He. Wanted. Her.

Today and tomorrow. And for all of the tomorrows to come. He hadn't planned it. He didn't understand it. No, he didn't understand it at all. But he could no more change the way he felt than he could make the water fall up instead of down.

Did she feel it, too? Her soft gasp when she had touched his hand must mean something. The way her eyes clung to his face—wide and searching—seemed to indicate similar emotions. Did she have the same sense of inevitability? Did she feel everything that had ever happened to her in her life had led up to this moment? He hoped so, because that was exactly how he felt.

If he was free—if he was able—he would fall to one knee, at that very moment, and propose, so certain was he that she was his destiny. But fate, he realized, was a feckless mistress. Darcie Finch may have taken possession of his heart, but the rest of him belonged to someone else.

Darcie was drowning in an awareness bordering on panic. Amazing, wasn't it? How one simple touch could change everything. She was drawn to this man. Attracted. Mesmerized. Connected. She had never expected her initial attraction to blossom into this. Why did it feel so inescapable? she wondered. And why did it have to be so irresistible? Why him? Why her? And why now? *Why is the one man I've ever wanted the one I can't have?* Her mind was screaming, but her heart couldn't resist.

She wasn't sure how long they stood there, each trying desperately to decipher the unspoken thoughts of the other. Her innocent gesture of comfort had turned into anything but.

"*Darcie.* There you are."

She heard the censure in Joey's voice before he came close enough for her to see it in his eyes. "It's time to cut the groom's cake, *sister dear*. And I know *you* don't want to miss that," he said through gritted teeth. "I know how much you *love* cake." He was across the balcony before he finished his sentence.

His flashy date, Honey—the actual name on her birth certificate—trailed behind more slowly. "Will you look at this?" she said aloud, gazing at the lighted waterfall. "It's *so* awesome!"

Joey ignored her. He took hold of Darcie's arm in a grip that was light, but firm. His unsmiling expression spoke volumes to Devin.

Amalie skipped up to the group, totally oblivious to the drama. "Mr. Joey? Is it time for cake now?" she asked hopefully.

Joey smiled. "Yes, ma'am. That's the reason I came out here. Tell your daddy to bring you back inside so you can have some." His smile disappeared as he glanced at Devin to make sure Amalie's daddy realized he wasn't making a suggestion.

Devin nodded once, reaching down for Amalie's hand. *Damn,* he thought, regretfully. *That was awkward.* And completely avoidable. He should have known better than to follow Darcie onto the balcony. He did know better. It just didn't seem to matter.

Honey latched onto Devin's arm. "Guess it's you and me now," she said, watching as Joey and his sister walked away. "Isn't this awesome?"

Devin wasn't at all sure what the clueless woman was talking about. Absolutely nothing about his present situation was in any way *awesome*. He was suddenly eager to return to the relative safety of the banquet hall. He tried to get moving by urging Amalie to take big steps. Honey—still staring at the glowing lights—trailed along at a snail's pace.

Darcie walked beside Joey, refusing to make a scene. Her overbearing brother still had a painless but ironclad grip on her arm. He had no intention of letting it go; of that, she was certain. She knew Joey well enough to know that he was determined to have his say. *She* was equally determined to have no part of it. Or of him. Not right now. She was twenty-three years old, not thirteen. She didn't need his assistance—or interference—at this particular moment in her life. Her beloved brother had just crossed an invisible line—a line no sibling had the right to cross. She would talk to him when *she* was ready. Not a minute before. And certainly not within hearing of Devin Merritt, his innocent daughter, and Joey's vacuous date.

As they came to the lighted part of the balcony, Honey's tactless words reached their ears: "Oh, you poor thing! What happened to your face?"

"Car accident," Devin muttered.

"Are they going to be able to fix it?" Honey asked, digging a deeper hole for herself. "I hope so. That would be awesome!"

Darcie couldn't hear Devin's reply. She turned to her brother. "Your date is a clueless idiot," she hissed.

"At least she's not *married*," her brother hissed back.

Darcie gasped. She shook off her brother's hand. Then she reached for the door handle, her eyes glittering with anger and hurt.

"We are *not* finished with this conversation, Princess," Joey said.

"Don't be so sure about that, Big Brother."

She opened the door, pinning a bright smile on her face before stepping into the dining room. The casual observer would have had no idea that the last five—very difficult—minutes had ever happened. Darcie did not, however, hold the door for her brother. Joey swore as the door clipped his elbow, but he followed his sister's example. With a wide smile, he strolled into the room, brimming with his usual effortless charm.

Their exchange would have gone unnoticed if not for the proximity of the head table. The lovely, green eyes of the bride—by no means a casual observer—narrowed in contemplation at the unobstructed view of her siblings' discord. Nor did it escape her notice that Devin Merritt entered several heartbeats later, holding his daughter's hand. He was trying to remove his arm from the clutches of Joey's empty-headed date. Grace bit her lip, determined to get to the bottom of the trouble.

Devin managed to untangle himself from Honey with a great deal of relief. He firmly directed her to her own table—and away from himself. He had no idea what words might have passed between Darcie and Joey. In spite of her valiant efforts, he could tell that his Pirate Queen was not happy. Nor was her brother finished with his lecture. Devin was sorry he had caused friction between the two. But he was not sorry for the stolen moments he had shared with the beautiful Miss Finch.

MACEE MCNEILL

The groom's cake was a lovely chocolate confection. Three tiers with elegant piping done in yellow. In the center of the top layer was a yellow oval, and in that oval was the black shape of a bat. The use of the Batman logo was a mystery to most of the guests, but the groom's eyes immediately lit with understanding. The answering glow in the eyes of his bride gave the impression that the logo meant more to them than something from the pages of a comic book.

As the cake was being cut and served, Grace took advantage of the lull to follow her sister into the ladies' room. Darcie eyed her warily but said nothing.

After checking to make sure no one else was in the ladies' room, Grace asked: "What was the big disagreement on the balcony all about, Darce?"

Darcie couldn't keep the frustration out of her voice, "I swear, Gracie. How did you—"

"I saw you through the glass doors," Grace interrupted. "I'm at the head table, remember?"

"You're the bride," Darcie replied, deliberately making light of what her sister saw. "You shouldn't be worrying about Joey or me. This weekend is about you and Blane and a lifetime—"

"Oh, no," Grace interrupted again. "Don't even think that's going to work." She crossed her arms and leaned back against the sink. "I know what I saw, and as the middle child, I've accepted that the position of peacemaker is mine for life. Married or not. You might as well tell me, sister dear. I'm not moving until you do."

She settled herself comfortably and waited.

Darcie grimaced and gave in. She kept her voice low and carefully even. "Joey made an incorrect assumption and I was correcting him."

"About Devin?" Grace asked gently.

Darcie regarded her sister incredulously. "What makes you think that?"

Grace put a comforting hand on her sister's arm. "Oh, sweetie, it's obvious. At least it is to me. You two are trying way too hard not to look at each other. But when your eyes meet…Darce, the sparks are flying. And you. You're distracted. You're not following anybody's conversation well. People keep having to repeat themselves. I've *never* seen you like this. There's something happening between you two."

"He's *married*, Gracie. Nothing can happen. Nothing is going to happen." Darcie gritted her teeth and proceeded to lie through them: "There is *nothing* going on between us."

Grace studied her beautiful baby sister. Darcie was undeniably tense. She stood stiffly, her left hand holding her right arm. Her right hand curled into a tight fist. She refused to meet Grace's eyes, keeping her head facing forward.

"Maybe there's nothing between you yet," Grace said, softly. "But there could be."

Darcie's eyes flew to her sister, denial poised on her lips. The words died when she saw the overwhelming love and understanding on Grace's face… and the tears.

Grace pulled her into a tight hug. "Guard your heart, Darce."

For a few seconds, Darcie allowed herself to relax. She would never love anybody quite the way she loved her sister. She tried not to think about Grace's words. She had no desire to ponder their significance. Or to remember that Grandma Sofi had told her the very same thing two months ago.

Guard your heart.

It was a moot point, anyway.

"I put butter in my coffee," Darcie whispered.

"I know," Grace said, kindly. "Having a nosy brother who is also ridiculously observant can be so inconvenient."

"Gracie," Darcie asked. "Have you ever met anybody and felt like you already knew him? Like your soul knew his? Like you didn't even have to try?"

Grace stilled for a moment, before pulling back so she could see Darcie's face. "Yes," she said, simply. "Yes, I have."

"What did you…? I mean, how did you…?" Darcie sighed. "What happened?"

"Oh, Darce…I'm marrying him tomorrow."

CHAPTER TWENTY-FIVE

A run was a good idea. A very good idea. Darcie felt better already. Not completely back to normal, but better. Well, she thought, at least she felt better than she had since her conversation with Grace in the ladies' room last night. Her head was clearer, and she was more in control of her emotions. After a few more miles, she would be good as new. Ready for anything.

It wasn't exactly daytime, yet, at least not in her book. It was dark and cold and five-thirty in the morning. The moon was still out. Even the roosters were sleeping in, but not her. Darcie Finch and sleep were officially estranged. That's all there was to it. She attributed some of the problem to time spent with the bride and four other bridesmaids. The rest, she decidedly refused to contemplate. Before a reasonable hour, it didn't bear thinking about.

Grace had lived in the gatekeeper's cottage on Blane's estate for nearly three years. On her last official night of occupancy—the eve of her wedding—the place had taken on the atmosphere of a college dorm. Complete with pizza, homemade brownies, somebody's playlist of songs from the nineties and early 2000s, and wine. It was fun. Darcie grinned now, remembering the stories and the laughter. For a while, the sheer nonsense had effectively distracted her from thinking of other things. Or other people. Handsome, one-eyed pirates, for instance.

But as soon as her head hit the pillow, thoughts of a certain one-eyed pirate loomed in the darkness, invading every corner of her brain. Thanks to a concerted effort on her part to recite the amendments to the US Constitution—in order—she finally fell asleep. She was, unfortunately, awakened by the bride's less-than-stealthy efforts to sneak out of their shared room around one-thirty.

"And just where do you think you're going, missy?" Darcie asked, sitting up in bed and crossing her arms.

"Shh," Grace said, putting her finger to her lips. "I have a rendezvous with a tall, dark, handsome man."

"You better go, then," Darcie advised. "It might be your last chance. I hear he's getting married tomorrow."

Grace grinned, heading to the door.

"Don't be gone too long, though," Darcie warned, shaking her finger playfully. "Exhausted brides with dark circles under their eyes don't make for the best photos."

"That's what makeup is for, little sister."

Grace winked and then she was gone.

Darcie wished she had a rendezvous with a tall, dark, handsome man, too. She tried to imagine what such a mystery lover would look like. But, after fitting him in the guise of multiple professions—from NFL quarterback to spy—she realized that no matter what he was wearing, the face was always the same. Strong jaw. Rugged lips. A single, gray eye. And, of course, an eye patch. That thought wasn't exactly conducive to sleep…so it was back to the Constitution.

She drifted off for a little while until Grace's return, two hours later, woke her. She pretended it didn't, being decidedly *not* in the mood for conversation. Besides, the bride deserved a little undisturbed rest before her big day. Grace was soon breathing deeply as her envious sister tossed. And turned. And tried to recite the Declaration of Independence in her head.

When Darcie finally dozed, her sleep was one long dream filled with pirates and fireworks and cake icing. A *great* deal of icing. She jerked awake. Falling over a swirling waterfall, made entirely of lemon buttercream, tended to jolt a person from her dreams. She sat up in bed, reaching for her phone. Five o'clock in the morning.

Longest. Night. Ever.

Well, she was finished with it, thank you very much.

She climbed out of bed, somehow managing to find her running clothes in the dark. Thankfully, she had packed a long-sleeve pullover. Shorts would be fine. She could deal with them. But the run was going to be chilly until the sun came up.

Running was a wonderful idea. The only sounds were her own footfalls on the drive and her even breathing. Peace. She planned to do four laps—from the bridge beside the gatekeeper's cottage to the edge of the circle drive at Heart's Ease, and back again. That would be four miles. Perfect. After that, she would head into town to pick up coffee from Jack's for the ladies of the wedding party. The order was already typed into her phone. All she had to do was press the button. She relaxed into the rhythm of her run, enjoying the freedom of the dark, invigorating morning air.

She reached the circle drive and turned around, picking up a little speed on the downhill section of the run. She was blissfully, completely alone…except that she wasn't. She realized about halfway down the drive that the sound of someone else's steps had become interspersed with her own. Whoever it was, he—or she—was behind her. She tensed, momentarily, before she remembered where she was. There was no safer venue in which to run than Heart's Ease, whether it was dark or not. She shook off the momentary anxiety, rationalizing that whoever was running behind her was somebody she knew. Maybe even Blane, although she doubted it. The groom, she knew, had had a busy night. Her breath seized in her chest. What if…?

The footfalls came closer. Whoever was behind her would catch up to her in a few seconds. A dreamy feeling of inevitability wrapped around her. She was gripped by the urge to laugh at herself. How had she conjured him out of thin air? Was she dreaming still?

Stop pretending, her conscience scolded. *You took a deliberate chance. Why else are you running out here in the dark? Who runs in the dark? You know you hoped it would happen. You, Darcie Finch, have developed some serious issues. Fight it, girl. You're stronger than this. Fight it.* Darcie kept running, refusing to look behind her.

He ran up on her right side. "Good morning, Darcie Finch," he grinned, behaving as if running into her while jogging—in a strange place, in the dark, at five-thirty in the morning—was a common, everyday occurrence.

"Go away, Laurence," she said firmly. "I'm busy."

She picked up her pace a little, even though she knew Devin Merritt's longer legs would have no problem keeping up.

Devin matched her strides easily. "Isn't this a little dangerous? Running in the dark? What if I was a diabolical criminal, intent on doing you harm?"

"At Heart's Ease?" She laughed. "This place has better security than the White House."

If he could act like nothing out of the ordinary had happened between them last night, then so could she. Was it wrong that her heart sank a little? What was she expecting, anyway? That he would declare his undying affection the next time they ran into each other? Ran *into*? Literally.

Oh, Darcie, she thought, mirthlessly. *You are so hilarious.* And, also, she knew, slightly pathetic. She cleared her throat. "For your information it is perfectly safe for me to run alone here. By myself. Without *you*."

"Probably," he said, making no move to distance himself from her.

Darcie glanced at him briefly. Changing tactics, she deliberately decreased her pace as they made the turn at the bridge. The gradual slope of the road leading to Heart's Ease was barely noticeable in a car. Running it, however, was a different story. Then, it felt like it was half a mile straight up. Her pirate stayed right beside her. "You don't have to run with me, Laurence," she chided. "I'll be fine by myself. Really."

"Is that so?" he asked, trying not to let his amusement show. She was flustered, he noted with satisfaction. And she was becoming extremely annoyed that he continued to disregard her wishes. She was also in very good shape. Even in the dark, he could see the muscles in the pale curves of her legs. She had called him *Laurence* twice, using her gorgeous voice. Yes, he decided, she was adorable. They were together again—alone, this time—in the dark. No, he thought. He definitely wasn't going anywhere.

"Hmph."

Darcie gave up. If he wanted to run with her, so be it. She had tried to discourage him. Sort of. Well, more or less. All right, she admitted. It had been a weak effort on her part. Her heart wasn't in it.

So, they kept running.

Her only outward acknowledgement of the fierce joy she felt running beside him was her inability to erase all traces of the tiny smiles that kept floating around her lips. Hopefully, the dark would hide them. Maybe he wouldn't notice.

Devin noticed, making sure to keep his answering grin out of sight.

They ran in silence, their attraction intensifying with each lap. By the time Darcie slowed down, the air practically shimmered with tension. She chose to stop in the final bend in the road, just short of her four-mile goal, but out of sight of the gatekeeper's cottage. She stepped off the road, walking about fifteen feet to the white fence that surrounded the expansive pastures.

Devin followed, watching as she placed her leg on the middle rail of the fence. Ignoring him, she leaned over to grab her foot. He bent down to touch his toes, enjoying the stretch in his lower back. He couldn't take his eye off of her, even though she flatly refused to look at him. He was completely focused on the *whatever it was* that ebbed and flowed between them.

When Darcie finished stretching, she climbed up to sit on the top of the fence, her back to the pasture. Devin walked to the fence. He propped his left arm on the rail beside her. He had no idea what to do now, so he waited. He was suddenly very uneasy. If she planned to tell him "Goodbye" or "Good riddance" or "Get the hell away from me," this would be the perfect time.

Darcie had yet to look at him. She hadn't looked at him since he ran up beside her, a little less than three miles ago. She wasn't quite sure what he was thinking. Last night, he hadn't spoken another word to her after Joey "escorted" her back inside from the balcony. Nor did he try to seek her out after the bus returned to Heart's Ease. She had *almost* been able to convince herself—as she tossed and turned last night—that she had blown their few moments on that balcony totally out of proportion. He kept her photograph in his desk drawer. So what? It was probably just what he said, a talisman that helped him remember he was not a monster. Encouragement from a friend. Devin's friend. *I am Devin's friend.* She tried saying the words in her head. She didn't like them. She felt as if she was standing in the ocean. No matter where she moved, the tide kept pulling the sand out from under her feet. Darcie had always had a strong dislike of uncertainty.

Well, she decided, there was one fact of which she *was* absolutely certain. She had *no intention* of admitting her own feelings without being sure of his. Talk about humiliating. She couldn't imagine anything worse. No, she was going to test the waters before she admitted anything.

"You're trouble for me, Laurence," she said. "Do you realize that? Nothing but pure trouble." She stated it as a fact—not a problem—as if she were talking about a toothache.

"Because of my dark, good looks and mysterious persona?" he asked, grinning.

"Of course not," she said, shaking her head as if he was an idiot.

Ouch. Why did he continue to think she would say the obvious thing? This was Darcie Finch, he reminded himself. Her mind never seemed to work quite like he expected it to.

"Because of your wedding ring," she said, bluntly. "Apparently I can't have a conversation with a man who wears one without raising eyebrows. Honestly. You should hear them. I'm talking about Grace and Joey," she clarified, barely pausing for breath. "It isn't like I haven't used better judgement than both of them so far. Grace almost married Roger, for heaven's sake. And Joey dates the most empty-headed girls." Her comment seemed to amuse Devin, so she elaborated on the dimwitted Honey. "Seriously, that girl he took to the rehearsal dinner didn't understand one thing anyone at our table said. The whole night. She just sat there, looking perpetually confused." She wrinkled her nose in disgust. "And *they* don't trust *me.*"

Ah-ha, Devin thought. So, that was it. Darcie was upset because her siblings assumed she was going to make a mistake. With Devin Merritt. He sighed. He certainly understood why her brother and sister were worried. His was a sorry situation. Any relationship with him at this point was clearly a risk. A bad risk. Maybe they thought he wasn't worth the risk, he surmised.

Was he? That point wasn't worth pondering, so he moved on to ask himself another, more disturbing question.

How in the hell had Grace and Joey figured out that there was something going on between him and Darcie Finch? It was a very complicated question, especially since *he* hadn't figured it out himself until last night. Well, he hedged, not really *last* night, but...okay. Yeah...well, maybe they had a point. The fact that something *was* going on between him and the irate woman currently sitting on the fence was obvious to anyone who saw them together for five minutes. Obvious to anyone except, possibly, Miss Finch herself.

Well, he would take care of that. "You mean because I can't take my eye off of you for thirty seconds? You mean because I've been sitting on that damn porch since four o'clock this morning hoping you would jog by?" Honesty was the best policy, after all.

Her eyes flew to his face for the first time. "What do you...?" She stopped talking and looked at him, overcome with giggles. "What are you wearing?"

"Excuse me?" He was spilling his guts and she was...giggling?

"What are you wearing on your face?" she sputtered. "Are those 'rec specs'?" She leaned in for a closer look.

"They are protective goggles," he said, with wounded dignity. "I can't just run around in the dark without wearing something. I only have one eye, remember?" He removed the offending goggles and handed them over for her inspection.

Far from inspiring the sympathy—or even worse, the pity—to which he had grown wearily accustomed, the sight of his goggles produced intense amusement. "But," she gasped. "You're wearing them over your eye patch. Oh my. I can't breathe." The sheer strength of her merriment forced him to join in.

It was a relief, he realized, to laugh with this woman. They had a problem. And it was a Big One. *His* circumstances were ironclad. *She* would never lower her standards. Both of them had ethics *and* integrity. But here they were. In the dark of an October morning. Standing beside a horse pasture. Laughing. What were they laughing at anyway? His ridiculous looking 'rec specs'? Her penchant for bluntness? That fate seemed to be playing some kind of twisted joke? Or were they laughing at the sheer folly of their situation? The fact that there was no right answer didn't seem to factor into their mounting hilarity. Or was it hysteria?

"Oh," Darcie choked. "Stop. My face hurts."

"I told you I can't stop," Devin said, his face full of wicked glee. At that Darcie collapsed into a new round of giggles, setting off a cause-and-effect chain reaction.

Her precarious position on top of the fence became even more so when she attempted to wipe her streaming eyes. She let go of the rail with her other hand…the one that wasn't holding his goggles. Letting go caused her to wobble. Wobbling caused the goggles to slip from her fingers. She made a grab for them, catching nothing but air. Her efforts overbalanced her on her perch. She would have fallen backward to the ground if not for Devin's quickness.

His right arm flew out to grab the other side of the fence, pinning her legs in place and steadying her torso. She frantically caught him by the shoulders and clung. His left arm came firmly around her, supporting her back. She drew flush against him, both of them taking deep breaths, as much from the remnants of their laughter as from her almost-fall.

I'm steady now, she told herself. Time to let go.

She's steady now, he told himself. Time to step back.

Yet, neither of them could move. They held on to each other, frozen in time, as all of the elements of the universe aligned. One perfect moment. Familiar in its rightness. Inevitable in its advent. Astonishing in its intensity. It was life-changing, because now they knew. And now, nothing would ever be the same.

"You feel it, too." She leaned her forehead onto his shoulder. "Thank God you feel it, too."

"How could I not feel it?" he whispered, tightening his arm to pull her even closer. His other hand let go of the rail to close comfortably around her nape. His thumb stroked the soft skin along her jaw.

"I don't know," she sighed, nestling closer into his arms. "Sometimes these things can be one-sided."

"Not something like this."

Devin closed his eye, breathing in her sweet scent. How could she still smell like flowers after a four-mile run?

"I've never even heard of something like this," he said. "It's…"

"Like love at first sight, only it's not." She was shaking with silent laughter.

He could feel it down to his bones. He opened his eye, pulling back a few inches to see her.

"Don't you get it?" she asked. "It's not love at first *sight*, because you couldn't. I mean…the first time we met you couldn't actually *see* me. So, it's really like…"

"Love at first fight," Devin finished, proudly.

She raised her head, her eyes brimming with laughter. "Love at first fight. We did that. We do that, don't we?"

"Fight?" he asked, softly, memorizing the way she looked. Hair tumbling down from her messy ponytail. No makeup. Cheeks flushed from the wind—or from something else—yet somehow more beautiful than he had ever seen her. "We strike sparks off each other, Darcie Finch. And we let them burn."

The sparks glowing in her eyes were threatening to start a fire that wouldn't be easy to extinguish. He touched his lips to the corner of her brow, moving delicately to her cheek and to her ear, where he paused and whispered, "You make me burn." He continued to nibble the side of her neck, working his way down to the sensitive place where her neck met her shoulder.

His words were the sexiest thing she had ever heard. They enflamed and terrified her at the same time, setting her world on fire. She wanted this. She wanted to burn. She felt her defenses slipping away under his tender onslaught until…

The alarm went off on her phone, startling her. She cursed and blessed the sound in equal measures. It doused the flames as effectively as a bucket of ice water. "Laurence," she whispered, pulling back a little. "Laurence."

"Darcie," he breathed, drunk on her intoxicating scent, on the exquisite feel of her in his arms. His lips returned to her cheek.

"Dev, Devin," she said, closing her eyes, but holding steady.

His lips were a hair's breadth from their glorious destiny when she opened her eyes. They were calm and serious. She wanted him to stop. He stepped back regretfully, understanding that their moment had come to an end.

Her arms reluctantly slid from his shoulders. Striving for normalcy, she sighed. "I have to pick up the coffee for the bride. And the bridesmaids. Maid of honor duties, you know." She hopped down from the fence. "Thanks for… well, for the run and…everything." Standing on her toes, she planted a kiss on his left cheek, the one *with* the scars. Before he could reply, she turned and walked away. Without meeting his eye.

He stood perfectly still until her footsteps receded. When nothing but silence remained, he picked up his rec specs, fitted them on his face, and set out for Heart's Ease. His pace was the only thing about him that was steady. The world as he knew it was permanently off-kilter. And it was all because of another unexpected—though desperately longed for—interlude with Darcie Finch, his Pirate Queen. He knew he should feel guilty for putting them both in an untenable situation. Instead, he could feel only a deep, abiding longing for it to happen again.

CHAPTER TWENTY-SIX

He hadn't meant to eavesdrop. Hell, he felt a little like Amalie, hiding behind the curtains, but he couldn't have moved if his life depended on it.

"Whatever it is that you want, Joey, will have to wait. We have to practice our song."

The sultry tones of The Voice wafted up to Devin's balcony on the light morning breeze. Hard to believe that just a few hours earlier he was holding The Voice—and all the rest of her—in his arms.

"No, it can't wait. I need to talk to you, Princess." Joey was very business-like, as if he faced a jury. "For the record, I was wrong about several things last night, and…"

"*You* were wrong? *Joey Finch* was wrong?" The Voice dripped with sarcasm.

Uh-oh. It sounded like Darcie's big brother was about to get an earful. Devin knew what that was like. He had a sister of his own. He felt a little sorry for poor Joey Finch, especially since the man had no idea he had chosen to have this conversation under the very balcony of the person he would be discussing.

"Now, Darce, before you get your back up..." Joey tried again. Unsuccessfully.

"Before *I* get *my* back up? You just admitted that you were wrong. Well, let me tell you something, Big Brother, the word *wrong* isn't going to cut it. *You* jumped to conclusions about what you saw on that balcony. *You* judged me without even letting me say a word. *You* basically accused me of being involved with a married man. And *you* don't even know anything about him. Or his situation. Or, apparently, about me. Because if you did—if you *really* knew me the way you seem to think you do—you would know that I would never...*never*...put myself or someone else in such a situation." The Voice, it seemed, had a lot to say.

"Princess."

Joey tried to calm the storm, but it was too late. She continued, unabated: "*He* has a daughter, Joey. A daughter that he adores. *He* would never do anything to hurt her. *He* has sacrificed so much for her. Yet, you stand there acting like he's some player. Some loser who cheats on his wife. You act like I'm too stupid to realize it. Or, maybe you think I'm just stupid enough to fall for it."

The Voice sounded hurt. Devin wanted to leap over the balcony and rescue her.

"Darcie. Sofia. Finch," Joey said. "*That. Is. Enough.*"

Devin heard a feminine gasp. Then, surprisingly, Darcie stopped talking. Apparently, Joey never called his sister anything but Princess. Hearing her full name must have stunned her into silence. Devin would have to remember that.

He listened to the footsteps on the travertine tile under the balcony. Joey must be pacing, probably trying to control his response. Once again, Devin was imbued with empathy. He knew, from experience, that Joey had better tread carefully.

The pacing stopped. "How could you *ever* say those things about me? I'm your brother, for the love of God, Almighty. One of the reasons I was put on this earth was to protect you and Grace, and I'll be damned if I walk away from you when you need me. Because you *do* need me, Princess, whether you know it or not."

The Voice tried to interrupt. "Joey, I'm…"

Not happening.

Joey, it appeared, could be as tenacious as his sister if he deemed it necessary. "As I said earlier, I was wrong about several things last night. I could tell you were off balance from the minute you walked into the house. You got worse during the rehearsal. I should have pulled you aside to ask what was going on, but I didn't. That was my mistake, and I'm sorry." His sincerity was unmistakable. "Instead, I watched you. And I watched Merritt. And I watched you watching each other. Then, I jumped to my own conclusions. But, when you put the butter in your coffee, I have to admit…well, it scared me a little, Princess, because you're always the one with all the answers."

She put butter in her coffee? No wonder Joey was so worried, Devin thought. He tried not to be so pleased that Darcie had been flustered enough to put butter in her coffee. It was a relief to know she was in the same state in which he found himself. He would never forget how he felt when she walked into the grand foyer…the first time he laid eyes—his eye—on her. Flustered had been the least of what he was feeling. Still, it was good to know that they were in this together. Whatever *this* was.

Joey was still talking. "All I knew about Merritt was that he was married, with a very young daughter. Imagine how that made me feel, Princess. When I thought that a man was taking advantage of my baby sister—any man, but especially a *married* man—I can't even tell you how upset I was. I was afraid you were going to compromise all of your principles, all of your beliefs, maybe even your future for some…*affair*. Well, as you saw, I just flipped out. And I'm sorry, Princess, so very sorry that I doubted you."

"Oh, Joe." The Voice was soft, velvety with emotion. "An affair? I wouldn't do that. I couldn't. You know me better than that. I could never…" She sighed, probably shaking her head.

Devin felt as if he was back in his bandages, trying to visualize her responses to make sense of the emotions of Darcie Finch.

"Come here, Princess."

That sounded like a hug, Devin decided. Yes, definitely a hug. So, there was to be peace between the Finch siblings. Good. He was happy for them. He doubted, however, that the peace would be extended to him. In fact, he expected some sort of confrontation with Darcie's brother in the very near future. Hopefully, *after* the wedding. He would count himself lucky if a verbal confrontation was the extent of it. Unfortunately, life had determined, thus far, that Devin Merritt wasn't a particularly lucky person. Finch was in good physical shape. He would be a formidable opponent. Surely, he wouldn't hit a man with one eye. Devin could only hope. *Maybe he'll let me wear my rec specs,* he thought philosophically.

Devin pondered that possibility before another pressing issue struck him. He didn't quite know where Darcie's unfinished sentence—"I could never..."—was going. That was bad. She could never...what? Have a relationship with a married man, however unhappily married? That's a good thing, he thought. For her, anyway, because it means she has integrity. But it was a bad thing for him because, well, he was the unhappily married man. Not that he would ever consider having an affair. Of course he wouldn't. He would *never* have an affair, because he had integrity, too. And a daughter. And the wife from hell.

Maybe Darcie was going to say that she could never let any man take advantage of her. *She's too smart for that,* he thought, approvingly. That's also a good thing. She would *never* compromise her principles. Or all of her beliefs. Or her future. Of course she wouldn't. *I'd be damned if I would let that happen anyway. She's much more important to me than that.* But, he thought, wistfully, if one day, I'm single. And she's single. Well, maybe, then....

Devin sighed. His demon wife was about as likely to end her financially profitable part of their sham of a marriage as Blane's uncle was to show up at his only nephew's wedding. There was no way in hell. Devin knew that Douglas McCallum's omission from the guest list had been deliberate, well deserved, and final. Thinking such depressing thoughts didn't last long, however. Devin was pleasantly surprised by what he overheard next.

"Look, Princess," Joey explained. "I had a long talk with Blane last night. He already suspected that something was up, by the way. Blane said the first time you met Merritt, you were at each other's throats. He said the sparks were flying between you two. He said that he figured you would either kill each other or, well..."

Devin pictured Joey shrugging his shoulders.

"Not kill each other, I guess," Joey finished, vaguely.

Devin imagined Darcie wrinkling her nose at her brother's revelation. She was probably extremely irritated that the feelings she and Devin had been so careful to keep secret from one another were, in fact, so transparent to others.

Joey continued: "Anyway, Blane explained a lot of things about Merritt and his sorry situation. I have to admit, Princess, that—after thinking about it—I kind of admire the guy. Anyone who willingly lives with that kind of wife for the sake of his child. Well, I have to say he has my respect." Joey's voice rang with sincerity. "And Blane thinks a lot of him. You know that speaks volumes."

Devin couldn't have been more surprised at this unexpected development.

"He's a good man, Joe," Darcie said, softly.

"Seems to be," Joey agreed. "Anyway, I trust Blane. And I trust your judgement, Princess. And the way I understand it, Devin needs to get out of his marriage with full custody intact. I don't know if such a thing is possible, but I'd like to help. That is...if you think you can trust me."

"I trust you, Joe."

The Voice sounded relieved. A little breathless, perhaps, but definitely relieved.

Devin was relieved, too.

"But..." Joey hesitated.

Damn it. Devin swore. *Why does there always have to be a* but?

Joey continued: "Until the time that he is free and clear. And until you both have a chance to decide if you want to do anything other than gaze soulfully at each other across the room. You. Be. Careful." The know-it-all big brother had returned. She must have wrinkled her nose, again, because

Joey added; "I mean it, Princess. I don't want to have to murder anyone in the near future."

"Hmph."

Devin listened as the sliding door opened and closed. Well, he thought, that was surprising. Surprising and enlightening. It seemed that Joey Finch was now something of an ally. He wondered if this meant Joey would stop glowering at him every time they were in the same room. Probably not, he decided. This was about the man's sister, after all. Devin wouldn't expect anything less from the brother of Darcie Finch.

Several hours later, Devin was still savoring the incomprehensible fact that Darcie Finch was as obsessed with him as he was with her. Why she would want someone with a scarred face, one eye, and tons of emotional baggage when she could have anyone—*anyone* else—was a mystery. But there it was. It was real and it was true. It was not, as he had feared, a product of too much pain medicine coupled with his overactive imagination.

Until this morning, he had half-convinced himself that the severity of his injuries had caused him to create a fantasy woman in his head. He had started to believe that the real Darcie Finch couldn't possibly be all that he remembered. And yet, several hours ago—for a few priceless moments full of sweet confessions and whispered words—he had held her in his arms. Just thinking about it filled him with renewed hope for the future. There had to be a way to end his marriage *and* keep his daughter. He would find it, if he had to go to the ends of the earth.

Roger Carrington's disgusted exclamation brought Devin back to a different part of that earth. The billiards room at Heart's Ease, to be specific. Roger had just been severely trounced in a game of pool. By Zack. Again.

"I don't believe it," Roger moaned. "That did *not* just happen. It's impossible. There is *no way* you made that." He walked around the table to get Zack's perspective of the last shot. "Damn it, Zack," Roger said in disbelief. "That was an impossible shot."

Devin had to hand it to Zack. That kid knew his way around a pool table.

Roger turned his incredulous face to the groom and his fellow groomsmen. Blane was grinning politely, but Joey and Evander were cracking up.

Roger shook his head, appealing to Joey. "Joey Finch, you have known me a long time, haven't you?"

"Oh yes," Joey replied, pleasantly. "I have known you a very long time."

Apparently satisfied by that answer, Roger continued: "And during the lengthy time of our acquaintance, you and I have played a lot of pool."

"We have played a lot of pool," Joey agreed.

Roger was warming up to whatever point he was trying to make. "And would you agree that I am a decent pool player?"

Joey nodded, the grin on his face widening. "We have played a lot of pool."

Evander's big booming laugh echoed through the billiards room. Devin exchanged an amused glance with Blane. Zack, he noticed, though silent, appeared to be enjoying himself thoroughly.

Roger glared at Joey. "Oh, ha, ha, Finch. You are so hilarious. Am I or am I not a decent pool player?"

Joey thought about it for a few moments before nodding his head again. "You, Roger, are a decent pool player."

That answer pleased Roger. "Thank you." He opened his mouth to say something else, but Joey wasn't quite finished.

"But Zack is an *exceptional* pool player." He couldn't help but add fuel to the fire.

Roger started again: "So, how is it possible that an eighteen-year-old kid…"

"Eighteen is considered an adult in a court of law," Zack chimed in, applying chalk to his pool cue.

"How is it that an eighteen-year-old *kid*," Roger continued, "plays pool like he's forty-five and on the professional circuit?"

"I guess I'm just lucky," Zack said with a satisfied smile.

Devin joined in the good-natured jeers and heckling. He could see why Blane enjoyed spending time with his groomsmen.

"Who's next?" asked Zack, raising his eyebrows in challenge.

"Not me," Roger said, throwing himself down onto the black leather sofa. "I need a break."

"You need to practice," Evander added cheerfully, carefully selecting a pool cue.

Zack tossed him the chalk and started racking up the balls.

"Watch him, Mayfield," Roger said. "I think he puts magnets in 'em when we're not looking." He laid his head on the back of the sofa, gleefully prepared to watch Evander's annihilation.

"We have to eat lunch after this *and* get dressed. Photos start at two o'clock for us," Joey added, glancing at his Apple watch.

"Yes, ma'am," said Zack, with a smart salute.

"Laugh if you want," Joey added. "But there is a schedule and I, for one, will not be responsible for messing it up. And neither will *you*."

"Yes, sir," Zack said, ruining the genuineness of his response by hitting himself in the head with his pool cue.

Joey walked to the window where Devin stood. "I didn't know being the best man meant I was responsible for the behavior of those clowns, too." He shook his head in mock sorrow. "How are you holding up? I know the situation with the wife could be better. Blane filled me in. Hope that's all right?" He was clearly making a point.

"Yeah. No big secret there," Devin answered honestly. He understood exactly what Joey *wasn't* saying: *I know all about you and I'm going along with this for now, but only because I trust Blane. However, the verdict is still out. Don't screw up. And don't hurt my sister.*

"And, apparently, no way out, either, huh?" Joey asked. "Well, nothing's ever completely hopeless...."

The rest of his statement was lost as Blane joined them at the window. "Speak of the devil." They followed his sober gaze to watch as a black Town Car rolled up the drive. Blane put his hand on Devin's suddenly tense shoulder and gave it a sympathetic squeeze. "Looks like they're here," he said kindly.

Devin sighed inwardly, trying to prepare himself. For the most part, he doubted his companions were aware of the turmoil roiling his stomach. He felt a moment of envy for their freedom from "wedded bliss." From his position by the window, he watched his parents step out of the car. He didn't, however, see his sister or his wife, but he assumed they were out there somewhere. Devin excused himself from the intense competition underway in the billiards room. Evander was giving Zack a game, and he hated to miss it. But it was time to do his duty. Mentally donning his Mallory-proof armor, he headed down the hall.

Devin met Robert and Allana Merritt in the entryway, hugging his mother and shaking his father's hand. He knew this happy reunion was only a prequel to the arrival of his own personal mistress of darkness. He watched the driveway, fighting the cowardly urge to run back to the billiards room. After a few moments of waiting in silence, he turned back to his parents with a questioning air. "Where are...?"

But before he could ask the question, his mother answered, "They're coming. In another car."

"There wasn't room in our car for all four of us," Robert Merritt hedged quickly.

Allana raised her eyebrows at her husband but said nothing. Clearly there was a story there.

"Guess it was too much to hope that Mallory changed her mind about coming," Devin said. *Or that she missed the plane. Or got on the wrong plane. Or fell out of the plane. No violence*, he sternly reminded himself. He promised himself long ago, not to let himself imagine Mallory's untimely demise. He started over. *Or fell out of the plane with a parachute which didn't open. No, which opened, but got stuck in the tallest trees of a deserted area of West*

Virginia. No, which opened and landed safely, but in a deserted area of West Virginia. With banjos. Yeah. That works.

"There they are now," said Allana.

The three of them watched through the still open door as the car approached the house.

"I'm sure it will all be fine, honey," his mother said, encouragingly.

Devin glanced at his dad, who had a strange look on his face. "Allana, I think I'll just run up to our room for a minute." He headed briskly down the two steps leading into the grand foyer, making for the west staircase. "I'll see you in a few minutes."

But his wife, it seemed, had other ideas. She followed him into the grand foyer. Devin trailed right behind her. "Rob, nobody has told us where our room is yet," Allana pointed out calmly.

But her guilty husband's pace didn't falter. He barely paused to greet Rafe, Ian, and Fergus, who were seated on the two sofas closest to the staircase.

"Robert Merritt," Allana said firmly, her voice slightly raised. "Don't you dare go up those stairs."

Robert stopped, his foot on the bottom step. He looked longingly up the stairs, before turning to face his charmingly adamant wife. "But, Allana, I can talk to Lydia privately after…"

"Don't you dare leave this room." Allana crossed her arms, glaring at her husband. "You can talk to your daughter right here."

Poor dad, Devin thought. He had been in trouble with his mother enough times to know that when Allana Merritt crossed her arms, negotiations were over.

"Allana," Robert wheedled charmingly, "perhaps *you* can talk to Lydia. You know, woman to woman…to explain."

Allana quashed that idea like a bug. "No, hon," she said. "This time you're on your own. You got yourself into this. Now, let's see if you can get yourself out of it."

Devin was enjoying the interplay between his parents. He looked at his red-faced father suspiciously. "Dad, what did you do?"

He didn't have to wait very long to find out.

Outside, before the driver came to a complete stop, Lydia Merritt leaped from out of the back seat. She practically ran onto the porch, through the front doors, past the startled housekeeper waiting to welcome her. She stomped across the entryway, stepped down into the grand foyer, and went straight to her brother. She grabbed his shoulders and pressed her face into his chest.

In a loud voice—with more drama than he had heard from her lately—she announced: "Thank God we're finally here. Thank. God. This has been the *longest* day of my life, and it's not even time for lunch." She lifted her head to look at her mother. "I could kiss the floor. I hope you know that I could kiss the floor."

She turned then, walking straight into her mother's awaiting arms.

Allana nodded, calmly. "I understand," she said, with a world of, well... understanding.

Lydia's gaze fell on Robert, who was still standing at the bottom of the staircase. Her hazel eyes narrowed. She walked slowly toward her father. "I can't *believe* you left me like that, Dad. You knew we were right behind you, but as soon as you got to the bottom of the escalator, you *ran*. You ran to that Town Car, dragging Mom behind you. You ran, and left me with, with... her. *Again*."

Devin sat down on the end of the sofa, out of the way. He inclined his head to Rafe, Ian, and Fergus. They were, he noticed, sitting absolutely still. He leaned his head back against the soft leather, preparing to wait it out. His sister's tirade seemed far from over.

Lydia turned to Devin. "I had to sit with *her* in *coach*. In. Coach." Lydia paused, dramatically. "Mom and Dad got upgraded. All right, I can live with that. Except I had to sit right beside *Miss Never Satisfied*. She complained so many times that I thought they were going to throw both of us off the plane. Without parachutes."

Lydia's voice changed into a shrill, nasally tone. Devin was impressed. His sister did a damn good impression of Mallory.

"'It's too hot,' " she whined, fanning herself vigorously. " 'It's too cold,' " she moaned, hugging herself with her arms. " 'I want *two* packs of peanuts. I want another drink. I want colder ice. I want whatever it is the lady across the aisle has.' " Lydia rocked her head from side to side with each *I want*. She looked like some kind of bizarre bobble-headed Barbie doll.

Devin wanted to grin. Lydia was unconsciously hilarious when she was in the Drama Zone, as he used to call it. Of course, he was remembering his sister in middle school and high school. This adult version, he decided, was even more entertaining.

Lydia's own sweet voice returned. "The worst part, relatively speaking, was that she kept pulling *me* into it," she explained. She began pacing around the grand foyer.

When she stopped moving, she planted her hands on her hips. Her voice immediately changed into the grating one of her nemesis: "'My sister-in-law needs a pillow' " she complained. "'My sister-in-law wants you to do something about the crying baby behind us,' " she wailed. " 'My sister-in-law has a headache.' "

Lydia paused, raising her hand to her forehead. "Actually, that one was true," she said philosophically. "I guess you can understand why. So, I finally got up—under the pretense of going to the bathroom—and told the flight attendants that I *wasn't* her sister-in-law. I told them that I was her caregiver and that we were transferring her to another facility. And they *believed* me. They believed she was a mental patient."

Lydia threw her hands in the air. "I've spent so much time with *her* today that I feel like *I* should find some nice facility to check into. Somewhere calm and quiet." She sighed, before continuing: "Anyway, after we *finally* made it through the flight, we had to wait for her checked bag. I don't know why she had to check a bag for one night. But after she picked it up, we went to meet *our parents*, Devin—yours and mine—to get a car. But when Dad saw us coming, he ran, Devin. He ran to the closest car, dragging Mom behind him. They got in that car. And they left. They *left*. They didn't wait for us. They left me all alone with *her*."

"*He*," said Allana, indicating her Mallory-avoiding spouse. "*He* left you. I was merely an innocent bystander." She smiled sweetly at Robert.

"I'm sorry, Lydia," Robert sighed heavily. He approached his daughter, enfolding her in a warm embrace. "I wasn't thinking. The idea of sharing a car with her, well...I just panicked. I don't have any other excuse. Forgive me?" He spoke to his daughter aloud, but also to his wife, raising his eyebrows in supplication. Allana nodded her approval.

"Oh, Dad," Lydia sighed. "Of course, I forgive you."

She planted a kiss on his cheek.

Devin felt he should applaud or something. Lydia was completely sincere, but her retelling of the story was priceless. He wanted to laugh, but he didn't want to hurt her feelings. He loved his funny little sister to distraction.

Suddenly, Lydia gasped as if she had just remembered something. She walked over to Carolina Mendez, Blane's head housekeeper. Carolina was acting as temporary hostess while Juli and Alina were getting their hair and makeup done. Holding out her hand, Lydia said, "I'm sorry for being so rude. I'm Devin's sister, Lydia." She shook Carolina's hand. "If it's not too much trouble, I need something to drink."

"There is sweetened or unsweetened tea, sodas, bottled water, and punch in the dining room," Carolina said into the silence. "All of you are welcome to have lunch at your leisure between now and one-thirty."

Carolina was the epitome of efficiency. She and Mrs. Hofmann were the only employees still on duty until after lunch. Blane insisted on hiring the catering company's entire staff, so his own employees could attend the wedding and reception as guests. It was just another perk for those lucky enough to work for Blane McCallum.

Devin noticed that Blane and company were standing near the east staircase, in the archway that led to the billiards room. They had apparently heard most of Lydia's soliloquy. Now they couldn't seem to decide what to do. *Amazing*, Devin observed, *how one little bit of irate woman can terrorize a colony of men.*

"No tea, thank you," said Lydia, holding the side of her forehead with her hand. "Or soda or water or punch. I need *something to drink*."

Carolina nodded in perfect understanding. "We also have mimosas in the dining room."

Lydia sighed. "That would be lovely. Please make mine heavy on the *mim* and light on the *osa*." She took a deep, cleansing breath. "Would something like that be possible?"

Carolina smiled, happy to help. She had difficult relatives, too. "Follow me. We'll find Mrs. Hofmann. Her mimosas are famous."

She led the way, with Lydia and Allana on her heels.

As soon as they disappeared into the dining room, Zack started a slow clap. "Wow," he exclaimed admiringly. "That was the best monologue I've ever heard. Maybe you should sign her up, Evander."

"She's too old for you, Zack," Evander observed.

"Damn." Zack lost some of his eagerness.

The other groomsmen exchanged amused glances.

Devin was glad they were enjoying themselves. He had the sinking feeling, however, that the show was only beginning.

Mallory Merritt had certain skills. There was no denying that. She could extinguish the light in a room faster than blowing out a candle. Quickly and efficiently, she imposed her own particular misery on her unsuspecting victims. She sailed into a place as if she owned it, as if she expected everyone to bow down and do her bidding. Devin knew from experience that more often than not, Mallory got *exactly* what Mallory wanted. He could almost admire the way she effortlessly manipulated those around her, if she wasn't so nasty about it.

He braced himself as his scheming wife burst through the front doors of Heart's Ease. Mallory's carefully orchestrated performance—although similar in action to Lydia's—was a marked contrast to his sister's genuine distress.

"This has, without a doubt, been the worst day of my life," she declared, posing herself prettily. She had paused in the archway leading to the grand foyer, her entrance carefully calculated to afford everyone in the house as unobstructed a view as possible.

Mallory was lovely, Devin grudgingly admitted to himself. She really was. Her blond hair was artfully arranged to look tousled and messy. Her makeup was flawless. Her clear blue eyes and porcelain skin were perfectly complemented by the stylish bronze color of her one-piece designer jumpsuit. Her four-inch heels and her matching handbag, both by Tory Burch, stood in immaculate contrast. She looked like a fashion plate, as if she had stepped out of a magazine.

"And I have *never* been subjected to such incompetence," she continued, breezing down the twin steps to hold court in the center of the room. "Those idiots outside dropped my bag. They actually dropped it," she announced with the same gravity an ordinary person would announce a death. "And," she continued, "there is a tiny scratch on the bottom corner. It's Louis Vuitton, too. I guess my *monster* will have to buy me another." She gave a superior little smile, advancing gracefully into the room…straight to her husband. "Hello, *Monster*," she cooed, presenting her cheek for his kiss.

Devin administered the kiss quickly, feeling more shame than usual at his obedient response. He was used to playing his role in Mallory's little performances. He didn't care how he came across in front of Mallory's friends, but, here, he was in the presence of people he genuinely liked. It cut his own self-respect to pieces.

Carolina came back in from the dining room, followed by Allana and Lydia. Allana carried two bottles of water, one of which she handed to her husband, who smiled gratefully. Lydia carried two mimosas, one in each hand. The drink in her left hand was in an oversized goblet. It looked to be suspiciously lacking in the orange juice department. As such, Lydia appeared much calmer.

Devin realized too late that somebody should have warned Carolina… strung up red flags or something. They really should have. It just wasn't fair. Poor Carolina approached Mallory without any caution, assuming she was dealing with a normal person.

As soon as the housekeeper introduced herself, Mallory exploded. "So, *you're* the one to blame for the incompetence of the baggage handlers. I'll have you know that I will be sending a bill for the damage that was done to one of my bags." At Carolina's startled expression, Mallory smiled cruelly. "If I find that any of my belongings are broken, I'll send the bill for that, too. I also insist that any monetary compensation I am owed be taken out of your salary. I know Blane well." She paused for effect, her eyes glittering with malice. "Oh, I forgot. He's *Mr. McCallum* to you, not Blane. Anyway, I'm sure that *Mr. McCallum* won't allow his guests to be treated with this kind of disrespect." Mallory's triumph was almost complete, but she couldn't resist one final taunt. "Why, I wouldn't be surprised if you no longer have a job tomorrow."

During Mallory's diatribe, Blane moved silently across the room to stand beside the shocked Carolina. He put a comforting hand on her shoulder, facing Mallory with eyes as cold as ice. "That's enough, Mallory," he said, in his CEO voice, the one that few men had the courage to oppose. "Listen and listen well. You are a guest in this house, and as a guest, you should expect to be treated with respect. Likewise, my family, my other guests, and *my staff* will be treated with respect by you. Is that clear enough for you, Mrs. Merritt?" Blane practically growled her name. "Those are my terms. If you cannot accept them, you—and your damaged bag—will return to Newport. Immediately."

Mallory froze at the tone of his voice. *Nobody* talked to Mallory Merritt like that. Devin watched the emotions flicker in her eyes. He saw surprise that anyone would naysay her. Anger that she couldn't respond as she wished. Frustration that she had put herself at odds with the one person she wanted to impress. And fear that Blane would follow through with his threat.

Devin was astounded. Rarely did Mallory go toe-to-toe with someone forceful enough to put her in her place. *Blane really is Batman,* he thought. At that moment, Blane looked like the Caped Crusader, dark and brooding, determined to protect his people from harm.

There was no doubt in Devin's mind, however, that Mallory would attempt to manipulate the confrontation in her favor. He braced himself for the fake emotional meltdown, the fake tears. He counted down in his head. Five. Four. Three. Two. One. Right on cue, Mallory burst into tears, throwing herself into Devin's arms. Well, in the general direction of his arms, anyway. She gave him two options. He could catch her, or he could watch her slide to the floor in front of their horrified audience. For a moment, he hesitated. He was tempted, he really was. She didn't deserve his support. But in the end, chivalry won out. He held her up as she sobbed on his shoulder. At least he didn't have to worry about an ambush from Mallory's ever-present bestie. Desiree was back in Newport. Far, far away. It slowly dawned on Devin that Mallory didn't have one single ally at Heart's Ease. She was all alone in a spectacle of her own making. He couldn't help but wonder how his spiteful wife would handle that.

"I'm so sorry for everything," she wailed, between pitiful sobs. "I don't know what I'm saying. I'm so tired and it's been such a terrible day. Our flight was one of the worst that I've ever experienced. After that, having to deal with the damage that was *accidentally* done to my favorite bag…well, it was just too much." She gazed up at Devin with blue eyes full of tears, fluttering her lashes in supplication. "Oh, Devin, don't let Blane think I'm a bad person."

Too late for that, Mal. The most Devin could manage was an awkward pat on her back.

At least she hadn't called him *Monster* again, but it was probably only a matter of time until that little "endearment" was repeated.

His token response seemed to satisfy Mallory. She pulled away, delicately dabbing at her eyes with the back of her hand. She looked to her much-maligned sister-in-law for help. "Lydia, dear, wasn't it just the most awful flight?"

Lydia took a sip of her champagne-with-a-tiny-drop-of-orange-juice-mimosa and smiled, wickedly. "Oh, I don't know about that. Personally, I thought it was a great flight. Out of all the flights I've ever been privileged to be a part of, it was probably the best flight I've ever been on. I really enjoyed myself," she said, managing to look sincere. "And everyone was so nice, too, especially the other passengers."

Mallory gazed at her in disbelief, but at least she stopped talking.

"What a woman," Zack said under his breath, gazing adoringly at Devin's little sister.

"Too old for you," said Evander, in a singsong voice.

"Out of your league, Junior," Roger added.

Lydia, fortified by another sip of champagne, finally took pity on her brother. She handed Mallory the smaller mimosa—the one with orange juice—and took her arm. "Come on, Mal, let's find our rooms and then we can come back down for lunch. I'm sure the guys have pictures soon, or something."

"Oh, Lydia," Mallory sniffed, piteously, leaning on the arm of her new best friend, "you're the only one who understands me."

Lydia's expression was priceless; if she rolled her eyes any harder, they were going to stick to the back of her head. Mallory had never treated her sister-in-law with anything but varying degrees of dislike. Now she was acting as if they had been friends for years. Devin wanted to laugh, but he really didn't dare.

As the pair walked toward the stairs, Mallory shot Devin a look of disdain over her shoulder. Then she turned away and very deliberately tossed her perfectly tousled locks. A final dismissal.

Good riddance, Devin thought.

Blane gave Devin an encouraging pat on the back as he passed by. "Time for lunch," he announced. Everyone moved at the same time, relieved to have something to do.

Devin stood perfectly still, rooted to his spot. This was the first time he had *ever* felt even remotely victorious after one of Mallory's tantrums. For once, he wasn't alone. He had friends and family here. People who were on his side. People who believed in him. Blane, for example, knew what Mallory was like. He had quickly and efficiently put the conniving woman in her place. Hell, Devin thought with wonder, even his baby sister—the same one he delighted in tormenting when they were growing up—had weighed in clearly on his side. And Lydia owed her big brother some grief. He was going to have to do something nice for his sister, like buy her a car or something.

Mallory had no power at Heart's Ease. The entire scenario made him think of *The Wizard of Oz*. Mallory was like the Wicked Witch of the West in Munchkinland, alone and in danger of having a house fall on her. Even though he could never expect to be that lucky, he did realize one thing. He had been so eager to hide the realities of his miserable marriage that he had shut himself off from the support he so desperately needed. It was eye-opening, to say the least.

Zack interrupted Devin's epiphany. "Can you put in a good word for me?" he asked, with the eagerness of a man barely grown.

Devin was confused. "A good word? With who? With my wife?"

"Hell, no!" Zack was emphatic on that point. "Your wife is The Devil. I'm talking about your sister." Zack grinned.

"My sister?"

Devin raised his eyebrows, studying his young friend. Zack was clearly smitten. Devin had an idea that he himself must look exactly the same way when he was thinking about Darcie Finch. "She's a little too old for you, pal," he said, kindly.

"See." Roger popped Zack on the back of the head as he walked by. "Better wait until you grow up."

"But I can be tried as an adult in a court of law," Zack said as he trailed after his mentor.

Roger stopped walking with a look of utter frustration. "Zack."

"Yeah?"

"Shut up."

Roger resumed his path to the dining room, Zack following in his wake.

Devin smiled. Those two were quite a comic pair.

He checked his phone for the time. Pictures with the wedding party were at three o'clock. In other words, at three o'clock he would be reunited with the maid of honor. He wondered what she had been doing for the last few hours. Probably sipping tea, buffing her nails, and enjoying herself.

CHAPTER TWENTY-SEVEN

*T*he title *Maid of Honor* didn't begin to encompass the myriad duties Darcie was currently juggling. She would add *Maid of Fetch and Carry*, *Maid of All Things Food*, *Maid of Table Decorations and Place Cards*, *Maid of Music to Do Hair and Makeup By*, and *Maid of Canine Appearance and Cooperation*. That last one had proven the most taxing so far.

She spent an hour with her doggie nephew, Atticus. Bathing him. Blow-drying him. And, most importantly, instructing him on the finer points of wedding etiquette and behavior. Atticus currently lay on the floor at Grace's feet, beautifully groomed and completely calm. He was wearing a tuxedo—his own canine version—and acting like a perfect gentleman.

But Darcie wasn't fooled for a minute. She knew Atticus too well. Granted, he seemed to understand the lecture she had administered during his bath—something along the lines of: Dogs who play in creeks do *not* get to attend formal events. He was frighteningly clever, that dog, and Darcie somehow sensed Atticus knew exactly what she was telling him. She could only hope for the best. She was absolutely inflexible on one point. No way was she giving Mr. Atticus Finch, Canine Esquire, another bath before the wedding.

She would have liked to leave the dog alone for the moment to ponder his future, but she wasn't quite finished with the mischievous canine. As *Maid of Footwear*—thus far, her least successful title of the day—it was her job to find Grace's missing sandal. The bride was determined to wear the emerald green Italian sandals Blane had given her during their courtship. No other shoes would do. Darcie was certain Atticus was somehow involved in *The Case of the Disappearing Footwear*. He and that sandal had a history. She was determined to find the little piece of Italy at all costs. And if that meant cajoling, threatening, and/or bribing Grace's sandal-obsessed mutt, so be it. This *Maid of (Insert Tedious, Time-consuming Task Here)* business was not for the faint of heart.

Darcie heard a girlish giggle. She looked around to see what the little princess was up to. Amalie seemed stress free, and having the time of her life. She was excited by everything that was happening. The girls had taken turns entertaining her all morning.

Juli and Alina let her help fold programs.

Grace taught her how to make a cup of tea. She was careful to use a caffeine-free herbal peach flavor. But she allowed the little girl to add so many sugar cubes to the cup that caffeine became a moot point. Amalie was so excited about the wedding, a bit more sugar was a nonissue.

Ana entertained her by taking funny pictures of everyone with her phone, promising not to post them on Instagram. Darcie doubted Ana would keep that promise, but Amalie was delighted to be included in the fun.

The wedding photographer, who was spending the morning with the girls, was wonderful. She let the little girl look at the pictures on her camera right after she took them. She even let Amalie press the button to take a few pictures herself.

Haven and Charlotte painted the little girl's nails the same maroon color the bridesmaids were wearing.

Lou braided and pinned Amalie's hair into a lovely coronet on top of her head. She sprayed it with the same cementlike hairspray the rest of the girls were using to assure it wasn't going anywhere.

Darcie hated hairspray and hairpins. The assemblage of hairpins currently being used by the wedding party would probably stretch across the state, from the mountains to the ocean, by now. "From Murphy to Manteo," as the saying went. When it was Darcie's turn, Lou took one look at the maid of honor's mutinous expression and raised her eyebrows in warning. *Don't speak*, Lou's look seemed to say. *You will not get out of this. Don't even try. This is Grace's day, and you will look the way you are supposed to, missy.*

Darcie got the message loud and clear. With a deep sigh, she allowed herself to be painted, pinned, and sprayed to within an inch of her life. She felt as if she was trapped once again in the despised role of Miss Honeysuckle Creek.

She glanced at Atticus, who gazed back empathetically, understanding in his wise, doggie eyes. *This is for Grace*, he seemed to say. *We can do this, you and I.* It was one thing to exchange an unspoken communication with Lou, but Darcie was suddenly making a genuine mental connection with a dog.

"Hmph."

Darcie grimaced as Lou pulled hard on a tangle in her hair.

"Sorry."

Lou smiled, not sorry at all, as she continued to stick pins straight into Darcie's skull. At least that's what it felt like. In a show of solidarity and silent protest, Atticus came to sit beside her. She promised herself they would both have a good roll in the creek when the wedding was over.

When everyone was sprayed and polished to perfection, they sat down together for a sweet moment with the bride. Grace gave her bridesmaids long, white button-up shirts to wear with leggings or jeans in lieu of robes, due to the fact that they would travel to Heart's Ease to don their dresses.

"We don't want to scandalize the horses," she said, referring to Blane's lovely thoroughbreds, the only potential witnesses to their trek.

The fashion-conscious ladies were thrilled with their thoughtful gift and happily wore the lovely shirts throughout the morning. The pocket of each shirt was beautifully monogrammed with each attendant's initials in the maroon color chosen for their dresses. Grace's pocket said, simply, *Bride*. She was so radiant, her joy so evident, all of the bridesmaids had difficulty holding back tears.

In the end, no one tried. The sentimental moments continued as the bride presented each bridesmaid with a delicate pearl bracelet, accompanied by a detailed explanation of what each of the women meant to her. Alina efficiently passed out tissues. And Lou expressed satisfaction that the spray she had used on their makeup really was tear-proof. The women—along with Amalie—ended the lovely interlude by holding hands as Juli prayed. A champagne toast followed, and then a delicious brunch provided by the Hearts and Flowers Tearoom.

Amalie received a gorgeous bride doll, complete with a tiny bouquet of silk flowers. Her delighted reaction confirmed that it was the perfect gift for a four-year-old flower girl. She made it a point to introduce her doll to Iggy, before leaving them both on the sofa to get acquainted while she went on her "big girl" errand. As Amalie, Diana, Darcie, and Lou headed to Lou's shop to pick up the wedding dress, the little girl continued talking about the cute, little sandwiches and tiny cakes they had enjoyed for lunch. Her main fascination, however, was with the delicious apple scones, which she had never seen before.

"Nanny Di, can we have *stones* at home? Can we make our own *stones*?"

"Scones," said Diana, trying not to laugh.

"Scones," Amalie said, skipping to the car.

"We don't want to eat stones, do we?" Lou asked, teasingly. "We might not have any teeth left if we did that." She folded her lips in and smiled, giving the illusion that all of her teeth were gone, much to Amalie's sugar-induced bemusement.

"Miss Lou! You're so silly! We can't eat *stones*, but we can eat *scones*." She articulated both words, carefully. "Nanny Di, can we make *scones* at home? I like *scones*!"

Diana helped her into the car, promising that they would check Pinterest for scone recipes on the way.

Lou was driving her dad's Escalade to allow plenty of room for the dress. Darcie's reprieve was over. As she climbed into the front seat, she tried to organize her to-do lists. At this point, she had checklists for her checklists. On any other day at any other time, she would have thrown herself into her role as maid of honor, enjoying the challenge.

But today, a large portion of her mind was consumed with the few breathless minutes she had spent earlier that morning on a dark, deserted road. She was having a great deal of difficulty keeping her brain from switching to the *All Devin, All the Time* channel. By sheer force of will, she had managed to address every detail so far and to do it with a smile on her face. To say she was distracted was the understatement of the year, but she refused to let Grace down on her wedding day.

She couldn't. She wouldn't.

So, she concentrated on her tasks by keeping a running conversation in her head. *Don't forget the clips for the veil,* she reminded herself. *You simply cannot forget the clips.* She wondered why the clips were waiting at Lou's when the veil was already at Heart's Ease. She didn't have the slightest idea. But she knew she could not forget them. *Clips, clips, clips....*

As Darcie tried to concentrate, she became aware of the curious glances Lou was throwing her way.

"You're awfully preoccupied," Lou remarked, with interest.

"Oh, you know," Darcie said, in as offhand a manner as she could manage. "I'm going over lists in my head. I can't afford to forget anything."

"You *never* forget anything," said Lou, suspiciously. "It's one of your most annoying traits."

Darcie tried to turn the conversation to a safe topic. "I love your doll, Amalie," she said, peering through the gap in her headrest. The little girl was seated directly behind her, strapped into her child safety seat. Darcie figured she didn't have to talk to Lou if she was talking to Amalie. *Good job, Darcie,* she congratulated herself. *Dolls are a safe topic. Completely safe.* "Have you chosen a name for her, Amalie?"

"Her name is *Queen Darcie*," Amalie announced in a proud voice.

Diana snorted. She actually snorted. Lou put a smug expression on her face.

Darcie blanched. She quickly turned back to face the front. Good Lord! She hadn't seen that coming. She glanced at Lou's face, then quickly looked down at her hands, so she wouldn't have to meet those intuitive eyes. Darcie knew that look. She could tell she was in for a full-scale question and answer session with the overly perceptive blonde. And Lou was a master. *Think, think, think*, she told herself, desperately.

Lou spoke first. "That's a beautiful name, Amalie. I would love to know why you picked it."

Darcie's lips pressed together in a thin line. *No fair, Lou,* she scolded her friend in her head. *Shame on you for picking the brain of a four-year-old.* Even as she fumed at Lou, Darcie had to admit that she, too, was a little curious. She wondered why Amalie hadn't chosen to call her doll Princess Darcie instead of…

Oh crap! The reason Amalie had chosen the name *Queen Darcie* was suddenly crystal clear, causing the real Queen Darcie to panic.

The photograph. The photograph in Devin's desk drawer.

"*She likes to keep it a secret,*" Devin had said about Darcie's title, "*so we can't tell anybody else about that photograph. Okay, Amalie?*"

Darcie had a sinking feeling that Amalie wasn't very good at keeping secrets. *Don't mention that photograph, Amalie,* Darcie silently pleaded. *Please, please, please, don't mention the photograph in your daddy's desk.*

"There's a picture of Miss Darcie in Daddy's desk drawer," Amalie announced, excitedly. "I saw it when I was looking for gum. Miss Darcie's wearing a crown. Daddy says she's a real live beauty queen," Amalie innocently prattled on. "But it's a secret, so we aren't supposed to tell."

Doomed, I am doomed. Darcie almost moaned.

"We aren't supposed to tell what?" asked Diana, for clarification.

"We aren't supposed to tell that Miss Darcie is a queen," Amalie explained in a whisper. "It's a secret. So, you can't tell anybody. Shhhh!"

Damn, damn, and double damn. Darcie knew she had to distract Lou and Diana. She had to do something. *Maybe when Lou slows down,* she considered, *I can jump out of the car.* Darcie casually looked out the window, her hand on the door handle, searching for a soft place to land.

"Am-a-lie," said Diana, trying to keep a straight face. "When Daddy asks you to keep a secret, you aren't supposed to tell anybody. You can't tell Daddy's secret and then ask the person you tell not to tell. Secrets don't work that way."

"Oh," said Amalie, her lower lip starting to tremble. "Am I in trouble, Nanny Di?"

Darcie couldn't stand it. It wasn't Amalie's fault that her daddy and his *whatever-Darcie-had-become* were a pair of imbeciles. She turned around and gave Amalie a bright smile. "Of course you're not in trouble, sweetie. You just told a secret to two of the *most* trustworthy people I know. In fact, I am *positive* that the two ladies in this car would *never* tell your Daddy's secret to *any*body else." Darcie congratulated herself for her quick thinking. *Darcie Finch, you are a genius.*

"Of course, we won't," Diana said, comfortingly.

Lou merely smiled at Darcie, fluttering her long lashes. *Don't look so smug over there, Darcie Finch,* she seemed to say. *You're not off the hook yet, sweetheart.*

Amalie beamed. "I like you, Nanny Di, and I like Miss Lou! You are the best secret-keepers."

Lou laughed. "Thank you, Amalie. I like you, too."

"And Nanny Di?" the little girl asked.

"And Nanny Di, and Miss…I mean, Queen Darcie. I like her, too," Lou announced, giving Darcie a wink.

Darcie wrinkled her nose. "Hmph."

"I like Miss Darcie, too," Amalie went on blissfully. "And so does my daddy. He likes Miss Darcie very much. I can tell."

"How can you tell, Amalie?" Lou asked, casually.

"Lou Ann Boggs…" Darcie breathed. She wanted this conversation to end almost as much as she wanted to find out what Amalie was going to say.

"I can tell because he smiles when he looks at her. She was Daddy's babysitter when he became a pirate. She gave him oranges to eat. He talks about her a lot. He likes to look at her photograph a lot, too. Daddy says Miss Darcie is very pretty on the inside. Daddy says that's the most important part. I think Miss Darcie is very pretty on the outside, too. She looks like a princess but she's really a queen. It's a secret and you can't tell, Miss Lou. So, you can't call her Queen Darcie." Amalie looked a little worried. "Please don't tell, Miss Lou."

"Don't worry, Amalie, I won't call her Queen Darcie anymore, okay?" Lou said kindly.

"Okay, Miss Lou." Amalie was smiling again.

"Let's talk about the wedding," said Diana. "I heard that each layer of the cake is a different flavor."

Darcie smiled at her, grateful for the change of subject

"I like cake! I hope one of the layers is pink," Amalie said. "Pink cake tastes good. Iggy likes chocolate cake best. Daddy likes pie better than cake. Miss Darcie made Daddy a pie when he became a pirate. It was chocolate and it was *so* good. He let me have a piece. Iggy really liked it. So did my daddy. He likes pie better than cake. I think Daddy likes Miss Darcie better than he likes my mommy." Amalie paused for breath, before continuing, "Miss Lou, Nanny Di says that my mommy is a selfish bitch."

"*Am-a-lie Rose Merritt!*" Diana began, anticipating Lou's shocked response.

But Lou was made of sterner stuff. She accepted the comment in the matter-of-fact way in which it was given. "Nanny Di must have been very tired the day she said that. I bet Nanny Di gets tired when she's with your mommy. I bet Nanny Di is tired a lot. I think Nanny Di deserves a medal and a month's paid vacation."

"And, maybe, a sainthood," Darcie added, under her breath.

Lou pulled into her parking place behind the shop. "C'mon, ladies," she said, gaily. "We've got a dress to pick up. And I have a little surprise for you, Amalie."

"A surprise for me? Hurray! Hurray for Miss Lou!" The little girl scrambled out of the car as Diana opened the door. Her face scrunched a little. "Nanny Di," she whispered urgently. "I need to freshen up. *Now!*"

Lou quickly unlocked the back door, motioning them inside. She flipped on the nearest lights. "Restroom is on the right after you go through those doors." She indicated the direction of the main fitting room.

"Hurry, Nanny Di! I need to freshen up *right now!*"

Amalie began hopping back and forth from one foot to the other. Diana grabbed her hand. They took off at a run for the double doors.

"She's such a cutie, isn't she?" Darcie asked, determined to behave as if the last few minutes never happened.

"So, tell me, Darcie," Lou said conversationally. "Why does Devin Merritt have a photograph of you in his desk drawer?"

Lou certainly didn't waste any time. "It's sort of a…joke," Darcie hedged.

Lou put her hands on her hips. "Not buying it," she said.

Darcie ignored her. "It started when he was at Heart's Ease, after he was injured. His face was covered with bandages. He couldn't see what I looked like. So, I made him a pie and put my picture in the box with it, so he would know…after the bandages came off, I mean."

"A pie is irrelevant," Lou said decidedly. "What I would like to know is why you chose your photograph as Miss Honeysuckle Creek? The Darcie Finch I know would rather cut off her nose than wear a tiara." Lou crossed her arms. "So, my friend, your explanation just isn't good enough."

Darcie looked at Lou uneasily. Lou looked back, completely focused on Darcie. She was prepared to be ruthless until she got the information she wanted. That much was apparent.

Darcie hadn't slept more than a few hours the night before. At this point, her emotions were stretched to the limit. She felt herself weakening under the intensity of that blue-eyed gaze. *Lou should interrogate prisoners for the FBI,* Darcie decided. *I'm surprised she isn't shining a light into my eyes.*

The pressure was suddenly too much for her. The dam burst. "I tried to tell him what I looked like and he didn't believe me, Lou. Can you imagine?

He didn't believe me. He didn't care. He said I had a beautiful soul." Darcie's voice cracked, and her eyes filled with tears. "He's brave and strong and he adores his daughter. And, oh, Lou, he's so funny and smart and crazy about his family. And he listens to what I have to say. He really listens. How could I not fall in love with a man like that?" *Love?* Darcie asked herself. *Did somebody say, "love"? Oh, God…it was me.*

"That's all I wanted to know, Darce." Lou relaxed, finally satisfied. "And now…"

"Thank the Lord!" The unexpected voice came from the doorway.

Lou and Darcie turned, surprised to find Diana standing so close. Her face was alight with joy. "You don't know how glad I am to hear you say that, Darcie. I was so afraid Devin's feelings for you were one-sided. I thought maybe you were only being kind because of his injuries. I couldn't bear to see him hurt by another woman."

"Devin talked about his feelings for me?" Darcie's rich voice was full of emotion.

"No." Diana shook her head, ruefully. "He would never have a conversation about feelings with me, unless it had some kind of funny punchline at the end. But it's obvious. He talks about you a lot. At least once a day. I mean, your name comes up in conversation all the time. Amalie talks about you, too. That's why she was so excited to meet you. She remembers everything you said on the phone that day. You made quite an impression. She craves that kind of special attention since she doesn't get it from Mallory."

"But, how do you know that he…" Darcie couldn't finish her sentence. She just stood there waiting for…what? She didn't really know what she wanted Diana to say. The fact that Diana appeared to be genuinely happy—not appalled—that Darcie had just admitted to having strong feelings for her married cousin spoke volumes. "Strong feelings" wasn't quite descriptive enough, but Darcie refused to use the "L" word again, even in her own head. It was too terrifying.

"Miss Lou! Miss Lou! I found the crowns!" Amalie came to the door of the fitting rooms, her eyes bright with excitement. "May I look, Miss Lou? Oh, please, may I try them on?"

"Yes, ma'am," Lou said, delighted with Amalie's eagerness. "We are going to find the perfect one for you to wear in the wedding. That's the surprise I was telling you about in the car."

"Oh, Miss Lou!" Amalie grabbed Lou's hand and pulled her toward the front of the shop. "Can I really wear a crown like a real princess? Can I take it home with me after the wedding?"

"Of course," Lou said. "But we are going to call it a tiara instead of a crown."

"Ti-a-ra," Amalie repeated, happily, as they disappeared through the door.

The sound of Amalie's childish chatter faded away, leaving Darcie and Diana alone. Diana reached for Darcie's hands, squeezing them in her own. Her eyes were shining with tears. "Darcie, I can't tell you how relieved I am. I truly believe that you are the reason Devin's accident didn't destroy him. Meeting you, I think it saved him. Whatever you did or said or…I don't know. It was a gift. A little miracle. I was so afraid that when he saw you again, he would find out you weren't the person he thought you were. I was so afraid that he would be disappointed." Diana paused in her confession. "He's lost so much," she said after a few moments. "I didn't know how he could stand to lose you, too. But, listening to you just now…well, I want to help. I mean, if you'll let me." Diana took a breath before giving Darcie a smile full of friendship and support. "If you want to get in touch with him or, I don't know, send a message or something, you can send it to me and I'll…"

"You're going to pass notes for me, Diana?"

Darcie was touched by Diana's sweet offer. She was still reeling from discovering, only a few hours earlier, that Devin returned her feelings. The realization that he had revealed so much about her to Diana was tying her stomach in knots. She had to ask about Mallory. Diana would tell her the truth, and she might not have another chance.

"How bad is it, Diana…with Mallory, I mean? Has it gotten worse since the accident?"

Diana grimaced. "It's always been bad, Darcie. Before the accident, she tried to manipulate him with charm. She pretended to be the perfect wife to get what she wanted, and, well…he gave it to her to keep the peace. It was better for Amalie, you see? Since the accident, it's gotten so much worse. She calls him *Monster* all the time, like he's her pet or something. No kindness. No compassion. Nothing for him. His scars and loss of an eye have been inconvenient. Inconvenient for her, not him. She really is a—"

"—selfish bitch," they finished together.

"And how are things for you?" Darcie asked, feeling more like herself, more in control. "It can't be easy, working for someone like that."

Diana sighed. "It's pretty awful. Please don't tell Devin I said that. I can stand anything for Amalie."

"Will you promise to let me know if I can help?" In a quick reversal, the comforted had become the comforter.

Diana nodded.

Lou appeared in the doorway. "It was love at first sight," she announced. She chuckled at the expression of shock in Darcie's dark eyes. "With the tiara, Miss Phi Beta Kappa. It was love at first sight with Amalie and the tiara. Honestly, Darcie," she said with an amused wink. "Everything isn't always about *you*."

"Hmph." Darcie scowled at the beautiful blonde.

"And now, Diana, if you will approve Princess Amalie's brand-new tiara, we can get Gracie Marie's dress and be on our way."

CHAPTER TWENTY-EIGHT

*A*fter lunch, Devin dressed for the wedding and joined the other groomsmen in Blane's study on the first floor. He was sorry to find he had arrived before the groom, because he was somewhat reluctant to face the others without Blane. He shook his head, refusing to be caught up in his own worries. The hopeful feelings of the morning had been spoiled by the appearance of his Diva of Darkness. He keenly felt the humiliation of allowing her free reign. He figured that, in spite of their initial support, the other men would keep their distance. To anyone unfamiliar with the techniques of Mallory Merritt, her performance no doubt cast great doubt regarding the existence of his manhood.

To his surprise, and to his sincere gratitude as well, the groomsmen continued to be supportive. He enjoyed his conversation with Evander and Roger about time spent in New York City. He was surprised to discover Roger had almost gone to work for an accounting firm directly across the street from McCallum Industries' city office. He also discovered he and Evander had several favorite restaurants in common in the theater district. Neither man mentioned the drama with Mallory.

Joey Finch was more direct, however, drawing Devin aside for what amounted to a private interview about his tragic mistake of a prenup. Joey listened to the explanation without censure. Instead of walking away in disgust, as Devin might have done in his place, he offered his help.

"Listen, Merritt, I would be more than happy to read over the prenup if you're interested. I'm not arrogant enough to assume I'll see something your family of lawyers missed, but sometimes an outsider can find a nuance here and there that might have been overlooked by those who are emotionally involved."

"I'd appreciate that, Finch," Devin said, and he meant it. "I'll email a copy on Monday." Not only was he appreciative of Joey's offer to help, and his willingness to withhold judgement on the situation with Darcie he was equally glad he wouldn't need to defend himself with or without his rec specs.

"Why don't you just get rid of her? Your wife, I mean."

Zack's question was loud—and completely tactless.

Devin didn't care. He thought Zack's penchant for plain speaking was priceless.

"I told you," Roger said, irritably, addressing the outspoken young man. "He signed a prenuptial agreement and he can't get out of it without giving up custody of his daughter." Roger turned to Devin apologetically. "Sorry. The kid's mouth gets ahead of his brain sometimes." He glanced irritably back to Zack. "We're working on it, aren't we, Zack?"

"I don't see why that was such a bad question." Zack was doing his best to understand. "We were all there. We saw her freak-out fit. Devin knows that."

"It's not about what we saw," Evander added, kindly. "He might not want to talk about it. It might make him feel worse."

"Oh, you mean because his wife is a…um…a bit high-maintenance?" Zack had pulled back just in time, looking at Roger, a question in his eyes.

Roger nodded his approval. "There may be hope for you yet, kid."

"It's all right, Zack," Devin said truthfully. "It's no secret. 'High maintenance' is a good way to put it. And I don't mind answering questions."

"Well, then, why don't you just buy her off?" Zack asked.

Evander and Roger looked at him in amazement.

"What?" the young man asked. "Did I say something wrong again?"

"No, you said something right," said Evander, encouragingly.

"That's not a bad idea. Have you tried it, Devin?" Roger wanted to know.

Devin sighed. "I've tried it. Several times, in fact, but she isn't interested."

"You're really that irresistible, huh?" Joey asked with a touch of sarcasm.

"It's my bank account," Devin confessed. "My bank account is pretty irresistible, as is my family's bank account. So is my family name and all of the bells and whistles that come with it. She also thought we made the perfect couple. You know, my *dark good looks* and her *blond beauty* and all that crap. But, now, well…the joke's on her, isn't it?" Devin tried not to sound bitter as he gestured to his scars and patch.

Joey looked thoughtful. "So, have you tried to buy her off *since* the attack?"

"Well, no. I just assumed that…" Devin's voice trailed off into nothing. Joey Finch was right. "Well, hell. What have I got to lose? It's pretty obvious she doesn't like being married to a monster like me."

"You're not the monster, dude," Zack said. He gave an overexaggerated shiver. "Your wife scares the hell out of me."

Zack's candor broke up the heavy tone of the discussion. When Blane finally arrived—looking like something straight out of *Bridal World* magazine—his groomsmen were talking sports and trying to figure out what to do with their floppy shirt cuffs. Their question was soon answered. Just as they had guessed, Blane presented each of them with a pair of solid gold, monogrammed cufflinks.

Zack was so overcome with emotion that he hugged the groom. "I don't know how to put these in my cuffs, but I love them."

The sincere expression of feeling from the usually overconfident teenager was a surprise, drawing forth smiles. His candor helped to further lighten the tone of their previous conversation.

UNMASKING THE HEART

Darcie breathed a small sigh of relief when Lou fastened the last of the endless buttons on her gorgeous design. Grace studied herself in the tall mirror of the dressing room. The room was part of the expansive master suite she was already sharing with her groom. She couldn't seem to stop smiling. Her green eyes once again filled with joyful tears. She reached out one hand to her sister and her other hand to her best friend, linking the three of them in a tableau of bridal splendor. The photographer quietly clicked away, preserving the moment for posterity.

"Thank you, Lou. Thank you, Darcie. You two have no idea how much you mean to me," Grace whispered. "I can't wait for the three of us to reshoot this scene two more times, with each of you standing in my place." She squeezed their hands before turning around.

The ladies of the wedding party gathered around their beloved bride. Blane's aunt opened a box lying on the ottoman, revealing a beautiful antique lace veil. Because the veil held such a special place in McCallum family history, Juli had invited a delighted Alina to assist.

Darcie felt a niggling worry. There was something about that veil. Something she was supposed to remember. Something she was supposed to do. Her eyes widened in horror. *The clips for the veil,* she thought. *I forgot to pick up the clips for the veil.* This, Darcie realized, was a disaster of epic proportions. It wasn't as if they could use bobby pins or zip ties or super glue. Those clips had been specially made to fasten this antique veil to that antique tiara…at least a hundred years ago. Using anything else might damage the precious heirloom—and it would all be Darcie's fault.

Alina placed the tiara on Grace's head. For Darcie, however, the beautiful moment was filled with true panic. What was she going to do when Alina asked for the clips for the veil? Admit that she forgot them? Admit that she was a failure as a Maid of Honor *and* a sister? Or admit that her brain was so befuddled with thoughts of Devin Merritt that she could barely remember her own name?

Before Darcie could figure out what to say, Lou came to the rescue: she pointed casually to the dressing table. Darcie didn't know how it was possible, but the forgotten clips were there. She grabbed them from the table, holding them as Alina fastened each clip in place. After adjusting the yards of lace until she was satisfied, Alina pressed a kiss to each of the bride's blushing cheeks. Only then did Darcie breathe a small sigh of relief. Crisis averted.

But her elevated heart rate had barely returned to normal before another crisis loomed on the horizon.

"Time for your sandals," Juli said gaily, after giving Grace's veil a final, motherly tweak.

Darcie's already overworked heart immediately went into overdrive. Again. *Sandals*, she almost groaned aloud. *You mean the emerald green Italian sandals that my beautiful sister wants to wear with her beautiful wedding dress?* she asked herself. *The* pair *of Italian sandals? And, by* pair, *I'm including the missing one I was supposed to find and didn't.* She had a mental picture of Grace hopping down the aisle determinedly, wearing a single sandal. *You can't have a heart attack today*, Darcie told herself. *It would ruin the wedding.* She looked around, frantically, for Atticus, who was, most assuredly, the responsible party. Before she took a single step toward him, she was surprised by another wedding-day miracle.

"And thank you so much for finding my sandal, Darcie," Grace enthused. "I don't know how you did it. Sometimes it takes me days to find something that Atticus has hidden. I don't know what I would have done without you today. You're the best," Grace said, giving her sister a fierce hug.

"Um…you're welcome," Darcie mumbled.

She returned the hug as her eyes flew to the devious canine. He was lying on a fluffy white rug, enjoying a lovely sunbeam slanting through the window. His freshly washed fur was still in pristine condition, not a hair out of place. He regarded her with a self-satisfied smirk that clearly said: *"You can thank me later."*

Darcie took a step back. She was somewhat in awe of her beautiful sister. Grace was ready. She stood there in all of her bridal glory. Her dress—the elegant flounces, flowing bits of tulle, and beautiful lace—was perfection.

The veil, clipped to the tiara—*Thank you, God!*—swirled around her like a delicate cloud. It was time for the photographs to begin.

Grace's eyes went to her sister. "I want some pictures with you and Mama, please."

Darcie's pounding heart relaxed, diminishing the chance of cardiac arrest for the moment. She joined the glowing bride and their exquisite mother for some sentimental photographs.

The photographer arrived on Blane's heels, along with Ian. Blane's grandfather, Fergus, came behind them, holding a bottle of beautifully aged Scottish whiskey. The groomsmen busied themselves finding glasses and preparing for a toast. Rafe joined the group just in time. The men took a moment to savor Fergus' excellent brew. Zack was particularly proud that the men included him in the ritual.

"Don't get too cocky, kid," Roger warned. "I asked your parents about this."

He whisked the unemptied glass out of Zack's hand as soon as the toast was over, impervious to the teen's request to finish it off.

"Can't have you staggering down the aisle, Zack, now can we?" Blane asked, raising one eyebrow. "Besides, Grace and Lou would kill us for allowing underage drinking. Not to mention what Maggie would say."

Zack figured he could handle Grace and Lou, but facing an irate Maggie was something else entirely. He shuddered at the thought. Grabbing his bottle of water, he took big gulps in an effort to hide the evidence on his breath.

Devin took a moment to touch base with Rafe. He hadn't had a chance to talk with him since they had stepped off the plane. With the exception of the rehearsal dinner, Rafe had been conspicuously absent since his arrival.

He was the picture of elegance now. His tux hugged his lean frame admirably. His silver hair added the right flair. He looked and acted the part of an aging James Bond. Devin knew Blane had asked Rafe to be his best man. He also knew Rafe had declined. The charismatic older man was more comfortable in his role behind the scenes. Still, Devin had seen him wipe his eyes afterward. Blane's offer clearly meant a great deal to him.

"I'm assuming all is well in Honeysuckle Creek," Devin began after Rafe motioned him toward an unoccupied corner of the room.

"Yes and no," Rafe said.

Devin didn't like it when Rafe was evasive. "Trouble with the wedding?"

"Douglas McCallum left Newport on a company plane a few hours ago. He just landed in Honeysuckle Creek."

"That bastard is going to crash the wedding." Devin wanted to punch something. "But, how can he? Guests have to present an invitation to be allowed on the bus." The wedding guests were parking at the now defunct Broad's Skating Rink. It was conveniently close by. Shuttle buses were scheduled to run every ten minutes.

"He'll drive right in with the paparazzi," Rafe explained. "It's a genius plan. We know Blane is allowing one reporter and one photographer from *Heathcliff's Personal Finance Weekly*, along with one cameraman from *The Celebrity Buzz*. Douglas can drive in behind them. Nobody will think anything about it."

"Isn't there something we can do?"

Devin wasn't dressed for battle, but he was willing to do his part for the Boss-man.

"Not this time, and Douglas knows it. The press would love to hear that Douglas McCallum wasn't on the guest list for his only nephew's wedding, especially since his nephew is his boss, etcetera, etcetera. They would have a field day with any negativity connected to this wedding."

"Does Blane know?" Devin asked.

He glanced at his friend. Blane looked relaxed and ready to marry his green-eyed girl.

"He knows," Rafe said. "And he doesn't want any negative publicity, either. We have to be especially careful, since Douglas is quite a fact-twister. Blane will put up with anything to protect Grace. Right now, they are the darlings of the media, but Douglas could change all that with a few well-placed words. Blane said to let his uncle in. We'll deal with him if there's any trouble."

"Let me know if you need me," Devin said, but Rafe's attention was already on the tasks ahead. He unobtrusively made his exit after exchanging a few, brief words with the other men in the room.

Maggie popped her head in the door. She looked striking in a lavender chiffon dress with a lace jacket, her red hair intricately piled on top of her head. Her eyes roamed the room, lighting on her anticipated target. "Blane, it's time for you to see your bride. You can come with me. All of the rest of you can watch from the ballroom, but don't touch anything." That last remark was directed to Zack, who nodded eagerly.

The men left Blane's study together, but Devin held back as they entered the ballroom. He needed a few moments alone to get his thoughts in order before the group pictures. Finally, he continued down the hallway with Blane. When they reached the door to the rose garden, Devin stopped and made a great show of glancing at his watch. "There's still time to make a break for it," he said.

Blane grinned. "Not a chance." He was finally marrying his Green Eyes. All was right with the world.

The two men shook hands. Devin was somewhat gratified when Blane paused, with his hand on the door handle, to take a deep breath. It appeared the bridegroom was human, after all. Devin needed to remember that.

"Good luck, Boss-man," he said with a smile.

Blane nodded. Then he opened the door and headed into the rose garden.

Devin walked from the hallway into the bedroom where had had spent so much of the past summer. He looked around, reacquainting himself with the place where he first heard The Voice. He was amazed to discover he possessed a heretofore unknown sentimental streak. The victim had returned to the scene of the crime, he thought, for it was in this very room that Miss Darcie Finch had stolen his heart. Was it possible that the enchanting thief would return as well? Was it wrong for him to hope she did? Right and wrong were all twisted up in his head, along with a pair of dark eyes and soft, kissable lips.

CHAPTER TWENTY-NINE

*D*arcie crept out of the ballroom without attracting anyone's notice. The bridesmaids were glued to the full-length windows. They were too busy straining their eyes to watch Grace and Blane's "first look" photographs to pay any attention to the errant maid of honor. She wanted to see the expression on her soon-to-be brother-in-law's face the moment he saw his beautiful bride, too, but her primary goal at the moment was preventing catastrophe. Grace's last request before going out the door with the photographer was for Darcie to keep a tight rein on Atticus. The dog hadn't seen his new daddy all day. He was liable to lose his recently acquired dignity in his haste to get to his second-favorite human.

Darcie did her best. She really did. She kept a death grip on the wayward dog's leash, holding on for dear life. Unfortunately, the leash mysteriously separated itself from Atticus' collar on the way down the stairs. That's when Atticus mysteriously separated himself from Darcie. The troublesome dog had gone rogue. He was now roaming the house and grounds, probably searching for his humans. Or looking for some water to roll in. Or—horror of horrors—searching for his humans *after* rolling in water. Darcie had a mental image of the creek-loving canine, covered in mud, crashing into her sister's gorgeous wedding gown.

This could *not* happen. She would *not* allow this to happen.

"Atticus Finch," Darcie whispered. "I'm coming for you, and if I have to tackle you myself, I will."

She walked through the deserted grand foyer and into the dining room, calling softly, "Atticus, come here, baby." *You rotten, scheming dog,* she thought. *You probably unhooked your leash yourself.*

"Here, sweetie. Here, sweet Atticus." *The only reason you found that sandal is because you were the one who hid it.*

"Here, Atticus. Good puppy." *I swear, if you're swimming in the creek right now, I will never give you another bath. Or blow-dry your fur again.*

She stuck her head into the kitchen, continuing to berate the maddening mutt in her mind. No luck. The kitchen was Atticus-free. She walked down the hallway behind the kitchen, opening doors and quietly calling the accomplished escape artist.

"Here, Atticus. Come out, come out, wherever you are." *Knowing you, you diabolical canine, you're smirking somewhere. Watching me look for you or...* Darcie took a deep breath. *No. I refuse to think you're already outside. Oh Lord, what if you're already outside?"*

She paused, listening for screams punctuated by hysterical barking. She listened for any sound that might point her in the right direction. But all was silent.

She couldn't help the memories that came rushing back as she opened each door. "At-ti-cus, here, boy. Sweet Atticus, I'll do anything you want if you come out now." *I won't hide your doggie bed. I won't nail your doggie door shut. I won't buy you a one-way plane ticket to somewhere far, far away.*

"At-ti-cus, if you come out now, I'll make you a pie. Any flavor you want, even if it's something doggie-disgusting."

She walked into the open door of the last room on the hall and stopped, unable to believe her eyes. Devin was looking out the window, his hands casually thrust into the pockets of his black tux pants. His broad shoulders showed to good advantage in the crisp, white shirt. His black bow tie added a touch of elegance. The highlights in his auburn hair reflected the light, glowing like fire.

Darcie couldn't breathe. If any man looked better in a tux, she had yet to meet him. She was sure such a person didn't exist. Even without his tux jacket, which was lying neatly on the bed, he looked devastatingly handsome.

She glanced again at the jacket on the bed. It had been carefully placed, so that the yellow rose of Devin's boutonniere lay on top, in no danger of being squashed.

He turned his head, as if he was expecting her. His eyebrow quirked up in the middle. The scars on his face moved in tandem with his lips as he grinned.

Darcie found Devin's eyebrow fascinating. Why wasn't he surprised? How could he *not* be surprised? She was dying, and he looked more amused than anything. She struggled to take it all in. Every thought had disappeared from her brain the moment she laid eyes on her pirate groomsman. Once again, she couldn't breathe.

Lack of oxygen, she decided. *That's what's making me stupid. No oxygen. Dying brain cells. No memory. Coma.*

She glanced down at the floor, trying to get control of herself. That's when her desperate gaze focused on Atticus, the goal of her quest. How quickly she had forgotten what she was looking for.

Devin didn't know what to make of the shocked look on Darcie's face.

"You found him," she gasped, the relief evident in her velvet voice.

Atticus was sitting on the floor, observing her with the same questioning look in his eyes as the man beside him. One look at the fluffy, perfect fur of the clean, dry dog who was still in the house—*still in the house*—and far away from the photograph shoot, made Darcie's knees a little weak.

"Actually, he found me," Devin admitted, giving her a look that warmed her from head to toe. "Do I still get a pie?" he asked.

"Hmph."

Darcie sank down onto the window seat, feeling a little dizzy. She forced herself to take slow, deep breaths. Her porcelain skin was devoid of color, her maroon lipstick in sharp contrast.

Devin's scars scrunched up in concern. "Say, are you all right? Your color is a little off." *But you're still the most freaking gorgeous woman I've ever seen.* He couldn't help the words that popped into his brain. They were the truth.

The maroon shade of Darcie's chiffon gown perfectly accented her coloring. Silver earrings dangled from her ears. Her dark eyes seemed even darker, making him more aware than ever of the haphazard sprinkling of caramel specks around her pupils. Her black hair was swept up into a stylish twist, showcasing the line of her neck. The one-shoulder neckline of the pleated bodice revealed her delicate collarbone as well as a pleasing expanse of smooth skin. The pleated waistband highlighted her trim waist. The chiffon skirt flowed smoothly over the contours of her hips, billowing behind her as she moved. The side slit in the material provided tantalizing glimpses of her legs. The subtle swirl of the dress's fabric was mesmerizing. Her dainty feet were encased in high-heeled silver sandals embellished with tiny, shimmering crystals.

She was a vision. Perfection. Something out of a man's most secret dreams and desires. The only thing that saved Devin from turning into a stammering moronic excuse for a human being was the fact that he had heard her coming down the hall, giving him time to prepare. Sort of. As usual, he fell back on humor. She inadvertently gave him the opening, and he had leaped on it. Asking about pie was pure genius, his way of deflecting the absolute paralysis that could result from an unexpected sighting of the goddess that was Darcie Finch. Right now, his goddess was babbling, and he was having a little difficulty following her nonstop monologue.

"I was afraid...Atticus and the creek. And the photos. And, I turned around, but he wasn't there. And I was supposed to watch him. And I forgot the clips for the veil, but they showed up anyway. I don't know how. And Grace's sandal...I was supposed to find the one that was missing but I forgot. And I don't know how it got upstairs or anything. It just appeared. By itself. And Grace thanked me, but I didn't have anything to do with it. It was that, that..." She paused and pointed at Atticus, sitting calmly beside Devin.

"Dog?" Devin asked politely.

"Yes. No. I don't even know anymore. Sometimes I don't think he's really a dog. He knows things. He's a step ahead of everyone."

Darcie finally paused, biting her lip in a gesture that usually belonged on her sister.

Atticus raised his doggie eyebrows at Devin in pure masculine sympathy.

Devin was amused in spite of himself, and more than a little concerned. He had never heard the self-possessed Miss Finch babble. He glanced out the window, searching for a distraction. "Darcie, it's time. Quick, or you'll miss it."

Hiking up her lovely dress so she wouldn't wrinkle it, Darcie turned around to sit on her knees on the window seat, leaning her arms on the sill. She was just in time because—as they watched—the bride came into view. "Oh, look, Devin! Aren't they gorgeous?"

You are gorgeous, Darcie Finch, he thought. And she didn't even realize it. She had absolutely no idea that the mere sight of her could turn him inside out with desire. Climbing up on her knees to look out of the window was something Amalie would have done. Devin found Darcie's eagerness to see her sister—and her total disregard for maintaining decorum—adorable.

Her elbows were propped on the windowsill, her nose practically touching the glass. Her gown flowed around her like a glorious waterfall. She was totally oblivious to her own allure. He wouldn't dare mention it when she was so worked up, but one day…one day he would tell her what she did to him. He was charmed…yet again. He was also in danger of missing the "first look," preferring his present view to anything he might see out the window.

She turned her head and met his eyes, her own sparkling with joy. He could see the worries of the last few hours had disappeared like morning mist ahead of a brilliant sunrise. He wanted to take the credit for that, but he sensed most of the credit belonged to a three-legged dog named Atticus.

"Here they go," she said.

She pinned her gaze to the path that separated the rose garden and the English garden. "Oh my gosh, I'm so nervous!"

She reached out, impulsively, and squeezed his hand.

Devin knew it wasn't planned, but instinctive. Just another piece of evidence affirming the strengthening connection between them. He took full advantage of her distraction, enveloping her small hand in his, enjoying the rightness of the moment. They watched as Grace, in a glorious display of lace, ruffles, and tulle, approached her groom, who stood with his back to her. On cue, Blane turned around to behold his bride. His eyes widened with masculine appreciation as he gently took her hand. Bringing it to his lips he planted a kiss on her palm, his eyes never leaving the enraptured eyes of his lovely bride. It was so blatantly possessive, so intimate that it felt almost wrong for them to have an audience.

"Oh, my." Darcie shivered. "I don't know if we should be watching this or not."

Her grip on Devin's hand tightened slightly. He returned the pressure, his thumb sliding rhythmically up and down the side of her hand in a gentle caress.

Blane leaned in to whisper something to his bride, breaking the sexual tension. Grace threw herself into his arms, hugging him for all she was worth. Both of them broke into delighted laughter…and a few tears. Blane handed Grace his handkerchief, and she dabbed lightly at her glowing eyes. The videographer and photographer worked feverishly to record every emotion.

Darcie turned to face Devin, a sweet smile blooming on her lips. Her eyes were shining with tears. "Oh, Devin, that was just perfect. *They're* just perfect, aren't they? And the wedding is going to be—"

"Perfect?" Devin raised an inquisitive eyebrow.

Darcie giggled, almost giddy with relief. The stress of the past few hours had miraculously disappeared in the presence of her pirate. "I was so afraid I would miss their first look, because I was searching for Atticus," Darcie confided. "Who would have guessed he would lead me to the perfect place to see the whole thing?"

"I think I owe him a debt of gratitude, too," Devin said softly.

"Why is that?"

"Because he brought you to me," he said simply, finally giving in to the desire to bring her hand to his mouth. He bypassed her palm—a man had to be original, after all—and placed a kiss on the inside of her wrist, just above the pearl bracelet.

Darcie stared at him, startled. His lips seemed to burn the delicate skin of her wrist. For once in her life, she was taken completely off guard. She didn't know what to say. Her eyes were impossibly wide, beckoning him closer.

Kiss her, you idiot, Devin told himself. *Kiss her. This is your chance.* But, he hesitated, held back by the force of his own conscience. *Well, hell. Sorry, Atticus,* he thought. *It's not that I don't appreciate the…*

Devin snapped back to the present. "Atticus," he said.

"What?" Darcie's head was still swimming in the wonder of his kiss on her wrist.

"Atticus," Devin said, urgently. "He's gone."

"Gone?" She looked around the room frantically. "Oh, no! He's gone! He can't be! We have to…"

The door to the rose garden slammed shut. They exchanged a horrified glance.

"The door, how did he…" Devin was shocked.

"I told you he wasn't really a dog!"

Darcie shrieked as she jumped off the window seat. She flew through the door of the bedroom, tugging Devin behind her. They ran into the rose garden just in time to see Atticus' scraggly tail disappear behind the last hedge of the English garden.

"We've got to catch him before he can get to the photographers," Devin said, loudly, as the rose bushes flashed by. He hadn't run in an unfamiliar area since he lost his eye…and the rose garden was full of uneven stones and furrows. He had to trust Darcie to lead the way. He had no choice but to follow her anyway. She had yet to let go of his hand.

They rounded the corner of the hedge, pausing to check out the terrain. To their left stood the site of the ceremony. One hundred and twenty white chairs were sitting in straight rows in anticipation of the guests who would be arriving shortly. To their right was a slight rise that dipped down the hill leading to the…

"…*Creek!*" they said in unison, their voices blending together in horror.

"There."

Devin pointed to the area farthest from them. They watched Atticus' hindquarters disappear over the rise.

Devin started off in pursuit. The lawn was expansive, with few obstacles. There was no danger in him taking the lead.

"Wait!" screeched Darcie, pulling on his hand to stop him. "My shoes!"

She let Devin support her with one hand while she slipped off her shoes with the other. She dropped the two shoes on a corner at the end of the cobblestone path. "Go, go, go!" she yelled, barefoot.

Devin started again. Somehow, Darcie managed to keep up with his long stride as they sprinted up the rise. They arrived at the top, breathing hard, attempting once again to sight their quarry. The serene, elegant scene before them was cringeworthy.

Grace and Blane stood quietly on the bank at the edge of the creek…a beautiful bridal couple, blissfully unaware of the charging, three-legged runaway train that was hurtling toward them. What a spectacular wreck it was going to be!

Lou was there, of course, guarding her creation like a lion guarding her cub. She had just finished adjusting Grace's dress: the beautiful white train was spread out behind the bride in waves of elegant ruffles. The photographer's assistant was holding the tip of the veil, with instructions to release it the moment the photograph was taken. It billowed behind the bride in a dainty cloud of lace. Blane looked the dashing hero in his black tux. The backdrop of autumn splendor was a wedding gift from nature that couldn't be bought. Or recreated.

"It's too late," Devin said, fatalistically. "There's nothing we can do."

Darcie wailed. "He won't be able to stop…They're going straight into the creek!"

Darcie's head was already filled with images of the aftermath. Grace's dress, ruined. Grace's beloved shoes, ruined. Blane's tux, muddy and unwearable. Lou, screaming like a banshee. Crushed by the destruction of her design. All of them blaming her. Pointing at her. Knowing it was all her fault.

She couldn't bear to watch. She released Devin's hand, covered her eyes with both of hers. Then she buried her face in Devin's chest. Devin's arms came around her in a comforting manner. He couldn't look away. Atticus was chaos personified.

Wrapped in Devin's arms, Darcie screwed her eyes shut. She waited for angry voices and shouts of anguish. Time seemed to stop. She waited. And waited. Until…

"Darcie, look," Devin said urgently.

"I can't look. I just can't…. How awful is it?" she moaned. "Just tell me."

"Look," Devin said again, relief evident in his voice. "Darcie…it's all right."

She turned her head, peering through her fingers. Then she lowered her hands. Opened both eyes wide. And stared at the improbable scene in front of her.

Somehow, some way—probably by the grace of God—Atticus had stopped in time. There was no collision. The innocent-looking canine sat on Blane's foot, posing for a formal family portrait. He looked as though he was *supposed* to be there, close beside his humans. Blane and Grace were smiling happily, unaware of how close they had come to total disaster.

"C'mon, Darcie."

Devin released her reluctantly from his embrace…everything but her hand. He towed her down the hill, her fingers securely entwined with his.

"Thanks for bringing Atta-boy," Blane said as they approached the group. "We should have thought of having a family portrait ourselves."

"Hope he hasn't been too much trouble, Darce." Grace leaned down to scratch Atticus' single ear. "I can't tell you how much I appreciate you taking care of him. You, too, Devin."

"No problem," Devin said, calmly, shaking his head at Darcie as she opened her mouth to speak.

She closed it without saying a word.

"Darcie Finch!" Lou exploded in outrage. "What the hell happened to your hair and makeup?"

"I'm…um…not sure," Darcie mumbled as all eyes turned to her. She heard the click of a camera. At that moment, she realized that the entire fiasco was being preserved for posterity. What she must look like, standing there barefoot in the grass, pieces of hair falling in her face....Lord only knew what state her makeup was in. She looked Devin straight in the eye and grinned. She didn't care. She really didn't care what she looked like. The only thing that mattered was that the bride and groom were perfect.

Devin grinned back, letting her know he understood, even if no one else did. "You look fine to me," Devin said, agreeably. In truth, he had quite a few words to describe Miss Darcie Finch in that instant. Fine. Very fine. Beyond fine. Sexy. Amazing. Sexy. Delicious. Sexy. Was he repeating himself? Part of him—well, most of him, actually—wished that *he* was the reason for her tousled state.

"Darcie Finch, you are coming with me. Now."

Lou grabbed Darcie's hand. She dragged her up the rise, fussing all the while.

"I can't leave you alone for five minutes..." she said, her voice trailing away.

Darcie paused at the top, turning to wave, before Lou yanked on her arm. Then, they disappeared over the rise.

Devin watched them go. After waving at Darcie he turned back to the Boss-man and his bride, slightly unnerved by their intense scrutiny. If they only knew. His eyes fell on Atticus. That self-possessed canine was sporting a self-satisfied smirk on his perfectly clean but very fluffy face.

CHAPTER THIRTY

𝒜 short while later, Devin returned to the scene of their narrowly averted disaster. This time, however, instead of his delectable Pirate Queen, he was accompanied by the male contingent of the wedding party. The bride and groom were already there, having just finished their respective family pictures. The photographer had to be thrilled to have the rippling waters of Honeysuckle Creek, beautiful fall leaves, and equally beautiful mountains as a backdrop. From any angle, the view was spectacular.

The wedding party looked fairly spectacular, too, Devin thought glumly, with one exception…the guy with the ruined face and the eye patch. He braced himself for the inevitable feeling of dread. For most of his life, he hadn't thought twice about being photographed. But since the attack, even harmless selfies with his daughter filled him with trepidation. Devin tried not to dwell on his appearance. He really tried. And, most days, he managed to forget about his scarred visage entirely. But there was something about having his photograph taken—the cameras, the posing, the smiling, the permanent record of his disfigurement—well…it was just…hard.

His dismal thoughts disappeared, however, the moment he once again caught sight of Miss Darcie Finch. He grinned. She was wearing her elegant shoes again. Her hair was properly pinned again, too: every strand was in place. She was perfectly polished. Completely put together. Stunning. There was no sign of the tousled, determined, shoeless beauty who chased out-of-control canines to protect her beloved sister and future brother-in-law's wedding pictures. Until she grinned, obviously reading his mind. Having a secret with Darcie Finch, Devin realized, was extremely satisfying.

Not looking at Darcie every second the photographer spent posing the wedding group, however, required extreme focus and concentration on Devin's part. Such a difficult challenge kept his mind relatively free from the fear that had haunted him for months, namely, ruining Blane and Grace's wedding pictures. He already felt like the ugly duckling in a group of beautiful swans. He didn't want to call any more attention to himself by staring at Darcie in every photograph, instead of smiling to the camera.

It had been a battle, but he had emerged the victor. Only after the ordeal was over did he realize that his efforts *not* to look at Darcie kept him from feeling self-conscious. Another obstacle overcome because of his guardian angel. *No,* he considered. *Not angel, exactly.* He watched Darcie engage in a spirited exchange with her brother during their maid of honor/best man photo. Judging by the disgusted look on Joey's face and the bright smile on Darcie's, he could see who had emerged the victor. Devin grinned. No guardian angel was half as spirited as his guardian…pirate. Yes, he decided, *guardian pirate* was better. Guardian pirate with a devilish sense of humor. Something like that.

After the photographer exhausted her ideas for photographs, there was nothing left to do but wait. The wedding party headed back to the grand foyer. They were to remain out of sight under penalty of suffering a heinous death until the time came to walk down the aisle. That order—it was not a request—was issued by Maggie Parker, wedding director extraordinaire.

The groomsmen were the first to arrive in the foyer; they were soon comfortably ensconced on the sofas closest to Mrs. Hofmann's seemingly endless buffet. The bridesmaids arrived next. They were standing together, a lovely group in their Lou Boggs' designer originals. One by one, each handed her gorgeous bouquet of yellow roses and mixed fall flowers to Charlie Ray and Evon, Honeysuckle Creek's legendary florists, for safekeeping.

"Hey, guys, look," Zack said with more enthusiasm than he had exhibited since seeing Devin's sister, Lydia.

"What now?" Roger asked irritably.

He stood right in front of Zack, adjusting the young man's bow tie, which was tilted slightly toward his right shoulder.

Zack indicated the bridesmaids gathered across the room. "Do you get it?"

Now Roger was annoyed *and* confused. "What are we supposed to get?"

"C'mon, y'all," Zack encouraged them. "This is easy. Don't you see it?"

"Give us a hint," Evander said evenly. He always enjoyed watching Zack's mind work.

"What color are the bridesmaids' dresses?" Zack asked.

"I think Lou said they were maroon," Evander volunteered. Then a grin broke over his face. "Good one, Zack." He glanced at Devin, who was smiling, too.

Roger was out of patience. "Would somebody please tell me what he's talking about?"

Devin took pity on him. "Five bridesmaids in maroon dresses. Maroon Five."

"Maroon Five, get it?"

Zack began his best Adam Levine impression of "Sugar," his antics starting to attract an audience.

Devin thought Zack's reference to the popular singing group was pretty creative.

Roger wasn't quite as appreciative. "That was a little weak, kid, even for you."

"Aw, give me some credit, Raj. You're just mad because you didn't get it," Zack said, unable to resist pointing out the obvious.

Roger raised his eyebrows in mock disapproval. "You're awfully busy checking out the ladies today. What's Emma going to think when she gets here?"

Zack's face fell a bit. "Emma's not coming to the wedding."

Joey and Darcie joined the group just in time to hear Zack's words.

"Why not?" Evander asked carefully.

"I guess because Emma was my *high school* girlfriend," the teenager said, trying desperately to act like his cool and casual self.

"Oh." Evander nodded, exchanging a glance with Roger. "When did this happen?"

"Last night, after the rehearsal dinner. She called me and told me she wasn't coming today and…" Zack shrugged his shoulders. "I figured it was better, you know, *for her*…since she's away at school. Didn't want her to feel she had to come home all the time just to see me. Thought it was time to let her go."

"She broke up with you, didn't she?" Joey interrupted, but kindly.

Zack sighed. "Yeah."

"Oh, Zack," Darcie said, giving him a hug. "I'm sorry. It's her loss, honey."

Lou and Dom wandered over, quickly gathering the gist of the conversation.

"It's okay." Zack tried to rally. "Lots of other fish in the sea, right?" he asked, hopefully.

"You bet," Joey said, punching his young friend playfully in the arm. "Whole schools of them." He was rewarded by Zack's first real smile since Roger mentioned Emma.

"Don't you worry about it, Zack," Lou said with a wink. "You're a catch."

"You're not alone, Zack," Evander said. "I bet everyone here has a high school breakup story."

"That's right," Roger admitted wryly. "My high school girlfriend's getting married today."

Zack perked up a little. "Oh, yeah. I forgot about that."

"My high school boyfriend broke up with me on the phone," Darcie added, shooting Dom a sideways glance.

Devin didn't like where this conversation was going.

"Who's the idiot who was dumb enough to break up with you?" Zack couldn't believe such a person existed.

"He's not an idiot." Darcie's eyes were brimming with wicked humor. "He's a pharmacist."

All eyes turned to Dominic Parker, who was studying the ceiling, trying to look as innocent as possible.

"*That* pharmacist?" Zack was amazed at Darcie's tidbit of information.

Devin was not. He had sensed all along there was something between them.

"To be fair, it was sort of mutual, Darcie," Dom said, in mock disapproval. "Don't make it sound like I broke your heart or anything."

Darcie patted his arm sympathetically. "I know, Dom. I was only kidding. I just wanted Zack to know that there's hope for a friendship with Emma someday, if he wants one."

The conversations fractured after that. The group broke up and spread out. Members of each family wandered in to wait with them. Dom and Darcie exchanged a lingering glance that no one else noticed. Devin, himself, wouldn't have seen it except for the fact that he was well on his way to falling in love with Miss Darcie Finch. Hence, he was constantly attuned to her every move. The look she exchanged with Dom was one of high regard, shared memories, and, perhaps, a little bit of an apology.

Maggie entered the grand foyer from the hallway just then, interrupting Devin's analysis. "The first shuttle is coming up the driveway," she announced with a smile.

Will and Rafe, seated by the fireplace, stood up to join her. They were the official greeters. Their job was to meet the shuttle bus at the covered walkway connecting the garage to the main house. After directing the guests toward the gazebo, Dom and his brother, Ric—serving as ushers—assisted with the seating of the guests.

On his way out, Dom winked at Darcie, touching her arm lightly. "Have fun, Darce. And don't you dare cry."

"Hmph."

She wrinkled her nose at Dom before crossing the room to answer her mother's summons.

Devin's initial suspicions that Dominic Parker was, or had been, important to Darcie Finch were spot on. The good news was that their relationship ended long ago. While that was a plus, his intuition was screaming. He knew he was being irrational, that he had no claim on any part of Darcie Finch at the moment. He wasn't part of her past. He couldn't be part of her present. Or, by virtue of his own ties to the self-serving Mallory Merritt, her future. Why, then, couldn't he stop the bone-deep desire to claim it all? He wanted all of her. He begrudged anything that might tie her to another man, no matter when it had occurred. Worst of all, his gut feeling was telling him that, once upon a time, his Pirate Queen and the mild-mannered pharmacist had been lovers.

Dom strolled by Devin, oblivious to his intense perusal. Dom's face was open and honest, his eyes without guile. He nodded in friendly greeting, his smile genuine and kind. Dom was obviously a man with a clear conscience. A good person. An all-around nice guy.

Devin's eye followed Dom's retreating figure as he walked out the door. At that moment—his own conscience conveniently absent—Devin embraced his pirate persona. He desired nothing more than to steal away with his lovely damsel while leaving the good-natured Dominic Parker to walk the plank.

Devin's fantasy was short-lived, broken up by the appearance of his own tiny princess. He hadn't seen his little girl since Diana whisked her inside for a snack after her part in the group photographs was complete. Amalie had been about as cooperative as a four-year-old flower girl could be, behavior Devin attributed to her nanny's vigilance. Diana made sure Amalie had ample time to rest, hopefully avoiding a tired-child meltdown later. She stayed with Amalie every minute. Devin was extremely thankful for Diana. The devotion of Amalie's nanny stood in sharp contrast to the indifference of Amalie's mother. Mallory had not sought out her daughter since her dramatic arrival.

Devin watched his daughter skip into the grand foyer. The way Amalie's face lit up when she saw him made his fatherly heart skip a beat. She ran to him, as oblivious to her fine attire as she was to his scars. He scooped Amalie up, swinging her around. The sight of his little girl filled him with joy, as it always did. She hugged him hard, chattering about her day so far. They hadn't been able to talk much during the photography session.

Amalie had spent so much time with Darcie during the session, the photographer assumed the little girl was hers. Hers and Devin's. If only, he thought, wistfully. After the photographer's assistant asked if Devin would like a picture with his wife and daughter for the third time, Devin finally understood her mistake. When he explained the situation, the embarrassed assistant apologized. She politely asked Devin if he wanted to text his real wife to see if Mallory might want to come down so they could take some family pictures. Devin graciously declined the offer. He knew—without asking— that Mallory would never willingly pose for a photograph with her Monster.

Amalie, however, was thrilled to be in photographs with her daddy. She looked adorable in a dress with a white satin bodice, scooped neckline, and elbow-length sleeves. A froth of white tulle skirts extended from her waist to the floor, and a maroon bow had been expertly tied around her waist by none other than the dress-designer herself. The longed-for tiara sat in the middle of her coronet of blond braids, much to the little girl's delight. According to Diana, Amalie had spent more time twirling in front of the big mirror upstairs than the bride. It was hard to imagine that any royal princess ever enjoyed herself more.

Darcie was enchanted. The fact that Devin unashamedly adored his daughter was another irresistible quality she added to her growing list, titled "Reasons Devin Merritt Might Be the Ideal Man." The contrast between the innocent child and Devin's piratical appearance made Darcie smile. She was drawn to the pair as a moth to a flame, but she held back. She still hadn't recovered from the assistant's error of thinking she, Devin, and Amalie were a family. Or from the realization that she would like nothing better than for that to be true.

Seeking a distraction from such wishful thinking, Darcie glanced around the grand foyer. Her eyes settled on her great-grandmother, currently holding court on the sofa closest to the fireplace and looking, for all the world, like a queen on her throne. Grandma Sofi was deep in conversation with curly-haired Ana Martin. If the look in Ana's eyes was any indication, the petite bridesmaid was awestruck—though slightly terrified—to find herself the recipient of Grandma Sofi's attentions. Darcie couldn't help but wonder if she, herself, would ever have the regal bearing and poise of Sofia Hanover.

The elderly lady was stylishly attired in a full-length gown of dark purple. The bodice and long sleeves were made entirely of lace over satin. The long flowing skirt covered the tips of her silver pumps. A jeweled belt encircled her waist. Very few wrinkles marred the smooth skin of her face. Her white hair—twisted into a complicated knot atop her head—was still thick and full. Her makeup was perfectly applied. Her nails were manicured. She was wearing a long string of pearls and matching earrings. She was elegance personified.

Grandma Sofi clutched her favorite cane, the one with the bird's head on the crown. The bird's eyes were brilliant green stones. Darcie's mother's eyes. And her sister, Gracie's. Once, long ago, young Darcie Finch had wished for green eyes, too. Grandma Sofi swore the bird's glittering eyes weren't real emeralds, but her youngest great-granddaughter had never believed her. Maybe that was why Darcie was still so fascinated by her great-grandmother's cane. Or maybe not. More likely, it was because she wasn't allowed to touch it. Then or now. Grace and Joey couldn't touch it either. That had always helped.

"Gamma Ollie! Papa Rob!" Amalie squealed, drawing Darcie's attention straight back to the little girl's father.

Devin chuckled as Amalie struggled to extricate herself from his arms. He put her down but not before planting a quick kiss on her cheek. She skipped away to be enveloped in the warm embraces of Allana and Robert Merritt.

Devin strolled over to Darcie, taking advantage of the opportunity. "And just like that, I'm second fiddle," he said, ruefully shaking his head.

"Oh, Laurence, you'll never be that girl's second fiddle to anybody, and you know it." Darcie shook her head, too. "Except maybe to the man she marries," she couldn't resist adding.

Devin drew himself up dramatically. "Marriage? Absolutely not. I have decided that Amalie will be four years old forever."

Darcie raised her eyebrows. "Little girls grow up, Laurence." Her voice took on the husky tone that never failed to fire Devin's blood. "I did."

"Is that why your father is looking at me like he wants to cut off my head and feed me to the squirrels?" Devin asked. He glanced at Joe Finch, who was, indeed, glowering at him from across the room.

"Bears," Darcie said, matter-of-factly.

"What?"

"Daddy would use bears. Squirrels don't eat people, Laurence. He would feed your body to the bears," she informed him with a sassy smile. "Don't take it personally. He looks at every male who talks to me like that. He's the same way with Grace. You can ask Blane. And if a guy looks too long at Mama, well…you don't want to be him." Her smile turned into a grin as she waved to Joe and blew him a kiss.

The warning in Joe's gaze melted into one of pure love as he observed his daughter's antics. As Amalie's father, Devin understood completely. He even felt a touch of empathy. As Darcie's whatever-he-was, however, Joe's fixed attention was just a bit disconcerting.

Juli floated over to her husband. She was adorned in her mother-of-the-bride dress of shimmering gray taffeta with long, sheer sleeves. The cuffs of each sleeve, also taffeta, were encrusted with rhinestones arrayed in an elegant, symmetrical pattern. The chiffon overskirt was iridescent with undercurrents of violet that rippled as she walked. The portrait neckline framed her lovely, oval face. Her black hair was piled on her head, with a few curling strands left at her nape. She wore a double strand of pearls at her throat, and on her wrists. Her ears were adorned with delicate dangling pearl earrings. Joe's attention was wholly diverted by the woman he cherished the most, leaving Devin free.

"You should have been there when…"

Darcie stopped. Her attention was captured by a flurry of activity on the balcony.

"Oh my," she said, her eyes widening.

Devin felt the malevolent presence of his wife before he saw her. It was as if a snake had slithered into their midst, stirring the stilled waters. The ensuing ripples would soon grow large enough to encompass the entire pond. Sure enough, when Devin looked up, she was standing there.

CHAPTER THIRTY-ONE

Mallory commanded attention as if she was Evita Peron on the balcony of the Casa Rosada. Devin wouldn't have been a bit surprised if she started to sing "Don't Cry for Me, Argentina." She gazed out over the grand foyer as if every person in the room was there just to see her. Her smile was calculating. Her shrewd eyes glittered. Every move she made as she glided down the staircase was deliberately done to draw the eye.

Mallory wore white. In Devin's opinion, it was a poor choice for an October wedding. Her Grecian dress was deceptively simple: sheer chiffon material over a white lining. The clean lines and pure, white color gave her a fresh, almost ethereal look…from a distance. On closer inspection the lining beneath the sheer fabric looked like cheap shiny spandex material. It was plastered to her every curve. It was also a few inches too short for good taste, skimming the tops of her thighs, barely concealing her derriere. A deep V-neckline slashed all the way to her waist, barely cover the sides of her breasts. Her blond hair was teased on top and pulled to the side in one long, blond curl. Long, gold earrings hung from her ears. She resembled a temple virgin, willing to sacrifice herself on the altar of pleasure.

What the hell?

Devin couldn't move. His wife looked like a high-class hooker. He was as horrified as everyone else, unable to do anything but wait to see what Mallory might do next.

"Precious," she called, almost halfway down the stairs. "Where is my precious baby? Come to Mommy, precious."

Mallory hurried down the remaining stairs, her hand lightly tracing the bannister. She stopped at the bottom of the staircase, gracefully extending her arms in the direction of her reluctant child.

"Come to Mommy!"

Amalie remained rooted where she stood. The happy, little princess of moments before disappeared. In her place stood a solemn, wary child.

Standing beside her, Robert set both hands on his granddaughter's shoulders, gently propelling her forward. Amalie dutifully walked from the safe haven of her grandparents, stopping to stand about two feet in front of her mother.

Diana casually moved nearer the hallway that led to Blane's study. "Excuse me," she said, softly, as she displaced Joey, who was leaning against the side of the staircase. Putting her hand on his arm, she pulled him toward her, neatly switching places. She backed up until she was almost hidden under the staircase.

Joey moved closer, obviously intrigued. "What are you doing?"

"Saving all of us a lot of unnecessary drama," Diana explained with a grimace.

Joey quickly surveyed the situation. "Okay," he replied agreeably.

As a result of the curving staircase, Amalie could see Diana, but Mallory could not. The next few minutes unfolded like a carefully choreographed dance.

Amalie watched her nanny's every move, as did the speechless occupants of the room.

When Diana nodded, Amalie walked into her mother's waiting arms. Mallory made a great show of hugging her child. She held the little girl loosely, however, preventing Amalie from touching her dress.

Diana held up the fingers of her right hand, one at a time, while mouthing the numbers: *One. Two. Three. Four. Five.* When her nanny got to five, Amalie released her mother, taking a step back.

Mallory straightened up, regarding her child expectantly.

Diana mouthed the words, *I missed you.*

Amalie didn't say anything.

Standing alongside Diana, Joey couldn't believe what he was seeing. "This is insane."

"Hush," Diana hissed. Then, to Amalie, she mouthed the words again: *I missed you.*

"I missed you, Mommy," Amalie said tonelessly.

"Oh, precious," Mallory gushed. "Mommy missed you, too. You look very pretty in your fancy dress."

You look pretty, too, mouthed Diana. She gave Amalie an encouraging nod.

"You look pretty, too," Amalie said, with all the enthusiasm of a child repeating multiplication tables.

Mallory preened at the praise. "Thank you, precious."

Joey asked disgustedly, "Does she call Amalie 'Precious' because she can't remember her name?"

Diana gave Amalie another nod. "Probably," she answered.

Amalie waited, patiently, her eyes on Diana.

But Mallory was tired of playing mommy. She straightened to her full height, relieved that her distasteful parental duty was behind her. She smiled, extremely pleased that Amalie had performed well in front of their audience. "Run away, precious. Mommy's busy." She immediately dismissed her child as if the little girl was an unwanted pet.

Amalie didn't move immediately. She didn't understand exactly where she was supposed to run. She didn't want to run away, the little girl decided. She wanted to be a flower girl and throw petals and stand with Miss Darcie and Miss Lou. She looked up at her mother, her blue eyes full of obstinance.

She wouldn't run away. She wouldn't. Her mommy couldn't make her! The determined little girl stuck out her chin.

Mallory's impatience threatened to burst forth, audience or no audience. Her displeasure with Amalie's failure to comply made her voice particularly harsh. "Why are you still standing there?" she hissed, looking around for the person who might rid her of her annoying offspring. "Di-a-na!" When her child's nanny didn't appear out of thin air, she glanced around again. Realizing that the majority of those in the room were still watching her—most of them with disapproval in their eyes—she quickly changed her compulsory voice to one of gentle criticism. "Poor dear, she's always so very busy doing *other* things just when I need her." Mallory smiled sweetly; but the expression on her face screamed her true opinion: Diana was the most unreliable nanny in the world.

"I'm right here, Mallory," Diana said politely, walking forward to join her ever-critical employer. To her amazement, Joey Finch moved with her.

Joey was feeling more sympathy for Mallory's unfortunate spouse than he would have thought possible a few hours ago. His deep-seated sense of justice—the one that made him such a passionate defense lawyer—was alive and well. He found himself itching to find a way to free Devin and his daughter—Diana, too, for that matter—from their untenable situation. Mallory had no idea that her display had just gained her husband a very powerful ally.

"I'd like a word, if you're not *too busy*." Mallory directed her remarks to Diana while giving Joey a speculative glance. "I can certainly understand your…distraction." Her taunting gaze looked with feminine approval at Joey's impressive physique, black hair, and snapping dark eyes.

Joey slipped his hands in his pockets, serious and unsmiling. He stared right back, sending Mrs. Mallory Merritt the clear message that he was neither interested nor available.

Unused to being rebuffed so blatantly, Mallory set her hand on Diana's arm. In response, Diana gently clasped Amalie's hand. Then Mallory pulled them both into the hallway for a whispered conference.

Devin had spent the last few minutes in an agony of shame. Mallory possessed the power in social situations like this, and she knew it. He couldn't stop her unless he wanted an ugly scene fraught with enormous consequences. A wedding was not the place for that…not that there was a good place for that. So, Devin was forced to stay on the sidelines, doing nothing. His hands were tied, and he hated it. He hated looking helpless. He hated losing the respect of people he cared about. But, most of all, he hated that his beloved, little girl had to watch her nanny's hand signals in order to interact with her own mother. How could he have a familial relationship like this?

All of his life, his family relationships had been solid as a rock. Not only did his mother and father adore their children, they adored each other. He had witnessed their mutual admiration and respect every day of his life growing up. He had always anticipated having the same interactions with his own wife and child. Instead, here he was in this pitiful farce. And, worse, he had pulled poor Diana into his mess. Mallory would kill Diana if she found out about the pantomime that had just occurred behind her back. The thought of the position his cousin was in, voluntary though it might be, sickened him even further.

He could almost hear the unspoken questions swirling around the room as the current episode of the reality TV show "Dysfunctional Families" played out. He could certainly imagine what they were all thinking:

Why doesn't Devin do something?

Devin knows what's going on. Why doesn't he stop this?

What kind of father just stands there…? And so on and so on.

Every person in the room—from Grandma Sofi to young Zack Kimel—liked children. It was obvious from the way they had treated Amalie ever since she bounced through the door. They were kind people. He was willing to bet every one of them would step up and stand as an advocate for any child who was in trouble or unloved. *Or neglected by her rotten, self-absorbed mother.* The only exception was, apparently, him.

Mallory glided back into the grand foyer. She had obviously finished her chat with Diana. *Uh-oh,* Devin thought with a sinking feeling in his stomach. *The viper is loose and searching for another victim to bite.* It was an ugly analogy, but he couldn't help it. He often watched silently as his wife worked a room. He had noticed it before; she did it to her own friends—even to Desiree. Mallory dropped malicious hints. She planted critical ideas in the minds of her victims. She landed subtle blows to their self-confidence. Of course, all of her toxic negativity was accomplished under the guise of genuine interest and friendship. She left each casualty pondering some new insecurity as she walked away.

Tearing others down to build yourself up, Devin thought. *That's how you do it, isn't it, Mallory?*

Today, she planned her attack carefully, avoiding those who had stood up to her in the past. He knew she would have only a perfunctory conversation with Joe and Juli. Ian and Alina would barely rate a greeting. Rafe's opinion of her was obvious; Mallory would ignore him completely. Even the bride and groom, whose wedding celebration she planned to enjoy, would not receive much notice. Mallory's unsuccessful bid to be a bridesmaid had revealed to her the steel behind Grace's sweet smile. And she was probably still smarting at Blane's defense of his housekeeper. Devin's vicious wife wasn't interested in the rules of the game. If she couldn't win, she wouldn't play.

Devin sighed. He was very careful to avoid the eyes of Darcie, who was still standing beside him. He wasn't sure he wanted to see the expression on her face, or to hear what she had to say about Mallory's performance. He could tell by her intense stillness that she was processing what she had seen. She, of course, would be the biggest child advocate of them all. Her save-the-world tendencies wouldn't allow for anything else. He had no doubt that, even now, her fine mind was running through various solutions. Or maybe not.

Maybe, he was wrong. Maybe she was repulsed by his blatant inadequacies as a father. Maybe she had decided he wasn't the man she thought he was. Or maybe…No, he decided. He wasn't going there. He would go somewhere else instead. He would play a little game in his head. A game that had gotten him through many social outings with Mallory. He called it "Places I Would Rather Be Than Here." He closed his eye, picturing the scene.…

MACEE MCNEILL

He would rather be on a tropical island, sitting on a beach chair and listening to the surf lap against the shore. He could feel the sun on his face and smell the tropical flowers. He noticed that his delicious tropical drink was gone. He looked around for a waiter, only to see a man in a white suit rapidly approaching.

"I have some bad news, sir," the man said.

"Seriously?" he asked in disbelief. What the hell? Who gets bad news in a daydream? Was he really that unlucky? "Lay it on me," he said, defeated.

"Your wife has been eaten by sharks," the waiter said. In his hand he held out one of Mallory's elaborately painted fake fingernails. "This is the only thing that was left."

No, no, no! Devin scolded, remembering his promise to himself. *Too graphic. Let's try that again....*

"I have some bad news, sir," the man said.

"Seriously?" he asked in disbelief. What the hell? Who gets bad news in a daydream? Was he really that unlucky? "Lay it on me," he said, defeated.

"Your wife wouldn't listen to the warnings. She and her friend took the boat out anyway."

"I see," he said, quietly nodding his head. How typical of Mallory to disregard all warnings.

The waiter continued: "We called the Coast Guard, but they can't rescue her until the Category 5 hurricane comes through. I'm sorry, sir, but it doesn't look good."

No, Devin thought. *That's not right, either. Too complicated. And the hurricane kind of lowers me to her level. Redo....*

UNMASKING THE HEART

"I have some bad news, sir," the man said.

"Seriously?" he asked in disbelief. What the hell? Who gets bad news in a daydream? Was he really that unlucky? "Lay it on me," he said, defeated.

"I'm sorry, sir, but I have a note from your wife. She's run off with her paddle-board instructor. She said to tell you the divorce papers will be in the mail."

He relaxed back in his chair, secure in the knowledge that all was right with the world....A beautiful woman walked down the beach toward him. She was wearing a white, flowing dress. She had flowers in her hair. She was holding the hand of a little, blond girl, similarly attired. His heart leapt. He knew exactly what was happening. He was a free man—and she was waiting for him. They would be a family.

She came closer, more beautiful than he could believe. She was so close he could see the caramel specks in her warm, luminous eyes. She opened her lovely lips to speak. He strained to hear the music of her glorious voice.

"Emotional abandonment," she said incongruously...."Devin. Devin, are you listening to me?"

He opened his eye to see her perfect features in the grand foyer of Heart's Ease. Not on some tropical shore. *Damn.*

Darcie's eyes were wide and determined. "The grounds are emotional abandonment."

Devin sighed, putting on the heavy yoke of responsibility once again, even while a small part of him was still enjoying her light, tropical scent. "Emotional abandonment is almost impossible to prove, Darcie. You know that."

"I know, but it seems so obvious." Darcie was frustrated. "There is no real connection between your daughter and her biological mother. It's all for show."

Devin raised his eyebrows. "I appreciate the thought, Darcie. I really do. But, well, my uncles, my cousins…we've all been through it so many times. Looking and looking for something. Anything. Some tiny loophole. There isn't one." *Which makes me the world's biggest idiot, by the way.*

Her face fell in disappointment. He wished he wasn't enjoying the rosy flush on Darcie's soft cheeks quite so ardently. He also wished he didn't want to touch her soft skin the way he had earlier. Had it only been this morning? It seemed like an emotional lifetime ago. He was so involved in his own thoughts that his legally espoused wife was standing in front of him before he realized it.

"Hello, Monster," Mallory said, her soft smile all for him. "Aren't you going to introduce me to this *terribly* entertaining woman who has so graciously *monopolized* your attention since I walked into the room."

Well, hell. What am I supposed to say to that? Devin knew then that he was doomed. "Mallory," he managed, "this is Darcie Finch, Grace's sister. Darcie, this is Mallory. My wife."

Darcie met Mallory head on, calmly hiding her initial reaction. Truth be told, she was surprised by the undercurrent of venom in Mallory's seemingly innocuous phrases. *"Terribly entertaining"? "Graciously monopolized"? Ooh, Mallory, you are good,* Darcie thought. What Mallory didn't know, however, was that any Southern girl who was worth her salt could play syntax games. And play them well. Darcie had learned that skill from the cradle.

Assuming her best Southern belle persona, Darcie pinned a bright smile on her face. She reached out, taking both of Mallory's hands in her own.

Ready. Aim. Fire.

"Well, bless your heart, honey, I'm not talking to a monster, I'm talking to your husband, Devin." She squeezed Mallory's hands gently. Her nemesis lost her balance for a moment at Darcie's unexpected kindness.

Direct hit.

Mallory recovered quickly. Her high-pitched giggle caused several guests to look around curiously. Satisfied that she had garnered some attention,

Mallory launched her next volley. "Then, Miss Finch, you must be a witch, because he's obviously caught in your spell. Aren't you, Devin dear?"

Devin had the good sense to remain silent.

"Maybe I am," Darcie agreed evenly, squeezing Mallory's hands once more before letting them go. *Oh, Mallory, if you only knew.*

Mallory hadn't faced many opponents who refused to back down. She let her gaze travel from Darcie's head to her toes. Her voice grew a little louder: "I have to admit that I am surprised at what I see, Miss Finch. I've heard about your brilliant mind and what a wonderful addition you're going to be to the law community when you pass the bar. The lawyers at Merritt never stop talking about wanting to hire you after you graduate. But after seeing you, I have to wonder exactly what it is they want to hire." Mallory's eyes glowed with malice, certain that Darcie would crumble under such an explicit onslaught.

Darcie wanted to laugh. *Oh, Mallory, is that the best you can do? I've seen better efforts at middle school cotillion.* She decided to sound dense. "Why, Mrs. Merritt. They're hiring me for my legal skills, of course. Why else would they want to hire me?" The very next moment she forced herself to gasp, as if the real import of Mallory's words had just dawned on her. "You mean..." She hesitated. "You mean because I'm...attractive?"

Mallory gleefully jumped on her question. "Miss Finch," she sneered. "You and I both know that you are not merely attractive. A beautiful woman like you will *never* be taken seriously by any man. Or woman, for that matter. Particularly in a legal setting. The talk will be devastating for you, poor dear. Innuendos. Rumors. Water cooler talk. Bedroom games. I'm sure you're already *very* familiar with that sort of thing, though. Aren't you?"

Mallory could barely contain her triumph. She was almost giddy with victory. Darcie Finch was putty in her hands. She repeated herself one more time, for emphasis: "It's a shame, really. All those brains hidden in all that beauty. So sad no one will *ever* take you seriously."

Darcie tilted her head, thoughtfully, as if pondering the sad truths the woman in front of her had just revealed. "Mrs. Merritt, do *you* think men—or *women*, too, for that matter—think that *you're* an attractive woman?"

Mallory's outraged vanity responded immediately. "Of course people think I'm attractive. How could you even ask such a question?"

Darcie almost smiled. *Mallory, you're such an amateur. You're making this too easy.*

"Oh, honey," she said, seriously. "That's the *real* problem, isn't it? Oh, you poor little thing." She spoke in a sugary sweet tone, full of pity. Devin had never heard her use it before. "Nobody takes *you* seriously, do they, honey? Men *or* women. That must be *so* hard to deal with. Now I understand why you're so bitter, bless your little heart."

Pftt. Darcie triumphantly blew away the smoke billowing from the barrel of her imaginary rifle.

Mallory looked at Darcie in stupefied shock, as if she couldn't understand what had just happened. She couldn't even speak coherently. "Why, you… you…you little…" She could only sputter,

"*Basta!*" Grandma Sofi said in her heavily accented voice. She rose, majestically, from her place on the sofa. Her face was expressionless as she clutched her cane and approached her granddaughter. "Bella," she said, firmly. "No mas."

Darcie regarded her great-grandmother uneasily. When Grandma Sofi said, "enough" and "no more, Bella" in that tone of voice—in any language—Darcie automatically obeyed. So, it seemed, did Mallory.

Devin was impressed. Grandma Sofi had presence. He would give her that. He was also grateful her timely interruption prevented him from taking Darcie's side, which wouldn't have been good for anyone. Sofia Hanover, Devin mused, was just as she appeared to be—a beautiful old lady dressed for a wedding. But only a fool would overlook the fire burning in her eyes.

Oh, Lord, Darcie thought. This was not going to be pretty. Grandma Sofi was currently wearing the same expression as the bird on the head of her cane, one Darcie could only call warlike. She hoped that her indomitable relation didn't make the truly awkward situation any worse. Darcie wouldn't put it past her feisty great-grandmother to use her cane if she deemed it necessary.

Darcie glanced around the grand foyer, telegraphing a panicked plea for help. Juli, always vigilant—particularly in social situations with her outspoken grandmother—was already making her way across the room, with Joe at her side. Grace and Blane were also moving in their direction.

Unfortunately, Amalie was skipping their way as well, followed by Joey and Diana. Lou, who wasn't a stranger to Grandma Sofi's sharp tongue, intercepted the little girl. "Why don't you and I go look at the pretty flowers in the ballroom?" the perceptive blonde offered. Darcie applauded Lou's quick thinking. Getting the innocent child as far from the scene as possible seemed imperative.

Seeing Darcie and her great-grandmother together for the first time, Devin was struck by their resemblance. He wasn't surprised to see the determined glint in Grandma Sofi's eye. *So, this is where Darcie gets it,* he surmised. *Good luck, Mallory.* The older lady would prevail. Of this, he had no doubt.

"Aunque la mona se vista de seda, mona se queda," Grandma Sofi said as she advanced on her unsuspecting foe. Grandma Sofi spoke fluent Spanish and Italian, but it was rare for her to address a stranger in the language of her birth. Unless she was so angry about something that she didn't realize she was doing it. An angry Sofia Bertolli Hanover was not to be trifled with.

Darcie didn't remember all of her college Spanish, but she knew the quote. She had heard it plenty of times growing up. *"Even if the monkey is dressed in silk, it remains a monkey."* Ouch. Grandma Sofi did have a penchant for bluntness. Too bad Mallory couldn't understand a word.

Devin glanced at Darcie, questioningly, but Darcie shook her head. She wouldn't dare interrupt Grandma Sofi. No one in her right mind would interrupt Grandma Sofi when she looked like this, her eyes blazing with the righteous anger of an avenging angel.

At Mallory's puzzled expression, Grandma Sofi shook her head in an irritated manner. She made a concerted effort to find the English equivalent as she looked directly into Mallory's eyes. "You can put lipstick on a pig, but it is still a pig, no?"

Mallory burst into delighted laughter. "Oh my God," she exclaimed, "you are hilarious. Just hilarious. Dementia," she assumed, wrongly. "You have dementia, don't you? You can say anything you want, and nobody cares." Mallory grinned at Grandma Sofi. "I can't wait to be old enough to say anything *I* want. Without the dementia, of course. Oh, I wish Desiree could meet you."

Grandma Sofi had an arrested expression on her face, as if she was trying to discern if Mallory's lack of comprehension was real.

Lydia chose that moment to take her brother's wife firmly by the arm. "Come on, Mallory," she said through gritted teeth. "We have to find seats before the wedding starts. Mom said to come *now*."

Still giggling, Mallory followed her long-suffering sister-in-law into the hallway that led to the rose garden.

Darcie looked at her great-grandmother blankly. Grandma Sofi couldn't have spoken any plainer than that. How had Mallory managed to miss the point? Because she had missed it. Darcie was certain of that. Mallory had missed it completely.

The atmosphere of the room lightened without the presence of Devin's venomous wife. The group gathered around Darcie so protectively relaxed, but only for a moment.

Grandma Sofi abruptly focused on Devin. "Your wife is a pig," she said in a flat voice, banging her cane on the floor. She had a habit of looking reality in the face, fearlessly expressing what everyone else was afraid to say. "Your wife is a pig," she repeated in her heaviest accent—the one she used for emphasis. "Your daughter, a precious pearl. 'Neither cast ye your pearls before swine, lest they trample them under their feet,'" she quoted. "This is from the book of Matthew in the King James version of the Bible. Matthew 7:6. You know the Bible, no?"

"Yes, ma'am, I know the Bible," Devin said gravely. He felt as if Grandma Sofi had punched him in the stomach.

"You have read it?" Grandma Sofi pressed.

"I'm working on that," Devin answered honestly. Who could be anything but honest in the face of such a forceful interrogation? Grandma Sofi had missed her calling as a prosecuting attorney.

"Good. Your nanny…" She pointed to Diana, who looked a little surprised to be pulled into the strange conversation. "She is good, but even she cannot protect your little pearl forever. Eventually, *you* must fix, no?" Grandma Sofi tilted her head, studying Devin.

"Yes, ma'am."

He nodded, once, in complete agreement. He was appreciative of her candor but shaken to the core by her observations.

Her face relaxed as if satisfied. "Bella?" she said. She turned her attention to her beautiful great-granddaughter, noting the pallor of her complexion and the haunted look in her eyes.

"Yes, ma'am?"

Darcie managed to get the words out, but her mind was spinning. Rolling through law cases. Child welfare stratagems. Instances of fathers retaining sole custody of their children. Searching for a solution. She tried to focus on Grandma Sofi, hoping her formidable great-grandmother would, unintentionally, give them the answer to their dilemma.

"I see now why you made the pie," the old woman said, matter-of-factly.

Darcie waited for more, but that seemed to be the end of Grandma Sofi's part in the drama.

Maggie bustled into the room before anyone else could speak. The vibrant redhead was a breath of fresh air, helping to clear the pall left by Mallory's malignant presence. "Why are you all standing around?" she asked, excitement making her voice more forceful than usual. "It's almost time! I need Fergus and Grandma Sofi. Ian and Alina. And Joe and Juli. In that order, please." She paused, waiting for those assembled to do her bidding. "Everyone else should follow us to the rose garden. Ladies, don't forget your bouquets!"

The focus was back where it should be; the members of the wedding party started to move. The groomsmen slipped into their tux jackets. Bow ties were adjusted. Boutonnieres were straightened. The bridesmaids checked each other's dresses. Lipstick was reapplied. Hair was fluffed. The ladies scrambled to pick up their flowers, pausing to sneak a last quick look in the mirror.

Darcie didn't move. She kept her eyes on the bleak visage of the man standing beside her. She wanted to reach out. To spout false platitudes. To make promises that couldn't be kept. Anything to erase the expression of brooding despair that had settled on Devin's face at Grandma Sofi's last words to him.

Devin was struggling to regain his equilibrium, still reeling from Grandma Sofi's observations. He had never before felt such a desperate sense of urgency to free his sweet child from the malignant influence of her mother. Emotional abandonment as the grounds for a custody battle didn't stand a chance against the theatrical efforts of a weeping, hysterical Mallory. She would have been wonderful on the stage playing a tragically misunderstood, emotionally fragile character. She could have made the role work as long as the audience was too far away to look into his wife's cold, hard eyes. Looking into those eyes was like looking into the soul of a boa constrictor. She lulled her victims closer, softly enfolding them in her embrace until it was too late to escape her choking grasp.

If this was a fairy tale, his cold-hearted wife would transform into a snake, slithering away by the end of the story. Or meet an untimely demise on the tip of Grandma Sofi's cane. *No untimely demise,* he quickly reminded himself. There had to be something. Something Mallory couldn't act her way out of. He needed evidence. Cold, hard evidence. But evidence of what? Maybe she would be open to some kind of payoff because he had become such a *monster*. He hadn't asked in a while, but, even then, he still needed tangible confirmation to get full custody, some kind of definitive proof that she…

The memory hit him in the face.

"The paddleboard instructor," Devin said under his breath. "The damn paddleboard instructor." It was so obvious. Why hadn't he seen it before?

After giving him a curious glance, Darcie looked quickly away, without commenting.

Well, Devin thought, it was official. He had finally done it. Even Darcie Finch thought he was crazy. Maybe she was right, but if he was…he was some kind of a crazy genius. The paddleboard instructor. The pool boy. Hell, the man holding a sign on the corner. He didn't give a damn who it was. All he had to do was prove Mallory guilty of infidelity. If he could do that, he and Amalie were free. *Devin Merritt*, he congratulated himself, *you are some kind of a friggin' genius.*

Lou reappeared just then with an excited Amalie in tow. The little girl ran to her daddy, chattering with innocent abandon about the candles and flowers and pretty decorations in the ballroom. "That's where we're going to have the 'cepshun, Daddy! I have a special place to sit. There's a card with my name on it. I'm sitting next to Nanny Di. Miss Lou showed me." She grinned at the tall blonde happily. Lou grinned back.

Amalie turned to address Darcie. "Daddy promised to dance with me! *And* he said we'll eat more cake! You can dance with us, too, Miss Darcie," she added generously, eager to include her friend in the fun.

"Thank you, Amalie," Darcie said, because what else could she say? She couldn't exactly give the answer that immediately popped into her head. *Yes, Amalie, I would love that. I would love to dance and eat cake with you and your daddy. I would love to take you upstairs to tuck you in bed when you get sleepy. I would love to come back downstairs to dance with your daddy some more and go back upstairs with him…before either of us get too sleepy. I would love that.* Darcie couldn't stop herself from thinking the words, she could only keep herself from saying them out loud. *Shut up, Darcie.* She was beyond annoyed at the selfish direction of her own thoughts. Amalie's welfare was the most important thing. Darcie resolved to remember that.

She was pleased to note, however, that Devin's scarred face had bloomed into a bright smile in the presence of Amalie's enthusiasm. She watched the two of them together, basking in the return of Laurence, her light-hearted pirate. She wasn't quite sure what caused the shift from despair to hope, but the positive light was back in his eye. She wanted to make sure it stayed there. Her own smile burst forth with all the brightness of stage lights on opening night.

Devin caught his breath at the sheer beauty of the woman standing beside him. The pharmacist was right. It was like jumping into a cold lake. If she kept smiling at him like that, he would need a cold lake. Or, maybe, a cold shower. Or a really, big popsicle or…something.

Since he couldn't stand around gawking like an adolescent, he forced himself to move. He forced himself to respond to Amalie's happy chatter until they made it all the way across the room. Taking his daughter by the hand, Devin turned down the hallway toward the rose garden. Only then could he shake off the devastating effects of Darcie Finch. Her smile was lethal, it really was. But…He smiled ruefully. He had to admit, he couldn't imagine a better way to go.

He caught up with Roger, Evander, and Zack in the rose garden. Listening to them banter back and forth took some of the edge off.

The Finch siblings suddenly found themselves alone.

"Well," said Joey, "I've got to hand it to Grandma Sofi. The old girl made her point, even if Monstrous Mallory couldn't think her way through the animal references to get it."

They exchanged glances, a combination of admiration and disgust. For as long as they could remember, Grandma Sofi had been mixing up the words in familiar idioms. They had all taken great pride in untangling the words to figure out what she was trying to say. The older they got, the more suspicious they became of the lengths to which that sharp-witted woman would go to make her point.

"She's a fraud," said Joey. "I always thought so, but now I know it's true."

"You're right," Grace agreed. "Three perfect quotes, and she didn't bat an eye."

"No '*His bite is worse than the sound of his bark.*'" Darcie did her best to capture the thick accent Grandma Sofi used on a regular basis. "No garbled phrases. She stood right there and said every word perfectly. All of these years, she's been playing us."

The three looked at each other and grinned.

"She's a legend," Joey said, respectfully.

"She is fierce," Grace agreed.

"I want to be just like that when I'm ninety-one," said Darcie, laughing at the look on her siblings' faces.

"I don't think you'll have to wait that long, Princess," Joey said, solemnly, putting his arms around both of his sisters as they walked toward the hallway. "C'mon. We've finally found someone to marry the Brat, and I don't think we should keep him waiting."

CHAPTER THIRTY-TWO

*M*ost of the one hundred and twenty white chairs arranged in front of the gazebo were filled with guests by the time Devin and Amalie emerged from the house. Father and daughter followed the cobblestone walkway to the edge of the rose garden to join Devin's fellow groomsmen. From there the walkway ran the entire distance—one hundred and fifty feet— to the gazebo, providing a ready-made aisle for the event.

Maggie's twins, Phoebe and Penelope, stood together behind the last row of chairs—on either side of the walkway—handing out programs. They looked like matching sentries in identical bronze-colored dresses standing beside identical bronze-colored mums. Dom and Ric loitered nearby, ready to help any late arrivals find a seat. General Maggie was determined to keep the wedding party out of sight as long as possible. None of those under her command dared step a foot out of the rose garden until she gave the word.

Devin noted that Fergus and Grandma Sofi were already in their seats in the front row. Ian and Alina were waiting for the string quartet to play the next selection, Pachelbel's *Canon*, which would signal the traditional seating of the mothers of the bride and groom. The first two chairs by the aisle on the groom's side remained empty, each adorned by a single, white rose in memory of Mac and Lily McCallum. Blane had asked his uncle and aunt to represent his deceased parents by joining his grandfather on the first row. Once they were seated, Joe and Juli would follow. After Joe seated Juli beside Grandma Sofi on the bride's side of the aisle, he would return to the rose garden to walk his oldest daughter down the aisle.

Devin noticed Blane talking to Rafe and Will, who were still standing around the covered walkway that connected the garage to the house. Coincidentally, this was the area through which all invited guests must pass. Will was frowning as he listened to Rafe, but Blane nodded his head, seemingly unperturbed. After the conversation ended, the smiling groom walked over to join the wedding director.

"All right, Blane, honey," Maggie said. "It's time."

She kissed his cheek and gave him a quick hug. She called for Joey and Pastor Faircloth, but not before Devin saw her swipe impatiently at the tears in her eyes. It looked as though Dom was right. General Maggie wasn't so tough, after all.

Blane shook Will's hand and then Rafe's, pausing to blow a kiss to his bride. He and the pastor stopped halfway to the chairs to wait for the best man.

"*Joey Finch*," hissed Maggie. "Come here. Now!"

Putting his arms around his surprised sisters, Joey posed for what was to become one of the Finch siblings' favorite photographs. Joey's lack of cooperation during family photos was almost a given. The last photograph that Darcie could remember in which her brother willingly posed with his sisters featured the three of them in their red-footed pajamas in front of the family Christmas tree when Joey, the oldest of the three of them, was seven.

"Love you, Brat," he said, with a little hitch in his breath. "You, too, Princess." The next moment he left to take his place as Blane's best man.

Darcie and Grace looked at each other in amazement. The rare sight of an emotional Joey Finch had robbed them of their ability to speak.

As Blane, Joey, and the pastor walked down the aisle toward the gazebo, the groomsmen followed Maggie. They had privately dubbed the area behind the chairs Checkpoint Parker Twins. Phoebe and Penelope were responsible for telling each member of the wedding party when to start walking down the aisle. Devin left Amalie with Maggie to take his place in line behind Roger.

While they waited for Clarke's "Trumpet Voluntary" to begin, Devin tried to focus on the nonsense going on in front of him; but he had difficulty resisting the temptation to turn around and gaze at the gorgeous lady standing beside the beautiful bride at the edge of the rose garden. Joe had rejoined Grace and Darcie a few minutes ago. Devin could well imagine that staring at Joe's youngest daughter like a lovesick teenager would not endear him to her formidable father. Being fed to bears would be the least of his worries.

"Dammit," Roger swore as a slight breeze blew nearby leaves their way. Devin glanced up from his intense study of the ground to see Roger wiping his right eye.

"What's the matter, Raj?" Zack asked, grinning mischievously at Devin. "All choked up?"

"Of course not," Roger said indignantly, wiping his streaming eye. "The wind blew a cinder or something in my eye. It's stuck to my contact."

Zack peered past Devin. "Hey, Evander," he said in an overly loud whisper, "do you have a handkerchief?"

Evander fished in his pants pocket. "Yeah," he said. "Why do you need a handkerchief?" He handed a neatly folded cloth to Zack. "Did you spill something?" He sounded suspicious because it wouldn't be the first time.

"Naw, it's not for me." Zack took the handkerchief and handed it to Roger. "Roger's *cry-ing.*"

"I am not crying," snapped Roger, wiping his eye with the handkerchief.

Evander grinned. "Awww, I think that's nice, Raj. I'm glad you're not afraid to show a little manly emotion."

"You two can just go—"

Roger never finished his retort because as soon as he said the word, *Go*, Maggie echoed his words.

"That's right," said Maggie. "*Go*. It's time to go."

After Blane, Joey, and Pastor Faircloth reached the end of the aisle, they turned to face the audience. A heightened sense of anticipation swept through the guests. The wedding was about to begin.

Devin glimpsed the back of Mallory's blond head; his wife was seated beside Lydia. He imagined the expression on his sister's face was one of supreme irritation. He wondered how many times Lydia would roll her eyes at Diana—seated on her other side—during the ceremony. He wondered if Diana would keep count.

The sight of his problematical spouse sent Devin's thoughts back to the never-before-accessible avenue to win sole custody of his daughter: infidelity. He had always passed over the possibility when studying their prenup to determine if he could identify a viable escape clause. Before his attack, it was a moot point. Mallory had been eager for sex, praising his prowess and abilities. Her apparent satisfaction in that domain of their marriage had never caused him to question her fidelity. He discovered, almost immediately, that sex was the commodity Mallory used to bargain for whatever object was her current heart's desire. Mallory wanted *lots* of things, which equated to *lots* of invitations for Devin to visit her don't-even-think-about-coming-in-here-without-an-invitation bedroom. He had to confess that—even after he figured her out—he had never denied her requests. Devin didn't know what that said about him as a person. He was honest enough to admit he had enjoyed the physical aspect of their relationship, devoid as those encounters were of softer emotions. She had always been proud to be seen with him in public, taking every opportunity to show the world what a *gorgeous couple* they were.

Since the attack, things had changed. Mallory never came out and said it, but her general abhorrence of the change in his appearance made it clear that sex with the *monster* was out of the question. She also stopped demanding that Devin accompany her to any of the myriad social events that cluttered her calendar. On the contrary, she simply told him where she was going and when she would be back. To some extent, this new development greatly improved Devin's quality of life, but—and with Mallory, there was always a *but*—she still wanted things. She wanted lots of things. So, as her new bargaining tool, she chose to remind him of the tragedy her life had become as a result of his attack. Devin usually gave in to her whims, so he wouldn't have to endure her whining and insensitive remarks.

He hadn't really thought about the change in the physical aspect of their relationship, so relieved was he to be rid of her unpleasantness. Now, however, it made him wonder. Had she managed to find a new lover? A part-time lover? A few one-night stands? Unfortunately, he doubted it. He really did. Mallory didn't seem interested in love, except for the all-encompassing love she had for herself. She still managed to get everything she wanted from Devin without sex. So, what was the point? Still, he wondered how much she missed it. Could the lack of bedsport lead her down the path to an affair?

Devin pulled himself out of his musings, realizing that Roger had started down the aisle. That meant he was next. What he hadn't counted on was the unexpected feeling of dread that took hold at the thought that all of the guests' gazes would now be directed his way. His initial reluctance about being a groomsman had disappeared due to the kindness and acceptance of everyone he encountered at Heart's Ease. But now, as Phoebe put a gentle hand on his arm to signal when he should move forward, the aisle looked long and lonely. He glanced behind him, but his Pirate Queen was nowhere in sight. Still, he could do this. He would do this. For Blane. And for himself. As Devin started down the aisle, he forced his mind back to his marital conundrum.

So, Devin wondered, how exactly, did one go about encouraging one's wife to commit adultery? He figured the main issue would be finding someone who was willing to commit adultery with her. *That's the tough part*, Devin thought. *I mean, I'm talking about Mallory. Once a man gets to know her, he'll run like hell if he has any idea of what's good for him. Unless he's a trusting idiot, like me.* Maybe he should just put an ad in the paper:

> **Narcissistic woman seeks narcissistic man for loveless relationship based solely on acquiring material possessions. Only those with annual incomes of $500,000 or above need apply.**

Or, maybe he could fill out a profile for her on one of those dating websites:

Hi, I'm Mallory. I enjoy having meaningless conversations, getting endless manicures, and spending somebody else's money. I also like to make people feel badly about themselves. My hobbies are making an entrance and ignoring my own child. Only those without a backbone need apply.

Devin had to give himself a little credit. He could be more than a little amusing under duress. The sheer irony of thinking about finding someone to cheat on him with his own wife *while* he was walking down the aisle as the groomsman at a wedding was not lost on him. His lip tipped up at one corner. He had always appreciated that kind of absurd humor, dark though it was.

An older woman with glasses that made her eyes look as big as an owl's returned his smile as he walked by. She appeared intrigued, rather than repulsed. Good. A little of his pirate swagger returned when he realized he had almost made it to the front row of chairs without making a single person scream or faint. Not a single one. He felt himself relax a little, realizing he had been overly concerned about the impact his scarred face might have on the wedding guests. Apparently, Blane had been right all along. Devin's face was a nonissue. Rather than staring, the guests were already looking past him to see who was next. He grinned at Blane before turning to take his place beside Roger.

As he watched Evander make his way down the aisle, Devin's eye searched for Darcie. He knew he had to be careful when he saw her. Too many eyes were watching. He tried to prepare himself. A sudden glimpse of Darcie Finch, in all her glory, could muddle any man's head. He saw Ana Martin at the back of the aisle, standing at the ready. Still no Darcie. But it was only a matter of time until she appeared.

He glanced at Mallory, who was busily texting, completely absorbed in whatever conversation she was having. She didn't have a lover. He was sure of it. *Maybe I can cancel her credit cards and make her think we're having financial troubles,* he mused. That would shake her up. Then she might start looking for another Sugar Daddy. Or not. *Damn.* Devin sighed as he felt the familiar sting of reality's sharp claws.

Mallory was about as likely to have an affair as Douglas McCallum was to suddenly appear at the back of the aisle. He remembered Rafe's absolute certainty that Douglas was going to crash the wedding. Devin searched the crowd as Ana started down the aisle. No sign of him anywhere, he thought. Looks like the infallible Rafe Montgomery was finally wrong.

CHAPTER THIRTY-THREE

When Maggie called for the bridesmaids to take their position in line, Darcie held back. Her senses were informing her that something was wrong. She noticed Rafe and Will talking to several new arrivals. She relaxed a bit, realizing the newcomers were members of the paparazzi Blane had hand-picked to cover the wedding. But still she hesitated, staying where she was so she could listen to their conversation.

Rafe explained the rules: "You are free to stay in the immediate area of the ceremony and the reception, but please don't get in the way of the wedding photographer and videographer."

"Thank you, Mr. Montgomery," replied a short blonde. She was tastefully attired in black. "All of us at *Heathcliff's Personal Finance Weekly* are thrilled to be covering the wedding. We're especially proud of the part we played in Blane and Grace's courtship. I'm sure that *The Celebrity Buzz* is equally appreciative of being chosen today. I'm *positive* they will be extremely respectful with their coverage."

Darcie surmised that the blonde—fearlessly staring down the *CB* cameraman until he nodded his agreement—had to be Serena Adams. She was the reporter who had helped Blane write the article that finally won Grace's heart. In a magazine that ran the gamut between hard news and sensationalism,

Serena could be depended on to tell the truth. Darcie respected her dedication to honest journalism. She watched as Serena and the *CB* cameraman hurried to find the best vantage point for the ceremony.

Maggie was already lining up the other bridesmaids, with Amalie in tow, but Darcie didn't join them. Her instincts were on high alert: one of the new arrivals was still lingering near the covered walkway. Her initial assumption that he was a member of the paparazzi must have been a mistake. But who was he? She couldn't recall where she had seen him before, even though he looked very familiar. He was appropriately attired in a tux, but the smug, almost taunting expression on his face gave her pause. Then she heard her father's quick intake of breath. She glanced back at her sister, who was wearing a worried expression that did not belong on the face of a happy bride.

"What...who is that?" Darcie asked, in a low voice.

"That's Blane's uncle, little sister. You might remember him: The Meanest Man in the World," Grace said. She tightened her hold on her father's arm. Her reference originated from another time and place, but to Darcie the meaning was crystal clear.

Douglas McCallum. Darcie was certain. She was only six years old at the time, but she had never forgotten that awful night. This was the man who burst into their home to take a twelve-year-old Blane, newly orphaned and grieving, away from the only place he wanted to be. The memory of Douglas' cruelty had remained with Darcie, making her heart particularly sensitive to legal cases involving children.

"Daddy," Grace said as Joe took a step toward the walkway. "Daddy. No," Grace repeated, refusing to let go of Joe's arm.

Grace's father raised his hand to touch her face. His eyes were kind but determined. "Let me have my say, Gracie."

She nodded reluctantly, releasing him.

Grace and Darcie watched their father confront his bitter enemy. Darcie had to admit she was rather glad that Rafe and Will stood beside him. She had no doubt, however, that—alone or not—Joe Finch could handle Douglas McCallum. She and her sister had both borne witness to that long ago.

Maggie came halfway down the walkway, waving frantically for them to hurry up. Her face was flaming. Her beautiful turquoise eyes huge. She hesitated, torn between directing the remaining bridesmaids and coming down the path to get them herself. Amalie's tug on her arm was the only thing that held her in place. She stooped down to hear what the little flower girl was saying.

Grace bit her lip, squared her shoulders and started toward the group of men. They seemed to be having a standoff on the walkway.

But Darcie was having none of it. "No, Gracie." She stopped her sister with a gentle hand. "I'll do it. You go ahead and tell Maggie we're coming." She was going to fetch her father and save the wedding, in spite of The Meanest Man in the World's malevolent presence. She strode toward the tense group, looking a lot more confident than she felt. Her sure stride faltered as she heard her father's words.

"You can stay, McCallum," Joe said graciously. "In fact, we were expecting you. Rafe will show you to your reserved seat in just a moment. But first, I want you to understand something. You are here because *we* have made the conscious decision to allow you to be here. That was up to us. Whether you remain is up to you. There will be *no* trouble. *No trouble.* And if you're standing there thinking you can do whatever the hell you want, allow me to point out a few critical pieces of information."

Douglas' face flushed a bit. His eyes shifted to take in Rafe. He detested Rafe Montgomery almost as much as he detested Joe Finch. Although Rafe's arms were casually crossed, he regarded Douglas as if he would like nothing better than to see him at his feet, lying flat on the ground. Douglas glanced at the other man, deciding immediately that his odds didn't seem any better with him. Parker looked quite capable of shedding his calm demeanor for all manner of mayhem, if necessary. As for Finch, well, Douglas had taken that path before. Twice. And under no circumstances was Douglas interested in going there again.

Joe continued in a hard voice that Darcie hardly recognized: "In *our* town you play by *our* rules. Among the guests today are several members of the local police force. Several county deputies. A few lawyers. Three judges, one of whom is a federal judge. Two SBI agents. One FBI agent. And a United

States senator. You. Are. In. Our. Town. Do you understand what I'm saying, McCallum?" Joe stopped talking, waiting to see what his enemy would do.

Douglas, who was outmanned and outmaneuvered, nodded, politely. He even held out his hand. Joe refused to shake hands, however, choosing instead to glare at the offending appendage. Douglas shrugged, withdrawing his hand and shoving it in his pocket.

Darcie made her move. She drew close enough to put her hand on Joe's arm. She squeezed it, surprised as always at the rock-hard muscles hidden under her father's dress shirt and jacket. "Daddy," she said, calmly.

Joe didn't respond, his eyes glued to the flushed face of Douglas McCallum.

"Daddy," Darcie said again. "It's time to go. Gracie is waiting. And Maggie's going to have a heart attack if we don't come *now*."

Joe met her eyes. He appeared almost surprised to see her standing there, so intent was his focus on the other man.

Darcie tried again. "Daddy, Gracie is biting her lip. The bridesmaids are going down the aisle. And Maggie says, '*It's time to go!*'"

Joe's eyes widened with comprehension. To Darcie's astonishment, he grinned, as if he had just remembered that he was the man who was giving away the bride.

He offered her his arm. "Well, Darcie-girl, looks like you're waiting on me for a change. Who would have expected that to happen?" he asked teasingly, once again her even-tempered father.

Darcie shook her head, wondering if she would ever understand the mysterious workings of the mind of her father. She took his arm, tugging him to the walkway. They arrived just in time. After receiving a hug from her grateful sister, Darcie allowed a relieved-looking Maggie to send her down the aisle.

She tried to appear calm, nodding and smiling, but the tense situation with Blane's uncle had tied her stomach in knots. She focused on the beautiful flowers, giving the gorgeous venue a chance to settle her nerves and soothe her pounding heart. But it wasn't until she fixed her eyes on the one person who truly understood her that she felt her spirit sigh.

Devin tried not to reveal how she took his breath away as she came toward him. Darcie walked the aisle with the gracefulness of royalty. He had never before experienced shortness of breath, but it was becoming a regular occurrence in the presence of his magnificent Pirate Queen. Everything about her—her hair, her eyes, her lips…her perfectly formed, perfectly soft, immensely kissable lips—called to something deep within him. Something possessive and primitive. Very, very primitive.

He wanted her with every fiber of his being. It wasn't even the fact that her beauty reduced him to a sputtering, laconic moron. It was the courage she showed when faced with adversity. The way she wouldn't give up, even when the odds were stacked against her. It was her kindness. Her compassion. Her determination. And, he had to admit, the completely disarming way she said whatever popped into her mind. It was the way she encouraged a scarred man who had lost an eye. The way she put an arrogant woman in her place. The way she enabled a child to keep dreaming.

He wanted her. He wanted all of her. He could tell that she was doing her best to avoid meeting his eye. *Don't you dare shut me out*, he demanded. *Look at me, Darcie. Look at me, love. Look. At. Me.*

Her eyes met his, as if she could hear his thoughts. He felt the intensity of her gaze like a punch in the gut. Everything he was thinking was reflected right back at him from the depth of her dark, dark eyes. She broke the contact as she turned to take her place beside Lou.

He doubted that anyone had noticed their heated exchange.…With the exception of Joey, who was regarding him with narrowed eyes, the attention of the audience was focused on the fairy-like flower girl slowly making her way down the aisle.

Devin's heart swelled with fatherly pride as Amalie came toward him. He saw her lips moving silently. He knew she was carefully counting steps and fistfuls of petals just as Miss Maggie had instructed her. When she reached the front row of chairs without running out of petals, she was so excited that she forgot the rest of her instructions.

She ran straight to Devin. "Daddy, look! I didn't run out of petals!" She grinned up at him.

He grinned back, leaning down to kiss her cheek. He gently turned her around, pointing her in the direction of Darcie, who was smiling and holding out her hand. Amalie skipped to Darcie, happily showing her the remaining petals. Darcie nodded her approval, taking the excited girl by the hand and positioning her so she faced the front. Lou leaned down to look in the basket as Amalie smiled up at the lovely blonde. Soft laughter and smiles played all around. Not a hint of disapproval marred Amalie's happiness.

Devin glanced toward Mallory, not the least bit surprised to see her still glued to the screen of her phone. She continued texting someone, probably Desiree, and she had missed the whole thing. He was glad to know neither Amalie nor Diana would have to hear Mallory's criticism of the child's innocent antics.

Devin chided himself on his lack of perception. Grandma Sofi had made him realize he needed to raise his own awareness regarding the interactions between Mallory and Amalie. Diana had born the bulk of that burden without complaint. But Devin now saw that her daily battles with his wife on behalf of his daughter were something he could no longer ignore. The time had arrived for him to assume more of his fatherly responsibilities.

A pause ensued before the entrance of the bride. The string quartet switched seamlessly to Wagner's traditional "Bridal Chorus." After Pastor Faircloth motioned for the audience to stand, the guests turned for their first glimpse of the gorgeous bride accompanied by her proud father.

Devin's eye, however, followed Rafe's progress. He and another man quietly walked along the far side of the chairs, finally joining Alina, Ian, and Fergus in the front row. Devin glanced at Blane to assess the groom's reaction to his uninvited, but not—thanks to Rafe—entirely unexpected guest. Blane calmly returned Devin's gaze with a slight nod. Although aware of Douglas McCallum's arrival, Blane flatly refused to give his uncle the satisfaction of acknowledging his unwanted presence.

As Rafe and Douglas reached the two empty seats awaiting them, Grace and Joe started slowly down the aisle. Devin wasn't certain whether to shake his head in admiration of Rafe Montgomery's uncanny ability to predict the future or in disgust at the unmitigated gall of Douglas McCallum to appear at a wedding to which he had not been invited. Instead, Devin smiled at the realization that—twice that day—he had considered the appearance of Blane's uncle to be as impossible as the situation in which he found himself. But now he could only see the appearance of the diabolical man as a sign. Douglas McCallum was a wedding crasher. Suddenly, all things were possible.

CHAPTER THIRTY-FOUR

*I*t was difficult to imagine a more beautiful setting for a wedding ceremony. The sky was on fire with the gorgeous reds, oranges, and pinks of an October sunset. The distant mountains—at the splendid peak of their autumnal glory—seemed to glow in the magical shimmer of pre-twilight.

The aisle between the rows of white chairs was lined with potted mums, each one an explosion of fall color. The white gazebo was elegantly draped in lace, dripping in tulle and yellow roses. The brilliant yellow mums lining the steps of the gazebo were surrounded by a multitude of glorious fall flowers interspersed with more yellow roses, all anointed with a delicate sprinkling of Charlie Ray's signature glitter. Evon had carefully supervised his glitter-loving partner's tendency to go overboard with the shiny adornment. The results were magical.

And, behind it all, flowed Honeysuckle Creek. Its gurgling waters made for a soothing addition to the melodies of the talented string quartet.

The maroon tint of the bridesmaids' dresses blended beautifully with the floral display. Each bridesmaid, with the exception of Ana, wore her hair up in an elaborate twist. Ana's short riot of curls had been deliberately pulled back off her face then fastened in jewel-encrusted clips. Pearl necklaces, earrings, and bracelets made for the perfect finishing touch.

The flowers the women carried were a tribute to Charlie Ray and Evon's expertise. Each bouquet was an individual work of art, combining shades of maroon and yellow to form a visual feast.

The groomsmen were equally impressive in their black tux and bow ties. Their boutonnieres of yellow roses had, thankfully, survived the day. In spite of their earlier high jinks, the groomsmen managed to comport themselves well. Even Zack was behaving himself under the tutelage of Roger and Evander.

The groom was the epitome of tall, dark, and handsome; he stood calmly beside Pastor Faircloth. Only the light glowing in Blane's eyes as he watched his bride walk down the aisle and the catch in his voice as he said his vows gave away the deep emotion he was usually so adept at concealing.

The bride wore her heart in her gorgeous green eyes for all to see. Grace seemed to float toward her groom. Her gown was a dreamlike confection of tulle and lace, her veil, a treasure from the past, irrevocably linking her hopes to the hopes of previous generations of McCallum brides. She carried a bouquet brimming with yellow roses. Her voice was full of joy as she responded to the pastor's prompts with absolute conviction.

The love and genuine devotion of the couple—so clearly and honestly displayed—made it difficult for the guests to avoid a tightening in their throats or a slight stinging in their eyes. Only the hardest-hearted souls in the audience remained unaffected.

Devin observed it all from his spot in the groomsmen's line. He couldn't help but smile, marveling at the change Grace had made in the life of the Boss-man over the course of the past year. He had watched, from his bird's-eye view across his desk, as Blane wrestled with his heart. He had been bemused and intrigued and, even, impressed by the effects of the green-eyed girl. But he hadn't understood, not really, not until the day he met...*her*. Miss Darcie Finch had walked into his lonely room at the lowest point of his life and changed...everything. She challenged him. She inspired him. And she refused to let him give in to fear or self-pity. She wouldn't give in, either. And she wouldn't back down.

What would his life be like if he hadn't met his Pirate Queen? Devin decided it didn't bear thinking about. He knew that the vivid colors, autumn breezes, and sharp details of Blane's wedding day would eventually fade into a pleasant memory. He, however, was absolutely certain he would never forget the vision of Darcie Finch, in a maroon bridesmaid dress, standing in the golden light of what had to be one of October's finest sunsets. The absolute perfection of the moment imprinted on his brain.

Nor was he likely to forget the way Darcie Finch's lovely voice blended effortlessly with her brother's as they performed Rascal Flatts' "Bless the Broken Road." The lyrics to the song were a perfect fit for the bride and groom. They had both been through a great deal of brokenness on the way to their happy ending.

As the glorious harmonies swelled and floated on the breeze, Devin was struck by the transformation of the brokenness in his own life. Amazing, how losing his eye had helped him to see with greater clarity. Colors were brighter. Music was sweeter. His heart was hopeful. And it was all because of *her*. He dared to dream of the future because of *her*.

Did she know what she meant to him? Did she have any idea? His eye sought her face, studying the emotions flitting across her features. She was watching her brother, her concentration on tempo and the blending of their voices. It was only as they reached the end of the song that she dared to look his way. He was shaken to the core by the perfect understanding he saw in her eyes. They didn't need words, he marveled. She knew exactly what he was thinking. *This is what it's like when you find your soulmate,* he realized. *This is what it's like.* The realization nearly leveled him. He forced himself to look away before he attracted unwanted attention.

He focused on the ceremony, watching as Blane and Grace exchanged vows and rings. After Pastor Faircloth pronounced them man and wife, Blane kissed his bride, employing just a little more enthusiasm than was absolutely necessary.

"Hot damn!"

Zack's trademark phase was mercifully drowned out by the applause and whistles of the guests.

The blushing bride and grinning groom faced their family and friends as the pastor announced, "I am happy to present to you, for the first time, Blane and Grace McCallum."

The instruments began to play Mendelssohn's "Wedding March," from *A Midsummer Night's Dream*, as the new Mr. and Mrs. McCallum made their way back to the rose garden. The wedding party followed, pairing off as they had practiced, to join the bridal couple for some final congratulations before they had to share them with the other guests.

Amalie ran to Darcie, throwing her arms around her waist with childish enthusiasm. "We did it, Miss Darcie! We did it! We helped Mr. Blane and Miss Grace get married!"

"We certainly did," Darcie replied, hugging the little girl. "And you did a great job, Amalie. You're probably the best flower girl ever."

Beaming with happiness at Darcie's words of praise, Amalie replied, "You're the best maid of honor ever!"

Devin's eye locked onto Darcie's gaze. They shared another moment of silent communication; then Darcie once again turned her attention back to Devin's blissful daughter. He felt a little detached as he watched Amalie chatter with Darcie. Several feet away, the newlyweds enjoyed a few moments respite. Their joy was infectious. The stress was over. Time for the real celebration to begin.

Devin was happy for Blane and Grace. He really was. But he also envied the way their broken roads had merged to become one smoothly paved, perfectly straight path filled with blue skies and sunshine. As much as he would like to believe otherwise, he was fairly certain the road in front of him—at least for the foreseeable future—would be filled with traffic jams, road construction, and plenty of potholes.

CHAPTER THIRTY-FIVE

*G*race and Blane joined the photographer on the far side of the lawn for a few final photos before the spectacular sunset faded to black. The guests mingled with the wedding party in the rose garden, enjoying a variety of hot beverages: apple cider, tea, or coffee. Servers in white jackets and black bow ties wandered the grounds with trays of hors d'oeuvres. Mini-quiche, stuffed mushrooms, bacon-wrapped dates, spicy cranberry barbecue meatballs, braised short ribs on garlic crostini, and miniature beef Wellingtons were plentiful. The informal atmosphere allowed the guests to relax and enjoy themselves.

For the florists, however, the next fifteen or twenty minutes were pivotal. They had to move the enormous amount of foliage from the wedding site to the ballroom where the reception would be. Charlie Ray and Evon had closed Honeysuckle Creek Flower and Gift at noon that day, because making this wedding happen required the efforts of all of their employees. They even enlisted the help of several of their friends at Blossom Florist in Pilot Mountain.

Not only were the floral arrangements complicated and exacting, the presence of the media, according to Charlie Ray, demanded perfection. After listening to Charlie Ray go on and on about opportunities and publicity,

Evon laughed. He knew the truth, and so did everybody else. Charlie Ray loved Grace and Blane to distraction; he had known them both since they were babies. He would never allow any kind of floral faux pas to mar their special day.

After congratulating a relieved Maggie on a job well done, Darcie made her way to the beverage station. She needed to find a drink with enough caffeine to get her through the next few hours. After looking things over, she chose a strong English breakfast tea, adding a few drops of honey for good measure. Her job wasn't over yet. As the maid of honor, she still had to make a toast before dinner.

Mallory made a beeline to Devin's side as soon as the wedding was over, clinging like ivy. Since Darcie had no desire for another uncomfortable encounter with Devin's legally espoused wife, she chose not to return to the rose garden. Instead, she wandered toward the gazebo to check on Charlie Ray and Evon's progress. But Mallory, she noticed irritably, was certainly acting the devoted wife now that she had a large audience of important people to impress. Devin, she also noticed, had assumed the stoic but watchful demeanor he probably assumed during every social situation he attended with his wife. She was sad to see his charming and witty personality disappear right before her eyes, but she understood.

She walked the cobblestone path, determined not to look back. But after a few moments, her determination disappeared. She couldn't resist chancing a quick peek. Just to check on him, she promised herself.

When she turned, he was watching her from the edge of the rose garden. Mallory stood in the center of a group consisting of several local lawyers and their wives. She appeared to be enjoying herself, if her animated hand gestures were any indication.

Devin stood with his hands in his pockets a short ways apart from the group. He looked so alone, standing there, that Darcie's compassionate heart turned over. She forced herself to keep walking away, however. With her usual insight, she realized that—under Devin's current circumstances—her presence would bring him nothing but trouble.

Determined to spare him, she hurried down the rapidly vanishing aisle: the chairs were quickly disappearing into the back of a large truck, and almost all of the flowers had been removed. Charlie Ray and Evon were loading the last of the mums into the bed of their John Deere Gator. They stopped working when they saw her approach.

Charlie Ray whistled with admiration. "Darcie Finch, you good-lookin' thing! Honey chile, there's not a woman here who can compete with you."

Darcie grinned. "Oh, Charlie Ray, you're such a flirt." She gifted her admirer with a quick hug.

"Except the bride, Charlie Ray," Evon said, in his soft Charleston accent. "You cannot forget our beautiful Gracie."

Darcie hugged Evon, too. He was always so sweet.

"Oh, hush, Evon," Charlie Ray chided his partner of more than thirty years. "Darcie knows what I mean. Don't you, honey?"

"Of course, Charlie Ray." Darcie winked at Evon before adding, loyally: "Nobody looks as beautiful as my sister."

Evon smiled, patting her on the shoulder.

"Want a ride?" Charlie Ray asked. "These are the last of the florals and, well, honey, why walk when you don't have to?"

He climbed into the driver's seat as Evon motioned for Darcie to take the other seat.

"Oh, no, Evon," Darcie objected. "I don't want to take your seat. I'll walk."

"I have to sit in the back, darlin', to hold onto the mums," Evon explained, helping her into the front seat. "Charlie Ray drives a tad too fast in this thing."

"Oh, my stars! Hush up, Evon."

Charlie Ray huffed at what he considered to be Evon's blatant exaggeration.

But, when he put the Gator into drive, it became apparent that Evon was *not* exaggerating. Darcie's only option was to grab the seat and hang on. For the first time, she was quite grateful that—thanks to a double treatment of Lou's hairspray—her stiff hair wouldn't have moved during a hurricane. She looked over her shoulder at Evon to find him holding on for dear life.

When they reached the fountain on the large terrace behind the ballroom, Charlie Ray stopped the Gator abruptly. Only the timely intervention of Evon's hand on Darcie's arm kept Darcie from tumbling out of the vehicle. She exchanged a relieved glance with her rescuer as Charlie Ray hopped out of the Gator with the boundless energy that always seemed to radiate from his person.

He surveyed the area around the fountain with satisfaction. "It's absolutely the right number of mums, Evon. I just knew it would be. Once we put the rest of them in that empty spot, it will be perfect. Don't you think so, Darcie, honey?"

"Oh, yes, Charlie Ray," she answered truthfully. "Everything is just gorgeous."

"I'll tell you who's gorgeous," Charlie Ray said, with a mischievous wink. "That pirate groomsman is *beyond* gorgeous. You think so, too, don't you, honey?"

Darcie looked at him in shock. How could Charlie Ray possibly know that? Did she have a flashing sign on her head? Was it written in lipstick on her face? Tattooed on her forehead? She had to play this off. If Charlie Ray gave her secret away, even accidentally, there would be hell to pay.

She fluttered her eyelashes, employing her best Southern belle drawl, "Now, Charlie Ray, whyever would you think something like that? Now, honey, don't you go startin' any unfortunate rumors!"

Charlie Ray was delighted with her little game. "Why would I think that? Well, honey, you know Evon and I were behind the gazebo during the wedding in case a floral emergency arose. I sat there the whole time and watched your pirate watching you. He had the same look in his one eye—bless his handsome heart—that your daddy still has in both of his when he looks at your mama. Why, honey, he could just eat you up."

After Evon placed the last mum, he stepped back to join them. He gave Darcie an understanding smile, and she knew he had heard the whole conversation.

"Charlie Ray," Darcie said softly. "You do know that pirate you're speaking of has a Mrs. Pirate, don't you?" Her fake accent faded away, along with some of her fake bravado.

Charlie Ray smiled, encouragingly. "Now, Darcie Finch, what does that have to do with anything? I would bet all of my Christmas poinsettias that he's *never* looked at Mrs. Pirate the way he looks at you. Evon had a wife when I met him, too, but that didn't stop true love. Isn't that right, Evon, honey?"

Darcie looked at Evon in amazement, noting the shy smile and slight flush rising toward his forehead. She had never heard this particular story before, and in Honeysuckle Creek, that was saying a lot.

Evon shrugged. "It's true, Darcie. My family expected me to marry her, so I did. I was too young to know any better and I hadn't, well…I hadn't figured myself out yet. As you can imagine, it wasn't exactly a match made in heaven. You saved me, didn't you, Charlie Ray?" he asked, fondly.

Charlie Ray nodded. "Well, of course, I did, Evon." For Darcie's benefit, he added: "From a fate worse than death. And you can save your pirate, too, Darcie," he encouraged, with a wink.

"He's not *my* pirate, Charlie Ray," Darcie said gently, wishing with all her heart that what the florist said was true.

"Pshaw! Just look at you trying to deny it. He might not be yours yet, but he wants to be," he said decisively.

To Darcie's relief, the well-meaning but all too perceptive florist finally stopped talking to make a final inspection of the fountain. "I swear, Evon, these mums look perfect. Let's do a final walk-through of the ballroom and then we can tell them it's time to open the doors." He swept into the ballroom, a devoted Evon trailing close behind. "Behave yourself, Darcie, but not too much."

Darcie stared at the water rolling over the sides of the Caterina tiered fountain. The happy gurgle did little to soothe her troubled spirit. She couldn't hide her feelings for Devin. Nor, it seemed, could Devin hide his feelings for her. They were too obvious. Too many people noticed too much. Eventually, their ticking time bomb was bound to blow up in their faces. She was going to have to make a concerted effort to keep her distance from Devin Merritt. It was the only option.

CHAPTER THIRTY-SIX

*E*ven the seating arrangement at the reception was against Devin. The bride and groom and their immediate family members sat at the head table near the back wall of the ballroom. Devin found himself in the middle of one of the long tables arranged diagonally around the head table. Miles from his Pirate Queen. Or it might as well be miles, for all the good it did him. He couldn't even see her unless he moved his chair or turned his head completely around. He was wise enough to realize that having his back to Darcie Finch during dinner was probably in both of their best interests. But he didn't have to like it.

According to the place cards, he was supposed to sit between Roger Carrington and Mallory. Devin's attention-seeking wife, however, had other plans. Before he could pull out her chair, Mallory insisted on changing seats. They needed to sit boy-girl-boy-girl, she explained with a girlish giggle. Devin saw no reason to argue. He had learned to choose his battles carefully. Roger looked less than thrilled, but Diana and Lydia brightened considerably. Devin ended up seated between Mallory and Amalie. Diana sat to Amalie's immediate right. Lydia sat directly across the table. Robert and Allana Merritt were seated directly across from Devin and Amalie. Their close proximity kept Mallory's behavior in check. For the most part.

So situated, the only glimpse Devin had of Darcie during dinner was when she stood to deliver her toast. He didn't really pay attention to the words she uttered…something to do with marshmallows, horses, and yellow roses. Instead, he focused on the way her lips formed the words. He let the sound of her rich voice wash over him, filling him with equal parts longing and lust. At the moment, he admitted to himself, a little heavy on the lust.

To distract himself, Devin focused on the members of his family seated around him. Robert and Allana were an attractive couple, but more than that, they were a happy couple. As if privy to his thoughts, his parents exchanged a warm, intimate smile. He was glad to see they were having a good time. They always seemed to have a good time together. Even after thirty-plus years—they had an ongoing but comical disagreement as to the exact number—it was obvious his parents still had more fun with each other than with anyone else. Watching them made Devin long for a marriage like theirs. Full of warmth, love, support, understanding. At the moment, such a goal felt completely out of his reach. He sighed, fighting an unwelcome wave of discouragement.

His heart lifted a little as Amalie burst into giggles over something her nanny was saying. He grinned, too, at the comical expression on Diana's face. Glancing at his sister across the table, he was glad to see that Lydia was, at the moment, smiling and relaxed. He had been encouraged earlier to see a little of her old sparkle return. After her initial outburst in the grand foyer, however, Lydia withdrew once again into herself.

His sister's joyful spirit and enthusiasm—two of her most endearing qualities—had been largely extinguished by her abusive marriage. Devin still wasn't used to the quiet, timid version of Lydia. Her desire *not* to call attention to herself was even reflected in her attire. She wore a long dark blue chiffon gown with a modest, scoop neckline. Too modest, in her brother's opinion. The bodice had a chiffon overlay and cascading ruffled short sleeves. The sleeves were the only part of the dress that was even reminiscent of his little sister's long-forgotten love of fancy feminine dresses. Devin had grown up teasing her about her frilly flounces and bows. Now, she barely wore jewelry. His spirits drooped further.

He glanced over Amalie's blond head at Diana. She, alone, knew what life with Mallory was really like. She, alone, shared his burden. Sometimes, he didn't know how he would keep his sanity without her. He gave her a smile. Diana smiled back. She was lovely in a dramatic turquoise gown with a bateau neckline and a keyhole back. The bodice was black lace over chiffon. The illusion-style half sleeves were made of the same black lace. The sweeping chiffon skirt billowed and swirled with every step, a feature Diana had enjoyed immensely throughout the wedding.

Unfortunately for Devin, the chiffon of his cousin's dress was an exact match for the turquoise eyes of Dominic Parker. Rather than dwell on that supremely annoying fact, Devin forced himself to pay attention to the end of—what appeared to be—the final toast. To his immense relief, the welcome distraction of dinner would soon be arriving.

And what a feast it was. The guests enjoyed a first course salad of cucumber wrapped mixed spring greens with cherry tomatoes, cheese, carrots, and pickled onion with sweet tea vinaigrette. Devin was amused to see that the menu placed neatly at each person's setting actually said "sweet tea vinaigrette." He chuckled with Lydia at that. They had spent many summers in Charleston with their very Southern grandmother, who, they knew, would absolutely love sweet tea vinaigrette. Devin made a mental note to find out where to buy the tangy salad dressing so he could surprise his grandmother the next time he visited.

Granny Rose would love Darcie Finch, too, Devin mused, as the servers cleared the first course from the tables. His grandmother and Darcie, in his opinion, had a lot in common: devotion to family, a love of baking, and—Devin smiled just thinking about it—*absolutely no filter*. Listening to a conversation between his Pirate Queen and Granny Rose would be immensely entertaining. But Devin only had a few seconds to enjoy such thoughts. His pleasant vision quickly disappeared, courtesy of the sound of his legally espoused wife's grating voice.

"Oh, Roger," cooed Mallory to the man seated on her other side. "You are so *funny*."

Damn. For all his good intentions, Devin realized his body was slowly turning, of its own accord, toward the head table. And the lovely Miss Darcie

Finch. Devin grimaced. Talk about calling attention to himself. None of the wedding guests would notice the fool sitting backwards in his chair staring at the head table, now would they? He blew out a breath of frustration at his own folly. Darcie would notice. Of that he was certain. And what would he do when he got her attention? Wave at her? Blow her a kiss? Gaze at her like a lovesick, pathetic loser? Devin silently berated himself. He was an idiot. He hastily returned to his former—and much safer—position…with his back to Darcie Finch.

The second course was soon served: seared scallops with minted pea puree. In spite of his inability to enjoy even a glimpse of his lovely Pirate Queen, Devin's appetite hadn't diminished in the least. His heart, however, was getting lonelier by the minute. Regardless of his personal situation, the food continued to impress. The scallops were seared to perfection. Fortunately, Diana was trying to save room for the third course, so Devin was the lucky recipient of her untouched scallop. He gave a little bite to Amalie, who pronounced it "super yummy, but not as good as the veggie pieces with dip or the smiling fruit."

As the only child present, Amalie enjoyed a specially prepared children's menu fit for a princess. Her first course consisted of carrot and celery sticks with Ranch dressing, followed by fruit cut into kid-friendly shapes. To his daughter's delight, Iggy Iguana was waiting when they arrived at the table; he was even honored with his own name card and special menu. The dashing iguana was also sporting a tiny bow tie.

Devin read Iggy's menu items aloud. Included were such inventive delicacies as sautéed flies with honey and something called "insect-ghetti." He couldn't hold back a smile as Amalie collapsed into peals of laughter. He lost count of how many times she had asked him to read it since they sat down. Devin suspected that Darcie and Mrs. Hofmann had put their heads together to plan the surprise. Iggy's menu was a small gesture, but one most people wouldn't have thought of. He appreciated the extra effort on Amalie's behalf.

The third course arrived. Filet mignon and butter-poached Maine lobster tail with whipped potato, veal reduction, and citrus butter. Diana was already in love with lobster tail. Devin couldn't help but laugh at the expression of pure bliss on her face. She seemed almost as excited as Amalie was about her choice of three different sauces for her chicken tenders.

All in all, the meal lasted nearly an hour and a half from start to finish. The expert wine selections were a delicious addition to the memorable culinary experience.

After dinner, the dancing began in earnest. Only a brief pause allowed Mr. and Mrs. McCallum to cut their gorgeous five-tier wedding cake. The Honeysuckle Creek Cakery had prepared a traditional cake, covered with a delicate cascade of buttercream flowers and crowned with an intricate buttercream magnolia. Each layer was a different flavor. From top to bottom: caramel apple, tiramisu, peanut butter cup, dulce de leche, and dark chocolate mousse. Blane had requested two pieces of cake from each layer be placed in a to-go box for the honeymoon. Coming from a man who hid banana bread in his desk drawer, the request was not surprising. But it still gave Devin and Rafe plenty of opportunity to make fun of the groom. After tasting the cake, however, Devin understood completely. The Cakery had outdone itself. When he had glanced at the table holding the cake a few minutes earlier—trying to talk himself out of a third piece—there was nothing left but crumbs.

Devin opted out of the dancing, preferring instead to make himself miserable watching Darcie dance with an endless number of partners who were *not* him. When she stood up with Dominic Parker for the fourth time, however, Devin couldn't sit still. He rose from his seat, leaving behind a very quiet Iggy—who had sunk into something of a food coma—and a very lively Amalie—happily chattering with her "Auntie Lyd."

Devin prowled the edges of the ballroom, trying to appear inconspicuous. *Because nobody would notice a scarred man in a tuxedo with an eye patch pacing the outside of the ballroom and muttering to himself,* he thought, sarcastically. *Yeah. Let's go with that.*

MACEE MCNEILL

If he had known that he would cease to exist the moment Darcie walked away from him in the rose garden, he would have done something to stop her. But…what? What exactly could he have done? Grab her and kiss her? Brilliant idea. He would lose his daughter and all of his worldly assets simultaneously. Not to mention the fact that Darcie would probably never forgive him for hurting Amalie. Hell, he'd never forgive himself. But, still, he could have…what? What could he have done differently?

Devin sighed, studying the mums surrounding the fountain on the patio to keep from studying Darcie. The mums weren't nearly as adept at holding his attention. Not surprisingly, his restless dissatisfaction had led him to this deserted corner of the ballroom. He was as far from the DJ and the happy, dancing throng as possible. Here, he could lean against the cool glass of the enormous windows that stretched from the floor to the ceiling across the back of the ballroom. Here, he could blend into the shadows and…brood while surreptitiously watching Darcie Finch enjoy her sister's wedding reception.

So far, she hadn't glanced his way. Not once. She hadn't acknowledged he was even in the ballroom. He found himself in familiar waters. He was used to being alone in a crowded room. He just hadn't realized that the yawning hole caused by his loneliness had briefly been filled with the knowledge of his and Darcie's shared attraction. He hadn't realized it, that is, until all evidence of that attraction vanished.

The worst part was, he couldn't do anything about it. He couldn't ask her what was wrong. He couldn't inquire if she had changed her mind. He could only watch as she moved from group to group, laughing and talking. She seemed perfectly content, perfectly happy to turn her back on a scarred excuse for a man. After all, he thought bitterly, the room was full of attractive, whole men who were single and free of unpleasant baggage. He had known from the beginning that Darcie could do much better than a one-eyed man trapped in a marriage with no way out. Not to mention that the one-eyed man had a child, however charming that child might be. It was a lot to ask of any woman, but especially a woman as magnetic and vibrant as Darcie Finch.

He couldn't make any promises or commitments. He couldn't allow himself to act on his feelings. He really couldn't do much of anything except telegraph his desperate devotion through longing glances and heavy sighs. *Merritt*, he rebuked himself, *you are pathetic.* It was true, he admitted. He was acting like some pitiful character in one of those romance novels Diana liked to read. He needed to get a grip. It wasn't Darcie's fault. It wasn't *anybody's* fault. And the least he could do was man up to it.

Devin scanned the room, squaring his shoulders. He had coddled himself as long as his conscience would allow. It was time to rejoin the party; time to face the music. His resolve faltered when he spied Darcie across the room dancing with...

Damn.

Dominic Parker. Again.

Of course she's dancing with Parker, he almost snarled. *They're lovers, remember?* Devin shook off the annoying commentary of his inner voice. *We'll just see about that.* He was halfway across the ballroom before he realized it.

"Daddy! Come and dance with us!"

Amalie stepped in front of him, squealing happily, effectively halting his progress.

He picked his daughter up automatically as his brain registered the worried glance exchanged by Diana and Lydia, his daughter's current dance partners.

"Dev," Lydia asked, gently. "Where are you headed?"

Devin looked around, almost as surprised as they were to find himself less than ten feet from his apparent target. He was a little embarrassed that his battle with his inner voice had propelled him toward Darcie, and a little concerned that he was having a battle with his inner voice. What the hell was he planning to do when he got to her anyway? Devin tried to smile. "I came to dance with my best girl, of course." He hoped his hasty excuse was believable.

Amalie grinned, hugging her father tightly as they spun around. She wanted down, however, as soon as they stopped spinning. She planted her feet on her daddy's shoes, positioning her arms the way he had shown her. Diana smiled at him before turning, with a pleased expression on her face, to accept an invitation to dance from Ric Parker. Devin watched her go, feeling quite confident that he had covered his ill-conceived lapse of judgement. When his eye met his sister's, however, he realized he was completely mistaken.

His sister was wearing the same expression of disbelief, mixed with disgust, he had seen on her face the day he told her the real identity of Santa Claus. She hadn't believed him then, either. She shook her head. "Darcie's doing it to protect you, you idiot," she hissed at his obvious confusion.

"Doing what?"

He didn't bother to deny his interest in Darcie. Lydia already knew. He wasn't sure how she knew—possibly Diana, or his sister's own uncanny intuition—but she knew.

"What exactly is Darcie doing?" he asked.

"Ignoring you. She's trying to protect you from your devil-wife. Mallory is on the alert, brother dear," Lydia explained. "She must have picked up on something when she talked to Darcie earlier."

Devin furrowed his brow, regarding his sister with respect. When had she gotten so wise? He had been so immersed in self-pity that he hadn't been able to see the obvious. All the pieces fell into place as he realized two things. Mallory wanted to catch him having an affair as much as he wanted to catch her. And Darcie had already figured that out.

CHAPTER THIRTY-SEVEN

"Stop looking," Dom whispered to his distracted dance partner.

"Oh, hush," Darcie whispered back. "I only looked for a second, nobody saw me but you. Anyway, they're so sweet, it's impossible not to."

Dom swung her around so her back was to Devin and Amalie. "Can't look now, can you?" he teased.

"Hmph."

She wrinkled her nose in annoyance. She didn't say anything, but he could see it building up inside her. It would only be another second before...

"What are they doing now?" she asked for the three hundred and twenty-seventh time in the last two and a half hours.

"Amalie is still standing on Devin's feet, and he is still dancing around in a circle." Dom felt like the narrator of one of those nature documentaries on the Discovery Channel, something like *The Mating Habits of Mammals*. He was torn between amusement at the fact that the independent, career-minded, no-nonsense Darcie Finch had fallen so fast and so hard for a man she barely knew and fear that she was going to get hurt. "I remember when you used to dance on your daddy's feet," Dom offered in an effort to distract her.

"I remember when I used to dance on your feet," Darcie quipped, trying not to listen for Devin's voice. He was dancing only a few feet away, but the music was too loud.

"Yeah," Dom agreed sadly. "It was like two minutes ago."

"That is not true, and you know it."

Darcie let go of his hand long enough to smack him on the shoulder.

"Ow," Dom said, rotating his shoulder in mock outrage.

"Hey, what did my pesky little brother do now?" asked Ric, grinning at the two of them, as he and Diana danced over to them. "Or was it Darcie's fault? Do you want me to tell Joe that she's picking on you, Nicky?" Ric asked, using Dom's childhood nickname.

"Ricky and Nicky. Together again," Darcie said, in a singsong imitation of a child's voice.

"Ricky and Nicky?" Diana asked. She began choking on laughter as she watched the look on Ric's face, which indicated he had momentarily forgotten his own nickname.

"Yeah," Darcie said wickedly. "They *love* to be called Ricky and Nicky. It makes them *so* happy."

"Is that right, Princess?" Ric fired back, laughing as Darcie stuck out her tongue.

"The Princess and the Brat," Joey intoned as he joined the group, effectively ending their efforts to keep dancing.

"The Princess and the Brat." Ric echoed his friend. Then he shook his head. "I never knew it would stick."

"You?" Grace gasped as she and Blane walked up at the end of Ric's admission. She looked at Ric in astonishment. "You mean it's *your* fault?"

"Of course it was me," Ric said, with pride. "You didn't think Little Joe thought it up by himself, did you?"

That was exactly what Grace and Darcie had been led to believe…by Little Joe himself. They glared at the innocent expression on their devilish brother's face.

Ric clamped a firm hand on Joey's shoulder. "This clown couldn't even tie his own shoes when I started calling you Brat, Gracie. And Darcie, you were such a diva, even as a baby, that Princess was the only choice." His grin widened at Darcie's annoyed expression. "When you got older, you hated to be called Princess. The more you hated it, the more fun it was."

Darcie grumbled, narrowing her eyes. "Hmph."

"You know what, though?" Ric asked, thoughtfully. "In retrospect, I think I got it backwards." He pointed at Grace, her beautiful eyes alight with laughter. "You, Miss Finch—"

"Mrs. McCallum," growled Blane, placing an arm around her waist and tugging her toward him securely.

"Sorry. You, Mrs. McCallum, are the Princess," Ric announced, delivering Grace an elegant bow from the waist.

She responded with a graceful curtsey.

"I told you so," Blane said with satisfaction. They exchanged a look nobody else understood.

Ric turned to Darcie, who was glaring at him with both hands on her hips. "And you, Miss Finch, you are definitely the Brat."

"Amen to that." Joey's remark was met with general laughter and smiles all around.

Darcie smiled, too, as she took aim and kicked her brother in the shin.

"Hey, wait a minute," Joey said, nodding his head in Ric's direction while leaning over to rub his throbbing shin. "Why didn't you kick *him*?"

"Shut up, Joey," Darcie said. She rolled her eyes as if her brother was the least intelligent member of the human race.

Grace and Diana giggled companionably. Ric displayed a pleased smile on his face. Blane and Dom seemed to be enjoying themselves immensely. Even Joey and Darcie shared a laugh as Joey bumped his hip against his sister's waist before giving her a hug.

Devin watched them, secretly wishing he was one of them. He glanced at Mallory, who was furiously texting someone who was somewhere else. It was quite clear. She didn't want to be anywhere she wasn't the center of attention. And that meant any wedding, other than her own, was unacceptable.

Of course, without the wife, the beautiful, little, blue-eyed blonde currently dancing on his feet would not exist. For the gift of his Amalie, Devin would always be grateful to Mallory. He would prefer, however, to be grateful to Mallory, his ex-wife who lived in another state, instead of to Mallory, the careless, self-absorbed woman who currently shared his name.

"Now it's time to change partners," the DJ announced. "Next dance is Ladies' Choice." His enthusiasm sent the dance floor into chaos as the ladies jockeyed for position, some enjoying the first opportunity of the night to dance with a special someone.

Darcie didn't move, but her eyes reflexively flew to the face of the one man she wanted to ask. Devin was studying her, questioningly. After a few seconds, his entire demeanor changed as relief flooded his face. He felt something tug on his hand. Amalie. He tore his eye from Darcie to his daughter, still standing on his shoes.

"What's Ladies' Choice, Daddy?" Amalie asked, her big blue eyes full of curiosity.

"That means the ladies ask the gentlemen to dance," Devin's mother answered, appearing just in time to answer her granddaughter's question. "*You* get to choose who you want to dance with next," Allana continued. "And I know someone who would love to be asked." She gestured toward her husband.

Rob was looking up at the ceiling, pretending he wasn't paying attention.

"Hurray!" squealed Amalie. She jumped off Devin's shoes to run to her grandfather. "Papa Rob, I choose you," she announced, dipping into a childish curtsey.

"Me?" Rob asked, trying to keep the grin off his face. He bowed solemnly, before holding out his arm to his granddaughter.

Allana watched them go with a delighted smile on her face. Devin smiled, too. But his smile was for someone else.

The wave of heat that rushed through Darcie's body made her feel reckless. Was this her chance? Could she ask Devin to dance without anybody noticing? How could she not? She took a tentative step in his direction, halting as Devin's wife stood from the table. Mallory had finally stopped texting—and she was heading straight for her husband. Darcie froze. How could she have forgotten Devin had a wife? Her disappointment turned to anger as she watched Mallory lightly skim her hand over Devin's arm, making a comment that brought a red flush to his cheeks.

The heartless woman turned from him quickly, a self-satisfied smirk on her face. She tracked down her chosen target, plowing over Lydia in her haste to latch onto Roger's arm. He looked less than thrilled to be chosen and a little unhappy with Joey, who had practically whisked Diana out of his grasp. Joey looked so triumphant at avoiding Mallory's grasping hands that Diana couldn't seem to stop smiling.

Mallory's callous shove propelled Lydia straight into Dom, who caught her arms and steadied her. She thanked him for the rescue without taking advantage of the opportunity to ask him to dance. Lydia's divorce had stripped her of her confidence with members of the opposite sex. She quickly returned to her seat.

Across the ballroom, couples were pairing off, their happy chatter echoing through the vast, open space. Ana Martin asked Dom the minute Lydia walked away. Lou came out of nowhere to grab Blane by the elbow with a mischievous wink to her best friend, the bride. Not to be outdone, Grace made a beeline for Evander, blowing a kiss to the leggy blonde.

But, to Darcie, the noise and movement faded away as she focused on one man. He was the only one she wanted. He was smiling at her, less than ten feet away, daring her to close the gap between them. She looked around the room noting that everyone seemed totally distracted with his or her own partner. Or hors d'oeuvres. Or wine. She narrowed her eyes as Devin's grin widened. He crossed his arms, raising his eyebrow. A clear challenge.

She responded automatically. *Careful what you wish for, Pirate,* she telegraphed back. Darcie Finch did not back down from a challenge. That wasn't a secret. He had forced her hand, and he knew it. She had to ask him now.

His mind filled with abject satisfaction; she had responded exactly as he hoped she would. A multitude of unlikely scenarios tumbled through his brain....

He would pull her into his arms and kiss her senseless.

No, that would be extremely careless and counterproductive. He wanted to catch his wife in an affair. Not the other way around.

He would pick her up and carry her out of the ballroom, where he would find a deserted room, pull her into his arms, and kiss her senseless.

Better, but still an asinine idea.

Hmm…He would tell her to pretend to faint, so he could pick her up, carry her out of the ballroom, pull her into his arms, and kiss her senseless.

Highly unlikely. He doubted Darcie had ever fainted in her life.

He would calmly share a dance, pretending it wasn't a big deal, while secretly arranging to meet her later…and then gently, lovingly, kiss her senseless.

Not bad. That one just might work.

He felt anything but calm as his Pirate Queen started toward him. He was so focused on the woman walking toward him that he must have missed the gentle tug on his sleeve. He saw Darcie hesitate, watched her expression soften with fondness. And regret.

Devin's mind screamed. *Don't stop. Please don't stop now. Don't you change your mind about us, Darcie Finch.* He felt the tug on his sleeve again, but more strongly this time. With great difficulty, he forced himself to take his eye off his Pirate Queen, who was now almost close enough to touch.

One of the Parker twins was shyly smiling up at him. He thought it was the quiet one—the twin who had asked about Iggy and had made Amalie smile—but he couldn't be sure. He didn't remember either of the red-headed girls' names anyway.

"Mr. Merritt, will you dance with me?" she asked in a trembling voice, glancing behind her anxiously. When she turned back, he felt the full force of her big brown, hopeful eyes.

Devin was filled with compassion. How could he say no? The brave girl was very young and very nervous, although she was trying so hard to summon a little bit of dignity. He met the gaze of the woman he wanted.

Darcie nodded. Her lips tipped up ruefully. *Maybe next time*, she seemed to say.

He held out his arm. "Miss Parker, I would be delighted."

Phoebe took his proffered arm with a sigh of relief, glancing back one more time before allowing him to lead her farther onto the dance floor. "Thank you so much, Mr. Merritt. I knew you were kind," she admitted with an amusing air of satisfaction.

That she had doubted his kindness stung a bit, but he couldn't blame her. He knew his scarred visage could be off-putting to all but the bravest souls. Usually he didn't care, but something about the brown-eyed teenager tugged at his fatherly heart. "Was that fact in doubt?" he asked casually, watching her for signs of fear or disgust.

She grinned, completely at ease. "Oh, no. Not to me," she said. "I was just trying to prove a point to, um…someone." She glanced over her shoulder again, unconsciously identifying the someone as her twin. Penelope was watching their dance with a shocked expression on her face.

"I appreciate your vote of confidence, Miss Parker," Devin replied, twirling the girl in a circle.

"Phoebe," she volunteered after completing the turn. "I'm Phoebe."

"Well, thank you for looking beyond my physical appearance, Phoebe."

He smiled at the girl, almost certain she was the one who had been so nice to Amalie.

"Oh, that's okay. Lots of people have scars on the inside, Mr. Merritt," she said confidently. "Yours are just easier to see."

He experienced a moment of alarm when she said that, searching her open, honest expression for evidence she was trying to tell him something serious. "Do you have scars, Phoebe?" he asked, carefully.

"Oh, no. I wasn't talking about myself. The only scar I have is this little one on my elbow. See." She showed him a tiny scar on the inside of her arm. "I got that from missing the last step coming out of the library. The steps were all icy that day," she confided. "I was talking about my brother, the one who's dancing with Darcie."

Devin turned his head, expecting to see Dominic Parker. Instead he saw the dark, good looks of Dom's brother, Ric. What was the deal with the damn Parker brothers? Did this Ric guy have something going on with Darcie, too? He had a sudden thought. "You don't have any more brothers, do you, Phoebe?"

"Oh, no, Mr. Merritt." Phoebe giggled. "Two is enough. That's what Mama says, anyway."

Devin watched the handsome Ric whisper into Darcie's ear. Whatever he said, it made her laugh out loud. He spun her in a wide circle before pulling her close. Too close, in Devin's opinion. He almost growled in frustration.

"Your brother looks pretty happy to me," he said.

"Oh, Ric likes to come home, but in a few days, he'll get that look on his face. Then he'll leave again," Phoebe added, sadly. "I miss him when he's gone." Her lips turned down, making her freckles stand out a bit more.

Good riddance, Devin thought.

"I'm sorry, Phoebe," he said, trying not to show his relief upon learning that good, old Ric wouldn't be around for long. "Maybe one day he'll decide to come home for good." *Let's hope he falls in love with an Australian woman and decides to settle down Down Under.* At any other time, Devin's clever turn of phrase would have amused him.

"I used to hope he would marry Darcie," Phoebe continued. "So she would be my sister, but I've given up on that idea."

"And why is that?" Devin asked absently, convinced he and Phoebe were dancing to the longest song ever recorded.

"Because I think she's going to marry you. After you divorce your um... wife, of course." She smiled sweetly, completely unaware that her honesty had knocked the breath out of her partner. When the music stopped, Phoebe practically ran off the dance floor to find her twin. She couldn't wait to tell Penelope that Mr. Merritt was, indeed, kind. And that she had been right all along.

Devin, still astonished by Phoebe's perception, saw Ric give Darcie a kiss on the cheek before they walked over to the group currently surrounding the bride and groom. He squelched the flare of white-hot jealousy that surged through his body, replacing it with the sudden urge to talk to his good friend, Blane. The appearance of his own little princess halted him in his tracks. Her arms and legs were draped over the shoulder of Papa Rob, and she yawned as she waved to Devin. As Rob handed her over with a kiss on the cheek, Devin was gifted with the most brilliant idea. He moved toward the group of chairs that were closest to the newlyweds. In other words, closest to Miss Darcie Finch.

Amalie poked him in the shoulder. She had surprising strength for a sleepy four-year-old. "No, Daddy," she said. "Not there. I want Iggy." She pointed to the seats they had occupied during the dinner...the ones on the opposite end of the long table.

Devin sighed. He might as well give up his quest for now. Telling an exhausted child that she couldn't sit with her iguana was not a battle he was going to win. He sank, gratefully, into a chair beside Roger Carrington. Lou, Evander, and Mallory sat close by.

Devin massaged his shoulder with his hand. Either he was getting weaker or Amalie was getting heavier.

After a brief perusal he regarded his daughter with some amusement. Her tiara was sideways on her head; her hair partially undone. There was an enormous hole in her white tights. At some point during the reception, she had lost the ribbon that wrapped around her waist. She more closely resembled a homeless orphan than a princess, but she smiled happily as she hugged her reptile.

Lou stood and took the pins out of Amalie's hair so that it hung down her back in one long braid. Amalie yawned several times during the process.

Not long after that, she crawled into Devin's lap, clutched Iggy to her chest, and promptly fell asleep. As he held his sleeping daughter, Devin realized Mallory had not had anything to do with Amalie since they entered the ballroom for the reception. *Emotional abandonment.* Darcie's words echoed in his head as he listened to the lively conversation proceeding around him. It was a sad situation for the little girl, especially because her mother was currently one seat away, on the other side of Carrington. Mallory made no move to take the exhausted child upstairs to bed.

Zack was, apparently, worried about the same thing. "So, why don't *you* put her to bed?" he asked Mallory, genuine curiosity in his voice. "You're her mama, aren't you?"

Mallory glared at the teenager for dragging her away from her phone, but before she could blast him for his impertinence, he continued: "My mama always said putting me to bed was her favorite time of the day."

"I can understand why," Roger said. He leaned back in his chair and put both hands in his pockets.

"Because she loved spending time with me."

Zack grinned, a young man secure in his mother's love.

"Nope." Roger laughed. "Because when you went to sleep you finally stopped talking. It was probably the only time of day the poor woman had any peace."

Zack jerked his head upwards then reached both his hands behind his shoulder blades, as though to pull out the bloody blade that had ruthlessly stabbed him. The group shared smiles of amusement…all but Mallory. She continued to glare in Zack's direction. Her disapproval did nothing to stem the young man's tenacity; if anything, her continued perusal egged him on. "So, why *don't* you put her to bed? Isn't that what moms are supposed to do?" Zack was like a dog with a bone.

Devin sighed, causing Roger to glance his way inquiringly. Mallory's husband simply shook his head and waited. He knew what was going to happen. Zack was about to be bitten by the snake.

Mallory stood, her lovely lips curving prettily. Her hand delicately covered her heart. She closed her eyes, taking a deep breath. Devin knew that this particular display had the twofold purpose of drawing the attention of the companions seated at their table *and* showcasing her plunging neckline.

Oh Lord, here we go.

Devin almost groaned, wishing he could think of something—*any*thing—to distract his wife. But, he knew, she loved nothing better than this. Any interference on his part would only result in an uglier mess.

Mallory opened her eyes. They were luminous, as if she could barely contain the joy she held within.

Devin felt sick. The only joy Mallory ever experienced was in causing the pain of others. He could do little more than stick around to perform damage control after his wife was finished humiliating poor Zack.

"Oh, Zeke," Mallory breathed, embarking on her performance.

"It's Zack," the teenager said, politely.

Mallory acknowledged the mistake with a silvery giggle, her hand coming to her mouth to cover her error. "Oh, Zack," she continued, still in that light tone. "You're so lucky. So very lucky. Sixteen years old…"

"I'm eighteen," Zack chimed in. But his bright tone belied the shrewd expression that had come into his eyes.

"Really?" Mallory said, in a tone of disbelief designed to strip Zack of any confidence he might still have left. "You act so much younger than that. Oh, well. You're very lucky, young man, to be at the age where you think you know everything. The sad reality, dear Zeke, is that you know *Ab-so-lute-ly No-thing.*" Her slight separation of syllables only emphasized her underlying meaning. "Oh, how I envy your ignorance. Enjoy this time, Zeke," Mallory whispered solemnly, "for it will not come again." She paused triumphantly, waiting for Zack's self-esteem to crumble in front of everyone's eyes.

Zack stared right back at his tormentor, undaunted, and savvy beyond his years. "You're right, lady," he said, leaning back in his chair so that it balanced on two legs. He slipped his hands into his pockets as Roger had done earlier, grinning wickedly. "You're one hundred percent right. It's damn good to be me."

Lou choked on her wine then started coughing. Devin suspected she was choking with laughter. Evander patted her on the back as he and Roger exchanged a satisfied glance. Their boy had done well. Devin kept a serious expression on his own face, as Mallory's eyes flickered to his. Let her think he was on her side. It would be better for everyone in the long run.

Mallory regarded Zack's unexpected aplomb with astonishment. Everyone else at their end of the table was watching her with varying degrees of displeasure.

"I'm going to get a drink," she finally said, withdrawing quickly from her defeat on this particular battlefield.

Nobody spoke for several moments.

"How about those Philadelphia Eagles?" Roger finally asked, deliberately changing subjects. "They're looking pretty good this year. They're going to be tough to beat."

General conversation quickly broke out. Everyone gradually relaxed.

At the conversation continued, Devin caught Zack's eye. He raised his glass in a silent salute. Zack grinned, reaching for Evander's wine glass. Evander's big hand came down, halting his progress. Undeterred, Zack picked up his glass of sweet tea and returned Devin's gesture.

CHAPTER THIRTY-EIGHT

𝒟ouglas McCallum stood beside the bar in his deceased brother's ballroom. No, that wasn't quite right, he argued with himself. The *current* owner of the stunning property was three-fourths of the way across the room, dancing with his new bride. No matter, Douglas decided. His nephew, Blane, would always be a sniveling twelve-year-old in his mind. And Heart's Ease would always be Donovan's. It was the end result of Don's marriage to Lily, the woman who was his brother's obsession. And his downfall. That obsession had brought Don to Heart's Ease. Living here had killed him. Yes, Douglas conceded. His brother and sister-in-law could have been hit by a drunk driver anywhere. But they hadn't been, had they? It had happened here. Well, he thought, heartlessly, good riddance to them both.

He glanced at his phone. Calli would call in a few minutes. *Damn.* His brilliant plan to crash his nephew's wedding hadn't turned out the way he thought it would. How he dreaded admitting that. It was always hell when he was wrong and Calli was right.

Douglas surveyed the elegant room filled with smiling guests enjoying themselves.

For the first time since he arrived, he allowed his eyes to settle on the laughing profile of the mother of the bride. Juliette Hanover. *Finch*, he reminded himself. *Juliette Hanover Finch.* She had seemed so trusting all those years ago. So sweet and kind, with a soft, Southern accent and eyes like twin emeralds. It was the accent that had caught his attention. He quickly discovered that—in addition to her hot, little body—Juliette was also just sassy enough to be interesting. She was a proper lady with a hidden fire. A true Southern belle. That made her irresistible to his ego. He was the conqueror and she, the unsuspecting object of his lust. Douglas absently rubbed the slight bump on the bridge of his nose. He still had that little memento from his unfortunate encounter with the fist of Joe Finch…the only physical defect on an otherwise perfect profile. That, alone, gave him good cause to hate the interfering son of a bitch.

No, things weren't going at all as he had planned. At the very least, he had attended his nephew's wedding in anticipation of tormenting Juliette. Her unattainable status still called to his overcharged libido. The never forgotten object of his desire, however, was untouchable. She was surrounded by sentries, cleverly dispatched by an unknown someone, probably her ever-vigilant husband. The occupants of the chairs changed, but the chairs were always occupied, leaving no doubt regarding the layers of protection currently surrounding his target. Joe hadn't been lying. Several very high-profile individuals were in attendance. Douglas' face curled into an ugly snarl as he recognized Senator Edwin Whitehurst as one of those engaged in conversation with the lovely Juliette.

"Enjoying yourself?" Rafe asked, politely.

Douglas started at the sudden appearance of Blane's watchdog, admonishing himself. While he was at Heart's Ease he would have to be more mindful of his facial expressions. Montgomery was the king of appearing out of nowhere…The damn man noticed everything.

Douglas took a deliberate swallow of his wine, giving his anger a chance to dissipate. It wouldn't do for Montgomery to become any more interested in the activities of his employer's uncle than he already was. Thanks to Rafe and the odd assortment of men and women that made up the security department of McCallum Industries, Douglas had been forced to step down as president of the North American branch of the company. No, that wasn't quite right. Douglas, himself, was at least partially to blame for the one unfortunate hire he had horribly misjudged. How had Douglas McCallum, of all people, made the mistake of hiring an honest man? The ensuing mess had forced him to make significant security adjustments of his own, which had severely curtailed his very profitable side business. The past six months would negatively affect his second income for some time to come. But his operation was up and running again, thanks to Calli. And to Bill, Douglas' less intuitive but no less lethal version of Rafe Montgomery.

Douglas forced his lips to smile. "Of course, Montgomery. What's not to enjoy? Beautiful setting. Beautiful ceremony. Beautiful bride. I'm just waiting for the right moment to welcome my brand-new niece into the family." He looked straight into Rafe's eyes, daring him to take offense to that.

"Hmph. Yes, well, make sure that's all you do, Douglas."

Rafe clapped his hand on Douglas' shoulder in an innocuous gesture that, to any observer, would appear as harmless as could be. No one could feel the intense pain that Douglas struggled to hide as Rafe's thumb and forefinger found the hidden nerve and pressed. Hard. Rafe's lips smiled benignly but his eyes were cold as ice as he released Douglas' burning shoulder and vanished into the crowd at the edge of the ballroom.

Damn the man.

Douglas gingerly moved his shoulder as the sting slowly receded. He had greatly underestimated not only Rafe Montgomery but his nephew as well. Blane hadn't been the least bit surprised or upset at his uncle's sudden appearance. Come to think of it, nobody had been caught off guard. Their plan to deal with his unwanted presence had obviously been in place for quite some time. From the minute he stepped out of the car, he was outmanned, outgunned, and completely out-smarted. He anticipated making a scene when they forbid him entry into the event, but they ruined those plans by saving him a seat. Douglas was so shocked that he obediently complied with their wishes, ending up uncomfortably seated between Montgomery and Ian, his bastard half brother. He would have been a fool to start anything from that position, and Douglas McCallum was no fool. Hell, one of the two would probably have snapped his neck at the slightest provocation. But quietly, so as not to interrupt the wedding vows.

To make matters even more impossible, Alina had been seated on the other side of Ian. She nodded her head coolly at Douglas, handing him a wedding program with all the disdain of a queen. At the sight of his sister-in-law, Douglas felt the familiar hunger course through him. The lithe and alluring Alina was blatant sex appeal wrapped in a sophisticated package. He had wanted to unwrap that package for years. His one futile attempt, soon after her marriage to Ian, ended with her knee in his chest and her knife at his throat. He never tried again but remained perversely attracted to the deadly woman.

Discovering, a few months ago, that Alina was Rafe's daughter inspired more questions than it answered. He didn't know where the hell Rafe and Alina had come from or what kind of special forces they, and his bastard brother, were involved in. He would probably never know. What he did know was that they were a lethal trio…one beyond the ability of even Douglas and his "associates" to eliminate. How he would love to make the three of them permanently disappear, he thought, wistfully. Well, maybe not Alina, at least not until he had…humbled her. Douglas smiled at the thought until a latent twinge in his shoulder decided to express itself, reminding him of the stark reality. No, he decided. His best bet was to fly under the radar when it came to those three. The alternative would win him nothing more than a free trip to the morgue.

He had to admit that he rarely experienced such a thorough defeat. Even though his arrogance preened at the effort they had made on his behalf, he couldn't help but feel a grudging amount of respect. On this one occasion, Douglas would give them credit for the victory. Montgomery was good, there was no denying that. But, in the great wide scheme of things, he hadn't been quite good enough. At least not yet.

Douglas finished his wine, a surprisingly pleasing vintage for the Middle of Nowhere, North Carolina. Or wherever the hell they were. His situation, he realized, was made considerably worse by another, very pressing problem. There were just certain things Calli couldn't or wouldn't do, and certain things Douglas couldn't or wouldn't do without. His longtime lover understood his sexual proclivities, turning a blind eye to the number of women that littered Douglas' nightlife. The illusion of the careless playboy was important. It kept the eyes of those around him firmly fixed on his public persona, and conveniently averted from his business "ventures."

That's why the tragic demise of his secret lover, Sheila, was so inconvenient. Poor Sheila. He missed her already. She was always so eager and willing to satisfy his basest desires, the more unusual, the better. Their one night had turned into…more nights. Before Douglas realized it, six months had passed. She lasted longer than any lover he ever had…except for Calli, of course. Douglas made sure to keep the number of times he visited Sheila a secret. Calli might countenance an occasional one-night stand but didn't like to share.

Poor Sheila. Poor overly possessive, overly confident Sheila. And such bad judgement. Attempting to bribe a lover was bad form. One might call it something of a fatal mistake. Drug overdoses were so tragically common these days. Such a sad reality.

Since Sheila's unfortunate death, Douglas had been bored. He needed a new toy. Two weeks with nothing to play with was making him restless and cranky. That was why he was standing here indulging himself with fantasies of Juliette and Alina. Damn, but this trip was a bad idea, he admitted to himself. He would wait for Calli's call, get the hell out of Disneyland, and… then what? Maybe fly to Vegas?

Just then a woman caught his eye. He blew out a breath of pure frustration, going on the alert. He recognized her immediately. Mallory Merritt, unfortunate wife of the forever damaged head of McCallum Industries' legal department. Douglas felt a rare twinge of regret for his part, however inadvertent, in the attack that had deprived the world of the masculine beauty of Devin Merritt. The poor man's face was a veritable wreck compared to the gorgeous visage he formerly enjoyed. And, according to rumors, his wife wasn't particularly kind about it.

Mrs. Merritt was approaching quickly, a hot little number in a low-cut dress. Totally inappropriate for a wedding, Douglas mused. She looked, well… angry. Like she needed to blow off a little steam. What a coincidence. Blowing off steam was Douglas' specialty. The party had just gotten interesting. Why would he want Snow White when he could have the Wicked Queen?

MACEE MCNEILL

Mallory elbowed her way through the crowd, indifferent to the annoyed glances she left in her wake. She needed a drink. Now. If she didn't have something to calm her nerves, she was going to scream. *That cocky little know-it-all teenager,* she fumed to herself. Nobody talked that way to Mallory Merritt and got away with it. Didn't he know who she was?

She placed both of her beautifully manicured hands on the bar. She cleared her throat. Twice. By the time the busy bartender finished serving the person who stood beside her, she could barely contain herself. Those lovely hands were balled into fists of sheer frustration.

"Yes, ma'am?" the bartender asked, a wary look in his eye. He had seen her type before. "What can I get for you?"

"You mean *me*?" Mallory asked sarcastically, slightly offended by his use of the word *ma'am*. "I can't believe you finally have time for *me*."

"What can I get for you, ma'am?" The bartender's grimace was barely visible.

Douglas would have missed it if he hadn't been paying close attention.

Mallory actually flinched this time. "I should not be addressed as *ma'am*," she instructed angrily. "The word *ma'am* should be reserved for a woman who is old or unmarried." She gestured to her flawless face and figure with a dramatic sweep of her arm. She ended by waving her enormous wedding rings in the expressionless bartender's face. He couldn't have missed them if he tried. "As you can see, I am neither old nor unmarried."

The bartender had developed a slight twitch in his jaw. "Yes, ma'am...I mean...I..." He paused, treading carefully this time. "You're not from around here, are you?"

Mallory looked at him in amazement. "What's that got to do with anything?"

The bartender sighed. "What exactly would you like to be called, ma'am?"

Mallory's eyes nearly rolled back into her head with frustration. They were obviously at an impasse.

Another bartender—sporting the name *Jeff* on his nametag—tapped Mallory's current opponent on the shoulder, unintentionally putting a halt to their syntax war. "Time for your break, Paul. There's a great buffet set up in the dining room just for the staff. You should check it out. You were right. Best wedding job I've ever worked. Mr. McCallum sure is a great guy."

Paul took one last look at Mallory's angry expression. Then, he fled.

The clueless Jeff took his place. "What can I get for you, ma'am?" he asked with a friendly smile.

Mallory's face crumpled in vexation, her clenched fists slowly rapping the bar. "Scotch on the rocks," she said through tightly clenched teeth. "And make it a double."

"I'm sorry, ma'am," Jeff said, completely oblivious to her anger. "We're only serving beer and wine today."

Mallory gripped the edge of the bar with both hands. She opened her mouth to give the hapless bartender a tongue-lashing he would never forget. But before she could speak, Douglas saw his opportunity to intervene.

He strolled over, leaning in until his mouth was very close to her ear. "Order club soda," he advised.

She turned her head angrily, her eyes widening in recognition. "Mr. McCallum," she gasped, surprised into silence.

Douglas turned to the bartender. "One club soda for the lady," he said smoothly. "And only half full." Taking Mallory's hand he raised it to his mouth, pressing a kiss on the tips of her fingers. He purposely allowed his lips to linger a moment longer than necessary. His calculated effort was rewarded by her soft intake of breath. Interest suddenly bloomed in her blue eyes.

Douglas took Mallory's club soda from the bartender. Without releasing Mallory's hand, he tugged her over to the end of the bar, tucked against the wall. And relatively out of sight. He reached into the inner pocket of his tux jacket, pulling out an overly ornate flask. After pouring a substantial amount of the contents into Mallory's club soda, he closed the flask, replacing it in his pocket. "Your scotch, milady," he said as he handed her the glass.

Mallory took an appreciative sip, arranging herself against the bar so that her assets showed to good advantage.

Douglas' heated gaze raked her from head to toe. "What's a lovely lady like you doing in a place like this?" He had found, over the years, that the oldest clichés were the quickest way to get what he wanted.

"It certainly is a substandard gathering," she agreed, sipping her drink. "Nothing like I'm used to, I can assure you of that." She all but quivered under his intense perusal.

Interesting, he thought. "I am surprised your husband is willing to let a gorgeous woman like you out of his sight for a second. How is he doing, anyway?"

She rolled her eyes at the mention of her absent spouse. "My husband?" Her flippant tone held an edge of contempt. "Oh, you're talking about my *monster*. It's a little harder for him to keep me in his sight now. He has only one eye, you know, and the rest of his face..." She shuddered before leaning closer to confide: "I have to tell you, Mr. McCallum—"

"Call me Douglas," he interjected smoothly, pasting a sympathetic look on his face.

"Douglas." She made a show of dabbing her dry eyes with the corner of her cocktail napkin before continuing. "I have to tell you, Douglas, that Devin's attack has wreaked havoc on our marriage. I mean, can you imagine how painful it is for me to look at those scars? Day in and day out? And that horrible eyepatch? His artificial eye is even worse. It never moves. It just sits there looking straight ahead. Thank goodness he decided to keep it covered. I just don't think I could have borne it for much longer."

"Mm-hmm," murmured Douglas encouragingly. "Tell me more, Mrs. Merritt."

"Mallory," she said, in a silky voice. "Call me Mallory."

"Mallory." Devin's wife was getting ready to amp up her performance. Douglas could tell. With a few well-chosen words and those luminous blue eyes, she managed to divert all of the sympathy that should have gone to her husband onto herself. At that moment he knew he was dealing with a professional.

Mallory continued her rant. "He also refuses to have more plastic surgery. He's going to look the way he looks right now for the rest of his life. I never thought Devin would betray me like that." The cocktail napkin was in use again. She also added a shaky breath for emphasis, looking away as if she couldn't bear to think about the cruelty awaiting her.

Douglas' hand came down on her arm, squeezing gently, letting her know she had his support. "How could he make such a choice? Doesn't he understand what you're going through?"

Mallory turned her head, surprised at his response. "That's exactly what I tried to tell him. He just kept repeating the doctor's warnings about fragile nerve endings and possible facial paralysis. Over and over again. He might lose the ability to chew his food. But, so what? Who cares about being able to move your mouth when you look like a monster? Another plastic surgery would be so much better for me…I mean, for him. But he just won't do it. He won't even try. He's so selfish. He never even thinks of me or of how I feel. Oh, Douglas, I just don't think I can bear it." She took a deep breath, raising hopeful eyes to the man standing beside her as if he was the answer to all of the problems in her world.

What a cold bitch, Douglas thought with approval. *She doesn't think about anyone but herself. No scruples, and even fewer morals. I think I'm in love.*

"There, there, Mallory," he said. "I can't believe your own husband could be so cruel. It might be too soon to admit it after such a short conversation, but I feel like I understand you completely. Like we have a special connection." By which Douglas meant: *I understand exactly what you are, my manipulative little temptress.*

"That means so much to me, Douglas," she said, breathlessly, her eyes clinging to his.

"I would be delighted to offer you a shoulder to cry on…or anything else you might need in the future. You only have to—"

Douglas' phone rang. *Damn.* He closed his eyes. He was so very close to arranging a fiery encounter with this woman with the icy heart.

Yes, he knew she had her own agenda. That's why he made himself appear so easy to manipulate. The cold, hard reality was that she had no idea who she was dealing with. When she was absolutely certain of her own imagined power…well, that's when Douglas would make his move. Subduing all of that indignant passion would be half the fun.

Douglas' phone rang again. He couldn't keep Calli waiting. An angry Calli wasn't an option. He pasted an apologetic smile on his face. "I really have to take this call. Business, you know."

Her smile was luminous. "Oh, I understand, Douglas."

"Until we meet again, Mallory." His voice caressed each syllable of her name. He squeezed her arm one more time then left her alone without a backward glance. He experienced a surge of triumph as he walked away, swearing he could feel her eyes watching him.

Devin watched as the other groomsmen left for the billiard room and, he imagined, a little liquid refreshment. He would be leaving, too, in a minute, but his destination was a different one. It was time to take his little princess upstairs to bed.

A soft hand touched his shoulder. He looked up into his sister's understanding hazel eyes. "Mom says she and Dad are going to say their goodbyes and head upstairs in a few minutes." Lydia's eyes twinkled with laughter. "She says it's past Dad's bedtime."

Devin couldn't help but grin at his sister's words. Robert Merritt was the first to admit that any charm he might possess disappeared the moment he got sleepy. It was a family joke.

Lydia grinned back. "She also said they would be happy for you to put Amalie in the extra bed in their room, so you can come back down for the rest of the reception."

"That sounds like a plan."

Devin nodded, grateful for his parents' support. Lord knew he never got any from Mallory, wherever she was. He hadn't seen her since she stomped away after her exchange with Zack. There had been something incredibly satisfying about watching a teenager put his self-important wife in her place. No, he didn't know where Mallory was. Furthermore, he had no intention of looking for her. To be honest, he didn't really care where she was. Or who she was with, for that matter. Unless she was with the imaginary paddleboard instructor that he had conjured up earlier…the one with the power to free him and his sleeping daughter from the snake….

Amalie hadn't moved since she crawled into his lap half an hour ago. His poor baby was exhausted. He hesitated, pondering how to stand up without waking her.

"Let me help," Lydia offered. Leaning over, she gathered her sleeping niece into her arms. "She's so much heavier asleep than awake," she remarked.

Devin struggled to his feet, chuckling. "Tell me about it." He gingerly shook his right leg. The pins-and-needles sensation let him know that his sleeping limb was coming to life. "Thanks, Lyd. I'll take her now."

Lydia hugged the little girl jealously. "That's all right, Dev. She's not that heavy. I don't mind helping you put her to bed." Her voice was wistful. Devin felt a momentary flash of anger toward the man who had broken his little sister's heart. And her spirit. The entire family knew how much Lydia longed for a child of her own.

"All right, sis. I'll just get her things."

Devin picked up the tiara and the other treasures Amalie had carefully piled onto the table before falling asleep.

"And Iggy," Lydia said. "Don't forget Iggy, whatever you do."

They both looked around for the errant iguana.

"There he is." Lydia saw him first. "There, on the floor. Your little princess would not be pleased."

"Look at him. Poor slob. He probably drank too much and passed out down there," Devin joked, as he bent down to pick up the stuffed animal. He stood up. Three tables away, Darcie stood up. Their eyes locked across the room. She gave him a sad, little smile before turning to make her way to the dessert table.

Devin's grip tightened around the iguana's tail. That was it. He had to do something. And, in this case, the solution was clear. It was easier than any proof from geometry class, as easy as it was obvious. Darcie was sad. Because of him. Which was unacceptable. Therefore, he had to talk to Darcie.

As he followed Lydia from the ballroom, his mind worked feverishly. Before they reached the guest wing, he had come up with the perfect plan. The only problem was that his perfect plan involved his skittish little sister.

"Hey, Lyd," Devin said, softly. "I have an idea and I need your help."

She eyed him suspiciously as they walked up the stairs. She knew that tone of voice, had lived through the fallout from her brother's ideas one time too many. She mentally ticked a few of them off in her head. There was the time Devin thought jumping off the roof of the chicken house was a great idea. He promised to catch her, but she ended up with a cast on her arm for the rest of the summer. And there was the time Devin thought playing barber with the dog was a great idea. The poor dog looked like some freakish beast from a nightmare. Worse than that, the wayward siblings lost all television privileges for two weeks. And there was the time Devin dared her to eat all of her Halloween candy at once. She still couldn't hear the words *trick or treat* without shuddering. And there were so many more examples of how following her brother's lead had been a terrible idea. Yes, she had always gone along with Devin's ideas. But this time, she hesitated. "I don't know, Dev," she said, "sometimes your ideas are a little…"

He stopped climbing the stairs. "Please, Lydia," he said, serious, for once.

And just like that they were children again. And she couldn't tell her beloved brother "no."

Lydia sighed. "All right, Dev, but I have a feeling I'm going to regret this. What do you want me to do?"

"Well, Baby Sister, it's like this. I need an alibi." He paused, his eyes intense in the dim light. "I need *you* to be my alibi."

CHAPTER THIRTY-NINE

"Thanks for coming with me, Darcie," Lydia said, trying to make sure the doors connecting the ballroom and the grand foyer were once again tightly closed.

"No problem," Darcie responded. "I know how annoying a broken strap can be. We'll get you all put back together in no time."

As she watched Devin's sister double-check the doors, Darcie's confusion grew. Lydia had refused to go to the ladies' room located in the ballroom, insisting instead on visiting the one by the front doors. Why? Darcie studied the young woman in front of her, noting her flushed cheeks and the way her hands were shaking as she fiddled with the door. Maybe Devin's sister was just overly cautious or OCD or something. Or maybe she was just a little…odd.

"That's good enough, hon," Darcie said, kindly, when she couldn't stand it another minute. "Nobody's using these doors, anyway, except the servers." She gently pried the nervous woman's hands off the doorknobs.

Lydia's gaze flitted past Darcie's shoulder to fix on the rounded arch of the entryway. The apologetic expression on her face turned to one of relief.

Darcie felt a little thrill run down her spine. She was certain Devin was standing behind her. She was absolutely certain. Lydia nodded her head, encouragingly. When Darcie slowly turned around, she found him watching her from the edge of the entryway.

He was standing in the shadows. She couldn't see his face, but she could sense his intensity. He didn't say a word. Instead he held out his hand, asking her to come with him. She understood immediately that it was her choice. If she walked back into the ballroom, he would not follow her. Darcie had never lacked courage or the ability to take a chance, but she hesitated. The consequences of being caught in the arms of this man—and she had no doubt as to her destination if she went with him—were huge. And far-reaching. They affected more than just the two of them.

She glanced again at Lydia. "Mallory?" she whispered.

"I can handle her," Lydia said, with a little less confidence than Darcie would have liked. Devin's little sister would be more convincing if she would stop wringing her hands.

Darcie looked at Devin again. He was standing all alone in the dim light. So very alone. And so very dear. He was asking her to take a risk. For him. The pounding of her heart effectively silenced the warning of her logical self. Darcie turned back to Lydia. "Thank you," she said, simply, leaning in to give Devin's little sister a quick hug.

Her jeweled heels clicked across the floor, echoing in the cavernous space as she made short work of the distance between them. She put her hand in Devin's, allowing him to pull her into the darkened entry. There wasn't another choice. There never had been.

"Be careful," Lydia said, softly, as she watched them disappear through the front door. She leaned back against the double doors of the ballroom, breathing a sigh of relief. *All right, Lydia,* she encouraged herself. It was time to go to work. She could do this. For Devin. She was determined to dig down deep to find the remains of her poise, the shreds of her courage. Both had been missing since the day she embarked on her disastrous marriage. This was not the time to fall apart, she reminded herself. She would deal with her hateful sister-in-law *and* give her brother a moment of happiness.

Lydia straightened her spine before returning to the ballroom. She was determined to find Mallory and stick to her like glue.

UNMASKING THE HEART

Come with me, Darcie. Come with me, love.

The litany had begun in Devin's head the moment he saw her. She was so luminous. So perfect. Devin struggled with self-doubt. How could she want to be with someone like him? Had he misjudged her? Had he made a mistake? He watched the play of emotions dance across her flawless features. He could tell she was struggling between head and heart. Between what was safe, smart, and prudent—and what she wanted.

Come with me, Darcie. Come with me, love.

His plan was dangerous. And foolish. But it was entirely necessary to his sanity. When he saw her hesitate, he actually stopped breathing for a few seconds. Or minutes. Or, what felt a hell of a lot like an eternity. Now, he found himself a little light-headed from lack of oxygen.

He watched her float across the grand foyer toward him, half-convinced he was dreaming. When she reached him, he took her hand, folding it in his. Her fingers were cold. They trembled slightly, but they were real. This was no dream, he thought gratefully.

They walked onto the portico, careful to stay in the shadows. The majority of the lights at the front of the house—inside and out—had been turned off to discourage guests from straying out of the ballroom. As they were doing, Devin thought, ironically. He led the way toward the steps at the end of the portico. Unbeknownst to Darcie, their romantic rendezvous was slated to occur in the least romantic location possible. The stables.

Devin's reasons for choosing the destination were sound. Nobody would be hanging around in the stables during Blane and Grace's wedding reception. All of Blane's employees were back in the ballroom, enjoying the reception. Devin had made sure of that immediately after hatching his ingenious plan. Even the intrepid Rafe appeared to have taken the night off. Of course, he was probably keeping an eye on Douglas McCallum, Wedding Crasher. Rafe rarely did anything without a motive.

But, perhaps the best reason for choosing the stables was that it was the only place he could think of that Mallory would refuse to go. His appearance-obsessed wife hated everything that had to do with stables…from the dirt and the smell to the horses themselves. Not surprising, he thought, since Mallory had a strong aversion to anything having to do with hard work. Or regular work. Or work of any kind. He realized that he had never seen her do anything remotely approaching labor since he met her. She was…

Not here. But, damn, if her spirit didn't linger. She was, he decided, like mold. She crawled her way onto a surface and stuck there, refusing to let go. Well, no way in hell was he going to let her malevolence ruin his few golden moments with his Pirate Queen. With a practiced effort, he purged his wife from his brain. He chose, instead, to concentrate on the way Darcie's hand felt in his. She clung to him. Willing to follow him anywhere. Trusting him implicitly as they continued down the portico. Her absolute confidence in his abilities made him feel like a king.

Darcie was trying to be patient. Really, she was. But he hadn't said a word about where they were going. He just kept pulling her behind him. And he wasn't slowing down. It wasn't surprising, she reasoned, for her overly developed curiosity to make an appearance.

"Where are we going?" asked Darcie, attempting, but failing, to whisper.

"Shhh."

Devin shook his head, wanting to laugh as much at his own presumptuousness as the idea that Darcie Finch would meekly follow anyone.

"Are you laughing at me?" Her ability to whisper was nonexistent. Her rich voice washed over him in the darkness. How could she sound so annoyed and so sexy at the same time?

"Shhh," he hissed, not trusting himself to speak.

She pursed her lips and raised her eyebrows. He knew, with a keen, amused satisfaction, that she was saying "hmph" in her head.

Devin squeezed her hand as they approached the end of the portico. Almost there. In a few more feet they would be home free.

A burst of laughter from the open window of the billiard room stopped Devin in his tracks. Darcie plowed against his back. She squeaked. That was the only term he could come up with for the sound she made. It seemed to echo in the quiet. He turned his head, looking into eyes wide with the fear of discovery. He felt his confidence waver. Maybe stealing off to the stables was a bad idea. Maybe they should give it up before…

Her eyes narrowed. She gave him a little push, mouthing the word, "Hurry."

Devin grinned, feeling his confidence return. He continued, more slowly this time. He realized Darcie was walking on her toes, trying to be as silent as possible, no easy trick in those heels.

As another huge round of laughter arose from the billiard room again, Darcie nearly jumped out of her skin. They froze, certain that somebody would look out the window this time. But nothing happened. Devin gave her hand a squeeze, speeding up a bit. He was, it seemed, quite eager to reach the end of the portico. They passed the last window; he helped Darcie navigate the steps, pausing to assess their next move. She let go of his hand when they reached the bottom. He studied the terrain. From where he was standing, several smooth pavers curved around to the brick path at the side of the house. That path continued all the way to the middle doors of the stables, about a hundred feet away.

Blane's parents had doubled the size of the existing stable when they purchased Heart's Ease. The middle doors opened onto a wide area that connected the original horse stalls on the east side with the newer addition on the west side. Walking straight through the connecting chamber led to a covered area that was open to the surrounding paddock. Although trees stood on either side of the path, their lower limbs had been trimmed. They, unfortunately, provided no protection for a pair of desperate fugitives. Not an option, Devin decided. He made the executive decision to steal through the darkened yard to reach the original portion of the stables. The darkness would afford them cover until the last few feet. Satisfied, he turned his head to explain his plan to Darcie, but she had disappeared.

"Laurence," she hissed from the darkness. "Hurry up! We don't have all night."

He joined her in the shadows. He was, once again, fighting the urge to laugh as she grabbed his hand, confidently taking the lead.

"We can go around this way and use the side door," she explained, tugging him along.

He liked the fact that she was usually one step ahead of him. He liked the give-and-take that had developed between them. A relationship with Darcie Finch would either be a true partnership or there would be no relationship at all. Lucky for him, he relished that idea.

Douglas McCallum stepped out of Blane's office. Silently, he made his way down the deserted hallway. He bypassed the rowdy billiard room, too angry to give it more than a perfunctory glance. Shoving open the side door, he stepped onto a small landing. He needed a few minutes alone to get over his unpleasantly heated conversation with Calli.

Inhaling deeply, he let the crisp autumn air cool his hot face. He closed his eyes, leaning against the railing. So, crashing the wedding was a bad decision. So what? he asked himself. Calli certainly wasn't the perfect one in their relationship. Not by a long shot. Assuming the role of condescending judge did not reveal his longtime lover in a pleasing light. How dare Calli question his motives. Such needless suspicions made him angry. And being angry made him reckless.

Perhaps it was time to return to the ballroom to further his acquaintance with Devin Merritt's bitchy wife. She might be just the distraction he needed. Before he could turn to go back inside, a movement at the end of the stables caught his eye. He quickly moved away from the light so he couldn't be seen. From his cramped position behind a prickly bush, he spotted the back of a groomsman's black tux jacket opening the stable's door. He couldn't make out the identity of the man. But the woman paused a split second to look toward the house just as the light from the open door illuminated her lovely face.

Well, well, well, Douglas growled with satisfaction. *So the lovely Miss Finch has a secret....* Her name, he recalled, was Darcie. And there was no doubt she was ravishing enough to make a man forget himself.

Douglas smiled. He envied the unknown man who was going to get his hands on that one. He wouldn't mind having a go with Miss Finch himself, but it appeared her opinion of him was already well-established.

Douglas' smile turned into a snarl as he recalled the way she had looked at him earlier. The coldness in her eyes mirrored the icy glare of her father. There was a fine line between hate and passion, but he decided it was better to let Miss Darcie Finch go. Still, knowledge of her assignation might prove useful. Maybe his first attempt at wedding crashing wasn't going as badly as he—or Calli—originally thought.

CHAPTER FORTY

Darcie leaned back against the closed door to the stables, her eyes shining with excitement. "Victory, Laurence. I declare victory. We made it!"

Devin's partner in intrigue grinned at him in triumph, her cheeks rosy with excitement. God help the lawyer who tried to oppose Darcie Finch in a court of law. She would annihilate him by the sheer force of her personality.

He watched her as she reached down and picked up the slightly overweight, yellow cat that had appeared out of nowhere. She took no notice of the fact that the floor was dusty, the cat was dirty, and the whole place smelled strongly of horse. She hugged the cat to her chest, crooning to it as if it was a baby. Only his Pirate Queen could look as drop-dead gorgeous holding a cat in a horse barn as she would at the coronation of a king. It was all part of the aura that surrounded Darcie Finch. He, for one, was completely captivated by her. He shook his head, realizing he couldn't seem to stop smiling.

She drew her eyebrows together and lowered her head. "What?" she asked the cat. "Are you talking about the fellow with the eye patch?" She paused, as if listening to the cat. "Yes, I think so, too." She addressed her next remark to Devin: "The cat thinks you're incredibly handsome standing over there."

"Um, tell the cat thanks?"

In truth, Devin wasn't sure what to say. Being called "incredibly handsome" had thrown him off balance. He had heard those words all the time, up until a few months ago. But now...well, nobody said anything like that to him anymore.

"What was that?" Darcie asked the cat. "You want him to what? Are you sure? That's a little up-close-and-personal. You haven't even been formally introduced." She looked at Devin, mischief in her eyes. "The cat wants you to pet her."

"What if she bites me?"

The look that then passed between Darcie and the cat was not encouraging.

Hmm. Maybe *bite* was too severe. Devin backpedaled a bit. "Not bite. I didn't really mean to say bite. But, well...what if she scratches me?" The last thing Devin wanted to do was catch cat scratch fever from some random feline.

Darcie raised her eyebrows in disbelief. "You really don't know anything about cats, do you?"

"I've never had the privilege. Lydia is allergic," Devin added, by way of explanation.

"Oh, well, that's different." Darcie addressed the cat again: "What do you think?" Apparently the cat came to a quick decision because Darcie leaned over, placing the animal on the ground directly at her feet.

Devin looked at the cat, who returned his gaze unblinkingly. Then he looked at Darcie. The challenge in *her* gaze was unmistakable. Devin felt himself relent. "Um...sure, okay," he mumbled. "Why not?"

Devin took a step toward the feral-looking animal, reaching out his hand as if he would pet it on the head. The cat eyed him suspiciously.

Darcie sighed in mock frustration, shaking her head as she walked over to stand beside him. "No, not like that. Slowly, so she'll learn to trust you." She tugged on his arm until he took a knee beside her on the dusty floor. "Let the cat come to you. Hold out one finger and wait," she instructed, taking his hand and showing him what to do.

Devin was willing to attempt anything if Darcie kept holding his hand, even at the risk of suffering heinous consequences. After a few seconds, the cat made its choice, touching its pink nose to the tip of Devin's finger. He watched as the cat sniffed him and then proceeded to rub against his pant legs. He reached out tentatively, rubbing the soft fur.

After a few moments, the cat wandered a few feet away, positioning herself in front of the wall near the side door. Devin watched her tail swish slowly back and forth, ridiculously pleased that he had risen to the challenge.

"Well, how about that?" he said. "It worked. I hate to admit it, Darcie, but this time, you were right," he teased, waiting for her outburst. "Darcie, I just admitted you were right. Don't you have something to say about that?" When nothing was forthcoming, he got to his feet, looking around. "Darcie?"

But Darcie had wandered up the aisle to the horse stalls. She appeared to be deep in conversation with a striking reddish-brown stallion. Perhaps bringing Darcie to the stables hadn't been the best choice, Devin thought. Brushing the cat hair from his tux, he hurried to catch up.

"This is Fen," Darcie said as he approached.

Devin read the nameplate on the stall. "This says his name is Fenugreek."

"That's right," Darcie agreed. "Fen, for short."

"Who would name a horse Fenugreek?" Devin was intrigued in spite of himself. "What do you suppose it means, anyway?"

Darcie chuckled. "It's a spice. They're all named after spices. Blane's mother started the tradition."

Devin studied the nameplates on the other stalls. "You're right," he said. "I see Cardamom. And Rosemary. And here's one named Saffron." He grinned. It was kind of fun. Talking about horses' names with Darcie Finch was fun.

"Of course I'm right, Laurence," she said, her eyes dancing. "I know stuff."

She paused at the next stall. "Hello, Rosemary." The big horse ambled over, eager for Darcie to rub her soft nose. Darcie addressed her first: "Rosemary, this is Devin." She turned back to Devin. "And may I present Rosemary?"

Devin gave Rosemary a formal bow. "Are you going to introduce me to all of the horses?" he asked the lovely lady standing beside him.

"Probably," Darcie said. "We're in their home, Laurence. It's the polite thing to do."

He nodded solemnly, mesmerized by the secretive smile that floated on her lips. Her mouth was almost irresistible. Maybe coming to the barn was the right choice after all. She seemed happy to be here with him. She appeared to be completely at ease. Her obvious love for cats and horses gave him previously unknown insight into the psyche of the endlessly fascinating Miss Finch.

After making the acquaintance of several more horses, he offered an observation. "You seem to know all of these horses pretty well."

"Only the ones in this barn," she admitted. "I'm not very familiar with the others. Since I've been away at school, I mean."

"Did you ride often, when you were younger?" Devin asked. "Do you have a passion for it?"

She stopped, surprised to find he was taking a genuine interest. "I used to ride some, especially when I was in middle school. But not so much now." She considered the question carefully again, before shaking her head. "I do enjoy it, but, no, I wouldn't say I have a passion for it."

Devin took a step closer. "What do you have a passion for, Darcie Finch?" he asked. *Because I sure as hell have a passion for you.* He stood there, watching her closely, so he didn't miss the moment her eyes flared with awareness.

You...you idiot, she thought. *I have a passion for you.*

"Oh, I don't know," she said aloud. "This and that."

They studied each other for a moment with the unspoken words thrumming between them. She thought he was going to kiss her. Her lips began to tingle with expectation. But...he didn't. When more than a few seconds passed, she moved to the next stall.

Devin felt a sharp pain between the thumb and forefinger on his right hand. On further inspection he realized a long splinter was poking through his skin. As he dug it out, he wasn't surprised. It was a direct result of the death grip he had employed on the front wall of Rosemary's stall to keep himself from reaching for Darcie Finch. He had to get control of himself, he realized, before he did something both of them would regret.

Well, that wasn't quite true. He was fairly certain he wouldn't regret whatever he did. He would never regret anything that happened between himself and this mesmerizing woman, but…he wanted to make sure she felt the same way. So, he watched her. She was elegance personified. The horses, it appeared, were as infatuated with Darcie as he was. As she approached each stall, each horse moved as close to her as possible, seeking her touch. Devin found himself in complete empathy with them.

"Do you see that pirate over there?" she asked a black horse with the name "Jasmine" on her nameplate. Jasmine snorted in reply. "Yes," Darcie said, "I said pirate. He kidnapped me and brought me to his lair." Jasmine turned her questioning eyes to Darcie, who stroked her nose softly. "Why? I'm not sure," she said, as if confiding to the horse a secret Devin didn't know. "I think he intends to ravish me."

Devin stopped walking. A wave of heat engulfed him. The part of him that would like nothing better than to act on Darcie's suggestion threatened to break free from his iron-clad restraint. He forced himself to breathe deeply. He forced himself to count the pieces of straw at the feet of the object of his desire. Her dainty feet. Her dainty feet in her sexy sandals. Her dainty feet in her sexy sandals connected to her elegant ankles. Her elegant ankles connected to her luscious legs. And those legs went all the way up to her…

He jerked his eyes back to her face, shocked at the struggle he was having to control his own lustful thoughts. He had *never* had trouble before; but then, he had never been alone in a horse barn with Darcie Finch.

"Oh, don't look so horrified, Laurence," she scolded, misunderstanding his reaction. "I was just kidding." *Stupid, stupid, stupid, Darcie,* she reprimanded herself. *He obviously has another reason for bringing you here.*

She tried not to feel deflated, but a little of her earlier sparkle disappeared. She forced herself to move on. Purposely putting a bright note into her voice, she addressed the next equine specimen. "Hello, Cori," she crooned.

Devin stood perfectly still, waging an internal war with himself. *I think she's disappointed. Did she think I asked her out here to ravish her? Does she want* me *to ravish her? Do I want to ravish her?* He liked the word, "ravish."

It was a very pirate-like word. *Hell, yes, I want to ravish her, but…I can't.* He dug down deep for something clever to say to break the strange tension that had enveloped them since Darcie said the word "ravish."

"Cori is not a spice," he announced, into what had become an awkward silence.

"What?"

Darcie looked as if she was struggling to follow his attempt at conversation.

"Co-ri is not a spice," he repeated very slowly.

"Coriander," she said, in an aggravated tone. "Honestly, don't you use anything but salt and pepper?"

Devin's effort was a weak attempt at best, but at least Darcie was talking again. And correcting him. It was better than nothing. "Where are they, anyway, Miss Spice Expert?"

"Where are who?" she asked in annoyance.

Devin was relieved to see the light had returned to her eyes. The lovely light of irritation. That meant he was winning. "Salt and pepper?" he asked, innocently.

"Back in the ballroom, where I'm sending you if you don't start behaving," she said, in satisfaction, pleased to have the last word. "Hmph."

Devin had a sudden glimpse of what Darcie Finch would be like as a mother. Loving, but a little bit terrifying. He couldn't help but be impressed. He was starting to realize that his relationship with this woman was unlike anything he had ever experienced. Whatever bound them together wasn't just physical or mental or emotional or any one force. It was every conversation. Every move. Every look. Every touch. It didn't matter where they were. Or what they were doing. They might talk about something silly. Or they might not talk at all. The only thing that mattered was being with her. Breathing her in. And wallowing—for lack of a better word—in the sensations she so effortlessly evoked. He wanted to take care of her. He wanted to be the recipient of her protective instincts. He wanted to possess her. He wanted to be possessed by her. He could be with her forever and never learn all there was to know about Darcie Finch. Of that he was certain.

Devin sighed. He wanted her heart. It was blatantly obvious to everyone, even the fine equine specimens in the Boss-man's barn. Darcie had been the keeper of his heart since they met. Maybe even before that. He knew that. And he realized that she knew that, too. *My God.* The implications of their situation hit him in the face with the force of a small explosion. *I'm in love with her. And she's in love with me. And I'm going to ruin her life.*

He fought to hide his feelings. He couldn't let her find out what he was thinking. He couldn't let her see. Because then it would be worse. And he flatly refused to make it worse. He couldn't bind her to a man like him, he realized, sorrowfully. Doing so would be like stealing her life. Years of her life in which she might accomplish magnificent things. Oh, who was he kidding? She was brilliant. Of course she would accomplish magnificent things unless…

Unless she gave it all up, he thought. Gave up everything for him. But if she did it merely meant she hadn't thought it through. It might be five or even ten years before his situation would change. How could he ask a woman like Darcie to give up that much time for him? It wasn't fair. It was wrong. Absolutely, unequivocally wrong. If he loved her—and he did—then he had to do the right thing. He had to let her go.

Darcie reached the last horse in the original portion of the stables. "Hello, Starlight, you gorgeous boy. How are you feeling tonight?" She pressed her cheek to the ancient horse's nose for a moment. She glanced over her shoulder at Devin. "Well?"

He forced himself to answer as normally as possible, even though he was reeling from his awful discovery. "Well what?"

"Aren't you going to ask me about Starlight?"

She waited, impatiently.

His relief was palpable. Darcie hadn't noticed anything was wrong. She was giving her full attention to the horse. Devin struggled to put an offhand expression on his face. "What about Starlight?"

She gave him the you-are-such-a-disappointment look. "Pay attention, Laurence. You didn't ask me why he's not named after a spice."

"Why isn't he named after a spice?" he asked, obediently.

"Because he was Blane's first horse." She rubbed Starlight's nose gently. "Blane trained him, so his dad let him name the horse anything he wanted."

"He has to be at least twenty years old," Devin said conversationally, but his voice sounded hollow, even to his own ears.

"Something like that." Darcie shrugged, her gaze on the horse. "Blane left when Starlight was three years old. Imagine that. This fine fellow had to wait sixteen years just to be with the person he loved best in the world again." She continued to stroke Starlight's soft nose as she spoke to the horse again: "It was worth the wait, though, wasn't it, boy?"

Starlight's wise eyes seemed to hold the answer Darcie was looking for because she turned around quickly to face the man who had been unusually reticent for the past several minutes. "I would wait for you, too, Devin. All you have to do is ask." Her dark eyes searched his, trying desperately to read his shuttered expression.

Devin was taken completely off guard by her unexpected offer. This was the opening he needed. It was time for him to do the right thing. The thing his conscience was demanding. The one thing he didn't want to do. It was time for him to walk away from Darcie Finch.

CHAPTER FORTY-ONE

*L*ydia did *not* like Mallory Merritt. Specifically, Lydia did *not* like the way Mallory treated her husband and daughter. She also did *not* like the way Mallory treated her nanny. Or her in-laws. She most certainly did *not* like the way Mallory treated her in-laws. Or the rest of the Merritt family. No, she certainly didn't like the way Mallory treated them, either. And, while she was at it, she may as well admit that she certainly did *not* like the way Mallory treated her sister-in-law.

Mallory talked to Lydia as if she was a small child. A small, annoying child with developmental issues. Or a dog. A small, annoying dog. With developmental issues. Lydia would give her sister-in-law high marks for consistency, however. Mallory was consistently awful to Lydia every time they were together. She would never forget the words that sprang from Mallory's lips the first time that they were introduced....

"So, you're Devin's baby sister," Mallory said, her tone dripping with disdain. *"What an adorable, fragile, little mouse you are."*

That moment set the tone for their less-than-stellar relationship. Lydia rarely escaped unscathed from a conversation with her sister-in-law. For years, she had made it a point to avoid one-on-one situations with Mallory. And she had been, for the most part, successful. Until their morning flight—

and the subsequent defection of her parents—forced her into close quarters with the devil herself. For *hours*. Lydia decided after the first five minutes that she would rather walk back to Alexandria than get on another plane with Devin's demon-possessed wife.

Lydia had honestly believed it wasn't possible to dislike her sister-in-law more than she had during their interminable journey to Grace and Blane's wedding. Unfortunately, she was wrong. Because in the past thirty minutes she had discovered a depth of loathing for her brother's wife that she had never before experienced.

"I know there's one in the entryway, but this one is bigger, with more mirrors," Mallory said as they rounded the corner of the bar. "See?" Mallory turned in triumph, squashing Lydia's toe in the process. "Seriously, Lydia. You need to back off. You've been under my feet for the last thirty minutes."

"Sorry, Mal," Lydia muttered, rubbing her sore toe.

She couldn't tell Mallory she would rather be anywhere else. With anyone else. Instead she forced herself to follow her pushy sister-in-law into the crowded ladies' room, apologizing for Mallory's rudeness in her wake.

Mallory wiggled her way to the nearest mirror to study her makeup. "Give me your eyeliner. I can't believe I left mine at home. Yours doesn't last nearly as long as mine. Must be a discount brand."

She held out her hand impatiently as Lydia dug into her tiny purse. Then Lydia paused in her rummaging. "Oh, I forgot. I gave it to Devin because I had too much in my purse. It wouldn't fit."

Mallory rolled her eyes in displeasure, turning back to face the mirror. "Well, I've *got* to have it. I can't walk around looking like this. We'll just have to find the *Monster*." She left the bathroom at a brisk pace, forcing Devin's little sister to trot at her heels.

Lydia was in a state of controlled panic. Mallory wanted to find Devin, but she wouldn't be able to find Devin because Devin was with Darcie. And Lydia was the only one who knew. Telling Mallory *not* to look for Devin would seem suspicious, she realized. But allowing Mallory to *find* Devin would be disastrous. *What do I do?* she asked herself. *What do I do?*

She blindly followed her snippy sister-in-law, completely overwhelmed with worry. For whatever reason, Mallory stopped suddenly, her eyes scanning the ballroom. Lydia barely avoided an embarrassing collision, managing to stop herself two inches short of Mallory. She was so busy congratulating herself for the near miss, she didn't step back.

"Well, he's obviously not in here," Mallory said impatiently. "Where do you think..." She turned to address Lydia, only to find her shadow inches away from her. "Lydia, what the hell are you doing? Why are you following me around like we're Siamese twins?" She stepped back, putting more space between them. "Why don't you run along and find someone else to play with?"

Lydia flinched. Mallory was doing it again...treating her as though she was the same age as Amalie. She would be only too happy to do as her hateful sister-in-law asked, but she couldn't. Devin was counting on her. She glanced around the ballroom before replying, "I don't know anyone here but you." She forced a fake smile on her face. "Looks like you're stuck with me."

Mallory let out an impatient huff of breath. "Suit yourself," she said. She rolled her blue eyes elaborately. "Just stay the hell off my feet."

Lydia couldn't hold back a genuine grin. Under the circumstances, she couldn't help but enjoy being the cause of the exasperation Mallory was unable to hide.

Maggie Parker walked by, pausing in time to hear their exchange. "Everything all right, ladies?" she asked, eyeing Lydia with concern.

Mallory smiled sweetly. "Just looking for my *monster*. You haven't seen him, have you?"

Maggie frowned at the use of the word "monster" but continued smoothly: "Most of the groomsmen and a few bridesmaids headed for the billiard room a few minutes ago. He's probably with them."

Mallory took off across the ballroom without a word of thanks. Maggie grimaced in her wake, patting Lydia on the arm. "Lydia, you're welcome to join us if you like," she said kindly.

Those clear turquoise eyes held the promise of relief from the venomous presence of Mallory Merritt, but Lydia knew she had to refuse. She had seen the determination on Mallory's reptilian features. Her sister-in-law was on a mission; she wouldn't give up until she found her husband. "Thanks, Mrs. Parker, but I better help her find Devin."

She hurried across the ballroom and into the grand foyer, catching Mallory right before she reached the hallway to the billiard room.

"Mallory! Wait a minute." Her sister-in-law paused so Lydia could catch up, all the while tapping her foot in vexation. "I bet he's still upstairs with Amalie. Why don't you call him?"

Instead of thanking her for the suggestion, Mallory responded angrily: "Well, why didn't you say that before we came all the way out here? Honestly, Lydia, sometimes I think you are more than a little dense."

Lydia tried not to cringe at her venom. She watched as Mallory found Devin's number. She wouldn't have been surprised if that phone suddenly burst into flames from excessive use. It was Lydia's private opinion that Mallory's obsessive relationship with the device bordered on lunacy. But then, she thought quite a lot about Devin's wife bordered on lunacy. She watched as Mallory waited for an answer. *Please pick up, Dev. Please answer.* She strained her ears, praying to hear her brother's voice, but she wasn't close enough. She wasn't going to risk being on the receiving end of more of her sister-in-law's wrath, so she waited.

"Allana?" Mallory said in surprise. "Why are you answering Devin's phone?"

Apparently, Allana launched into a detailed narrative, which her daughter-in-law impatiently interrupted. "Oh, never mind all that. I don't need the details. Just tell him I need to speak with him. Now." She glanced at Lydia, before adding a belated, "Please," as an afterthought. She almost forgot that being sugary sweet to her in-laws reaped the greatest reward.

Lydia fought the urge to groan. Mallory's assumption that Devin's parents were too stupid to see through her fake persona couldn't have been further from the truth. In the name of family peace, however, Robert and Allana kept pretending.

Lydia couldn't hear a thing that her mother was saying. She could only watch the expression on Mallory's face quickly change from mildly inconvenienced to downright angry. *Great,* she thought dispiritedly. *What else has gone wrong?*

Mallory's blue eyes narrowed. "Tell him to call me if he comes back for his phone." She hung up, glaring at Lydia as if she was to blame. "He forgot his phone when he came back downstairs," Mallory announced. "How can he be so inconsiderate? I can't believe your brother. He's the most selfish person I've ever met."

Lydia's mouth fell open in disbelief. Mallory's perspective was completely distorted by her narcissistic fog. One day, Lydia promised herself, she would inform her sister-in-law, in no uncertain terms, that the world did *not* revolve around her.

"Hurry up, Lydia. I swear. One minute I can't get rid of you and the next you're in slow motion." Mallory hurled her comment over her shoulder as she hurried down the corridor toward the billiard room. Lydia could hear the excited voices and laughter through the closed door. Mallory pushed it open without knocking.

They were greeted by stunned silence. Lydia glanced around the room quickly, her heart sinking as she saw no glimpse of her brother or Darcie. Some of her concern must have been visible, because she saw Diana narrow her eyes.

Lou was standing beside the pool table, holding her cue stick and looking like the cat that found the cream. Zack stood directly opposite, studying the table as if he couldn't believe what had just happened. The faces of everyone else ranged from mild amusement to complete elation, the last belonging to Roger Carrington. It appeared that Zack, the pool shark, had finally met his match.

"Ladies," Evander said politely, breaking the silence. "What can we do for you?"

Mallory's lips curled into a disdainful smile as her gaze swept the group. "I'm looking for my *monster*." She laughed a tinkling little laugh.

No one joined her.

"We haven't seen any *monsters*," Joey said firmly.

"Well, just the one," Zack muttered, returning Mallory's hateful glare. Lou poked him in the shoulder with her pool cue. "Ow," Zack said, and rubbed the spot while looking as if he wanted to say more. When Lou raised her eyebrows, he subsided.

"If you're looking for your husband, we haven't seen him either," Evander said.

Mallory let out a frustrated breath. They watched as she stalked out of the room.

"He's probably hiding from the monster," Zack's voice echoed into the hallway.

"Za-a-ck," Lou hissed. But Zack's comment had broken the momentary tension. The billiard room returned to the happy cacophony of before.

Lydia smiled apologetically. She turned to follow her sister-in-law, until a gentle hand on her arm impeded her progress. Diana pulled her over to the door where they could hold a whispered conversation without the danger of being overheard.

"What's going on, Lyd?" Diana asked suspiciously.

"What...um, do you mean?" Lydia stammered. She was trying desperately to decide whether she could confide in Diana. She looked longingly at the door, something that didn't escape her cousin's notice.

"I know you, cuz. You wouldn't hang around with that spawn of Satan for fun. What's wrong? Is it Dev?" Diana was suspicious and perceptive...a deadly combination.

"Just make sure Devin stays with you if he comes in here," Lydia whispered. She had to make sure Mallory didn't get away.

"Why?" Diana asked. Her face was worried.

"I don't have time to explain. Just, please, make him stay with you."

Lydia disengaged her arm from Diana's grasp. She returned to the hallway, only to draw up short at the sound of voices coming from the grand foyer. She crept quietly down the shadowed corridor until she reached the last open doorway. She stepped into it quickly. It seemed to be somebody's office and was, fortunately, deserted and dark. She pressed herself against the doorframe to listen.

"I'm sorry you can't find your husband, Mrs. Merritt," said a deep voice Lydia couldn't identify. She was convinced, however, she had heard it before.

"Mallory," her sister-in-law simpered.

Lydia frowned. Mallory obviously considered this man to be important, whoever he was. She was giving him the whole show.

"Mallory," said the man, sadly. "Dear, trusting Mallory. I hate to mention this, but I feel obligated to tell you what I saw. Keep in mind, my dear, that it might not have anything to do with your husband. But, on the small outside chance that it does...Oh, my dear..." The man paused dramatically.

Lydia would have laughed if the stakes weren't so high. From the sound of the conversation, it seemed Mallory had finally met someone as fake and manipulative as she was.

"What is it, Mr. McCallum?" gasped Mallory.

"Douglas," said the man.

"Douglas. Tell me, Douglas." Mallory's voice sounded so delicate. So very, very frightened.

Lydia grimaced. She could almost picture her sister-in-law's face. Big blue eyes wide and vulnerable. Lips slightly parted. It was only a matter of time until she would start dabbing at those fake tears. But... Douglas McCallum was a surprise. Since when did Mallory have a reason to talk to Douglas McCallum? Lydia was puzzled. Her sister-in-law had never once mentioned the association. Strange, she realized, especially since Mallory loved to brag about her important acquaintances. Lydia had met the man once before, and immediately picked up on his penchant for cruelty. Her instincts were, unfortunately, finely honed by experience. She shivered. She knew from hearing her brother talk about him that Douglas McCallum was bad news.

She felt another knot of anxiety form in her stomach, accompanying all of the other knots of anxiety permanently residing there. She gathered her courage to peek around the doorframe. When she did, she breathed a silent sigh of relief. Mallory and Douglas stood with their backs to her, facing the ballroom doors. Lydia braced herself because she had a bad feeling about what Mr. McCallum was going to say.

"My brave, brave Mallory. I'm sorry to have to tell you…"

Lydia didn't think he sounded very sorry at all.

"I'm sorry to tell you…I saw a man in a tuxedo going into the stables about half an hour ago. And I'm almost certain it was your husband."

Oh, damn, damn, damn. Lydia knew she was wringing her hands, but she couldn't stop. This was bad. Very bad. Maybe the worst possible situation for someone who was supposed to be protecting her brother from discovery by his evil, nasty, wicked witch of a wife. But wait a minute, she thought, grasping at straws. Maybe Douglas saw Devin, but he didn't see Darcie. That would be good, wouldn't it? It was a small spark of hope, but she took hold of it with both hands.

"And," Douglas added, finishing with a flourish, "Darcie Finch was with him."

The spark died. And Lydia's hope died with it.

CHAPTER FORTY-TWO

"I would wait for you, Devin." Darcie was holding on to her own hope with both hands. "All you have to do is ask," she repeated.

She tilted her head to one side, studying the man standing across from her. He was, obviously, waging an internal battle with his own damn conscience. That was bad, she decided. Very, very bad.

She understood completely. She wasn't sure what was wrong or right anymore, either. Her morals were all tangled up in the myriad ways of looking at their situation. She only knew, with frightening clarity, that it would be this man or no one. Something primitive at the very core of her being kept telling her: Devin Merritt was her soulmate. It was that intuition—which she had never before had cause to doubt—that compelled her to fight for this man. He was prone to self-sacrifice. He had willingly given up his own happiness for his daughter. This bit of evidence was terrifying. Because if it came down to a choice between her or his self-sacrificial tendencies…well, Darcie felt an awful certainty that she would lose.

His whole posture changed when he reached his decision, becoming stiff and unyielding. The hand that was lying on top of the railing, only minutes before, was gripping the wood so tightly that Devin's knuckles were turning white.

She steeled herself for his words, drawing on her own reserve of strength. She thought she was ready. She was certain she wasn't going to like what he had to say, but…

"I can't ask you to wait for me," he said grimly. The verdict was in.

"Can't…or won't?"

She watched him carefully. He paused for a moment before answering. "Won't."

"Won't…or don't want to?"

She couldn't breathe. Would he tell the truth? Would he lie? Would the truth be worse than a lie?

Devin was going to lie. He could do this. It was the only way to save her.

"Don't want to."

There. He had said it. Now all he had to do was watch her walk away. But she didn't. She didn't move. She simply stood there looking at him, the shock of his betrayal written all over her face. Devin berated himself in the harshest terms possible. *I am a liar. And an ass. I am a lying ass. And a coward. I am a lying coward. I am a lying, cowardly ASS.*

Three little words. *"Don't want to."* Darcie wasn't ready for the pain caused by those three little words. It nearly took her breath away. She concentrated on remaining calm. She closed her eyes. Striving for composure, she drew on her father's training. Joe Finch wouldn't send his daughter into a fight unarmed.

"Never let them know when they score a point, Darcie. You can't let it show. Pull back to your corner. Take a deep breath. Regroup. And come out swinging."

She hadn't expected to need that particular piece of advice outside of the courtroom. But she was currently in the fight of her life, the fight for her future happiness…as well as the happiness of the man in front of her. The selfless, noble, make-the-wrong-choice-for-all-the-right-reasons man in front of her. The man who was going to break the railing in half if he gripped it any tighter. *All right, Daddy,* Darcie thought. *I'm your girl.*

Devin was in trouble. He could see the determined light in Darcie Finch's dark eyes. She wasn't giving up. She wasn't giving in. He wondered, soberly, if he had the strength to withstand the desires of his own heart. Rejecting her was killing him. He expected her to walk away in the face of his words. Anyone else would already be gone. But, of course, he wasn't dealing with anyone else, he reminded himself. He was dealing with Darcie Finch. She never did what she was supposed to.

Darcie narrowed her eyes. "Liar," she whispered, her rich tones increasing in volume as she reiterated: "Devin Merritt…you are a liar."

And a coward and an ass, he thought. *Don't forget that.* He waited for her to continue, but she said nothing. She merely stood there, looking at him, her eyes blazing.

He couldn't stand the silence another minute. "Darcie," he said, softly. "It could be five years. Or ten. It could be ten years. I can't ask you to wait that long. It isn't fair. You have a life to live. I can't let you waste it waiting on me."

Her knees nearly gave way, so great was her relief. He *was* trying to save her. He still wanted her. She grabbed hold of that piece of evidence and hung on. "Ten years for a lifetime." She shrugged her shoulders. "Doesn't seem like such a bad trade to me."

He could feel himself acquiesce. *Well, if you look at it like that…NO. Focus, Merritt.* What was she doing to him? "No, Darcie," he said firmly. "I can't ask. I won't ask. And I definitely don't *want* to ask you to wait."

There. She would be angry now and she would leave.

But Darcie didn't budge.

Of course not, he thought in equal parts aggravation and admiration. He had been fooling himself. Nothing with Darcie Finch would ever be easy. That was one of the qualities about her he most respected. But, now, he was in trouble. He watched her warily as she paced in front of him, looking for all the world as if she was preparing to present the closing arguments in a trial.

The fire was back in her eyes. "*You* can't ask? *You* can't let me '*waste my life*' waiting for *you*? Well, it seems to me *you* have taken it upon *your*self to decide what's best for *me*. How considerate of you. How kind of you. Especially since I'm clearly *incapable* of deciding such a thing for myself." Her gorgeous voice was filled with righteous indignation. "And what a sacrifice *you're* making. Stepping aside to do what's best for *me*. Even though it hurts *you*. Don't you dare stand there and try to tell me this isn't killing you." Her eyes went to the railing and his bloodless hand. "If you squeeze that post any harder, it's going to snap in half."

"Darcie."

He tried to ease his grip on the railing, but her next words put an end to his efforts.

"You're good at being a martyr, aren't you, Laurence?" she asked evenly. "First, for your daughter? And now for me? You're not worth the trouble. Are you? Especially with those scars and that eye patch? Why should *anyone* wait for you?"

Devin flinched at her words.

Darcie's expression softened. "I'll tell you why, you stupid man. You see more with one eye than most people do with two. You're intuitive. And loving. And you have a brilliant mind." She didn't even try to hide the emotion shining in her eyes. "You're loyal. Kind. And funny. You have more integrity and character than almost anyone I've ever met."

"Darcie."

"But you are also opinionated. And presuming. And stubborn. And selfish."

Selfish? Devin asked himself. She had gone too far. "Now, wait just a minute." How could she call him selfish when he was giving up every dream he could ever imagine? For her.

"Yes, Laurence," she confirmed. "You're selfish. You've made yourself my judge and my jury. You've decided my fate without putting me on the stand. Without even thinking about the sentence you seem determined to give me. You're so hell-bent on being a martyr and doing what you deem is the right thing, that you can't see what's in front of you. Do you want to know what the end result will be if I do what you have decided I must?"

"Darcie," he said, desperate to make her stop.

"I'm going to tell you."

"Of course you are."

"Now, don't get sassy with me, Laurence. Your ridiculous assumptions are sentencing me to life as a trophy wife." At the shock on his face, she continued: "That's right. A trophy wife. Married to a man who views me as a prize. Nothing more than a pretty face. Someone to show off when it suits him. Someone to put back in the box at the end of the day."

Devin was horrified. "Darcie, it won't be like that. You'll find someone…"

"No, I won't," she objected. "And do you know why? Because *no one* really sees *me*. No one can get past this," She gestured to her flawless face. "They can't get past my face long enough to figure out what's in here." She pointed to her head. "It's easy with *you*. *You* get me. *You* understand me. And, Laurence, there isn't anyone else who will."

Devin stood perfectly still. He didn't say a word. He couldn't allow himself to speak because he wanted more than anything to give in.

She threw up her hands in frustration. "Oh, all right, fine. You win. Do you hear that, *Devin*?"

He winced when she called him Devin. Laurence was no more.

"I'll do what you want," she said. "I'll find some man who will allow me to hang on his arm. And warm his bed. And do the pretty. Because that's what will make you happy. See? I can be a martyr, too."

She flounced toward the door that led to the area between the stables.

Devin took a deep breath, holding to his rapidly vanishing control by a thread. He had to be strong. He had to let her go.

Darcie played her last card. Her last, desperate card. If it didn't work, he was lost to her. She raised her chin and turned, her hand on the doorknob. "Give me a fifteen-minute head start." Her eyes were blazing. "I guarantee that by the time you get to the ballroom, I'll have found a man who will take me home tonight. And take me to bed. Isn't that exactly what you want me to do?" She raised her eyebrows in challenge. "You should enjoy thinking about that since it's what you want so badly. Think about it tonight, Devin. Me with another man. In a bed. In the dark. Another man's lips where yours should be. Another man's hands…"

That was as far as she got. Devin's self-control snapped. In two strides he had reached her. He grabbed her shoulders, turning her around to face him.

"You *will not*, Darcie Finch. I swear to God above, no other man's hands will *ever* touch you." His eye was burning with the twin flames of anger and desire. His scars were red on his pale face, his breath emerging in rapid pants. His fingers bit into her shoulders.

"What do you want me to do, Laurence?" she whispered. "What do you *really* want me to do?"

"This," he breathed, as his mouth came down on hers. It was a claiming. His lips searing. Possessive. All-encompassing. He gave in to the urges of his primitive self. His battered heart rejoiced. Finally.

The impact on her heightened senses turned her wobbly knees to water. She would have fallen but for his strong arm, wrapped around her waist. He pinned her to him, kissing her as if he could absorb her. Drink her in. As if she was the last drop of water in the middle of the desert. His passion was raw. Impatient. Needy. Completely lacking his usual finesse.

He needn't have worried. She reveled in his strength, submitting to a force stronger than logic for the first time in her life. She was his willing conquest. The role was foreign to her…but incredibly appealing. His tongue tangled with hers, turning the fire of their desire into a raging inferno.

He couldn't get enough of her. His hands were everywhere, exploring her glorious curves and tropical flower-scented skin. So soft. So warm. The small gasps and delicate moans she released in response to the slightest caress drove him wild. Each release was a sweet surrender to the inevitable. That sudden realization came to him, in the last sane portion of his brain. This—Darcie Finch, Devin Merritt, alone together, finally unleashing their desperate passions—was inevitable. Everything that had happened before—every conversation, every glance, every thought—had been leading up to this moment. He gave himself up to destiny.

Nothing had ever felt so wonderful. Or, if she was honest, so decadent. So absolutely right. She was well on her way to getting drunk on the emotions and feelings she had never experienced with anyone else. Burning up, yet she gloried in the flames.

His caressing hand moved down her chiffon-covered thigh. Grabbing a fistful of the material of her dress, he slipped the soft material up. Slowly. She clung to him, her kisses almost frantic. He could feel her melting against him, becoming more pliant, completely at the mercy of her own passionate nature....

Devin wanted this woman. Now. He had to make her his. He had to possess the glorious vision in his arms. And he was certain: she wanted this, too. She would deny him nothing. *Yes,* he thought. *Yes. How can I refuse this? How can I live without this? How can I not make love to this amazing woman in a...barn?*

A barn? He felt the impact of the thought like a slap in the face.

He released her skirt, pulling back slightly to study the face in front of him. Her cheeks were flushed. Her lips swollen and lush. Her eyes, under heavy lids, were drowsy with desire. She clung to him in abject surrender. Eager to continue. Desperate for what only he could give her. He touched his forehead to hers. He could hear his own harsh breaths as he fought for control enough for both of them

"What's wrong? What is it?" she whispered, a touch of fear coming into her eyes.

Did she think he had changed his mind? As if he ever could. "The first time I make love to you, Darcie Finch," he said, punctuating nearly every word with a kiss, "it won't be in a stable." He kissed her neck. The tender spot below her earlobe. But when he said her name, he took her lips tenderly, swirling her tongue around his in a way that made her shiver. He drew away to look at the luscious woman in front of him. Unbelievingly, she wanted him.

She gazed back. "How about the second time?" she asked, hopefully.

He pulled her to him, cradling her in his arms. She was his future. No matter how long it took, she would be his. They were in this together.

He met her gaze seriously. "I love you, Darcie Finch."

"I know," she said, smiling that secret smile he was coming to treasure.

Lydia remained where she was, frozen in horror.

"Darcie Finch?" Mallory snarled in reaction to Douglas' words. "*Darcie Finch*? Why that little…" She hesitated a bit, catching herself. "Surely, it can't be true." She stretched out a trembling hand, once again the fragile victim. "Douglas, what should I do?"

Douglas clasped Mallory Merritt's hand in both of his. "If I were you, I would confront them. I would demand answers." He raised her hand to his lips. "And then, my dear Mallory, I would make them pay."

"I'll do it," Mallory said, vehemently. "I'll catch that lying, cheating *monster* in the act."

Lydia heard the sound of her sister-in-law's ridiculously high heels tapping across the parquet floor. She moved farther into the darkened office, trying to stay hidden. She expected Mallory to storm by on a mission to ruin Devin's life. But the oily voice of Douglas McCallum halted the clap of Mallory's heels.

"Wait a minute, my impulsive flower. You aren't using your resources."

"What do you mean?" Mallory asked. Curiosity infused her voice.

"A bored *CB* cameraman is standing in that ballroom right now…I'm certain he would love to shoot some juicy footage from this wedding. How much better will it look in a court of law if you catch your cheating husband in the act? Millions of viewers will see it. Every single one of whom will feel so much sympathy for the beautiful wife who was wronged. Doesn't that sound better than his word against yours? Better than some desperate attempt at taking a video with your phone?"

Lydia blanched, closing her eyes. Her sister-in-law would love the idea. She would love the chance to play the victim. The results would be devastating. For Devin. For Amalie. Lydia could hardly breathe. She had to stop them. She spoke impulsively, hurrying into the grand foyer. "Mallory, wait!"

Douglas and Mallory turned in surprise.

Mallory's scornful gaze swept Lydia from head to toe. "There you are. I should have known you'd catch up eventually." She glanced sideways at Douglas McCallum.

The look they shared gave Lydia the feeling that they considered her too stupid to figure out what was going on. For once, she was thankful to play dumb. Until Mallory continued....

"You and I have finished our game of 'Follow the Leader,' dear. It's time for you to find a new friend to play with. Run along back to the billiard room. I'm sure someone there has time for a little mouse like you."

Lydia didn't move. Mallory's eyes took on a malevolent glint.

"Don't be afraid, Lydia. I'm sure nobody in the billiard room wants to *hit* you."

She tossed her head triumphantly before she and Douglas disappeared into the ballroom.

Although Lydia stood perfectly still, the floor seemed to tilt beneath her feet. The lights took on a funny hue. She could almost feel her pupils shrink. Those deliberately malicious words were going to send her into a full-blown panic attack. She hadn't had one in months. She tried to fight it, tried to remember what her therapist had said about breathing and counting and focusing on something else. *I can't pass out here. I've got to find Devin,* she thought desperately.

With more determination than she had felt in ages, she carefully crossed over to the entryway. The floor continued to buck and roll beneath her feet. The lights continued to flicker. The perimeter of her vision began blackening, but still she pushed toward the door. The cool air outside might help. It had helped before. Of course, that was when she had someone to talk her down. Her breath was coming in quick, shallow pants. She grabbed the door handle, to no avail. She was too far gone, it seemed, to open the large door.

Breathe, Lydia, breathe, she encouraged herself. *You can do this.* She struggled with the handle. *I can't do this. I'm going to...* She rattled the door handle desperately as the room closed in around her.

CHAPTER FORTY-THREE

"*G*ood night, Kayleigh."

Dominic Parker stood on the porch, staring at his phone. Well, that was that, he thought philosophically. Another in the series of increasingly unsatisfying phone conversations with his girlfriend in New York City.

Dom sighed. The distance was a problem, just as he feared it would be.

He slipped his phone into the inner pocket of his tux jacket, glancing around for Atticus. The dog had followed him outside after suddenly appearing in the grand foyer. Dom was certain the wily canine was supposed to be safe and secure in another part of the house. But that was Atticus, he decided. The dog was a conundrum. And, currently, the conundrum was pacing back and forth in front of the side door to the stables. A little odd, Dom thought, but then, so was Atticus. He put two fingers to his lips to get the dog's attention. In Dom's opinion, his piercing whistle was one of his few standout skills.

His attention was diverted from the dog by the rattling sound coming from the stately front doors of Heart's Ease. Someone was having quite a bit of difficulty trying to get out. He knew from personal experience the doors weren't the easiest doors to open. Reacting with an ingrained courtesy, Dom walked over, turned the handle, and gave the door a strong push.

The door flew back, nearly knocking Lydia over. She managed to hang on to the door handle by sheer force of will. Dom thrust his head inside just in time. He took one look at her pale face and switched into the role of medical professional.

"Lydia? Are you all right?"

Before she could say anything, she was sitting on the front steps of the portico with her head on her knees. Dominic was sitting right beside her, his hand, warm and comforting, set on the back of her neck.

He calmly encouraged her to breathe. "Come on now, Lydia. Breathe in and out. Slowly. That's it. Fight it. You can beat this."

Her clammy hand clutched his arm. "Don't leave," she gasped.

"I'm right here, Lydia," Dominic said evenly. "I'm with you."

She concentrated on the soothing quality of his voice and the warmth of his hand at her neck. She jumped as she felt a large animal bump against her leg.

"Easy, Lydia," Dom said soothingly. "It's just Atticus. He's with you, too."

Lydia reached down to clutch Atticus' soft fur. The tingling in her hands began to subside. She focused on inhaling and exhaling, nothing else, just as the therapist had recommended. All thoughts of her brother's dilemma faded from her mind.

Devin was astonished by his own self-restraint. The fact that he had been able to put any sort of distance between himself and Darcie was an outright miracle. His thwarted desire was screaming for a return to the sizzling moments of passion. "We better get some air," he suggested, in a voice he barely recognized.

He opened the door to the stables. Hand in hand, they entered the pass-through area, which was open to the cool night air of the paddock. They felt the light breeze brush their faces as they stepped off the concrete and walked onto the grass.

They walked toward the fence, the fallen leaves crackling beneath their feet. Overhead the stars shone through the trees' thinning canopy. Someone had left the outside speaker on. Music from the reception poured into the enclosed space.

"Oh," Darcie said, twirling in a circle. "It's our own private ballroom."

She looked almost ethereal. The moonlight and her radiant beauty made it hard for Devin to believe she was real. She was, though. She was very real. His heart rate attested to that. It had yet to return to normal. Nor had anything else about him, for that matter. The heated kisses they shared were like nothing he had ever experienced. Or ever imagined. She enchanted him. She challenged him. Sometimes, she infuriated him. But that was all part and parcel of the breathtaking woman spinning in the moonlight. His woman. And she wanted him. *Him*. He sent his Maker a quick word of thanks for this precious, undeserved gift.

"Listen," he said, as the opening strains of the love song from *Beauty and the Beast* filled the air. "They're playing our song."

"Lau-rence," she said, raising her eyebrows in disapproval, just as he knew she would. "I'm disappointed in you. Not only have you forgotten that you are *not* a beast, your comment reveals a disappointing gap in your fairy-tale education. If you remembered the story, you would know that the beast was really a prince in disguise."

Her triumphant expression quickly turned to annoyance at his next words. "I guess that makes you a princess," he said, trying to hide a teasing smile. He failed miserably.

"Oh, not that again." She threw her hands in the air and glared at the grinning man in front of her. "Why does it always have to come back to that? Every time I…"

"All right. All right. Settle down, Da-rr-cie Finch." He stopped what was sure to be a lengthy tirade by lapsing into pirate-speak.

"Hmph."

She glared at him. Crossing her arms over her chest, she waited.

"Hmmm. What a-rre you waiting for, Da-rr-cie Finch? A-rre ye planning to run me through?"

When she didn't reply, he moved closer, raising his hand to tuck a stray curl behind her ear. The curl was as contrary as the woman, refusing to stay put despite a double dose of Lou's cement-like hairspray. Moving his hand to the side of her neck he brushed her cheek with his thumb, pleased by her quick intake of breath. She was obviously as affected as he was. Leaning in, he whispered in her ear, "You a-rre my treasure, Da-rr-cie Finch."

Her stern demeanor dissolved instantly. "Spoken like a true pirate," she said, her husky tones a little deeper than before. Her eyes shone more brightly than the stars. He couldn't resist the opportunity, touching his lips to hers in a gentle kiss. The kiss was as devastating in its sweetness as the passionate embraces they had shared earlier. Her eyes flared. He reluctantly forced himself to step back before he gave in to the demand of his unruly senses to deepen the kiss.

Tilting her head, she looked at him under her eyelashes, a flirtatious gesture that made him take a shaky breath. She was beyond amused by something he had said. Eagerly, he waited to hear what thought was going to pop out of her mouth next. Grinning mischievously, she said, "Pirate's treasure. An excellent, and safe, word choice, Laurence."

He was so perfectly attuned to her quick mind that he answered without missing a beat. "Oh, no, Da-rr-cie Finch, my treasure you will be. I have no desire to walk the plank. No man who values all of his body pa-rrts would ever say that you are any pirate's—"

"—*Booty*," they said together, as he pulled her close, swinging her into the dance. They were laughing again, moving to the music, lost in the joy of their stolen interlude.

Her presence was intoxicating. Her tropical flower scent teased his senses. There was no way he could resist the soft place where her neck met her shoulder. His lips lingered there in a gentle caress, one that made her shiver in his arms.

"Are you trying to seduce me?" She tried to whisper, failing miserably. Her glorious tones wrapped around him like an embrace.

"And if I am?" he asked, raising his head to look into eyes that shimmered with desire.

"You're very close to obtaining your goal," she purred, pressing against him in a way that made him curse the thin material of her gown.

"Seduction is preferable to ravishment, then. I'll make a note." He tried to be offhand about it, but hell, this conversation was killing him. The music changed to Christina Perri's haunting "A Thousand Years." The romantic lyrics failed to improve his situation. "At least I'm not a vampire," he whispered, returning his attention to her neck.

"If you leave any marks, Daddy will put a stake through your heart," Darcie replied, pertly. "Then you won't have to worry about *what* you are."

Devin reluctantly raised his head. "Moonlight makes you sassy, Darcie Finch." He spun her around, careful not to pull her quite as close this time. Even a vampire had his limits.

"Vampires don't sleep," she said. It was a random comment to be sure, but one perfectly in line with the thoughts spinning through her head. Her brain was all jumbled up with flashes of color and music, and the all-encompassing, completely intoxicating presence of Devin Merritt. She felt drunk, giddy with sensation, loving the way his arms cherished her as they closed around her protectively.

His warm breath tickled her ear. "I don't sleep much, either, but when I do, I dream of you, Darcie Finch. I have since I met you."

Her rich voice sounded amused: "It must have been difficult to dream about someone you've never seen. Oh, wait. Did I have a horse's head and extremely large feet in your dreams? Tell me the truth, Laurence."

He laughed softly, nodding his head.

Her eyes narrowed in mock disapproval. "While that vision of me is terribly appealing, I'm glad you know what I look like now. At least you can close your eyes without seeing the horse-faced woman of your dreams."

"Oh, you're not just in my dreams. I think about you when I'm awake, too." His lips brushed her cheek delicately. He continued to voice his heretofore unspoken thoughts. "Lying in my bed, in the dark, I wish…"

Darcie froze, stepping back to regard him in horror. "No, Devin. Don't say it."

He looked at her in alarm as well as confusion. "What did I—"

"Don't say that you think of me when you're with her."

She took another step back, regarding him as if he had slapped her.

"Darcie, I would never…"

"Don't, Devin. Just don't."

He saw the sheen of tears in her glorious eyes. He started to reach for her, stopping himself only when he realized what had brought the pain of betrayal to those eyes.

"Darcie, no."

He let his arms drop down to his sides, speaking with as little emotion as possible. He had to make her understand how it was. "It's not like that. Mallory and I don't…well, we used to, but we don't anymore. At least not since the attack." Devin sighed. This was going to be humiliating, he realized. But if it would erase the hurt from her eyes…

"Actually," he began. "I think the last time we had sex was a couple of weeks before my attack. I remember because Mallory wanted to buy the shoes that she's wearing tonight. They're Yves Saint Laurent and cost nearly a grand." He paused, waiting until understanding dawned on Darcie's face. "That's what Mallory does, Darcie," he continued. "She bargains with her body. Sex for whatever she wants. I'm ashamed to admit that it took me a while to figure it out. But, I'm even more ashamed to admit I went along with it. I mean, I figured she was my wife, so…what the hell?" He ran his hand through his hair in frustration, his face a mask of regret. "We don't sleep together. We never have. We've always had separate bedrooms. You see, entry into Mallory's is by invitation only. Since the attack, I've been removed from the guest list." He looked down into the indignant face of the woman who was…well, hugging him, for lack of a better word. Her reflexive defense of him warmed his heart. Her instinctive loyalty was another precious gift.

"She's a fool," Darcie said, fiercely, her arms wrapped around him as if she could protect him from the world. "Nothing but an ignorant fool. If I was her, I would…" She gasped, catching herself before she could say more.

"What would you do, Darcie Finch?" Devin whispered. "What do you think about when you're all alone at night, lying in your bed? What did you think about when you were with…Dom?"

"Dom?"

She didn't move, just stood there, staring at him in shock.

"I know you were lovers."

The words seemed to linger in the air between them. He hadn't meant to say it at all. He had meant to let whatever happened in the past stay there, unless she wanted to bring it up.

She continued to gaze at him in horror, giving him momentary hope. Maybe he was wrong. Maybe she would tell him that he was crazy.

"How did you know?" she finally gasped. "Nobody knows but Dom and me…and, well, Mama."

She walked out of his arms, pacing back and forth, the leaves crackling beneath her feet. Something made her pause as her eyes widened incredulously. "Did Dom tell you?"

"Of course not," Devin said, but his heart sank. Damn his intuition.

"It wasn't his fault. It was all my idea…my stupid, stupid idea."

She turned her back to him, leaning on the fence. The dreamy music from the ballroom continued playing. The chilly air made her feel the absence of his warmth keenly. She refused to look at him as she told her story with characteristic honesty. "When I was a senior in high school, I overheard a conversation between Mama and Daddy that I wasn't supposed to hear. It was an honest mistake on my part. I wanted to borrow one of Daddy's law books. The door to his office was open. They were sitting on the sofa with their backs to the door. They had no idea that I was there.

"They were talking about an assault. A sexual assault. And it was…Mama. Somebody tried to rape Mama when she was in college." Darcie still didn't like to think about hearing those words. "Apparently, Daddy got there just in time to save her. He broke the guy's nose. I still don't know who the guy was, but it was somebody they both knew."

Devin didn't move. He couldn't. He was horrified and angry at the same time. "Darcie," he said, softly.

But she shook her head without turning around. He realized there was more. She continued her explanation.

"The same thing happened to Grandma Sofi and her sister during World War II. The Nazis. Grandma Sofi got away. Her sister didn't." Darcie continued to study the pasture in the dark, her voice vibrating with emotion. "I also knew that Maggie was the victim of a date rape when she was studying abroad in Madrid. She got pregnant, then, with Ric. She has no idea who drugged her drink. She never even knew his name."

Devin came to stand beside her, his forearms propped on the top of the fence. He was careful not to touch her, but to offer his unspoken support. He was surprised about Ric, but it explained why his coloring was so different from the rest of the Parker family. It also explained the age gap between Ric and Dom.

Darcie sighed. "So, anyway, after I heard Mama and Daddy talking, I got scared. I didn't want to take the chance that my first time would be like that. With a stranger…or worse.…"

"So you told Dom and he offered to help you out," Devin said. *That damn bastard. She trusted him. How could he take advantage of her like that?* He tried to relax, but what he really wanted to do was to haul Dominic Parker out of the ballroom and plant his fist squarely in the other man's face.

"No," Darcie objected vehemently. "It wasn't like that at all. Dom and I weren't madly in love or anything. He was my safety net. It was all my idea, and it took me a while to talk him into it." She finally dared to face him. "Look, when I said he was my boyfriend, that was probably stretching it. It's sort of our joke. We've known each other since we were babies. Dom has always been one of my best friends. We went out together all the time in high school. We were always each other's fallback date for dances and stuff. And then he kissed me…the Christmas when we were seniors. Under the mistletoe, of course. It was romantic and fun. And we decided maybe we should date each other and see how things went. We had only been going out for a few months when I talked him into being my…well, partner. On prom night, of course. It only happened once and…" She wrinkled her nose. "…I didn't exactly enjoy it."

"But he did," Devin interjected. There had to be *something* he could blame on Dominic Parker.

"Yeah, I guess." Darcie shrugged her shoulders. "He seemed pretty happy, but when he asked me if I wanted to do it again, I said no. He never told anybody. And he never asked me to again, or even mentioned it. No pressure whatsoever. Dom's like that. He's a really good guy. Anyway, we dated until after graduation, and then he went to the lake for a month. Dom's grandparents have a house at Lake Norman, near Charlotte. About two weeks after he left, he called me and said he had met a girl, and would I mind if we stopped dating for the summer. I was getting all of my college stuff together and had other things on my mind. To be honest, I didn't really care one way or the other. So, we broke up. I like to tease Dom about it, but it was really mature of him to tell me the truth. For an eighteen-year-old, I mean."

Devin smiled. He couldn't help it. Who but Darcie Finch would think of having sex for the first time as a preventative measure? He was very sorry that they lived in a world where such a decision was necessary for her peace of mind, but he was glad Dom had been kind to her. Good, old Dom really was good, old Dom. Devin had misjudged him, and for that he was sorry.

Darcie, however, wasn't finished with her confession. "So, you see, Laurence, he didn't know what he was doing, and I didn't know what I was doing and I...well, I'm not very good at it." Her eyes were fixed on the ground. He could make out a faint flush on her cheeks in the dim light.

"And you never did it again. Because you weren't good at it," he surmised.

"Something like that," she murmured, twisting her hands in her skirt. "And now, if I were to go to bed with a man—I mean, go to bed with"—she hesitated—"you, I'm afraid...I mean..." She raised her hands helplessly. "I'm not very good at it."

"Darcie Finch," he said softly. "Look at me."

She refused. Her eyes were glued to the faintly colorful leaves under her feet.

"Darcie."

He brushed the back of his hand slowly down her smooth cheek, feeling the heat from her skin. His hand reached her chin and he cupped it, gently forcing it up until she had to meet his gaze.

Darcie's eyes met his unwillingly, unsure of what she would find. Disappointment? Censure? Disdain? Pity? Instead, she saw an intense heat he didn't try to hide. She was mesmerized by the light glowing in his eye. The warmth in her face rapidly spread of its own accord to other parts of her body.

"Darcie Finch," he whispered. "I *know* what I'm doing." Devin was shocked at his own confession. He never said provocative things like that. Yet, he couldn't seem to stop the words coming out of his mouth. And why was that? he asked himself. The reason was standing right in front of him.

Darcie's eyes went wide as she processed the meaning of his words. He could see the rapid rise and fall of her chest. Her hand came up to touch his scarred cheek. She was tentative, hesitant. Hope and fear warred in her gaze. He leaned even closer. His breath brushed her ear, drawing goose bumps to the surface of her skin that had nothing to do with the cold.

"And do you know what else, Darcie Finch?" he asked in a husky whisper that even he didn't recognize, "I'm *good* at it."

She was lost, unresisting and as desperate as he.

He tilted her chin, devouring her luscious lips with his own.

CHAPTER FORTY-FOUR

Sandwiched between the comforting presence of Dominic Parker and the warm weight of a three-legged dog, Lydia started to feel better. The steps were solid beneath her and she no longer felt like she was suffocating. After a few more quiet moments, she slowly raised her head, relieved to find that the world had stopped spinning. She looked around in surprise. She had beaten it this time. She had actually beaten it.

Dom regarded her kindly. "Better?" he asked.

She nodded shakily. "Thank you," she whispered.

"Do you want me to find Devin?" Dom asked, searching her face with concern.

Her eyes widened. "Devin!" She grabbed his arm with both hands. "We've got to find Devin. He's with Darcie. I mean, she's with him. They're with each other."

Dom looked at her in alarm. "Slow down, Lydia. What are you saying?"

She took a deep breath and began again. The presence of the unflappable Dominic Parker gave her the strength. "Devin and Darcie are in the stables and Mallory is looking for them and she's bringing the cameraman with her. If she catches them…"

"That's why Atticus has been sniffing around the barn. He knows they're in there." Now it all made sense. Well, they might as well take advantage of the intrepid canine. "Atticus," Dom said. "Find Darcie."

The dog took off at a run, headed straight for the barn.

Dom stood up, starting down the steps.

"Where are you going?" Lydia asked, frantically.

Dom paused. "I'm going to warn them." He held out his hand. "You can come with me, if you're feeling up to it."

Her near miss with the panic attack was immediately forgotten. Lydia scrambled to her feet, taking Dom's hand. They hurried through the darkness, making their way toward the old section of the stables. As they approached, they saw Atticus standing on his back feet, scratching at the door. His front paws had already left long marks on the pristine red paint.

They were almost to the door when Dom heard Lydia gasp. He stopped to inquire what was wrong. She pointed toward the back of the house. He looked just in time to see Mallory striding across the lawn; she was followed by a cameraman. They were heading to the side door of the new section of the stables, the end opposite to where Dom and Lydia were standing.

"Hurry up!" Mallory hissed, pausing—for the *third* time, no less—so that the cameraman could catch up. "How does anyone as slow as you ever get a story?"

The disgruntled cameraman had no intention of moving a millisecond faster. If anything, the incessant whining and criticism of the woman who was impatiently tapping her foot, had him *slowing* his steps, even though they were barely creeping along as it was.

Todd should have known something wasn't quite right when Douglas McCallum refused to accompany them on their quest. During the past few years, the devious man had been instrumental in quite a few of the cameraman's choicest exposés. The way he disappeared into the ballroom tonight should have set off warning bells. Mr. McCallum usually stayed around to watch the fireworks.

Todd would have realized, a little sooner, that something was a bit off if the woman he was currently stuck with had been less attractive. She hadn't told him her name, nor who the man he was about to film in flagrante was. No! She had merely dazzled him with her blinding smile, blue eyes, and gorgeous, blond hair. Todd had always had a weakness for blondes…an unfortunate malady, especially in the case of this particular blonde. The more time he spent in her malignant presence, the more sympathy he had for her husband, the one who was supposed to be cheating on her. Poor guy. Todd didn't blame him a bit.

"Will you hurry up?" she demanded. "You are the worst excuse for a professional I've ever seen. You are incompetent. *Completely* incompetent. Just look at you." Her disdainful gaze swept over him. "Your slovenly appearance and general bad manners are a crime against your profession. Your boss will hear from me after this is over." She threw those words out without thinking them through.

Todd stopped in his tracks. "Listen, lady." No story was worth the abuse he was suffering. "I don't know who you think you are, but I do *not* work for you. You aren't paying me a dime. And if you think I have to stand here and listen to you…that I'm so desperate to score some footage of some guy—a guy nobody cares about—caught in the act with some woman—a *woman* nobody cares about…well, lady, you've got another think coming."

Mallory's mouth fell open in shock. Todd turned and started back to the house. This could not be happening. She was close, so very close to getting rid of Devin Merritt and having all that she had ever wanted. She would *not* let some asinine cameraman ruin it for her. Time to change tactics, she decided.

She ran after the cameraman, touching his arm softly when she reached him. He turned to regard her with disgust.

"Look, lady, it's over. I'm going back to the house."

She smiled, almost pityingly. "You don't know who I am, do you? What's your name…Todd?" Her eyes had glanced discreetly at his badge. "Well, Todd, for your information, I am Mrs. Devin Merritt."

Todd raised his eyebrows in surprise. Everybody had heard of Merritt Brothers Law Firm. He actually knew one of the Merritts…the one who handled the most high-profile cases. He had worked with…hmm, he thought the man's name was Lance. Yes, Todd was certain. Lance. He had worked with Lance multiple times. He was always respectful to the press and seemed like an okay guy. But, as far as Todd knew, Lance was single.

"Now you're getting it. I'm married to Devin. The one who had the ac-ci-dent," she added. "You know," she said impatiently. "One eye. Hideous disfig-urement. Monster face…."

Todd nodded, thoroughly disgusted by her words.

Mallory continued: "The *monster* appears to be cheating on me." She dabbed at her eyes, which, as far as Todd could tell, were completely dry. "I know, Todd, I can't believe it, either." She obviously mistook his surprise for something else. She reached out and touched Todd's arm again, leaning in so he could get a good glimpse of her cleavage.

It wasn't hard to get a good glimpse at that cleavage, Todd thought. It had been on display the whole night. A closer look, then. She leaned in to give him a closer look. He did remember hearing about the hit-and-run case, though. Merritt had been hit by an Uber, or something like that. What a freak accident. Now the man was disfigured *and* married to a woman who called him a monster. Todd wanted to return to the house and spare the man more embarrassment, but he had to admit that this was pretty good stuff. Maybe there was an angle to this story that would generate sympathy for the unfor-tunate Mr. Merritt.

"And," whispered the blonde, who wasn't nearly as attractive as she had seemed half an hour earlier, "he's in the stables with the *maid of honor*. Just think of the exposé you could have on your hands…Devin Merritt—Blane McCallum's right-hand man—found cheating on his long-suffering wife with the *sister* of the bride. That's McCallum's new *sister-in-law*." She enunciated the words as if Todd's small brain couldn't possibly figure out the relation-ships in this little fiasco. "Won't that be better than a story about the nause-atingly happy newlyweds sipping champagne and doing the Cupid Shuffle with all of their nauseatingly happy friends and family?"

Todd held up his hand. "Please don't say *nauseatingly* again," he requested politely. He thought it over while Mallory waited. He hated to admit it, but Blondie—for all her ridiculous posturing and maliciousness—had a point. The devoted fans of *CB* loved this kind of crap. They couldn't wait to hear dirt about someone in the public eye. Funny thing that Douglas McCallum would throw his nephew's head of legal to the wolves, but most of those playboy types didn't have much loyalty anyway. Damn. He really needed to find a new line of work.

"All right, lady," he said, "lead the way."

Mallory's smile of triumph almost made him turn around, but the temptation of a big exposé was too much to resist. They hurried to the side door of the newest section of the stables. Todd positioned himself behind the smirking blonde as she flung open the door with a flourish.

"Ah-ha! I knew it!" she said. She hurried into the…

Deserted barn.

Mallory stood there, looking around in obvious disappointment. Nearly half of the stalls were occupied. Their equine audience regarded the intruders with utter disinterest.

"What now, lady?" Todd asked, politely.

"We go to the other side of the stables, you idiot," she snapped. "Haven't you ever done this before? Pick up your feet and hurry up!"

Oh, great, Todd thought. They were back to that.

She started toward the opposite door at a clipped pace. Even though he followed, he held out hope that Blondie's husband was, at this very moment, sipping nauseatingly bubbly champagne and dancing the Cupid Shuffle with his nauseatingly happy friends in the nauseatingly beautiful ballroom.

"Hurry!" Lydia whispered.

"If they're in the new barn, we're already too late," Dom said, grimly. He gently nudged Atticus aside and opened the door.

Lydia glanced around hopefully, but the stable was empty. Atticus appeared momentarily flummoxed, sniffing the ground. Dom could only hope that the variety of scents—earthy and otherwise—wouldn't distract the canine from his original intent.

"Damn it, Darcie," Dom muttered under his breath.

Atticus made a beeline to the door that led to the outside area between the old barn and the new. Tugging Devin's sister—who was doing an admirable job of keeping up in spite of her heels—they followed the dog.

Halfway down the barn, Lydia slowed, bringing them to a halt. Her eyes were wide with worry. "What are we going to do if we find them?"

"I have an idea, but we have to find them first," Dom said. He squeezed her hand encouragingly. "All you have to do is get Devin back to the ballroom. I'll take care of the rest." He concentrated on keeping Lydia as calm as possible. All they needed was for her to have another panic attack. That would add a completely new dimension to their already bizarre situation. "Let's hope they're on the other side of that door," he said, with a reassuring nod of his head. Atticus was scratching and sniffing at the wood, sending imploring looks over his shoulder.

Lydia held up the hand he wasn't holding and crossed her fingers. Dom found the girlish gesture charming. Just then, Atticus let out a bark of rare frustration. He began pawing at the door with renewed vigor.

"C'mon, Lydia," Dom said.

As they raced for the door, he could only pray that the resolute canine was right.

Devin was warm, solid, supremely well-built. Darcie was all but plastered to him for the second time in the past thirty minutes. She was drifting in a blissful, sensual haze until, out of nowhere, a familiar furry beast came crashing into them. Atticus seemed intent on shoving his body between them. No easy feat, considering finding an inch of space between Darcie's hips and Devin's waist was difficult. Darcie squealed at the impact, grabbing at Devin's shoulders, trying desperately to stay on her feet. He caught her around the waist, steadying her and realizing, too late, that they were not alone.

Atticus sat down heavily on Devin's foot, pinning it to the ground. Devin struggled to comprehend what was happening. He was off-balance, almost dizzy, but the feel of the heavily panting dog against his leg was helping to steady him. He didn't like the look of shock on Darcie's face. He followed her eyes to the corner of the barn. His baby sister was standing in the darkness with none other than good, old Dom. The four froze for a few seconds, staring at each other. Each drew his or her own conclusion, none of which were good. Devin's brilliant plan was unraveling quickly.

Lydia spoke first, her voice hushed. "Thank God we found you first. Mallory's coming this way. With a cameraman from *The CB*." She rushed to Devin, tugging on his arm. "Come with me, Dev. We've got a plan. Hurry."

Devin and Darcie reacted to the desperation in Lydia's voice. Operating like puppets, they did exactly what they were told, too stunned by the urgency of their rescuers to argue.

Devin disappeared with Lydia into the older portion of the stables. Dom approached Darcie.

He took Devin's place, looking into the eyes of one of his oldest, dearest friends. "Sorry, Darce," he whispered, right before he pulled her into his embrace, kissing her as if she was his heart's desire.

Darcie's head was spinning. She didn't know whether to laugh or scream. Or try to push Dom away. He had obviously lost his mind. Something, she didn't know what—perhaps a latent survival instinct—prompted her to go along with his insanity. She tried to breathe, but Dom was having none of it.

She heard a triumphant, "Ah-ha! I knew I would find you here!"

The next moment an unexpectedly bright light lit up the sides of both barns, and the fence, and all the area in between.

Dom stopped kissing her. He turned his head, shielding her body with his own as much as possible. "What the *hell* do you think you're doing?" he asked angrily.

Mallory's triumph turned to abject humiliation.

"Oh, my...I thought, I mean...I assumed that you were...and..." she stuttered, completely at a loss.

"This is your big story?" the cameraman asked. He stared at Dom and Darcie, then turned to the woman. "You're crazy, lady. I'm going to leave these poor people alone and go back to the house. It would probably be a good idea for you to do the same." He turned to face Dom and Darcie again. "Sorry, you two. If you want to report me for being unprofessional, my name's Todd. But I hope you won't. Report me, I mean." He flashed a final look of disgust at the woman who had summoned him to the barn. "I received some flawed information!" he explained. Then he flipped off his light and left without a backward glance.

Mallory stood in the dark, glaring at Dom and Darcie.

"Again," Dom stated, clearly. "What the *hell* do you think you're doing?"

Mallory smiled coldly. "I'm just looking for my *monster*. That's all. And I thought he was out here doing, you know...*monster* things." Her tinkling laugh fell on deaf ears.

"The only monster I've seen out here is you," Darcie said, stepping out from behind Dom to face the blue-eyed demon.

Mallory's beautifully manicured hands curled into tight fists. "Why, you little..." She actually took a step toward Darcie, but paused, controlling herself with difficulty.

"Darcie!" Dom hissed in warning.

"Don't go there, Miss Finch," Mallory resumed. "I assure you...*you* don't want to go there. You've never dealt with the likes of me."

Darcie's eyes glistened with anger. "How do *you* know that, Mallory?" she asked, softly. Her velvety voice was deceptively calm.

Dom saw the fire in her eyes and knew he was in trouble. He had seen that look before. "Oh, Lord," he said under his breath.

"Because you're still standing there," Mallory hissed. "Make no mistake. If you knew what I could do, you'd be running back to the house in those tacky rhinestone heels."

Darcie gasped. "Are you threatening me?"

"Darcie, enough," Dom said, a note of alarm in his voice. He tried to take her arm, but she shook him off.

"Not a threat, but a warning. Stay away from me and mine, Miss Finch." Mallory sneered. "Or you'll regret it."

Her cold gaze remained on Darcie for a few seconds. She seemed poised to attack if given the slightest provocation.

Darcie raised her eyebrows, returning Mallory's pointed glare. Dom braced himself to intervene if necessary. Privately, he wondered why he invariably found himself in situations that required intervention.

Mallory finally tossed her head, ending the standoff. She stalked to the door she had entered so victoriously only minutes before. She paused long enough to spear Darcie and Dom with a hateful stare before making her customary spectacular exit. She failed in spectacular fashion, however: one of the heels of her Yves Saint Laurent shoe caught on the door jamb. She tripped, stepping involuntarily out of the shoe to land hard on her left knee. Dom, ever the gentleman, picked up the shoe and handed it to her. She jerked it out of his grasp, struggling to stand. When she finally regained her balance and stood somewhat confidently, her attempt to reunite her foot with her shoe proved to be an exercise in futility.

"Mallory."

Darcie couldn't resist the chance to have the last word.

Devin's treacherous wife paused, vibrating with anger. Her dress displayed a streak of dirt from her knee to the edge of her hem. She was still holding her shoe in her hand, having yet to manage the elaborate fastening while balancing on one foot.

"My shoes are Italian," Darcie snapped with great satisfaction.

"Go to hell," Mallory hissed.

She limped off to the new section of the stables, clutching one five-hundred-dollar shoe in her hand. Atticus, for some reason known only to Atticus, trotted at her heels. Dom and Darcie listened in silence until the sound of Mallory's uneven gait faded away.

"That went well," Dom said without heat, nodding his head philosophically.

Darcie turned to glare at her oldest friend in the world for a moment before punching him in the arm. Twice. She turned without saying a word, choosing the middle doors that led straight back to the house. She had spent enough time in the stables for one night.

"Hey," Dom said, scrambling after her. "What was that for? I was the one who helped you, remember?" He rotated his shoulder. He had forgotten that Darcie Finch could really throw a punch.

Dom knew better than to ask questions. Catching up to Darcie, he simply waited for the dam to break, confident that, in true Darcie-fashion, he wouldn't have to wait for long. And he didn't.

"You kissed me," she burst out, still in shock. "I mean, you *kissed* me. With your…tongue and everything."

She couldn't believe what had happened.

The horrified look on her face wasn't doing a lot for Dom's ego. "Well, what did you expect me to do? I had to make it look realistic." He looked genuinely affronted, as if she had crossed an invisible line and stomped all over his masculine pride. "I'm sorry it was such an *unpleasant* experience for you," he said.

"Oh, Dom, I'm sorry. I didn't mean it like that. I wasn't criticizing the quality of your kisses." She shrugged her shoulders. "You just, I don't know… surprised me, I guess. You haven't kissed me since high school." Giving him a quick sideways glance, she couldn't resist adding, "I have to say that your technique has greatly improved since then."

"Yeah, I guess I just overwhelmed you with my superior skill and expertise."

He was doing his best to appear serious, but a small smile hovered at the corner of his mouth.

Darcie smiled back. He was one of her best friends. He didn't deserve to be her punching bag. He deserved her gratitude. "Thanks, Dom," she said softly.

"Anything for you, Darce. Just don't tell Kayleigh. Kissing an old girlfriend comes under the category of *Ultimate Relationship Killers*, even if it was for a good reason."

Darcie laughed. "My lips are sealed," she promised.

She wasn't lying. She would never betray her friend. And, although his kissing abilities were impressive, she wasn't in love with Dominic Parker. She had given her whole heart to Devin Merritt. His kisses were the only ones that would ever leave her wanting more. He loved her, she thought, dreamily. He actually said he loved her. Out loud. And even though the horses were her only witnesses, she would never forget that moment.

And in response, she said...

Darcie frowned, trying to remember. Her overheated brain was still trying to cool down. What did she say? Did she say anything? Surely, she had said something. She tried to focus. Devin said, *"I love you, Darcie Finch."* And she said...

Her brain refused to cooperate. What *did* she say? She knew what she *didn't* say. She didn't say, "I love you, too." She was certain she hadn't said that.

Think, Darcie, think, she encouraged herself. *What did you say? He said, "I love you, Darcie Finch," and you said....*

..."I know."

She gasped aloud, stopping at the bottom of the steps that led to the small portico at the side of the house. She cringed as she remembered her words. *"I know."*

I. Know.

Why, oh why did she have to say that? Why didn't she just say, *"I love you, too"* like a normal person? Who says *"I know"* when somebody tells her he loves her for the first time? The answer was easy. Darcie I'm-The-World's-Biggest-Romantic-Loser Finch, that's who. She had to fix her mistake. She had to tell him.

Dom looked at her with some concern. "Darce, are you all right? Why don't you sit here on the steps for a minute?"

She appeared frozen in place. So he helped her sit down, watching her carefully. Surely, he wasn't going to have to deal with *two* panic attacks in *two* different women in less than *two* hours. Of course, the way Dom's night was going so far...

He brushed straw from the bottom of her dress. She didn't seem capable of taking care of that small detail at present. The least he could do was to try to make her look a little less like a woman who...well, like a woman who had spent some time with a man in a barn. She finally pushed his hand away, assuming the task herself.

"You need to fix your hair, too," he suggested in a neutral tone.

"I don't know why I should bother," she grumbled. "The hair of half the women in the ballroom will be falling down by now."

"Appearances," Dom said firmly. "Speaking of which...I have no intention of letting you out of my sight for the duration of the reception."

"But, Dom, don't you think that's a little extreme?" How was she going to tell Devin she loved him if Dom was tagging along all night? Talk about an uncomfortable situation.

"No, Miss Disaster-Waiting-To-Happen. That cameraman from *The CB* will be lurking around, and you can't take any chances."

Dom watched her face fall as the reality of what he was saying sunk in.

She sighed "You're probably right."

Dom was surprised by her easy acquiescence. She was being awfully agreeable. Too agreeable. Uh-oh, he thought, uneasily. An agreeable Darcie almost always led to trouble. She was quiet for a few seconds, too. Too quiet. That never boded well for anybody, but particularly for him. She was plotting something. He would bet his last dollar on it.

When she finished brushing off her dress and tidying her hair, she stood up. Dom waited, bracing himself for the worst.

She looked up at him, hopefully, "Dom, I was wondering…"

"No. Whatever it is, Darcie, my answer is no."

"But…"

"No, no, no. An emphatic *no*. A *no* with capital letters and an exclamation point. Make that two exclamation points."

"But, Dom…"

"*No*, Darcie. N-O. *NO!*" He crossed his arms to emphasize his point.

"You're right, Dom," she agreed in defeat. "You're exactly right. I can't ask you to do one more thing for me tonight. You've done more than enough already. I'll just have to do it myself."

She ran up the steps to reach for the door handle. But before she could open the door, Dom's hand pressed against it from behind her, holding the door closed.

"Oh, no you don't, Darcie," he said in a resigned tone. "I don't know what you're planning, but it's not going to happen without me. I told you that I was sticking to you for the rest of the night. And I meant it."

She wrinkled her nose, still tugging on the door handle. It wouldn't budge.

Dom sighed reluctantly. "What do you want me to do?"

"Just ask Devin to meet me in the gazebo at midnight. I need to tell him…" She paused, looking a little flushed. "I need to tell him something important."

"Are you crazy?" Dom couldn't believe it. "You almost got caught meeting him in the stables." Darcie had lost her mind. That was the only explanation for it. Or was it love? If so, Dom hoped he would *never* fall in love like that. He sighed again. Louder than before. He was going to give in eventually. He may as well save them both some time. "All right, Darcie. I'll deliver the message, but you have to promise to be careful."

She threw her arms around her oldest friend. "Oh, thank you, Dom. I promise."

Her beautiful smile was blinding. Dom was once again thankful for his ninety-five percent immunity to that smile.

As they headed back to the reception, Dom considered the implications of the "favor" he was about to do for Darcie. Sometimes her requests played havoc with his good intentions, but, somehow, he always managed to do the right thing. Dom was known for making good choices. He was That Guy. He had always been That Guy. The kind of person fathers want their daughters to date. The kind of person loved by grandmothers near and far.

The monikers had followed him for most of his life. *Dominic Do-Right. Do-good Dom.* And the ever-popular *Dom, the Dependable.* He didn't mind it too much. A man had to follow the dictates of his conscience, after all. He had made his decision. He was going to do what Darcie wanted. He would do the right thing. And God help them all.

CHAPTER FORTY-FIVE

Seated beside Lydia, Devin watched them come back into the ballroom. He had been seated in this position for the last ten minutes. Dom led the way. Darcie's hand firmly in his. He walked confidently, completely at ease, as if disappearing for half an hour with the maid of honor during a wedding reception was no big deal. The woman at his side, however, practically shimmered with romance.

Devin couldn't help but notice the myriad reactions caused by the unexpected entrance of Darcie Finch and Dominic Parker. Together. Maggie appeared delighted by the turn of events. She had never given up on the dream of having Darcie as a daughter-in-law. Joey and Grace shot each other speculative glances. Juli watched her daughter with genuine concern, while Joe looked downright suspicious. Blane nodded encouragingly, letting Devin know he had his support. Devin was careful to keep his own expression blandly neutral, a skill he had mastered some time ago. Let them think what they wanted. Darcie Finch belonged to him now. She knew it. He knew it. That was all that mattered.

He gazed at her hungrily, taking in the rosy flush of her cheeks. She was almost too sexy, with her hair slightly mussed and that wayward curl still teasing the side of her neck. She looked just rumpled enough to hint at misbehavior. His pulse leaped in response. There had been a bit of misbehavior all right. But with *him*. Damn it. With Devin Merritt, the one-eyed pirate lawyer. Darcie Finch was in the stables with *him*. *He* was the one who had put that sparkle in her eyes. He wanted to go to her and pull her into his arms. He wanted to kiss those sweet lips. But, most of all, he wanted to let everyone know she was his.

But he couldn't, because he was back to his existence as a helpless animal. He was trapped in the coil of a boa constrictor that was slowly squeezing the life out of him. Once again, he had to sit on the sidelines and act as if he didn't care. He was getting damn tired of it.

The DJ's next words caused a flurry of movement. "And now let's take a little trip down to Ocean Boulevard."

The song was "Carolina Girls" by General Johnson and the Chairman of the Board. It was obviously an old favorite of the Honeysuckle Creek crowd. Dom and Darcie had learned to dance the shag in middle school cotillion. It didn't take much urging for them to join their family and friends on the dance floor.

As partners, they were well matched. Moving effortlessly to the music, they executed a number of different moves with confidence and a smooth, natural vitality. But to Devin, well…he didn't like it. He was rational enough to understand that Dom and Darcie were trying to give him the alibi he so desperately needed. He was, however, irrational enough to resent the man currently holding Darcie Finch's hand. He should be more grateful, he kept admonishing himself. That man—along with Devin's timid little sister—had, unselfishly, saved his ass less than an hour ago. In spite of Dom's assistance, Devin admitted to himself, he would like nothing more than to plant his fist right in Dom's smiling…

"Devin," Lydia hissed, planting a very firm elbow into his side. "Stop it."

"Stop what?"

Devin refused to take his eyes off the smiling pair of dancers.

"Stop looking like you want to punch Dom in the face. He's a nice man, Devin. Really. A very nice man," she finished softly. Her quiet defense of

Dominic Parker brought Devin's head around to study his sister. She appeared in earnest.

"How do *you* know he's such a *nice man*?" Devin asked perversely. "And how the hell did he get involved in all of this, anyway?" He was acting like a jerk. Worse than that, he knew it. But Lydia was his sister. She was supposed to be on his side. Wasn't she?

Lydia put a soft hand on his arm, meeting his eye seriously. "I almost had a panic attack after I figured out what Mallory was going to do. He helped me, Devin. If he hadn't been there, we wouldn't have made it in time. You owe him a debt of gratitude, not a broken nose."

Devin sighed. His sister's soft words took all of the bluster out of him. "I know. You're right, little sister. It's just…"

"I'm sorry," she blurted out, looking as though she wanted to cry.

"What are you talking about, Lydia?"

"I'm sorry I messed up. This is all my fault. I should have kept a better eye on Mallory. I should have…" Her pretty, hazel eyes filled with tears.

"Lydia, hush," Devin said, hating the way she tried to blame herself for everything. She had never behaved that way when they were growing up. He should never have let her marry Kyle Follansbee, he thought, regretfully. At the very least, he should have beaten the hell out of the abusive bastard when he had the chance. Devin caught himself. He sounded just like Lydia, blaming himself for something he couldn't control. Damn if it wasn't contagious. "You didn't mess up anything, Lydia," he said softly. "You're the one who saved us all. If you hadn't…"

An ear-splitting cry filled with rage and frustration stopped him midsentence. Devin and Lydia exchanged a troubled glance. Something about that cry sounded familiar. By mutual agreement, they rose and unobtrusively made their way toward the source of the commotion.

Another shrill shriek, louder than the first, quickly followed. The sound rippled across the outdoor patio, through the outer doors of the ballroom—thrown open to catch the cool night air—and then into the ballroom itself. Heads began to turn as the guests closest to the doors exchanged glances. The third scream—more like the howl of an infuriated animal—was followed by the appearance of a three-legged canine running toward the large fountain in the center of the patio as if his life depended on it.

Blane motioned for the DJ to stop the music. "Oh, Lord," Grace gasped into the silence.

Every eye in the crowded room watched Atticus race to the side of the fountain closest to the house. He paused, glancing behind him, warily.

"What has that dog done now?" Grace's voice echoed in the cavernous ballroom.

The bride and groom rushed toward the open doors. Darcie, Dom, and Joey hurried quickly behind them. Blane reached the patio first, Grace at his heels.

"Atta-boy," Blane called in a firm voice. "Come here."

Atticus rarely ignored a direct order from his second-favorite human. But this time he refused to comply.

Blane changed his tactics, kneeling down on one knee. "Come on, Atta-boy," he cajoled. "You're scaring your mama."

Atticus wagged his tail but didn't budge. Moving nothing but his head, he glanced at his new master, apologetically. The light glinted off something he was clenching between his teeth.

Grace knelt behind Blane, peeking over his shoulder. "What's that in his mouth?"

Atticus turned his head again, searching the darkness behind him. The object in his mouth suddenly became easy to identify. A lady's high-heeled shoe.

"Oh, no! Not that!"

Grace's loud remark was heard by every person in the ballroom. The bride faced her family and friends. "Is anyone missing a shoe?" she asked apologetically.

The women—those who had slipped off their shoes for the dancing—moved around the room, looking under tables and beside chairs to check on their own footwear.

When nobody raised a hand, Darcie chanced a glance at Dom. The look on his face confirmed her fears. "Oh, Dom, you don't think..."

Dom nodded. "It has to be Mallory's," he said, torn between laughter at another ridiculous turn of events and concern for his deathly pale co-conspirator. "Atticus started following Mallory right after I handed her that shoe."

"Oh, Lord," Darcie moaned. Could this night get any more complicated?

Dom grinned. "Don't worry, Darce," he said. "The star witness can't talk."

Darcie ignored him. "Maybe it's not Mallory's," she said hopefully.

"Oh, it's hers all right. Look."

Dom pointed to the other side of the fountain.

Sure enough, Mallory came limping out of the darkness, a fallen angel in search of vengeance. Her dress was soiled from her earlier tumble in the barn; it had acquired a long stain of mud and grass as well. The stain stretched from her low-cut bodice, across the dress' waistline, and down the side to the hip. It was difficult to imagine what had caused that stain, unless she had rolled down a hill. Several leaves and a few pine needles adorned her formerly pristine locks. Her single long blond curl was a matted mess. One side of her face had a smudge of dirt that stretched from her nose to her ear. The expression in her eyes was pure fury.

"Give me that shoe, you hound from hell! Or I'll take you to the pound myself!"

She had snarled the threat the moment she spotted Atticus. So focused was she on her quest that, for once, she failed to notice that every eye in the ballroom was riveted to the spectacle going on beside the fountain.

Mallory continued with even greater venom: "And don't think I won't demand a front row seat to watch while you're being euthanized!"

Grace gasped, poised to intervene. Atticus was her baby, after all.

"Hold on, Green Eyes," Blane said, under his breath. "Atta-boy can take care of himself."

It did appear that the vexatious dog had some sort of plan. They watched him almost crawl toward Mallory. He was, for the moment, visibly humbled, his head hanging low to the ground. He dropped the shoe two feet in front of her. Backing up a step, he eyed her steadily.

"That's right, you despicable excuse for a dog," Mallory said, her syrupy tone in complete opposition to her words. "If you give me my shoe, I might tell the pound to let you have something besides dogfood for your last meal." She took a tentative step toward her expensive footwear, stretching out her hand. Her fingers had almost achieved their goal when the wily dog snatched the shoe in his mouth again. He headed straight for the fountain. Mallory hurried right behind him, screeching in anger. Atticus planted his front feet on the edge of the fountain, regarding his nemesis steadily as she crept closer.

"Don't you dare!" Mallory whispered. "Don't you dare drop my Yves Saint Laurent shoe into that fountain, you three-legged fiend!"

She approached the unpredictable dog, moving slowly until she was nearly close enough to touch him.

Atticus glanced back, regarding her calmly. He actually looked a little bored. Lulled into security, Mallory reached out carefully, preparing to pluck her property from the dog's mouth. She had, however, underestimated her opponent. She played right into his devious paws. At the last moment, Atticus turned back to the fountain, leaned forward slightly, then gave his nose a little toss. He opened his mouth and watched the high-heeled shoe sail through the air. Mallory lunged but missed it, barely catching herself on the side of the fountain. Her eyes followed her Yves Saint Laurent shoe as it disappeared under the swirling waters.

She, however, had no intention of letting the shoe go. She plunged her arm into the water, stretching as far as she could, but to no avail. She couldn't quite reach her shoe from where she stood by the side of the fountain. Still, she refused to give up. Those shoes were the most expensive pair of shoes she had ever owned, and she wasn't letting them go.

She climbed onto the side of the fountain, precariously perching on her knees. She set her left hand down into the cold water for balance and reached out as far as she could with her right. Her effort was rewarded as her hand grasped the heel of her shoe. "Got it!" she announced, triumphantly, to no one in particular.

Before she could pull her shoe out of the water, Atticus made his final move. He crept stealthily behind Mallory; as stealthily as a three-legged dog could creep, anyway. Then he paused, throwing a look at his spellbound audience. The glint in his eyes seemed to say "Checkmate." He opened his mouth, barking at the top of his lungs. So unexpected was Atticus' outburst that Mallory lost her balance. She fell headfirst into the fountain. Several moments later, she came up sputtering. And swearing. *And* clutching her shoe to the bodice of her nearly transparent gown.

Atticus trotted back to his humans. He sat down on Blane's foot, surveying the chaos he had created with a maniacal smile on his canine lips.

Somehow Mallory managed to crawl out of the fountain, dripping wet and vibrating with anger. She brushed past the few brave souls who stepped forward to assist her: Devin and Lydia, out of a sense of duty and obligation, and Charlie Ray, for the sheer enjoyment of being part of the drama.

Mallory ignored them all. Her only goal was reaching her victorious foe.

Devin managed to halt her progress. "Mallory," he said, stepping in front of her, "put this on." He slipped out of his tux jacket and held it out to her.

"Go to hell, *Monster*," Mallory hissed. She jerked the jacket out of his hands then threw it back at his face.

Devin caught the jacket, his face devoid of expression. He saw in his wife's eyes the dawning realization that she was suddenly the center of attention. He knew that look. Only Mallory could take joy in the fact that she finally, *finally* had the chance to take center stage. He also knew there was absolutely nothing he could do about it. "As you wish," he said, bowing his head slightly. He stepped back, resigned to the knowledge that an ugly scene was only moments away.

The vindictive woman advanced on Atticus, basking in the knowledge that she had captured the attention of her audience. She was five feet from her prey when Grace planted herself squarely in her path. The contrast between the beautiful bride—intent on protecting her beloved dog—and the soaking wet woman—thoroughly ensnared in a drama of her own making—was striking.

Grace's hands set firmly on her hips. Her undaunted green eyes glowed with the primitive light of battle as she faced her enemy. "Don't even think about it," she said.

Mallory took a step back, changing her tactics. "Oh, Grace," she gushed. "I can't even begin to tell you what I've been through. I went down to the stables to see *Blane's* beautiful horses and, well, I got lost and stepped in a hole. I'm sure that *Blane's* groundskeepers didn't *intend* for their *careless* negligence to result in a *devastating* fall for one of your guests, but that's exactly what happened." She shook her head sadly, gesturing this way and that as she told her tale of woe. She made sure to position herself in the most flattering light.

Devin shook his head and sighed, feeling Lydia's slight movement beside him. He was as uncomfortable as she was. At least Amalie was safely tucked into bed. The little girl didn't need to see another of her mother's unfortunate performances.

Grace crossed her arms. She raised her eyebrows. She said absolutely nothing.

Many of the guests drew closer, perhaps out of concern for the bride. Or, perhaps for the dog. Or, perhaps, purely for the unadulterated entertainment value of the farce taking place outside the ballroom. The truth was hard to tell.

Mallory employed every skill she possessed to implicate and manipulate while exonerating herself. She was completely engrossed in her tirade. The fact that Grace had yet to say anything only added more fuel to her overblown sense of impending victory. She blithely continued: "And your poor, sweet dog. How tragic that he must now be put down for mauling a guest in your home. And for destroying personal property. I would be happy to make the necessary arrangements. I'm sure it would be too emotionally difficult for you. I'll take care of everything while you and Blane are enjoying your honeymoon." She dabbed at her eyes with the back of her hand, smiling as she prepared for the bride's heartfelt tears. And apology.

Grace smiled, too, but her smile was more feral than anything else. She looked as if she would like nothing better than to bite Mallory herself. Darcie and Joey exchanged a knowing glance. They knew better than anyone how fiercely protective their gentle sister could be when someone she loved was threatened. After Mallory's menacing offer to euthanize Grace's beloved canine companion, it was little wonder the bride stood regarding the heartless woman the way a fireman regards a fire…right before putting it out.

"Mallory," Grace said, her voice deceptively calm. "While I'm certain that your *kind* offer to kill *my* dog was made with the best of intentions, it isn't necessary. I firmly believe that Atticus is better off alive than dead. You can rest assured, however, that Atticus and I will discuss his unfortunate obsession with women's footwear."

She glared at the guilty canine comfortably ensconced on Blane's left foot. Atticus refused to meet her gaze. His eyes were firmly focused on the bushes at the edge of the patio. His attempt to appear innocent, however, was negated by the remnants of straw and fallen leaves sticking out from his fur.

Grace turned back to her adversary. "So, you see, Mallory, there is absolutely no reason for you to worry about *my* dog anymore." She paused to sweep her eyes over Mallory's revealing ensemble. "What you do need to worry about, honey, is covering yourself up. At this moment, your wet dress is quite transparent." Her voice oozed with pity. "And besides that, you're going to catch your death of cold standing out here. Soaked to the skin. In the night air. Bless your soggy little heart."

With great dignity, Grace turned her back on the gaping woman. She walked into the ballroom without another word, Atticus at her heels.

Still reeling from the shock of the most efficient set-down she had ever received, Mallory barely managed to close her mouth. "Well, I never," she gasped.

"Yeah," said Blane agreeably, putting his hands in his pockets. "But you would probably be a better person if you had."

He headed into the ballroom in search of champagne to toast his lovely bride.

Mallory glared at the retreating groom's back until he disappeared inside. She stood there by the door, pouting, as the remaining spectators on the patio filed by in twos and threes. No one, including her monster-faced husband, stopped to offer a single, commiserating word. Even her pathetic sister-in-law avoided her gaze as she passed by.

Quite unexpectedly, Mallory found herself alone. She waited until the music started up again before stomping into the ballroom. The bright interior lights made her sodden dress more appropriate for a wet T-shirt contest than a wedding reception.

Mallory stalked quickly by a table occupied by several locals from Honeysuckle Creek. Seated in one of the chairs, Evon calmly took hold of each end of the maroon-colored tablecloth. With a quick flick of his wrists, he whisked the tablecloth out from under the cake plates, wineglasses, and goblets. Not a single one had been upset. Gasps of admiration arose from the other guests around the table. "He trained with a magician," Charlie Ray proudly explained.

Evon tossed the tablecloth to Mallory as she passed by. She gave him a glare that could have melted the glasses on the table. But she wrapped the cloth around her shoulders as if it was a robe for a queen. Right before reaching the doors that led into the grand foyer, she paused to deliver one final disdainful glare around the ballroom. Her eyes widened with shock when she discovered no one was interested in her grand exit. She tossed her head anyway, and flounced out.

Had she turned around at that moment, she would have seen Todd—her much-maligned cameraman from *The Celebrity Buzz*—step into the ballroom, coming in from the patio. He was grinning gleefully from ear to ear. And why not? He had just filmed every moment of Mallory's unfortunate display.

Only one person in the ballroom truly appreciated Mallory's dramatic exit. Douglas McCallum wanted to applaud. He felt a wicked thrill at her out-of-control display of emotions. He enjoyed watching her failed attempt to manipulate the observers of her situation. With a less savvy crowd, she would have been right on target.

Now, however, she must be filled with a desire for revenge. And who better to be the recipient of her vengeance than her very own husband? The one she called the *Monster*? Douglas discreetly followed Mallory from the ballroom. She was so distracted by the failure of her own performance that trailing her was easy. He watched her until she entered the last door on the east side of the guest wing.

Douglas smiled. His wedding-crashing had just taken a turn for the better.

When Mallory opened the bathroom door a short while later, she had calmed down enough to appreciate the fact that she was warm and dry. She had not, however, recovered from her humiliation. She rarely failed to capture her audience's adulation. It was so easy to do in Newport. A little drama, a few fake tears, and soon they were all eating out of her hand. Not so in Honeysuckle Creek. She felt angry and reckless, eager to make someone pay for her troubles.

She paused to study herself in the large mirror over the double vanity. Her freshly blow-dried blonde hair fell in soft waves down her back. Her blue eyes were wide and clear. She turned back and forth in front of the mirror, admiring how desirable she looked wrapped in nothing but a towel.

They were fools. All of them. Nothing but fools. And she was going to make them pay.

She walked out of the bathroom and stopped, sucking in a breath of surprise. There, reclining comfortably in the middle of her bed, was Douglas McCallum. He had untied his bowtie. The ends were hanging on either side of his open tux shirt. His back was set against the headboard, cushioned by two fluffy pillows. His ankles were comfortably crossed. He held a glass filled with a pale, sparkling beverage. It looked suspiciously like champagne.

She studied him for a minute. Her cold but appreciative gaze took note of his well-toned physique, his handsome features. He was ridiculously attractive for a man in his fifties, she realized. He was still ruggedly masculine. And tremendously appealing. The way he was looking at her screamed sex. The reason he was here was quite obvious…and quite flattering to her wounded ego. He was playing some kind of game with her. That was okay. Mallory liked games.

"Oh, pardon me, Mrs. Merritt…" he began.

"Mallory," she reminded him, not bothering to hide her pleased reaction to his presence.

"Oh, yes, Mallory. I seem to have gotten lost. I didn't realize this was your room." He smiled, his eyes raking her body from head to toe as if he could see right through her towel.

She deliberately let the towel slip a bit over her right breast. A game was a game. "Mr. McCallum…"

"Douglas," he said, smiling in anticipation.

Mallory's heart started to beat a little faster. "Really, Douglas," she chided him. "I imagine you've never been lost in your life. Why are you *really* here?"

She crossed her arms, making all but the tips of her breasts visible for his perusal.

"Why, Mallory, I've come to make you feel better. That's all."

He smiled, but his innocent expression was spoiled by the hunger in his eyes. The same eyes that couldn't stop staring at her breasts.

Mallory felt an instant response. Douglas McCallum was handsome. And wildly rich. And lying in her bed. Why not? she asked herself. Why the hell not? She deserved a man's attention after all that she had been through tonight. *A handsome and powerful man,* she amended, *who obviously knows what he's doing in the bedroom.* She had read the articles. His prowess was legendary. She owed it to herself to experience the skills of Douglas McCallum. She made the decision then and there that she was going to play.

His eyes bored into hers. "Join me, Mallory. I promise you'll be glad you did."

Mallory dropped her towel. Let the games begin.

CHAPTER FORTY-SIX

The anticipation was killing Darcie. She didn't even have the chance to tell Devin goodbye. All she managed was a quick glance behind her as she left the reception with her family. The Parkers left with them, and a large group of friends of the bride and groom—mostly the younger set. The group headed to the London County Airport to send the happy couple off to their Scottish honeymoon in style.

Devin's decision to stay behind was largely attributed to his desire to check on his wife, who had not returned to the party after her debacle in the fountain. Darcie was certain his decision had more to do with self-preservation. His inability to hide the molten desire flaming in his eyes was doing all sorts of things to her pulse rate. He was right to stay behind. It was the safer option.

Heaven knew she had been under the silent scrutiny of her parents since returning to the ballroom with Dom. From that point on, she and Devin had carefully avoided all contact save for an occasional brief glance. She hoped Dom's presence was enough of a buffer to distract attention from Devin. It wouldn't be enough to save her from an interrogation later about Dom. Or about Devin. Or both, she thought, gloomily. She was sure of that. But she wasn't worried about later. All she needed was to postpone the inevitable until *after* she met Devin at the gazebo.

True to his word, Dom had barely left her side for the past hour. That, in itself, was causing raised eyebrows and wagging tongues in another quarter entirely. Speculation about the rekindling of her and Dom's brief high school romance was rampant. Darcie could tell. Memories were long in Honeysuckle Creek.

Dom's family was particularly interested. Maggie—barely held in check by the continued vigilance of her husband—was practically vibrating with curiosity. Phoebe was silent and disappointed. But Penelope appeared smug, as if she had been right all along. Out of all of the Parkers, only Ric appeared completely unconcerned by the strange turn of events. He was Darcie's unknowing ally of the moment because his hilarious comments distracted Joey from delving too deeply into his sister's business. Darcie was beyond grateful.

She was also appreciative of Roger and Ana, who were equally oblivious. By staying close to them Darcie could pretend to ignore the sympathetic glances from Lou and Evander. She also tried to ignore Zack's open speculation. That sharp-witted young man never missed anything.

The bride and groom inadvertently provided the most effective distraction of all. Their going-away ceremony at the airport was the most unusual anyone could remember. Grace and Blane ran from the small airport office to the boarding stairs leading up to the plane, racing through a shower of yellow rose petals. After pausing for a few quick photographs, the happy couple ascended the stairs. Blane went first, holding his bride's hand protectively in his. Negotiating stairs with ruffles and tulle was no joke. When Grace finally reached the door of the sleek, private jet, she turned around, preparing to throw her bouquet.

All of the laughing single ladies on the tarmac jostled each other, vying for the most advantageous position. Grace gave her best friend, Lou, a mischievous wink before turning around. She and Lou had planned this moment since they were seven, after all. Their plans, however, were not to be. Atticus, who had been patiently awaiting his humans inside the plane, poked his head from the doorway of the jet. The unexpected appearance of Grace's beloved canine startled the bride just as she released the bouquet. The bouquet sailed through the air, passing quietly over the heads of the waiting ladies. Straight into the hands of...Zack.

"Touchdown!" he said, grinning at the ladies. The next moment he launched into his version of an NFL celebration dance.

"Don't you dare spike that bouquet!" Lou screamed, racing toward him.

Pandemonium ensued. Lou playfully tried to wrestle the bouquet from the proud young man. Her comic attempts were unsuccessful. Much to his audience's delight, the victorious Zack immediately insisted on having his picture taken. Standing in the middle of the single females. Holding the bouquet.

"How about the garter?" Ric yelled over the joyous cacophony.

"Not a chance," Blane yelled back. "That garter belongs to me." He waggled his eyebrows at his blushing bride. And as if to emphasize his words, he bent the bride back over his arm in the most romantic kiss imaginable. His efforts drew envious sighs and heartfelt laughter from the onlookers. When the kiss ended, the grinning groom escorted his flustered bride onto the plane.

Darcie watched the door close with a wistful sigh. Grace and Blane would be spending their honeymoon in the cottage on the McCallum estate where Ian was raised. She had visited the lovely place during Grace and Blane's engagement party. The stone cottage surrounded by ancient trees reminded her of something out of a fairy tale. Darcie was quite happy for her sister, but she couldn't help feeling a bit envious. She could only wonder how long she was going to have to wait for a fairy tale honeymoon of her own.

Dom stepped beside her. "Stop it," he hissed.

Darcie was startled out of her reverie. "Stop what?" she asked, surprised at the urgency in his voice.

"Stop looking like you're ready for a honeymoon of your own. Enough people are talking about us already."

"What's the matter, Dom?" she teased. "Can't stand a little small town gossip? I always thought your skin was thicker than that."

"Not me, genius," Dom said ruefully. "Kayleigh. If she hears any rumors about you and me there'll be hell to pay."

Darcie's eyes widened. She finally realized the kind of trouble Dom's assistance might cause him. "Oh, Dom, I'm so sorry! I didn't even think."

"You're doing that a lot lately, aren't you, Darce? Not thinking?" He regarded her shocked expression, amused in spite of himself. Darcie was rarely accused of not thinking.

"Hmph," she said, before wrinkling her nose at her oldest friend. Even though his words were true, she couldn't resist punching him.

"Ow," said Dom. "Damn it, Darce," he swore, frowning. He began rubbing his sore appendage. "That's three times tonight. I do have another arm, you know."

And just like that they were out of the limelight. The exchange was so normal for them, so completely unromantic, that their watchers relaxed their surveillance. Maggie looked at Will…disappointed but resigned. Phoebe tossed her head, smiling smugly at her twin. Juli got caught up in a conversation with Lou. Only Joe Finch continued to study his daughter in silent speculation.

As the group broke up, arrangements were made for the younger crowd to meet at their favorite karaoke bar to continue the celebration.

"Are y'all coming?" Ric asked as Dom and Darcie reached her Jeep.

"Not this time," Darcie said, shaking her head. "I'm headed back to school in the morning." *And I have a meeting*, she added to herself, trying desperately to keep the exhilaration that was pulsing through her veins from showing. *No, a date. No, that's not good, either. A clandestine rendezvous.* She shook her head. *Shut up, Darcie.*

"I'll be there," Dom told Ric. "See you in a few."

Ric squeezed his brother's shoulder in response and headed to the car.

Dom opened the passenger-side door for Darcie before walking around to the driver's side. Dom liked driving her Jeep. He always had. Darcie didn't mind. At the moment, she was a little too distracted for driving.

He started the engine and pulled into the line of cars leaving the airport. Darcie didn't say anything for the first mile. Dom thought that might be some kind of record until…

"I just don't understand why Kayleigh still doesn't like me," Darcie said, genuine puzzlement in her voice. "I mean, it's been seven years since you and I..." She trailed off, obviously deep in thought.

Dom had to grin at that. He was always amazed by Darcie's inability to comprehend the effect her devastating beauty had on others. Or the envy it roused in all but the most secure females. Every time he tried to explain, she flatly refused to believe him. To Dom, Darcie's naivete regarding her beauty was one of the most charming aspects of Darcie's character. She was his friend for life. Of this he had no doubt. The knowledge made him feel a bit better about what he was getting ready to do. Because Dominic Parker was about to stress that friendship severely.

A few minutes later, Dom pulled into the driveway of the gatekeeper's cottage.

Darcie regarded her oldest friend curiously. "Why are we stopping here? You don't have to walk all the way to Heart's Ease in the dark," she observed. "We'll switch places so I can drive you to your car."

"Ric has my car, Darcie," Dom said patiently.

"Oh, yeah, I guess he does," she agreed. "Then, I suppose he's picking you up here?"

"No," said Dom. "He's taking the bridesmaids to karaoke."

What was going on? Darcie frowned in confusion. She must have missed something. Her brain suddenly felt thick and slow. She studied her friend for a few seconds. Dom looked tired all of a sudden, she realized. Something was wrong with him. She could tell. Maybe he was upset about Kayleigh. Sometimes—most of the time—Darcie didn't like Kayleigh very much. In her private opinion, Kayleigh simply wasn't good enough for Dom.

Darcie sighed. Maybe Dom was upset because he had been pulled into this mess by his own Good Samaritan qualities, she speculated. Poor Dom.

Always the good guy. And always to the rescue. And usually because of her. Maybe he was upset with *her*. She wouldn't blame him a bit if he was.

Darcie continued to scrutinize Dom's neutral expression. He didn't look upset…and he wasn't acting upset, either. As a matter of fact, he was being perfectly pleasant, answering her questions with his usual patience.

Maybe it's not him at all, she decided. Maybe it was her. Maybe *she* was imagining things. It had been an extremely long day. Maybe she was distracted. And nervous. And not thinking clearly. That's probably what it was. Maybe all Darcie needed was to see Devin and to tell him…

"How are you getting home?" she blurted out, without realizing how she sounded.

Dom sighed without answering. His expression was a mixture of resignation and dread.

Darcie's heart began to beat faster. "Are you sure Ric isn't coming back to pick you up here?" she asked hopefully, trying not to glance at her watch.

"No, Darcie, he isn't."

The way he said it gave Darcie a twinge of unease. She couldn't take Dom home. She didn't have time. She had to meet Devin, and…wait a minute. Darcie was starting to get alarmed. Dom knew that she had to meet Devin. *He* was the one who delivered the message, unless…

She had an awful thought. "Dom, did you or did you not give Devin my message?"

Dom looked a little taken aback. "Of course, I did, Darcie. I told you I would." He paused, before continuing carefully. "And now, I have a message for you."

Devin isn't going to meet me, she thought. *Oh, Lord, he doesn't want to meet me. And Dom is afraid to tell me.*

"A message from *whom*, Dom?" she asked, correctly.

"From Joe."

Darcie's heart sank. "From…Daddy?"

"Yeah," Dom said, softly.

"But, Dom, we just saw him." She was watching her friend carefully. "Why didn't he tell me himself?"

Dom shrugged halfheartedly, already hating the task he had been given.

Darcie's face was a mask of anxiety. "Go ahead and tell me. You might as well. What did Daddy say?"

"He said to tell you that it would be hard for a man to forgive the woman that caused him to lose custody of his child."

There. He had said it. He had followed his instructions to the letter. Now he could only watch as all of the color drained from her face.

Her grip on the door handle tightened as she struggled to control her breathing. There wasn't anyone she respected more in the world than her daddy. There wasn't anyone whose opinion mattered to her more than his. His words were crippling, but they had the effect that he had intended. They ripped her out of her rosy haze and thrust her straight into the blinding light of reality.

She had heard Joe's words before, seated in the big chair in his comfortable office. *"Never mince words when a man's fate is on the line, Darcie. It will be hard. But you must have the strength to administer the verbal blow, however devastating, that may ultimately save a man from himself."* She had pondered Joe's advice, trying to understand its practical application. But she had never understood it until the moment she herself was the recipient of her father's blunt speech. It would be foolish, she realized, to attempt another meeting with Devin. Foolish and selfish. Amalie's safety and well-being were more important than romantic games. Joe Finch was right, of course. He always was. But, oh, how she wished—just this once—he was wrong.

She steeled herself. She trusted her father. And, she decided, she would respect his wishes. It was amazing, really, how he always knew just what to say. She wondered if she would ever be like him. If she would ever have all of the answers. He always knew…But how?

Darcie narrowed her eyes. How did he know she was supposed to meet Devin? She certainly hadn't told him. And she was certain Devin hadn't. The only other person who knew about their ill-fated rendezvous was…*seated behind the steering wheel of her Jeep.*

"*Dominic! Parker!*" Darcie exploded, giving him a glare that could melt a glacier.

Dom shifted uncomfortably in his seat. "Now, Darce, let me explain...."

But he wasn't given the chance for that.

"Don't say anything, Dom. I know exactly why you told him." Darcie crossed her arms in frustration. "*You* were worried about me. And *you* didn't think it was a good idea for me to see Devin again after we almost got caught. And *you* just had to do the right thing. And blah, blah, blah..." She paused, regarding him through accusing eyes.

Dom didn't say a word. He simply sat there, watching the fire in her gaze turn into icy acceptance.

"Am I right?" she asked haughtily.

"You are," he replied calmly. "And..."

"And?" she asked, throwing her hands up into the air. Ice turned to fire in an instant. "Seriously. There's an 'and'?"

Dom cleared his throat. "Joe wants you to get your suitcases from the cottage. He wants you to allow me to drive you home. He said he would like a word with you in his study. He asks for you to please wait until he gets there." Dom looked at her consideringly. "He said, 'please,' Darcie. He said 'please' twice. He was very polite."

A word in his study. Oh, Lord. She disliked very few of her father's phrases more than that one. Dominic Do-Right had done it again, she thought, accusingly. No, that wasn't exactly fair. Darcie Do-It-Wrong had done it this time.

Dom cleared his throat again. She wished she had a damn cough drop to shove in his mouth.

"And..."

Darcie blew out a frustrated breath. This was getting ridiculous. "You better say everything this time, Dominic Parker. Because after this, I'm not listening to one more word that comes out of your mouth. Maybe ever."

Dom was extremely heartened by her use of the word *maybe*. And by the fact that part three was indeed the final part of Joe's message. "And he said to tell you that doing as he asks is your choice, but…" Dom paused, trying to anticipate her response. "He is certain that you will decide to…"

"Do the right thing," they said in unison.

It was a calculated blow. A one-sided choice. Joe Finch had effectively stripped her of her options. Darcie felt an icy calm take hold of her emotions. Her hand pulled on the handle, and the door of her Jeep swung open. She jumped down and headed to the cottage without a backward glance.

Dom stuck his head out the window. "Darce, listen…" He couldn't stand to see her freeze up like that. For the first time, he honestly wasn't sure what she would do. He figured he didn't have much of a choice but to wait and see. At least she hadn't punched him in the arm again, he thought, hopefully, deciding to be grateful for small favors.

Ten minutes later she stomped down the steps of the gatekeeper's cottage. She stalked across the yard, carrying a garment bag and dragging her suitcase behind her. Dom climbed out of the Jeep to help her stow her baggage. After they got back into the Jeep, Darcie gave him one long, sorrowful look from the passenger side of her vehicle. Then she crossed her arms, refusing to meet his gaze.

Dom shrugged. He backed out of the driveway, heading toward town. He knew better than to open his mouth again. He didn't want to be the target for her bottled-up emotions. He figured he had already said enough, anyway.

Neither one uttered a word, even when his house came into view. He pulled into his driveway, put the Jeep in park, and climbed out. She jumped down from the passenger side. They met in front of the Jeep, facing each other. Darcie looked up into the compassionate eyes of her oldest and most trusted friend.

"Oh, Darce," Dom whispered. "It'll be okay."

He tried to be encouraging. He meant to make her feel better. She was always so brave and so strong. The strongest person he knew, really. She was still so beautiful—standing there in the moonlight—even after all she had been through. He was proud of her, proud of the way she held herself together in the most difficult of circumstances. He could send her home now, in good conscience, knowing Joe and Juli could take it from here. Dom had done his part. His unexpected and extremely stressful role in the drama was over.

He sidestepped so Darcie could make her way to the driver's side of the Jeep. She didn't move. Dom felt a small niggling of dread. She shifted her right foot from side to side, her eyes pinned to the ground. She sniffed once. Her shoulders hitched. She sniffed again. Dom knew he was in trouble. He took a step toward her as Darcie Finch—brave, strong, beautiful Darcie Finch—fell into his arms, crying as if her heart would break.

Devin swore under his breath as he tripped over another root of another tree on his interminable journey to his midnight rendezvous. Having only one eye wreaked havoc with his perception. Sneaking through the heavily wooded area on the west side of the gazebo had seemed like such a brilliant idea...*before* he actually attempted it. His only other option was strolling across the cobblestone path in plain sight. In other words, he had no other option. Creeping through the dark was taking him twice as long as he had imagined it would. He was pretty sure, however, that arriving a few minutes after midnight wouldn't be a problem.

According to reliable sources, his Pirate Queen was notorious for being *just a little bit late*. While the groomsmen were having their group pictures taken, Joey had relished telling several stories about his sister's penchant for tardiness. Darcie's obvious annoyance at Joey's tales told Devin that most of what her brother said was true. With that piece of information fresh in his mind, he couldn't imagine that she was already in the gazebo, waiting for him.

He still couldn't believe he was meeting Darcie Finch. In a gazebo. At midnight. He questioned his sanity even as his heartbeat quickened at the thought. His attack must have destroyed the part of his brain that knew better, he rationalized. He used to be smarter than this. And to think Mallory said he never did anything exciting. Wouldn't she be impressed if she could see him now? Of course, he reminded himself, everything would be ruined if she could see him now.

The thought stopped him in his tracks. This was a crazy risk. It was stupid *and* dangerous. He should turn around *now*. He should go back the way he came before taking such a gamble.

He stood perfectly still for a few seconds, pondering the wisdom of returning to his lonely room at Heart's Ease. Abandoning his quest was an excellent choice. A wise choice. A safe choice. The best choice. But, of course, he mused sardonically, he wasn't going to make the best choice, now was he?

So, Devin started walking again. Maybe Darcie would have more brains than he did. She would probably assess the pros and cons and decide not to come to the gazebo. At midnight. To meet him. That would be a good decision on her part, he decided. That would be exactly the right thing for her to do. As a matter of fact, he hoped she changed her mind. He hoped she didn't come. *And I am a terrible liar,* he informed himself.

He tripped on another root and stumbled, his knee landing hard on the ground. Again. He picked himself up, cursing all the while. After a few more minutes of plodding through the darkness, his persistence was rewarded. Finally.

He stepped out of the trees onto the edge of the side lawn. Before him was the gazebo; the large house loomed in the dark somewhere out of his limited line of sight. He turned his head toward the rose garden, pleased to discover that no one lurked on the expanse of lawn between the gazebo and the side of the house. He paused, listening for any noise indicating he wasn't alone. The only sounds he heard came from the creek, bubbling and churning its way over rocks and into the night.

He took the steps two at a time. "Hello," he called, over the rippling water. "Is anyone here?" He was certain the sound of his beating heart was louder than the rushing water. Peering into the darkened gazebo, he thought he detected a shadowy movement. "Darcie," he said urgently. "Darcie, are you there?"

"Hello, Devin."

The disembodied voice did not speak in the rich, melodious tones he was anticipating. Nor was the figure that emerged from the darkness the one he was expecting to see. Oh, no, Devin wasn't expecting this at all.

CHAPTER FORTY-SEVEN

"Hello, Joe," Devin said, softly, as he watched Darcie's father stroll toward him. Joe leaned both forearms on the outer railing of the gazebo. Clasping his hands loosely, he gazed at the rolling waters of Honeysuckle Creek.

Neither man spoke for a few moments. Devin's mind conjured and rejected a variety of reasons for Joe's appearance, all of which ended badly. Finally, he dared to break the silence, voicing the reason he feared the most. "Did Darcie send you?"

Joe shook his head. "No, Devin. Darcie didn't send me." He paused, apparently to let that bit of information sink in. "As a matter of fact," he continued. "I doubt she's figured out I'm keeping her appointment for her."

Devin was surprised to hear a smile in Joe's voice.

"Yet," Joe clarified. "She hasn't figured it out yet. She will, though. The way that girl's mind works is terrifying." He spoke in an even voice, quite at odds with the voice Devin would expect from a father deliberately interrupting his daughter's midnight rendezvous with a married man.

"How did you…?" Devin blew out a breath as the answer hit him. "Parker."

He paced away from Joe, running his hand through his hair in frustration. Of course, it was Parker. Darcie's defender. *Dominic the Good.* Riding in on his white charger to save the princess from the beast. *Damn, I hate that guy.* His pacing brought him right back to the railing beside Joe. He leaned on the railing, mimicking the relaxed stance of Darcie's seemingly relaxed father.

"Dom means well," Joe said easily. "They've been friends for a long time. He's just trying to *protect* her."

His emphasis on the word *protect* wasn't lost on Devin. In other words, Dom was not alone in his quest to protect the lovely Miss Finch. Case in point…the presence of Joe Finch, her formidable father.

Devin opted for honesty. "Look, Joe…"

"I've always liked you, Devin," Joe interrupted, keeping his eyes on the water. "I remember the first time I met you. I was working on something with your dad. For McCallum." Joe turned his head, meeting Devin's eye for the first time. He had a slight smile on his face. "You were just a little guy, maybe seven or eight years old. You watched me do a magic trick with a quarter. I made it disappear and reappear, and you loved it. You must have asked me to do it again at least a dozen times." Joe chuckled at the memory. "You refused to go to bed until I showed you the secret so you could do it, too. You might not remember that."

"I remember," Devin said, sharing a smile with Joe. "Amalie loves that trick as much as I did."

Joe nodded, pleased with Devin's words. "I like your determination, Devin. And your drive to succeed. And your desire for knowledge. I consider your dad a friend, and your mom, too. And I have the greatest respect for Merritt Brothers Law. I also know that the work you do as head of legal at McCallum Industries is exemplary. Moreover, I believe you are a man of integrity. I do, however, have one question for you."

Joe paused, as if to choose his next words carefully.

Devin didn't give him a chance to continue. He knew where this conversation was going. "What are my intentions toward your daughter?"

"Your intentions?" Joe actually chuckled. "Sounds a bit old-fashioned, doesn't it? Your intentions...like we need to negotiate cows and chickens for a dowry."

Devin felt himself relax a little. Apparently, Joe Finch didn't want to feed him to bears after all. Not yet, at least.

"Oh, no, Devin," Joe continued. "I think your intentions are very clear. Make no doubt, son, I understand exactly how you feel. You've found the woman you want, but you can't have her because you're tied to another. And you have a confidence problem. Because you don't think you're worth the wait."

Astonishment was written all over Devin's face. How could Joe Finch possibly have surmised so much in such a short time?

"You see, Devin," Joe Finch observed, "I understand you better than you think."

There was no rancor in Joe's words. No warning, either. Only a bone-deep understanding from one man to another.

Devin's eye returned to the rushing water. Maybe Joe did understand. Devin hoped so. He didn't want to put Darcie in the middle of a bad situation.

"There is one thing, however, that doesn't quite make sense," Joe said.

Devin leaned his arm on the railing, facing the intuitive man. "What is that, sir?"

"How the hell did one of the best contract lawyers in the country end up signing such an inane excuse for a prenuptial agreement?"

Devin flinched at the question.

Joe, who was watching him carefully, didn't hold back. "I cannot fathom why you would put pen to paper on such a farcical document. Were you so overcome with lust that you would sign anything to have her? Were you drunk? Were you taking some kind of hallucinogenic drugs? How could anyone with a mind like yours possibly agree to sign something as foolish as it is binding?"

Joe seemed genuinely perplexed. Devin made his decision. He had held his silence long enough. Joe deserved to know his reasons. If he was going to have any kind of future with the man's daughter, Joe deserved to know.

Devin straightened to his full height, blowing out a breath. "She threatened to have an abortion if I didn't sign the prenup."

"Oh." Joe was momentarily speechless. This was definitely not the answer he was expecting.

Devin found a little satisfaction in shocking the imperturbable Joe Finch.

"Are you sure she would have gone through with it?" Joe asked. He was clearly horrified.

Devin nodded slowly. "I didn't know if she was serious, either, so I followed her. I signed the prenup papers in the waiting room of the clinic. She had an appointment, Joe. She had already completed the bloodwork. At that point, I would have signed anything. Hell, I would have done anything she asked to save my child." Devin began to pace again. "When I look at Amalie and I think of how close I came to losing her…" He shuddered. The thought still gave him nightmares.

Joe was completely taken aback. "Good Lord, Devin. I had no clue. No one has any idea, do they? Even Robert doesn't know. Did you tell anyone?"

Devin saw the compassion in Joe's eyes. He was sincerely troubled by Devin's revelations. "Roman," Devin admitted. "Roman knows. He's the only one. He went with me to the clinic. He was there." *And thank God for that*, Devin thought. For years, the knowledge that Roman knew the real reason behind the damnable prenup was Devin's saving grace. At least he had one person who understood. One person who didn't think he was an out-of-control hormonal fool.

Devin realized Joe was still watching him, still waiting patiently for the rest of the story. The man's silent support was encouraging. "Mallory went out with Roman a couple of times before she started seeing me," Devin explained. "I think she really wanted him. He was already an associate at the firm. His career was off to a more prestigious start than mine. But, unfortunately for Mallory, my cousin was more perceptive—and a whole lot smarter—than me. He saw right through her. He warned me over and over. But I was blinded by her…well…" Devin shrugged. "I guess I don't have to explain. You've seen her. Manipulation is her middle name. By the time I figured it out, she was pregnant. It was too late. And, well…here we are."

"But why not tell your father?" Joe asked, clearly puzzled. "He's worried over it for years, and your mother, as well. Robert sent me a copy of the prenup right after you signed it, hoping I could find some kind of loophole. I don't really understand your need for secrecy." Joe was trying to find some reason for Devin's willingness to look a fool to protect his undeserving wife. "Your parents don't like her, you know. I can imagine there aren't many people who do."

Devin went back to the railing to gaze unseeing into the night. "They don't like her. But they have no idea how manipulative she can be. How cruel and self-centered she really is. I don't want anyone to know, because, well… she's Amalie's mother. I don't want people to make those comparisons. I don't want them to look for those tendencies and inclinations in Amalie. I'll never let anyone say, 'like mother, like daughter.' Amalie doesn't deserve to grow up that way."

Joe nodded, soberly. "Sins of the fathers, huh? I also understand that. All too well." He sighed. "I'm sorry you've had to live with such a difficult secret, but you're right. People are like that. They tend to judge based on heredity. 'The apple doesn't fall far from the tree,'" he quoted sarcastically. "I've heard it all. In court and out. You're a good father, Devin. And a good man."

"I have to be honest, sir, in case you were wondering…" Devin looked Joe in the eye. He would make no apologies for what he was about to say. "If I had a choice, I would do it the same way all over again just so I could have Amalie."

Joe smiled, apparently satisfied. "I respect that, son. You would do anything for your daughter."

"I would."

"So, would I," Joe replied. "And I have a request for you. From one father to another."

Well, hell. I walked right into that one. Devin waited, tensely, impressed in spite of himself at the efficient way Joe Finch had brought the conversation back to its original focus.

"I would ask that you refrain from continuing your relationship with my daughter until—"

Devin jumped in before Joe could finish: "I am free and clear of my sorry excuse for a wife and mother. I understand, sir, but…"

Joe studied Devin's face, shaking his head at the younger man's impatience. "*Until* she finishes law school and passes the bar, which should be sometime in July. She has worked too hard to allow anything to keep her from reaching those goals. I am biased, I know, but she is a remarkable young woman. And she will be a remarkable attorney. She deserves to finish well. If both of you still feel the same way in nine months, then it will be up to the two of you to chart your own course."

Joe held out his hand. Devin took it, the handshake strong and firm.

"And, Devin," Joe said, "if you and my daughter are as committed to each other as I think you are, you risk nothing by waiting."

Devin's expression was full of resignation. And regret. His admiration for Joe Finch—always strong—had grown in the last thirty minutes. The trust that he saw in that gaze fortified him. "I understand, sir, and I agree with you. I promise that I will never stand in her way. But I can also promise you that my feelings won't change in the next nine months." Or nine years. Or nineteen years. Or, even, ninety years, he added to himself.

At that moment, Devin acknowledged one fact with absolute certainty. His promise to Joe Finch was as sacred as a vow. For the next nine months, he would stay away from Darcie Finch. Even if it killed him.

Amalie woke with a start, reaching instinctively for Iggy. She wasn't used to waking up in a strange place, but the soft snores of Papa Rob coming from the other bed made her giggle. She covered her mouth so he wouldn't hear her. Papa Rob was funny, she thought. No wonder Gamma Ollie slept with those silly things in her ears so she couldn't hear.

Amalie's giggles faded as a thorough search, under the covers and on the floor, revealed no sign of her best friend.

Where was Iggy? A terrible thought made her frown. Iggy must be lost.

Amalie's little feet hit the floor. Poor Iggy!

"Don't worry, Iggy," she said in a loud whisper. "I'll find you."

Oops! She forgot that she had to be quiet. Looking at herself in the big mirror on the wall, she held up one finger and put it to her lips. "Shhhh!" Then, she crept out of the door and into the hallway.

Daddy's room was beside Papa Rob and Gamma Ollie. She headed toward it, happy to discover she was the only one in the hallway. She didn't want to get into trouble, but she wanted Iggy. Her little heart beat faster when she thought of Iggy. All alone. Iggy would be very sad that he couldn't find her. Poor Iggy! He might not know where *she* was, but Iggy knew where Daddy's room was. She hoped that her loyal iguana was waiting for her. She hurried to the door, turned the knob, and pushed.

The door swung open, hitting the wall with a loud bang. It sounded loud to her, anyway. She ran into the room and jumped on the bed. "Daddy, Daddy...."

The bed was empty.

Oh, no, Amalie thought. Daddy was lost, too. Now, she would have to find both of them.

Amalie decided to find Iggy first. The iguana would help her find her daddy. Then, they would all be together again.

When she looked at the other bed, sure enough, her best friend was waiting for her. "Iggy!" she squealed. Nobody was sleeping in this room, so she didn't have to be quiet. She hugged the stuffed iguana. "Oh, Iggy, I'm so glad I found you! Now, you can help me find Daddy! Come on!" She jumped off the bed with the iguana tucked securely under her arm. She padded out of the room and into the still-deserted hallway.

Amalie looked to the left and to the right. The hallway was enormous. It seemed a little scary in the dim light. "Which way should we go, Iggy?" she asked, holding the iguana's mouth to her ear. "Oh, what a good idea! You're so smart, Iggy," she told him. "We'll ask Nanny Di. She'll help us find Daddy. Come on, Iggy."

Nanny Di's room was on the other side of Papa Rob and Gamma Ollie at the end of the hall. It was across from Mommy's room. Amalie knew better than to ask Mommy for help. Mommy would get mad if Amalie woke her up. And Mommy didn't like Iggy very much.

"Shhh, Iggy," Amalie whispered, tiptoeing as slowly and quietly as she could.

She had almost reached Nanny Di's room when the door to Mommy's room opened. Amalie watched as a man dressed in black backed out into the hallway. The Man in Black didn't see her because he hadn't turned around. She watched him shut the door carefully, as if he didn't want to wake Mommy up. She knew what that was like. She wondered if the Man in Black was lost. Maybe he had asked Mommy for help. Poor Man in Black! Mommy wasn't very nice. But Amalie was nice. She decided that she and Iggy would help the Man in Black.

"Hello," she said, looking up into the startled face of Douglas McCallum.

The man paused. "Hello," he replied, watching her carefully.

"Are you lost?" she asked, with a friendly smile. Nanny Di said smiling at people made them feel happy. Amalie liked to make people feel happy. "Iggy was lost," she continued, conversationally. "He was in Daddy's room and I found him. My daddy is lost, too. Iggy and I are going to find him. Do you want us to help you find someone? Your mommy or your daddy?"

The Man in Black didn't say anything. He must be too sad to say anything, Amalie decided. Poor Man in Black. "I'm going to ask Nanny Di to help us. She's right in here." Amalie motioned to her nanny's door.

Douglas lunged to grab the knob before she did. "No, thank you, little girl. That won't be necessary." He was starting to sweat a little. All he needed was for this little demon to call attention to his presence in the hallway.

"Amalie," she said clearly. "My name is Amalie. Amalie Merritt."

Ironic, Douglas thought. The little brat was Merritt's spawn…and Douglas had spent the last several, very enjoyable, hours screwing her mother. He had to silence this child, that much was certain. But short of throwing her out of a window—one was conveniently located at the end of the hall—he couldn't seem to think his way through this. Good sex had a tendency to scramble his nefarious brain. And the sex had been good. *Very* good.

He swiftly discarded the window idea. Too messy. And there was always a possibility that someone was still outside. Maybe he could scare her into silence. It wasn't much, but it was the best his tired brain could do at the moment.

He lowered his voice, speaking slowly and clearly. "Get away from that door, little girl." He leaned closer, trying his best to be terrifying. It must have worked, because her mouth fell open in shock. She even dropped her stupid stuffed toy. Douglas picked up the animal by its tail, swinging it back and forth.

"I am the Grim Reaper," he intoned. "I eat little girls for breakfast and their…" He glanced at the animal in his hand. An iguana? Who played with a stuffed iguana? What happened to dolls and teddy bears? "And I eat their iguanas for dessert." He laughed cruelly at the terror on Amalie Merritt's face. "If you tell anyone you have seen me, I will…" *What's the worst thing that can happen to a child?* "I will hurt your mother. And your father. And your…nanny?"

"Nanny Di?" She gasped in horror. Her crystal blue eyes filled with tears. "And Daddy?"

"Do not tell anyone about the Grim Reaper." Douglas sneered. "This is your only warning. If you tell anyone you have seen me, someone you love will die."

Douglas tossed her iguana toward the window then took off in the opposite direction. He paused at the end of the hallway, just in time to see the little girl open the door to her nanny's room. The frightened child rushed inside, dragging her precious iguana behind her.

Good, Douglas thought, as he hurried down the staircase and entered the deserted grand foyer. He felt confident that his plan would work. Even if the little brat decided to tell, nobody would believe her. They would assume her story was the by-product of an overactive imagination.

He chuckled to himself, feeling the usual adrenaline rush that came with a display of power. Scaring children was more fun than it ought to be. Maybe his own son wouldn't be such a pain in the ass if the Grim Reaper had been around to scare him every now and then. Too late for that, he decided, philosophically.

He reached the front doors without incident, congratulating himself on his stealth. It had been a very enjoyable weekend. *Very* enjoyable. Calli was wrong this time. Crashing Blane's wedding had been a very good idea. Douglas had found a new toy. He couldn't wait until he could play with it again.

Amalie shut the door so quickly that Iggy's tail got caught. She tugged and pulled, but to no avail. Her struggles and sobs grew louder and louder.

Diana rolled over, then sat up, coming instantly awake. "Amalie? Amalie, sweetie, what are you doing in here?"

She climbed out of bed and hurried to the door. Amalie stopped struggling with Iggy to throw her arms around her nanny's legs, burying her face against her hip. Diana got down on both knees and hugged the little girl tight. "What's the matter, 'Malie?" she asked, soothingly. "Did you have a bad dream?" She brushed the child's tangled hair from out of her eyes. "It's all right, sweetie. Nanny Di's right here."

"IIII-gggy," Amalie wailed, pointing to the door.

Diana turned the knob, opening the door enough to pull Iggy into the room. Amalie pressed her back to the door, closing it as quickly as possible.

"Don't open the door," she begged. "He's out there."

"Who's out there?" Diana asked calmly.

"The Grin Ripper," Amalie sobbed. "He's going to hurt you and Daddy," she wailed. "And Mommy, too," she added almost as an afterthought.

"The Grin Ripper?" Diana thought it over for a minute. "Oh, you must mean The Grim Reaper," she said. Honestly. She wondered what kind of television shows Devin and Mallory let Amalie watch when her nanny wasn't around? She would have to speak to Devin to make sure Amalie wasn't hiding behind the curtains watching *Friday the 13th* or something like that. It was hard to tell what the frightened child had seen. She picked Amalie up and hugged her close. "All right, Amalie. Do you remember how we talked about facing our fears?"

The little girl nodded. Her sobs died away to an occasional, watery hiccup.

"What would Mara Lee do?" Diana made reference to the little girl character in her books based, loosely, on the little girl in her arms.

"Mara Lee would tell the Grin Ripper to go away," said Amalie, tightening her hold on Diana's shoulder. "But Nanny Di and Iggy would go with her."

"All right, then, let's go tell the Grim Reaper to go away." She opened the door and looked at Amalie. "Ready, 'Malie?"

"Ready, Nanny Di!" Amalie nodded her head, determined to be brave.

"Is Iggy ready, too?"

Amalie nodded again.

"One. Two. Three. Go!" Diana rushed into the hallway, turning this way and that while waving her arms around. "Go away, Grim Reaper! Go away, and don't come back!"

Amalie waved Iggy in the air with the hand that wasn't clutching Diana in a death grip. "Go away, Grin Ripper!" she cried.

After a few more spins, Diana looked at Amalie, who nodded in approval. They returned to the room. Diana let Amalie lock the door.

Fifteen minutes later, the little girl was sleeping peacefully in the middle of Diana's bed. Diana sighed. She loved Amalie to distraction, and she always would. But sometimes, being her surrogate mother was exhausting. Diana tried not to think of Mallory, who was probably enjoying a good night's rest right across the hall, blissfully ignorant of the fact that her daughter needed her.

No matter, now that Diana was wide awake, she may as well get some work done. She took out her computer, settling herself comfortably on the other bed. A Halloween story might be just the thing. She hadn't written a holiday story before, hadn't even considered it. But now, she had the perfect idea. She opened a new document and typed the title of her latest inspiration: *Nanny Di and the Grim Reaper*.

It was a little before three o'clock in the morning when Juliette Finch stole into Joe's study. She quietly closed the door and turned the lock. Resting her back against the door, she looked across the room. She found him exactly where she knew he would be…at his desk. Deep in thought. His chair was turned toward the window and his eyes were fixed on the darkness, seeing nothing, she was sure. His hands were steepled over his chest and his index fingers were tapping together in a rhythm only he could hear.

How many times had she found him in this position over the years? This room was Joe Finch's personal sanctuary…the place where he drew internal conclusions, pondered his options, and cleared his head. All before allowing his wife to share the burden. Juli had learned that Joe needed time to wrestle with himself. Only then could he resume his position as her partner in all things. She always gave him that time.

But Juli also knew when enough was enough. And that was where she came in. If given the opportunity, Joe would shoulder the weight of the world. He would take the blame for original sin, if she would allow it. That was his nature, and his weakness. She was his balance; she loved this imperfect man to distraction.

"Brooding, are we?" she asked softly, from the doorway.

Joe turned his head, his intense gaze softening at the sight of her. He held out his hand, in wordless invitation. She crossed the space that separated them and took his hand, allowing him to pull her close. He hid his face in her robe. His muffled voice came from the depths of the soft fabric. "How is she?"

Juli's hand settled on his hair in a comforting gesture. "She's not angry with you, Joe, if that's what you're worried about. She's not angry with anyone. She understands why you did what you did. And why Dom did what he did.

And Joey...." Juli sighed in commiseration. "And every other protective male in her life. Even Devin. She understands."

Joe's face came up, his expression bleak. "She was just so damn stoic sitting here. And calm. And, well...accepting. I was expecting..."

"What, Joe?" Juli asked, patiently. "What were you expecting?"

He shrugged his shoulders. "Tears. Maybe anger. Shaking her fist at fate. Some kind of response."

"She won't cry in front of you, Joe. You know that," Juli said. "How many times have I heard you say, *'Never let them see you cry, Darcie. If you break down, they win.'* How many times have you told her...?"

He was quick to interrupt. "I had to give her some armor, Juliette. You, of all people, are well aware of that. She's too beautiful to survive any other way. They would have crushed her spirit...would still crush her."

Juli nodded in agreement. "And she learned that lesson well. You're an excellent teacher."

"Damn it." Joe leaned back in his chair, rubbing both hands through his hair. "I didn't want her to use my own advice against me."

His lovely wife smiled at that. "She wants you to be proud of her, Joe. Of her strength and her resilience."

He reached out, pulling her to him, his face once again hidden. "I *am* proud of her. Damn it."

"She knows, Joe." Juli smoothed his hair back into some semblance of order. "She knows. She's dealing with a lot right now...a lot of random emotions. On one hand, she's elated. Absolutely elated that she's fallen in love with someone. And not just someone, Joe. *The One.* Do you remember what that was like, Joe? Do you remember what that felt like?"

"What that feels like," Joe corrected, his hands busily working on the knot of her robe. "Juliette, did you lock the door?"

Juli ignored his question.

"On the other hand, she's devastated that she can't have him. That it might be years before they can be together. She didn't say *never*, but it's there in the back of her mind. Do you remember what *that's* like, Joe? I imagine knowing that he feels the same way she does makes it a little easier." She paused to make her point. "Don't you think so, Joe? Wouldn't *that* have made it a little easier?"

His hooded gaze studied her deliberately innocent expression for a few seconds, before returning to the knot.

Juli took pity on him, leaving the veiled reference to their own past to return to her daughter's present. "Darcie's determined to wait for Devin. No matter what."

Joe blew out a breath without looking up this time. "That's the part that worries me, Juli, the *'no matter what.'*" His hands paused. He was making no progress whatsoever. He studied the knot before reversing his strategy.

"Oh, Joe, you worry about Gracie because she wears her heart on her sleeve. And you worry about Darcie because she doesn't show enough emotion. What about Joey?"

Joe sighed. "God help us all with that one. Joey's too damn charming for his own good."

Juli raised her eyebrows at her charming husband, trying not to laugh.

"Juliette Hanover Finch, if you say *the apple doesn't fall far from the tree*, I swear I will tear this blasted robe in half."

"It wouldn't be the first time," Juli mused.

Joe huffed out a frustrated breath. "I would bet everything I own that your grandmother taught you to tie these knots for the sole purpose of driving me insane."

Juli smiled a secret little smile. His statement wasn't far from the truth. She had a clear memory of that knot-tying lesson on her eighteenth birthday. It wasn't an accident that all of the women in the family received a new robe every Christmas.

"Juliette, did you lock the door?" Joe asked again.

"Joey's snoring away upstairs, and there's no way that Darcie will come down any time soon, so…"

"Juliette, did you lock the door?" He looked up at her, his eyes burning into hers.

She caught her breath, as she always did. Oh, how she loved this man. Her eyes held his. "You know I did."

"Thank God."

Her robe fell open as he tugged her onto his lap, bringing a sudden, mutually satisfying end to this particular conversation.

CHAPTER FORTY-EIGHT

Seven months later
Newport, Rhode Island

Shopping for groceries was, in Devin's estimation, an acquired skill. Unfortunately for him he had yet to acquire it.

"*Buy some ice cream,*" they said. "*It'll be easy,*" they promised.

That's how Devin—poor, trusting sap that he was—allowed himself to be coerced by the pair of big, blue eyes that lived in his house. And by the amused gray ones who took care of the blue ones. Devin, personally, blamed FaceTime for the whole debacle.

He felt guilty about going into the office on Memorial Day, so he called home to see how things were going. Amalie insisted on showing him her new dance steps—Iggy had a solo—before making her request. To their credit, both pairs of eyes suggested that he visit the specialty market close to the townhouse.

But traffic was heavy, and it was raining. So, he pulled into the first mega-huge-good-luck-finding-anything-you're-looking-for-store he saw. It was no surprise that—after wandering through sporting goods, cosmetics, clothing, and the camping section—he was delighted to finally stumble upon actual food. He could ask someone for assistance, he reasoned, but that was like admitting defeat...something Devin refused to do.

Asking for help in a store was like asking for directions when driving. It offended his masculinity. Or something. He finally found the frozen foods on his own, and, subsequently, the ice cream. But, of course, he did *not* find Amalie's "flavor of the moment." He looked high and low—literally—before waving the white flag of surrender.

Hating to admit he needed help, he approached the teenager with the man bun, at the end of the aisle. Man Bun was unpacking a case of frozen yogurt bars. He had a pair of earbuds in his rather large ears. He was also very involved in the drum solo of whatever he was listening to, much to the detriment of the yogurt.

"Excuse me," Devin said loudly.

Man Bun kept right on drumming.

Devin tapped him on the shoulder, finally gaining his attention.

Man Bun jumped back from Devin in horror. He took out an earbud, studying the scarred man in front of him. "What happened to your face?" he asked with interest. "Did you get mauled by a bear or something?" He appeared oddly fascinated.

"Nothing happened to my face," said Devin dryly. "I'm a pirate."

"Oh," Man Bun said agreeably. "I guess that makes sense." He started to put the earbud back in, pausing as if it had just occurred to him Devin might need help. "I bet you're looking for this," he said, holding up a package of YOHOHO Yogurt bars. The pirate on the box sported a colorful parrot on his shoulder. And an eyepatch. "Ar-re you interested in these?" Man Bun was enjoying himself a bit too much.

"I'm having a bit of trouble finding the Cotton Candy Crunch ice cream," Devin said, politely. "And I was wondering if you might know where it is."

Man Bun's grin grew wider. "Cotton Candy Crunch? Some woman sent you to buy ice cream, didn't she?"

"Yeah, that's right," Devin conceded. "Two women, actually...a big one and a little one."

"And I bet they told you *not* to come here, didn't they?" Man Bun asked smugly.

"Yeah." Devin hedged. "I think they did."

Man Bun nodded, unsurprised. "But *you* didn't listen to them, did you?" The teenager was obviously wise beyond his years. "Guess why they told you not to come here."

Devin didn't say a word.

"Aren't you going to guess, mister?" Man Bun looked disappointed.

Devin sighed. "I figured you were going to tell me anyway," he said before giving in. "All right, then. You tell me. Why did they tell me *not* to come here?"

"Because we don't *have* Cotton Candy Crunch ice cream." Man Bun shook his head at Devin's stupidity. "You have to get it at the specialty market down the street. You know, the fancy one with all of the organic stuff. It's really expensive, mister. Wouldn't you rather have a couple of boxes of YOHOHO Yogurt bars?"

"No, thanks," Devin said, politely.

Man Bun simply shrugged his shoulders, popping his earbud back into his ear. Before Devin could turn around, however, the helpful teen changed his mind. He took his earbud out again. "Cheer up, mister," he said. "There are always a lot of women at that marr-ket. Maybe you'll get lucky and get some booty." He cracked up at his own piratical humor. His laughter followed Devin back down the aisle.

As Devin walked to his car, he realized that he missed more than just his eye. He missed Darcie Finch. The pirate conversation made the ache that had lodged in his heart seven months ago sting a little more. He was certain Darcie would have made short work of Man Bun. First, for daring to mention Devin's scars and eyepatch. And second, for making his first offense worse with the tactless offer of YOHOHO Yogurt bars. After that, she would have given the young man a talking to for his thoughtless comment about booty at the specialty market. Yes, Man Bun would probably have preferred walking the plank to tangling with Devin's redoubtable Pirate Queen. He couldn't help but smile as he pulled into traffic on the way to the specialty market… the one he should have gone to in the first place.

True to his promise, Devin had not made an effort to continue his relationship with Joe Finch's daughter by attempting to see or talk with her since the night of the wedding. Other means of communication, however, were available. Devin and Darcie managed to keep in touch with the help of Lydia, Diana, Grace, and, occasionally, Blane.

Every two weeks Devin received a pie. The flavors varied according to the season, but each pie was a precious expression of shared longing and love. To the outside observer, absolutely nothing appeared odd about those pies. Every pie arrived professionally packaged in a plain, white box—the type of box that might be found in any bakery anywhere in the country.

Looking inside the box would offer the casual observer no insight either. The pies were beautifully made. Some had fancy crusts that were woven or braided. Some were covered with delicious crumb toppings (and on one momentous occasion, golden brown meringue). They were also delicious, although most people in Devin's immediate circle remained unaware of that fact, because Devin was reluctant to share the bounty. No one, however—not even his fellow conspirators—knew about the words of love and terms of endearment that awaited him, securely taped to the bottom of each aluminum pie pan.

Growing up in the world of text messages, Devin had never learned to truly appreciate the value of the written word. Until the past seven months. Reading a letter from Darcie Finch was an experience unto itself. How she managed to put so much of herself on the page was a mystery. Reading a letter from his Pirate Queen was like having a conversation with the writer herself. She wrote exactly what was in her head, jumping from topic to topic. The way her brain worked fascinated him. Her quick mind was always, it seemed, ahead of her hand. Devin didn't enjoy her absence, but he did enjoy her words. Through her letters he gained even more insight into the woman he loved. What she was thinking. What she was doing. And, most importantly, how she felt about it.

Every other week, Darcie received her own official-looking missive from the offices of Merritt Brothers Law Firm or McCallum Industries. The official mailings were usually delivered to her apartment. Occasionally, they arrived via the law school. If anyone wondered why Merritt Brothers Law Firm was so anxious to hire an untried law student like Darcie Finch—one who hadn't even passed the bar—he or she chose not to mention it.

Devin tried to vary the source of his missives as frequently as possible. No use taking unnecessary chances. The argument did exist that any communication was an unnecessary chance. But he didn't think he could make it through the required period of abstinence if he didn't have those biweekly missives to look forward to. He had a feeling Darcie Finch felt the same way. By an unspoken but mutual agreement, the letters weren't love letters in a traditional sense. There were, after all, some things that should be said only in person. However, Devin had little difficulty reading between the lines.

In spite of his promise, he found holidays and special occasions irresistible. He was unable to ignore Darcie's birthday, sending a gift certificate for a dozen Cinnamon Whip Lattes from Jack's in Honeysuckle Creek. In addition, she received an umbrella with a tropical flower motif. Devin was assisted in this endeavor by Zack and Grace.

And who could resist Christmas? Certainly not Devin. He was unable to stop himself after a lovely silver necklace caught his eye in a local jewelry store. The delicate, long-stem rose charm reminded him of the rose in *Beauty and the Beast*. The secret gift was discreetly deposited in Darcie's Christmas stocking by the Boss-man, himself. Devin understood from Blane that Santa received all of the credit.

The reference to *Beauty and the Beast* didn't escape Darcie's notice, of course. Even though he was treated to a chocolate mint pie the next week, she let him know exactly what she thought. The single sheet that fell from the envelope taped to the bottom of his pie pan read: *HMPH*. He chuckled at that. His Pirate Queen was no mere beauty. Nobody was more aware of that than Devin.

He noticed, however, that Darcie was wearing the necklace in this year's Finch family Christmas photograph...the one that usually lay facedown on Blane's desk. The Boss-man "adjusted" the photograph when Devin was in his office, blaming it for his head of legal's inability to concentrate.

Valentine's Day inspired a bouquet of lovely tropical flowers. Charlie Ray secretly ordered the gorgeous blooms for Devin. A local florist in Chapel Hill delivered them to Darcie's family law practice class. The card was signed *Your Secret Admirer.* Darcie was, apparently, quite pleased by that card. She couldn't wait to brag about her secret admirer in her next letter, taking great pains to describe his imaginary attributes. She also described the ways she wanted to reward her secret admirer's devotion. Devin had to take a cold shower after that missive.

For graduation, he anonymously paid for her lifetime membership in Carolina's general alumni association. He was surprised and gratified to receive a T-shirt and a mug from Darcie the next week. Both sported the words *Carolina School of Law Alumni.* Devin added the intense love of their alma mater to the unending list of commonalities he shared with Darcie Finch, the woman of his dreams.

The rain was falling harder by the time Devin reached the crowded specialty market. He waded through the customers, most of whom seemed annoyed that rain on Memorial Day had ended their aspirations for hosting their planned outdoor barbecue. Patrons were lined up four-deep at the Butcher's Block, making Devin thankful that he wasn't buying anything that mooed, oinked, or squawked.

After skirting his way around the small mob at the meat counter, he made a beeline to the frozen foods. The ice cream section was, mercifully, deserted. He perused the long freezer after his first quick glance revealed his quest wasn't going to be as easy as he had anticipated. For a minute, he almost missed Man Bun. He began his search again with renewed determination. The idea of going home with YOHOHO Yogurt bars and disappointing his baby girl was unacceptable. *Man up, Merritt,* he ordered himself. *Are you a pirate or what?*

Of course, being a pirate made him think about Darcie again. In pirate garb. Now that he knew that she didn't have a horse's head or overly large feet, the mental image was a lot more pleasing. Too pleasing, actually. If he continued thinking about her, he would melt every bit of ice cream in the freezer in front of him. He forced himself to focus. Just then, out of the corner of his eye he caught a woman pushing her grocery cart directly toward him.

He reacted immediately. One corner of his brain was extremely thankful that the woman with the cart was coming toward the side with his good eye. With both hands, he grabbed the front of the cart, stopping it before it could do him any damage. The cart pusher wasn't so lucky. The impact threw her into the handle of the cart, knocking the breath out of her. She immediately doubled over, gasping and wheezing.

What the hell was wrong with him? Did he have some kind of magnet in his body that attracted foreign objects? Devin was pretty sure, at this point, that he was running out of lives.

The woman continued to sputter, finally heaving an enormous breath. Still hanging onto the handle of her cart, she lifted furious eyes to Devin. She obviously intended to blast him for being in *her* way.

Devin couldn't believe his eyes. The angry woman with the overly large, still heaving bosom was none other than Mallory's bestie, Desiree. Unlike the pirate from his dream, she was beardless. Devin wondered, idly, when she had decided to shave.

"Devin!" she snarled, her distaste for him apparent in her tone. She thrust out her bosom, glaring at him. "Get out of my way!"

Devin sighed. If Desiree was standing right in front of him, Mallory must be around the corner. The last thing she had told him before leaving the house for the long weekend was that she and Desiree weren't planning to come home until very late on Memorial Day. His heart sank. Their plans must have changed. He would have to get some raspberry sherbet in addition to the Cotton Candy Crunch. Raspberry was Mallory's favorite. If he didn't get something for her, she would whine the rest of the night.

Desiree wiggled the cart, but Devin didn't let go. He regarded his wife's friend with resignation. "Nice to see you, too, Desiree. Where's Mallory? I know she must be around here somewhere."

Desiree's botoxed lips pursed in hurt. "How should I know where Mallory is? She hasn't spoken a word to me in months."

Devin looked at her in surprise. "What do you mean she hasn't spoken to you in months?" he said. "She's been with you all weekend."

Desiree's eyes went wide with shock. "All weekend? Is that what she told you?"

He nodded, studying the overwrought woman and trying to figure out what kind of game she was playing. He felt cold, as if something momentous was about to happen. Or it could possibly be because he was standing in the frozen food section with the best friend of the original Ice Queen.

Desiree regarded him seriously. "I haven't seen her in months, Devin, not since that wedding in North Carolina. Mallory"—she sniffed pitifully—"she...she dropped me." A fat tear ran down Desiree's cheek to hang on her protruding lip.

Devin watched that tear, absently, noting that the tears that followed had begun forming a small puddle on Desiree's expansive upper lip. His heart began to pound. "Let me get this straight, Desiree." He struggled to remain calm. "You mean to tell me that Mallory hasn't been anywhere with you in the past seven months even though she claims to spend all of her time with you?"

"I haven't seen her once," Desiree said, a frown forming between her excessively plucked eyebrows. "Not once. That little bitch has been lying to you."

Devin's brain was working furiously, but he still couldn't process what was happening.

Desiree was having no trouble, whatsoever. When she arrived at her awful conclusion, the hurt in her eyes changed to malice. "Well," she said icily. "Looks like she's cheating on both of us."

Devin looked at her, mute with shock.

"Poor Devin," said Desiree. But the next moment, her expression changed again. Her eyes filled with the light of opportunity. "If I were you, I'd divorce her lying ass tomorrow. Your prenup is null and void if one of you commits adultery, isn't it?" She leaned toward him over her cart handle. The movement forced her enormous breasts up and nearly out of her too tight T-shirt. "I've read your prenup, you know," she whispered loudly. "It's a piece of crap. I never understood why you were fool enough to sign it. Mallory couldn't have been *that* good in bed." She leaned a little closer. "There are plenty of other women who are, you know…better. And completely…available."

After that startling bit of information, Desiree winked.

Devin couldn't have said what repulsed him more: her unnecessary display of flesh or the fact that she was propositioning him two minutes after he discovered that his wife was having an affair. He quickly muttered his thanks, suddenly needing to remove himself from her unwanted presence before any more ideas came into her head. He let go of her cart and moved, intent on getting as far away from her as he could get. And as quickly as possible.

"Bye, Devin," Desiree called after him. "Give me a call sometime."

"See you around," Devin said over his shoulder. Only when he reached the end of the aisle did he remember the ice cream. He glanced back to find Desiree watching him…Well, at least watching his posterior. No way in hell was he was going back to get the Cotton Candy Crunch ice cream. He grabbed two boxes of YOHOHO Yogurt bars and headed straight to the check-out counter.

If the information that Desiree had just revealed was true, he had a lot of work to do before his errant wife arrived home. It appeared Mallory had finally found her paddleboard instructor.

He was waiting in his home office around two o'clock in the morning when she opened the front door. Sitting in the dark with the office door thrown wide open, he had a good view of her as she struggled to roll her suitcase over the front threshold. It would have been easier to pick it up, but

Mallory was above that. The suitcase had wheels, it was *supposed* to roll. And roll it would.

Devin had to admire Mallory's tenacity. When she finally managed to drag the suitcase inside, she went back outside. She returned with two garment bags, an overnight bag, and a huge leather tote. She had certainly had a busy weekend if she had worn even half of the clothes in those bags. He moved to the doorway of his office, watching Mallory close the front door quietly. She turned around, leaning her back against the door. She was obviously exhausted by the unusual bout of manual labor.

"Hello, Mallory."

Devin flipped on the elegant, ridiculously pricy chandelier Mallory had insisted upon for the two-story foyer of their townhouse.

She jumped, letting out a squeak of surprise. Her eyes narrowed into a glare that looked like it wanted to slice him in half. "Hello, Monster," she snarled. "How fitting to find you lurking about in the dark. Cut the lights off again and spare me your monster face." She stalked by him on her way to the stairs.

Devin didn't move. So accustomed was he to her cruelty he no longer so much as flinched. Her words fell far short of their mark. He continued, unfazed: "I ran into a friend of yours this afternoon at the specialty market."

Mallory's sure steps faltered. She paused two feet short of the bottom step. "Oh?" She turned her head, doing her best to appear completely disinterested. "And which friend might that be?"

"Desiree," Devin said softly.

She drew in a quick breath of surprise before she could stop herself. But she just as quickly recovered. "Desiree decided to come back early! She…"

"Don't bother, Mal. She told me she hasn't seen you since Blane's wedding."

Devin was watching her carefully. For the first time in their marriage, he had the serpent backed into a corner. And just as he expected, she tried to strike.

"What the hell are you implying?" she cried. "I cannot fathom you would believe Desiree over me. Why…why…". Her face was pale. For once, she was struggling to come up with a diversion.

Devin had *never* seen Mallory work so hard to be convincing. Lying came as naturally to her as breathing. It was second nature. That was the moment he noticed, for the first time, that something wasn't quite right. Mallory looked—for lack of a better word—rough. Her eyes were bloodshot. Her lips were swollen and puffy. Her hair was messy. Her clothes were wrinkled. She wasn't wearing her usual scarf, and there appeared to be bruises on her neck. She didn't look rough, he amended. She looked like she had been roughly handled.

"Desiree is in love with you," his duplicitous spouse announced, her eyes flashing in her pale face. "She's desperate to break us up. She manufactured this whole situation. I never thought she would betray me like this. What happened to our friendship?" She covered her face with her hands for a bout of pretend sobbing. She even went so far as to peek at Devin between her fingers to see how he was taking it.

Devin crossed his arms patiently. "Although I applaud your effort, I'm not buying it. I know you have a lover."

She dropped her hands from her face, raising completely dry eyes toward his. What she read there made her own eyes widen in shock. He knew. There was no way out. He was forcing her hand. All right, then. She faced him proudly and attacked. "You think you're so smart, don't you? Just look at you, standing there all smug and self-righteous. With your hideous scars on your hideous face, and behind that eyepatch…well, you are a monster. *You* know it and *I* know it. How could any woman want to spend the rest of her life with such a pitiful excuse for a man? This is all *your* fault. You've compelled me to find someone else. And I have." She paused for dramatic effect. "He's powerful and rich and better in bed than you ever were. The things he does to me…you have no idea. He can give me everything I've ever wanted. How could I choose to continue with this nightmare when I've found a way out?" Her eyes glittered with malice as she carefully enunciated the words Devin thought she would never say:

"I. Want. A Divorce."

She didn't try to hide her blatant satisfaction at delivering the final blow to the man she so loathed. Looking at her triumphant face, Devin realized he felt nothing for her. Absolutely nothing. Not anger. Not regret. Not pity.

Nothing. He couldn't even muster the emotion to enjoy this moment. There was nothing enjoyable about his marriage, or his relationship with the viper in front of him. There never had been, even in the early days of his blind ignorance.

He found himself, with no little surprise, on the cusp of freedom. But—and it was a big *but*—he had to be careful. For the first time since meeting Mallory, he had the upper hand. He felt strangely calm, almost detached, as if all of his emotions were contained in a block of ice. The only thing in his head were the words of Darcie Finch. *"Repeat after me, Laurence. You are not a monster."* No, he thought, he was *not* a monster. He was *not* a monster who crawled into his lair to nurse his wounds, quietly giving up in defeat. And he was certainly *not* a monster who tore his victim to shreds after a heady victory. He was a man. A man with a child. And he would not walk away from the serpent without taking that child forever out of striking distance.

Mallory was watching him, waiting for his response. Her eyes, beneath their puffy lids, glittered in frustration. "Don't you get it, *Monster*?" she sneered. "I'm walking away." She said it again, very slowly as if he was very stupid:

"I. Want. A. Divorce."

Devin met her gaze. He studied his faithless wife in silence. Her impatience was palpable. Her contempt absolute. She was so confident, so certain that he would bow to her will. Again. Devin couldn't help but feel a fleeting satisfaction at the astounded expression on her face. Because when he opened his mouth, he said the very last word she ever expected to hear.

"No."

CHAPTER FORTY-NINE

To say that Mallory was wide awake and restless was the understatement of the year. In spite of being exhausted from her weekend with Douglas, she slept very little. This morning she was bleary eyed and dull. She hadn't been up before eight o'clock in the morning in years, but her restless night propelled her out of bed. She sat at the kitchen table—clutching a mug of very strong coffee—trying to fight off the panic induced by Devin's uncharacteristic use of the word *no*.

She found herself in unfamiliar waters. Devin was always endlessly predictable and easy to manipulate. She knew exactly which buttons to push to achieve the desired results. At least, she always had…until last night. Last night he caught her completely off guard. Why would any man want to remain married to a woman who continually reminded him that she was repulsed by his appearance? She had expected him to be relieved, if nothing else. She never dreamed that her demand for a divorce would be met by one emphatic word…*No*.

She still couldn't believe it. Devin actually said, "*No*." Then, he had turned around and walked back into his office. After numerous attempts to get him to open the door—from begging and pleading to a rare bout of very real tears—she had finally given up. She retreated to her room to worry about the unforeseen roadblock to her happily-ever-after. And to pace. And to resist the urge to call Douglas.

For months, her clandestine lover had flatly refused to give her the number of his cell phone. Douglas told her over and over that it was too dangerous for her to contact him. Too risky, he said. Too reckless. *He* would call *her*, he informed her. And that was the end of that…or so he thought. But Mallory was not a woman who put herself at the beck and call of any man. So, last Saturday night, she had gotten the number from Douglas' phone…while her secretive lover was in the shower. She was quite proud of her subterfuge. Douglas had no idea she had his number. She had no plans to enlighten him, either. Somehow, she knew that he would not be pleased with her little secret.

Douglas was odd about things like that. So, she resigned herself to calling him at McCallum Industries as soon as they opened. Nine o'clock. She was certain she had nothing to worry about. He had told her over and over how much he wanted her. He reminded her quite often just how much he enjoyed what they had together. He would be so pleased when she told him she was getting a divorce. She was sure of it. But, she realized, a divorce depended on the *monster* and…

She gasped as the thought hit her. Of course. It was obvious, and it explained everything. Devin didn't want a divorce because he was still in love. With *her*. He loved *her*, in spite of her constant abuse. What a fool he was! Suddenly, Mallory smiled. She was back in control. Now, she knew exactly what she was going to do.

Devin knew the climate had changed when he walked into the kitchen. Mallory smiled, softly, and handed him a cup of coffee. The fact that Mallory even knew how to make coffee was a surprise. *Damn it.* He almost groaned. Was it possible he had overplayed his hand the night before? He watched her warily as she pointed to the chair across the table from the seat she had just taken.

"Please," she said, her blue eyes pleading and innocent.

Devin sat, feeling a little sick. He knew what was coming. He knew she wanted something, but he wasn't sure what. The uncertainty wasn't doing a lot for his nerves. He took a long swallow of coffee, surprised that she remembered he took it with cream and sugar. "Thanks," he said.

She propped her elbows on the table, clasping her hands together. She hoped he wouldn't notice how they were shaking. "Devin, I had no idea," she began. "Why didn't you tell me?"

"Tell you what?"

She hadn't called him Devin in months. She was trying to relate to him, human to human instead of monster to snake. At that moment, he preferred the latter.

"That you're still in love with me," she explained. "I'm so sorry. You have to believe that I didn't set out to break your heart. What happened with my lover and I was, well…it was fate. It was meant to be, Devin. There wasn't anything either you or I could have done about it. Do you understand?" She dabbed her napkin delicately at her eyes.

Devin was almost blindsided. He should have expected Mallory to view the situation through her narcissistic vision, but he absolutely had not seen this coming. Relief and trepidation mingled through his veins. *Careful, Merritt,* he chided himself. *Be very careful.* Devin was well aware that everything—*everything*—depended on the way he handled this conversation. Freedom was within his grasp. Suddenly, he knew exactly what he had to do. If Mallory preferred *her* version of events, he was damn well going to go along with her.

Forcing his face into a tragic expression, Devin sighed dramatically. He got up from the table. He ran his hands through his hair in—what he hoped—looked like, a gesture of helpless frustration. He paced around the kitchen as if coming to terms with her words. He knew what he had to do. She thrived on drama. Their entire relationship was based on drama, so it was quite fitting that it end with drama. He dug down deep and gave her what he thought she wanted.

"Beautiful, beautiful, Mallory," he began. "I can see that your heart belongs to someone else." He shook his head in defeat. He managed another heartfelt sigh. He hesitated a few seconds before turning away from the growing satisfaction in her eyes. His heart beat faster. He could almost hear the rusty hinges squeak as the door of his prison slowly swung open. He gave her the words she was waiting for. "And I know, in my heart, that I have to let you go."

Her lips burst into a smile. This was exactly what she wanted. He was putty in her hands. She could barely hide her triumph. "Oh, Dev, thank you for understanding." She rose from her chair, intending to go upstairs for some much-needed sleep.

"But," Devin continued, firmly. He was determined to finish their agreement here and now. "If I can't have you, sweet Mallory…if I have to live the rest of my life without you…" He paused, as if struggling to continue. "Then I feel compelled to ask for the one thing that will always remind me of you."

Mallory sat back down, regarding him warily. "What is it, Devin? What do you want?" Her eyes automatically flew to the enormous diamond engagement ring and matching wedding band on her left hand. When she looked up, there was fear in her eyes.

Devin wanted to laugh. *You can keep the damn ring, Mallory, and everything else I ever gave you. They don't mean anything to me.*

"I want Amalie."

"Amalie?" she asked, in surprise. "What do you mean?"

This was it. This was the most important part. Everything he said from this point on was pivotal. "I want full custody," Devin said, keeping his tone even. It wouldn't do for her to get even a hint of his desperation.

Mallory's eyebrows rose as she thought this over. Free from the monster *and* their demon daughter? And she got to keep her beautiful diamonds? Could she really be that lucky? She did have a slight pang when she thought of the high society mother-daughter events that she would miss. However, the attention she would garner was appealing. A grieving mother who, through no fault of her own, lost custody of her only daughter to her cruel ex-husband. Yes, she could totally work with that.

Devin kept his relaxed stance, barely daring to breathe. The rest of his life—and Amalie's—hinged on what Mallory would say.

"All right," Mallory agreed. "But I would like to take her to events every now and then. And I want to sponsor her as a debutante when she turns eighteen, of course."

Devin nodded his head. "Of course. I won't deny you anything as long as you let us know in advance. And as long as it doesn't interfere with her education. I imagine that we will spend most of our time in North Carolina when Blane opens the new headquarters. I hope that won't be a problem." There would be no misunderstandings or false expectations. Devin wanted all of the cards on the table.

"Of course," Mallory murmured. "You know, Devin, hard as it is, this is all for the best. I wouldn't have been happy in North Carolina. I belong in Newport. You can let me know when you have something for me to sign." She started to rise from her chair again, surprised when he reached behind him to open his briefcase. It was, conveniently, lying on the counter. He pulled out a folder and a pen.

"Please sit down, Mallory." His tone was firm and businesslike.

Mallory sat, watching as he opened the folder and handed her the pen. He sat down in the chair across from her.

"You can sign this agreement right now," Devin said, trying to calm his racing heart. "I will be happy to file the separation papers this afternoon."

She looked at him, slyly "Hmmm you didn't waste any time, did you?"

"On the contrary, I had *a lot* of time while I was waiting for you to come in this morning. I had a feeling our marriage had reached an end." He tried to look tragic, difficult to do when he was so close to victory. "I can go over each bullet if you like."

She shrugged her shoulders. "Don't bother. Surprisingly, I trust you." As she reached for the pen, the long sleeve of her robe fell back to reveal her slender wrist. It was completely ringed with purple bruises.

Devin felt a sharp jolt of alarm at the sight. He reached, automatically, for her arm. "Mallory, did *he* do that to you?" He eyed her now with genuine concern. "And what about your neck? Did he…"

She pulled her arm back, her eyes glittering with annoyance. "Don't worry about it, Devin. I'm not your problem anymore."

He looked at her steadily. "But, Mallory, nobody has the right to hurt you. If you need help, I…"

"Let it go, Devin." She was quick to interrupt him. "There was nothing we did that I didn't want to do and…" His worry seemed to please her. She leaned forward and almost purred, "I enjoyed it."

Devin couldn't seem to wrap his head around what she had just revealed. He abhorred men who justified violence against women by saying they deserved it. He was especially sensitive to that fact since his own little sister was the victim of a violent man.

But Mallory's situation was different. He had no idea what to do about a woman who seemed to enjoy such violence. His inborn instinct to protect wouldn't allow him to walk away as if nothing was happening. He knew some psychologists. He would have to consult with a few of them to see what they recommended. If nothing else, maybe he could talk to Mallory's mysterious lover, just to make him aware that someone else knew what was going on. Regardless of their past history, his wife had given him a priceless gift. Because of their daughter, he would try to help her…whether she wanted his help or not.

Devin tried not to show the revulsion he felt at her careless confession, keeping quiet as she reached for the pen. She signed her name to the papers that he had carefully prepared last night. She placed the pen on the table when she was finished. As she stood up, Devin saw her wince. Thoroughly alarmed at the evidence of the physical abuse she had supposedly enjoyed at her lover's hands, he was compelled to try one more time.

"I was thinking, Mallory," he said, slowly. "Of how I would feel if somebody did that to Amalie." He paused at her surprised expression. "If you need any help, don't hesitate to call."

She studied him, almost pityingly, before saying sincerely, "You're a good father, Devin." She nodded her head to affirm her words before adding, "I never wanted to be anybody's mother, you know?"

"I know," he said.

They looked at each other across the table, aware their relationship was ending exactly where it began. After five years together, they were still nothing more than two strangers who shared a daughter.

"I hope you find someone who wants you in spite of your scars." Mallory considered her words before shaking her head. "Of course, having a daughter in addition to that face, well…" She shrugged, callous as always. "Good luck with that." Without a backward glance, she headed out of the kitchen, intent on finding her bed.

Freedom.

Devin glanced at the papers on the table. F-R-E-E-D-O-M. It was within his grasp. Mallory's signature represented freedom from the snake pit. Not only for him, but for his beloved Amalie. He refused to let himself think of what it would also mean to the raven-haired beauty who had captured his heart.

And wouldn't Darcie be furious to know that I called her a beauty, even in my head? He almost chuckled at that, feeling more hopeful than he had since their memorable night in the stables. *Focus, Merritt,* he admonished. *Amalie, first. And then…*

He forced himself to read through the agreement one more time. Word for word. He scoured it for loopholes, once again finding none. The document appeared sound. Still, he wasn't taking any chances. He was not going to file the papers until they were approved by the best and most trusted expert in family law that he knew…his cousin, Roman.

It was a short flight to Alexandria. Blane, loyal to the core, had already arranged for private transportation. Devin checked his watch. If he left now, he could be there by eleven-thirty.

He stood up, feeling weak in the knees. A lot had happened in the last twenty-four hours. *"I hope you find someone who wants you in spite of your scars,"* Mallory had taunted, cruel to the end. Devin's heart began to beat a little harder. Wouldn't she be surprised to know that he already had?

CHAPTER FIFTY

"There's not one person in this room who doesn't understand what it means to be part of a family business, Darcie."

Robert Merritt's smile was kind as he looked into the serious face of the woman he hoped would one day become his daughter-in-law.

"We are Merritt *Brothers* Law Firm," Garrett Merritt agreed, albeit regretfully. Darcie was, by far, the best fit for the position she had just declined. So much so that Garrett was going to suggest they hold off hiring anyone until they received a new crop of applications.

"I bet old Joe Finch is the happiest man in Honeysuckle Creek," Barrett Merritt added. "And Will, too. I tell you, Darcie, you couldn't be taking a position with a better firm. Well, unless you were working for us. I'm not saying that because it's expected, either. I have the greatest respect for Parker and Finch."

Darcie's voice rang with sincerity. "I can't thank each of you enough for everything you've done for me. What I learned during my internship has been invaluable. Your encouragement has, also, meant a lot to me personally." She rose to her feet, the picture of professionalism.

Her hair was pulled back into a simple twist that accentuated the elegant lines of her profile. She was wearing a perfectly appropriate black sheath, matching jacket, and black pumps. Her nails were expertly manicured, painted in a neutral shade. She limited her jewelry to an onyx class ring, a watch with a black leather band, and small, silver earrings.

Roman Merritt watched her say her goodbyes. *She tries so hard to downplay her looks,* he thought. *But it's no use. Damn, but she's stunning.* In spite of his appreciation for her beauty—he was only human, after all—Roman had never been romantically attracted to Darcie. While they had worked together during her internship, he was impressed with her legal prowess and the intuitive way her mind worked. If he was being honest, he would have to admit that, sometimes, working with her was intimidating as hell.

Roman's request to be present when his father and uncles offered Darcie an associate position was twofold. His specialty was family law. The job Darcie had just turned down would have fallen under his domain. That was the professional part, but the real reason he was there was because of Devin.

Roman still blamed himself for Devin's miserable situation; he was the one who introduced Mallory to his cousin in the first place. There was no way Roman could ever atone for that. The fact that he had done it purely for reasons of self-preservation didn't go a long way toward making him feel any better. Pawning Mallory off on Devin was the only way Roman was able to get rid of her himself. How was he to know that his cousin would end up ruining his life by marrying the egotistical bitch?

The least Roman could do now was to look out for the woman Devin loved. Darcie had appeared during the lowest point in Devin's life. Roman gave her all the credit for putting his cousin on the road to emotional recovery. He knew Devin expected the lovely Miss Finch to accept the prestigious position with Merritt Brothers. But Darcie had informed Roman otherwise as soon as she arrived. Now, he couldn't help but grin. Devin was wrong this time. And Roman would love to see his cousin's face when he found out.

Darcie shook the hand of every partner. Each one of them stood up, respectfully, when she did. In spite of the fact that she had been raised to expect such a courtesy, she was aware it didn't happen everywhere, especially when someone had just turned down the position of a lifetime.

Robert gave her a warm smile. "Feel free to contact us at any time, Darcie. We hope to see you again very soon."

She was confident there was a double meaning to his words. The fact that she had won the approval of Devin's father made her feel unexpectedly emotional. "I hope to see you, too," she said softly.

"I will go so far as to say that there is a standing offer with this firm for you, Darcie," Garrett said, nodding. "What do you two think?" he asked his siblings.

Robert agreed immediately. "Any hour, any day."

Barrett chimed in, "Absolutely."

Their genuine good will drained some of the tension that had been Darcie's constant companion since making her decision. The last thing she wanted was to offend the Merritt brothers. They were, incidentally, the father and uncles of the man she loved. She rewarded their comments with a bright smile, unaware, as usual, of its devastating impact. Even the highly articulate men in front of her were struck speechless with admiration.

Garrett recovered first. "Roman, you may show her the way out."

"Sure thing, Dad," Roman agreed. He took Darcie's elbow and lead her into the hallway.

Darcie took a deep breath as the door closed behind them. It was the first breath she had managed since walking into the room to discover that all three of the Merritt brothers would be conducting the interview.

"See," Roman said encouragingly, as they walked down the hallway. "I told you they would understand. They're disappointed, but they understand."

Darcie breathed a sigh of relief. "I can't tell you how much better I feel. I was so afraid they would think I'm ungrateful."

"No way," Roman said. "To those three, it's family first. It always has been." They stopped at the elevator doors, which opened as soon as Roman pushed the button. "Good luck, Darcie Finch."

"Thanks, Roman, for the support and..." She shrugged one shoulder, the one that wasn't supporting the strap of her black satchel. "Well, you know.

Thanks for everything." She stepped into the empty elevator. "Give Devin my love." She said it quietly, with a wistful little smile that tugged at Roman's heart.

"Funny thing," Roman replied with a wink. "He told me to tell you the same thing. Great minds, you know." He grinned as her serious expression dissolved. The perfect vision in front of him promptly wrinkled her nose and stuck out her tongue, much to his amusement. In that moment, she reminded him of Amalie Merritt. He squared his shoulders and saluted, chuckling as the elevator doors closed. Darcie Finch was a study in contrasts. *More power to you, cousin,* Roman thought. *You are a braver man than I am.*

Five minutes later, Roman was seated in his comfortable chair behind the desk in his office. He opened his laptop, reluctant to return to the case on which he was currently working. It was a difficult one, referred to him by his grandmother in Charleston. The woman involved was the granddaughter of Nana's dearest friend. No way Roman could tell his grandmother, "No." No way under the sun. Determined to make Nana proud, he clicked on the file and began to read.

He had barely skimmed the first document when his door flew open, crashing against the wall. He looked up in surprise. Nobody created a commotion at Merritt Brothers Law Firm. Commotions were not allowed. Equally surprising was the person causing the commotion.

"*You* are not going to believe this." Devin approached his cousin's desk, breathing hard. He was clearly emotional. "Hell, *I* don't even believe this." He dropped his briefcase on the floor, clutching Roman's desk with both hands.

To Roman, the answer was obvious. Devin had just run into Darcie Finch when she was getting out of the elevator. She had probably told him she had turned down the position at Merritt Brothers in lieu of taking a position in her father's firm. Because of Blane's decision to move the headquarters of McCallum Industries' North American branch to North Carolina, Devin would, himself, be spending a lot of time in the small town of Honeysuckle

Creek. Roman had anticipated that Devin would be thrilled at the news. Now, if Mallory would only vanish into thin air, they could all live happily ever after.

After seeing his cousin's flushed face, however, he decided he must be wrong in his assumption. Roman was used to gauging Devin's emotions. The cousins had always been close. Devin usually hid what he was feeling with humor, forcing Roman to dig it out, something at which he excelled. He probably knew his cousin better than anybody. But, damn it all. He could see that Devin's hands were shaking. This was serious. What was going on—and what could possibly have caused his cousin's current state of anxiety? One of them needed to stay calm, and from the looks of things, Roman figured it would have to be him. He clasped his hands atop the keyboard in front of him. "Enlighten me," was all he said. He motioned for Devin to close the door, noting that his cousin still had the wherewithal to follow instructions.

Devin ran his hand through his hair in agitation as he paced back and forth in front of Roman's desk. "Last night, Mallory asked me for a divorce."

Roman looked at him in astonishment. This was certainly not what he was expecting Devin to say. It was turning out to be one hell of a day, he thought. The surprises just kept on coming. He stretched his leg out under his desk to kick the chair that was in front of it. "Sit," he ordered.

Devin sat down, but two seconds later, he was up and pacing again. "I still can't believe it," he said, as he proceeded to explain the details of the last twenty-four hours.

Roman listened with growing astonishment. He was particularly amazed that someone existed who actually *wanted* a relationship with Mallory. The fact that someone would choose to devote his time, energy, and love to Mallory of his own free will was astounding. Roman couldn't think of a single reason why anyone would want to be involved with Mallory if he didn't have to be. This was fantastic news for Devin, and for Amalie. After five years of misery, the jailor had willingly handed the prisoner the key to his cell.

"And she actually agreed to sign the papers?" Roman asked, finally understanding Devin's distracted excitement.

"She didn't even read them. She said she trusted me." He looked at Roman in amazement. "I asked for full custody and she didn't even blink. This makes the prenup null and void. *Null and void*, Roman. She has *no* hold over me at all. She didn't ask for anything. *Nothing*. No money. No property. Nothing."

"That, in itself, is hard to believe. Mallory's the greediest, most grasping woman I've ever had the displeasure to know," Roman said with distaste. "She didn't ask for her jewelry? Or anything of a material nature?" Mallory was a material girl, after all.

Devin wrinkled his brow. "Come to think of it, she did seem concerned, at first, that I wanted her engagement ring and wedding band. But since I asked for Amalie instead, she relaxed."

"Bitch," Roman hissed. "How typical."

Devin nodded in agreement. "No surprise there." He finally sat down in the proffered chair.

"There is one thing that I can't figure out." Roman leaned back in his chair, moving it ever so slightly from left to right. "Who is she having an affair with? The Prince of Wales?"

"He's already married," Devin said, absently, referring to the Prince of Wales. His initial burst of adrenaline was wearing off, allowing him to study his miracle somewhat objectively.

Roman continued his musings, as if Devin hadn't spoken, "But what kind of an idiot would actually *want* the narcissistic little demon?" Too late, Roman realized what he had unwittingly implied. "Um…no insult intended, cuz," he murmured apologetically.

"None taken," Devin said. "And I have no idea who wants her. Or why." He felt a reluctant degree of empathy with Mallory's unknown, but clearly deluded lover. "Whoever he is, he must be fabulously wealthy."

"How did she describe this *dream lover*?" Roman wanted the facts.

"She said he's powerful, rich, and better in bed than me," Devin admitted ruefully.

"Powerful and rich. That sounds like the Mallory we know so well." Roman grinned at the look on his cousin's face. "That last part is relative, Devin. Let's take that one out of the equation. As a matter of fact, let's delete the whole equation. The important thing is that you're getting full custody of Amalie. And, best of all, Mallory is somebody else's problem. The poor, unsuspecting bastard." They digested that statement for a moment before Roman added, "So, what did Darcie say?"

"I haven't told her yet," Devin said. "I came straight here as soon as I got Mallory's signature. I want you to go over the separation agreement word-by-word to make absolutely certain this whole thing isn't going to blow up in my face."

Roman was puzzled. "So, you didn't say anything about this to Darcie when you saw her?"

"I haven't seen Darcie since Blane's wedding, Roman. I promised Joe Finch. You know that."

Devin picked up his briefcase. Setting it atop the desk, he opened it and took out a folder. He handled that folder carefully, as if it was made of the most delicate crystal; as if it held all his hopes for the future. Maybe it did, at that. He placed the folder on the desktop, closing his briefcase.

Realizing that Roman had a strange look on his face, Devin paused. "What?" he asked.

His cousin held up the single sheet of paper lying beside his computer. A resume. The name on top of the page made Devin suck in a quick breath. "Darcie's interview," he said. "I knew it was this week, but she didn't tell me the date. So much has happened that I forgot all about it. Is it today?"

"It ended right before you got here," Roman explained patiently. "That's why I thought you ran into her coming out of the elevator."

"You mean she just left? Damn it!" Devin swore. "The one time I take the stairs. I can't believe I just missed her."

"Well, that explains why you were breathing so hard when you came in. I thought you were going to have a heart attack. You must have run all the way from wherever you parked your rental car," Roman quipped, filing Darcie's resume for future reference. "Your timing is impeccable," he continued. "I think she's staying at Joey's apartment. You can probably catch her if you…" Roman looked up, stopping midsentence because he realized that the room was empty. And because he looked like a fool, sitting there, with the door open, talking to himself.

UNMASKING THE HEART

Darcie smiled as she stepped onto North Washington Street. A gentle May shower had rolled in—but to Darcie the morning was the loveliest day imaginable. She had done it. She had reached the goal she set for herself at the beginning of her sophomore year in high school…a position at one of the country's most prestigious law firms. Working for Merritt Brothers would prove beyond a shadow of a doubt that Darcie Finch was more than just a pretty face. Nobody would ever again assume the only thing that filled her beautiful head was inconsequential fluff. They would never doubt her *substance*. Being offered a position at Merritt Brothers was the culmination of every dream she had ever had.

Today, she had turned it down. And she couldn't be happier.

One year ago she would have laughed if anyone told her she would refuse a job offered by not one, but three of the partners of Merritt Brothers. She would have pronounced that individual crazy. She might even have been a little offended with the unlucky person simply for mentioning the possibility. But that was before. All of that was before a one-eyed pirate turned her world upside down. Meeting Devin Merritt changed everything. The way she saw the world. The way she saw her future. The way she saw herself. And all because of the way he saw her.

After months of struggles, prayers, and tears, she had come to an amazing conclusion. She had nothing to prove. She was exactly the person she set out to be. She was *not* a beautiful woman with a brain. She was a woman with a brain who just happened to be beautiful. She didn't need a prestigious position to be the person God made her to be. The time had come to stop questioning the judgement of her Maker. Instead, it was time to listen to her heart. And her heart was telling her to return to the last place her youthful ambition would ever have considered.

It was time to go home. Home to Honeysuckle Creek. It was time to take her place at Parker and Finch. Time to learn from her father and Will, and, hopefully, to continue their legacy. Oh, she hadn't lost one ounce of her fierce desire to help people, particularly children. Her passion for justice was as strong as ever. She couldn't wait to be an advocate for the innocent, a voice for the voiceless, and all of the other idealistic clichés she had heard all of her life. She didn't care what anyone said. At this moment, she was absolutely certain she was headed in the right direction.

Except that she wasn't. Headed in the right direction. She wasn't headed in the right direction! She had walked nearly two blocks in the rain, which now was pouring down upon her. She was carrying the lovely umbrella Devin gave her for her birthday—the one with the beautiful tropical flowers—and wearing a silly grin on her face. And she was going the wrong way. She looked around to see if anyone had noticed. She realized the rain was falling too hard for anyone to pay attention. And, then, she decided she didn't care anyway.

She thought about getting a cab or calling an Uber, but quickly discarded the idea. It was a new day. She was Darcie Finch—and if she wanted to walk in the rain she would. She thought about dancing around a lamppost and jumping in the puddles like Gene Kelley in *Singin' in the Rain*. But she figured that wasn't a good idea either. So, she turned around to retrace her steps, the title song now firmly stuck in her head. She started to hum.

The last time she watched *Singin' in the Rain* was with her dad. Joe Finch loved musicals, but always pretended not to. He amused himself by making little comments and complaining about all of the singing. His father's supposed disdain for musicals was a family joke, one he enjoyed using to torment his musical-loving family immensely.

Darcie grinned. It seemed like Joe Finch was always one step ahead of everybody else. Catching her intuitive father off guard was a rare and satisfying occurrence. That was why Darcie—and Will, for that matter—had so enjoyed the expression of shock that had appeared on Joe's face when he walked into Will's office to meet the person whom Will had called the "perfect applicant for the new associate position."

UNMASKING THE HEART

Will had already shared with Darcie—during their informal conversation—the fact that Joe continued to find fault with every single person they interviewed. The office space upstairs had been redone to accommodate not one, but two new associate lawyers—one of whom was Darcie's big brother, Joey Finch. In spite of the extra space, Joe flatly refused to hire anyone who wasn't the perfect fit.

"So, there have been applicants that you really liked, Will? And Dad didn't?" Darcie asked, surprised. Joe and Will were the best of friends. The two men were almost always on the same page.

Will grinned. "No. I haven't liked a single one of them, either."

Darcie laughed. "Why did you make it sound like Daddy was the bad guy, then?"

"Because I'm the partner who's doing the preliminary interview. You're supposed to think I'm the nice one. Both of us can't come across as a couple of tyrants."

"You two are terrifying."

A knock on the door signified the arrival of the other partner. Will stood up, motioning for Darcie to move to the side of the room, away from the door. She was anxious, in spite of herself, to see if her father would approve of the latest applicant.

"Come in, Joe," Will said, shooting Darcie an encouraging glance.

Joe's eyes were locked on Will. He never even glanced Darcie's way. The frustrations of the day had obviously erased Will's promise of the "perfect applicant" from Joe's mind. He walked straight into the room, throwing himself into the chair in front of Will's desk. He slipped his arms out of his coat and loosened his tie. He closed his eyes, rolling his neck from side to side before exploding.

"Damned clerk of court nearly destroyed the entire transcript of the last two witnesses. I told Judge Harrell he ought to lock her up and throw away the key. I've never seen such an incompetent excuse for an elected official in my life." He leaned back in the chair with a sigh. "Well, that part probably isn't true, *but you know damn well what I mean. Anyway, if you still have that scotch in your bottom drawer, it would probably be a good day to finish it off. You aren't going to believe..."*

He stopped talking, his face a puzzled frown as he watched Will jerk his head to the side. It was Will's not so subtle effort to turn Joe's attention to where Darcie stood waiting. "What's wrong with your neck, man? Looks like you need a drink worse than I do."

Will sighed, setting his elbow on the desk. He rubbed his forehead with his hand as Darcie tried not to giggle. "The newest applicant for the associate position is standing over there," Will said, patiently.

Joe froze. His demeanor changed immediately. He slipped his arms back into his suit coat, straightened his tie, and stood up with great dignity. He took two steps toward Darcie before looking up. "Good afternoon," he said. "I'm Joe Finch. I apologize..." His brows rose nearly to his hairline as his eyes widened in surprise. Other than that, he made no other indication that anything out of the ordinary was about to occur. "I apologize for my outburst, Miss...?"

"Finch," she said. "Darcie Finch."

She had to admire her father's implacable calm. She knew that she was about to be interviewed within an inch of her life. She squared her shoulders, resolving to give as good as she got.

She was Joe Finch's daughter, wasn't she?

Fifteen minutes after Darcie finished her interview, Joe walked into his office to find her waiting for him. She was sitting exactly the way she used to sit when she was a little girl. She was spinning around and around in his big desk chair, her legs tucked comfortably under her. She stopped the chair midspin, grinning mischievously.

He couldn't seem to stop himself from grinning in reply, even though Darcie could tell he was trying not to. She was fairly certain that she had blindsided him. She was ridiculously pleased with that rare accomplishment. Even better had been the obvious pride he had taken in her responses to his rapid-fire questions. Nothing warmed her heart more than making her daddy proud.

"Cocky little thing. Aren't you, Darcie-girl?" he asked. "Already sitting in a chair that belongs to a partner."

"Nope," she replied, smugly. "I'm sitting in my daddy's chair." She resumed spinning around in circles.

Joe laughed at her sass. Darcie was aware that having his children become part of his firm was one of his fondest dreams. Joey had always planned to return after acquiring some more experience with Merritt Brothers. He was slated to join Parker and Finch in mid-August: his name was already on the door of his second-floor office.

Darcie knew that her father had never even considered the possibility of having his daughter as well. To his credit she had never felt any pressure to turn to law as a profession, or even to return to her hometown after graduation. Her choices were her own. Joe had always encouraged his children to follow the path that was right for them. He was just as proud of Grace's decision to become a teacher as he was of the way Joey and Darcie were following in his footsteps. With those thoughts in mind, she knew what was coming. He wanted her there for the right reasons. His thorough mind had to be sure.

"Darce..." he began, waiting for her chair to come to a halt.

"I know," she interrupted, lapsing into an excellent imitation of the man in front of her. "'Darcie-girl, if you're taking this job for Devin. Or for me. Or for anyone other than yourself, you're not going to be successful. Or happy, for that matter.'" She smiled at the surprised expression on her father's face. "That's what you were going to say, isn't it, Daddy?"

Joe merely crossed his arms as he looked into the face of his all-too-perceptive daughter.

"You're a good teacher, Daddy," she continued thoughtfully. "Did you know that? You always taught me to do my best and to stand up for myself. You also taught me to stand up for people who can't stand up for themselves. You taught me to be tough, Daddy. And to be kind. You taught me that integrity is what you do when nobody's looking. You taught me that, contrary to the opinion of the world, honesty and character do matter. But you did more than that,

Daddy. You didn't just say the words. You lived them every single day. And I was watching you." She smiled at her father. "I'm still watching, you know. I see the way you live your life. And the way you love your family. But there's one more thing that you taught me, Daddy, and you never even realized it." She paused, watching him. "You taught me that sometimes it's okay to follow your heart instead of your head. And that's exactly what I've done. I've followed my heart and it's led me right back here. And this is exactly where I'm supposed to be."

"Well, then," Joe said gruffly. "Welcome aboard, Miss Finch."

He tried to maintain a businesslike persona, but his eyes were suspiciously shiny.

It was a moment Darcie would always treasure. She paused on the sidewalk, enjoying the memory. The surprise of being doused by a large amount of cold water hauled her out of her reverie. She stood there in shock, gasping as she glared at the taillights of a black SUV. The increasingly strong downpour had come on so quickly that standing water had collected in large puddles on every street. The driver of the SUV had run through one of the largest of all the puddles, sending a wave of water onto the sidewalk and its lone unfortunate occupant.

She resisted the urge to jot down the license plate. What kind of citation would they get anyway? She couldn't help but wonder. Failure to refrain from dousing oblivious woman walking in the rain? That charge probably wouldn't hold up in court, she decided. Total destruction of professional-looking and very expensive business attire? That particular charge actually might work. On the other hand, she would probably be fined for being a visual distraction to drivers. After all, she was, presently, the only pedestrian insane enough to be walking on the sidewalk in the rain.

At this point, the term *rain* was probably a stretch as the weather had taken on a definite hurricane-like feel, with strong wind gusts and decreased visibility. Darcie glanced around, not surprised that the number of people currently on the street had diminished to two: herself and some poor man about a block behind her who appeared to be running. *I salute you, Random Running Man,* she thought. *And your devotion to extreme physical fitness.*

Darcie turned and continued slogging along, refusing to give in to nature's fury. She couldn't be more than half a block from Joey's apartment building. She was, she rationalized, soaked to the skin anyway, so she might as well keep going. She did take a moment to stop and fold up her umbrella. It wasn't doing her any good at this point, and it did seem determined to turn wrong-side-out in the wind. If she couldn't have Devin, at least she could have his umbrella. And she would protect it at all costs.

Devin. Just the thought of him made her heart beat a little faster. Nobody else on the planet would have given Darcie Finch an umbrella with brilliant, tropical flowers. They would all have assumed that she wanted a nondescript, serviceable black one. But, oh how she loved that umbrella, with its beautiful colors and bright red handle! She loved it passionately. He had known that she would because he *knew* her. He understood the way her mind worked. And he thought she had a beautiful soul. What would he think about her decision to take a position with Parker and Finch? How she wished she could tell him in person. Darcie sighed, wistfully. If this was *really* a movie musical, Devin would appear at this precise moment, calling her name.

"Darcie Finch!"

Well, she thought. That was unexpected. She froze, glancing from side to side. *Oh, Lord. Now I'm hearing voices.* She really needed to get to Joey's apartment, which was, thankfully, in sight. She picked up her pace.

"Darcie Finch!"

She stopped again, because she hadn't imagined that. She hadn't imagined that at all. She turned around as Random Running Man caught up with her, only to discover that Random Running Man wasn't. Random. He wasn't random, but he was running. And he was running after her.

Darcie couldn't breathe. It was impossible. It was as if she had conjured him out of thin air. Her brain couldn't seem to comprehend his sudden presence. Her heart, however, was beating madly, already well ahead of her thought processes. She met him halfway. Her pirate reached out and hauled her into his arms.

CHAPTER FIFTY-ONE

"I'm leaving now, Mrs. Merritt," Lois Tredway called up the stairs.

Mallory heard the front door open and close. She forced herself to open her eyes. Mrs. Tredway always left right after making breakfast, slipping something for lunch and dinner in the refrigerator and straightening up the house. She didn't clean, though. Mallory had a very pricy maid service for that. They came on Mondays and Fridays. Mrs. Tredway was Mallory's compromise in exchange for the maid service. She had originally wanted to hire her own chef, one of the few things Devin had denied her during their marriage.

Mallory put both her arms over her head, stretching like a cat. It was Tuesday, the day Diana took Amalie to Providence after preschool for her dance lesson. Amalie spent the rest of the day with her grandparents. Devin went to their house after work for dinner. He and Amalie usually didn't get back to Newport until eight or nine o'clock, giving Mallory the entire day to herself. In the empty townhouse. Alone.

Or, lately, not always alone. Douglas had recently discovered that Tuesdays around noon were an excellent time for a lovers' rendezvous. He appeared in numerous guises. The cable guy. The HVAC repairman. And, once, a political candidate. The role-playing games that followed made

Mallory look forward to Tuesdays with breathless anticipation. Douglas was quite a creative lover.

Today, she was a little nervous. This morning she had ignored Douglas' specific instructions not to call him at work. He was more than annoyed. She could tell. Her lover's voice—usually so smooth and urbane—was clipped and hard. He didn't even respond when she told him what had transpired the night before. His unexpected silence was unnerving, leaving Mallory terrified that she had made a mistake. That she had misread his feelings for her.

He hadn't spoken for such a long time that she almost hung up the phone. Almost. But then, she heard the silky tones she had come to expect. He told her he would be over around twelve-thirty. He told her to leave the back door unlocked for him. He was coming by boat, this time, he said, to celebrate the good news of her divorce. She finally relaxed when he told her to chill a bottle of champagne.

After a quick shower, Mallory came downstairs around noon. To her surprise, she found her daughter seated on a bar stool in the kitchen, swinging her feet back and forth. The little girl was eating what appeared to be a peanut butter and jelly sandwich.

Mallory stopped in her tracks, fighting panic. "What are *you* doing here?" she asked.

Amalie regarded her skeptically, without answering.

"What are you doing here?" she repeated, her voice rising slightly in volume.

Amalie sighed. Her mommy *never* remembered anything. Maybe that was because Mommy wasn't very smart, she decided. Nanny Di said Amalie had to be nice to Mommy anyway. The little girl finished chewing before she answered, because Nanny Di said it wasn't good manners to talk with food in her mouth.

"Because I'm an *M*," Amalie said politely, before taking another bite of sandwich.

Mallory was completely confused. "What does that mean?"

Amalie chewed and swallowed. She wished Mommy would stop asking questions, so she could finish her sandwich. Mrs. Tredway had left some cookies for dessert but made Amalie promise to finish her sandwich first. Amalie knew that the cookies wouldn't taste very good if she broke her promise. Nanny Di said so.

"*Merritt* starts with the letter *M*," she explained, taking another bite of her sandwich.

Mallory wanted to scream. "I know that *Merritt* starts with the letter *M*, but *why aren't you at preschool*?"

Poor Mommy, Amalie thought. Not being very smart must be hard. She looked at Iggy, who was sitting on the counter beside her. He seemed to agree. Amalie chewed and swallowed before she answered. "The big-kid school is having 'valutions for kindergarten. The *M*'s go tomorrow. I'm an *M*, so I go tomorrow."

Amalie was almost halfway through her sandwich. Those cookies were going to taste good.

Mallory relaxed. She would tell Diana to take Amalie to her dance lesson early. That way, they would both be gone before Douglas arrived.

She walked into the hallway. "Diana," she yelled up the stairs. "Get down here now!"

Diana was probably hiding in the spare bedroom, working on one of her stupid, little books. "*Diana*," she yelled again. "*You have to take Amalie to dance class now*." When she didn't receive an answer, Mallory returned to the kitchen.

"Nanny Di can't take me to dance class," Amalie politely informed her mother. "Dance class is over until school starts again. We just had our recital, Mommy. Don't you remember?"

Poor Mommy, Amalie thought. She couldn't remember anything.

"*Di-a-na!*" Mallory yelled desperately.

"She's not here," Amalie mumbled, her mouth full of peanut butter, her manners forgotten.

"What?" Mallory whirled around, regarding her daughter as if she was speaking another language. "What do you mean she's not here? Where is she?" Her voice was growing louder and louder.

"She'll be here soon," Amalie whispered. At least she hoped so. Mommy was scary when she yelled like that. Amalie looked at Iggy. Iggy thought Mommy was scary, too, even though he didn't say it out loud. Amalie didn't like to be scared. She didn't ever want to watch scary shows on TV or hear scary stories. Unless Nanny Di told them. Nanny Di's scary stories always got un-scary at the end.

"Nanny Di has a meeting with her book person today," Amalie said. "But she's coming after that." Amalie hoped she was coming very, very soon.

"Oh, that's great! Just great!" Mallory paced around the kitchen. What the hell was she supposed to do now? Everything was ruined. How could she celebrate with her lover when her five-year-old daughter was in the house?

The room turned silent after Mallory's outburst. Silent except for Amalie's chewing.

"Can't you chew without making so much noise?" she asked her daughter, leveling Amalie with a hostile glare.

Amalie glared right back. Mommy was mean. All Amalie was trying to do was finish her sandwich so she could eat her cookies. She watched her mommy walk up and down the kitchen. She didn't look very scary now, and she wasn't yelling.

Amalie kept right on chewing.

Honestly, Mallory fumed to herself. Would that child never finish her sandwich? Glancing at Amalie's Disney-themed plate she noticed that the untouched half of the sandwich was covering up half of Cinderella's head. At that exact moment, Amalie took another bite, smacking her lips as loudly as she could. Mallory made a very unmaternal decision. She really didn't have time for this.

"All right, you little demon, that's enough." Mallory took Amalie's plate and tossed it into the trashcan under the sink. "Now, you're finished. Get down off that stool and go to your room. It's time for a nap."

Amalie's eyes were huge. Nobody had *ever* thrown her lunch into the trashcan before. Or her favorite plate, either. Poor Cinderella. Amalie wanted to cry. And she wanted Nanny Di. She looked at Iggy. *"Be brave,"* he seemed to say. It was what Iggy always told Mara Lee in the Nanny Di books. It's what the real Nanny Di would tell Amalie if she was there right now.

Amalie grabbed Iggy's tail and jumped down from the stool. "*You* are the meanest mommy in the world!" she yelled, defiantly, before running up the stairs to her room. She closed and locked the door.

. Mallory had followed Amalie up the stairs to her room. "Oh, you haven't even seen *mean* yet, you little demon," she yelled. She tried the door, only to find it locked. Good, she thought. "Stay in there and be quiet until Diana comes!" she yelled through the door. She barely paused before adding, "Or something very, very bad will happen to you."

There. That was the best she could do, she decided. If Amalie came downstairs while Douglas was in the house, so be it. And if Diana came home, well…whatever. Now that Mallory was getting a divorce, there was nothing to prevent her from marrying her imaginative, insatiable—and very, very wealthy—lover. Mallory couldn't wipe the smile of delight that accompanied her thought from her lips. It was almost time to tell the world that *she* was going to be Mrs. Douglas McCallum.

What did it matter if it was sooner or later?

Amalie sat on her bed holding Iggy. Iggy was hungry, she realized. Poor Iggy. She was hungry, too. She wished she had the rest of her sandwich, but what she wanted most of all were her cookies. There were four of them: chocolate with chocolate chips. Mrs. Tredway made good cookies. Mommy didn't make cookies or cakes. She didn't even make pies like Miss Darcie did. Mrs. Tredway cooked all of their food and straightened up their house. Mommy couldn't cook *or* clean. She didn't know how to do anything, and she wasn't smart enough to learn.

Amalie decided that she didn't feel sad for Mommy anymore, because Mommy was mean. Mommy was like the mean step-mommies in her princess books. But Mommy wasn't Amalie's step-mommy. She was her *real* mommy. Amalie knew that *real* mommies weren't supposed to be mean. But Amalie's real mommy was very, very, very mean.

Amalie's stomach growled. She looked at Iggy. *"I want cookies,"* he seemed to say. *"Be brave."*

"I want cookies, too, Iggy," she whispered. They would be brave together. She slid off the bed and tiptoed to the door.

CHAPTER FIFTY-TWO

𝒯he answer came to Darcie in a flash. She was dreaming. It explained everything. The surreal landscape. The rain. Her ability to make Devin appear out of the mist. All of it. It didn't matter that they were standing in the middle of North Washington Street in plain view of the cars passing by. It was *her* dream and she could do anything she wanted. So, she kissed her pirate with all of the longing that was in her heart.

Devin's relief rolled through him in one powerful wave. Having Darcie Finch in his arms was like finding the missing piece of his puzzle. Her lips found his, and that first spark burst into a brilliant flame. Her lips, cool and wet from the rain, did nothing to douse the fire raging in his blood. When he pulled her soaking wet frame against his burning chest, he half-expected to hear a sizzle as steam rose from their torrid embrace. He couldn't get enough of her. He kissed her again and again. Hotter and hotter. Kisses that were more appropriate for a bedroom than the middle of North Washington Street. Even in a pelting rainstorm.

A cold splash of water and a shouted, "Have a little class! Get a room!" finally pulled them from their sensual haze. Another SUV. Another puddle. Another dousing.

Darcie gasped from the shock of the water. This was *no* dream. This was as real as could be. She looked into Devin's eye to find him equally stunned by their sudden jolt back to reality. They shared a guilty grin. Neither of them had ever heard the words, "Get a room," directed at them. They were usually the ones who *tsked, tsked* public displays of affection.

As Darcie stepped back, Devin let her go reluctantly. "What are you doing here?" she shouted over the rain.

"I'm free," he yelled back. "Darcie, I'm free! Mallory wants a divorce!"

He watched her face for every nuance, every change of expression. This was important. Her perfect brow furrowed with concentration as she tried to comprehend his words. He could almost see the thoughts racing through her mind. She looked up at him, her eyes full of caution. His stomach twisted with anxiety, until she spoke the three words he would never forget.

"What about Amalie?"

Dear God, how he loved her. She was as different from Mallory as the sun from the moon. Her first thoughts weren't even about herself, but about a five-year-old girl who thought the amazing woman in front of him was a princess. His voice shook with emotion as he answered, "Full custody, Darcie. I get full custody."

She reached for his hands, clutching them in a tight grip. "Thank you, dear Lord." She closed her dark eyes in relief. When she opened them, he could see the tears running unheeded down her cheeks to mix with the raindrops. Her smile was bright enough to dry up the rain. On any other day, it seemed, except this one.

He didn't know how long they stood there, her hands gripping his, but another dousing of water from the damned ditch planted them firmly in reality.

Devin grinned. "We should probably get out of the rain," he suggested.

"Oh, I don't know," she said happily, shrugging her shoulders. "I'm kind of enjoying it."

"You heard the guy that splashed us," Devin reminded her.

"Which one?" Darcie asked.

Devin had a wicked glint in his eye. "The first one. The one who told us to get a room." She looked gorgeous, even soaking wet. "Maybe we should take his advice."

"We're about fifty feet from Joey's building. And I'm always up for taking advice from strange men in SUVs that splash water on me. Shall we?"

She held out her arm, and he took it, each of them wildly aware of the almost unbearable sexual tension raging between them.

Don't be at home, Joey. Please don't be at home. I will kill you if you're at home. Those were the only thoughts in Darcie's head as they walked into the apartment building. They headed straight for the elevator, exchanging heated glances until the doors opened. Joey lived on the fourth floor. Darcie reached out to punch the button.

As soon as the doors slid closed, she found her back against the wall of the elevator and her lips once again being devoured by her lusty pirate. He had one hand on either side of her head, but the heat and friction from his body were driving her crazy. She could feel the slight pressure of his hard muscled thigh between her legs. The thin material of her summer suit only heightened the exquisite sensations. She clung to her pirate, stunned by her own helpless response. Every brush of the wet material against her skin was turning her to a molten pool of lava.

When the elevator stopped on the third floor, Devin stepped away. He was trying to appear calm and collected. The fact that his breath was coming in short, hard pants as if he had just finished running a marathon was spoiling the effect. Darcie wore a dazzled expression. She seemed incapable of any movement. She just stared at the doors as they slid open like a rabbit caught in a trap.

The little, old lady that was waiting for the elevator looked from one to the other. Her bright eyes regarded them both with interest. She took in the fact that they were soaked to the skin. She saw Darcie's guilty face and Devin's attempt at a nonchalant stance with both hands casually in his pockets.

A delighted grin lit her wizened face. "Enjoy yourselves, loves. I'll take the stairs." They heard her happy chuckle as she vanished down the hallway.

Devin grinned as he reached for the button; this time, he kept his hands to himself. The doors opened onto Joey's floor. With his hand firmly clasped in hers, he followed Darcie to the third door on the left.

She opened her overly large satchel, searching desperately for the key Joey had given her yesterday. Of course, she couldn't find it. Devin stood right behind her, so close she could feel his hot breath on the back of her neck. She couldn't help the shiver that ran down her spine. His heat against her wet jacket and dress was doing all sorts of things to her already rapid heartbeat. Her hands were shaking so badly she could barely hold on to her heavy bag. Where was that damn key? Why couldn't she think?

She felt Devin's lips delicately brush the back of her ear. Oh, she thought. *That's why.* His warm lips trailed down from her ear to the spot where her neck met her shoulder. She closed her eyes, entranced by the feel of him. She tilted her head slightly, leaning back a little. *Key, key, key,* she admonished herself. *Focus, Darcie, focus. Oh, where is that stupid key?*

Devin's arms came around her waist to tug her back against him. His lips became more insistent, as he continued to nibble up and down her neck. His hands crept up her torso, under her jacket, hesitating just below her breasts. Darcie froze in exquisite anticipation of his touch. His hands continued upward, gently cupping her breasts. She gasped as every nerve ending she possessed came to life. Her hands worked feverishly to find the key.

Devin wasn't lying, she realized. He was good at this. *I'm going to die right here in this hallway,* she thought. She arched her back as he continued his gentle massage, his lips never ceasing their lovely torment. Maybe they should go back to the elevator, she mused. Where was that damn... Her hand closed on the key.

As she pulled it out of her satchel, she heard Devin's mumbled, "Thank God." She tried to fit it in the lock, but her hands were shaking so badly that she couldn't even make contact.

Devin took the key from her trembling hands. He inserted it in the lock with a satisfying *click*. He turned the door handle and pushed. *If Joey Finch is here*, he decided, *I might kill him and throw his body over the balcony.* Devin had never—*never*—wanted a woman in his life the way he wanted Darcie Finch. His control was hanging by a thread. Everything about her called to his most primitive self. Her scent. Her taste. Her inability to control her reactions to his slightest touch. His body was screaming. The delicate gasps she made when he touched her breasts nearly sent him over the edge. Only extreme strength of will kept him from making love to her against the door in the hallway.

Now, they surveyed the obviously unoccupied room in abject relief. Joey wasn't at home. His life was spared. The serious look they exchanged was a shared recognition of the significance of this moment. Together, they silently acknowledged their mutual decision to continue on life's path together. It felt right as nothing else ever had.

"It feels like we're on our honeymoon," Darcie whispered solemnly, filter absent as usual.

"I should have picked a better hotel," Devin answered, his recently dormant sense of humor coming alive in the presence of his Pirate Queen.

"It's more comfortable than the doorway," Darcie quipped.

"Or the elevator."

"Or the sidewalk." Her lips quirked up in a little smile. "All right, Mr. I'm-Good-At-It. What do we do now?"

The wave of desire that slammed into Devin sent his senses reeling. His reaction was swift and decisive. He swept her up into his arms, closing the door behind them with his foot. He strode toward the bedroom on the right.

"Other one," she gasped, clinging to his shoulders. He disregarded her words, entering Joey's bedroom without hesitation. After a swift perusal of the space, he walked to the bedside table.

"What are you doing?" she asked, as Devin set her gently on her feet.

Devin grinned, ridiculously sure of himself…and of what he knew about Joey Finch. He reached in the drawer and pulled out a pack of condoms. He had guessed correctly.

Darcie's eyes widened in surprise. "How did you...oh, never mind." There were just some things she did *not* want to know about her brother. Before she could give too much thought to Joey's questionable love life, Devin picked her up again, striding across the room. Her arms crept around his neck as her heart began to pound.

Crossing the hall, he entered the doorway to the guest bedroom. Once again, he closed the door with his foot.

"Did you play soccer?" she whispered.

"No, football. Why?"

He regarded her curiously, as he carefully set her on her feet.

"You're pretty good with that foot." *Say something stupid, Darcie. Ruin the moment, Darcie.* She almost groaned aloud. *Feels like we're on our honeymoon. Shut up, Darcie.* She realized he was watching her. His eye burned with heat. And something else. He looked hungry. For her. She shivered again as his expression changed to chagrin.

"You must be freezing in all of those wet clothes. I'll be happy to help you out of them." The gleam was back in his eye. "I'll be happy to warm you up..." He leaned closer to whisper in her ear, "From the inside."

She sucked in a shaky breath, watching him with glowing eyes. How could he possibly be so sexy? If he looked this good in soaking wet khaki pants and a polo shirt, what would he look like...wearing nothing at all?

"Take off your jacket, Darcie."

He took a step toward her, only to be stopped by a hand on his chest.

"Oh, no, Laurence." Some heretofore unknown sassy imp prompted her to tease him. "You promised to warm me up. Not freeze me to death." She gestured to his wet clothes. "Those clothes are not warming me up."

He grinned, happy to oblige.

She watched with hooded eyes as he kicked off his shoes before removing his shirt and khakis. *Oh my,* was all she could muster as her entire body was consumed by a wave of heat. She was certain her brain was melting. She held onto rational cognitive thought with her fingernails, fighting the powerful urge to tackle him to the floor.

He glanced up to see if his efforts had met her approval, only to find her waiting with her arms crossed under those delectable breasts.

"Those, too," she demanded, waving her hand at his navy-blue briefs.

"You, first," he teased. It appeared his Pirate Queen was firmly in control, as long as he wasn't touching her. Well, he would just see about that. "Take off your jacket, Darcie."

She obediently pulled her arms from the sleeves and tossed the jacket onto a nearby chair. He watched her every move, wondering if she would be as obedient to his *every* request. The thought made him hotter, even as he dismissed it. Darcie Finch and the word *obedient* didn't exactly mesh.

"Turn around, Darcie," he said, his voice hoarse, almost unrecognizable. She did as he wished, so she had no idea that his hands were shaking as he reached for her zipper. He unzipped her dress slowly. The sound of the zipper and their harsh breathing were the only sounds in the room. He put both hands on her shoulder, gently pushing the sleeves down her arms. The dress dropped to her feet.

Darcie stepped out of it, kicking the material out of the way. As she turned to face him, her eyes were nearly black with emotion. She stood there in a lacy bra and panty set, just sheer enough to wreak havoc on a man's imagination. Devin froze as he struggled to draw breath. Her lingerie was red. Of course, it was. He should have known that Darcie Finch was wearing erotic red underthings beneath her plain, black business attire. Devin closed his eye, striving desperately to control his reaction to her firm, tempting breasts. She was going to be the death of him. How much more could he take? How did a scarred mortal like him make love to a goddess?

"What's the matter, Laurence?" she asked, softly. "Don't you like what you see?"

His eye snapped open when he heard the note of worry in her husky voice. She stood in front of him in all of her incredible glory. The vulnerability in her eyes, however, called for reassurance. Devin was an idiot. How could he make her doubt herself? She had no idea what she was doing to him—a situation he could easily rectify. Even so, he felt like a sixteen-year-old again as he admitted, "If I look too long, I'll be finished before we start."

"Oh," she gasped in sudden understanding. A lovely flush covered her cheeks. "I think I like that."

Devin made a concentrated effort to stop focusing on Darcie's seemingly untouchable beauty. He chose instead to focus on the woman. *His* woman, he corrected with supreme satisfaction. Her skin was like porcelain. Smooth as silk. Her figure was perfect. Her hair—hanging in wet rivulets around her shoulders—would have seemed messy on any other woman. But on her—on Darcie Finch—it looked enticing…as if she had just stepped out of the shower.

If Devin got any harder, he wasn't going to make it to the bed. The longer he looked, the more paralyzed he became by the vision before him. He remembered vestiges of the feeling from the first time he saw her…in the grand foyer of Heart's Ease. Sort of. What he was feeling now was a more intense version. A thoroughly all-encompassing emotion. *Mine.* His frozen brain could only produce one word at a time. *Mine.*

He reached out a hand, stopping in midair. "You are too beautiful to touch," he whispered.

"Too beautiful to touch?" She let out an exasperated breath. "What good is that, for either of us? Seriously, Laurence? That's the *best* you can do?" Darcie was having none of that *you're so beautiful* nonsense. Not here. Not now. And *never* with this man.

She took his hand in hers, placing it over her pounding heart. "Do you feel that, Laurence? In an X-ray, my heart looks like everybody else's. It isn't *more* beautiful or *less* beautiful than any other heart. But—listen carefully to this part, Laurence—my heart belongs to *you*. Only to *you*. And since *you* have the heart—which is the most important part, by the way—the body comes with it." Her lips turned up in a mischievous grin. "Think of it as an added bonus."

Her wry observation was so very Darcie. Everything she said was true. And so very, very right. She was beautiful, but she was real. And she was *his*.

Her arms dropped to her side. Her eyes held a question. His frozen limbs thawed instantly, as his hot gaze moved from her flushed face to his hand, still resting on her heart.

He studied that hand objectively, noting that it was only inches away from a semitransparent covering of red lace. That erotic lace rose and fell with her quick breaths. Her nipples were puckered with something other than the cold. He was happy to take credit for that. He slowly brushed the back of his knuckles over the soft flesh at the top of her breast. He trailed the tips of his fingers very deliberately over her tightened nipple. Her gasp of pleasure caused his swollen member to throb in reply. He closed his eye, determined to regain enough control of himself to make every touch, every kiss, every action good for her.

Darcie was quickly losing her grip on reality. And she knew it. Dying of pleasure, perhaps? She blissfully wondered if such a thing was possible. Because she was pretty sure she was dying right now. She watched Devin close his eye and breathe. She knew he was trying to calm himself. She tried to do the same, even though her lungs would not cooperate. If he didn't hurry up, she was going to have a serious stroke and expire before he got to the really good part.

He raised his other hand, his knuckles repeating the delicate touch on her other breast. This time, he lingered to trace a circle around her nipple. She felt her knees weaken a bit more. He was teasing her. That was all. *Hurry up. Hurry up.* She leaned toward him eagerly, but he had other plans. He put his hands on her shoulders, turning her to face the full-length mirror on the back of the door. She studied their reflection, unable to look away from the hot light that was burning in his eye.

Devin had never imagined that any woman could look so sexy. Even in his wildest fantasies. He raked her reflection with his gaze, starting with her bare feet. For some odd reason, he found her red toenail polish wildly arousing. His hungry eye took in her shapely legs, rising to a vee, covered with a wisp of sheer red lace. He focused on that part of her for so long that she moved against him, desperate for contact. She pressed back against him, her tight, little behind undulating slowly against his bulging member.

His eye moved upward to the pert breasts, begging for his touch. *Mine,* his primitive-self growled. *She's mine.* His hands rhythmically massaged her shoulders. *Now,* his libido screamed. *I want her now.* Her head fell back against his chest in complete surrender. Devin inhaled again, reeling in his primal urges. He forced himself to slow down. To savor. To linger. His fingers traced her lacy, red straps, leisurely. One at a time.

Darcie raised her arms to encircle his neck. She tugged eagerly, bringing his hot mouth closer. He planted heated kisses up and down her neck and shoulders. He held off as long as he could, but he wanted those sweet breasts in his hands, wanted to hear those sighs from her lips. His hands encircled her waist, moving slowly upward. He wanted to draw out every sensation possible before reaching his desired destination. When he finally cupped her breasts—filling his hands with her lace-covered flesh—his sigh of relief was echoed by the woman in his arms. He couldn't look away from her face, entranced by the play of emotions. Her dark eyes widened briefly with surprise before nearly closing in supreme pleasure. *Beautiful. Beautiful. Beautiful.* His mind was stuck on the word, but he didn't dare to say it out loud.

Darcie was surprised he couldn't hear her pounding heart. She decided that her breathy gasps were probably drowning it out. The lace, scraping gently over her sensitized flesh, caused cravings she had never before experienced. She wanted more. She wanted his hands on her bare skin. "Take it off," she moaned, hoarsely. "Touch me, Laurence. Touch my skin."

His hands searched desperately for the clasp of the lacy obstruction, pulling his gaze away from the erotic vision in the mirror to study her back. He saw the strap, but he didn't see the clasp. Where was it? Where was the damn clasp? He ran his fingers under the back strap from one side to another. "How the hell does this come off?" he murmured in frustration. "What kind of twisted lunatic made this thing?" It was his own voice he heard. He had spoken his thoughts aloud. No filter. He was starting to sound just like Darcie Finch.

"Laurence," she sighed.

"Yes," he whispered, unable to keep himself from kissing the warm flesh of her back. It was right in front of him and too tempting.

"The clasp is in front," she whispered. Well, she tried to whisper. Her rich voice rang out in the tiny room, the answer to all of his dreams.

Devin tried to listen to what she was saying. He really did, but he was standing behind her with his lips on her neck, watching the reflection of her alluring body clad only in red lingerie. It was impossible to pay attention. "Hmm..." he managed to say.

Darcie took matters into her own hands. She reached down and unhooked her bra, dropping the wisp of lace to the floor. Replacing her arms around the neck of her pirate lover, she waited.

Devin never imagined anything like this. Darcie Finch in a lacy bra and panties was stunning. But Darcie Finch minus the bra, well...he thought his heart might explode. His hands moved of their own accord. He cupped her bare breasts, massaging gently. He used his knuckles to lightly caress her nipples. Her gasps and small sounds of pleasure shook his control.

With a growl, he turned her to the side and bent her back over his arm. His mouth found her breasts, nibbling them, tasting them. His lips closed over a nipple, suckling gently. His other hand trailed down her stomach to toy with the scrap of lace still hiding her delicate curls. He covered her soft flesh with his fingers, stroking her through the lace. He pressed the heel of his hand into her most sensitive flesh. She pressed against him, urging him on. He moved his hand to the top of her lacy panties before sliding inside.

"Yes, oh, yes, please," she gasped, moving against him. "Do that. Yes, right there and...oh, just like that."

Devin wasn't so far gone that he couldn't smile at her chatter. Of course Darcie Finch would start talking the closer she got to completion. He should have expected it. His fingers brushed through her soft curls to find her folds. He stroked her, finding her hot and wet. She clutched him tightly. He pressed inside her with his finger. He could feel her inner muscles twitch in response. He withdrew, pleased by her huff of impatience. With a swift tug, he relieved her of her lacy panties. Returning to his original objective, he sought her soft folds, pressing in again. So focused was he on his objective that he was only dimly aware of her encouraging narration.

Darcie was burning up. Devin's hands and lips evoked sensation after sensation that she never knew existed. Her whole body was coiled tight, increasingly desperate for release. She could hear herself begging for him to continue. She felt his finger brush a spot on the inside that made her toes curl. His thumb played with the sensitive nub at the top of her folds while his finger found the perfect rhythm. She nearly cried out when he brushed that internal spot again. He lingered there, moving back and forth until she thought she would die from the pleasure of it.

Devin raised his head from her delectable breasts to look into the mirror. "Open your eyes, Darcie. I want to see you."

It took an effort, but she opened her eyes. The reflection that met her gaze was the most erotic thing she had ever seen. His finger caressed the spot that drove her wild at that exact moment. Darcie let go, with a scream of pleasure.

Devin reveled in her responses, keeping a rhythm as the spasms went on and on. His masculine pride—which had taken such a hit after his accident—came roaring to the surface. He, once again, felt strong. Whole. Undamaged. For the first time since his accident, he felt as if he lacked nothing.

Just as Darcie's knees would have given way, he picked her up in his arms. Striding across the room, he deposited her gently onto the bed. She flopped back on the mattress, gazing at him. Her beautiful eyes filled with amazement. She was glowing with the aftermath of the glorious moments in front of the mirror. Her body still strummed with a few aftershocks in some very unexpected places. And she couldn't stop smiling.

The sight of a sated—and naked—Darcie Finch sprawled on a bed put a severe strain on Devin's already tenuous control. His libido was screaming for release, but he wanted Darcie to make a decision that wasn't clouded by passion. He was determined to give her a minute to catch her breath. Determined to let her decide what happened next…even if it killed him. And if he had to wait much longer, it just might. Still, he couldn't resist the chance to tease her just a little. "I told you I was good," he said, puffing out his chest.

She pushed herself up so that she was leaning back on her elbows. "You'll get no arguments from me, Laurence." Her lips quirked up in a sly smile.

"No arguments from Darcie Finch? This is a day for firsts," he said, loving the belligerent light that appeared in her eyes.

"Hmph," she said, sitting up straighter and puffing out her chest in a perfect imitation of his earlier stance. She lowered her lashes in unmistakable invitation.

Unable to resist the siren song of his lovely Pirate Queen, he closed the distance between them to brush her lips with his. He teased her with a series of soft, light kisses, until she gave a little groan of frustration. Only when her arms closed around his neck to pull him closer, did he deepen the kiss.

Her hands explored his upper body eagerly, before coming to rest on the waistband of his briefs. She tugged, causing him to pull back, inquiringly.

"Yes, may I help you?" he asked politely, waggling his eyebrows in a wicked gesture.

"These have to go," she stated, tugging again.

"Oh, really?" he asked.

It appeared that Miss Finch had made her decision. *Thank God.* Devin leaned over her, his hands on the unmade bed on either side of her shoulders. "So, Darcie Finch doesn't make her bed? I have to admit that I'm a little surprised by that, Miss Finch."

She once again found herself breathless, and for good reason. She was pinned to the bed by her pirate lover. "For your information, Laurence, I *always* make my bed. But today, I didn't have time because I was afraid that I was going to be..."

"Late," they finished together. He smiled charmingly. She wrinkled her nose, stuck out her tongue, and busied herself by plucking at his waistband.

"But we're not talking about me and my unmade bed, Laurence," she informed him. "We're talking about you and your briefs. Or more importantly, getting you *out* of your briefs and *into* my unmade bed." She was all sassy confidence again.

Devin stepped back to do her bidding. How could he refuse his Pirate Queen anything? Darcie rose to her knees, coming to the side of the bed to watch. He was beyond pleased to hear her swift intake of breath at the sight of his inspired member. He moved next to her, standing beside the bed. She threw her arms around his neck. "Is this where I'm supposed to say, '*Take me, now,*' or '*Make me yours,*' or something like that?" she asked, mischievously.

"Say whatever you like," he smiled. He leaned in to kiss her, surprised when she stopped him with a gentle hand on his chest. He looked at her inquiringly.

"I want you to take off the eyepatch," she said, seriously.

Her request was so unexpected that he attempted to recoil from her. Anticipating his response, she held fast, both arms secure behind his neck.

"Why now?" he asked, the last of his insecurities roaring to the surface. He wasn't even wearing his artificial eye. Sometimes, it just wasn't comfortable. How could he let her see that? He quirked his lips, attempting to distract her. "Ar-re you saying that you don't want to make love to a pirate, Dar-r-cie Finch?"

She looked him in the eye, determined to make him understand. "I love you, Devin Merritt. You are everything to me. I want to share your joy *and* your pain. I want you to believe me when I say that I love all of you. So please, take off that eyepatch and make love to me."

He looked into those dark eyes, brimming with overwhelming love and trust. At that moment, he couldn't have denied her anything. He removed the patch. As he tossed it to the side, he braced himself for those beautiful eyes to fill with disgust. He could barely draw breath. Would the staggering hideousness of his face make her change her mind? He wouldn't blame her if it did. Still, he hoped....

She studied him for a moment, one soft hand on either side of his face. Her expression betrayed nothing. She pressed her lips to the scars on the good side of his face, kissing him thoroughly before moving to the other side. She kissed his nose, before working her way to his mangled eye socket. When she pressed a gentle kiss to the part of him he considered the most hideous, he was undone, both by her sweet caresses and her honest devotion.

"I love your scars, Devin," she breathed softly. "Because they brought you to me."

Darcie's unflinching acceptance of his greatest physical flaws nearly sent him to his knees. He was overcome by a wave of tenderness. He didn't deserve the luscious woman kneeling on the bed with her heart in her eyes. That thought was followed by a wave of the strongest desire he had ever experienced. The tsunami of emotion snapped the fragile hold he had on himself. He gave up and gave in, letting his instincts run wild.

Darcie once again found herself flat on her back. Her pirate lover was all encompassing, his hands moving with expert precision. She was completely entranced. Completely under his passionate spell. Her entire world was reduced to feelings. And the feelings were exquisite. His lips were thorough—teasing, tasting, arousing—until she was once again lost in the spinning vortex of emotions. When he entered her, she braced herself for the remembered pain of her one youthful experience. Instead, she was swept away by the intensity of pleasure as wave after wave of blissful sensations coursed through her.

Devin held himself back until he felt her inner muscles contract around his aching member. Only then did he allow himself to let go, his powerful thrusts building to the most remarkable release of his life. Careful not to crush his treasure, he rolled onto his back, tucking her against his side.

She snuggled next to him, sighing the sensuous sigh of the sated female. "Oh, Lau-rence," she crooned, lengthening his name in delight. "You were so right. You know *exactly* what you're doing. And you are very, very good at it."

Devin grinned. What man wouldn't enjoy hearing those words from his lover? Devin had heard lying lips deliver similar phrases before. Many times. This was different because Darcie Finch's lips were saying those things. As always, her words rang with sincerity.

"Darcie, I want you to know something." He propped himself up with his elbow, so he could look into her face. "This isn't the first time I've had sex, but it's the first time I've ever made love."

Her face lit with joy. "I love you, Devin Merritt. I can't even begin to tell you how much."

"Marry me, Darcie." The words burst from his lips without thought, finesse, or preparation. *Well, that was smooth, Merritt,* he admonished himself. He hadn't filed the separation papers yet. He would have to wait a year for the divorce. And he didn't even have a ring. In fact, he had nothing to offer this woman.

Darcie, of course, took it all in stride. To her his request was the next step in a logical progression. "I just did," she said, matter-of-factly.

Devin thought she must have misunderstood him. "What did you say?"

She smiled at the confusion on his face. "Oh, Laurence, don't you understand? You have my whole heart. I belong to you now. I couldn't feel any more married to you than I do right at this very moment. But, yes, I will happily become Mrs. Darcie Merritt. In a lovely ceremony. With a long, white dress.

Flowers. Music. Friends. Family. And a beautiful, little flower girl named Amalie. *After* your divorce is final. Until then…" She shrugged nonchalantly. "I guess I'll just have to be your girlfriend."

He couldn't resist kissing her smiling mouth. "Don't move, Darcie Finch. I'll be right back."

He jumped out of bed and began looking through the pile of wet clothes he had haphazardly tossed onto the floor. Darcie watched him curiously, appreciating the view.

"Ah-ha," he said in satisfaction, holding his eyepatch up triumphantly. He put it on and returned to the bed. "And now, wench, ar-re you ready to be ravished by a pirate?" he asked, a challenging light in his eye.

"Wench?" she asked, in mock outrage, sitting up against the headboard. "I think the real question is, ar-re you ready to be ravished by a pirate queen?"

Devin grinned. There was only one right answer for that question.

Roman pounded on the door at three o'clock in the afternoon. "Devin," he yelled. "Devin, are you in there?" He was breathing hard and struggling to prepare himself for the task ahead.

Joey caught up with Roman as he resumed his pounding. "What are you doing?"

"I'm knocking on the door," Roman answered, annoyance in his voice. "What does it look like I'm doing?"

"Well, genius, it is *my* apartment." Joey held up his apartment key, dangling it in front of Roman's face. "Why don't we just use the key?"

Roman glared at Joey, already a little put out. Even though his friend had also run all the way from Merritt Brothers, Joey wasn't the least bit out of breath. "I'm trying to give them a little…time," Roman said, fixing Joey with his stare. He didn't want to say what he was thinking since the woman involved was Joey's baby sister, of whom he was very protective.

"Time for what?" Joey asked, before the underlying meaning of Roman's words dawned on him. "What the hell, Roman, you don't think they're…" He blew out a frustrated breath. "Damn it. Now, I'm going to have to kill him." He paced back and forth as Roman continued to pound on the door. "And in *my* apartment, too. Damn it."

"Sorry, Finch, you're going to have to put that thought on hold," Roman said firmly. "We've got a lot more to worry about than my cousin and your sister."

"You wouldn't consider him married anymore, would you?" Joey asked, clenching and unclenching his fists.

Roman paused, thinking it over. "Technically, no," he said, changing hands to continue his pounding.

"I'm going to kill him anyway," Joey announced, before unceremoniously shoving Roman out of the way to insert his key in the lock.

"It can't be Joey," Darcie argued as she and Devin walked out of the guest bedroom. "He would use his key."

She was wearing jeans and a flowered shirt with long sleeves and embroidery around the square neck. Her hair was in a bun on the top of her head. She looked beautiful.

Devin had slipped on a long-sleeve T-shirt and khaki pants, both of which belonged to Joey. The chest of the shirt was too tight. The sleeves were too short, as were the legs of the khaki pants. He looked like hell.

"It has to be him," Devin said, logically. "Nobody else knows you're here."

"Good point," Darcie said.

"He's come to kill me." Devin appeared resigned to his fate.

"Or me," Darcie added. "He might want to kill me, too."

"Probably, but he'll kill me first," Devin said. "And he'll make you watch."

Darcie grinned at that. "I don't care. It was worth it."

Devin gave her a quick kiss on the lips. She was right. He would rather have one day with Darcie Finch than a lifetime with anyone else. They approached the door with more than a little reluctance.

"Who is it?" Darcie asked as Devin looked through the peephole.

He sighed, heavily. "It's your brother, all right. And Roman's with him."

"Roman must be here to keep Joey from killing you…Us. That makes sense. But, why are they beating on the door? Why doesn't Joey just…"

Her voice trailed away as the knob began to turn.

Darcie and Devin stepped back, waiting while the door swung open. She reached out her hand and he took it, folding it firmly in his grasp. Whatever happened next, they would face it together. Perhaps it wouldn't go as badly if they presented a united front.

Joey came barreling in. He stopped when he saw them, his eyes going straight to his sister. Darcie looked good, in Joey's estimation. Maybe, just maybe, he and Roman had arrived in time. Maybe they had interrupted nothing more than a long conversation. His gaze moved to Devin. The man looked like he had just gotten out of bed. He was rumpled. And happy about it. Great. "I may have to kill you," Joey said to Devin. "I can't believe…" He paused, looking the man up and down. "Hey, wait a minute, are those my khakis?"

"Shut up, Joey," Darcie said, clearly annoyed at her protective older brother. She turned to Roman. "Why are you here?" she asked politely.

"We, um…have something to tell Devin…and you. I mean, mostly Devin, but it involves you, too. I mean…" Roman seemed unable to express himself.

Joey interrupted him, coming straight to the point. "Mallory's dead."

CHAPTER FIFTY-THREE

*J*oey's blunt announcement was followed by a minimal number of details. The only information Roman could offer was what he had been able to gather from his sister's hysterical phone call. Diana had arrived at Devin's house after a late lunch to discover Mallory lying on the sofa in her sitting room. After several unsuccessful attempts to awaken her employer, Diana called 911. When the EMTs arrived, they confirmed that Mallory was dead. Diana found Amalie under the bed in her own room with the door locked. The little girl was, thankfully, unharmed. That was all Diana had been able to tell him.

After a brief, whispered argument, Roman persuaded Joey to accompany him to his apartment to pack a bag for the trip up to Newport. Joey's obvious reluctance to leave Darcie at that moment was equal parts sweet and annoying to his baby sister. She needed a few quiet moments to wrap her head around what had happened to Devin's wife without the terribly helpful voice of her big brother. She had a decision to make. Even though she desperately wanted to accompany Devin to Newport, she wasn't sure if it was the wisest choice.

Roman made up her mind for her. He didn't give her an option. "Devin might need an alibi," he suggested gently.

Darcie nodded soberly. Until that moment, the idea that Mallory could have been murdered hadn't occurred to her. She attributed her lack of clarity to the glorious hours she had spent with her pirate lover. All of that joy, she thought regretfully, brutally snuffed by a dose of hard, cold reality.

Joey surprised her with a kiss on the cheek on his way out the door with Roman. Darcie breathed a sigh of relief once they were gone. Getting rid of Joey wasn't easy when his protective hackles were roused. She practically had to push him out the door. Thank the Lord for Roman's good sense.

Darcie eyed Devin with some concern. He hadn't said a word since Roman mentioned he might need an alibi. She had to figure out how best to help the man she loved. The very pale man. The man that had a what-the-hell-is-happening look of shock in his eye. Devin's scars stood out starkly against his colorless face. Darcie moved quickly to his side, afraid he was going to pass out. As she watched, his face suddenly suffused with color. The beads of sweat popping up on his brow prompted her to tug his unresisting form to Joey's guest bathroom.

Devin's body had gone completely numb when Roman said the word *alibi*. Initially, he had assumed that Mallory's death must have been caused by a careless accident. Or the sudden onset of some unknown congenital condition. But murder *never* crossed Devin's mind. The thought that someone might have murdered his wife chilled him. The thought that someone might have murdered his wife while his daughter was in the house rocked him to his very foundation. He became violently ill, hanging over the toilet bowl in Joey's guest bathroom. For a very long half hour, he remained there on his knees. So very, very, sick. And cold. He couldn't seem to stop shaking. Every time he thought of what might have happened to his baby girl, he could barely breathe. Darcie never left his side. She rubbed his back. She held a cold washcloth against his neck. She whispered encouraging words. She was a rock. His saving grace.

When Devin finally felt well enough to leave the cursed bathroom, Darcie helped him to the couch in Joey's living room. He was grateful for her strength—he felt weak as a kitten—and her steady presence. Grateful for her compassion and understanding. Just…grateful. When she sat down beside him on the couch, he gathered her into his arms, holding her close. The feel of her, silently supportive, helped him to recover his equilibrium.

By the time Roman and Joey returned, Devin was once again thinking rationally. Roman—being of a similar height and build as his cousin—brought Devin some decent clothes to wear on the plane. After donning a pair of long-enough khakis and a shirt that didn't look like the buttons were going to pop off at any moment, Devin was ready to head to the airport.

They didn't talk much on the short flight back to Providence. Everyone was still too stunned by Mallory's death to engage in much conversation. Devin figured he wouldn't remember much of what was said anyway. He would, however, remember holding Darcie's hand during the entire flight.

Grace and Blane met them at the airport. Devin received a tearful hug from Grace. He hugged her in return, thankful for the support. He watched as she enveloped her sister in a protective embrace before he allowed Blane to pull him aside. The Boss-man offered his support as well as any of the resources currently at the disposal of McCallum Industries. Devin was heartened by his loyalty. He was blessed to have a friend like Blane, one who always had his back. Even Joey—who had a better reason than anyone to question Devin's motives—shook his hand and promised legal help, if necessary. With a reassuring nod, he, too, stepped back.

Darcie was the last to say goodbye. The general consensus was that she should remain in Providence unless the police needed her statement. The others tactfully gave them a bit of privacy. Darcie was calm but composed. She reached out, enfolding both of his hands in hers. She peered into his eye, as if searching for a glimpse of his soul. He gazed back, feeling her love wrap around his heart. It was a moment that needed no words.

She nodded her head, apparently satisfied by what she saw. She stood on her toes, pressing her soft lips to his scarred cheek. "Courage, Laurence," she said, and then she was gone.

And Devin was all alone.

Well, not totally alone, he realized, as he felt Roman's hand on his shoulder. Together they walked to Devin's car. Buoyed by the encouragement of the woman he loved and the solid presence of family, Devin headed to Newport.

When they walked into the townhouse, Diana launched herself at her brother, collapsing on his shoulder with heartrending sobs. Roman wrapped his arms around her, a grim expression on his face. He listened to her, as best he could, through her strangled gasps, whispering every comforting word he could think of.

Allana was sitting on the sofa with Amalie. The little girl was sound asleep, her head comfortably pillowed by her grandmother's lap. The compassion in Allana's loving gaze made Devin long for the innocent days when his mother and father had shielded him from the ugly side of life. That was no longer possible, but as he looked from his mother's eyes to his father's sober expression, he could tell that they still wished it was. Rob gave Devin a quick, bracing hug, before delivering the shocking news.

As it turned out, nobody needed an alibi. According to the coroner, Mallory had died from an accidental drug overdose.

Diana lifted her face from Roman's shoulder. Her eyes were red. Her face was splotchy. Her freckles stood out in sharp relief. She looked pitiful. The tears started again as she looked at Devin. "I'm so sorry, Dev. If I had come home earlier, maybe I could have…"

"Diana," Devin said firmly. "This is not your fault."

"I tried to tell her that," Roman said. "Maybe she'll believe it if you say it."

"Diana," Devin said firmly again. "Listen to me. Mallory was a grown woman. She made her own decisions. I'm absolutely certain that there wasn't anything you could have done to change what happened."

Diana sniffed, dabbing at her eyes with the back of her hand. "Thanks, Dev," she whispered, managing a wobbly, little smile. She took a deep breath. "I think I'll go get a bottle of water from the kitchen. Does anyone else want one?"

Allana waved from the sofa. Diana nodded before disappearing down the hallway. Her color was better, and she seemed calmer now. Devin and Roman exchanged relieved glances. Poor Diana had borne the brunt of things, as usual.

"About what the coroner said…" Rob began. But before they could get that particular discussion under way, the doorbell rang.

When Devin opened the door, Pamela Gagnon, Mallory's mother, threw herself in his arms. She immediately proceeded to sob all over his borrowed shirt. Devin had no choice but to grit his teeth and bear the histrionics of his grieving former mother-in-law. Over the next few hours, the townhouse filled with Pamela's friends and family. Devin bore it all stoically. He wasn't callous enough to tell the rapt audience that—contrary to the image she was projecting—Pamela Gagnon hadn't spoken to her deceased daughter in four and a half years.

In spite of the coroner's decision, Devin couldn't shake the feeling that Mallory's death wasn't as simple as it appeared. The next day, he and Diana, along with Rob and Roman—for moral support—made an appointment with the local police department to discuss their suspicions.

Their grim, little party was escorted into an office and introduced to Detective Tim Ross. He was a middle-aged man with twenty-seven years of experience on the force...the last ten months as a detective. Although he quickly hid the distaste caused by his first sighting of Devin's face, he wasn't quick enough. His initial response didn't endear him to any of them.

After the detective got his expression under control, he arrogantly told the men to leave so he could interview Diana. *She* was the one he needed to address, he explained, smugly, since *she* was the person who found the body. He motioned for her to take a seat in the single chair in front of his desk. He settled himself behind the desk, waiting, confidently, for them to do his bidding.

Devin glanced at Diana, who nodded bravely to let him know she was willing to be interviewed alone. He and Rob returned to the hallway to wait. But Roman refused to budge. His thoughts were written all over his face. *Leave my sister in here alone with you? Like hell I will.*

Roman very deliberately moved another chair beside Diana's, sat down, and crossed his arms. He raised his eyebrows and returned the detective's glare, almost daring him to do something about it. Roman could be intimidating when he chose. After a few tense moments, Detective Ross backed down. Roman, it seemed, would be allowed to remain.

Devin enjoyed the expression of pure irritation his cousin threw at him as the detective shut the door. It sparked the first genuine humor he had felt since finding out Mallory was dead. He paced the hallway while Rob checked his messages on his phone.

Fifteen minutes later, Detective Ross opened the door to invite Devin and Robert to join them in his office. Roman was standing by the window, his arm around Diana's shoulders. Her longing expression was fixed on the parking lot as if she couldn't wait to get in a car and travel as far from her current location as possible.

The detective looked at Diana, gesturing his head toward the door. "Thank you, Miss Merritt, that's all we need from you today," he said dismissively.

Roman took Diana's arm, leading her toward the door. "Detective," he said, returning glare for glare as he passed the pompous man.

"Mr. Merritt," the detective replied, shutting the door behind them. As soon as he turned, he was all business. He asked Devin and Rob to be seated. They complied, planting themselves in the chairs vacated by Diana and Roman.

When they were arranged to his liking, the detective expressed his condolences. "Tragic loss," he said. "So very tragic, and all too common these days."

Devin thought his words sounded hollow, lacking in genuine sympathy.

Detective Ross continued, his voice oozing with superiority. "Opioid abuse is running rampant in our society and it's only getting worse. Your wife died of an *overdose*, son. We'll probably never know whether it was accidental or not. *You* are going to have to accept that."

Devin took immediate umbrage at his accusatory tone and the imperious way he used the word, *son*. "I'm sorry, sir," he said, politely. "But I'm finding it difficult to believe that my wife died from a drug overdose. She didn't take drugs of any kind, except an occasional headache powder. And that was pretty rare."

The detective sighed deeply. He looked at Devin pityingly. "I know it's hard, son, but sometimes *we* don't know the people *we* live with as well as *we* think *we* do. As a matter of fact," he continued patronizingly, "in this particular case, it was entirely unnecessary for any of you to contact the police."

Devin started to interrupt, but the detective dismissed his concerns with a wave of his hand. "I realize Miss Merritt was frightened when she found your wife. Discovering a dead body is never easy, especially for a fragile young woman like your cousin." He shook his head regretfully. "It's understandable that she would overreact. I recommend intensive counseling for her. You don't want to risk her getting lost in her own delusions."

Devin stared at him in amazement. Diana was anything but fragile. She was strong and confident. As a matter of fact, he couldn't *remember* the last time she overreacted to anything. Her ability to be rational in the face of nonsense was one of the reasons she could stand working for Mallory.

The detective continued in a bored tone: "This case, gentlemen, is cut and dried. Having a 'bad feeling' about your wife's death because Miss Merritt never saw her take drugs is not grounds to open a murder investigation. Your cousin is clearly overwrought."

"But, sir," Devin repeated, more insistently, "I *agree* with my cousin. I'm *certain* my wife didn't take drugs. I've never seen her under the influence of anything but, maybe, a couple of martinis or a glass of champagne. She was *very* conscious of her appearance. She didn't do anything to affect that, including smoking, excessive drinking, and drug use. And to imagine that she would accidentally overdose…well, it doesn't even seem possible to me."

The detective's eyes narrowed slightly in irritation. His tone became more than a little condescending. "Look, Mr. Merritt," he began firmly. "I know you're upset, but there is *no* evidence of foul play. There was no sign of forced entry. All of the doors were locked when Miss Merritt got home. And your daughter—who was there the whole time—didn't see or hear anything. As I said before, *we* don't always know everything about the people *we* live with."

"But," Devin tried to interrupt, "my daughter hasn't spoken a word since Diana found her. Not one word." Devin tried not to show how worried he was by Amalie's persistent silence. "So, we really don't know if she saw anything or not."

Detective Ross leaned back in his chair. "I didn't want to bring this up, Mr. Merritt, but I see that it's going to be necessary." It was obviously his coup de grâce. He seemed to be enjoying himself as he relayed the information. "I have looked through the coroner's report. He found bruises on your wife's neck, wrists, ankles, and torso. They appeared to be around three days old. I know they weren't put there by *you*, because *you* spent the weekend with your family in Alexandria, and your wife wasn't with you." At Devin's raised eyebrows, the arrogant man explained. "Miss Merritt just supplied us with the details of your whereabouts." He looked Devin right in the eye, a knowing gaze on his face. "Bruises of this type usually indicate some kind of sadomasochistic behavior. Your wife obviously had other"—he paused to clear his throat, before continuing—"acquaintances and interests that you knew nothing about. By the look on your face, I can tell that this information is a shock. I'm sorry to be the one to have to tell you the truth." Contrary to his statement, he didn't seem sorry at all.

Devin met his father's eyes, noting the imperceptible shake of his head. He understood Rob's unspoken message. There was no reason to continue his argument. As far as the authorities was concerned, the case was closed.

Rob, his expression grim, stood up. He politely extended his hand to the overbearing detective. "Thank you for your time," he said in a clipped tone.

Devin followed suit. "Thank you," he echoed, extending his hand. What he really wanted to do was plant a facer on the smug face of the pretentious man.

The detective shook Devin's hand firmly. "I'm sorry, son." Having regained his position as the ultimate authority in the room, he had also regained his sympathetic demeanor. He glanced at his watch. "And now, if you will excuse me, I have a great deal of work to do." He walked to his door, opened it, and motioned them into the hallway.

They heard the *click* as the door shut behind them. No one spoke until they were seated in Roman's shiny, silver BMW 7 series.

"He was a cocky little asshole, wasn't he?" Roman asked, putting the car in gear and pulling into traffic.

Devin nodded in agreement. He still wasn't satisfied. Instead of putting his fears to rest, the detective's dismissal of their suspicions only made him more certain something truly heinous had happened to Mallory.

CHAPTER FIFTY-FOUR

*D*evin couldn't shake the sneaking suspicion that he had wandered into the wrong funeral. He glanced around surreptitiously. His discomfort had nothing to do with what he was wearing. He fit right in with the other mourners in the church. His black suit and solid black tie were perfectly appropriate. His shoes were black, too. In the cuffs of his crisp, white shirt, he was wearing the cufflinks he had received when he graduated from college… black onyx with a monogrammed *M*.

His location wasn't the problem, either. He was sitting with the appropriate people. Amalie was beside him, swinging her feet—in their shiny black shoes and lacy white socks—back and forth. She wore a black headband around her blond head. Allana had curled the little girl's hair so that it hung in ringlets down her back. Her black dress was sleeveless; white bric-a-brac trim circled the sleeves, skirt, and neckline. Amalie gently grasped Iggy, who sported one of Devin's black bow ties. That bit of whimsy was Roman's idea, an attempt to bring a smile to Diana's pale face.

Seated next to Amalie, Diana was riddled with guilt. She had convinced herself she could have acted to prevent Mallory's tragic end. If she had only returned to the townhouse earlier, then, maybe, she could have…what? What could she have done? She would probably never know, but the struggle not to feel somewhat responsible was real.

Devin studied his cousin for a minute, noting her tightly clasped hands and bowed head. Her black peasant dress—with its sweeping skirt and flowing sleeves—accentuated her small waistline. A long, silver necklace hung on either side of the V-necked bodice.

Diana looked good in the trendy Boho style that was currently so popular. She didn't like wearing black, however. Devin noted that his cousin did look extremely pale. He sighed, resolving to talk to her again. She had to stop blaming herself for Mallory's death.

He surveyed the occupants of the rest of his pew. Mallory's mother, Pamela, had walked down the aisle sobbing, so overcome with grief she required the assistance of her son and his wife to reach her seat. Her tragic performance was a far cry from the childish tantrum she had thrown on the church steps minutes earlier. Devin's former—thanks be to a merciful God—mother-in-law exploded in rage when she realized the nanny would enter the sacred building in front of the woman who gave birth to the deceased, as Pamela called herself.

Her outburst was ugly. And inappropriate. It proved quite upsetting to "the nanny." In Diana's mind, Mallory's mother was right. She was *only* the nanny. After listening to the deranged woman's outburst, Diana was, understandably reluctant to sit in the same row. She attempted to disengage herself from her small charge. But Amalie refused to let go of her hand. In the end, the crocodile tears pooling in Amalie's pleading blue eyes overrode Diana's misgivings. Devin was glad she was there, for Amalie's sake. And for his own.

The so-called "bereaved" cousins and other presumably "close" family members were seated in the reserved pews behind the immediate family. They were, without exception, people who Devin had never met—or even heard Mallory mention—in the five long years of their marriage. The rest of his former mother-in-law's entourage and what amounted to a large number of curious spectators packed the church.

The reverend conducting the funeral—a man Devin had never laid eyes on until the previous afternoon—spoke at great length about accepting the will of God. He read a famous passage from the book of Ecclesiastes, the one that began: *To everything there is a season...* The solemn man gave particular attention to the phrase, *A time to be born, a time to die."*

Devin wasn't a theology expert, by any means, but he felt fairly confident that dying of a drug overdose didn't figure into God's will for anybody's life. Did he believe God could make good things come out of bad? Of course he did. He was living proof of that, but he also believed that people weren't puppets. God gave them the freedom to make choices. With choices, came consequences. The wrong choices often resulted in tragic consequences. Blaming Mallory's choices on God's will didn't seem quite fair to Devin's way of thinking.

He was relieved when the reverend finally sat down. The soloist—also someone he had never met—sang one of Mallory's "favorite" hymns. At least, that's what he said. Diana glanced at Devin in surprise, before quickly turning away. In all the time Devin had known her, Mallory had rarely attended religious services. If she did, she did so only because she had some ulterior motive. It was highly likely, in Devin's opinion, Mallory hadn't heard Horatio Spafford's beautiful hymn *It Is Well With My Soul* more than a couple times in her life. It was also quite possible she had been texting one of her friends during those few occasions.

Diana passed Amalie a stick of gum. Amalie took the gum, regarding her nanny patiently until Diana pulled out another stick of gum for Iggy. She held it out, but Amalie made Iggy shake his head. Apparently, the iguana preferred another flavor. Diana smiled mildly. She offered the unwanted gum to Devin instead. He took it, in spite of the fact that what he really wanted was a nice stiff drink.

The reverend stood after the solo, giving Devin a moment to hope the ordeal might almost be over. Instead of dismissing the congregation for the graveside service, however, the reverend launched into his own personal history of Mallory's "pure and virtuous" life. It was, without a doubt, a fictitious history; the person he was talking about was a figment of the reverend's own imagination. This realization brought Devin back to his original supposition. This had to be the wrong funeral because he had *never* met the devoted wife, loving mother, and selfless daughter whom the reverend was currently describing.

Even Amalie was confused. Under different circumstances, Devin would have laughed at the expression on his daughter's face. She was gaping at the reverend who had just made a remark about the loving care Mallory had lavished on her only daughter. Amalie's gum fell out of her mouth, causing a temporary crisis. Diana quickly fixed the situation by producing another stick.

After several moments of intense chewing, Amalie looked up at her father. Her blue eyes were filled with disbelief as the reverend launched into another made-up example of Mallory's doting affection for her daughter. Devin held his breath. Amalie hadn't spoken a word to anyone since the day Mallory died. His little girl opened her mouth like she wanted to ask a question but changed her mind. The question, however, remained in her eyes. *Whose mommy is he talking about?* Devin sighed again. Amalie finally shrugged her shoulders and went back to kicking her legs.

The blatant hypocrisy of this farce of a funeral made Devin want to stand up, walk out of the church, and never look back. Two things prevented him doing just that. His daughter needed him to be a role model of proper behavior. Of grace under fire, as it were. He had no doubt that one day, Amalie would have to deal with the fact that her mother never wanted her. Or loved her. He was prepared for that. He hoped only that Amalie's self-esteem and self-worth had not already suffered permanent damage.

His second reason for remaining was more complicated. Somewhere in that church sat his entire family. Aunts. Uncles. Cousins. Even his grandmother from Charleston. Most of the employees from Merritt Brothers were present, from the main office in Alexandria as well as from the New York office. A large contingent from McCallum Industries was in attendance, including his secretary. Even the custodian who cleaned his office was present.

Blane and Grace were there. So were Joe and Juli Finch, who flew up earlier in the day. The show of support from Darcie's parents meant a lot, particularly in light of the circumstances of his last conversation with Joe. Joey Finch had decided to stay in Newport for the funeral, as well, rather than returning home. Devin hoped that gesture signified some kind of truce. And, of course, somewhere in that church sat Miss Darcie Finch, the woman who had captured his heart. *"Have courage, Laurence,"* she had said. Remaining in his current position required more courage than he had ever imagined.

The reverend droned on and on, his words punctuated by the strategically placed sobs of Devin's former mother-in-law. Her Oscar-worthy performance as a grieving mother was sure to win her an Academy Award: Best Supporting Actress at a Funeral.

Eventually, those who lived with her found it next to impossible to listen to any more statements about the make-believe Mallory. Their attention waned. Amalie straightened her legs, letting Iggy slide down them. Before the loyal iguana hit the floor, Amalie pulled him back by his tail. She repeated the process seventy-three times, according to Devin's count. Diana had a far-away look in her eyes, probably writing her book in her head. It was time for Devin's dependable escape. It was time to play *Places I Would Rather Be Than Here*.

He began as he always did. *I would rather be...*

Devin blinked in surprise. He found himself unable to complete the thought. He tried again.

I would rather be...

Nothing.

Damn it.

For the first time that he could remember, Devin's game had failed him. The next moment, however, it hit him. *I would rather be with Darcie Finch.* Well, of course, he would. Why would he want to be anywhere else? *Places I Would Rather Be Than Here* had turned into *Places I Would Rather Be with Darcie Finch*. He liked the sound of that. It was a game he could play all day. And all night.

Diana cleared her throat. Devin realized he was sitting in the pew at his deceased wife's funeral with a lovesick grin on his face. Diana and Amalie were looking at him expectantly. As was the usher standing beside the pew. The expressionless man was waiting for Devin to stand up. The time had come to go. The ordeal had finally ended. Devin hastily wiped all traces of the smile from his face. He stood up, nodding politely to the blank-faced usher as he stepped into the aisle. He paused until Amalie and Diana joined him.

Together, they made their way toward the honest sunlight and fresh air that waited on the other side of the open church doors.

For Darcie, the last hour had been interminable. The whiny voice of the reverend grated on her already overwrought nerves. The imaginary accolades he continued to heap on a woman he had obviously never met made Darcie want to scream. With every word, he led the congregation farther and farther away from a true portrait of Mallory Merritt. It was a travesty of justice, she fumed silently. Worse than that, the inability to do anything about it left her feeling increasingly frustrated and utterly helpless. She, along with the rest of the congregation, was trapped in a hell of Mallory's making. And at the moment, there was no way out. Even death seemed unable to rid the world of Mallory's twisted spirit. The evil woman continued to torment and manipulate from the grave. Darcie prayed that Mallory's last, tenuous grip on the mortal world would vanish after her funeral, her fingers pried loose by the magnitude of lies the reverend spouted so effortlessly.

The unusually dramatic turn of Darcie's thoughts made her a little uncomfortable. And nervous. And, well…angry. How dare that pompous, little man stand in this beautiful church and pontificate on the fictitious virtues of such a selfish, vindictive woman. A woman who went out of her way to belittle, humiliate, and exploit the weaknesses of everyone she met. She called her injured husband a monster. *A. Monster.* How could she speak such cruel and callous words to a wonderful, caring man like Devin?

Darcie would never forget the aftermath of that awful phone conversation. Those words had hurt Devin. It had been obvious to her even though she barely knew him at the time. He was devastated after talking to his wife. Darcie bristled at the thought. Not only that, she added to herself, Mallory was a horrible excuse for a mother. She ignored the needs of Amalie, tossing her aside as soon as she was finished using her. Everything the manipulative woman had ever done was for show. She deserved to be charged with crimes against…well…against something. Darcie would have loved the chance to put Mallory on the stand and cross-examine her. She pictured the scene in her mind....

So deeply involved was she in her imaginary quest for vengeance that she jumped when a shoulder bumped against her arm. Joey's warm hand covered her cold ones in a firm grip. Her startled eyes looked into her brother's face to find that he was studying her with concern. Only then did she realize her right hand was clutching her left in a death grip. He turned her left hand over, shaking his head when he saw the half-moon shaped indentions her nails had made on her palm. He enfolded her hand in his comfortingly. Darcie felt tears prick her eyes. The hard, little knot of misery that had lodged in her stomach uncoiled a bit. Sometimes her overprotective brother did just the right thing.

As the organ music swelled, Darcie allowed Joey to pull her to her feet. She felt Grace's gentle grip on her other arm as she stood with the rest of the congregation to watch Mallory's family exit the church. Darcie could only watch as Devin walked slowly down the aisle, Amalie's hand in his. He was careful, she noticed, to keep his head down and his eye on the carpet under his feet. Darcie's heart hurt for him and all that he was going through. She wanted to shield him from the blatant curiosity and heartless scrutiny of strangers. But circumstances—and the firm grips of her siblings—kept her where she was. She was glad Diana also accompanied Amalie. At least her pirate wasn't completely alone.

She felt sorry for Amalie, too, uncertain of how much the little girl knew about what happened to her mother. The fact that she refused to speak was telling. But from what Darcie could see, Amalie looked more confused than sad. She clung to her daddy's hand. She held her stuffed iguana firmly under her other arm, tail first.

That unfortunate fellow's stuffed head bobbed up and down with Amalie's every step. His precarious position placed him face to face with Mallory's family members, following directly behind him in the procession. His sightless, plastic eyes were the only thing that spared him from the spectacle of Mallory's mother pretending to wipe away tears while she proceeded down the aisle and walked slowly to the front doors of the church.

MACEE MCNEILL

After the burial, Devin's personal support system gathered on the side of the cemetery that overlooked the ocean. The beautiful view and fresh ocean breezes were a welcome relief after the cloistering atmosphere of the funeral. They all needed a little fresh air after witnessing Mallory's mother's elaborate display of grief. After throwing herself across the coffin at the graveside service, the hysterical woman had to be carried to her car.

Darcie had never witnessed such an uncontrollable outpouring of grief firsthand. "I had no idea that Mallory was so close to her mother," she remarked to Diana in a low voice.

"She wasn't," Diana said. Her mouth twisted in disgust. "Mallory couldn't stand her mother, and the feeling was mutual. They hadn't spoken to each other in years, probably since Amalie was born. Amalie didn't even recognize her grandmother today. And Pamela didn't say a word to her."

"That's horrible," Darcie said, trying to imagine growing up without the wisdom and advice of a grandparent. "I was also surprised by the number of people at the funeral. I wouldn't have expected so many for someone with Mallory's, um…" She hesitated, not wanting to sound petty.

"Warm and loving personality?" Diana quipped.

"Yeah," Darcie agreed. "Something like that."

"These people aren't Mallory's friends. They're only here because of Pamela." This bit of helpful information was supplied by Allana, who had joined them. "From what I understand, she invited several hundred people to a lobster bake on Goat Island after the funeral. She's calling it a 'celebration of life.'" Allana's smile was bitter. "She invited all of us, too, but I declined." She glanced toward the gravesite. "Looks like Devin is finally *finished* with Mallory's family, one way or another."

Darcie felt certain the meaning of Allana's words was twofold.

The three women watched as Devin stepped away from the cluster of people near the funeral tent.

After shaking hands with Mallory's brother for the last time, Devin's eye found Darcie. Mentally assessing the shortest route to reuniting with her, he started walking. Pamela called his name, but he was having none of it. He pretended not to hear her as he picked up his pace. He had played his role in Mallory's dramas for years. He would *not* be a part of her mother's. Instead, he kept his eye fixed on the one who held his heart.

Darcie watched his approach, pretending to listen to the conversations swirling all around her. She forced herself to wait. What she really wanted to do was run to him and pull him into the protective circle of his friends and family.

When he finally reached the group, Devin found that he could breathe easily again. There was no judgement here. No ridicule. And no false emotions. Only support. He silently thanked God for that support. Diana and Allana stopped talking, looking to him expectantly.

"None of Mallory's friends came to the funeral," Devin said. "Not a single one." It was the first thing that came out of his mouth. It had bothered him since he entered the church. It was remarkable, really. After all of her jostling for social position. All of her posturing. All of her token expressions of affection. All of it was for naught. Of the users and players with whom Mallory had spent the majority of her days, not one had taken time to attend her funeral, not even Desiree. They were going on with their lives as if she never existed. The users would keep using and the players would keep playing. Damn it. The whole of Mallory's existence had been summed up with a fake eulogy delivered to a church packed with strangers. In spite of all Devin had suffered at her hands, he could still see the tragedy of her wasted life.

A soft touch on his arm brought his thoughts back to the present. He looked into Darcie's worried eyes. She was wearing the same black sheath and jacket that he had last seen discarded on the floor of Joey's guest bedroom. Even though he could use the distraction, he refused to allow himself to wonder what she was wearing underneath.

"Are you all right?" she asked, softly, her lovely voice filled with concern.

"If I can hear your voice, I'm all right," he answered, covering her hand with his own.

She looked into his eye for a moment before nodding, apparently satisfied with his answer. "How is Amalie?"

Devin's face fell. "She still won't say a word. We've tried everything. The doctor says she's suffering trauma induced by the death of her mother, but…"

"I don't believe that for a minute," Diana interrupted. "Iggy Iguana is more of a mother to her than Mallory was. It has to be something else."

"Maybe she needs a change of scenery," Juli Finch suggested. She and Joe had wandered over in time to hear the last part of the conversation. "Why don't you send her home with us for a couple of weeks?"

Devin nodded slowly, considering their offer. "That may be the best thing for her. We've talked about getting her away from here. She had a wonderful time in Honeysuckle Creek at the wedding. Blane and I will be there in two weeks, anyway, to start the initial setup for the new headquarters. What do you think, Darcie?" Her opinion was the one that mattered to him the most.

"I think it's the right decision," she said confidently. "I've talked to several child psychologists that Dad and I know. They all suggested removing the child from the scene of the cr—. Um, trauma." She nearly groaned aloud. *Way to go, Darcie. Way to keep your suspicions to yourself.*

A quick glance around the group, however, confirmed that each one of them had picked up on her omission of the word *crime*. She also noticed that nobody spoke up to disagree with her. Nor did anyone seem the least bit shocked.

Darcie felt a little better. She apparently was not alone in her assumption that something more sinister than an accidental overdose had occurred in Newport the day of Mallory's death.

"We would *love* to have Amalie with us, Devin," she said, getting back to the most important topic. "I can stay with her at Heart's Ease, if you like."

Thank God. Devin was more than a little relieved. Amalie would love spending time with Darcie. He was counting on her to help his baby girl, especially since the always dependable Diana was having troubles of her own. He glanced at his cousin, glad to see the relief on her face. He even caught the hint of a smile.

According to Roman, Diana was making herself sick over Amalie's refusal to speak. Devin had immediately insisted his nanny take a couple of weeks off. After a stoic attempt to deny that anything was wrong, Diana finally broke down, admitting she needed a break from the trauma. She was going to spend some time with her parents in Virginia.

Devin could see in Darcie's eyes that she was committed to helping his daughter. He wanted to be sure, however, that his baby wasn't going to be homesick. She had been through enough already. "I think it will be good for Amalie, but I'm not going to make her go if she doesn't want to," Devin said. His little princess had stayed very close to her daddy the past few days, refusing to be alone any time they were in the townhouse.

"Here she comes now," Darcie said.

Lydia and Amalie were making their way toward the group, after having spent some time getting a closer look at the ocean. They watched the little girl's face light up at the sight of Darcie. She dropped Lydia's hand and sprinted across the grass. "Miss Darcie! Miss Darcie!" she yelled, excitedly, speaking for the first time since Mallory's death. She threw herself into Darcie's outstretched arms. The glances the adults exchanged were in complete accord. Amalie was going to Honeysuckle Creek.

CHAPTER FIFTY-FIVE

Honeysuckle Creek, North Carolina
Two weeks later

The June morning was glorious. The kind that causes all but the hardest of hearts to pause a moment and bask in the endless blue of a cloudless sky. After giving Rosemary a farewell pat on the nose, Darcie climbed down from her perch on the fence. She watched the spirited horse lope across the pasture to join several of Blane's fine equine stock, happily munching on clover. She closed her eyes for a minute, enjoying the gentle breeze that wafted through the trees.

According to the local TV weatherman, sweltering temperatures were on the way. But for now, all was perfection. Darcie's eyes surveyed the space that joined the two stables. She would never stand in this spot again without remembering the dance she shared with her pirate. She had come here often since that moment, seeking solace whenever her soul was troubled. She had come at other times, too, when her heart was sad or lonely.

She was not, however, troubled at the moment. Or sad. Or lonely. Because, in a little while, her pirate would be here. With her. Darcie's heart beat faster every time she thought of it. They would be together. In broad daylight. And it didn't matter who saw them. She was still having difficulty believing there was nothing—*nothing*—to keep them apart.

The last two weeks had been filled with countless texts and phone calls between Devin and herself. The decision to send Amalie to Honeysuckle Creek had been a good one. Amalie's determination not to speak quickly decreased the farther away she drew from Newport. Darcie and Amalie were staying at Heart's Ease for security reasons, on the outside chance that Mallory's death wasn't accidental. The watchful eyes of the extra "employees" Rafe had put in place was a little unnerving. As was the constant surveillance. On the plus side, Darcie and Amalie were enjoying the pool and the stables. They were also free to wander the grounds of the beautiful estate to their hearts' content.

Other than Amalie's adamant refusal to enter the upstairs guest wing, she had reacted positively to every other part of Blane's lovely home. Darcie didn't ask any questions. But she did arrange for she and Amalie to stay in rooms on the first floor. Coincidentally, they were the very same rooms she and Devin had occupied when they first met. Whether or not the residual aura of love in those rooms had anything to do with Amalie's recovery—and Darcie liked to think it did—good things happened quickly.

The morning after their arrival, Darcie overheard Amalie having an animated conversation with the horses. That night at dinner, the little girl asked for more ketchup before clapping her hands over her mouth in horror. Darcie could sense they were close to a breakthrough. Determined to help the innocent child who had won her heart, Darcie sat down on Amalie's bed after dinner for a little girl-talk. In the end, Amalie took very little convincing. Darcie smiled when she remembered their conversation.

"Are you having fun at Heart's Ease, Amalie?" she asked, brushing the little girl's hair off her forehead with a gentle hand.

Amalie nodded, her blue eyes never leaving Darcie's face.

"What's your favorite thing about being here?" Darcie asked encouragingly.

Amalie sat up excitedly, opened her mouth, and hesitated before closing it tightly. She sank back into her pillow with a discouraged sigh.

Darcie wasn't giving up, however. "Oh, Amalie, I know that you have so many wonderful things to say and I want to hear every single one of them. Aren't you getting tired of not talking, honey?" she asked gently.

Amalie's blue eyes filled with tears as she nodded her head. Her little face was so full of sadness that it broke Darcie's heart.

"Oh, sweetie," Darcie crooned. She pulled the child into a comforting hug, striving to say the right thing. "You're scared to talk about your mommy, aren't you?"

Amalie's face was hidden in Darcie's shoulder, but she could feel the child's tentative little nod, the first indication that Darcie was on the right track. She continued in a soothing voice: "I understand, 'Malie. I don't like to talk about scary things, either. What if we decide together not to talk about that day at all?"

Amalie looked up, a little ray of hope blooming in her eyes.

Darcie smiled. "Would you like that?"

Amalie nodded.

Darcie continued encouragingly: "That means we can talk about anything else in the whole world."

Amalie sat up, the first hint of a smile on her face. "Like horses?" she asked.

"And ice cream…" Darcie added. "And Atticus."

Amalie grinned at the mention of the quirky canine. "And princesses!" she added, starting to giggle.

"And ticklish little girls…" Darcie said, tickling Amalie's ribs. Much to her delight, the child burst into peals of laughter.

UNMASKING THE HEART

From that moment on, the bright, confident child that was Amalie Merritt had returned. Darcie couldn't wait for Devin to see his happy little girl again. To her everlasting delight, Darcie discovered Amalie possessed even less of a filter than she did. The little girl revealed all kinds of interesting facts and delicious secrets about her daddy. Darcie couldn't wait to use her newfound knowledge to tease her pirate unmercifully.

Amalie, with Iggy tucked securely under her arm, came flying through the door of the stable. It appeared the long wait was over. The little girl ran up to Darcie, eyes wide with excitement.

"Miss Darcie! He's here! Daddy's here! He's coming *right now*." She ducked behind a large, wooden barrel against the wall, peeking over it to admonish: "Shhhh! Don't tell him where we are."

Darcie nodded in agreement, watching Amalie's blond head disappear behind the barrel. Iggy's tail, unfortunately, didn't quite make it. Before Darcie could remedy the situation, or attempt to draw a calming breath, Devin's powerful frame filled the doorway. He had dressed casually, in jeans and a dark blue polo shirt with burgundy stripes. The spattering of sunlight caught the burnished bronze highlights in his hair. His intelligent gray eye took in the scene at a glance. He was the most striking man Darcie had ever seen in her life. The way he was staring at her stole her ability to speak. She simply stood there, gazing at the man like a lovesick teenager.

Devin was equally stunned, unprepared for the sheer poetry of her presence. Today, his lovely lady was wearing cutoff jean shorts and a tight, little T-shirt. Her hair was caught up in a loose ponytail. The pair of running shoes she was wearing had seen better days. But it didn't matter. She was gorgeous. Breathtakingly gorgeous…not to mention In. Cred. Ibly. Sex. Y. He wouldn't mention either, though, if he knew what was good for him. So, he stood there, letting everything he was thinking radiate from his one, good eye.

"Hello, Laurence," she finally breathed.

Her lovely vocals wrapped around him, igniting the spark that propelled him to action.

He strode toward her, stopping a foot away. "Hello, Darcie Finch." He slowly raised his hand, gently brushing the backs of his fingers down the side of her cheek. Her swift intake of breath radiated to his very soul. She made the sun brighter. The sky a deeper shade of blue. The breeze sweeter. Everything in his life was better because of the rare, incomparable woman in front of him.

And now she had saved his daughter. The little girl he followed into the barn was laughing and giggling and happy. She was a better version of the pale, sad little girl he had last seen two weeks ago. Just as Devin was a better version of the man he used to be. All because of Darcie Finch.

"Have you seen my lovely daughter?"

He winked, gesturing to Iggy's rapidly disappearing tail with his head. He knew exactly where his little girl was. The muffled giggle from the space behind the barrel confirmed his guess.

Darcie smiled. "Oh, I think she's around here somewhere. I bet we can find—"

"Darcie."

He was quick to interrupt her. She looked at him, surprised at the sudden seriousness of his tone. "Yes," she said, tentatively.

It was time. He couldn't wait another moment. Couldn't make small talk or silly jokes or teasing comments. The rest of his life, and Amalie's, depended on Darcie's answer. Even though he was one hundred percent certain of what that answer would be—well…at least ninety-nine percent certain—asking the question was terrifying. He took a deep breath. The glow in her dark eyes encouraged him. The dam burst. The words he had prepared—had repeated over and over in his head for two long weeks—poured out.

"Darcie Finch, you are the beauty to my beast," he began. "The princess to my prince."

She opened her mouth to protest, just as he expected. But he was ready. He silently held up his hand, asking her to listen. She closed her mouth, crossing her arms in front of her. She looked mildly annoyed.

Not an auspicious beginning, he thought with some amusement. He forged ahead anyway. "Will you also be my Pirate Queen? My partner in all things?"

The corners of her lips lifted. Her eyes began to sparkle.

Devin knew, then. He had won. "Will you stand beside me, Darcie, all the days of our lives? Will you be my lover? And my friend? The other half of my heart?"

She was smiling now…the smile that made him feel like he was a king.

His voice was hoarse with emotion. "And will you teach my daughter—and any children we may have—to be fierce and strong and fearless? Like you?"

"Oh, Laurence, you know I will." Her eyes were bright with happy tears. "But it's too soon for this. I mean, isn't it?" More than anything, Darcie wanted him to be sure that he was ready. She found herself on shaky ground, eager to forge ahead into the future, but unable to dismiss the niggling worry that it was too much too soon. She needed his reassurance more than she needed to draw her next breath.

He cupped her beautiful face with his hands, gently wiping her tears with both thumbs. "There's nothing sudden about this, Darcie."

Her heart nearly melted into a puddle of mush at the certainty of his words. They were the exact words she needed to hear. Imagine that, she thought.

His confidence did not abate as he continued: "I've felt this way since the first time I heard your voice. We were meant to be together, Darcie Finch. Please tell me that you feel it, too."

"Oh, Devin," she said, breathlessly. "You know I do."

Devin relaxed as his world fell into place. Whether she called him Laurence or Devin, this woman was his. To have and to hold. To love and to cherish. For all time. "I need six months, Darcie," he explained. "Six months to get everything in order. Then, I can go down on one knee and make it official. Until then, I was hoping you would take this…" He fumbled in his pocket, suddenly nervous. His cold fingers struggled to grasp the object he was searching for.

"Try the other pocket, Daddy," said the voice behind the barrel.

"Thank you, Amalie," Devin said, politely.

"You're welcome, Daddy." She popped up from behind the barrel long enough to answer, only to disappear again.

He shoved his hand into his other pocket. His fingers found the prize.

Darcie was trying not to giggle as Devin cleared his throat. "I hope you will take this ring as a symbol of my promise to, well…keep my promise," he finished with a flourish. It had sounded better in his head. He looked at her anxiously as he held out the ring resting in his palm.

She took the ring, studying it from all sides. It looked like a gold signet ring, but in place of the monogram was a gold coin. A very old coin by the looks of it.

"It's a gold doubloon, from the sixteen hundreds," Devin explained. "Pirate's gold. I thought it was appropriate because…"

"Yes," she interrupted.

"Excuse me?" Now, he was confused.

"Pay attention, Laurence," she instructed, her eyes sparkling with joy. "You asked if I would be your Pirate Queen and all of those other lovely questions. The answer to all of them is yes. Yes!" She slipped the ring onto her finger, holding it out for him to admire.

"Daddy," said the voice behind the barrel. "You forgot the other thing."

"What other thing?" Devin asked, leaning down to confer with his very helpful daughter.

After a whispered conference, he stood up. "It has come to my attention, Darcie Finch, that I have conducted our whole relationship out of order. I have asked you the most important question first. Now, I have six months to make it up to you." He paused, looking a little embarrassed. "Miss Darcie Finch, will you go out with me?"

"And me?" asked the voice behind the barrel. "And Iggy?"

"On a date?" Darcie asked, for clarification. She was trying not to laugh.

"Yes," Devin smiled. "Will you go out on a date with me?"

"And me?" the barrel added. "And Iggy?"

Darcie did laugh then, a rich, lilting sound that rang out like bells. "I would be delighted to go out with all of you," she announced.

"Hurray!" Amalie popped back up, hugging Iggy to her chest excitedly. "We're going on a date!" She promptly disappeared again. Iggy, however, chose to remain, his plastic eyes looking on in approval.

"Hurray," Devin echoed, chuckling from the sheer joy of the moment.

"Aren't you going to kiss her?" asked his very mischievous daughter. She was peeking at her daddy and his Darcie again, over the rim of the barrel. "Iggy says you're supposed to kiss her."

Devin looked into Darcie's eyes, brimming with laughter. He took her hand and brought it to his lips, pressing a kiss against her knuckles.

"No, Daddy," Amalie objected. "Iggy says you're doing it wrong. Iggy says you're supposed to kiss her on the lips."

Devin looked at Darcie, a mischievous light in his eye. "Iggy says I'm supposed to kiss you on the lips."

Darcie grinned back, "Then you better do what Iggy says."

Devin leaned over and planted what he intended as a brief kiss on her lips. He couldn't, however, prevent himself from lingering. Her lips were so very soft. Soft and delicious and...

"Yuck," said Amalie. "Iggy says kissing is *nasty*."

The look in Devin's eye as he pulled his lips from the perfect lips of Miss Darcie Soon-to-be-Merritt-Finch held a promise. Their kiss would resume later, in an iguana-free location, yet to be determined. And it would be anything but nasty.

Devin reached behind the barrel to help his daughter stand up. "That's right, Amalie," he agreed, deciding to take advantage of a teachable moment. "Iggy is absolutely correct. Kissing is nasty. You should *never* kiss a boy until you're somewhere around, oh, maybe thirty-five years old."

He nodded his head decisively as Darcie looked at him in amazement.

She took Amalie's hand. "Don't listen to Iggy, Amalie. Or to your daddy, either, for that matter. He's just teasing you."

"No, I'm not," said Devin indignantly.

Hand in hand, Darcie and Amalie walked toward the doors. "One day," Darcie promised, "you'll find a nice boy and you'll fall in love. Then you'll want to kiss him all the time. And you won't think it's yucky at all."

"Is that what happened to you and Daddy?" Amalie asked.

"Of course."

Darcie threw Devin a sexy smile over her shoulder. He couldn't help but smile back. She was the keeper of his heart. His Pirate Queen.

Amalie stopped walking. "Miss Darcie," she squealed in excitement. "If you're a pirate queen, then that makes Daddy your Pirate King, right?"

"You are absolutely right," Darcie agreed, enjoying the pleased expression on Devin's face. Her pirate had become a king.

"And if you're a queen and Daddy's a king, what does that make me?" Amalie was breathless with anticipation.

"Why, that makes you a princess, of course," Darcie said. She blew a kiss to her Pirate King.

"Hurray," said Amalie. "I'm a pirate princess!" She threw her beloved iguana into the air with joy, sending a beaming smile in the direction of the Pirate King.

He winked.

Amalie, having established her own royal title, efficiently directed her attention to the most pressing business of the moment. "Miss Darcie, where are we going to go on our date?"

Darcie tore her gaze from her pirate and the promise in his eye. "Well, I thought we might go to Honeysuckle Creek Pizza and Karaoke," she said. "Unless you have a better idea."

"Hurray! I love the pizza there. And maybe we could get ice cream, too."

Amalie always made the most of her opportunities.

Darcie gasped in make-believe shock. "Pizza *and* ice cream? That's quite a first date."

"Well." Amalie compromised: "Maybe we could go to the market instead, to get some YOHOHO Yogurt bars. They are soooo yummy, Miss Darcie. They're made especially for pirates, but regular people can eat them, too."

Darcie nodded encouragingly as Amalie continued to elaborate on the merits of YOHOHO Yogurt bars.

After giving a mental shout-out to Man Bun, Devin watched his Pirate Queen and his happy, little Pirate Princess disappear through the doors of the stable. The Pirate King was left holding the iguana.

Literally.

He was, literally, holding the stuffed iguana he had rescued from the stable floor. He looked into those alert, plastic eyes. "So, Iggy, where do *you* think we should go on our date?" Devin waited for a moment but wasn't a bit surprised when that usually articulate fellow chose not to reply.

Still, Devin nodded in commiseration. "Good decision. It's probably best to let the females decide. I imagine we'll be doing a lot of that, my friend." *And loving every minute of it,* he thought happily.

Devin tucked the iguana under his arm. He followed his lady pirates into the bright, summer morning, unable to stop himself from whistling the melody that was stuck in his head...The love song from *Beauty and the Beast*.

EPILOGUE

Honeysuckle Creek, North Carolina
Two weeks later

*A*malie stood behind the overly large recliner in Mr. Blane's office. Her back was flattened against the wall, and the right half of the curtains hid her from view. It was the best hiding place ever. She could hear everything. *And* she wasn't breaking her promise to stop hiding behind the curtains. She wasn't *behind* the curtains. She was *beside* them. She almost giggled but stopped herself in time. She put her finger on her lips so Iggy would stay quiet, too.

Some of Amalie's favorite people were here in Mr. Blane's office. Her daddy was here. And Miss Darcie. They were her two *most*, most favorite people. Except for Nanny Di, Amalie thought. If Nanny Di could be here too, then Amalie's three *most*, most favorite people would be in Mr. Blane's office. Miss Darcie said that Nanny Di was taking a little vacation. Amalie missed Nanny Di. She missed Nanny Di a lot. So did Iggy. Miss Darcie said Amalie would see Nanny Di soon. Amalie couldn't wait. Neither could Iggy.

Mr. Blane was sitting at his big desk. Mr. Blane's big desk drawer was always full of candy—tiny candy bars, candy kisses, and, sometimes, the candy with chocolate *and* peanut butter. Amalie liked that kind the best. Mr.

Blane liked chocolate. He always shared his candy with her. He even gave her extra for Iggy.

Miss Grace was sitting on the sofa beside Miss Darcie and Daddy. Miss Grace was so much fun. She taught Amalie songs to sing, and she and Amalie made up dance steps together. But, best of all, Miss Grace let Amalie play dress-up with her fancy clothes. And Miss Grace *never* got mad if her dresses got wrinkled *or* dirty. Miss Grace was very, very nice. She let Iggy play dress-up, too.

Amalie felt the recliner move. She almost giggled again. It moved because Mr. Rafe was sitting in it. She liked Mr. Rafe. He always smiled when he saw her. And he always talked to Iggy. Iggy liked Mr. Rafe, too.

Mr. Roger Carrington was in Mr. Blane's office. Amalie called him Mr. Roger. Amalie liked Mr. Roger a lot. He sang funny songs and, sometimes, he danced with Iggy.

And Mr. Dominic Parker was in Mr. Blane's office. Amalie called him Mr. Dom. He had "turkey-eyes." Amalie thought Mr. Dom had the most beautiful eyes in the whole world.

Amalie wasn't sure why they were all here in Mr. Blane's office, but she figured it must be important. She was glad she wasn't left out. She didn't like to be left out. She was glad that Iggy wasn't left out, either. After reminding Iggy to be quiet, Amalie settled back to listen.

Rafe had just returned to North Carolina after three weeks in Belize. It was, he informed them, a last-ditch effort to find out who had hired the person or persons complicit in Kenneth Wade's death. Whoever tampered with the harness of the zip line had, apparently, vanished from the face of the earth. It had been over a year since Wade left the mysterious message on Devin's voicemail. Over a year since the unfortunate man fell to his death.

Rafe had tried on three separate occasions to discover who was behind Wade's murder. But the perpetrators' steps had been well covered, even when faced with someone possessing Rafe's particular skillset. This time, however, he had taken Roger Carrington along. Roger had the inside track with many upper-class foreigners living in Belize—his parents owned a house there—and his help had proved invaluable.

Together, Rafe and Roger had managed to pry a confession from the owner of the zip line company. He had knowingly allowed a man whom he had never seen before to impersonate one of his employees and tamper with the harness. The despicable owner was currently residing in a Belize prison. No bail, no trial pending. A little cash in the right hands had accomplished the arrangement in no time.

Roger was actually quite good at the intrigue game—to his surprise. "I think I'm working for you, now, Blane," he said with a grin. "Who saw that coming?"

Blane grimaced, shaking his head sadly. "Certainly not me." He laughed then and stood up to shake Roger's hand. The hand (he thought, ironically) of his wife's ex-fiancé. Moreover, Roger was also Blane's closest neighbor in Honeysuckle Creek. Their respective estates shared a border. The two had become very good friends, contrary to everyone's initial expectations. "Welcome aboard," Blane said good naturedly.

"And now for the bad news," Rafe said, forcing the conversation back to its original topic. "We still have absolutely no idea who made the deal with the owner of the zip line company. The owner flatly refuses to talk."

Roger spoke up next. "The only description we have is of a rich American. Medium age, medium height, medium build." He stopped.

"That's it?" Devin asked in frustration.

"That's it," said Rafe. "Except for the fact that he wore a Panama hat, dark glasses, and had a tan." He crossed his arms, leaning back against the sofa. "I don't know how we'll ever discover the identity of a man who looks exactly like every other tourist on that island. There isn't any point in continuing the search. We've exhausted every lead."

"And we have no idea who impersonated the employee. He apparently vanished into the rain forest," Roger said, grimly.

Devin sighed. "Thanks for making such an effort."

"I don't like dead ends," Rafe admitted. "You've worked with me long enough to know that, but this end is as dead as it gets. By the way, I'm sorry I missed the funeral."

"Don't be," Devin said. "It was as unpleasant as the marriage."

Rafe leaned forward, propping his elbows on his knees. "Blane says you don't believe Mallory's death was an accident."

All conversation ceased. Rafe always cut to the chase. The tension in the room thickened as every eye fixed on the elegant, lethal man who was sitting on the sofa.

"No," said Devin slowly. "I don't. None of what happened adds up. Mallory was on the verge of getting everything she ever wanted. Why would she mix herself a lethal cocktail? Even if she had been dabbling with opioids, she would have known not to mix those drugs with champagne. She wasn't stupid, and she always took very good care of herself. It just doesn't make sense."

Devin reached into the backpack he had placed beside the sofa where he was sitting. "And when I went through her things, I found these in the drawer of her bedside table." He held up a plastic bag filled with unlabeled pill bottles.

Dominic Parker took up the tale: "I sent a sample from each bottle to a friend of mine who works in a pharmaceutical lab in the Research Triangle. Opiods. All of them."

"They're pills," Devin said. "Not liquid. Not capsules. Pills." He glanced around the room to make sure everyone would understand what he was about to say: "Mallory couldn't swallow pills. She absolutely *couldn't*. No matter how small. Whenever she had a headache she had to take those powders because she just couldn't swallow a pill. I saw her pull capsules of Tylenol apart and mix them with water when she didn't have any powder. And she always bought liquid medicine if it was available."

"I'm assuming you reported your discovery to the police," Rafe said into the silence.

"I did," Devin said in a disgusted manner. "I called the detective we talked to a couple of days after Mallory's death."

"I gather it didn't make any difference," Rafe commented.

"No, it didn't," Devin replied.

"What did the detective say?" Rafe's face was grim.

"When I told him Mallory couldn't swallow pills, he said she must have 'acquired the skill.'" Devin's face was devoid of expression.

Roger spoke up: "Yeah, right. So what was she doing with seven unlabeled bottles of opioids in her bedside table?"

"Because someone put them there," Darcie interjected. "They were a plant to make everyone accept the fact that she was an addict, when in reality…"

"…Somebody wanted her dead," Rafe finished. "But who? Who planted pills so it would appear she had died of an overdose? Why not just make it look like a robbery? Why not steal a TV or some jewelry to make it look random? Why put extra effort into hiding the evidence that a crime was even committed? Who would go to so much trouble?"

The tense group fell silent as each one pondered the answer to Rafe's question.

"When we figure that out, my friends," Rafe added, "we'll know who killed Mallory Merritt."

Amalie sat very still behind the recliner. She covered Iggy's mouth with one hand and her own mouth with the other in an effort to keep both of them quiet. Amalie knew the answer to Mr. Rafe's question. She knew exactly who fixed Mommy the drink that made her sleep forever. She and Iggy saw him do it from their hiding place behind the curtains in Mommy's special room.

Amalie would like to tell on that mean, nasty man very much. But she couldn't. She couldn't say his name ever again. He had warned her that bad things would happen if she told anybody about him. She hadn't listened to him the first time. She told Nanny Di after he scared her in the dark hallway the night of Mr. Blane and Miss Grace's wedding.

Now, Mommy was dead.

Amalie didn't want anything bad to happen to Daddy or Nanny Di or Miss Darcie or anyone else. She couldn't tell anybody that she knew the man who put the powder in her mommy's drink. He wore black clothes. He ate little girls for breakfast and gobbled up their iguanas for dessert. He was a bad, mean, scary, terrible man and she knew his name…

The Grin Ripper.

The End

ABOUT THE AUTHOR

*M*acee McNeill is a retired high school teacher who happily traded grading papers for writing novels. She lives on a large lake in North Carolina with her husband and two overly enthusiastic poodles. She adores spending time with her husband, their two grown sons, and their families. When she isn't writing, Macee sings harmony, bakes pound cakes, runs, and cheers for the University of North Carolina at Chapel Hill, her alma mater.